Una Horne lives in Saltburn-by-the-Sea in Cleveland. Trained as a nurse, she gave up a career to raise a family but began writing when her two children were grown up. Her wonderful regional sagas set in the North East have won a faithful following.

The Marble Clock

Also by Una Horne

A Time to Heal
Under the Rowan Tree
Come the Day
Bright is the Dawn
Lorinda Leigh
When Morning Comes
The Jewel Streets
A Blackbird Singing

The Marble Clock

Una Horne

This combined edition first published in Great Britain
in 2002 by Judy Piatkus (Publishers) Ltd,
5 Windmill Street, London W1T 2JA
Email: info@piatkus.co.uk
Website: www.piatkus.co.uk

A catalogue record for this book is available from the British Library

ISBN 0 7499 3263 5

Printed and bound in Great Britain by
Mackays of Chatham Ltd, Chatham, Kent

To my aunt, Mary Walker, one of the Aycliffe Angels, who worked in the Royal Ordnance factory there. Also my uncle, the late Sergeant Joseph Howe, Croix de Guerre.

Though this book is a work of fiction I drew heavily on their experiences during World War II to create the atmosphere and background material.

Chapter One

1938

'Sing as you go and let the world go by . . .'

The high, sweet voice of Gracie Fields rang out over the clatter of the sewing machines on the factory floor and the girls in the long line on the belt bent over the cloth racing under the needles, singing along with her.

Molly Mason finished yet another side seam and flung the pieces in the bin at her side. She hardly lifted her head to look as she picked up two more pieces and deftly fitted them under the needle. Enid Parker, the line overseer, was nearby, walking up the line collecting the bins of finished work to take to the next line where the shoulder seams were sewn.

Molly's fingers were a blur. She could sew this simple straight seam over and over, barely thinking what she was doing. Neither did she hear the wireless for she was thinking of clocking off time and if she would make her bonus this week. Oh, she needed it, it was the only way she could afford new winter shoes. The toes of her stockings were still damp and gritty because it had been raining at seven-thirty when she'd walked to the bus which took her to work and her old shoes let in the water.

Consequently, it was a minute or two before Molly realised that the music had stopped. She looked up in surprise. It was only a quarter to five, there were fifteen minutes left of the working day.

'We are going over to our news room at Newcastle for an important announcement,' said the radio announcer's plummy disembodied voice. The girls looked at each other. Had the war started after all? But what about Chamberlain's visit to Munich? Peace in our time and all that? The thoughts raced through Molly's head while her fingers holding the cloth stilled on the machine.

There was a crackling noise from the wireless and all heads turned to the set, which was on a shelf on the wall above their heads.

'This is John Grage, speaking from Newcastle. News is coming through of a major mining disaster,' said another voice suddenly and Molly's heart plummeted. It's not likely to be Eden Hope, she told herself, we're miles from Newcastle, even as the voice continued: 'There has been an explosion at Eden Hope colliery, a mine near Bishop Auckland in County Durham.' There was an audible intake of breath along the whole of the line. 'A number of miners are trapped behind a roof cave-in. We are not at present able to ascertain the number of casualties. Further bulletins will be issued as more news comes in.' After a moment the music started again, not Gracie now, more solemn, classical music.

Enid Parker was standing by Molly, one hand on the pieces bin. 'Your dad works there, doesn't he?' she asked, in an interested, conversational sort of tone. Molly stared at her.

'Mine an' all,' Joan Pendle chipped in from the next machine. One or two other voices joined hers. 'My dad's off shift, thank God,' someone else said.

Mine isn't. No, he's not. He went to work this morning when I did. We left the house together, walked down the street, parted at the bus stop. For a second or so Molly didn't know whether she had spoken aloud or not but then she realised the voice was in her head. The scene this morning ran through her mind. They had walked in silence as usual, Dad and her, a companionable silence, though.

'Doesn't he?' Enid repeated, and this time Molly heard her.

She nodded, but still didn't speak. She had a feeling of unreality. Maybe this was just a dream, a nightmare. The classical piece was finished and Gracie was singing again, about her aspidistra.

Molly's dad liked that song, always hummed snatches of it while he was shaving. She shook her head. No, nothing could have happened to him, of course not. This was the first year he was back at work, the first year after the long lay-off of the depression years. The depression which had killed her mother, or so he always said though the doctor maintained it was meningitis. The depression which had sent Harry, her brother, into the army to escape from it. Harry was in India now, he and his mate Jackson.

Dad's hands had been too soft when he went back to work; they had blistered and bled and he had suffered intensely with them at first. Molly had treated them with methylated spirits to harden them. The cuts had healed now, in their place calluses. And Dad was bringing in a proper wage now, held his head high, even joked and laughed as he used to do. He was changing back from the dour, silent man he had become after her mother died.

The manager, Mr Bolton, came on to the floor. The girls turned back to their work as he spoke to Enid Parker. Molly looked down at the piece in her hand but she was moving so slowly she never actually got it under the needle. Then suddenly all was quiet, the power had been switched off.

'Righto, girls, you can go now,' Enid called though it was only five to the hour. There was a buzz of conversation as the women bustled about, collecting their bags, going to the cloakroom for their outdoor things. But it was subdued. There was no light-hearted relief that the day was over, just solemn glances at the girls from Eden Hope.

'Your dad will be all right, I expect,' said Enid. 'Go on now, Molly, the factory bus is going five minutes early, you don't want to miss it.' The floor was almost empty. Joan Pendle hadn't waited for Molly even though they were next-door neighbours. But then, thought Molly, with that twinge of hurt puzzlement which she always felt when the girl ignored her, Joan wouldn't wait for her, they had never got on.

All the way home on the bus there was a ball of dread in the pit of Molly's stomach. It was no good telling herself that her dad stood a good chance of not being caught in the fall – after all, the mine employed 700 men, there were different levels being worked, why should it be the one where Bill Mason was working? It was no use. When at last the bus reached the village and stopped close by the pityard gates, Molly was first off to join the knot of people standing there.

'Any news?' 'Which face?' 'How bad is it?' the newcomers questioned, but before they could be answered there was a buzz of activity around the shaft. The driver of the green Union ambulance which had been waiting by the offices drove forward.

'They've got someone out alive!'

The cry went through the crowd, hope springing up in them all. Molly closed her eyes and prayed then tried to be glad that it was Mr Morley they were taking out of the cage, Mr Morley who lived in Eden Terrace. It was his son Jackson who was in India with Harry. Mrs Morley slipped through the gate and ran to the stretcher, went in the ambulance with him.

'His back,' the murmur went through the crowd as they made way for the gate to open fully and the ambulance to drive off. 'His back and face cut open. His bonny looks will be gone now.' The Morley men were famous for their good looks.

A few minutes late the manager appeared, a list in his hand. The crowd fell silent, watching him intently. He spoke to someone in an expensive suit who looked incongruous in the pit yard. 'The owner,' the whisper went round, and everyone gazed at this alien to their community. The man nodded and the manager, Mr Hill, walked towards the group by the gate. Halting, he cleared his throat before beginning the roll call of the dead. William Mason's name was halfway down the list.

'You get a good night's sleep, lass, and you'll feel better.'

'I'll try, Mrs Pendle.'

Molly closed the door after her neighbour and turned back to the empty house with a sigh of relief. She was grateful to Ann Pendle who'd done all she could for her in the days leading up to the mass funeral in Eden Hope Methodist Chapel, even gone to the inquest with her beforehand. (Accidental death, the coroner had said.) Ann had brought her broth afterwards which Molly had politely accepted but couldn't eat.

This was the first time she had been on her own since the disaster. It was very quiet, the only sound the ticking of the marble clock which stood on the high mantel over the crash mantel frill which Mam had embroidered before she died, three years ago now. Molly's thoughts touched on that and skimmed away. Not now, she wasn't going to think of that now. Rising from her chair by the fire, she picked up the rake and pulled small coals from the shelf at the back of the fire on to the flames, banking it as her father had always done before bed. She turned the mat away from the range just in case anything spat out, seeing in her mind's eye Dad doing it. She turned the key in the back door lock and climbed the stairs to bed.

'I'll not be able to sleep,' she said aloud, more to break the silence which was so profound she could almost hear it than anything else. Dad had been the noisy one, always whistling or humming something. 'Little Old Lady' or 'The Lambeth Walk' or that Fred Astaire song from *Top Hat*. He liked keeping the wireless on until last thing at night or until the accumulator batteries ran down and had to be taken to Eldon to be recharged. Except when he was on night shift. That was it. Molly would pretend he was just on night shift. Illogically she was comforted by that. Her restless, rambling thoughts shut off and she drifted into sleep.

There was a letter from the manager of Eden Hope Colliery when she came downstairs next morning. It had a crest on the envelope and on the top of the single sheet of paper the words *Hope Estates*, all curlicues and fancy lines.

Dear Miss Mason,

On behalf of the owners and management of Eden Hope Colliery, I wish to convey the Company's deepest sympathy for the loss of your father in the tragic accident which occurred last week.

The Company will pay in full any funeral expenses. As Mr Mason had no dependants, being a widower with grown-up children earning their own living, there will be no compensation payable according to law. However, the Company is prepared to offer you £25, without obligation, to help you with removal costs.

If you have any questions concerning the above, you may call at the colliery office at your convenience and I will endeavour to answer them.

Molly stared at the letter, uncomprehending. There was an unrecognisable scribble for signature. She felt no alarm but was dimly aware that she would have to do something about this. Go to see Mr Hill, that was it. She glanced at the clock. It was nine o'clock, she could go today, Friday. If she didn't she would have to put it off until Monday and she was going back to work then. She had to, they wouldn't keep her job open forever.

Glad of something positive to do, Molly put the letter down on the table. She stirred the fire and grey ash fell through to the box underneath. There was a hint of red so she added a few sticks from the box by the fire, raked cinders on top and a few good lumps of coal. Then she filled the kettle and put it on the gas ring.

Ten minutes later, sipping milkless tea, she picked the letter up again and read it through once more. Three hundred pounds was the usual compensation for a miner killed in the pit; she knew that, had heard the men discussing it. It had not occurred to her that she was no longer a dependant because she was working at the factory. And in the back of her mind she had known she would have to move, that the house would be wanted for a working miner, oh, yes, she'd known that. But she had put off facing the knowledge until after the funeral; hadn't been able to think beyond that.

The tea tasted acidic on her tongue, churned in her stomach. She would have to eat something, she thought, and found the heel of a loaf, buttered it and spread on blackcurrant jam. Methodically, she chewed and swallowed, chewed and swallowed. She was not angry or upset at the letter, just felt disconnected, as though it was happening to someone else.

She felt vaguely angry at Harry, her brother. He was three years older than she was and should have been here to see to things. But, no, he was in India. India! He probably didn't even know yet that Dad was gone. Though how could he, she hadn't written to him? She was being unfair, she knew it.

Sighing, Molly rose from the table and cleared away the breakfast things. She washed and dressed in her grey costume, the Sunday one, the only one she had really. There was nothing for it but to wear her old shoes, she hadn't got into West Auckland for last week's pay yet. She brushed her straight brown bobbed hair and clipped it over her right ear with the tortoiseshell slide which Mam had bought for her years ago when she was still at school. She didn't have another. As an afterthought she pulled on her velour hat with the brim and gazed in the mirror of the press. Did it make her look older? She decided it did. Picking up her handbag, imitation leather and cracked now but all she had, she went out of the door and down the yard, turning to where the black path led off, a shortcut to the pit used by generations of miners.

'It is the agreed policy of the Owners' Association,' said Mr Hill. 'I'm sorry, I'm afraid it is all I can do.' He looked away from the slight young girl sitting before his desk. She reminded him of his own daughter, away at the Friends' School in Great Ayton now, and the comparison made him slightly uncomfortable. The two girls were of an age. He dropped his eyes before Molly's direct gaze and walked to the window, staring out across the yard to the stack of new pit props just come from Norway.

'You have a brother in the army, don't you? Have you written to him yet?'

'He's in India,' said Molly. 'Won't have got the letter yet. In any case, he can hardly get back from there by next week, can he?'

The manager coughed, bit his lip, sought for a handkerchief in his trouser pocket and held it to his lips to conceal a momentary shame. But there was nothing he could do. He turned back to the desk.

'Take the cheque, my dear,' he said. His tone, which had been business-like up until then, sounded softer. 'I'm sure someone in the village will take you in. Or why don't you get a room closer to your place of employment? Think of the bus fare you would save.'

He meant to be kind, she knew. He had sounded almost fatherly. And Molly couldn't bear it suddenly. She jumped to her feet, picked up the cheque and stuffed it in her bag though she would rather have stuffed it down his throat.

'Don't worry about me, Mr Hill,' she said. 'I'll manage fine.'

'Got a plan, have you?' he asked, relief showing in his face. 'Oh, good, you –' He broke off as she turned on her heel and hurried to the door, banging it shut behind her. Oh, well, he thought, he certainly didn't need to worry about that little madam. That was all the thanks one got for trying to be kind.

Molly began to walk back along the path. Oh, Dad, she cried silently, what am I going to do? On impulse she cut off to the side and made her way to the cemetery, to the fresh-turned earth of the new graves. The flowers were already beginning to wilt, she saw, even the large wreath of white lilies which had come from the owners. Her own bunch of dahlias was lasting better, she thought, and bent to straighten a large sunshine yellow head. Dad had loved his garden, the dahlias were his pride and joy. He had grown these himself. She bent down and moved the bunch into a more prominent position, pushing the lily wreath to one side. There was going to be a big memorial one day, there was a subscription fund already.

'Dad?' she said tentatively. 'Mam?' For she was laid in this grave, too, though there was no headstone. It was something Dad had been going to do once he was back at work. 'As soon as we're back on our feet, pet.' Though, of course, that couldn't happen now.

After a minute or two Molly became aware that it had started to rain. She walked away, slowly at first then briskly, out of the cemetery and down the path to the houses. There was no sense in catching pneumonia on top of everything else. And besides she had work to do, a new life to arrange.

'Don't let the buggers get you down,' Dad was always saying, and by heck, she'd be blowed if she did.

Chapter Two

Harry marched smartly out of the Adjutant's office and stopped abruptly on the edge of the verandah. He stared out over the dusty parade ground, the officer's voice still echoing in his ears, though the words hadn't sunk in, not yet.

'It's ruddy hot,' he observed to no one in particular. Even though it was barely eight o'clock in the morning, the air shimmered with heat. The sky glared white above the roof of the barracks on the opposite side of the square. Suddenly Harry's shoulders slumped and he looked at the paper in his hand, an official communication from headquarters.

No matter how often he read the few typewritten words, they told him only the bare fact that Dad was dead, killed in the pit. He stared in front of him, seeing not the parade ground but the pithead buildings at Eden Hope; smelling not the heat and dust and multifarious smells of India but soot and engine oil and damp coal.

The day when he was thirteen and had first gone down in the cage with his dad returned vividly to Harry's mind. The steep drop, and the feeling of having left his stomach somewhere up there in the light. Then trembling dread as he had followed his dad to the coalface, ducking when his father said duck, too late once or twice so that he had banged his head on low-slung battens; a dread he had tried valiantly to hide because that day he was finally a man, a miner like his dad.

Not that he had worked in the pit for long. Six months after that day he had been laid off, never to go down the mine again as the depression of the thirties bit deep into the coalfield. He remembered the day he'd joined the army as a boy soldier at sixteen, along with Jackson Morley, his mate at school and his marra in the pit. At least it was employment and money in his pocket.

All those years Dad had fretted to get back down the pit. And now the pit had got him. Harry couldn't believe it. He wiped his brow with a khaki handkerchief, adjusted his hat and started out over the parade ground. He was halfway across it before he thought about young Molly. She was on her own now. God, and she was just a kid! There were no relatives left at home; his mother had been an orphan, and Gran, his father's mother, had died before Mam. Harry halted, thinking about going back in to see the Adjutant. He had to get home, he realised desperately.

Then he saw Jackson come to the door of the barracks, lifting his hand to shade his eyes as he looked over towards Harry. He'd talk it over with Jackson, the only one who would understand exactly because he came from Eden Hope too. There was still time before he had to go on guard duty at the main gate.

'Your old fella? No! Are you sure?'

Jackson Morley stopped buttoning his tunic and stared at Harry. Shocked, he thought of Bill Mason, his cheeky, lopsided grin so like Harry's and wavy black hair only just touched with grey. A man so full of life couldn't be dead, it had to be a mistake.

'Here, read it,' said Harry and thrust the piece of paper into Jackson's hand. He studied the few words written there. No ambiguity, no room for doubt. Bill Mason was gone, poor beggar.

'But what about Molly? What will she do?' Little Molly, only fifteen when they had left England. Bonny little Molly. Jackson was going to marry her when she grew up – that was what he'd always told her, jokingly of course.

'I'll have to try for home leave,' said Harry. 'The Company won't let her stay in the house on her own, there's nowt so sure.'

'No,' Jackson agreed. 'But she'll be taken in by somebody in Hope, you know she will. Folks'll rally round.'

'It's up to me, she's my sister,' said Harry. 'I must try to get home. I'm off to see the Adjutant again.'

'I'll walk over there with you.' Jackson bit his lip. 'Oh, man,' he said, 'I'm right sorry.'

'Aye.'

The Adjutant, Lieutenant Carey, was just coming out of the office.

'Private Morley,' he said, 'I was about to send for you.' He had a paper in his hand similar to the one he'd given Harry and Jackson's heart sank to his boots. He cast a quick glance at Harry.

'I'll wait here,' said his friend.

Five minutes later, Jackson came out of the office. 'Dad was injured,' he said, 'he's in hospital. Come on, I've asked to see the Colonel, we can ask for home leave together.'

They waited around the verandah for ten minutes before being summoned into the office only to be told that home leave was unlikely to be granted.

'I'm sorry, men,' said the Colonel, a dapper little man with steel-grey hair who, in spite of the heat, looked as though he had never sweated in his life. 'With the situation as it stands at the moment – well, you have my sympathy, I'm sure, especially you, Private Mason, for the loss of your father. But after all your sister is an adult, she is not dependent on you, is she?'

'She's sixteen, sir,' said Harry. 'And we have no other relatives.'

'Sixteen? Well, there you are. Earning her own living, I presume?'

'Yes, sir.' Despair ate into Harry. Outside a Sergeant-Major began to bark orders; there was the sound of marching feet. Harry opened his mouth to ask what the Colonel would do in his position but the habit of deferring to a superior officer was too strong. He merely stood to attention and stared straight ahead.

'Well then, request for compassionate leave denied.' The Colonel turned to Jackson. 'I hope your father recovers, Private Morley. However, your request is denied also, for the same reasons. You men have to realise these are troubled times. We have to be constantly on the alert. A number of our men have problems at home but this is the army. We must all do our duty.' He nodded a dismissal and the two men from Eden Hope marched smartly out of the office.

'I'll put in for a transfer to the Durham Light Infantry,' said Harry as they walked over the parade ground.

Jackson glanced at his friend; Harry's face was set, his eyes steely. 'We both will,' he agreed. 'I'm fairly sure war is coming, no matter what Chamberlain says. The Durhams will have us, I don't think the Colonel can stop that.'

'It's my bedroom, Mam, and I'm not sharing it! Especially not with that toffee-nosed Molly Mason. Let her find somewhere else to live.'

'But, Joan, in simple Christian charity . . . You know her mother was my friend.'

'Aye, well, Molly isn't mine and I want nothing to do with her. Or her good-for-nothing brother!'

'That's it, isn't it? It's because Harry jilted you?'

'He did not! I didn't want him!' shouted Joan. 'Don't you go saying he jilted me . . .'

Molly, just about to turn into the back gate of the Pendles' house, paused, clearly hearing the raised voices. She flushed, hesitated for a moment, backed away from the gate and leaned against the coalhouse wall. The sun shone brightly, low on the horizon this December day, blinding her. She closed her eyes tightly.

'Are you all right, pet?'

The concerned voice was that of old Tom Bailey who worked in the lamp cabin at the mine and lived in one of the older, single-storey cottages on the end of the rows.

Molly did her best to summon a smile. 'I'm fine, Tom,' she mumbled.

He leaned on his stick and gazed at her with faded but shrewd blue eyes.

'Aye, well, you don't look fine to me,' he pronounced. 'Still . . . I was right sorry about your dad, Molly. A grand man.' He coughed and she looked away quickly, her eyes filling. 'Aye,' he said and went on, his stick tap-tapping and his pit boots ringing on the cobbles.

'Pull yourself together!' Molly said fiercely, her words loud in the empty house. She had run back into her own kitchen and closed the door, wiped her eyes and blown her nose. She had to plan her next move. She could ask Mrs Morley, she supposed, but though Jackson was Harry's friend she didn't know his mother all that well. Mrs Morley was a woman who kept herself to herself. No doubt one of the other families would take her in but she couldn't offer much for her board, her usual wage was only 12/6 even with bonuses. Now the pit was working there were single miners coming in and they took up most of the spare rooms in the village. The mining folk had been poverty-stricken during the long slump and were struggling to pay back debts even now.

Taking a pencil and piece of paper from the press drawer, she wrote a 'room wanted' sign. She could ask the paper shop to put it in the window, she thought. In the end she left it lying on the table while she put on her coat and hat and, picking up her bag, went out for the bus into Bishop Auckland.

She met Mrs Pendle at the door. 'Look, Molly,' she said. 'Don't you think it would be a good idea to get a place near the factory? Think of the bus fare you'd save. The thing is, pet, I don't think I can take you in. I've thought about it and it's not fair to ask Joan to share her room . . .'

Mrs Pendle was the picture of embarrassment. Molly decided to take pity on her.

'Just what I was thinking myself,' she said. 'In fact, I'm going there now. Do you want anything brought from Bishop? I'll be going through.'

The relief showed on Ann Pendle's face. 'Eeh, no, I don't think so, ta, not today.' She put out a hand and laid it on

Molly's arm. 'I think you're doing the right thing, I really do. Get away . . . that's best.'

'Ta-ra,' said Molly, walking off for the bus. Ann Pendle looked after her as she strode purposefully up the street. Waiting at the bus stop at the end of the rows, she calmed the butterflies of panic in her stomach by counting the number of people who crossed over the street rather than walk by her, averting their faces, pretending they hadn't seen her.

Molly sighed. Oh, she knew they weren't unfeeling, the trouble was they were *too* feeling, just didn't know what to say to her. But most of them had been to the funeral, had paid their respects. The trouble was there were so many bereaved in Eden Hope just now, misery was all pervasive. They wanted to get back to normal. And everyone wasn't the same, she thought, remembering old Mr Bailey.

In Auckland the wind blew down Newgate Street, built on the line of the old Roman road and providing no corners for shelter. In Hardisty's, the greengrocer's and florist's, there was a Christmas tree in the window, strung with coloured lanterns and tinsel. Christmas? When was that? she thought vaguely. Not that it mattered. Christmas was nothing to her now.

Lockey's bus for West Auckland and St Helen's Auckland was standing waiting, only a few passengers already aboard. Molly sat at the back on her own and stared fixedly at her hands so that no one getting on the bus could catch her eye and talk to her.

'Where are you going, love?' asked the conductor after waiting patiently for her to look up.

'Oh, St Helen's.'

'Tuppence ha'penny return.'

He took a ticket from his board and handed it to her, and went off whistling to the front of the bus. Molly looked out of the window, seeing nothing until the line of new factories came into view, built on the site of an old colliery. The bus stopped right beside the clothing factory. She got off and walked in.

'I'm afraid you'll have to wait, the wages aren't made up until four,' said the girl behind the desk. She looked uncomfortable. Of course she had heard about the disaster and Bill Mason being one of the dead. Molly felt like telling her not to worry, she was fine, everything was fine. And everything would have been if it wasn't for the leaden feeling somewhere inside her.

'I'll come back,' she said instead, and went to look in the newsagent's window to see if there were any single rooms to let at a price she could afford. Or even some live-in digs, with a family.

The newsagent's was closed for dinner, which surprised Molly, she hadn't realised it was after twelve. But there were cards in the window. She took her indelible pencil out of her bag and jotted addresses down on the back of the envelope she had received from the mine manager. Peering through the window, she saw it was twelve-twenty-five. She didn't have a watch, that was what her dad had been going to get her for Christmas, he'd promised her.

Molly walked along to the fish and chip shop. She should eat, she told herself. But the line of girls from the factory made her shrink inside herself and the smell of the grease took away any appetite she had. Instead she turned and walked down a side street.

Adelaide Street – that was the first address on the envelope. It was cheap too, only 8/6 a week, and she'd have no bus fares to pay. Cheaper than any of the others. When Molly saw the house she was heartened. The lace at the windows was clean and white and the front door step scrubbed and sand-stoned. She lifted a hand to the shining brass knocker. The door was opened by a girl who looked to be about twelve, wearing a green gym slip and cream-coloured blouse and over them a pinafore that was much too big for her. Her hair was tied back severely with a length of green tape.

She stared at Molly through thick-lensed glasses with large, nervous eyes.

'What do you want?' she asked baldly.

'I've come about the room,' said Molly, and smiled to show she was friendly and harmless.

'My dad's at work,' said the girl. 'And I have to go back to school in ten minutes.'

'Well, can I come in? When does your dad get in from work? Where's your mother?'

'I haven't got a mother and Dad doesn't get in until four o'clock.'

Molly looked at her and after a moment the girl opened the door wide, revealing a passage with brown linoleum polished to a gleaming finish. There was even a length of carpet in the middle and a side table. Oh, yes, Molly liked the look of this house.

'I'll leave my name, shall I? I can come later. Four o'clock, did you say?'

The girl looked even more nervous and glanced about her hesitantly. 'Er, I haven't got a pencil,' she murmured.

'I have, I've got one here,' said Molly. Taking charge, she walked past the girl and wrote her name swiftly on a piece of paper torn from the envelope, laying it on the table. She looked around her. The door to the living room was open, there was a smell of beeswax. 'I'll be back tonight,' she said. 'By the way, what's your name?'

'Betty. Betty Jones.'

'I'll see you later, Betty.'

By, thought Molly as she walked off, that girl's as timid as a mouse. But she felt some fellow feeling with the poor kid. After all, she hadn't been much older when she had lost her own mother.

The line outside the fish shop had disappeared, the factory only allowed thirty minutes for dinner. Molly went in and bought a penny bag of chips and walked along to where the Gaunless stream ran alongside the road. She sat on a low wall by the water and ate the chips. Already she was feeling slightly better. With luck she would get the lodgings at a shilling or two less than she had expected to pay. Nice, clean lodgings an' all.

Chapter Three

'I'll be back at work on Monday, I promise, Mr Bolton,' said Molly.

'Yes, well,' he answered, standing up to show that the interview was ended, 'I hope you are. You understand I have every sympathy with your position, my dear, but I can't keep your place open any longer. We have a lot of orders to fill and there is a national emergency.'

'Yes, Mr Bolton.'

Molly left the factory, her wage packet safely tucked away in her bag. He hadn't *looked* very sympathetic, she thought to herself, but as though he wanted rid of her so that he could get on with his work. She took deep breaths of the clean cold air as she walked out side. The atmosphere in the office had been hot and stuffy despite the winter weather.

She would have liked to have told Mr Bolton where to put his job, she thought rebelliously. She'd had every intention of starting on Monday anyway but he'd implied, by his tone at least, that she was slacking, the tone of a manager who knew there were plenty more where she came from. But Molly's innate caution had stopped her from rising to the bait. During the long depression she had seen what being out of work did to people. Too many friends and neighbours had been broken by it.

Molly turned her collar up against the bitter wind and walked over the road towards the streets on the other side. She would pass the time until four by looking at the other houses with rooms to let.

It was half-past four when she stood once more outside the door of number 44 Adelaide Street and knocked. Her feet ached and her stomach felt empty, reminding her that a bag of chips was all she had eaten since breakfast. This time the door was opened by a thin little man in a suit, his meagre hair smoothed flat against his skull and shining with Brylcreem.

'Good afternoon,' Molly began, 'I've come about the room, I–'

'Aye, I know, our Betty told me a lass had been looking. Come on in then,' the man said impatiently. 'Don't stand there on the step for all the neighbours to gawp at. I won't have them gossiping about me and my doings.'

A bit surprised, Molly glanced about. The street was deserted, not a soul in sight, but she stepped inside the passageway obediently. He opened a door to the left and went in, motioning her to follow. There was electric light. When he switched it on the harsh glare showed her a square room with an empty grate, a brown leather three-piece suite shining with polish, and a sideboard with nothing on it except for a picture of him with a woman holding a bouquet of flowers. The Joneses' wedding picture she presumed. There was a faint smell of damp; obviously the room was not lived in.

'Sit down, sit down,' he said, and Molly sat on the edge of the sofa, knees together, handbag clutched nervously in her hands. I've nothing to be nervous about, she told herself firmly and lifted her chin. Mr Jones took up a stance, legs apart, hands on hips, before the fireless grate and stared at her over the top of rimless spectacles.

'Now then, young lady,' he said, rather in the tone her old headmistress had used when confronting a recalcitrant pupil. 'I haven't much time, my tea's nearly ready. You want to rent the room, do you?'

'Yes, please,' said Molly, though she was beginning to wonder if she did. But only one of the other houses on her list had been as clean as this one and it had been 1/6 extra per week.

'It's 8/6 a week, including breakfast but not including evening meal. You can use the kitchen to cook your own food for that. But mind, I won't have anything which stinks the house out. Let's say between five and six? We'll leave you to it for that hour.'

'That will be all right,' said Molly, perking up a little. She hadn't realised the price included breakfast. Perhaps if she ate a good breakfast she wouldn't need much during the day. His next words disillusioned her on that score.

'I'll leave bread and margarine and jam out for you before I go to work. I leave the house at six o'clock every morning. Now, I suppose you want to see your room?' He was already leading the way out of the sitting room. Molly got to her feet and followed him meekly up the stairs.

It was quite a large bedroom at the back of the house. A single bed stood in solitary splendour in the middle of an expanse of highly polished linoleum. It was covered with a white cotton bedspread. But there was a dressing table in the corner with a plain wooden chair in front of it, and in the corner a cupboard. Mr Jones opened the cupboard door and showed Molly a row of hooks with a shelf above. 'You can put your things in here,' he said, and turned and stared fiercely at her. 'I can't abide slovens,' he snapped. 'I won't have things laid about, do you understand?' Without waiting for an answer he went on, 'That'll be two weeks in advance, you can move in when you like. Seventeen shillings, please.'

'Is there a fire?'

He looked affronted. 'If you must have a fire, you'll have to find your own coal. I don't hold with fires in bedrooms. I can't have you using electric either, I'm not made of money. It's a coal fire or nothing. An' you'll have to see to getting the chimney swept yourself an' all.'

Molly hesitated. She looked about her. There were floral curtains at the window and a tiny cast-iron fireplace with a paper fan in the grate. But there was a key in the lock; she could shut herself in at least. She wouldn't have to see a lot of Mr Jones. And if she hated it she could always move out. 'I'll take it,' she said, and fumbled in her bag for her purse. 'I'll be back with my stuff on Sunday, I have to work Monday.'

'I won't have the place cluttered up, mind,' he warned. 'And I don't know about Sunday. Me and Betty go to Chapel on Sunday, ten o'clock service. Are you Chapel?'

'I'll be bringing just a few things,' Molly insisted, thinking that for two pins she would tell him what to do with his room. 'I will be cleaning it after all. And since you ask, yes, I'm Chapel.' Not that she'd been to service much since Dad died, she thought dismally.

'Aye, well. Just mind what I've told you,' said Mr Jones, and marched off down the stairs leaving her to follow.

Molly caught the bus back to Eden Hope, it came along just as she approached the stop. She sat staring out of the window, wondering if she had done the right thing. Maybe not, she thought, chewing on the corner of a thumb nail. As she had walked down the stairs in Adelaide Street the door to the kitchen was open. She had smelled boiled cabbage and over-done meat.

'Haven't I told you to keep this door shut, you gormless fool? The place will stink of food,' she'd heard Mr Jones snap as he banged the door to behind him. She thought she'd heard a muffled cry too but was letting herself out of the house by then.

Molly caught sight of her reflection in the darkened window of the bus and put her hand down on her lap. It was years since she'd chewed her thumb, Mam had always been telling her off about it. Suddenly she felt such an intense desire for her mother, her father, Harry, any of them, that it cut into her like a knife. She blinked, blew her nose, and stared fixedly out of the window. The bus had just stopped. Shildon, she thought, it's Shildon. She forced herself to think of that. Home of the railways, most of the men hereabouts worked in the wagon works. There were Christmas lights in the windows of some of the shops, shining out on to the pavement. What was she going to do to celebrate Christmas? Suddenly she dreaded the thought of it. Her first Christmas on her own. Oh, Harry, where are you? she thought sadly.

'Fares, please.'

The conductor had to say it twice before it registered with Molly.

'Sorry. Return to Eden Hope Colliery,' she said. The bell on his ticket machine tinkled. She put the ticket in her bag, alongside the return ticket she had got on the bus from Bishop that morning. Oh, well, she would use both of them up, she supposed. But there was a frighteningly small amount of money left in her purse, she would have to dip into her £25 soon. And she couldn't afford to do that too often.

Ann Pendle looked up at Molly, arrested by the sudden look of desolation which had crossed the young girl's face. 'You do understand, don't you, Molly?' she asked yet again. Ann felt guilty. She knew she should have made more of an effort to get her family to accept the girl, at least for a while. For the sake of Molly's mother at least. But it was Joan . . . she had loved Harry Mason since she was a tiny girl. Her face had always lit up when she saw him. If he had smiled at her, talked to her, she had been in seventh heaven. Ann had felt her daughter's pain when Harry had jilted her. She'd tried to comfort her but Joan would not be consoled. Harry had tried to let her down lightly, told her that she wouldn't want to be tied to him when he was going away for years perhaps. But she couldn't forgive or forget.

Well, I have my own family to think of first, Ann told herself.

'You'll be all right in West Auckland? You've got nice clean digs, haven't you?' she asked for the third time.

'I'll be fine,' said Molly. Her mind was on other things, like the brass poker stand in the form of a prancing horse which had been displayed on the hearth ever since she could remember. And the marble clock, a wedding present from her grandparents to her parents. She touched it with her fingers. The marble was smooth and cool. It ticked away as loudly as it had done ever since she could remember.

'Granma took out a Universal club for it, two an' six a week it cost her,' Mam used to say. She had loved that clock. Maybe Molly should take it with her to West Auckland. She tried to visualise it on the meagre mantelpiece in the room in Adelaide Street but her imagination failed her. Still, she would take it, she couldn't just let it go. It was part of her life.

'The flat cart's here,' Ann announced. By the gate the horse snorted, nodding its head up and down with a jangling of brasses. The second-hand dealer from Shildon had arrived.

Molly had a kind of numb feeling as she stood by the window and watched him carry things out to the cart. Her dad's wooden-ended bed with the rose carved in the middle of the head. Harry's cheap black iron bedstead and her own. The bundles of bedclothes, the press, a chest of drawers. Even the best of the clippy mats. She been given £11 for the lot. Well, it could keep her for a month and buy a pair of winter shoes, at least.

Ann Pendle tied a knot in the string round the box of kitchen bits and pieces and stood back as Mr Robson, the second-hand dealer, came to the door.

'Everything's ready,' she said.

'Righto. I'll get loaded.'

Mr Robson glanced at Molly's white, set face and looked away again. He felt sorry for the lass but business was business. He went through these scenes almost every day and couldn't be constantly thinking of the tragedies which usually went before.

'I'll give you a hand,' said Ann, and picked up a box. It didn't take long to load the cart and Molly stood watching as her home was dismantled around her.

'Where's the marble clock?'

She started at Mr Robson's question. 'I'm not selling the clock, I'm keeping it,' she replied firmly. 'I told you I wasn't selling the clock.' Her heart beat wildly. For a minute she thought he would insist on taking it. He couldn't, could he?

Mr Robson pursed his lips, opened his mouth to say something then thought better of it and nodded acquiescence. Taking a wallet out of his inside pocket, he counted out £10, hesitating as he considered deducting £1 at least for the clock. But he didn't. He added the £1 to the pile of notes on the table, reckoning he must be going soft in the head.

The house seemed strange, empty as it was but for the few things Molly was taking with her. Ann Pendle looked around at the patch of unfaded wallpaper which had been behind the press. She had forgotten that the roses on it had once been that particular shade of pink, the trailing ivy so darkly green. She took Molly by the arm.

'Howay, pet,' she said, 'you're coming round to us for a bite of dinner.' She couldn't let the lass go off without her Sunday dinner. After all, Joan was out today, off visiting her aunt, so couldn't object.

Chapter Four

'Only six more shopping days to Christmas,' the voice on the wireless boomed out between records. Enid Parker, walking down the line handing out fresh batches of dress parts to be sewn, grinned.

'To tell you the truth, I could do all my shopping in one go on Saturday. All I need is the money, I'd soon make the time,' she said.

There was a murmur of agreement from the girls on the line. Molly bent her head over her machine, slickly slipping the seam to be sewn under the needle, throwing the two pieces into the box beside her and picking up yet another two pieces of navy blue rayon cloth.

Shopping? she thought. She hadn't even thought about shopping. But then what shopping did she have to do? There was no one but Harry to buy for. Harry! With a sense of shock she realised she hadn't sent him a Christmas present, nor even a card. He wouldn't get it now. Usually she sent one weeks before Christmas. Still she would go into the town tomorrow and get something, send it at the main post office.

Her fingers busy as ever as she bent over her work, Molly's mind wandered off on to thoughts of her brother and his friend Jackson. Where were they? Why hadn't she had a letter since Dad died? Irrational though it was, as well she knew, she felt resentful that he wasn't here but at the other side of the world. He should come home, really he should.

The air was filled with the tinny sound of the wireless, the volume turned up. Christmas carols resounded off the walls, the girls singing along with them. Only the bright and brisk carols, of course, it wouldn't do to have slow, melodic ones. The BBC was well aware that bright and breezy music was needed in factories to push production levels as high as possible. The threat of war had ended the depression, there was leeway to make up.

The threat of war . . . People said that Chamberlain had ended that with the Munich Agreement but the fear still lurked. Molly shivered, she didn't want to think of it. Harry was a soldier. If there was a war . . . Her thoughts stopped there, she couldn't bear to go on.

Luckily the whistle blew just then, the wireless was switched off, the power to the machines stopped and the room was suddenly silent but for the chatter of the girls as they rose from their machines in relief, stretched, picked up bags and tin boxes holding sandwiches and walked out to the canteen or over the road to the fish shop.

One or two of them smiled uncertainly at Molly as they passed, still uncomfortable with someone who had been so savagely bereaved. Joan Pendle, though, didn't even look her way as she went out, surrounded by her cronies. Joan knew how to keep people about her. She was a pretty girl with fair hair and blue eyes, and a curvaceous figure with big breasts she liked to show off under tight sweaters.

Molly wanted to ask her what the people were like who had got the Masons' old house. Was it a big family or just a young couple? Did they look after the place? Was the man a gardener and would he keep the long narrow strip of garden trim? Dad had been a gardener. He'd loved his flowers, had a special trench where he grew his prize leeks, winning a prize for them at the club last year. But of course she couldn't ask. Sighing, Molly picked up her bag and followed the rest of the girls out of the room.

She didn't go into the canteen. That was one blessing of living in St Helen's Auckland, she only had to cross the road and walk along to Adelaide Street to be back in her lodgings. She saved money there. Mr Jones was always out at work during the day and Betty didn't mind her boiling the kettle for tea. In fact, Betty was usually glad of a cup herself, so long as the spoonful of leaves came from Molly's caddy. Mr Jones kept a strict watch on his own.

Over the days since Molly had come to Adelaide Street, she and Betty had become quite friendly, though the girl was still reserved and quiet. Today they sat at the kitchen table eating fish paste sandwiches. Molly finished hers and picked up her cup, holding it with both hands and leaning her elbows on the table. She was grateful for the warmth of the cup as it seeped into her chilly fingers and sipped at it slowly. Ten minutes before she had to go back to work. Her thoughts strayed back to Harry, wondering what she could get for fifteen shillings including the cost of postage to India. Not much, she suspected.

'By, it's cold today,' Betty volunteered suddenly, and Molly forgot about the problem of Harry's present as she looked properly at her companion for the first time. With a shock she realised that the girl was pale – well, she was always pale but now she was even more so. Yet even as Molly gazed at her a pink flush began to suffuse her cheeks. It wasn't a healthy flush, though, Betty looked decidedly feverish. There were shadows under her eyes and her hand trembled as she held the cup. The sandwich on her plate had only one bite taken from it.

'You look poorly,' said Molly in concern, berating herself for not noticing as soon as she came in.

'I'm all right. Just a bit of a cold, I think. Any road, I have to go back to school,' the girl replied, and started to stand up before sitting back down abruptly. Her eyes had a glazed look about them.

'I don't think you should,' said Molly. All of her attention was focussed on Betty now. She looked really ill, shivering uncontrollably. The girl tried picking up her cup but tea slopped into her saucer and she put it down again.

'I'm bad,' she admitted. 'I have to go to school, though, what would me dad say if I stayed at home?'

'He would likely tell you you'd done the best thing,' said Molly firmly. 'Look at you, you're not fit to go out.'

'He'll play war with me if I don't go to school,' whispered Betty. 'I have to go.'

'No, don't —' said Molly, but she was too late. Betty had stood up again and promptly fallen to the floor. Molly rushed around the table, her heart beating rapidly in alarm. She bent over the girl, put her arm under her shoulders, patted her cheek. 'Betty!' she cried. 'Oh, please, God! Please, make her wake up!'

Betty moaned and opened her eyes and Molly breathed a prayer of relief. The linoleum was icy. She had to get the girl upstairs into bed, there wasn't a fire on in the house. Mr Jones believed it was a waste of money during the day when there was no one in.

Molly bit her lip as she sat on the floor, supporting Betty's limp form. She had had a fire in her room the night before, just a small one, perhaps there was still some lingering warmth. If only she could get Betty up the stairs.

'Come on, pet, let's have you,' she said. 'You must help me, I've got to get you into bed.'

'Dad says it's pure laziness to . . .' Betty began but Molly interrupted her.

'Never mind what your dad says, he's not here now,' she cried, exasperated. 'Do you think you can walk upstairs if you lean on me? I promise I won't let you fall.'

'I'll try.'

It was a struggle, Betty twice faltering and clinging to Molly, almost bringing them both tumbling down the stairs. But eventually they were on the landing. Betty turned towards the tiny boxroom which was her bedroom but Molly stopped her.

'No, I think you'll be better in my bed,' she said. 'It's warmer there.' By this time Betty was past arguing. She allowed herself to be led into the warmer room and put to bed.

'Thank you,' she murmured, lying back on the pillow, her eyes closed and face as white as the pillowcase once again. She was shivering uncontrollably by now. Molly gazed at her and bit her lip. She had to get back to work, couldn't afford to take the afternoon off which would mean she'd have to break into Harry's Christmas box money to pay her rent.

'How do you feel now?' she asked, and Betty opened her eyes briefly, attempted a smile.

'Warmer.'

'I'll get the doctor,' Molly said, but Betty became agitated. Her eyes flew open in alarm.

'No!' she cried and her breathing became laboured until she was gasping for breath. 'No, me dad will have a fit if you do,' she managed to say.

'All right, all right, I won't,' Molly said hastily. 'Don't get upset, it's bad for you. Lie quiet, man, will you? I'll get you a hot water bottle. I think you've got the 'flu, though.'

She rushed downstairs and found an ancient stone hot water bottle under the sink, heated water and filled it. Upstairs once again, she wrapped it in her own woollen scarf and put it at Betty's feet.

The girl was quieter now, her breathing seemed easier, she was dropping off to sleep. Maybe she would sleep herself better, thought Molly. She went to the fireplace and, using her own precious store of coal, lit the fire. Oh, to think that she should actually have to count lumps of coal! It was the only thing they'd always had enough of in Eden Hope; the miners' coal allowance had been delivered every third week there. Heaps had been dumped on the pavements outside the back gates, a familiar sight, waiting to be shovelled into coal houses. She pictured it in her mind – the street winding upwards, stepping out carefully into the road to avoid the coal – and wept inside. The emotion took her by surprise. What a thing to be nostalgic about!

Molly blinked rapidly, closing her mind against the memory. She looked at the meagre fire she had built, sighed and added another small shovelful of coal. So she would have to do without a fire for the rest of the week. Well, it wouldn't hurt her, *she* was healthy enough.

Molly looked at the marble clock, perched slightly

precariously on the narrow mantelshelf above the fire. It was one o'clock already, the line would be starting up in the factory soon. She went back to the bed. Betty was sleeping. Maybe Molly could just go back to work. After all, Betty's father would be home in three hours, wouldn't he? She felt the girl's forehead, which was hot and dry, tried to feel for a pulse but couldn't remember where to find it.

Betty moved, turned over on to her side, seemed to settle into an easier sleep. Molly decided to go back to work. The girl would probably sleep for hours, sleep herself better. She tip-toed to the door and down the stairs and let herself out of the house.

At three o'clock she was back. She hadn't been able to concentrate on the work at all, had actually spoilt two pieces and Enid had been very annoyed, even when Molly had told her the reason.

'You'd best go back then and make sure the lass is all right,' the charge hand had finally said. 'Mind, Mr Bolton will dock the time off your wages. He might fine you for these pieces an' all. I don't know, Molly Mason, if you're going to take on the woes of all and sundry and let them affect your work, you're not going to be much good to anyone, are you?'

'No, you're right,' she had agreed humbly. 'I wouldn't normally, but she's only thirteen and in the house on her own, she's got no mother.'

'Away with you then, if you have to,' Enid had said, her voice edged with bad temper, and Molly had left while the going was good.

It was very quiet as she let herself into the house. Betty must be asleep, she thought, and took off her shoes before climbing the stairs though the cold from the thin cotton carpet seeped straight through her lisle stockings and her toes curled against it.

'Betty?' she murmured from the doorway. There was no movement from the bed. The fire was nearly out, the room chilly. Molly moved quietly to the grate, tried to poke the flames to life with as little noise as possible. Ash fell with a plop into the box beneath, a small plume of smoke rose. She added a couple of sticks, blew on the ashes until the sticks crackled then put on a couple of lumps of coal.

Tip-toeing to the bed, Molly looked down at the still figure. 'Betty?' she said. Then louder, 'Betty?'

Oh, God! Betty was so white and still, her eyes not properly closed. She looked as though she wasn't breathing. She had pushed back the eiderdown which Molly had brought from Eden Hope. Molly put a hand on her shoulder, her bare arm. Don't let her be dead, she prayed. There was some slight warmth there, of course there was. Betty couldn't really be dead. By heck, I'm getting morbid, Molly berated herself, and pulled the eiderdown up around the girl's neck, tucking it in. She patted her cheek. 'Betty!' she cried, loudly now. 'Betty!' And she stirred, opened her eyes, tried to sit up.

Molly was weak with relief. 'Oh, Betty, you scared me half to death,' she said, laughing almost.

'My throat hurts,' whispered Betty.

'Wait, I'll get you a hot drink,' said Molly, and ran downstairs to the kitchen. She put on the kettle and rummaged in the press for Ovaltine, cocoa, anything.

'What do you think you're doing, young woman?'

Molly hadn't heard the door opening and was startled when the angry voice spoke right behind her so that she almost dropped the packet of cocoa she was reaching for.

'Oh, I'm so pleased to see you —' she began as relief flooded through her.

'Aye, I bet you are. I caught you nicely, didn't I?' Mr Jones was angry. His narrow nose quivered pinkly, his lips were moist with spittle. 'Going through my press, eh? I suppose you've already been through all the drawers. Well, you can just pack your things–'

'Shut up! Just shut your flaming mouth!' Molly shouted, all the worry and agitation of the past few hours finding release in fury. 'Do you think I want your measly groceries? You're nothing but a mean old . . .' She bit off the rest of the sentence, forcing herself to calm down as her eye fell on the cocoa and she remembered Betty.

'Don't you speak to me like that,' Mr Jones began, but Molly broke in, her voice quieter.

'Betty's poorly. I think she needs the doctor.'

'What, Betty is? She's never bad. If this is just some excuse, I'll soon find out.'

'It's no excuse. She's in my bed upstairs. I put her there because it's warmer. This house feels like an igloo.'

'We'll see about that! A daughter of mine in bed during the day . . .'

Molly watched in disbelief as he marched up the stairs with the air of a teacher about to sort out a recalcitrant pupil. The kettle boiled and she made the cocoa, adding milk and two spoonfuls of sugar from her own supply. Putting on her shoes, she followed him up to her room.

He was standing by the bed, looking stricken. Molly glanced at him and went round the other side with the cocoa, putting it down on the night table. Betty was lying with her eyes closed, her mouth slightly open, breathing fast in shallow breaths which barely raised the covers. She was unconscious.

'I'll get the doctor,' Molly said.

'No, I'll go. You look after her, will you?'

The man's manner had changed completely. He seemed to have shrunk, gazing at Molly in appeal before turning and running for the door. She heard the front door bang and then there was silence but for the laboured breathing coming from the unconscious girl in the bed.

Chapter Five

'National Emergency!' said Harry, his voice full of disgust. He sat on his hunkers in the typical miner's resting position in the poor shade of a sparse bush. 'Isn't that just like the army? There could be a war in Europe any day and the powers that be think we should stay in India playing war games because of the National Emergency!'

Jackson leaned back against a dusty rock, his long legs stretched out in front of him, his helmet tipped slightly forward to shade his eyes from the ever-present and pitiless glare of the sun. He grinned but there was no real amusement in his face.

'And wouldn't you think they would have had the two best soldiers in the entire British Army back there ready to defend old Blighty to the death? That would frighten old Hitler to death, wouldn't it? He'd think twice before–'

'Aw, shut up, Jackson, this is nowt to laugh at. What about our Molly? Poor lass, in that house all by herself. Why, man, she's just a kid, isn't she?'

'I'm far from laughing, Harry. I just don't know what we can do about it apart from what I've already done. We can't just desert. How the hell would we get back anyway if we did? I've asked my mam and dad to keep an eye on her. I'm sure we'll be going home soon at any rate.'

Jackson stared grimly out at the dusty road, flanked with rocky outcrops. The platoon was strung out along it, taking what shade they could from the rocks as they ate their hard biscuit and bully beef, drank sparingly from their water bottles. There would be no more water until they got back to camp in six hours' time, five if they were lucky.

'Let's have another look at that letter, lad,' he said, and Harry rummaged in his top pocket and pulled out the well-thumbed sheets of cheap ruled paper. Jackson read it through, though he practically knew it by heart. Mind, she was a plucky one was Molly, he thought. This had been written very soon after her father's death; the pain of her loss was clear to see in every sentence and yet she had tried to soften the blow for Harry. She'd written it must have been instantaneous, their dad hadn't suffered, though the writing wavered a bit here. She'd asked if Harry could come home, but told him not to worry if he couldn't.

'I can manage fine, you know, I'm working at the clothing factory now, Mrs Pendle is very good too.'

There was a round water mark right at the bottom of the page, though. Jackson fingered it. It had to be made by a teardrop.

'I asked Mam to write back and tell me how she's getting on,' he said as he folded the sheets up carefully and handed them back to Harry. Jackson chewed on his bottom lip. 'We won't be long, you know, they will be sending us back,' he went on as he rose to his feet, lifted his helmet and wiped his brow before settling it firmly back on his head.

'Right then, you lot,' he called along the line of men. 'Let's be having you. We have to make camp before dark.' Jackson had only recently been promoted to corporal and Harry to lance-corporal. There were a few muttered grumbles which the men considered obligatory but they got to their feet readily enough and the column set off down the dusty track.

There was post in from England when they finally arrived at the gates, just as the sun sank beyond the hills in the distance and dark descended with startling suddenness. Nothing for Harry but a letter from Mrs Morley, Jackson's mother. He skimmed through it then handed a page to Harry.

. . . Molly Mason, poor lass, you were asking about her. She had to get out of the colliery house, you know. The pit's working full strength and it was wanted, the gaffer said. He's a hard manager that one. Any road, as to Molly, I can't keep an eye on her because she's left Eden Hope. According to Ann Pendle, she's got a room over West Auckland way, near the clothing factory.

I would have taken her in, I would, Jackson, but with your dad the way he was after the accident I didn't realise till she'd gone. But likely she'll be better off not having to take the bus to work and no doubt she'll be sending word to Harry. Ann Pendle had a Christmas card from her . . .

Harry handed the page back to his friend, saying nothing, thinking that this was the first time Molly hadn't sent him a card and a present in time for Christmas.

'She'll be all right, I know she will. Right as rain once she gets over the first few weeks,' said Jackson, and Harry nodded.

But later, as Jackson collected his soap and towel and headed for the showers, he wondered about Molly. What sort of a Christmas had she had? Lonely, he dared to bet. She was a lovely lass but didn't make friends easily. She was quiet, reserved, had been since the death of her mother. Surely they would get their orders to go back to Blighty soon? He had lied when he'd told Harry he thought Molly would be fine. In fact, he felt anxious about her.

A strange sort of Christmas, Molly thought as she stood at the window of her bedroom and gazed out over the street. The familiar feeling of unhappiness was lodged in her chest. 1939. She hoped it would be a better year than 1938 had been for her but somehow she didn't feel very optimistic.

At least the holiday was over. Like Christmas, the celebrations had been subdued this year. She looked over to where her gas mask lay in its cardboard box on the bed beside her sewing basket. She was making a waterproof cover for it out of an old macintosh. It had been half-finished since Dad had died, now she was getting on with it at last. She drew the curtains across the window and went over to the bed. Picking up her needle, she threaded it and began to sew.

She had stayed in her room over Christmas, apart from Chapel on Christmas morning. But the congregation was strange to her; only a few people and the minister had spoken to her, wished her a Merry Christmas. She had come home afterwards and locked herself in her room, putting on the wireless which she had brought from Eden Hope quietly, not wanting to disturb Mr Jones.

Her needle faltered. If only Betty were still here they might have been friends. But she had gone into hospital with pneumonia and not come back. Instead she had been sent to the sanatorium high in Weardale. A shadow on the lungs, the doctor had diagnosed. It had come to light in the hospital and a good thing too, he'd said. He had said a lot of other things, such as the girl was too thin, almost undernourished, it was a miracle she had survived pneumonia. She was still very ill. Even if Molly could have afforded the fare, Betty wasn't allowed visitors.

Molly sighed and decided to play some music now, patiently twiddling the knobs on her radio until the crackling subsided and the sound of a dance band came out. They were playing a Noël Coward tune. What was it called? But there was a knocking at the door, loud over the music. She went to it but didn't open it. Somehow she disliked being in the house alone with Mr Jones now Betty was away, always felt uncomfortable.

'Yes? What is it?'

'Turn that damn' thing off, will you? I'm off to my bed and I want to sleep, not listen to that racket all night!'

'Righto. Sorry, Mr Jones.'

Molly switched off the wireless and stood for a minute, curling her bare toes against the cold linoleum. She might as well go to bed too, she thought, and began tidying away the sewing things. The fire was almost out anyway and she couldn't afford to use any more coal.

In bed she picked up her library book from the night table

and opened it. It was a Sherlock Holmes mystery. She would finish it and then be able to change it tomorrow. The branch library at West Auckland only opened three days a week.

She was on the last chapter when the knocking came again. Startled, she jumped out of bed and pulled the coverlet round her.

'What is it?'

'Put that light out, do you think I'm made of money? The electric's dear enough without wasting it. Any decent lass should be asleep by now any road.'

Molly sighed. 'Righto. Sorry, Mr Jones.' Snuggling back under the bedclothes in the dark, she began to think about looking for different lodgings. Mr Jones wasn't human, she thought. What a rotten life Betty must have had living here alone with him. She was probably better off in the sanatorium. At least she wouldn't have her father carping on at her all the time. And once she felt better, of course, Molly reminded herself with a prick of conscience.

Over the next week or two there was a subtle change in Mr Jones's attitude. Molly was spending quite a lot of her dinner hours looking about for a new place. There were several rooms to rent but all of them were beyond her purse and she was beginning to despair of ever getting away from Adelaide Street. She even thought of going back to Eden Hope to see Mrs Morley and begging Jackson's mother to take her in, if only on a temporary basis. (Oh, why wasn't there a letter from India?)

She picked up the small photograph of Harry and Jackson, replendent in their new uniforms, arms round each other's shoulders, both smiling out at her with well-remembered cheeky grins. It had been her Christmas present to herself, having the photograph framed. It had been taken by Taylor's, the photographer's in Bishop Auckland, not long before the two men sailed for India.

Molly smiled at it, touched each tiny black and white face with her finger tip. They had always been together like that, the two lads, all through school and starting work together down the pit. The grins were wiped off their faces on the day they were both turned off in the depression. Molly had ached for their despair that day, hoped with them every time they went after jobs, shared their disappointment when work failed to materialise. Cried when they decided to go into the army as boy soldiers.

Molly put the photograph back on the mantelshelf. Dear Lord, she was getting maudlin. She glanced at the marble clock. Five o'clock. It was time to go downstairs and start her meal, Mr Jones should be out of the kitchen by now.

But was not. He was hovering around the sink, doing something with the tap.

'Oh, you're not finished, Mr Jones. I'll come back,' said Molly.

'No, no, lass, come on in, I'm just putting a washer on this dripping tap. But I filled the kettle for you before I turned off the water.'

'Oh . . . er, thanks.' Molly was surprised at this consideration. Even more so when he turned to her, a spanner in his hand, and took a step or two forward.

'Why don't you call me Bart? Here we are, living in this house together, just the two of us. Mr Jones is a bit formal, isn't it?' His smile was unctuous.

'Er . . . yes,' she mumbled, and turned her back to rummage in the cupboard where she kept her few groceries. What was he up to? She felt decidedly uncomfortable now, her face burning as she moved a packet of dried peas aside, looking for the tin of beans which she had decided to have on toast. There it was, she had been looking at it all the time. Grabbing it, feeling all fingers and thumbs with embarrassment, she nearly dropped it as she looked round and found he was still standing by the sink, watching her. She looked down at the tin, pretending to read the label.

'I'll take this up to my room, I can easily make toast by the fire up there.'

The half smile which had been playing round his lips disappeared. 'No, you won't, young lady,' he snapped. 'I won't have the smell of food in the bedrooms.' For a second or two he was back to his old self.

'Sorry, you're right,' said Molly, not sure why she was apologising. She took a small pan from the rack and put the beans to heat on the gas ring by the range. Sticking a slice of bread on the toasting fork, she held it before the bars, glad of a reason to keep her back to him. Formless fears crowded coherent thought from her mind so that the toast was smoking by the time she snatched it away from the fire and the beans were bubbling furiously. She turned off the gas and looked over her shoulder at him.

'Mr Jones,' she began but he had gone. Relief flooded through her. She scraped the burned bits off the toast and ate her scanty meal quickly, washed up and practically scuttled upstairs. This time she locked the door and put a chair under the door handle too though she smiled wryly to herself as she did so. Nothing has changed, she told herself. It was all in your imagination.

The next day there was no chance of looking for somewhere else to live, the girls' dinner hour was reduced by half as a rush order came in.

'We're changing over to uniforms, girls,' said Mr Bolton, sounding eager. 'There'll be no slacking, we have to get the order out as soon as possible. Now, anyone who can stay back and work overtime tonight, put your name down on the list I've pinned on the notice board.'

There was a buzz of conversation among the others on the line. Molly heard Joan Pendle's jubilant voice above the rest. 'Now I'll be able to buy that dance dress in Doggart's window. By, it's lovely, an' only five shillings down and a shilling a week. Are you going to the station dance on Saturday night, Enid?'

There was a dance hall next to the station in Auckland, a five-piece band regularly playing there. Molly had never been but she had heard a lot about it from the other girls. For a moment she wondered what it was like to go to a dance like that then dismissed it from her mind. She had more important things to do with her money. Maybe she could even afford different lodgings.

Enid had moved on down the line and the girls were quiet as the wireless started to play and they bent over their humming sewing machines. Molly's thoughts were with the boys, Harry and Jackson. She still hadn't had a reply to her Christmas card or a thank you for the tie pin she had sent Harry. Nine-carat gold it was, with a minuscule red stone in the middle which the shop keeper had assured her was a ruby. Nice and light too, it hadn't cost much to post. Soon it would be time to find him a birthday present, get it off in good time for his birthday in July.

It was not until six-thirty that evening when she came out of the factory to face a bitter cold wind which seemed to blow in her face no matter which way she turned, that Molly realised she had missed her hour in the kitchen. Cold and hungry, she paused in the lea of the gable end of the house. She could ask Mr Jones if she could use the kitchen now, though she knew he couldn't abide the the smell of food in the house in the evening.

Molly was reluctant to ask any favours of him but she was so hungry her stomach felt like a great empty hole. She'd had only had a tomato sandwich and an apple at dinner time. Pausing at the door, she changed her mind about going in and made her way back to the fish shop where the smell of frying fish made her feel dizzy. She spent half her overtime on a fish and a bag of chips. Putting the newspaper-wrapped parcel inside her coat and buttoning it up, she sped back to the house. As she let herself in she prayed Mr Jones wouldn't smell the fish. Luckily there was no sign of him and she hurried up the stairs and into her room, locking the door after her as usual.

She sat on the clippie mat she had brought from home and ate the fish and chips out of the paper, leaning forward to let the smell go up the chimney as far as possible. The fish was piping hot and flaky, the batter crisp and light, the chips done to a turn. Molly enjoyed them more than she had enjoyed any meal since before her father was killed.

The newly lit fire flamed and crackled, started as it was by the outer layers of the newspaper parcel. Warmth crept through her bones. Though it was late-spring already according to the calendar, the north-easter still swept down the Wear valley and drew the flames upwards.

Replete, Molly screwed the inner paper into a ball and added it to the flames. She sat back against the chair and gazed at the fire, rubbing her neck which was aching after bending over the sewing machine for such long hours. She was tired. When she had drunk her Tizer she would wash and go to bed early with her book.

Relaxed now, her mind wandered off. She was back in another time, years before, when she and Harry were children and had pinched pea pods from the row in Dad's garden, ducking down out of view of the house to eat sweet, not yet fully grown peas from the pod. She smiled now as she pictured it, the two of them giggling and laughing, thinking they were safe from detection, out of sight of the windows of the house. And there Dad had been, standing at the end of the row, trying to look stern. He had been out and come in by the garden gate.

'But . . . why have you come this way?' Harry had stammered, jumping to his feet, scattering pea pods. 'You always use the back gate.'

'I didn't today, though, did I?' Dad had asked, and the corners of his mouth had twitched. He hadn't really been mad, thought Molly now. Not like Mr Jones would be if he found out about tonight's meal.

'Oh, what the heck!' she said aloud. She had enjoyed it. Jumping to her feet, she began to prepare for bed.

Chapter Six

'HITLER AND MUSSOLINI SIGN PACT OF STEEL'. The headlines were on the board outside the newsagent's window. Molly saw it as she rounded the corner from Adelaide Street and waited for the bus to go by before crossing the road to the factory. She was heavy-eyed this morning, had slept badly after last night's greasy supper. Mr Jones had knocked on her door again after she had gone to bed and she had been startled out of her first sleep. Standing by the closed door she had asked what he wanted. Could he smell the faint aroma of fish which hung in the air?

'Let me in a minute, Molly, I just want to talk to you,' he had said.

'I can't, Mr Jones, I'm not dressed,' she'd replied.

'Aw, come on, do you think I haven't seen a lass in her pyjamas before?'

Molly had stood there, shivering with cold. 'I'll see you in the morning, Mr Jones.'

'Why can't you call me Bart? It's only friendly like.'

'Goodnight, Mr Jones,' Molly had said firmly and went back to bed. She pulled the covers up over her ears, determined not to let him bother her, but despite that her heart beat fast and she was trembling. Was that the door handle turning?

'I'll speak to you in the morning then,' he called.

'Yes.' It was a few minutes before she heard him shuffling

away and another hour before she was relaxed enough to sleep after getting up and checking that the door was locked.

This morning she had been late in waking and had had to rush to work without her breakfast. Her landlord had already gone, thank goodness. But, oh, she knew she had to find somewhere else to live very soon.

There was a parcel by her sewing machine postmarked India. Molly forgot all her troubles when she saw it. She didn't even wonder how it had got there, just sat and stared at it, her happiness intensified by her previous misery until she thought she might burst.

The parcel was still there unopened when the power was switched on and the wireless started churning out 'Whistle While You Work' from Disney's *Snow White*.

'Howay now, girls,' Enid shouted, and the line settled down to work, heads bent over machines, khaki cloth whizzing under needles. For the minute it was enough for Molly to keep glancing at the parcel. Its brown paper covering was scuffed and torn in places after its journey halfway round the world. She was eager to open it when the morning break arrived at last. Some of the girls crowded round, curious about it.

'Your birthday, is it, Molly?' asked Enid.

'No.'

Someone offered her a pen knife and she carefully split the paper and opened the cardboard box inside. On top there was a card with a picture of Father Christmas, mopping his brow as he staggered beneath a sackful of goodies under a blazing sun. 'Merry Christmas' was written in Harry's handwriting.

'Blimey!' one of the girls said. 'It's a Christmas present. Nearly six months late an' all.'

'You brought it, didn't you, Joan?' asked Enid. 'Where did you get it?'

She sniffed and didn't reply for a moment.

'Well?' asked Molly.

'It came to your old house a while ago. I just forgot to bring it.' In fact her mother had been on at her over and over to take the parcel for Molly and Joan had only pretended to forget.

This morning there had been a shouting match in the Pendle household about it.

'You'll take that parcel to the lass or I'll come with you and take it myself!' Ann had said.

'Aw, why should I have to run about after her?' Joan had retorted. 'If she wants it, she can come over and get it!'

'You'll take it!' Ann had lost her temper thoroughly and thrust the parcel into Joan's arms. 'Get along with you now, and you give it to her, do you understand me? I'm ashamed it's been here so long.'

'All right, all right,' Joan had said in martyred tones. 'I'll take it.'

Now the other girls were looking at her strangely and she didn't like it. It was all that stuck-up Molly's fault. Joan glared at her. She was so like Harry. Her hair and eyes were lighter but she had the same straight nose and firm chin. Joan felt a pang of misery and turned sharply away.

'Oh, get on with it,' she said crossly. 'I'm going to have my tea. I've got better things to do. It'll only be rubbish any road.' And she walked away, not wanting to think about Harry any more.

Joan looked over her shoulder, however, as there was a gasp from the girls. Molly had lifted out a shawl of palest blue silk, edged with a wide fringe. There was another gasp as a matching dolly bag emerged with a picture of the Taj Mahal embroidered in silver on the side.

'Eeh . . . it's lovely!' one of the girls breathed. 'By, you are lucky, Molly.'

Lucky? For a minute Molly's happiness dimmed. Was she lucky after all that had happened to her? She shook her head. No, she mustn't be bitter. It was a happy day, she was lucky to get such beautiful things. Surely such a lovely shawl had never been seen before in Eden Hope or West Auckland?

'Now then, girls,' said Enid, brisk again. 'Get your tea or you won't have time before the break is over.'

The girls moved away and Molly pulled out a letter from Harry. She would save it for the dinner hour, take it back to Adelaide Street and stow the beautiful shawl and dolly bag safely in her bedroom. She was packing it in the box carefully when she noticed there was something else: a letter from Jackson. Her happiness intensified. He hadn't forgotten her. She was so happy she even smiled at Joan.

'Thanks for fetching it in,' she said. 'How is your mother, by the way?' She well knew it would be Ann who had insisted on Joan's bringing it. But in her present mood she could even forgive the long delay.

The second half of the morning seemed interminable but at last Molly was free to pick up the parcel and run over the road and round the corner into Adelaide Street. She was panting as she opened the door and raced up the stairs to her bedroom. Leaving the door ajar, for she knew her landlord wouldn't be in from work for hours yet, she sat on the bed and unpacked the box again, laying the presents carefully on the bedspread. Then she took the letters and went over to her chair by the fireplace and settled down to read Harry's first.

> I'm worried about you, petal. I don't like to think of you alone in the house. Travelling to work too. You should watch out for yourself, there are some funny folk about. And can you afford it? You can't be making much money. I've enclosed a money order for five pounds, it's not much but it will help. Let me know if you need any more. I can let you have an allowance from my pay if you can't manage, as I told you in my letter.

What letter? Molly wondered. Had there been a letter gone astray? For a minute she suspected Joan, but no, she wouldn't do that. And why didn't Harry know she was living in St Helen's Auckland now? She had written to him, sent a Christmas present too. Molly shook her head and read on.

> I don't know when we'll be coming back to Blighty but it can't be long, not with the way things are over there. In the meantime, look after yourself and eat properly. You were always too thin, so don't stint on food. And *don't* go with

any lads. You're just a young lass, remember. And *I* know what lads are like, believe me. You're my kid sister and I will be back soon to look after you. Think on it and be a good girl. You know Mam and Dad would expect it.

Your loving brother, Harry

P.S. I hope you like the shawl, pet. When we come home we'll find a posh dance where you can wear it.

Molly had a grand bubbly feeling inside her. In one morning she had gone from black depression, where she'd felt completely alone and unloved, to a mood of bright optimism which had once been her usual outlook on life but which she hadn't felt since her dad was killed. She carefully folded the letter and put it back, glancing at the clock. Goodness, she only had five minutes to get back to her machine. It was amazing how fast half an hour could go. Promising herself she would save Jackson's letter until the evening, she rushed back to the factory, completely forgetting that she'd had no dinner.

By six o'clock Molly was light-headed. The noise of the machines and the wireless still rang in her head as she crossed the road towards Adelaide Street. Calling at the grocer's on the main road, she bought a couple of eggs. She would do herself scrambled eggs or an omelette, she thought. Her empty stomach ached almost as much as her head.

Mr Jones was in the kitchen, sitting by the oil-cloth-covered table and reading the *Evening Gazette*. Molly hesitated in the doorway.

'Can I use the kitchen, Mr Jones?' she asked. 'I have to work an extra hour at the factory nowadays and I've just come in.'

'Aye, go on then,' he replied with a grudging sort of sigh. 'I hope you're not going to cook anything smelly?'

'Oh, no, Mr Jones,' said Molly, thinking regretfully of the onion lying in her cupboard which she had been going to put in an omelette. Scrambled eggs it was then.

He sat at the table, looking at her over a pair of reading glasses from Woolworth's. 'I've told you to call me Bart,' he said mildly. Molly smiled vaguely. She couldn't imagine calling him by his first name, not in a million years. And tonight, as soon as she had eaten, she would go to the newsagent's and take the address of another house with a room to let, even if it cost ten shillings or more. She thought of the five-pound money order which Harry had sent with a warm glow of gratitude.

She whisked eggs, cooked them in a pan on the fire, sat at the table and ate them with bread and butter rather than spend more time making toast. All the time she could feel Mr Jones's eyes on her, though she kept hers on what she was doing. After she had washed up she escaped to her room, looked regretfully at the letter from Jackson and decided to leave it until she came back in. Feeling decidedly better with something in her stomach, she washed her face and combed her hair. This was a good day with the parcel coming and now she was going to find other lodgings, she was sure of it.

Going to her bedroom door, she realised the key was missing. She looked about on the floor, even turned back the rug, but it wasn't there. It wasn't outside on the landing either and it wasn't in her bag. She couldn't remember if she had used it to get in this evening. She racked her memory but knew she had been feeling slightly dizzy then. Everything before she had eaten was hazy.

Oh, well, she would find it eventually, she told herself. Now she had to go before it was too late. It was already seven-thirty and people didn't like callers too late in the evening when they had settled down to listen to the wireless. Molly closed her door and hurried down the stairs.

'Going to the pictures, are you, Molly?'

Mr Jones was standing in the doorway of the kitchen, watching her.

'No, just to see a friend,' she fibbed.

'I'll treat you to the pictures one night, maybe on Saturday,' he said with a benevolent air.

'Hmmm.' Molly couldn't think of anything else to say. She turned smartly and went out of the door. No, you will not, she thought savagely as she walked down the street. If you think I'm going anywhere with you, you're out of your head.

There were two addresses in the newsagent's window. One of them in West Auckland, about half a mile away, the other in Front Street. Molly considered it worth the extra walking distance to be away from Adelaide Street and set off along Manor Road, past the ancient church and over the bridge which spanned the Gaunless river and into West Auckland. She found the house easily enough. It was in a small row of old two-storey houses with elegant Georgian fronts. There was a bell, too. She pressed it and heard it ring inside the house.

'Answer that, Jimmy,' a female voice called and a moment later the heavy front door opened and a boy of about seven poked his head round. He stared at Molly.

'What do you want?'

'Can I speak to your mam?'

He closed the door and she could hear him shouting at the top of his voice behind it.

'Mam! Mam!'

'Who is it, Jimmy? I'm busy with the baby, you know I am.'

'It's a lass.'

'Ask her what she wants,' the woman yelled back at him.

The door opened again. 'What do you want?' he asked again. 'Mam wants to know.'

'I've come about the room. Can I come in?'

The door closed for a moment again as he held a shouted conference with his mother. Then, 'Aye. Howay in then,' he said and Molly crossed over the high step and into a hall with a high ceiling and varnished dado rail, the floor covered with a worn carpet runner, a piece of coco-matting acting as a door mat. There was a smell of meat pudding from the back of the hall; a door which must lead to the kitchen, Molly surmised, stood beside the narrow staircase. The smell reminded her of her mother somehow. A pair of roller skates lay on their sides just inside the door and a shabby pram stood to one side of the hall.

A woman was coming down the stairs, sandy hair like the

boy's drawn back from her forehead, cheeks rosy beneath laughing blue eyes.

'Come on in,' she said, striding forward and holding out her hand. 'I'm Cathy Grimes and this tearaway is Jimmy.' Her handshake was firm, her smile friendly. 'After the room, did you say?'

'Yes. I'm Molly Mason. I work at the clothing factory in St Helen's.'

The room which Cathy led her into was large and airy, with a bay window through which rays of a sinking summer sun shone, speckling the air with dancing dust motes. There was a leather suite, shabby and with sagging cushions, an ancient sideboard and corner cupboard. It had a lived in air, unlike most of the sitting rooms Molly had known. Most mining families spent their time in the kitchen-cum-living room, the sitting room kept tidy for visits from the minister or other important personages.

'Run along and make sure your sister's all right,' Cathy said to her son, reaching out a hand and tousling his hair.

'Aw, Mam,' he grumbled, but went all the same, and Cathy motioned Molly to a seat and perched on an armchair herself.

'You don't live with your family, then?' she asked. 'Not had a fight with your dad, have you?'

Molly's throat constricted. 'No. My dad's dead, my mam an' all.' She coughed, put a hand to her mouth. 'Dad was killed in the disaster at Eden Hope.'

'Eeh, I'm that sorry! Take no notice of my big mouth, love. Look, I'll just get us a cup of tea then we'll have a talk and I'll show you the room.'

'Don't make it just for me,' protested Molly.

'I'm not. Believe me, after seeing to the kids' teas and struggling with the little 'un – he's cutting a tooth, poor bairn – me own tongue's hanging out.'

Molly looked around when Cathy left the room. The wall-paper was faded. In one place there were crayon marks which someone had attempted to wash off. But there were a couple of nice prints on the wall, one of High Force in Teesdale, the water tumbling over the falls in full spate. The other was an engraving of Stephenson's Locomotion No. 1. Cathy came back in with a tea tray as Molly was studying it.

'My man's an engine driver,' she volunteered. 'He's daft on the old engines.' She poured tea and handed Molly a cup and saucer. 'He's away a lot, on the London run. That's why I wanted a lodger, a woman for preference. Company, you know. That and the money, of course. I'd best tell you it's ten shillings a week. We had to spend some to get it ready, you know, it's a new bed.'

'I can manage ten shillings. As I said, I'm in regular work. I'd like it here, I like children.' Molly sounded too eager, she knew she did.

Cathy laughed. 'You haven't seen the room yet! It's in the attic, mind. And when you've been pestered a bit by my lot, you might change your mind about kids. Come on, I'll show you the room.'

There were three flights of stairs and then a shorter one to a door at the top of the house. Inside the room was large and airy, with a dormer window looking out over the green and the roofs of Post Office Square.

'Oh, it's fine,' breathed Molly. It was too: a single bed with a bright patchwork coverlet, even a square of carpet on the floor. There was a wash stand with basin and jug, and a walnut dressing table. There was a gas fire on one wall with a meter by the side.

'I hope you don't mind, paying for your own gas? We couldn't afford . . .'

'I'll take it,' interrupted Molly. 'When can I move in?'

Chapter Seven

Molly walked back to Adelaide Street in the gathering dusk, so happy she had to stop herself from skipping along. Cathy was very friendly and sympathetic; Molly had found herself telling her all about Eden Hope and her dad and Harry, away in the army in India.

'I bet you have a boyfriend too, a pretty girl like you?' she had said, teasing. Molly thought about Jackson. Not *really* a boyfriend, she had been too young when he went away. But still . . .

'He's in the army with Harry,' she had replied.

Now she thought of Jackson's letter, still unread. It was something to look forward to, she would read it in bed tonight. By, it had been a lovely, lovely day. And she was moving to Cathy's at the end of the week, would give in her notice to Mr Jones now. It was a load lifted off her mind.

The house in Adelaide Street was dark, Mr Jones was out evidently. Well, she would tell him tomorrow. Molly let herself in and ran upstairs to her room. The door wasn't quite closed. Had he been nosing around? She shivered, hating the thought of him touching her things. Closing the door after her, she put the chair under the handle. That should keep him out anyway. And in a few days she would be gone from this house forever.

In bed she opened Jackson's letter. There wasn't a lot in it and he had written similar things to her brother except for the last sentence. *'We'll be home soon, I promise you. Look after my best girl till then.'*

He meant her! He had to mean her. Maybe it was just a saying but he had written she was his best girl, or that was what it meant. Molly slipped out of bed and checked the chair under the door handle. Was it strong enough? She wasn't sure. But maybe she was worrying about nothing. She wouldn't let it spoil this wonderful day. Putting out the light, she slipped under the covers and curled into a ball.

Today she had found a new friend, she thought drowsily. It was almost like being part of a family again. And there had been letters from the two men she loved most in the world and those lovely things from Harry. Everything was going right for her at last. The sun was shining on her, thank God. Molly slipped into sleep.

She was walking along the promenade at Roker, Mam on one side and Dad on the other. They were holding her hands. She had to reach up to them she was so small.

'Look at that, Molly, will you just look?' Mam cried, and she saw a small cottage all lit up around the roof, a light shining from the tiny window. The roof was orange and the walls white; roses climbed over the front door.

'It's a fairy house, Molly,' said Mam, and she was awed and delighted for her mam read fairy stories to her every night before she went to sleep and she knew what a fairy house was. And as she gazed and gazed, a fairy flew round the front of the house, smiled directly at her and disappeared inside.

'Howay, pet,' said Dad. 'We have to get on, the bus will be waiting.' They were on a bus trip to Roker to see the illuminations. But Molly didn't want to go. She tugged away from his hand and hung on to the railing around the little house. So he picked her up and carried her and suddenly she was frightened. It wasn't really her dad . . . no, he was killed in the pit, wasn't he? Who was holding her? Who?

She struggled to wake up and pull away, hit out at whoever it was and rolled out of bed and on to the floor. Dashing for the bedroom door, she tripped on the mat, almost fell, then blundered into something else. A chair? But she managed to keep to her feet and reached the light switch. Her hand on the door knob as the light came on, she glanced over her shoulder and there, just picking himself up from the floor, was Mr Jones, blinking in the light.

She could almost have laughed at the sight of him, his hair all awry and feet bare. He was dressed in a voluminous nightshirt. She had been going to flee out into the street but he looked so pathetic somehow that she stood still and gaped at him.

'What did you do that for?' he asked.

'Never mind that, what are *you* doing in my room? How did you get in anyway?' Molly looked at the chair, lying on its side. That was what she must have stumbled over. She couldn't have put it under the knob the right way, she hadn't even heard it fall.

'Aw, come on, Molly, you know well what I want. A young lass like you, staying in a man's house, just the two of us! Well, tonight's your lucky night, I'm here to give it to you.' He smiled, showing broken crooked teeth. 'Howay, back to bed, it's still a bit cold on a night. We might as well be cosy,' he coaxed, and Molly began to laugh. She couldn't help it. She laughed and laughed until tears streamed down her face. To think she had been nervous, not to say frightened, of this silly little man!

'Come on, I mean it, I'm not just having you on,' said Mr Jones, still not understanding. His tone implied he thought he was doing her a favour, Molly realised, and laughed the more, released tension making her a little hysterical.

'Stop that!' Mr Jones suddenly shouted. He crossed the room and slapped her hard across the face. Molly stopped laughing and stared at him. He slavered slightly, lips wet. 'Now then, come to bed when I say, do you hear?' He had raised his voice, was almost shouting. He caught hold of her arms and dragged her towards the bed.

'No! Don't be silly, I don't want to!' cried Molly, finding her voice and pulling herself free.

'Don't be so bloody coy and come to bed when you're told,' he shouted. 'Don't you realise all the neighbours think we must be at it any road? If you didn't want me you would have gone somewhere else when Betty went into hospital. Now come on, you've protested enough. Come to bed when I tell you.'

'I'm not! I didn't . . . I locked the door and you took the key. You must have forced your way in here tonight, I put the chair up against the knob.'

'Bloody games. I've had enough,' he shouted, and grabbed her again, practically throwing her on the bed with him on top of her. The breath was knocked out of Molly. He wasn't very big but strong enough to hold her slight form down, her arms pinned. One of his hands was clutching at her hair, the other scrabbling at her breast. His face was close to hers. A drop of spittle fell on to her chin. She felt as though her hair was being torn out at the roots, the pain agonising.

'This is what you want, isn't it?' he said hoarsely. 'This is what you've been angling for ever since Betty went to hospital – wiggling your arse at me every time you went past me, looking at me with those big come-to-bed eyes. Well, now you're going to get it, slut! Now . . .'

In a desperate burst of energy Molly heaved and managed to catch him off balance. He fell off her, teetering on the edge of the bed for a second and falling heavily on to the floor. As he fell his fingers dug into her breast and she cried out with the pain.

'Stop that flaming noise!' someone was shouting. There was a banging on the wall. Molly heard it as from a distance. She was too busy scrambling off the bed, grabbing her coat from the hook and covering herself. She stood at the dooway, poised for flight, then realised Mr Jones was saying nothing, lying on the floor beside the bed. Oh, God, had she killed him? Had he hit his head on the fender? No, he was moving, sitting up, groaning. He put a hand to his head and held it there for a moment before getting heavily to his feet.

Molly took a step through the door, the linoleum cold under her bare feet. She was wary of him but he did not look at her as he walked past her, nightshirt billowing round skinny ankles. At his own bedroom door he turned.

'Get out of here, you slut! Take your things and get out. Never mind the rent, I want shot of you.'

'It's the middle of the night!' gasped Molly.

'I don't care what time it is. You can sleep on the street for all I care. Get your things together now or get out without them. Either way, if you're not out of here in ten minutes, I'll throw you out.'

He stood there, holding his head and trying to look dignified, succeeding only in looking ludicrous so that Molly felt a bubble of hysterical laughter rising in her in spite of her predicament. Hurriedly she went back into her bedroom and closed the door, leaning on it and hiccuping with laughter. But it died almost immediately and tears took its place.

She dashed them away angrily and dressed before gathering her things together. She could only take her case, she thought. What about the bits and pieces she had brought from Eden Hope? Dumbly she put the parcel she'd received that morning, the one which had brought her such happiness as she hadn't known for months, in her suitcase. It stuck up a bit, the case wouldn't close properly. She'd have to be careful with it, she told herself. She'd have to leave her other things, her sewing basket and such. She carried the case to the door, paused and looked back. She had no idea where she was going, she realised. Could she turn up on Cathy's doorstep in the middle of the night? No, she rejected the idea. After all, they had only just met.

Going back into the room, she picked up the marble clock from the mantelshelf. She couldn't leave that. With the clock tucked under one arm and her suitcase, which felt as heavy as lead, in her other hand, she went downstairs. Mr Jones was waiting at the door.

'I'll come back for my other things.'

'You will not,' he replied. 'I'll get them myself and put them outside. If they're not gone by morning I'll take them to the tip.'

'You can't! I'll get the polis . . .'

'You'll not, lass. It'll be me that gets the polis,' he said grimly, and gave her a push out of the door and on to the pavement. Molly dropped her case and grasped at the clock to stop it falling. The case burst open. She must not have closed it properly.

A light came on in the bedroom of the next-door house, the window opened and a man stuck his head out.

'What the hell is all the racket about?' he shouted. 'I have to go to work the morn!'

'I'm sorry, Joe, really I am,' said Mr Jones, and Molly was amazed at his change of tone. He sounded conciliatory now. 'It won't happen again. It's this thieving lass I took in off the streets. She's been pinching the wife's things!'

'I have not!' Molly cried, shock and disbelief making her shout. 'I haven't touched anything –'

'What's this then?'

Mr Jones was bending over the open suitcase. When he stood up he had a bangle in his hand. It sparkled in the light from the open door.

'Do you see this, Joe? Do you see it?' He held it up and Joe nodded.

'Aye, I see it. It's that gold bangle your wife was so proud of, isn't it? Why, the thieving little bitch!' He leaned further out of the window and glared at Molly.

'I didn't take it, really I didn't,' she said. She looked from the neighbour's face to that of Mr Jones. He had a nasty little smile playing round his lips; his eyes were filled with vindictive glee.

'You're my witness, Joe. You saw me take it out of the case, didn't you? I knew she had it somewhere, I missed it out of the dressing-table drawer tonight so I tackled her about it. If she'd give it me back I'd have let her off, but she's a hard-faced little slut, you know. Will you watch her, Joe, while I go for the polis?'

Molly was struck dumb. She stood there, her open case at her feet, the marble clock under her arm. She looked down at it. It was one o'clock in the morning. Surely this was just a bad dream? It couldn't really be happening, of course it couldn't. She closed her eyes tight, prayed that she should wake up then opened them again.

Someone had taken a firm hold on her arm. She almost dropped the clock. It was the man from next door.

'Now then, don't you think you can get away,' he snapped. 'I wouldn't be surprised if you'd done this before, arriving here out of nowhere and trying to take honest folk down.'

'I didn't – I haven't!' moaned Molly. Up the street other windows were opening. Some front doors even had people peering round them.

'What's going on, Joe?' someone shouted.

'It's this lass that was lodging with Bart,' he explained, speaking loudly so everyone could hear. Molly felt herself shrinking inside with the shame of it. 'She's been pinching stuff from him, that's what's going on.' His fingers dug painfully into her arm again.

'I haven't! I didn't!' cried Molly, but hopelessly now.

'May the Lord save your lying little soul,' someone shouted piously. 'Make you see the error of your ways.'

'I did nothing!' she screamed, beside herself now with an anger which rose up inside her and burst out. 'It was him! He got into my bed . . . he . . .'

'Eeh, I tell you what . . .' said a woman from up the street. She came walking down towards Molly, a coat on over her nightie, old shoes thrust on her feet and her hair done up in steel curling pins. 'I tell you what . . . folk like her'll say owt but their prayers. An' who would've believed it? She looked a meek little thing, butter wouldn't melt in her mouth. Aye, but you've been found out, haven't you?' The woman thrust her face close to Molly's. 'You didn't think you would, did you? Lasses like you should have their fingers chopped off, that's what I think!' She folded her arms across her enormous chest and nodded her head to emphasise her words.

'I didn't do it! It was him, he got into my bed!' shouted Molly, and a growl went up amongst the crowd which was now gathering round.

'Will you listen to her? Will you?' one man cried. 'Isn't that what they all say when they're caught? Blame it on the fella. Oh, aye, it must have been *his* fault. Tried to take you down, did he? An innocent little virgin, are you? I just bloody well *bet* you are!'

The crowd murmured agreement, their mood growing ugly. They moved forward, hemming her in. Someone grabbed her other arm, the one holding the clock, and she dropped it.

'Me mam's clock!' she cried, and pushed and shoved, taking Joe by surprise so that he let go of her and she bent down on the pavement, crying over the clock as though the world had come to an end.

'It was me mam's,' she cried brokenly. 'Look at it now, the marble's all chipped. I bet it won't work neither.'

The old woman laughed. 'It's only an old clock,' she said. 'You won't be needing a clock where you're going, me lass.'

'Now then, what's going on here?' a new voice said, and the crowd melted away as it by magic. Molly was left bending over the clock, trying to fix the glass door back on for it had come off in the fall. Miraculously, it hadn't broken. She hardly heard what was being said by the men above her. The door on the clock went back on, albeit a bit crooked. She stood it carefully on the pavement and turned to her suitcase, pushing her things back into it, trying to get them even so she could close the lid. The catch wouldn't work at first. She tried and tried with it and at last it clicked into place. She nearly cried with frustration. She should have a belt round it, she thought, that would work. One of her father's belts, that was it.

The policeman bent down and pulled her to her feet.

'It's no good taking on like that, lass,' he said mildly. 'You'll just have to come along o' me now. I want no fuss, mind.'

'Where are we going?' asked Molly. Suddenly she was exhausted, couldn't fight any more, feeling like a bird in a trap.

'Well, where do you think? The police station in Bondgate. You can't go pinching things and get away Scot free, you know. A night in the cells will do you the world of good.'

On the pavement, the clock began to chime, its tone sweet

and silvery. It chimed six times. 'See what they did,' said Molly, more to herself than the policeman. 'That can't be right. It's not six o'clock, surely?'

'The lass is off her head,' Bart Jones remarked.

'Never mind that. You're coming along an' all, I want a statement from you. You, too, whatever your name is.' He nodded at Joe.

'I have to go to work the morn!'

'Me an' all,' said Joe.

'That's matterless, you're coming down to the station,' the policeman said calmly. 'Come on, the Black Maria's at the end of the street.'

'Why, yer bugger!' said Joe, glaring at Molly. 'I could be fast asleep in bed if it wasn't for you. A fella's just doing his duty and now I'm going to lose a morning's pay for it. What's the world coming to, I ask you?'

'It's the law,' said the policeman. And, picking up Molly's suitcase, led the way down the street.

Chapter Eight

At least she didn't have to worry about where she was going to sleep, thought Molly. She sat on the hard bed in a police cell in Bondgate and looked about her in total disbelief. How could this have happened? The cold struck through the bare stone walls but she didn't feel it; she didn't feel anything. There was a barred window set so high up the wall it was impossible to see through, a metal door with a peephole which denied her all privacy, a battered table and a chair.

'Lights out in five minutes, lass,' a policeman said through the peephole. 'If I were you I'd try to get some sleep.' He sounded quite kindly, she thought, and opened her mouth to appeal to him but he had gone. She could hear his footsteps retreating down the passage.

She looked at the bed. A hard flock mattress. A lumpy striped pillow with no pillowslip. A brown blanket, clean but worn almost away in patches. She took off her shoes, thought about removing her dress but decided against it. She lay on the bed, covering herself with the blanket. Her mind felt blank, she couldn't even think. She stared at the door. The light from the bare bulb in the middle of the ceiling shone in her eyes and she closed them against the glare. The next minute it was suddenly dark, a dense blackness relieved only by bars of lighter grey near the ceiling and coming from the window.

'Dad,' she whispered. 'Oh, Dad.' She needed him here so

much but he was dead. And then a moan she hardly recognised came from her lips. 'God help me. Please, God, please.'

She became aware of noises. Someone in the next cell was drunk. He was singing a song from the Great War. 'Mademoiselle from Armentières', that was it. Someone else, a woman's voice it was, shouted, 'Stop that ruddy racket, will you?' And a policeman walked in heavy boots outside the door.

'Quiet in there!' an authoritative voice shouted and the drunk was quiet for a few minutes then started up again with 'Keep the Home Fires Burning'.

Suddenly Molly was desperate to pass water. There was a lavatory pan in the corner. She got up and went over to it, moving hesitantly in the dark, her hands out in front of her, feeling her way. She sat on the lavatory, finding herself at first unable to use it. There was no seat and the cold of the pottery pan bit into her. At last she managed and made her way back to the bed, stubbing her toe on the leg. The pain was agonising. She fell into bed, pulled the blanket over her head and sobbed and sobbed, shoulders heaving. No one was going to help her, no one at all. She was completely alone. Eventually the storm of crying passed and she fell into an uneasy sleep.

It was morning when she awoke and the cell looked worse in the daylight than it had in artificial light. Molly sat up, disorientated for a moment. Her head throbbed, her throat was dry. A tin mug stood on the table. She pulled on her shoes and went over to it. As she had thought, it held water and she drank thirstily, stale though the water tasted.

A policeman opened the door and came in with a tray which he put down on the table. There was porridge, bread and butter and jam, and a mug of tea, strong and brown.

'I don't want anything,' said Molly. She felt dirty and dishevelled, her dress creased from sleeping in it. The policeman looked at her, considering. He was about the same age as her father, she thought. Did he have a family?

'You should eat something, lass,' he said. 'Howay now. And drink the tea, I put two sugars in, it'll give you strength.'

'I want to wash.'

'All right, I'll bring you a dish of water and a towel. But drink the tea at least.'

He went out, the door clanging behind him. Molly took a spoonful of porridge. It was lukewarm and sweet. She drank the tea because the policeman seemed kind and had told her to. When he came back she washed and combed her hair, rubbed at a mark on her dress with the soapy water.

At ten o'clock, feeling better, she followed the policeman upstairs to the magistrates' court and stood before the bench. The magistrates would let her go, she told herself. Surely no one would believe Mr Jones?

'Remanded in custody until Monday next,' said the chairman.

'Why? I didn't do anything!' cried Molly.

The chairman sighed. 'No one ever has,' he remarked to his neighbour, a white-haired lady in twinset and pearls, who nodded sagely.

'You have no fixed address,' he went so far as to explain to Molly.

'But I have. I have a room in West Auckland,' she said eagerly, filled with relief. 'I told the officer–'

'Take her down, Constable,' said the magistrate. 'Bailiff, call the next case.'

As Molly was led away, an old man shuffled in, his eyes bleary with drink, his movements unsteady. He took her place before the bench. The bailiff was saying something about him being drunk and disorderly.

For the rest of the day, Molly sat in her cell, going over and over the hearing in her mind. Mr Jones had appeared an upright citizen, worried to death about his daughter in a sanatorium, allowing Molly to keep on her room out of the kindness of his heart. His neighbour had testified to seeing him bring the bangle out of Molly's suitcase, said he recognised it as once being the property of the late Mrs Jones. The evidence was all against her, Molly conceded, but it was lies. She'd protested her innocence, told them that Mr Jones had come into her room and attacked her, but they had cut her off. 'That's enough of that!' the chairman had said sharply. 'You can get into serious trouble if you take that line, my girl.'

'But–'

'Take her away,' said the chairman.

'Have you not got anyone who will testify as to your good character?' asked the kindly policeman later on. 'Where did you say you come from? Eden Hope? Well, there must be someone there, surely?'

His name was Constable Hardy and he was the only one who tried to help her. She learned he came from Coundon, his father a pitman there. His daughter was a teacher now and he was very proud of her.

Molly shrank within herself at the thought of asking Ann Pendle to testify for her. Mrs Morley might have done, but Molly was too ashamed to ask. She didn't want anyone in Eden Hope to find out, anyone who had known her family in better days. But surely when the magistrates heard the whole story she would be set free, they would know they had made a mistake? British justice was the best in the world, her dad had always told her so, and she believed him.

In the end, Molly decided not to ask anyone from Eden Hope. She would stand up in court, tell the truth and the magistrates would have to believe her, of course they would. She would be set free and would go to Cathy's house in West Auckland and then, with a room in a decent house and Cathy for a friend, the nightmare would be over.

Wearing a clean dress which Constable Hardy had had pressed for her, and with her hair brushed back from her temples and gleaming almost chestnut in the overhead lights of the court, Molly faced the magistrates once more. Her heart beat so fast she could feel it in her throat and she clasped her hands behind her to still their trembling. It would soon be over and she would go free, she told herself. A disturbance took her attention. It was someone coming in late and sitting down on the Press bench. The chairman of the magistrates frowned down at him.

There was a report in the local paper next day.

*

Before Bishop Auckland Magistrates yesterday morning, Molly Mason, of no fixed address but previously of Eden Hope, was sentenced to three months' imprisonment for the theft of a gold bangle, value fifteen pounds and ten shillings, from her then landlord, Mr Bartram Jones. Mr Jones said the bracelet belonged to his late wife and was of great sentimental value to him. In sentencing, the chairman, Sir John Hume, made the following remarks to the defendant.

'Mr Jones trusted you in his house and you betrayed that trust and stole from him. I am aware that you are of previous good character and also that you recently lost your father in the mining disaster at Eden Hope colliery. Nevertheless I have consulted with my colleagues and we are agreed that three months in prison could be just the shock you need to force you to see the error of your ways.'

Molly had climbed into the van which was to take her to prison, sat beside a policewoman, did what she was told automatically. It was a nightmare, she told herself, a nightmare which went on and on. And now she was sitting in a workroom with a number of other women, dressed in a stiff grey dress, sewing thick calico bags which the other girls said were to hold gun powder. The sewing machine she was using might have been the first one ever invented. She was in a line not unlike the one in the factory at St Helen's Auckland, but here there was no wireless, the women weren't chattering and laughing or singing along to music. There was just the clattering of the machines, the wardresses walking up and down, and the ache in Molly's fingers from handling the stiff fabric all day long.

Chapter Nine

The troopship nosed its way into Southampton and came to a slow, lumbering halt alongside the quay. A band of marines was playing far below them as Harry and Jackson stood to attention on deck with the rest of their platoon, part of this army of men returning to Britain to defend the homeland.

They were sunburned a dark brown by the Indian sun in contrast to the civilians below, waiting for the gangplank to be lowered and the soldiers to come on to dry land. They had been in transit for weeks, going the long way round by Cape Town rather than risk coming through the Suez Canal and crossing the Mediterranean Sea. There was no war as yet but the threat of it was ever present though some members of the government still thought it could be averted.

The August sun was shining, a pale imitation of what they were used to in India. But to the men on the deck of the ship it was infinitely preferable to what they had left behind in Bombay.

England, thought Jackson. Everything about it was different. The smells, the feel of the air, the noises. They would be in barracks for a few nights, but next week, always supposing war wasn't declared, they'd be on their way north, with rail vouchers which would take them all the way home. Or at least to Bishop Auckland which was as near as made no difference at all. Two whole weeks at home! Time enough for them to make sure Molly was managing on her own and coming to no harm.

The order to fall out was given, the men were beginning to file down the gangplank, and eventually the recently promoted Sergeant Morley was at liberty to talk to Corporal Mason. They threaded their way through the crowds of wives and sweethearts come to meet their men and onlookers who were simply curious or liked the atmosphere of excitement when a troopship came home.

'Molly's not here,' said Harry. They had searched and searched again, just in case they had missed her in the crowds.

'Oh, come on now, Harry, you didn't expect her to come all the way down here to meet the ship? The train is expensive. And besides, Molly will be at work. She has to make her living, hasn't she?'

Harry nodded. 'I know. But I still looked for her somehow.'

Jackson knew exactly how he felt. He too had felt a moment's disappointment when he had scanned the people meeting the ship and not seen Molly. They couldn't have missed her either. Both Harry and he had been looking and they had keen eyes.

'Five days and we'll be on our way any road,' said Harry as the soldiers came together again and the order rang out to form ranks. A step nearer home, he thought. They marched through the town to their temporary barracks, led by their own regimental band. It was August and the sun beat down on them but to men who had been in India for two years or more the air felt fresh and clean, the familiar scents of England carried on a breeze from the west. Yet it was not quite the same as the breeze which would be blowing down the Wear Valley, straight from the moors, Jackson mused. And five days suddenly felt like an awful long time.

The Northumbria, the Newcastle express train, was packed with soldiers as it left King's Cross and picked up speed as it steamed north. Harry and Jackson sat together in a compartment reserved for non-commissioned officers where they could relax, their kitbags stowed on the rack above their heads. They talked little as the train sped through the northern outskirts of

London and on into the dark countryside. They were due in Darlington at five past six in the morning. There would then be a wait of half an hour or so for the local train to Bishop Auckland.

There was little talking among the men, each of them had their thoughts fixed on home and family. Jackson settled down to sleep. The compartment light was dim. With his long legs stretched out in front of him and his cap over his eyes he took only minutes to drop off, waking only briefly as the train pulled into Peterborough and later on Doncaster. When it arrived in York he sat up, as did most of the others. There was a buzz of quiet talk. They all gazed at the Minster as it fell behind them in the grey light of early morning.

'It has the Taj Mahal beat, mate,' said a burly corporal, and Jackson agreed, grinning, aware that they were a tiny bit prejudiced. He took out his comb and tidied his hair, stroked his chin where he could begin to feel stubble. It didn't matter, though, soon be home. Harry and the others were also tidying themselves up. Jackson looked across and grinned.

'Not long now, mate, Molly will be waiting at the station, I bet.' They had sent a telegram to her and one to Jackson's mother. 'Everything will be all right,' they assured each other, though both had misgivings which intensified the nearer they got to home. It was such a long time since they'd heard from Molly, Harry hadn't even had a Christmas card. But mail could go astray so easily . . .

'Darlington in ten minutes,' said the conductor, sliding open the door of the compartment. 'Next stop Darlington.'

'By, that sounds grand,' a soldier remarked. 'I've been dreaming someone would say that.'

There was no one to meet them at the station at Bishop Auckland. Jackson hadn't expected his mother, not when she had his father at home an invalid, but he had been hoping against hope that Molly would be there. This time he had no words of comfort to offer Harry.

'Let's walk through the woods to Eden Hope,' he said

instead. 'It'll be almost as quick as going down the street for the bus. It's no good you going off to West Auckland when you don't know whereabouts Molly lives.'

'Righto.'

Newgate Street was a mile long. If they cut across country they could be halfway home before they'd even have got to the bus stop. Shouldering their kitbags, they set off.

The wood was pleasantly cool and the Gaunless flowing through it tinkled and splashed, a sound they hadn't heard often in India. They emerged on to a hill where they could see a number of colliery villages, all clustered round a winding wheel and chimneys. The countryside was green apart from patches of gold where corn was ripening. And, of course, the black heaps by the pits, slag heaps. But even the mineheads were beautiful to the two homecomers, pale smoke curling from the tall chimneys.

They hadn't far to go to Eden Hope and soon Jackson was turning into his own back gate while Harry went on to the house where he had been brought up. Or rather to the house next door to question Ann Pendle about Molly's new address.

'Eeh, I've been looking out for you for hours,' Mrs Morley cried, running to Jackson, her arms outstretched. He could feel her bones, he thought as his arms enfolded her, she'd lost weight. He realised why when he heard his father's voice, calling weakly from the sitting room. Frank Morley was laid in a sort of large perambulator, more like a wooden box bed on wheels. His back really was broken, Jackson realised. His mother had written to say so but somehow he couldn't believe it until now. His dad was such a solid, strong man, had always been so. God damn the pit, he thought, filled with helpless anger.

'I'm all right, son,' Frank said quickly, seeing the horror which Jackson had been too late to disguise. 'An' we've got the house and a bit of compen to live on, dinna fash the'self.'

Compensation? thought Jackson. No amount of money could compensate for what had happened to his dad. But he smiled and bent over him, almost kissed him but stopped himself in time. You didn't kiss men, not unless they were dying. And he knew his father wasn't about to give in just yet. But he was only a third of the weight he had been. The muscles of his arms, which Jackson remembered as being so powerful, were wasted away, his neck scraggy, cheeks fallen in.

'Why, no, man, I didn't think you were ready to pop your clogs yet a while,' was all he said.

'How've you been doing?' his father asked eagerly. 'Maggie, have you got the kettle boiling? I dare wager the lad'll be glad of a proper breakfast now he's home. He likely hasn't had anything worth eating since he went in't army. Hey, a Sergeant are you now? That's grand!'

As the kettle had been kept on the boil for the last couple of hours and bacon and eggs were already on the table ready to cook, Maggie was soon bustling about, smiling broadly but with suspiciously wet eyes. She looked up as she was breaking an egg into the pan as there was a knock at the door and Harry Mason walked in, his kitbag on his shoulder. Her smile became a look of concern. In the excitement of Jackson's homecoming she had forgotten about the Masons and their trouble. Had Harry heard about Molly?

'Harry, lad, howay in,' she said now. 'How would you like some breakfast? I can soon do enough for two.'

'No, thanks, Mrs Morley,' Harry replied. He wasn't hungry, simply bewildered and upset. The story which Ann Pendle had told him couldn't be true, it was quite unbelievable. Maggie saw he was white as a sheet under his tan.

'Sit down, lad, you look all in,' she said swiftly, pulling the pan off the fire and going to him. Her heart sank. Obviously Ann had told him. She only hoped that cat Joan hadn't been in to add her ha'porth of spite.

Harry put down his kitbag and she led him to an armchair by the fire.

'What is it? What?'

Jackson had come back into the kitchen, alarm making his voice sharp. He gazed from his mother to Harry. Something had happened to Molly, he knew it. Oh, he should have tried harder to get home before now. Both of them should have. No one answered him for a moment.

Maggie thrust a mug of hot strong tea into Harry's hand. 'Drink that, lad, go on,' she said, and stood over him until he had taken a few sips. 'Right then, come on now, you'll both eat something. There's nothing to be done this minute, nothing at all. You can get something in your stomachs and we'll talk about it.'

'What? Talk about what?' Jackson demanded, frustrated. Why didn't they tell him?

'Our Molly is in prison,' said Harry. He looked up at his friend. 'Ann Pendle says so any road.'

'In prison? Don't be so flaming daft!'

It was unbelievable, someone was having them on was all Jackson could think.

'It's true. They said she robbed the house where she was lodging. Took a gold bangle.'

'No!' Jackson said flatly. 'That's a lie, Molly wouldn't rob anybody.'

Harry looked up at Mrs Morley who was standing biting her lip, her face red. 'You knew about it?' he said.

'Aye, I did. Everyone did. I didn't see it in the *Echo* but Joan Pendle made sure we knew. She told anybody who would listen.'

'You believed Molly had done it?' asked Jackson, staring at his mother, and her face went redder still, as though she had been caught out in some wrongdoing herself.

'I . . . I didn't know what to think, that's the God's honest truth, son. That fella was a respectable man, like, and they said his neighbour saw it in Molly's suitcase.' She sighed heavily. 'I blame meself, really. I should have made time to go and see the lass. She was on her own like, must have been hard up . . . I don't know. But your dad was so poorly at the time . . .' Her voice trailed away.

'Well, I know!' said Jackson. 'An' Harry does an' all. She didn't do it. We'll never believe it, no matter what anybody says.' Without his meaning it to happen, his voice had risen, emphasising his words.

'Hey, lad, you've only been home a minute and you're shouting at your mother. I won't have it!' his father was calling and Jackson subsided immediately.

'Oh, Mam, I'm sorry. I didn't mean to shout at you, you know I didn't.'

'I know. I know, lad. It's all right.' Maggie looked at the food beginning to congeal in the pan. 'Look, eat this afore it spoils. Howay now, we can't waste good food, we'll be short enough of it if the war comes. Harry'll have a bit an' all, won't you, lad? Please, for me. Then we can sit down and decide what's to be done.'

The soldiers sat at the table and ate the food before them though neither of them could have said what it was they were eating. It was just a matter of getting the meal out of the way. Both their minds were working on how they were going to get to see Molly.

Mrs Morley wheeled the ungainly carriage through and stood it by the side of the table so that Frank could join in the talk.

'Thanks, Maggie,' he murmured. They were quiet until Jackson and Harry had finished the meal and laid down their knives and forks.

'More tea?' asked Maggie but they shook their heads.

'Well then,' said Harry, sounding more normal as the initial shock wore off, 'I think the first thing I've to do is telephone the prison.' There was a murmur of assent from the others.

'I'll come with you,' said Jackson. The nearest telephone was three-quarters of a mile away, by the post office in the next village.

'Mind, I think it was May or June, you know,' said Maggie. 'Joan Pendle said Molly got three months. She might be out by now.'

'What I can't understand is why they put her in gaol when she had a good character? The lass hasn't done a thing wrong in her life, I dare swear she hasn't,' said Frank.

Maggie flushed. 'They said in the Co-op that it was because she had no fixed address,' she said in little more than a whisper. 'I blame myself, I do. I could have let her stay here but she was gone before I had the chance to say. I thought she was all right, honest I did, Harry.'

'I'm sure you had enough on your plate, Mrs Morley. It's not your fault.' A terrible anger was replacing his initial sense of shock, an anger he kept well under control, the only sign being the white line around his lips and the set to his chin. 'Is it all right if I leave my kitbag here, Mrs Morley?'

'Why, lad, you know it is. An' you can stay here an' all, I'll make a shakey down bed up in Jackson's room. Now, I'll have no arguments, that's what you'll do.'

Harry nodded, he had had no intention of arguing. 'Thanks, Mrs Morley.'

The soldiers crossed over the field to Jordan, the next village, taking the path well worn by the miners and their families. At the phone box they both went in, their broad shoulders squashed against the glass. Jackson looked up the number and they scrabbled between them to find the six pennies the operator asked for.

'Who's enquiring?' the male voice at the other end asked.

'Does that matter?' Harry was exasperated. This was wasting time and they had no more change between them.

'We can't give out information–'

'All right, all right! I'm her brother. I've just returned from India and I have to find her,' he shouted down the phone.

'Steady on, Harry,' Jackson murmured. 'Losing your temper isn't going to get us anywhere.'

'If you hang on a minute, I'll look it up. What did you say the name was? And what was she in for?'

'Molly Mason. She was in for theft, though she didn't . . .'

'Right then, here it is. Molly Mason, age eighteen years. Discharged 20th August. You've just missed her, son.' The man was beginning to sound almost human.

'Your time is up, caller. If you want to continue, please put another fourpence in the box,' the operator butted in.

'But where? Where did she go?' shouted Harry.

'Why, home, I should think, wouldn't . . .' But the line was disconnected.

'I'll get some change at the post office,' suggested Jackson as they eased themselves out of the box. 'Or maybe we should just go to West Auckland and see if she's gone there? After all, she might have got her job back.'

'We could ask Ann Pendle first. Or Joan might be home now.'

'Any road, we'll go back and ask around Eden Hope. Tell Mam where we're going too,' Jackson decided, and they set off back across the field. They walked in silence, each man's thoughts on the young girl and what had happened to her. What might still happen to her if they didn't find her and help her put her life back together. For both of them knew what it could be like for anyone coming out of prison into the small enclosed mining communities. Molly could be in for a rough ride.

Chapter Ten

Jackson and Harry were on the Eden bus bound for West Auckland by one o'clock that afternoon. They could have gone through Bishop Auckland, changing buses in the town, but Mrs Morley advised them to go on the Eden. 'You won't have to change,' she said. 'It'll likely be quicker.' She couldn't do enough to help them, she felt so guilty over Molly. She could have got someone to sit with Frank when the lass was up before the magistrate; she could have gone and backed her up, told the chairman what a good lass Molly had always been. Aye, she said to herself, she could have done. But her thoughts had been centred on her husband, on his pain and looking after him night and day. She had been so tired those first few months after the accident.

'Bring her back with you, Jackson,' she said as the two soldiers went out. 'Bring her back, she can stay with us, I'll find space for her.'

He gazed at his mother for a long moment but it would be cruel to tell her she could have taken Molly in before now, and probably asking too much of her anyway. Maggie looked so careworn, he knew he was being unreasonable even to think it.

The bus passed the old coach house at Shildon which had been the very first railway ticket office in the world, a fact which always gave him a thrill of pride. But today he only wondered where Molly was. Was she in trouble? A nagging anxiety about her had grown inside him ever since he'd heard she had been in prison, innocent, and alone. For he had no doubt at all that she was innocent, he was as sure of that as Harry. But where was she?

At that moment Molly was walking down Newgate Street in Bishop Auckland after leaving the small damp room down by the Wear where she had been living since she came out of prison. She was on her way to the Labour Exchange where she went every morning searching for work. The money from the colliery, the £25 which she had received after her father's accident, had run out, careful though she'd been, eating only one meal a day and that as frugal as she could possibly exist upon. Now she *had* to get work, had to!

She rounded the corner into South Church Road and then again into Kingsway. The bus was just coming in from Eden Hope. She paused for a moment and gazed at it. It came from another world, it seemed to her, the world of her childhood where, even when the depression was at its height, she had felt safe because there was her dad and her mam and Harry.

The bus pulled up, people alighting, Molly hunched her shoulders and bent her head. Oh, she didn't want them to see her, no, she did not!

'Isn't that Molly Mason over there on Kingsway?' a housewife asked her friend. They were off to the store, the Co-op, to see if they could find any tinned food they could afford to buy to stock up against the threat of war, for everyone said there would likely be rationing.

'Is it?' her friend replied, looking, but Molly was gone. 'I felt sorry for that lass all right,' she went on. 'I would have offered her a place wi' me, but she was away afore I had the chance.'

'Aye. Do you know, I saw their Harry in the street the day. A fine upstanding lad he's grown into an' all. I wonder if she knows he's back?'

'Well, we can't go chasing after her. She must know, surely? But if she doesn't, no doubt she'll soon find out. Howay then, there'll likely be a crowd in the store.' And the two women bustled off into Newgate Street.

‘There’ll be more chance of work for you shortly, especially if the war does come,’ the clerk in the Labour Exchange said to Molly. ‘Nothing at present.’ He looked over her shoulder at the queue: shabby, down at heel, depressing. ‘Take this chit over to the cash desk for your money.’

‘But I must get something!’ she said, desperation making her tone sharp. ‘I can’t live on the dole, it’s not enough.’

‘Well, it’s all you’re going to get,’ the clerk said wearily. ‘Next, please.’

Already the next person in line was moving forward, nudging Molly out of the way. She took her chit and went over to the cash desk. Eight shillings and sixpence. It barely covered her rent. Out on Kingsway once again, she stood for a moment irresolute. She had tried all the shops in the town the day before, there was nothing there. Lingford’s the baking powder factory, too. They had vacancies but when they’d asked where she had been working last and where her references were Molly had backed away. ‘Excuse me,’ she had said. ‘I must go, I . . . I forgot . . .’ she’d left the manager looking after her in astonishment. Did she want work or not?

‘I’ll walk to West Auckland, St Helens at least,’ she said aloud.

‘Eh? What did you say?’ A man was turning into the Labour Exchange. He paused and stared at her.

‘Nothing, sorry, just talking to myself,’ replied Molly, blushing.

‘Aye, well, pet, it’s when you begin to answer back that you have to worry,’ he said, grinning. He was an older man. His shirt collar was clean but threadbare, his suit shiny with age. His grin slipped a little as he looked into her face, saw the shadows under her eyes, how thin she was.

‘Are you all right, pet?’

It was the first time anyone had spoken to her with any sort of concern for such a long time that her eyes filled and she had to turn away in case he saw it. ‘I’m fine, really,’ she mumbled, and fled down Kingsway and round the corner into South Church Road.

It was a fine day at least, she thought as she got her emotions under control and strode out for West Auckland. She paused at a butcher's shop in Cockton Hill and bought a penny dip, a bread bun dipped in the juices from roasted meat. Once away from the houses and on the open road she stopped at a stile and sat down to eat it. She had to force herself to take it slowly, savouring every bite. She had been so hungry she had felt sick with it, and light-headed too. She sat for a short while until the food made her feel better before resuming her journey. She was approaching Tindale Crescent, close to the factories which had been built on the site of an old colliery. Not far to go now. The sun was warm on her face, her spirits lifted. Perhaps Mr Bolton would give her her job back? After all, the factory was working full pelt, she knew that, turning out khaki uniforms for the troops.

Molly was hot and dusty by the time she reached the factory. She hesitated at the gate, her heart thumping in her breast as she tried to raise the courage to go in. It had been one thing thinking about it but now she was actually here . . . She lifted her chin and went into the reception area.

'Molly Mason!' exclaimed the girl behind the desk. 'By, I never expected to see you.'

'Hello, Alice.' The receptionist hadn't been hostile, merely surprised, and Molly felt slightly better. 'I'd like to see Mr Bolton, if I may?'

He kept her waiting for half an hour before calling her into his office.

'I suppose you want your job back,' he said with no preamble. He sat back in his chair and stared at her, no expression on his face.

'I would, yes,' said Molly in a small voice. She looked down at her clenched hands. He wasn't going to give her work, she could tell by his attitude. By, she wished she hadn't come back, wished she were anywhere but here.

'I don't know if it would be wise to take you on again.'

'But I'm a good worker, you know I am, I always kept my production up!'

'Aye, I know that. I wouldn't be seeing you otherwise.' He drummed his fingures on the desk, the first and second stained brown with nicotine. She was a bonny lass, he thought, and wondered if there had been hanky-panky in that house when she was alone with her landlord. Maybe he had given her the bangle for favours received and then said she'd stolen it when she would no longer perform.

Molly rose to her feet. 'Well, if you don't want me, I'll be on my way,' she said. She had had enough humiliation, she wasn't going to beg him, not Bolton.

'Hold your horses, woman, I never said I didn't want you.'

Molly paused on her way to the door and looked back at him.

'Where would you live if I did take you back?' he asked. 'No one round here would have you, I'm certain of that.'

'I have a room in Bishop,' said Molly. She was so filled with a mixture of embarrassment and humiliation, she could hardly see straight.

Mr Bolton studied her for a moment. A bonny lass she was. There was no doubt she was a good worker, had always earned her bonuses in the past. And he didn't think the other workers would care that she had been in prison. At least most of them would not. And what would it matter if they did? None of them would want to lose their job. There was the added advantage that she would probably work harder than anyone to prove herself, and keep her head down too. She was just the sort of experienced machinist he needed to fill the government orders. He came to a decision.

'Righto. You can start tomorrow. But mind, you'll have to keep yourself out of trouble.' He stood up and came round the desk to pat her on the shoulder, a move which caused her to jump and back towards the door.

'Thank you, Mr Bolton,' she managed to say, her cheeks flushed yet again. 'I'll be here at eight o'clock.'

Outside she took a deep breath of air, laden with the scent of new-mown grass where the gardener was trimming the lawn in front of the building. She couldn't believe her luck in being taken on again at the factory, had shrunk initially from trying there where she was known. But now she felt as though a load had rolled off her shoulders. She would be able to keep herself, no more hated dole office.

The afternoon sun was shining along Manor Road. She walked along in the opposite direction to Bishop Auckland with a fancy to see the house in West Auckland where she would have been living now if it weren't for Mr Jones. She felt the familiar twinge of hatred and despair as she thought of him but put it firmly from her mind. This was turning into a good day, the best for ages, and she wasn't going to spoil it. She walked past the entrance to Adelaide Street without even looking down it.

Cathy's house was still there, its windows dusty in the sun. She wondered about her. What had she thought when she'd heard about Molly? That she'd had a lucky escape, could have had a thief in the house? As Molly watched the house from across the street the little boy, Jimmy, came out and picked up the bicycle which had been laid down on the cobbles. He glanced across at Molly and she smiled tentatively but he simply looked at her and pedalled off along the street. Of course, she thought sadly, he had only met her for a few minutes that night.

So had Cathy. Molly had thought of knocking at the door, maybe apologising for not being able to take up the room, telling her the true story. But no, Cathy didn't know her either, it might just embarrass her. Molly walked back the way she had come with a sense of loss which dimmed the happiness of getting her job back.

Next day as she went into work it felt as though she had hardly been away, at least for the first few minutes. She was anxious and therefore earlier than the other girls who worked on the line. Enid was there, though. She said nothing, just allotted Molly a machine. She hung up her coat on the rack in the cloakroom, put her bag with her sandwich box in the small space by the side and waited for the electricity to be switched on. Her machine was at the far end of the line now. When the other girls came in she was sitting with her back to them.

‘Well! Will you look what the cat’s brought in?’ The hated voice exclaimed, the voice she had been dreading ever since Mr Bolton had told her she had got the job. Joan’s.

‘It’s the little sneak thief!’

Molly cringed. She wanted to curl up and die. She concentrated hard on threading her machine needle. The other girls fell quiet. One sniggered in embarrassment.

‘That’s enough of that! I’ll hear no more of that or whoever it is they’ll be out on their ear. Now get on with your work.’

Mr Bolton was standing in the doorway. The girls hurriedly sat down at their places on the band, the electricity began humming, the machines zipped away and the wireless came on: Fred Astaire singing ‘Dancing Cheek to Cheek’.

Molly felt grateful to Mr Bolton even though she knew he hadn’t said it to protect her but to ensure the work went on smoothly. She concentrated on her sewing. She was stitching the bands on battledress jackets, more interesting than sideseams and more complicated too. But Molly soon got the hang of it.

At dinnertime she took her sandwiches outside and sat on the low wall which bounded the factory. The sun was shining and the air felt fresh after the stuffiness and lint-laden atmosphere of the machine room. There were a number of girls doing the same thing. Some of them were laughing and flirting with the male cutters and pressers, Joan Pendle among them. She was smoking a Woodbine, holding it up in the air and gesturing with it, her elbow cupped in her other hand. Molly took care not to catch anyone’s eye but looked down at her sandwiches and the apple she had bought on the way to the bus.

There was a burst of laughter from the group of men and girls on the corner, Joan’s laughter ringing out over the others’. Involuntarily, Molly glanced quickly over at them to find they were looking back at her and grinning. Joan’s expression was pure malice, she thought, flinching. Molly took a bite of fish paste sandwich and chewed doggedly but somehow it refused to go down for ages and when it did she almost choked, coughing and spluttering.

'Get yourself a cup of tea, lass,' one of the men said. He was older, about forty, with kindly eyes.

Joan's jeering voice rang out. 'Don't tell me you're taken in by her big brown eyes an' all, Tom?' She looked round the group, inviting the others to laugh with her.

'Don't be so bloody soft!' he growled, and turned his back on Molly.

She put the remains of her sandwich back in her box and went inside, not to the canteen but to the cloakroom where she got a drink of water from the tap. After all, a cup of tea cost tuppence and she couldn't afford to waste money like that.

All in all, she reflected on her way home at six o'clock that evening, it hadn't been so bad. While she was working on the machine no one had bothered her. Enid had taken the sewn pieces away and left her fresh batches, not speaking to her while she did. But then, Enid was busy. They all were. Only one or two girls actually spoke to her but it was difficult what with the wireless being on and her being at the end of the line. Things would get better, she thought, surely they would? If it wasn't for Joan Pendle . . .

She had a potato to bake for her tea and a piece of hard cheese she'd picked up cheap at the store to grate over it. She washed the potato and put it in the ancient coal oven in the basement of the tumbledown old house which she shared with half a dozen other people down on their luck. While she waited Molly toasted her feet at the fire, glad to be able just to relax. No one was going to make snide remarks here. The fact that she had been in prison wasn't so remarkable in this house; she wasn't the only one.

Sitting in the rickety armchair Molly began to doze, what with her tiredness and the heat from the fire. She awoke with a start when a door banged somewhere in the house and a draught blew in under the kitchen door. Disorientated, she looked round apprehensively, thinking she was still in prison. The horror of that first night was still with her. The loneliness, the feeling of being abandoned by God and everyone else.

She could never go through that again, she told herself. Harry, where are you? Jackson, help me! She was still caught up in the dream she had been having. She saw Jackson running towards her and she was trying to run to him but somehow they never drew any closer no matter how fast they ran. The wall of the prison loomed between them suddenly. She sobbed. It was hopeless. And Harry, Harry was calling to her over Jackson's shoulder, calling her name . . .

Molly woke up properly. She could smell the potato now, it must be ready. He heart still beat fast and her head throbbed but she was awake and no longer behind the prison wall. She took the cloth which was singed brown with oven marks from the line under the mantelshelf and retrieved the potato from the oven. She was hungry, that was all that was the matter. She cut the potato and grated the cheese on to it and ate. She would feel better when she had her stomach full, she told herself.

She missed the old relationships she had had with her workmates. Though she hadn't been close friends with any of them at least she had felt part of the crowd. Now she was excluded, she thought sadly. But given time, and if Joan Pendle didn't stir things up too much, she would be accepted again.

Climbing into bed in her damp little room in the basement, she said a prayer for Harry and, of course, Jackson. She had grown used to thinking of them together. She wondered where they were now, yearned to see them. She felt so lonely. She hadn't written to either of them for months, had been unable to bring herself to while she was in that awful place. She was ashamed to, shrank from letting them know what had happened to her, felt degraded somehow.

At first she had been confident that Harry would believe her, Jackson too, surely they both would? But now she had doubts. Had Jackson's mother written to him, told him of the scandal?

Perhaps she had. Maybe that was why Molly hadn't heard from them. Perhaps even they didn't want to know her now. Restlessly she turned over in bed, trying to find a comfortable spot on the lumpy mattress. She must get some sleep. She had to catch the seven-thirty bus in the morning – couldn't afford to miss it. If she lost her job again she didn't know what she would do.

Most of the time Molly couldn't bear to think about what it was like in prison but tonight the memories wouldn't go away. Why were people so hard, so spitefully cruel? It wasn't just the wardresses, who were only doing their job, she supposed. The other women were worse, some of them at least. And then there was Bertha. Oh God, Bertha! She'd had to share a cell with Bertha. Only for one night but that had been enough. Molly had really reached rock bottom that night. She had fallen asleep from sheer exhaustion and when she woke it was like the night when Bart had put his slimy hands on her. Only this time it was a woman, Bertha.

Molly shuddered, tried desperately to think of something else, anything else. She jumped out of bed and walked the floor, backwards and forwards. Her skin crawled. She could still feel Bertha's hands on her, hear that voice whispering obscenities in her ear. Things she had never heard before, couldn't even comprehend.

Slowly, painfully slowly, Molly regained control of her thoughts, forced herself to push the memories out of her mind. Eventually numbness crept over her, brought on by extreme exhaustion. It allowed her to go back to bed and at last she slept.

Chapter Eleven

'You've both been called back, lads,' said Mrs Morley as they walked into the kitchen. Her voice wobbled slightly with disappointment and apprehension at what was to come.

'What? You must be joking!' cried Jackson, unbelieving.

'No, your mother's not having you on,' his father said, his voice coming through the door from the room beyond. 'It's come over the wireless. All troops to return to barracks. There's a telegram an' all.'

Jackson slumped into a chair, despair rising in him. They were so close to Molly, he knew they were. In another couple of days they would surely find her.

'What are we going to do, Jackson?' asked Harry. He too sounded thoroughly dispirited. But his question was rhetorical. He knew they had to go back to camp. War was coming nearer all the time and they were in the regular army. Jackson didn't even bother to answer, he knew too.

'Have you got any news of the lass?' asked Maggie. As she had asked every evening when they'd come in from searching the area for Molly.

'Oh, aye, we have,' said Harry. 'We know she started work back at the clothing factory three or four days ago. Worked the first two days then didn't go back.'

'Harry! You asked at the factory three days ago, or Jackson said you did any road.'

'Yes,' said Jackson. 'Evidently we asked only an hour before she was set on. I tell you what, Mam, anyone would think we weren't meant to find her. We seem to keep missing her all the time.'

Maggie sighed. 'Well, howay, lads,' she said, taking the oven cloth from the line. 'Come and eat your dinner. I've made a nice steak pie. I reckon we won't be getting a lot more of them if the war comes what with rationing an' all.'

She served the pie, rich with onion gravy and succulent steak, which had cost more than she usually spent on meat in a week. There were mashed potoatoes and vegetables from the garden, the pie crust was thick and savoury, and the men tucked in with a will in spite of their anxiety over Molly, a feeling which worsened as the days went on.

Today they had become desperate enough to knock on doors at random in West Auckland. And thought their luck was getting better when one woman had said yes, she had seen her.

'Come after the attic room,' she had said. 'A nice lass an' all, I thought, though that's not what folk said about her, not when she was sent down for thieving. I didn't think she looked the type at all. I was looking forward to having her living here but she never came back. I would have took her in an' all, I don't care what other folk think or say.' Cathy looked speculatively at the two soldiers. 'You her brothers, are you?'

'I am,' said Harry. 'This is my friend, we're both from Eden Hope. Molly didn't do it, you know. She wouldn't, she's an honest girl. Look, if you see or hear from her, will you let us know? This is Jackson's mother's address.' He handed her an envelope, addressed and stamped.

Cathy took the envelope and studied it for a second or two.

'I'll do that,' she said. She bit her lip and hesitated before going on: 'I know that Bart Jones – he's a flaming hypocrite, always was! They chucked him out of the Chapel once, some goings on they hushed up. Now *that* never got told to the magistrates. His own daughter went about like a timid mouse before she went into the sanatorium up Weardale. But there's no justice, is there?'

The men nodded in agreement. They were both silent at first as they walked on to the bus stop. There was no point in knocking on any more doors and it was almost tea-time.

Jackson couldn't bear to speak, in fact, his emotions were so mixed. Anger that the magistrates had taken the word of Bart Jones against a girl like Molly, frustration that yet another day of their leave had gone and they were no nearer to finding her. Worst of all was the anxiety of wondering where she was, if she was all right, always hoping nothing had happened to her.

Now they had to go back to camp without finding her. The order said immediately which meant the overnight train to King's Cross where they would get their connection. Suddenly he'd had enough of his mother's steak pie and pushed his plate away.

'Now then, lad. You have to eat, keep your strength up. Don't you go wasting good food, not after all the years we were short during the slump.'

With an effort he managed to clear his plate. Leaving food was indeed a sin in Eden Hope. And then the two friends had to pack their kitbags and go dashing through the wood to the station at Bishop Auckland, to catch the train by the skin of their teeth.

'I'll watch out for Molly, I will, son, I promise,' Mrs Morley called down the street after them. She stood gazing after them long after they had turned the corner.

'You've had the lad home on leave then?'

Turning, she saw Ann Pendle coming towards her and was just in the mood to give her a piece of her mind.

'Aye, I have,' snapped Maggie. 'The both of them. Not that we saw much of them, mind, they've been out looking for young Molly most of the time. I blame your Joan for most of it an' all, the spiteful little cat!'

'Well! How could it be Joan's fault, eh? *She* never pinched anything.'

'No, and neither did Molly Mason. You should be ashamed, Ann Pendle, an' you her mother's best friend. Your Joan spreading lies about her, just because she was jilted by Harry. If you ask me, he had a lucky escape there!'

'By, you have a flaming nerve, talking like that about my lass! I'll have you know–'

But what she was going to let Maggie know was lost as that lady stalked up her yard and went into the house, slamming the door behind her.

At Darlington, Harry and Jackson found the train full of soldiers returning to barracks and had to settle down on their kitbags in the corridor. Neither of them caring much about it, they sat there and stared at the floor or their boots, occasionally standing to stretch their legs and staring out of the window at the darkening landscape. Jackson lifted his eyes to see Harry, a Woodbine in his fingers, the ash on the end growing longer and longer as he forgot about it. Jackson got to his feet and stood beside him.

'We did all we could,' he said.

'An' not very much, was it?'

'No.' Jackson spoke heavily, feeling defeated.

The train was slowing down as it came into York station. It was crowded with men in uniform and women seeing them off but Jackson stared out unseeingly.

They had gone to Adelaide Street, found the house where Bart Jones lived, but there'd been no one in. The man next door had come out, angry at being woken.

'Can you not let a man sleep when he's on night shift?' he had snarled.

'Sorry, mate,' said Jackson. 'I wonder, though, now you're awake, when does Mr Jones get in from work?'

'He'll be here any minute,' the neighbour had replied. 'Ah, look, here he is now. Now if you don't mind . . .' He went inside and closed the door behind him.

'Yes?' Bart Jones had asked, his head cocked to one side. 'Are you looking for me?'

'We are if you're the man Molly Mason used to lodge with,' said Harry. 'We want to know where she is.'

Bart's demeanour changed. He looked about him before

gesturing them closer. 'Aye, I am,' he said. 'An' a sorry day it was too when I let her into my house. Stole from me, she did.'

'You're a liar!' Harry had suddenly yelled at him, and Bart Jones visibly paled and jumped away from the two soldiers. 'My sister never stole a penny in her life! She's just a young lass, brought up right an' all, she wouldn't steal anything.'

'Harry, calm down,' Jackson had cautioned, though his own blood was boiling.

'Aye, you tell him, coming here, threatening a poor chap like me. I've got a bad leg, let me tell you, and if you go for me I'll have the polis on you, I will!' As if he had been summoned, a policeman appeared at the top of the street. 'Constable Horton! Constable!' Bart Jones yelled, suddenly sounding more confident. 'These soldiers are threatening me!'

'What's all the commotion?'

The policeman was middle-aged and portly. He walked slowly up to them and frowned at the soldiers.

'It's about that young lass what stole from me. You know, the one who got sent to prison. They want to know where she is. I'm sure I don't know, I don't want anything to do with the likes of her again.' Bart sniffed and pursed his lips in disdain.

'He was saying things about my sister,' said Harry, his fingers itching to squeeze Bart's throat.

'An' you threatened me! I have a good mind to lay you in, threatening innocent citizens . . .'

Jackson took a step towards Bart and he hurriedly backed into the house, ready to close the door on him.

'Aye, well, I'm sure it was in the heat of the minute. We don't want to be putting our soldier lads in gaol, do we? Not just now, we might need them,' said the constable mildly. 'Howay then, lads, time to be away, I think.' He gave them a friendly nod.

'Aw, come on, Jackson,' said Harry. 'We're going to get nowt out of him, the dirty little bugger. I suspect he was sniffing up our Molly's skirts and when she turned him down . . .'

'I didn't! I never did!' shouted Bart Jones, his head peeping out from behind the door.

'Never mind that,' said the constable. 'Inside wi' you now. An' you two, away wi' you.'

And Jackson and Harry had turned on their heel and marched up the street.

'I didn't expect to find out anything from him any road,' said Harry. 'I just wanted to see the man who put the lass in prison.'

'Aye,' Jackson agreed. 'I think you hit the nail on the head too. That was likely the way it happened, he'll have made up to her.'

'Aye.'

They lapsed into silence. Jackson was thinking of Bart Jones with his hands on Molly and his skin crawled. There were plenty of Bart Joneses out there, ready to take advantage of young girls. Pray God nothing more happened to her before they found her.

He sat down on his kitbag and leaned his head and shoulders against the side of the train. He closed his eyes, unable to get out of his mind a picture of Molly, frightened, at the mercy of men like Bart Jones. Or else in gaol, trying not to show how humiliated she was. For she would have been humiliated. Molly was a proud girl. Even as a little 'un she'd held her head high like a queen.

The train was steaming into Peterborough when on impulse he got to his feet and worked his way to the door through the crowds already on the train and the crowds beginning to get on, most of them soldiers with kitbags.

'Watch it, Sergeant!' a voice protested as he pushed his way out, bumping into a sailor and knocking the kitbag from his shoulder.

'Sorry,' Jackson muttered and jumped down from the train.

'Jackson!' Harry was shouting through the open window of the carriage.

'You go on, Harry,' he shouted back. 'I'll be there in a couple of days. Nothing will happen before then but there's no need for two of us to get into bother. With a bit of luck, I'll find her.'

His last words were lost as the whistle blew and the London train chugged out of the station. Jackson ran over to the opposite platform and jumped on the train standing there, this one half empty. He couldn't just go away like that, war or no war. He had to have another try at finding her.

Molly woke in black darkness. For a moment she thought herself back in prison and fear of the morning overwhelmed her before her mind cleared of nightmares and she sat up in bed. There was the sound of water. Rain was drumming against the small window at the top of the basement wall. There was more, though, not just raindrops. Water was lapping against something, it sounded close. She got out of bed, putting her feet directly into her shoes for the floor was of stone slabs and bitterly cold even at this time of the year. Groping her way over to the light switch, she slipped and almost fell. She was treading in water!

The light came on briefly and went off with a crackle. She had to find the mantelshelf and the candle and matches she kept there, for the electricity here was always going off. The hem of her nightie was wet, she realised, it flapped coldly about her legs. Something else brushed against her legs, something furry. She felt a scream rise up from her throat and forced it down again.

Her fingers closed around the box of matches. She fumbled to open it, almost dropped it, managed at last to take out a match and strike it to light the candle. Lifting it high, she gazed around the room: the dank walls, the steps leading up to the ground floor of the old house, the door with the bottom rotted away and a hole as big as a fist. Water was running down towards her.

Molly jumped on to the bed in a panic as she saw two, no, four, rats thrashing in the water, one of them actually swimming. For a moment she stood on the bed, frozen into stillness, then her brain began working again. She jumped down and grabbed her coat from the hook on the back of the door, lifting the latch.

The door swung open with the force of the water; the passage outside was completely covered. There was no sound but for the rushing of the water, the drumming of the rain, and from a room upstairs a man snoring, oblivious to it all.

'Get up! Get up! The place is flooded!' Molly shouted at the top of her voice. No one answered. She climbed up the stairs and shouted again,' There's a flood! Wake up – wake up, all of you!'

'What the hell's all that noise?' a man's voice shouted, the landlord's voice it was. 'Has Hitler invaded or what?'

'There's a flood,' cried Molly, 'the river must be up!'

'Aye, well, it does that now an' again down here,' the voice said. 'I'm going back to bed. It won't reach me up here. We'll deal with it in the morning.'

'But what about me?' she screamed.

'Oh, aye, you're in the basement, aren't you? Well, you'll just have to sit it out at the top of the stairs. I'm away back to bed, I have work the morn.'

Molly stared after him as he went back into his bedroom. She heard the springs creak as he got back into bed. Then she ran up and knocked on his door in total disbelief.

'What about me, I said? What about me? I pay my rent!'

'Aye, well, there's nowt to be done about the Wear. I'm not Moses, I can't hold back the waters,' he replied. The bedsprings creaked again, the door opened and he threw out a blanket and pillow. 'I told you, bed down on the landing, will you? And don't disturb me again.'

Someone shouted from the floor above. 'It's all right, go back to sleep!' the landlord shouted back, and closed his door.

Molly stared at the blanket and pillow, neither of them too clean. Then she rushed back down the stairs. The water in the basement was up to the level of her mattress. She waded in and grabbed her underclothes and skirt and jumper, wet though they were. Her teeth clenched against screams as more furry bodies brushed against her. She waded to the chest of drawers and took out her spare underclothes, all wet, and took them up the stairs to the dry landing. As an afterthought she went back for the marble clock which had come from Eden Hope.

Shivering, she lay down on a strip of carpet on the landing, pulling the blanket over her. Her mind was numb. She was past worrying about anything, even managed to doze a little. When she awoke, the light of morning was creeping on to the landing from an open bedroom door. The rain had stopped. Someone was moving about downstairs. Molly stood up, pulling the blanket round her.

'You can give us a hand here, if you like,' said the landlord. He had a yardbroom in his hand. As she watched he opened the front door and began sweeping water out. It cascaded over the steps, brown river water, dark with peat and full of debris. The rats had disappeared or perhaps were still in the basement.

The grass in front of the house was bedraggled and sodden, bits of debris caught in patches of nettles and ground elder.

'We get flash floods like that every time it rains up the dale,' the landlord said, making conversation. 'It soon goes down, though. But mebbe you should look somewhere else for lodging. The basement will be flooded for days now. I knew I shouldn't have let it.'

Chapter Twelve

'Just get out of here, will you?' Mr Bolton said. Molly gazed at him. His face was as hard as nails, she realised. He obviously wasn't going to change his mind.

'But it wasn't my fault! I've told you, we had a flood,' she protested. What was she going to do? She had had to spend the last of her reserve money to buy a second-hand dress and jacket on the market, she'd had nothing dry. She had got to the factory as soon as she possibly could and only to be given the sack. And at the back of her mind was the ever-present fear that she would not find any place to stay tonight, and she couldn't stay out on the street, could she?

'Aye. You'll tell me anything but your prayers, won't you?' Mr Bolton said. He picked up some papers from his desk and flipped through them. 'Go on now. I told you, I don't want you back. I'll say nothing about it, that's fair enough, isn't it? I'll even give you a reference if that'll get rid of you.'

Molly gave up. She might as well save her breath, he wasn't going to believe anything she said anyway. She felt utterly defeated. 'All right, I'll go,' she mumbled.

'Hang on,' said Mr Bolton. He picked up a piece of headed notepaper and wrote on it, slipped it in an envelope and handed it to her. 'Mind, you're lucky I'm doing this, do you realise? I told you, didn't I? Just one slip and you're out.' It was a pity, he thought, she was a tasty piece. Maybe if he'd kept her on . . . No, it was tempting but better leave it alone, that way only trouble lay. Molly Mason was bad news. Look at that fellow in Adelaide Street . . .

Outside Molly took the sheet of paper from the envelope.

'*Miss Mason proved to be a good and efficient worker*,' it said. What good was that? Any prospective employer would wonder why, if she was so good at her job, she had lost it. Putting the reference away in her bag she walked out on to the street, hesitating over which way to turn. She was drawn towards West Auckland where the only woman to give her a kind word in recent months lived. She wondered whether Cathy's attic bedroom was still for rent. No, it would have been snapped up months ago. Sadly Molly turned in the opposite direction.

The Eden bus passed her, making her think of Eden Hope. She felt a sharp longing for her home village, the rows, the Chapel, the colliery winding wheel and chimney towering over everything. Even the slag heap where, in the depression, miners who were out of work had searched for small coal. The bad old days had turned out to be the good old days for her.

She had to stop thinking about it, she told herself, setting her face for Bishop Auckland and the Labour Exchange. She would walk the couple of miles, it was a nice day and anyway she couldn't afford the bus fare.

In spite of her troubles her spirits lifted a little. The sun was shining. A group of pit ponies galloped about in the field by the side of the road. Their pit must be on holiday, she thought. They jumped and kicked up their sturdy hind legs in play, charged playfully then stood and blew gently on each other's necks. Little ponies, Shetlands, for the seams in the South-West Durham coal field were small.

Molly thought sadly of the contrast between their lives in the pits and what they would have been on the islands. She tried to rub the nose of one who came close but it backed away, no doubt fearful it would be caught and taken back down under the ground.

Fanciful, she thought, that was what she was, too fanciful. Her dad had always said so. Molly walked on, to the old road which had first been built by the Romans and led straight as a die to the centre of the town.

'They want girls at the Royal Ordnance Factory,' the man behind the counter at the Labour Exchange said. He gazed disapprovingly at her. 'I don't know, you don't seem to be capable of keeping a job, do you?' he commented.

Molly lifted her chin and stared back at him. Little tin gods, her dad had called the men at the dole office. Thought they were better than most just because they had good jobs.

'Was it my fault there was a flash flood on the Wear? I'm supposed to go to work in wet clothes, am I?'

Something about her direct gaze, the glint of defiance in her eyes, made him smile in spite of himself. Here was a lass who had been through the mill. He knew her history, it was all down on her file. And even if she had done wrong, she had had an awful lot of provocation it was true. He struggled but couldn't help softening his tone.

'Well, we'll say no more about the past,' he said. 'Now, about this job at the Royal Ordnance Factory . . .'

Molly fairly danced down the stairs of the Labour Exchange, the precious paper which she was to present to the manager of the factory clutched in her hand. Workers at the munitions factory were well-paid. She could make thirty shillings a week, maybe more. She would be able to afford a nice room somewhere fresh. It was a new beginning for her, she knew it in her bones, the bad times were past. Hope sprang up in her, she fairly bubbled with it, smiling brightly and standing aside to let a bent old miner go past. The factory would take her on, she thought. They must be going full pelt now, what with the war coming and everything. Not that she wanted the war to come, not when Harry and Jackson were in the army . . .

'Jackson!'

As if by magic, as if he had been conjured up by her thoughts, there, in the bright sunlight, was Jackson Morley, just turning into the entrance of the Labour Exchange.

They both stopped dead in their tracks. Molly blinked. After the comparative darkness of the stairs and entrance the sunlight was blinding. Perhaps it wasn't him, maybe she was fooled because she'd wanted it to be so much. She closed her eyes and wished.

'Molly.'

Jackson sighed, stepped forward, took her in his arms. He was hungry for the feel of her, couldn't believe that after all their efforts in the last few days he had actually found her by accident. He was filled with a profound sense of thankfulness. They stood quietly in the doorway, holding each other. Molly was drowning in the sweetness of the moment. After all that had happened, all the longing, here was Jackson. She clung to him as though he might disappear into thin air if she let go of him.

'Howay then, put her down, man, there's a time and a place for that sort of thing,' a man's gruff voice said. 'Come on, let a bloke in. You're blocking the doorway, man!'

'Sorry, mate.'

Jackson drew Molly outside. They stood to one side, her face radiant, eyes glazed with happiness. She looked about her eagerly.

'Where's Harry? He's not hiding, is he?'

Harry had often teased her when they were small. He would hide behind a bush or the furniture, jumping out at her when she least expected it.

'He's not here, he . . . he had to go back to barracks,' said Jackson, a shadow falling across his face. So the welcome hadn't all been for him, he thought with a sense of loss as he saw the disappointment on her face.

'Without coming to see me? You mean, he was here and he didn't come to see me?'

Molly couldn't believe it, Harry had been here and she had missed him. She looked up at Jackson, her brown eyes wide, waiting for him to tell her why.

'We didn't know where you were. We were looking for you, we only had a few days.'

'But I wrote to him – I wrote twice.'

That had been an age ago, before she went into *that* place. As usual she couldn't even think of prison, her mind shied away from it. She hadn't written since, she'd been too ashamed.

'Look, come into Rossi's, we'll have a cup of tea and talk about it.'

They walked down to South Church Road, turned the corner back into Newgate Street and went into Rossi's ice-cream and coffee shop. It was practically empty at that time of day. They took the booth furthest away from the counter so that they could talk in peace. Of course Molly was disappointed because her brother wasn't here, Jackson chided himself, she hadn't seen him for years and in the meantime she had lost her father in the pit. She was only a child when they went away, of course she was, she couldn't have been so excited just to see her brother's friend. That was it, he was her brother's friend. He'd been a fool to believe she thought any more of him. Still, now she was older . . . and so bonny, he mused as he stirred sugar into his tea.

'I'm that glad to see you,' Molly said simply, and his spirits lifted. She smiled at him. His face was lit up by a beam of light coming in from the high window. By, he was like Harry, yet different too. The same colouring, the same dark eyes, but Jackson had a look of his dad, that was it. But the two lads could have been brothers, she mused.

'Seen enough?' he asked softly, and Molly blushed and looked down at her tea. She took a sip. Ugh! You could tell Mr Rossi was Italian, his tea tasted funny.

'Tell me what happened, Molly?' said Jackson, and her heart dropped into her shoes. She didn't want to have to tell him, not Jackson, it was so humiliating. Maybe he wouldn't believe her.

'You can tell me, Molly. I already know some of it. We asked about in St Helens and West Auckland. You poor kid, what was it like in that place?'

He meant prison, she realised, and her mind closed up as it always did when she thought about it. Oh, she would never tell anyone what it had been like! No, she would not.

He put a hand across the table and took hers. She stared down at their two hands, his so brown, hers white.

'Tell me, Molly?'

'I got a place in St Helens when I had to leave the house,' Molly began, her tone expressionless. 'It was cheap at Bart Jones's and I couldn't afford any more.' She paused and he waited quietly. 'It was all right when his daughter was there. Betty was a nice kid, we got on. But she had to go to the sanatorium, she got TB. And then he began to pester me.'

'Don't go on if you don't want to, I can imagine the rest.' Jackson's grip on her hand tightened. It was firm and comforting. 'Why didn't you go to my mother's when you had to leave your place? She would have taken you in, I know.'

'I didn't like to ask. Not when she had your dad the way he is.'

'But you should have gone back. The folk at Eden Hope would have helped you. Anyone who had known you all your life would know you couldn't have stolen anything.'

Molly thought about Joan Pendle. She would have told the tale *her* way, poison dripping from every word, oh, yes, Molly was sure of that. She stared at Jackson and sighed. 'I was ashamed,' she said simply. She drained her cup and got to her feet. 'Now I have to go after this job, I can't afford not to.'

'But Harry was arranging to make you an allowance out of his pay, if he'd only had your address . . . Come home with me, I'm sure Mam will welcome you with open arms. She's been worried about you an' all.'

'No, I can't do that. Not yet. Not until I have a job and can make something of myself.'

'Well then, come on, I'll go with you. You'll get that job and I'll help you find a room. Where is it you're going?'

'The munitions factory.'

'The train then, that'll be the fastest way.'

They walked up to the station, caught the Darlington train and settled into a shabby compartment. Jackson held her hand like a lover and it felt so good to have someone with her, someone on her side. He meant no more than that, oh, she knew he didn't, but she could pretend, couldn't she? At Shildon other passengers got on. A couple looked into the compartment, saw the soldier and his girl, and went further down the train. That pair would have to part soon enough, they told each other, the way the news was going on the wireless.

They alighted at Aycliffe. The factory was easy to find it was so big. The gatekeeper wouldn't let Jackson in.

'I'll wait here, don't worry. Then, when you've got the job, we'll go looking for lodgings.'

He strolled backwards and forwards along the perimeter wall. Pulled a packet of Players from his top pocket, took out a cigarette and lit it with the flat lighter his mother had given him for Christmas. As soon as he had Molly settled he would catch the next train from Darlington, he thought. It was only forty-eight hours he had been AWOL. Surely he wouldn't be in too much trouble? Probably lose a stripe but it was worth it. He was so relieved to have found Molly, he felt relaxed for the first time in ages. Leaning against the wall, he crossed his feet at the ankles, blew out a cloud of smoke into the air which was already tinged with a touch of autumn though it was still August. Autumn came early in the North East. He wasn't complaining, though, not after the torrid heat of India.

Jackson glanced idly at the army truck coming up to the gates of the factory. He was so relaxed he failed to notice the red caps of the Military Police which the soldiers inside it were wearing.

'That's him, lads,' said the gatekeeper, nodding towards Jackson about fifty yards away. 'Durham Light Infantry. I know the badge, of course. My lad was called back a couple of days ago, they all were.'

Molly came out of the Administration building and ran towards the gate, past the keeper who stared straight-faced at her as he unlocked it for her.

'Jackson!'

She looked around eagerly. 'I've got the job, Jackson –' she went on before trailing into silence. Two redcaps had him by the arms, were frog marching him towards the truck. Molly ran towards them. 'What are you doing? He hasn't done anything!' she shouted at them. 'Leave him alone!'

'He's AWOL, miss,' the redcap nearest to her said. He looked down at Molly. Her face was flushed, her eyes flashing. Beneath her thin dress he could see the outline of her breasts, rising and falling rapidly as alarm took hold of her.

'Mind, looking at you, I can't say as I blame him,' he commented admiringly as his eyes raked up and down her.

'Don't worry, Molly, it's nothing,' said Jackson, talking over his shoulder as they hustled him into the truck. 'I'll be back soon as I can, me and Harry, we both will. Look after yourself, pet. Don't forget, if you need to, go to my mother.'

'Jackson! Jackson!'

But the redcap who had spoken to her closed the door of the truck. It was moving away, turning smartly and going off down the road. Molly was left gazing after it, the euphoria which had been with her all morning draining away. Tears rolled down her face unheeded. Jackson was gone.

'He didn't do anything,' she said to the gatekeeper, who was standing just inside the gates from where he had been following the proceedings with interest.

'He should have been in barracks,' snapped the man. 'Absent without leave – it's just another name for desertion. In my day they shot deserters.'

'He's not a deserter! Any road, there isn't even a war on yet!' Molly shouted at him.

'Not yet mebbe,' said the gatekeeper. 'Any day now, though. An' if my lad had to go, so should that one. Just trying to get out of it . . . scared to death likely.'

Molly turned to him furiously. 'He's not! He's not!' But the gatekeeper grinned and went inside his hut, well satisfied with the results of his telephone call.

Chapter Thirteen

Molly went on looking for somewhere to live, preferably near the factory, in a sort of daze where everything seemed unreal. She trailed about the surrounding villages all afternoon, gazing in newsagents' windows, chasing after the few notices which said 'rooms to let'. She couldn't allow herself to think of anything else. Not Harry, not Jackson. She used her search for a room as a buffer against such thoughts.

'Nay, it went last week, love,' was the usual reply she got as she stood on yet another doorstep. Or sometimes a man was wanted or the rent was far too high. There was a hostel but it was full to bursting.

It was hopeless, she knew it was hopeless; making her way to the train station Molly tried to think logically. What was she going to do? But somehow the fact that she had found Jackson only to have him snatched away before she had even found out where he and Harry were stationed was an agony which insisted on filling her mind, making even the necessity of finding a bed for the night seem of little importance.

The day was already turning to twilight and the trials and emotions of it had wearied her so much she sat in a stupor on the platform, moving like an automaton on to the train when it finally came.

She had bought a ticket for Bishop Auckland though she had no idea where she was going to sleep in the town; her money was practically gone. But what did it matter? Nothing was going to go right for her, she knew it now. She must have offended God somehow, Molly thought dully.

At Shildon a young mother came into the compartment with two children, a tiny boy sucking a lollipop and a girl of about six, holding him tightly by the hand, her face anxious. The woman was heavily pregnant, her abdomen sticking out in front of her, forcing open her cheap coat to reveal a cotton smock.

The boy sucked on his lollipop, staring gravely at Molly with big blue eyes. His nose began to run, the mucus shining in the light of the dying sun. Molly watched as it ran down his upper lip to meet the lollipop.

'Wipe Eddie's nose, Alice,' the mother said, noticing Molly's stare. She herself sat listlessly, legs apart, hands curved under her belly, as the little girl pulled out a grubby rag and wiped it across the boy's face. Eddie took the lollipop out of his mouth to protest loudly.

'Noaw, noaw, noooaw!' he screamed.

Suddenly Molly jumped to her feet. She had to get out into the fresh air. Nausea rose in her. Gagging, she flung herself on to the platform just as the station master came along, banging the doors closed.

'Hey, you want to watch it, miss,' he shouted, but she didn't hear. She was running to the side, gagging, gulping air. Gradually the nausea subsided, her vision cleared, her heart-beat slowed.

'Are you all right, lass?' the station master asked and Molly nodded, forced herself to smile, he looked so concerned.

'I . . . I just forgot I wanted to be off here,' she lied.

'Well, be a bit more careful in future,' he warned, clicking his teeth in disapproval. 'You could have had a nasty accident, you know.' He stumped off towards the barrier and looked expectantly back at her. She walked over and handed him her ticket. 'This is for Bishop, there's no refunds, you know,' he remarked.

Molly nodded without really registering what he had said and walked off up the path which led to Shildon town. She would just walk home from here, she thought, it wasn't all that far. She felt calm and peaceful now, going home. As the twilight turned to black night she trudged along, turning off at the stile which was the beginning of the shortcut to Eden Hope Colliery. The dark didn't matter, she knew all the footpaths around. She was thinking of nothing now, nothing at all, it was better that way. She was simply going home.

'Eeh, Mrs, will you come round our house a minute? There's somebody says she lives there. She asked me what I was doing in their house, the cheeky monkey!'

Mrs Hardy had knocked on her neighbour's door and walked straight in. The Pendles were having their tea. Ann had made a meat pudding and the gravy oozing from the suet crust gave off a wonderful smell, rich and meaty. She put down her knife and fork and got to her feet.

'Sit down, Mam, it can't be that urgent,' said Joan sharply. 'Eat your dinner first!'

'No, lass, I'll go now,' she replied mildly. Jim, her husband, looked up but went on eating his tea calmly. 'I'll put it in the oven, it'll keep hot,' Ann decided.

Molly was standing just inside the door of the house in which she had been brought up, looking around her in bewilderment. She must have made a mistake was her first thought, this must be the wrong house. Where was her mother's press, the marble clock? She felt as though she was in the middle of a nightmare. She swayed with tiredness, slumped, pulled herself together as the door opened behind her and Ann Pendle and the woman who had been in the house when she arrived came in.

'Eeh, Molly pet, what's the matter?' asked Ann. Somehow she was not surprised. She had heard from Joan how Molly had lost her job yet again and as usual had felt a twinge of guilt.

'Hello, Mrs Pendle,' said Molly. Memory was flooding back to her. What a fool she had been! How could she have thought she still lived here? Was she going out of her mind? She had to take a hold of herself, had to. That woman behind Ann was gazing at her as though she were a candidate for Sedgefield

Asylum. 'I'm sorry, I don't know what came over me, I'll go–'

'Howay along o' me, Molly,' said Ann. 'Mrs Hardy did the right thing coming for me. I bet you haven't had your tea neither? There's a bit of meat pudding left, we're just having ours. Come on, pet.' She put an arm around Molly's shoulders and drew her to the door.

'I'm all right now, I am,' said Molly. Looking over her shoulder, she apologised to Mrs Hardy, who was standing open-mouthed. 'I'm sorry, I was so tired, I just forgot–'

'Howay now,' said Ann.

Next door Jim Pendle had finished his meal and was sitting by the fire in the act of lighting a cigarette. He paused, the piece of paper which he had torn from the edge of his newspaper and lit from the fire still black and smoking in his hand. He raised his eyebrows at his wife.

'What's this? Young Molly Mason?'

'Mam!' Joan snapped. 'What's *she* doing here?'

'Aw, shut up, will you, the pair of you,' said Ann. 'Can't you see the lass is at the end of her tether? I'm just going to give her a bite to eat, that's all.'

'You know she got the sack again the day? I told you, didn't I?'

'Aye, you did. Strikes me you took a delight in telling me an' all,' said Ann.

She took a clean plate from the press and spooned on vegetables from the pans still standing on the fender then scraped the last of the meat pudding on too. 'Come on, love,' she said to Molly, 'get that down you.'

'It's all right, Mrs Pendle,' said Molly, blushing bright red as she caught the venomous look which Joan was giving her. 'Really, I'm not hungry.' But the smell was wonderful. Her stomach rumbled as if in direct contradiction of her words.

'Don't be daft, pet,' said Ann. She took her own out of the oven and picked up her knife and fork. 'Come on, tuck in.'

Molly sat at the table and began to eat. The meat was tasty and tender, the suet crust delicious. Though she hadn't felt hungry before, she now realised she was. After all, she had had practically nothing to eat all day. She cleared her plate, wiping the last piece of pudding around it to mop up the gravy.

'Eat the plate, why don't you?' said Joan. Molly looked up, startled, to see the other girl glaring at her with open animosity. Molly blushed yet again and put down her knife and fork.

'Thank you, Mrs Pendle,' she said quietly, 'I enjoyed that.'

'That's all right, pet,' said Ann. 'I'll make a nice cup of tea now. Then we can sit on the settee and have a long talk about what you've been doing all this while.'

'Huh, we know what she's been doing! Probably spent the day thieving, gaolbird that she is,' Joan commented.

'That's enough of that,' Ann said sharply. 'Leave the lass alone. Do you not think she's had enough to put up with?'

'Leave her alone after what she did?' Joan demanded, her voice rising so that Jim Pendle, who had been buried in his newspaper and appeared to be taking no notice of the women, suddenly flung it down and jumped to his feet.

'If there's to be no peace in this house, I'm off out!' he roared. Striding to the door, he took his coat from the hook and pulled it on. 'I'm away down the club,' he snapped over his shoulder.

'There now, look what you've done,' said Ann. 'If he comes in with a skinful I'll never get him up for fore shift then me wages'll be short again. I don't know, our Joan–'

'Oh, aye, it's all my fault, it always is,' she said while Molly sat embarrassed, studying her empty plate. 'I suppose you'll want the gaolbird to stay an' all, share my room? Why don't you give her my bed an' be done with it?'

Molly got to her feet. 'No, I can't stay. I have to go now. Thank you very much for having me, Mrs Pendle.' She moved towards the door. 'And for the supper, it was really good. Me mam always said you made the best meat puddings and she was right.'

'You don't have to go, Molly,' said Ann, but she glanced at Joan as she said it and Molly, intercepting the glance, thought she saw a touch of relief in it.

'Yes, I must. I only came to Eden Hope to . . . to see

Jackson's mother.' It was said on the spur of the moment but as Molly said goodbye again and walked down the yard and out on to the street, she realised that that was what she was going to do. Oh, not to stay, she wouldn't impose on Mrs Morley for the world, but just to look in, enquire after Mr Morley. Now she had eaten she felt better. She could visit Jackson's parents and not be too ashamed, for hadn't he and Harry been home and spoken for her?

'Eeh, lass, I'm that glad to see you! Father! Father! Will you look who's here!' Maggie called through to Frank.

It was heartening to stand at the door of the Morleys' house and be ushered in by Jackson's mother, her face wreathed in smiles. Molly allowed herself to be divested of her coat, to sit in a chair by the fire. It was such a luxurious novelty to be made a fuss of, to accept a cup of tea from the pot which stood on the hearth. It was black, strong, and laced with sweet condensed milk. So reminiscent of the tea her mother used to make that Molly almost broke down. She watched as Mr Morley was wheeled through to the kitchen in one of those long carriages she remembered seeing occasionally in her childhood, the ones which carried men who had had their backs broken in pit accidents, and her heart went out to the couple. But Mr Morley was smiling broadly, alert and happy to see her.

'You've just missed our Jackson and Harry, they've been on leave. Eeh, what a shame! Just by a day or two,' Maggie said, full of regret for what might have been.

'I saw Jackson, Mrs Morley, this –' Molly broke off. She couldn't tell his mother of the circumstances in which she had last seen him. It would worry her to death to think that he had been carted off by the military police because he had overstayed his leave. 'I saw him just before he went back,' she said instead.

'Did you? In Bishop? An' did you not see Harry?'

'No, he was already on the train, but I had a quick word with Jackson.' Molly looked down at the cup in her hand. She moved it slightly on the saucer, embarrassed that she'd had to lie, and not very convincingly either. It was her fault Jackson was in trouble, she thought guiltily, and she couldn't tell his mother that.

'Aye, well, that would relieve their minds any road.' Mrs Morley looked puzzled for a minute though she didn't question the tale.

'Now then, lass, we've heard all about your trouble,' said Mr Morley. 'You got yourself into a right pickle, didn't you?'

Molly's eyes prickled. He sounded so kindly, so concerned for her. 'I didn't do it, you know. I didn't rob that man.'

'No, we never thought you did,' Mrs Morley put in quickly. 'Not for a minute. But I wish you'd come to us, lass. I couldn't come looking for you, not with Frank the way he was. It must have been hell on earth for you in that prison. I've heard tales . . .' She broke off as she saw the expression of acute distress on Molly's face. 'Never mind, you're here now,' she said. 'I'm right glad you came an' all. So tell us what you're doing now?'

Molly almost lost her composure as a picture of the prison rose in her mind. She pulled herself together, back from the horror. 'I've got a job at the munitions factory. I start Monday.'

'Well, that's all right then, if you're working,' said Frank. Like a lot of pit folk after such a long depression he thought that to be working at least was halfway to paradise.

'Where are you staying?' Maggie asked. 'In Bishop, is it?'

'I was. Down by the Wear. But my room was flooded when it rained last night, and I can't go back there.'

'You mean, you haven't got a place?' Maggie glanced at her husband and he nodded slightly. 'Well then, you'll have to stay here. No, don't say a word, I insist. You can have our Jackson's room.'

'Oh, can I? Are you sure? I mean, I know you have a lot on–'

'It's settled. You bring your things tomorrow, pet. It'll make me feel a bit better an' all, I know I should have looked for you before.'

'I can help you when I'm home from work,' Molly said eagerly. 'An I'll pay for my board, of course. I've got a good job now, I can afford to.'

'We'll talk about that later,' Maggie said comfortably. 'You can stay here tonight, go get your things the morn. I'll lend you a nightie.'

Molly could hardly believe it. How could so much happen in one day? As she lay in Jackson's bed, a double bed for it had once held his brother Harold too, long since emigrated to New Zealand, she felt that at last her luck had changed. She snuggled down under the patchwork quilt, wrapped in Maggie's voluminous flannelette nightie, her feet on the warm oven shelf wrapped in an old sheet. Oh, her mam had done that always, put the solid oven shelf in the bed to air it. The pillow slip smelled of Sunlight soap, just as the pillow slips had always smelled at home. But there was also a faint something else there, a male smell, the smell of Jackson.

Oh, dear, Jackson. How selfish she was. She had actually forgotten the trouble he was in, she had been so happy to be here, in his house, with his family. And they'd actually believed her when she'd said she wasn't a thief. By, she was so grateful to them, she was. Molly closed her eyes tightly and prayed as she hadn't prayed in months. That Jackson wouldn't be in too much trouble. That he would be all right. And most of all that if the war came – and there was nothing so certain but that war was coming, everyone knew it, it was just a matter of how soon – please God, let nothing happen to Jackson. Or Harry. 'Look after them both, God, I beg you,' she cried in her heart, her whole being concentrating on the prayer. And then, as suddenly as walking off a cliff in the dark, she was asleep.

Chapter Fourteen

Molly was happy for the first time since her father had died. Even though the war had finally begun, and even though she was working in a room by herself filling trench mortar bombs with explosives. Her hair was tied up in a turban, her face smothered in face cream to protect it and her slim body wrapped in an enveloping overall. Yet still the all-pervasive yellow powder dyed the roots of her hair at the front, got under her finger nails, put a mustard-coloured 'V' in the neck of the thin jumper she wore underneath the overall. She couldn't wear a hair grip or slide to hold her hair back in case friction caused the powder to ignite so wisps escaped and yellowed too. But she was happy.

Today, 1st December, 1939, was a red-letter day. Today was going to be Christmas and New Year and all her birthdays rolled into one, for today, when she went home from the day shift, or back shift as her dad would have called it, Harry and Jackson would be home. They were coming for a week, a whole week! Maggie and Frank were beside themselves with joy, had been talking of nothing else since the letter came. Jackson had only been away a few months this time but the dangers of war made them deeply anxious for him. Now they were going to have him home and that anxiety was eased for a short while at least.

'We can have Christmas early,' Maggie had said to Molly. 'By, isn't it a good job I have the cake and pudding all ready?

'Cause I don't suppose they'll get home for proper Christmas, not this year.'

'No, nobody thinks it'll be over by Christmas this time,' said Frank. 'Only silly buggers thought so last.'

'Less o' that swearing, Frank Morley,' said Maggie automatically. But he had made her wonder how long it *was* going to go on. She thought of the carnage of the last war and shuddered. Please God, not that again, not four years of it.

Molly was going to have their bedroom while Maggie slept in the front room beside Frank. Harry was to share with Jackson. They were going to be a proper family, almost like it had been at home, Molly thought happily as she stopped the stream of powder going into the bomb and sent it on its way into the next room to be fused.

Music came over the radio: '*We're going to hang out the washing on the Siegefried Line*'. Molly sang along with it under her breath. It wasn't so bad working here, even though she was on her own. No one knew much about her past. Thousands of girls worked here, bussed in from all parts of the county, and those in her group were friendly to her. She'd even joined the fledgling concert party. Someone had heard her singing to herself in a sweet soprano she hadn't even realised was good before, no one had ever commented on it. But then she hadn't had much occasion to sing for a year or two, she thought, without self-pity.

The buzzer went and the belt slowed to a halt. It was four o'clock already, Molly realised with a tiny surge of elation. Were the boys home now? Sitting at the kitchen table eating parkin made yesterday with Golden Syrup and some of Maggie's precious hoard of powdered ginger?

By, she hoped they were. It would be grand having a natter tonight, all of them round the fire in the kitchen. Maybe the lads would go out for a drink at the club but they would be coming back for supper and she and Maggie would have it ready for them, they would do it together. There was tomorrow, of course, and Saturday morning too when she had to come to work, but she had the evenings and the whole of Saturday afternoon and Sunday with them.

Dreamily Molly went through to the changing rooms, took off her overall and turban, shook her hair out and washed her face and hands in the basins provided. Her street clothes were in her locker. She changed quickly and rummaged around in her bag for her comb and the slide which held back her thick brown hair from her forehead. She combed it before the mirror on the wall, turned her head this way and that to get a better view of it. It was all right, she supposed. She'd washed it last night with green soft soap and rinsed it with vinegar water to make it shine.

'Got a date, Molly? You're not usually so particular.' Mona, the girl with the locker next to hers, gave her a friendly grin. She was a small blonde girl, no more than five feet, with plump, round breasts and hips. She worked in the fusing room next to Molly, and told comic monologues with the concert party. *Me Mother's Duck Eggs* was Molly's favourite, Mona was a scream telling that one. They rehearsed for the Christmas show in the dinner hour.

'My brother's home on leave,' said Molly. 'Just back today.'

'Eeh, I thought it must be your lad and it's just a brother! I wouldn't bother just for a *brother*,' teased Mona. 'Got a sweetheart have you, Molly?'

Most of the girls talked all the time about their boyfriends, about the boys they would like to be their boyfriends, or, failing that, about Clarke Gable or Ronald Colman or whichever heart throb was on at the pictures that week.

Molly felt the heat rise in her cheeks but said nothing as she turned for the door.

'You're blushing! Hey, girls, Molly has a sweetheart!' called Mona.

'No, I haven't!' said Molly as she turned for the door.

'Ooh, is it a secret?' Mona kept pace with her then relented as she saw Molly's face. 'Oh, go on, I was only kidding,' she said. 'Take no notice of me, pet.'

'I don't, you daft ha'porth!' Molly smiled and ran for the

gates, taking out her pass to hold aloft as she joined the inevitable crush to get through. The train was already standing at the station. She pushed her way through the crowds of girls and men queueing to get on the buses which would take them home. Luckily the railway line went to Shildon and Bishop Auckland. It was faster and easier to get a bus from there to Eden Hope. Or sometimes she walked from Shildon.

Tonight she would have to go all the way to Bishop, it was too cold and wet to get off at Shildon and take the footpath home. The train was crowded too, as it always was. And they had to stand in the station as a troop train went through. All the girls cheered as the soldiers went past though truth to tell there was little to see of them through the blacked out windows. Molly wondered if Harry and Jackson were on the troop train. She felt thrilled to think they might be. Well, Harry was her brother, wasn't he? She kept telling herself it was because of him. But the picture in her mind was of Jackson: that lopsided grin on his face, the dark wave of hair falling over his forehead when he took off his cap, the way his left eyebrow lifted sometimes. She smiled secretly and stared out at the dark countryside, relieved only by the blue lantern of the station master as he waved it and their train chuntered slowly out of the station, following the troop train. And the tiny wink of the green light up the line.

The bus from Bishop was full too. It halted at every stop until Molly could alight at Eden Hope and run along the row and up the back yard. And at last she could open the back door, closing it quickly behind her in case the air raid warden saw the light. And then she was overcome by sudden shyness so that she stood rooted there, just inside the door, smiling foolishly as the two tall figures in khaki got to their feet and came towards her. Harry got there first and, taking hold of her under the arms, whirled her off her feet so that her gas mask fell to the floor unheeded then put her down, dizzy and laughing, before planting a kiss on her cheek.

'Mind, our Molly, you've gone and grown up while I had my back turned,' he cried. 'You're a sight for sore eyes, pet.'

Then it was Jackson's turn and he held her tight, her head against his chest so that she could feel the imprint of a brass button against her cheek. He turned his broad back to the others and she was hidden from their gaze as he kissed her, swiftly, but not at all as her brother had kissed her.

'Molly!' he whispered. 'Molly, my love.' At least that was what she thought he said but it was so low a whisper it might only have been wishful thinking on her part.

'Put her down, Jackson,' said his mother. 'Let the lass get in. She must be fair clamming for her tea and half frozen an' all.'

The table was set with Maggie's second best table-cloth which had unlikely-looking roses embroidered round the edges. The best one was reserved for Christmas Day. There was smoked haddock, poached in milk in the oven, and mashed potatoes and cabbage. For afters there were fairy cakes with the wings stuck on with real butter icing.

'It looks grand, Mrs Morley,' said Molly. 'An' you're right, I am starving.' She was too, she realised. It was a long time since pie and chips in the canteen.

'I'll just mash the tea, pet. We were waiting for you.' Happiness lit Maggie's face, spilled over and softened her voice and movements. She kept looking at Jackson then smiling at Frank as he lay against his pillows and smiled back, his carriage drawn up to one side of the big square table.

'What happened to your other stripe?' he asked suddenly, his brow knitting. Jackson looked up quickly, a forkful of haddock halfway to his mouth, but before he could say anything Harry butted in.

'He got lost on his way back to camp, didn't he? No sense of direction your Jackson, man. I'm sure if I wasn't going with him he'd never find a German to fight.'

'You lost a stripe for being late back?' Frank asked, incredulous. 'You hadn't been drinking, had you, lad?'

'No, no, I never had a drink,' said Jackson, 'it was nothing really.' He concentrated on eating his meal. Molly stole a glance at him but his expression betrayed no emotion. He chewed on. She had a vivid picture in her mind of him with a military policeman to either side of him as they pushed him into the van.

'He'll soon get it back, man,' Harry was saying. 'Good sergeants like Jackson are hard to find. An' this lot coming into the regiment now – by, they're keen but green as grass! They need someone like Jackson and me to knock them into shape, look after them, wipe their . . .' Hurriedly he changed what he had been going to say. 'Tuck them up in bed at night an' all.'

Molly kept her own head bent but the awkward moment soon passed and Maggie was telling the boys about the number of young miners who had joined up the minute the war had broken out, even some of the girls.

'I had a letter from Lancashire an' all,' she said. 'After all these years! That woman I went to work for when I was but a lass of fourteen wanted to know could I recommend anybody?' Maggie shrugged and pulled down the corners of her mouth. 'As if I would if I could, the stuck-up bitch! Won't hurt her to get her own hands dirty. Any road, the lasses are all off to the factories, nobody has to skivvy nowadays.' She nodded in satisfaction. It might have been a while ago but she remembered it well. 'That woman thought she was better than honest Durham folk, she did.'

'Now then, lass, Christian charity,' Frank admonished.

'What about the Pendles?' asked Harry, remembering the time he had gone to see them on his last leave. 'Did they not help you at all, Molly?'

'Ann wasn't too bad,' she said. 'But . . .' Her voice trailed off as she remembered Joan's bitter dislike, the way she'd seemed to delight in Molly's troubles. It still hurt after all this time.

'Aye, I know,' Harry said quickly. He couldn't understand how he had once thought Joan attractive, even gone out with her. Spiteful, that was what she was.

'Never mind, everything's all right now,' said Frank, thinking it high time the subject was changed before anyone mentioned prison. He couldn't bear to see the haunted look in Molly's eyes if the talk ever went anywhere near *that*.

'Molly's fine with us, isn't she, Mother? The past's best forgotten. When are you expecting to go to France then, Jackson? Chase the Hun back to his own country?'

'We can't tell you that,' he said solemnly. 'Walls have ears, you know.'

'Fifth columnists all over the place,' said Harry. He lifted the table-cloth and bent to look underneath.

'Aw, go on, you daft ha'porth!' Molly exclaimed.

'No, we mean it,' Jackson protested.

'Aye, well. I'll make a fresh brew to have with the fairy cakes.' Maggie put her knuckles on the table and heaved herself to her feet. 'You get them, Molly.'

'Nice and strong, mind,' said Frank. 'I daresay we'll be drinking it like dishwater soon when it has to come all the way from India. Blooming rationing! We saw enough of that in the last war.'

Later Maggie took her husband away to ready him for the night. Molly brought out the enamel washing up dish and tray and washed the dishes while the two men dried. Later still they sat around the fire, listening to Tommy Handley on the wireless. When the programme was ended, Jackson got to his feet.

'I think I'll take a walk,' he said. 'I feel like some fresh air. Anyone coming?'

'Going to the club?' asked Harry.

Jackson looked at Molly. She couldn't go to the club. 'No, I don't think so. Just along the lane, around the village, like.'

'Well, I think I'll have a quick one at the club,' said Harry. He glanced from his little sister to his best mate. It was plain to see what was happening there. Well, he couldn't wish a better lad for her. And not so little now, he reminded himself. Molly was growing up.

'I won't be long, just a quick half, see if any of our old mates are in.'

Outside the wind was rising but it had stopped raining. Molly didn't feel the cold. She walked between the men, each holding one of her arms, huddling in together, laughing and joking. At the club Harry left them and Molly and Jackson went on up the lane, away from the houses and the colliery, dodging the dark street lamps, the only lights their flashlights, the dimmed beams bobbing along in front of them. At the top of the bank Jackson stopped. They were in the lea of the old engine house which had once housed the standing engine which hauled the corves of coal up the hill and down the other side to the railway.

'We'll stand a minute,' he said. 'Come here, Molly, we'll keep each other warm.' He opened his greatcoat and pulled it round her so that they were both enveloped by it. She could feel the beat of his heart as he held her and for a minute felt panicky. She wasn't ready for this, no, she wasn't.

But he was sensitive to her feelings and said quickly, 'Don't worry, I'm not trying anything on. I wouldn't do anything you didn't want me to, petal.'

'Oh, Jackson, I do love you.'

Surely she hadn't said that? Overcome, she hid her face in the rough serge of his tunic. Mam had always said never to tell a man you liked him, not until he'd said it first. Had he said it in the house or had she imagined it? Any road, here she was standing in the dark with a man, even if it was Jackson and she'd known him all her life. But not like this. Not standing breast to breast, her head on his shoulder, his arms around her, making her feel warm and safe. Eeh, what would he think of her? She tried to move back, away from him, but his hold was unyielding, he wouldn't let her.

'Say it again,' he whispered, his lips against the nape of her neck, just below the brown beret she had pulled over her hair.

'I don't think I can.'

'Oh, Molly!' He laughed softly, caught her tighter in his arms and lifted her off the ground until her face was on a level with his. He kissed her lightly on her cheeks, her chin, her lips last of all, and small tremors of delight ran through her body. A new and strange excitement began somewhere deep inside her and rose up, threatening to engulf her. It was so dark she couldn't even see his eyes but she knew he was smiling. He moved his hand. His thumb brushed against her breast and her nipple sprang erect in response. She closed her eyes and leaned further into him, completely bewitched. But the next kiss never came. Instead she found herself back on her feet, he took a step back away from her, she knew he was no longer smiling.

'Come on,' he said, his voice suddenly rough. 'I'll get you back home. It's going to rain. And anyway, you have to go to work in the morning.'

The shock was like a slap in the face. She'd been too forward. Oh, aye, she could almost hear her mother's voice: 'A man won't respect a lass as is too free with her favours, you mark my words!' She had been talking about a girl from the other side of the village at the time. Molly had only been twelve and had puzzled about what was meant by 'being free with favours'. Now she knew. Her face burned. She had offered herself and Jackson had backed away. Not altogether, though. As she stood deep in misery a bus went past and in its dim lights he saw her downcast face. She saw his expression change from a frown to a grin. He stepped forward and pulled her beret on straight, her collar up around her neck.

'Howay, our Molly,' he cried, grasping her hand and pulling her after him in a run down the lane. 'We'll dodge the drops, eh?' As he had cried so often when they were children and she'd trailed after Harry and him, 'making a proper pest of herself', as Harry would tell her.

They arrived at Eden Hope, breathless and laughing, running past the pit yard to the rows of houses thrown up by the mine-owners at the smallest cost possible to house the workers for their new mine.

Harry was already back from the club as they went in. There was a faint smell of Federation Ale in the air. He looked from one to the other knowingly.

'Where've you two been then?' he asked, but didn't wait for an answer. 'There's tea in the pot if you want a cup. Your mam's gone to bed, Jackson.'

'No, thanks, I'd best get up. I've to be out by six in the morning,' said Molly. She could hardly look at her brother. Suppose they'd done more, her and Jackson? 'Gone all the way' as folk said. Would Harry have known and despised her for it?

Long after she'd gone to bed she could hear the soft murmur of the men's voices downstairs. Molly tossed and turned on the deep feather mattress which had been a wedding present to Maggie and Frank. Eventually she dropped off and dreamed confused dreams of Jackson and her going into Bishop Auckland to buy a ring. They stood before the counter in the jeweller's and she was ecstatically happy, so brimful of joy she couldn't contain herself. And then she looked down through the glass top and there, among others, was the bangle. The one which had put her in prison.

'You brought that bangle in,' the jeweller said accusingly. 'I'm going for the bobbies.'

'No, I didn't!' Molly shouted. 'I didn't, Jackson!'

But he was stepping away from her, looking at her with accusing eyes, hard as nails. 'The man should know,' he said. 'Oh, Molly, how could you do it?'

She woke in a sweat, still murmuring denials. Her head ached, her heart pounded with fear. There was a terrible noise. Molly turned on her back and took a deep breath. She reached over to the bedside table and pushed down the button on the cheap tin alarm clock she had bought in Woolworth's. The horrible noise stopped and after a moment or two the pain in her head lessened. It was morning, time to go to work.

Molly climbed out of bed and lit the gas jet on the wall above the fireplace. These dark mornings were a bane. She put on her overcoat in case one of the lads should wake and get up. Then, gathering her clothes together, crept downstairs.

The privy was across the yard. Slipping out of the back door and running across with her shoes unlaced on her bare feet, she shivered in the nagging, bitter cold. Back in the kitchen, still warm as the fire had been banked up the night before, she washed in a ladle of water from the boiler in the range and dressed hurriedly. She hadn't time to make a cup of tea. The fire was sluggish, reluctant to come back to life. Never mind, she'd get one in the canteen during her break.

Soon she was speeding down the road to where the bus was just pulling up at the stop on the end of the rows. Jackson would be there when she got back tonight, she thought, a warm glow suffusing her so that she hardly felt the cold. And Harry too, of course.

Chapter Fifteen

Saturday morning went on and on until Molly thought it would never come to an end. She was filling cordite bags for the navy, bag after boring bag, except that she couldn't be too bored, couldn't let her mind wander much. This stuff was dangerous.

George Formby was on the wireless singing 'Mr Woo' and Molly sang along with him softly, her voice sounding hollow in the small room on her own.

This afternoon she was going only as far as Bishop and Jackson was coming into town to meet her. The whole lovely afternoon stretched before her. They were going to have something to eat at the King's Hall café. Then, if the weather was cold or wet, and she couldn't really tell where she was working, they would go to the matinee at the King's Hall picture house. Or, if it was nice, they would walk in the Bishop's park. She didn't care which, she was going to be with him. There was happiness bubbling inside of her at the thought of it.

They could do exactly as they liked because Harry had a date. He was going out with a girl – was being evasive about who she was exactly.

'Fast work that, mind,' Jackson had said last night when her brother told them he had a date. 'You haven't been home two days yet.'

'Can I help it if I'm irresistible to women?' Harry had grinned and put on what he called his Clarke Gable look. He'd taken out his comb and combed back his dark hair with exagerated care, pushing it back slightly at the front to make a quiff.

Molly smiled at the memory. Tonight they would worm out of him who the girl was. So far all they'd got was his hands describing curves in the air and a long wolf whistle.

For the thousandth time she wondered what time it was. Surely it must be twelve o'clock by now? She started on another bag but at last the buzzer went, George Formby was cut off in the middle of asking Mr Woo what he could do, and Molly was free to go.

They ate pie and peas and chips at the King's Hall. Jackson had half a beer and Molly had a shandy, pale amber and sweet from the added lemonade. It tasted like nectar.

'Now what?' asked Jackson as they finished their meal and the waitress brought the bill. 'You choose, I'll do whatever you want to do.' He delved into his pocket and brought out a pound note and gave it to the waitress. 'Sixpence for yourself,' he said and smiled at her. She blushed and walked away hurriedly to get change at the desk. 'Some girls have all the luck,' she commented to the cashier, who followed her glance to the dashing soldier and his girl.

'I see what you mean,' she replied. 'It makes your heart flutter to look at him, doesn't it?' She held a hand dramatically over where she thought her heart to be and they both giggled.

'The sun's shining, we'll go for a walk,' Molly decided.

'Walking in December? Folks'll think we're off our chumps.' Jackson raised an eyebrow but she knew he was joking. He took hold of her hand and drew her out and down the stairs to Newgate Street, busy with Saturday shoppers.

'The park it is then.'

They walked slowly down the street, looking in shop windows, not exactly hand in hand but close enough to be touching each other sort of accidentally all the time. Jackson paused by the jeweller's window, 'Look, Molly, what sort of ring would you like? Always supposing, of course, that we were going to get engaged, you'd like a ring, wouldn't you? Or if you don't want to get engaged, we can pretend, can't we?' He was laughing but his eyes were serious, watching her.

Suddenly she was short of breath. Her hands fluttered in front of her, she couldn't keep them still. She bit her lip. Was this a real proposal? No, she told herself, he's joking, he doesn't mean it. If I said yes and picked out a ring he would run a mile, of course he would. She stared up at him.

'Oh, Molly, if you're not ready we'll wait,' he said, the smile gone from his face. They stood close together in the middle of the pavement as people pushed past them on their way to the market.

'You're having me on,' she said, forcing herself to look away. 'Come on, let's walk, it's too cold to stand about.' She made to walk on but he caught hold of her shoulders, his firm grip holding her still.

'No, Molly, I've never been so serious in my life,' he said, and suddenly a great elation filled her, shining out of her eyes.

'You're asking?' she said, for all the world as though they were at the church hall hop and he had come over for a dance.

'I'm asking,' he said. And it didn't matter at all (or just a little bit) that they had to come down to earth when they saw the prices in the window. Seven pounds ten shillings for a ring with three minuscule diamonds set on the slant on a golden band!

'You like it, don't you? I can't buy it today,' he said regretfully. 'But I will, now I know what you want, I promise you, my love.'

'Are you going to stop blocking the blooming pavement or have I to batter me way through with this pram?'

A strident voice cut into their dream. A tired-looking woman with dull untidy hair was trying to get by, pushing an enormous old pram with two toddlers hanging on to the handle on either side. They sprang into the shop doorway to clear the pavement.

'Love's young dream, eh?' the woman said as she passed.

One of the toddlers started to wail, 'Can I have a ride, Mam?

Me legs're tired. Howay, Mam, lift us up, I won't sit on the babby's legs.'

She stopped and lifted him on to the bottom of the pram, glancing again at Molly and Jackson. 'Aye, well, just you wait a year or two an' see what happens,' she said to Molly. 'I'd think twice if I was you.' But Molly wasn't looking at her any more, she was gazing through the window at the glass counter just inside the jeweller's with a sense of *déjà vu*. It was just like in her dream, the nightmare she'd had the other night when the jeweller had accused her of bringing in the bracelet. Oh, dear God! Suddenly all her old terrors rose to the surface.

'Molly?' Jackson took her arm, pulled her to him. 'What's the matter, Molly? You're not that upset because I haven't got the money with me to pay for a ring now, are you?'

She shook her head, shaking away the terrors. It had just been a nightmare, she told herself firmly.

'Nothing. Nothing's the matter,' she said, and smiled brightly up at him. She tucked her hand in his arm, feeling the warmth and strength of him beneath the rough khaki cloth. 'Come on, let's go to the park or it'll be dark before we get there.'

The market place was filled with stalls and thronged with shoppers hoping for bargains. Late Saturday afternoon was the time for those, the traders dropping their prices before packing up to go home. 'Now then, missus, two cauliflowers for the price of one . . . three pounds of carrots for the price of two . . . a proper bargain. Why, man, I'll be out of pocket . . .'

Jackson and Molly strode on to the gothic archway and the gate which led to the bridle path past the castle and on to the deer park. There were few people about though the sun still shone, slanting its rays through the railings of the castle gardens and pointing up the ancient battlements. But the lovers weren't interested in the castle, they were in a world of their own, going through the cattle gate at the end and on up the grass to the square deerhouse then back down into the valley where the Gaunless ran, hurrying to meet the Wear, brown and peaty and swollen now in winter time.

A wind had sprung up, keen and promising a frost later on, but here, in the small valley, they were sheltered from it though it soughed and whined through the high, bare branches of the trees. Molly felt as though they were the only people in the whole world. They could stay here, hidden away from everyone else, the war and all its dangers.

They paused beneath the branches of one of the oaks which had given the town its name, a thick, ancient tree with branches low and spreading, its carpet of dry brown leaves rustling under their feet. And it was all so perfectly natural, so *meant* to be, as Jackson's arms went around her and Molly lifted her face for his kisses. He loosed her coat and his, undid the top button of her blouse and kissed the swell of her breast. She sighed in ecstasy, feeling the two of them cocooned in the warm blanket of their love.

'You will marry me, won't you, Molly?' he asked urgently.

'I will,' she replied, and to her it was a dedication as binding as if she had said her vows in church.

'My next leave? Even if I have to get a special licence?'

'Your next leave.'

For a while she could think of nothing but the feel of his hands on her body, the surge of her response taking her by surprise at the strength of it. She was filled with the need to sink down on to the carpet of leaves with him and make love, full, total love.

An aeroplane went by overhead, then another. She heard them only as part of the background: the waters of the Gaunless rushing over stones, a lorry going up Durham Road in the distance, the wind. But for Jackson the engine noise brought him back to reality. He lifted his head, moved his hands back to the comparative safety of Molly's waist. She moaned softly with her need, leaned even closer in to him.

'We have to be sensible,' he whispered. 'You're so young.' That wasn't really what he meant. He meant that he was going to war and couldn't just make love and leave her. Suppose she was expecting a baby? Suppose he didn't come back? What would she do then? She was just a girl herself, nobbut a bairn.

When she opened her eyes they were dark with the want of him and his resolve almost went. But another flight went past. Five, no, six planes this time. He looked up to the sky. Hurricanes they were, flying low enough for him to see the rondels on their sides. The war was real and where would he be in a couple of weeks' time?

'Come on, Molly, it's getting dark,' he said and fastened her buttons again, then his own. They walked out of the park against the stiffening wind, apart now, not touching. He didn't think he could bear to touch her without making love, not yet, not until his blood had cooled down.

The aeroplanes had had their effect on Molly, too. She didn't know whether they were fighters or bombers but it had suddenly occurred to her that there were factories in Germany with girls filling bombs just as she was doing, and the thought of them dropping on Jackson and Harry and the rest of the Durham Light Infantry, and all the other soldiers going over there to Belgium or France or wherever they were going, filled her with unspeakable dread.

They caught the bus back to Eden Hope and sat close together on the narrow seat, holding hands. The bus filled up with people they knew; housewives with full baskets, men running to join the queue from Kingsway Football Ground, talking loudly of the match, arguing about the results. It had been a local Derby, Shildon versus Bishop, and there were supporters of both teams. The bus was packed, men standing in the aisle, shouting across the heads of those sitting down. 'The ref wants his eyes tested!' being the mildest of the comments. Some of the men, young miners, looked at Jackson in his uniform with a mixture of envy and respect. Some spoke to him: 'Good luck, lad.' Or, 'On leave are you, mate?'

A few of the women gave Molly peculiar looks and whispered to each other but she didn't care, not now, not when she had Jackson beside her. Most of the folk in Eden Hope had accepted her back among them anyway. The scandal had been a nine days wonder. There were more important things to talk about now.

Alighting at the end of the rows, most of the women joined the men in calling 'Goodnight!' to them. It was already black dark as they walked down the back street, bumping into each other between the blacked out houses for both of them had forgotten their flashlights. Jackson took her arm and led her into the yard and she felt cherished and looked after. Something of a novelty for Molly.

'There's a dance at the church hall the night,' said Harry after they had got in and were eating their tea. Sausages and mash it was, with brown sauce, and dire warnings yet again from Maggie about how these would probably be the last they saw before the meat rationing came in.

'There's them that's hoarding tins as fast as they can get a hold of them, but not me,' she said self-righteously. Then had the grace to add, 'I haven't the money to do that any road.'

'We'll go, won't we, Molly?' Jackson said in answer to Harry. 'A military two-step'll go down a treat, eh?'

'Oh, man, don't be so old-fashioned,' said Harry. 'A nice why-dance is what I like.'

'Why-dance?' said Molly, puzzled.

'Aye, you know, a slow waltz and a crowded floor and me just to say moving, me arms round a girl . . .' He held his arms in front of him as though round a girl, his head on one side, his eyes half-closed, and they all laughed.

'You haven't got a partner,' said Molly.

'Who needs a partner? They'll be falling over each other to dance with me, our Molly.' He paused. 'Any road, as it happens I'm meeting a lass inside. Wait till you see her an' all. A blonde, just as high as my heart, curves in all the right places . . .' His hands drew a figure of eight in the air.

'Well, we'll have to go now, pet, if only to see this beauty.' Jackson grinned at Molly.

'Aye, go on. Me an' your dad are going to have a night by the fire listening to the wireless,' said Maggie. Time was when Frank was down the club every Saturday night with his mates but things were different now.

*

The church hall was filling up nicely when they arrived. Molly left her coat in the cloakroom and combed her hair in front of the looking glass, surprised at her own reflection. Her eyes shone, her cheeks glowed. Why, she was almost pretty!

'Well, look who's here!' a familiar voice said and there was Mona from the factory, standing beside her as she applied poppy red lipstick to her pert mouth.

'Mona! What are you doing here? You live at Ferryhill, don't you?'

'Visiting me auntie,' said her friend, pressing her lips together then inspecting them critically in the glass. 'I'm here for the weekend, did I not tell you?'

'You at the dance on your own?' asked Molly. If she was then in all civility she had to let her friend keep them company.

'No, I'm with a fella.' Mona grinned triumphantly. 'Fast work, eh? A soldier an' all, home on leave. I met him last night. By, he's lovely an' all, Molly, I think I've fallen for him. He likes me too, I can tell.' She put a hand to her nape and flicked her long blonde hair back from her shoulders, arranging the front so that a lock fell forward in the manner of Veronica Lake. Her eyes twinkled up at Molly. 'Right, let's go. We'll knock 'em dead, eh?'

Molly laughed and followed her out of the cloakroom to see her walk straight over to where Jackson and Harry were waiting by the side of the stage where a five-piece band, most of whom were members of the colliery brass band, were striking up the first dance. Jackson's face was a study as Harry seized Mona round the waist and took a whirl round the floor, completing almost a whole circuit before other couples joined them.

'You dancing?' asked Jackson, and took Molly in his arms. They too began quickstepping to 'Dancing Cheek to Cheek'. The hall was crowded, mostly with miners and their girls but there was a sprinkling of khaki and Air Force blue, a couple of sailors standing out in their navy blue.

Molly was in heaven with Jackson's arms around her. They danced a Boston two step followed by the quickstep and then a waltz and a veleta, and then it was a ladies' excuse me quick-step. Molly hardly heard the announcements from the stage, she was in a world of her own, dreaming away, not wanting the evening to end, she was so happy. So it was a bit of a surprise when she felt a tap on the shoulder.

'Excuse me!'

Jackson's arms loosened reluctantly and Molly found herself left at the side of the floor while he whirled away with a girl with long black hair hanging down her back over a bright red dress which swirled out as they spun round. Feeling bereft she watched the dancers until she was caught up herself by a tall gangly youth who took her round the floor with more enthusiasm than skill. But it was not the thing to refuse to dance with anyone when you were without a partner, and anyway, she was so euphorically happy she even smiled when his foot descended with some force on hers.

'Hey, watch what you're doing!'

They stopped abruptly as the boy cannoned into another couple, knocking the girl from the arms of her partner.

'Sorry, did I hurt you?' the lad mumbled, his face bright red.

'What do you think, you clumsy oaf?' snapped Joan Pendle, rubbing her shoulder and wincing theatrically. For that was who it was, Joan Pendle, and she was dancing with Harry. Molly gazed up at him in surprise. He looked stiff and uncomfortable.

'No harm done,' he said. 'Come on, Joan.' He pulled her away and set off dancing again. There were only a few bars of the music left and Molly and her partner didn't get started before it came to an end.

'Blooming cheek, hasn't she?' Mona was at Molly's elbow, gazing at Joan. 'Who is she any road?'

'Nobody,' said Harry, hearing her as he came up. 'She's nobody. It's the interval now, how about lemonades all round?'

Chapter Sixteen

'That lass has her sights fixed on you,' Jackson commented. He didn't say which lass, he didn't have to. They were sitting at the kitchen table having breakfast and for once the two of them were on their own for it was Monday morning and Maggie was out in the wash house in the yard, the rhythmic thumping of her possing the clothes in the zinc tub loud and clear.

'Aye, well, she's wasting her time,' said Harry. He picked up the *Daily Herald* and glanced through it, quickly put it down again. 'Funny war this, man,' he said. 'Nothing's happening.'

'It will soon enough,' said Jackson. 'Aye, but you want to watch yourself, Harry, she's a determined sort. Look how she butted in for that excuse me quickstep. Brass-faced I call it after all she's said about your Molly.'

'Well, it'll do her no good, will it?' asked Harry. 'Any road, I've a fancy for little Mona, she's promised to write to me.' He grinned at Jackson and changed the subject.

'You going down to Bishop to buy that ring?'

'Yes.' He glanced at the clock on the mantelpiece and got to his feet. 'I'd best be off, catch the bus.'

'I'll come with you, I've nothing else to do, not 'til Mona finishes work. We're going to the pictures after.'

The girls were on first shift and Mona was still staying with her aunt in Eden Hope. She'd only known Harry for four days yet they were going steady. It was happening all around them for a lot of young miners had been in the territorials before the war and had recently been drafted. There was a sense of urgency somehow, a feeling of time being short.

The girls had travelled in to work together on the train, gravitated towards each other during the break.

'I wish we were getting engaged the night,' Mona said as they drank lukewarm tea and ate currant buns in the canteen. 'By, you never told me you had a dream boat for a brother!' She grinned, eyes sparkling over the rim of her mug.

'Well, I can't let everyone know, I might get knocked over in the rush,' said Molly, laughing before turning serious. 'Aw, come on, you've only known him four days. You can't get engaged to a fella when you've just known him four days.'

'I could!' Mona said fervently. 'If he asks me, I could. We're going to the pictures this afternoon. I'm going to take him to see a love story if I can. Do you know what's on at the Majestic or the Hippodrome?'

'Can't say I do,' said Molly as the buzzer went and they joined the crowd going back to work.

If anything the rest of the shift dragged by even more slowly than the one on the Friday before. Molly's hands were busy but the work came to her automatically now. Her mind was left to wander happily on thoughts of Jackson and the future. Because, she told herself, nothing was going to happen to Jackson or Harry. They were experienced soldiers, weren't they? Just occasionally Joan Pendle came to her mind, the way she'd butted in on Harry and Mona in the dance. Why had she done that? Probably it was just an urge to make mischief, thought Molly, Joan was a nasty piece of work all right.

There was a surprise for the two girls as the train pulled into Shildon. There were Jackson and Harry on the platform, running up and down, looking for them through the windows. Neither girl saw them at first. Mona was still talking about Harry. It seemed as though every other sentence had to be about him.

'Are those soldiers waving at you?' someone asked, and the two girls just managed to jump down from the train before the guard's flag went down and the other girls cat-called and wolf-whistled, emboldened by their numbers.

Harry grinned, not at all put off, and swept Mona into his arms. He gave her a smacking kiss then bowed to his audience on the train as it pulled away from the station.

'You daft ha'porth!' cried Mona when she could get her breath, and he swung her round and off her feet before putting her down again. 'Now we'll have such a ragging when we go in tomorrow!' But she loved it and so did Molly as Jackson took her hand and kissed her gently, his lips brushing against hers.

They walked down the path to Eden Hope, not noticing that the distance between the two couples grew longer and longer until they disappeared from each other's view. Skirting a wood by the corner of a ploughed field, brown and with dank dead grass sticking up in tufts in places for this had been a meadow before the war but now was needed to grow crops, Jackson drew her to a halt. It was sheltered here, halfway down the bank side, the sun shone, it could almost have been spring.

'I've been to Bishop this morning and bought you something,' he said softly, and drew a small box out of the breast pocket of his uniform. A ring box. Molly was speechless. She hadn't expected it yet. In fact, she'd thought it would be during his next leave.

He opened the box and put the ring on her fourth finger. The tiny diamonds sparkled and shone in the sun looking twice as big as they were. She gazed at it and it was the most beautiful ring in the whole world. Oh, yes, it was, it was!

They ambled along, arms around each other, sometimes stopping to cuddle closer. Molly couldn't help thinking that in three days he would be gone away, out of England even, to that menacing place the continent. It was a shadow on her happiness, one which took more and more of an effort to push to the back of her mind. She couldn't let him see how much it upset her.

The winter sun had disappeared by the time they reached the end of the rows at Eden Hope, the pit hooter had sounded and the back shift men were coming out of the pit yard making for home and a bath and hot meal. Smoke curled up towards the sky from the chimneys, visible in the star light. But the houses themselves were already blacked out, shutters up, blackout curtains drawn together.

'Where the heck have you been?' asked Maggie as they went into the kitchen. 'Harry was back hours ago. They've gone to the first house pictures. I've kept your meal hot in the oven but . . .'

Molly held out her hand, holding it under the gas mantle so that it caught the light. 'We're engaged.'

'Eeh, will you look at this, Frank! A ring – our Jackson's given Molly a ring! By, I'm right pleased for you both,' Maggie cried and flung her arms around them both. 'Congratulations, son,' she whispered into Jackson's ear, 'you've got a good 'un in Molly. An' you an' all, pet,' she nodded to the girl. 'Now, come on, sit yourselves down an' I'll dish up or it'll be kizzened to a cinder.'

As she turned to the oven she wiped her eyes with the corner of her apron. If she could have wished her lad had picked someone without the shadow of prison hanging over her, even if it had been a big mistake, she was wise enough to hide it.

Later, Jackson and Molly had the front room to themselves as befitted their engaged status while Maggie and Frank listened to the wireless in the kitchen. They sat on the imitation leather chesterfield in front of the fire and made plans for what they would do when the war was over. For both of them had decided they had to live for the present, it was no good meeting trouble before it happened. The Germans would be sent back to their own country, and Jackson *would* come back. How could it be any other way when men like him were there to make it happen? With his arms around her, Molly felt safe, confident, optimistic. The war might have just begun but her own bad times were over.

Somehow she was not so sure the day before they had to report back to their unit. The reality of the impending separation hit her. There were twenty-two hours left, twenty-one, nineteen. And she had to spend precious hours at work filling bombs, the sharp smell of the TNT getting up her nose, shrinking from the knowledge that the two men she loved most in the world could be killed. They were *soldiers*, for goodness' sake. But somehow she had to batten the dark thoughts down, show a cheerful, loving face to Jackson and to Harry.

Mona was cheerful enough when they met in the canteen, giggly in fact.

'We went to the King's Hall pictures – you know, those seats made for two in the back row? Eeh, it was lovely. Deanna Durbin it was. She's gorgeous, isn't she? Harry wanted to go to see a cowboy but I told him this was a gangster picture. Well, it was set in the twenties, wasn't it?' Mona sighed. 'She's got a gorgeous voice an' all, hasn't she, Molly? Molly, are you not listening to me?'

'I am, yes, I am,' said Molly but soon went back to studying her mug of tea. The buzzer went and she still hadn't drunk it. She put it down and went back to her work room and the band started up again and she worked away for the rest of the shift, trying hard to keep her mind a blank and succeeding to some extent.

At the end of the shift Mona was waiting for her in the changing room. She was going back to Eden Hope to stay with her auntie again, just until Harry went back from leave. 'Auntie June doesn't mind,' she had said to Molly, 'she likes me to stay, only she wants to know all about everything.' Molly knew Mona's auntie by sight. She lived on the other side of the village, her husband was a postman.

'Harry and me, we're going into Darlington this afternoon. There's a tea dance on at the Grand, very grand it is an' all.' Her eyes twinkled at Molly but then, all of a sudden, the grin left her face as Molly took her engagement ring from its hiding place at the back of her locker and put it on, saying nothing.

'Aw, Molly,' said Mona. 'Don't look so worried. They'll be all right, I know they will. I'd go mad if I didn't have a laugh. I can't stand the glooms, I can't.' Molly glanced at her. Mona's normally bright little face was pale, her eyes frightened.

'I'm all right, really,' she said. 'You're right, the glooms never did anyone any good. Come on, let's run for the train, see if we can get a seat for once.'

By the time they were sitting in the carriage, breathless from the race through the crowds, Mona was her old self, looking as though she hadn't a care in the world. 'Blondie and Dagwood!' she cried, and the whole compartment burst into laughter.

And then it was the last afternoon. Molly and Jackson had the house to themselves. Harry was round at Mona's auntie's: 'Getting his feet under the table,' as Maggie put it. And she herself had gone with Frank in the ambulance to Durham County Hospital where he was going to be re-examined by the surgeons to see if there was any sign of improvement.

The whole family was excited about it, swinging between hope and resignation. Not many men with spinal injuries such as he had suffered ever walked again.

'But if he could just sit up, you know,' Maggie had said to Molly the evening before. 'Sit in a wheel chair, get out a bit in the fresh air – by, it would do him the world of good.' And when he went out of the door, the stretcher manoeuvred expertly by the ambulance men, Frank had had such a look on his face, a look of desperate hope which Molly prayed wouldn't be dashed before the day was out.

In the street men and women stood at their yard gates to see him off, calling out to Frank as he was lifted into the ambulance. 'Good luck, Frank!' 'All the best, lad!'

Maggie climbed in beside him and waved her thanks to the well-wishers before the door was closed and then the ambulance was off, down the street and round the corner, on its way to Durham.

So Molly and Jackson were left alone in the house. Neither of them felt like going to the pictures and there was a wind outside sharp enough to cut a person in two. Molly jobbed about, changing the sheets on Frank's carriage, tidying the kitchen. Jackson carried in coal for the fire in the front room, and then they were free to sit together on the chesterfield, the doors closed, cocooned in a small world of their own.

The sense of urgency, of time fleeting, was in both their minds as Jackson took her into his arms, his kisses all the sweeter for it, her response all the stronger. Everything outside his arms faded to insignificance for Molly, the touch of his hands so unbearably exciting, the feel of his body sweet against hers. And for all their good resolutions, Jackson's in particular, they were carried away on the strong tide of their love, sinking to the thick clippie mat which lay in front of the fire. Somehow her dress was open, discarded, the straps of her satin cami-knickers down from her shoulders until her breasts were bare, the rosy tips standing firm and erect. And then they were lost altogether, drowning in such a depth of feeling that nothing mattered except the two of them together, expressing their love, taking it to its limits.

When he entered her the sharp pain gave her only momentary pause before it was forgotten in the triumph of fulfilment. Molly held him to her, her love for him heightened if that was possible, such a feeling of contentment as she had never experienced before washing over her, filling her with peace and a quiet elation.

'Oh, God, I'm sorry,' Jackson said brokenly. 'I am, Molly, I'm so sorry. Did I hurt you? I never meant to go that far, not when I'm going . . .'

'Shh, don't say it,' Molly whispered in his ear, 'don't. Not now. Don't spoil it, this is our time.'

Jackson was quiet. He lay by her side as his blood quietened, his breathing returned to normal.

'I'm not sorry,' said Molly, her voice soft with love. 'I'm glad, I am. So glad.'

She could be pregnant now, Jackson thought, what had he done? He was going to war, God only knew when or even if he would get back to Eden Hope, hadn't she had enough trouble in her short life without him going and adding to it? He groaned and Molly rose on one elbow and looked down at him. His face was lit by the firelight. Outside on this short winter's day it was already dark. The firelight lit the strong planes of his cheeks, the straight brows above the dark eyes, hidden in shadow now.

A coal flared in the grate and she caught a glimpse of the uncertainty and pain in those eyes. Oh, she didn't want him to feel pain, she did not!

'Don't be sorry, please don't be sorry,' said Molly.

The firelight made her skin glow with a rosy light, glinted on her hair which hung down over her shoulders and glorious breasts, and in spite of his resolution he felt himself responding again, the blood rising in him.

Abruptly he sat up, kissed her lightly on the tip of her nose, forced himself to look away. 'I'm not sorry, Molly, not if you're not. But we have to be sensible, my love. Come on, Mam and Dad will be back soon. And if we don't draw the curtains the warden will be knocking at the door. The firelight will be showing through the window.'

Feeling slightly rejected, Molly stood up, pulled on her underclothes and frock, keeping her back to him as he too dressed, unsure of herself. Until she felt his arms around her as he turned her to face him.

'I love you, Molly,' he said. 'More than anything in the world. You know that, don't you?'

She sagged against him. 'I love you too.'

'It's just, well, suppose you were to have a baby and me not here to look after you? I don't want you to be in trouble because of me, Molly, you've had enough of that.'

She thought of having his baby. The prospect didn't frighten her, she longed for it in fact. But she knew she had to be sensible. When they were married would be time enough, she told herself. When they were married. By, those four words sounded grand. But when?

'My next leave,' said Jackson. 'I'll get a special licence. Everything will come right, you'll see. Then when this war is over . . .' He stopped, thinking of the war. It was hardly begun, never mind being over.

Chapter Seventeen

It was almost six o'clock when the ambulance returned with Maggie and Frank. Molly and Jackson were back in the kitchen by now. She had the tea all ready, the mince cooking nicely in the oven just waiting for the dumplings to go in for the last ten minutes, vegetables coming to the boil on the fire. They had worked together, Jackson peeling potatoes surprisingly expertly, something he said he had learned in the army, not mentioning that it was when he was in detention after being absent without leave.

The table was set and Molly was just beginning to worry that the meal would be ready too soon when the door burst open and there was Maggie, her face wreathed in smiles as she almost danced into the kitchen.

'Come and see! Come on, you two, come and see!' And she took hold of both of them and dragged them out, down the yard to the back street, not even noticing or caring that the back door was left open and light was spilling out into the yard. The ambulance men were just opening the doors and putting down the step and then, instead of a stretcher with Frank laid flat on it, they were lifting out a wheel chair and he was sitting up.

'Dad!' cried Jackson. 'Dad, what's happening?'

'Hey, lad, let me get in the house first,' said Frank jovially as he was wheeled down the yard and over the step through into the kitchen. 'Thanks, lads, you've done a grand job,' he said to the ambulance men. 'How about a cup of tea now?'

'No, thanks, mate, we have to get back,' one said. 'See you next time.'

It wasn't until they were gone and his wheel chair settled by the fire in the place where his old armchair used to be, Maggie by his side, still beaming all over her face, that Frank spoke.

'Me back's getting better! There now, what do you think about that eh? A bloody miracle it is! I thought it was, I could feel me toes. I wiggled them a bit when I was on me own but didn't want to say anything 'til I'd been to see the specialist. Why, man, I might even get back on me feet – mebbe not digging coal just yet, but you never know!'

'That's grand, Dad, grand,' said Jackson. He didn't go so far as to throw his arms around Frank or kiss him but his grasp on his father's arm was eloquent enough. Molly, though, did bend and kiss and congratulate him, and Maggie stood back, content as a queen.

In the excitement Molly forgot to put the dumplings in among the mince but no one minded that the tea was late. It gave Jackson time to go down to the Miner's Arms in the village and bring back a jug of brown ale and a bottle of lemonade, and they all toasted Frank's health, and when Harry came in with Mona they celebrated all over again.

They sang songs from the old war and 'Roll Out the Barrel' from this one and then there was a knock at the door and their neighbour walked in to complain that her man was on first shift and could they have some quiet, please? Then she got him out of bed to come and join the party when she saw Frank in a wheel chair, the hated long carriage pushed into a corner of the room, abandoned.

Jackson and Molly didn't have another minute to themselves. She was called from making sandwiches to sing 'When I Grow Too Old to Dream', and the applause brought the neighbours in from the other side, and so the party went on until the air raid warden came to complain that the back door was opening so often it was almost like a light flashing and were they *trying* to signal to the Germans? Frank said there wasn't a cloud in the sky when he came in and not a German either but the party broke up then and Molly went to bed for a couple of hours until it was time for her to catch the bus into Bishop station and another day's work.

Before she went she slipped into the bedroom to whisper cheerio to the men. Jackson got out of bed and went downstairs with her. He pulled her into his arms and kissed her. 'Watch yourself, kid,' he said. 'Don't get into any sort of trouble 'til I come back. And I promise you, I will be back. We'll be married, you'll see.'

Mona was at the gate calling softly to her and reluctantly Molly went out.

'I love you, Jackson Morley,' she said softly as she went.

'Me an' all,' he replied. 'I mean it.'

The girls were quiet as they hurried down the road for the bus, both of them deep in their own thoughts. Mona had lost her sparkle, there were no jokes on the bus, none on the train.

'War is hell,' was her only comment as they separated to go to their work stations. 'Who would have thought it, eh? Me mooning over a fella I've only known a week.'

'We're beginning to look like Chinese,' said Mona, gazing critically into the mirror on the wall of the changing room.

'We're all turning a bit yellow, it's true,' said Molly. 'They say they're going to supply a special cream to stop the powder affecting the skin. It'll form a sort of barrier.'

'I can't see it meself,' said Mona gloomily. 'The powder might just mix with it and soak in all the more. Harry won't know me when he comes back.' She still hadn't returned to her usual bouncy self, Molly thought. Mona's brows were usually knitted nowadays; her smile wasn't to be seen so often as it once had been. She was worried about Harry, Molly supposed, but then she was herself. Most of the girls were worried about the brothers and sweethearts who were in France.

No, Belgium they were now, if the wireless was to be believed. The British Expeditionary Force was in Belgium anyway and the DLI were part of it, weren't they? She looked up at the poster on the wall:

KEEP IT DARK,
FOR THE DURATION!

And the other one alongside it:

WALLS HAVE EARS!

There was a picture of a brick wall with an ear growing grotesquely out of the bricks.

Everyone talked about fifth columnists or spies. Maggie had been saying only last night that she had heard it as gospel in the doctor's waiting room where she had gone to collect Frank's tablets, for his slow recovery wasn't all a bed of roses, she told anyone who would listen.

'No, he has terrible pain and you would think in this day and age they could give him something strong enough to help him sleep through the night at least,' she had remarked to Molly. Anyway, she'd heard that Hitler had sent hundreds of spies with the refugees who had come from Germany and all over. No, she had nothing against the poor souls, they'd lost their homes and some had lost their families, but it made you wonder, didn't it? Molly was brought back to the present by Mona.

'If you don't get a move on you'll miss the train,' she said as she went out of the door. Mona herself was going on the bus to Ferryhill. She had no reason now to go back to Eden Hope to see her auntie, not when Harry wasn't there.

'Righto,' Molly replied. 'See you tomorrow.' She went out and set off for the gate, not noticing that someone was walking by her side until he spoke.

'Molly?' he said and she looked up in surprise, seeing it was the foreman on the band, a man in his thirties, she supposed, no taller than she was herself and podgy with it. He was sometimes sharp with some of the girls but had always been civil to her, smiling when he asked her to do something and adding, 'If you don't mind, Molly?'

'Oh, hello, Mr Dowson,' she said, wondering what he wanted with her. The next minute she found out.

'I was thinking, Molly, how about going to the pictures, on Saturday? We could go to the Hippodrome in Shildon, or if you like we could go to . . .' He stopped speaking as he saw that she was shaking her head. His eager smile slipped a little.

Molly was taken aback. For a minute she couldn't think of an answer, simply shook her head.

'We can go somewhere else, if you'd prefer,' he said, recovering. 'How about a dance? There's one on at–'

She stopped walking. 'No, I'm sorry, Mr Dowson, I can't. I'm engaged to a soldier, didn't you know? I have to catch my train now.'

She set off at a smart pace, leaving him standing frowning after her.

Mona needn't have worried. The train to Bishop Auckland was held up on a branch line. There was a munitions train standing by the platform of the tiny station and it was still being loaded. By the time the workers' train actually got moving it was thirty minutes late and the tired passengers were low and dispirited.

Molly found a seat in a corner and stared out of the window at the dark shapes as they rushed by. The train was unlit although once they were through Shildon tunnel and away from the munitions factory a tiny blue light came on, giving an eerie glow.

Snow had begun to fall earlier in the afternoon, a desultory sort of fall, starting and stopping and not lying except in small patches near the side of the line. But now it suddenly thickened until the windows of the compartment were blotted out with white.

'Oh, heck, I hope the buses aren't stopped before we get home,' someone moaned. 'It can snow as much as it likes tomorrow, maybe we won't get to work in the morning and can have a day off. But not tonight, please, I have a date the night.'

When the train arrived in Bishop Auckland it was a slipping, sliding struggle to get down to the bus stop. The bus was crowded, the conductor shouting to the queue, 'Workers only, please, workers only!' Somehow Molly managed to squeeze on and it lurched off on its way round the mining villages to the east of the town.

'Sorry, folks, we're going no further tonight!' the driver called, sounding quite cheerful as he climbed the steps into the bus. 'I'm not going to chance it any road.'

There was a chorus of groans from the passengers who only a minute before had been congratulating themselves that no one had been hurt when the bus had skidded and slithered to a sudden stop in a snow bank at the side of the road. At least there'd been no standing passengers by this time, the bus was only a few stops from its terminus.

Those left sat and looked at one another until the driver, sounding impatient, went on, 'Let's be having you, you'll have to walk the rest of the way. Come on, it cannot be far. Got your flashlights, have you? Well then, you'll be fine. Worse things happening to our lads, you know!'

Molly got to her feet, thankful that she had invested in a pair of rubber over-shoes to go over her shoes only last Saturday. Outside the snow was driving down, freezing cold. It stung her face and drove under her collar, flung open the bottom of her coat, needled her knees.

She set off up the dark hill, one of a crowd which gradually grew thinner as people came to their homes. Eden Hope was the last village in the string. Down into the valley she trudged, where there was at least some relief from the biting wind, up the other side and at last in to Eden Hope, past the colliery to the end of the rows.

'Eeh, come on in, lass,' said Maggie when at last Molly reached the house and pushed her way through the drift of snow which the wind had blown against the back door. It came over her rubber over-shoes, and soaked wet and cold through her already wet stockings. 'A rotten night. Eeh, did you have to walk? You look like Nanouk of the North!'

'We had to walk the last bit, the bus was stuck.'

There was a letter propped on the mantelpiece, Molly saw with a sudden lift of her spirits. The warmth of the blazing fire filled the kitchen together with the smell of liver and onions cooking in the oven. She took off coat and scarf, both encrusted with snow, sat and undid her shoes and only then did she walk over to the fire, to see that it was Harry's handwriting.

Not that she was disappointed, she told herself. Only last year she would have given anything to hear from her brother. But it wasn't from Jackson.

'Oh, aye, a letter from your brother,' remarked Maggie as she opened the oven door and took out the steaming dish of liver and onions. 'We haven't heard from Jackson either,' she added as she read Molly's expression. 'There'll be a reason, pet. But mebbe Harry has some news of him.'

'Nothing much,' said Molly as she tore the envelope open and scanned the single sheet. 'Most of it's been crossed out by the censor. He says the two of them have become attached to something, but what that something is has been blotted out. And he says they're both in the pink. Jackson is a sergeant again. He says . . .' She looked up to see both Maggie and Frank watching and listening eagerly.

'I knew he'd get his stripe back,' said Frank. 'Can't keep a good soldier down, can they?'

'Here,' said Molly, handing over the letter. 'You read it, if you like.' She attacked her meal, feeling the heat of the fire seeping through to her chilled bones, her feet aching as the circulation returned to normal.

At least there had been a letter from one of them and both were fine when it was written, she thought. That was a bit of a relief. Finishing her meal, she got up to clear the table and wash up, which had become the accepted routine since she came to live at the Morleys'. Maggie did the cooking, Molly the washing up.

Afterwards she sat with them round the fire, listening to the wireless, Maggie knitting a pullover and Molly darning the elbows of one. At nine o'clock there was the BBC News. Both women's hands stilled as they listened.

There was fighting in Belgium, near the border with France, the news reader announced. Was that where Jackson and Harry were? Molly stared into the fire, her mending forgotten.

Maggie rose to her feet afterwards, lifted the kettle to see if there was enough water in it for the cocoa and settled it on the fire. She went to the window and lifted a corner of the blackout curtain, peering out.

'It's stopped snowing any road,' she remarked. 'I reckon you'll be able to get to work the morn, Molly.' She made the cocoa, put a careful spoonful of sugar in each cup and handed it round.

'In the Co-op today I heard that women with more money than sense were coming round from the towns and asking to buy folk's sugar ration.'

'No one sold, did they?' Molly looked up from her cocoa. Sugar rationing had begun just after Christmas, other foodstuffs in January.

'Well, one woman was going to, but they soon put her right according to Mrs Wright. You know, her from the top row. Sent the lah-di-dah one off with a flea in her ear an' all.' Maggie grinned at the thought. The men were all working now, women had a bit of money in their purses, no need to give up their precious sugar to the better off, nor anything else, neither. Why, she remembered a time just before the war when a woman had come to the village and bought up the whole stock of sugar in the shops, filling a car with the stuff. The miners' wives had been up in arms over that.

'In a motor car an' all, she were, Mrs Wright said,' Maggie reverted to the present. 'How did she get the petrol, that's what I'd like to know?'

Molly drained her cup. 'I'll just wash these up then I'll be off to bed,' she said. 'At least I'm on second shift, the roads will likely be cleared by then.' She smiled at the older couple, feeling a surge of affection for them. With all their troubles they had taken her in, treated her as one of the family. She would always be grateful to them for that. She touched the ring on her finger with the other hand, looked down at the stones glinting in the gaslight. When this war was over . . . Her eyes were alight with dreams.

*

Next morning, as Maggie had predicted, the roads were fairly clear. The bus grunted and groaned its way into the town then Molly easily caught the train to work. The snow covering fields beside the line shone in the pale sunshine, the cleared track snaking out before the train.

Even the sprawling mass of the factory buildings looked clean and attractive under the snow. It was so big now that there was a bus to the Administration building at the far end. Eight square miles, Mona said it was, though how she knew Molly hadn't an idea.

'Hello, Molly,' a man's voice said as she came out of the clean room, once again swathed in an overall, her hair tied up under a turban.

'Hello, Mr Dowson,' she replied and quickened her pace. As she turned to go into the room where she was working, she glanced back. He was still standing where she had left him, gazing after her. He smiled and gave a little wave. Molly wished he wouldn't, he made her feel so uncomfortable.

'I think he's smitten with you,' one of the girls walking past in a group said, and they all burst into giggles.

'Don't talk so daft,' said Molly. Even if he was, she thought as she started work, she'd told him last night she was engaged, hadn't she? She dismissed him from her thoughts, humming along with the Andrew Sisters on the wireless. Today was a good day, she told herself. Today there would be a letter from Jackson sitting on the mantelpiece when she got home. It was lovely, getting a letter from him, almost as good as actually seeing him. Almost but not quite.

Chapter Eighteen

Refugees streamed along the country road. Jackson watched one grandmother with a baby in her arms, the mother pushing a baby carriage filled with clothes and household goods wrapped up in bedding and dragging a toddler with the other hand.

'Hell's bells, I wish they would get off the road,' said Harry feelingly. 'It's bad enough trying to get the lads moved along without fighting your way through this lot.'

Next minute the whole column were fleeing for the ditch at the side as a twin-engined ME110 German fighter plane swooped out of nowhere and began strafing them. Harry grabbed the old woman and screaming baby and dived with her for safety, Jackson close behind with the mother and little boy. They huddled together in the scant cover and after what seemed an age and another couple of runs by the plane, the pilot tired, or perhaps his fuel was running low, and turned to go back where he came from. The sound of the engine died away in the distance. It was very quiet except for a baby crying and someone moaning a few yards away.

'Come on, we can't help them.' Before the refugees could gather themselves together Jackson was back on the road, shouting for the men of his patrol. 'Fall in! Come on, lads, we have to make the river by nightfall.'

They had been seconded to a French Army unit which was defending a small hamlet on the River Dyle. The roads were choked with refugees. The only way through was on foot. Why they were going to aid the French neither Jackson nor Harry knew, but they had had their orders and were determined to carry them out. Even more determined now even though they had to pass by a group of crying children clustered round a woman lying on the ground, wounded if not dead. Surely others among the refugees would help?

Setting off at a quick march the soldiers of the DLI moved down the road, at times detouring into the fields beside it to overtake a group of refugees. They were silent mostly, grim-faced after what they had just witnessed.

'I keep thinking, Jackson,' Harry said after the first mile, 'if that lot should get to England it could be our Molly on the run with your parents. My God! They could be being strafed by . . .'

'Neither Hitler nor the Luftwaffe nor his bloody army is going to get to England,' snapped Jackson roughly. 'I don't want to hear that sort of talk.'

Harry glanced quickly at his set face and away again. He was right, it couldn't happen. It didn't bear thinking about.

They reached the French position by seven o'clock. It was a warm May evening, the sun casting long shadows on the fields surrounding the cluster of houses. The French soldiers welcomed them quietly, gave them bread and slices of Belgian sausage, spicy, with lumps of fat in it, and completely alien to the lads from Durham.

'I'll be up half the night with this lot,' one of them grumbled though he went on ploughing his way through it, washing it down with rough red wine. 'What I wouldn't give for a bit of meat pudding and a glass of Newcastle Brown!'

'Get away, man,' said Harry. 'This is nothing to what we had to eat in India. The food there was hot enough to take the roof off your mouth. Why –'

What he had been going to say none of them discovered because at that precise moment three German dive-bombers, the noise of their engines muffled at first by the hill which they came over, zoomed down on the hamlet and strafed everything in sight. There was only the one run and after it Jackson picked himself up from under the bush where he had dived and looked around to assess the damage.

A few yards away a French ack-ack gun had opened up from its cover behind a clump of bushes. Now the gun barrel was lifted to the sky, waiting for the return run which never came.

'Harry!'

Jackson ran to his friend who sat slumped against the trunk of a tree, a lump of French bread still in his hand, his mouth hanging open slackly. Even as Jackson got to him, a dark red stain showed through the rough khaki of his battledress, spreading, turning almost black, beginning to drip on to the bare earth under the tree.

'Harry!' Jackson cried again. He was rifling through his kit, searching for a field dressing. He found one at last and the man who had been grumbling about the food barely a minute before was helping him get the battledress open.

'He's not dead, Sergeant,' the soldier said. 'Look, he's breathing.'

Jackson had control of himself now. He found the place, the entry wound deceptively small considering the amount of blood Harry had lost already. But it didn't look as though it was anywhere vital. He managed to put on the dressing, binding it tightly, and the flow of blood slowed.

'What the hell was that?'

Relief flooded Jackson as he looked up quickly to see that Harry's eyes were open. He was pale but his eyes were focussing properly. He tried to sit up and winced, his hand going to his side.

'It's all right, just a nick in your side. You were lucky that time, Harry,' he said. 'Help me get him inside, Private, will you?'

'Aye, Sergeant. That lot will be back, nowt so sure.'

Behind them was a cottage, its windows dark, the owners long gone. Probably they had passed them on the road earlier in the day. They got him inside, Harry walking at least though supported on either side by the other two. As soon as he could, Jackson would get him back to a First Aid post. It would have to be a French one, they were too far away from their own lines.

'I'll see the French officer, Harry.' Jackson got to his feet. 'Get you back to the–'

He broke off at the sound of gunfire, not in the distance but close, too close, coming nearer all the time, on the other side of the hill.

'Go on. I'll be all right,' said Harry. But Jackson and the Private were already at the door, rifles at the ready. The Germans were coming.

The concert party, mostly girls with a sprinkling of men, were rehearsing for the first works concert. Molly and Mona were there. They had rushed their dinner to allow as much time as possible for the rehearsal, though even then half an hour was about the most they had.

'Now then, lads and lasses.' Mr Dowson banged his baton on the music stand importantly, calling them to order. There was some giggling and a few remarks made in undertones but most of the concert party turned to listen.

Mr Dowson had surprised them all, turning up for the first rehearsal in response to a leaflet pinned on the notice board asking anyone interested to join the party. Not only could he sing in a fine tenor voice, he had a talent for acting which transformed him. When he was on stage everyone forgot his short stature and podgy figure. His voice rang out pure and true, mesmerising all who listened. He could play the piano too with an impressive ability so that straight away he was voted in as leader of the concert party.

Today they were rehearsing 'Kiss Me Goodnight, Sergeant-Major'. The girls were going to be dressed up in battledress, the Sergeant-Major would be Mr Dowson, sporting a large false moustache. He strutted up and down the stage as they danced, not exactly like the Tiller Girls as yet but they were getting there.

'The thing is, it's hard to sing *and* dance,' Mona complained. 'I can't get me breath, I'm like a stranded trout.'

'Shouldn't smoke so much,' said Molly. But she grinned at

Mona. Most of the girls smoked. She herself had tried it once or twice but couldn't understand what they saw in it. Anyway, it seemed a shame to start when there weren't enough cigarettes for the men as it was.

'They're getting so scarce we'll all be cutting down,' Mona said gloomily.

'Will you two girls at the back there stop gossipping and get on with it?' enquired Mr Dowson.

'*Kiss Me Goodnight, Sergeant-Major*,' the girls sang, in a line, kicking their legs in unison, arms along each other's shoulders.

'Just like that picture that's on at the Majestic. You know, *Ziegfield Follies of 1938*.'

Molly hadn't seen it, she didn't get to the pictures much. Usually she was doing jobs for Maggie when she was on the right shift.

The half hour sped by and she was soon back in her little room, filling shells with TNT from the hopper once again. Her movements were automatic by now but she had to concentrate, it was too dangerous not to. Nevertheless thoughts of Jackson sneaked into her mind. She wondered where he was, what he was doing, had he written to her?

There was a letter when she got back to Eden Hope. As always her eyes went straight to the mantelpiece and there it was. And Maggie and Frank were both smiling, they too had had a precious letter.

'He doesn't say much, lass, not about where he is. But according to the wireless, they're fighting in Belgium. I tell you what, our lads'll soon see the Huns off, you mark my words.'

'The main thing is, he's all right. Harry an' all, he reckons,' said Maggie.

Molly kept the letter beside her as she ate her tea. She kept looking at it, a warm glow suffusing her whole body. When she had finished she left the washing up and went up to her room. Jackson's room, it still was really, his things were still about, comforting to her.

'*My love . . .*'

Molly was lying on her bed, gas jet turned up high so she

could see to read by its flickering light. (The mantle was about done, it had two holes in it and the flame hissed and licked at it. Gas mantles were getting scarce along with everything else. The houses had been about to be wired for electricity but the war stopped that.) She kissed the words. She was his love, she thought. '*As soon as this campaign is over, I'll get some leave and we'll be married . . .*'

There was no real information. Harry was well, so was he. There might not be a letter for a while because he was going . . . The rest was blanked out by the censor, the only bit in the letter which was. Jackson was always careful what he wrote.

But at least it was a letter. He had held it in his hands, written the words. It was the only link Molly had had with him for weeks. She closed her eyes and imagined the feel of his lips on hers, him lying beside her.

Oh, well, she'd best go down and see to the washing up. And she'd promised to turn the pantry out for Maggie who had little time to spare now she took Frank out in the wheel chair every day. Up to the pit yard where he could meet the men coming off shift and have a few words with them. Or down to the Miners' Welfare, where there was a ramp for the chair and the chance of meeting some of his old mates for endless talks of wet seams and cavils and, nowadays, how the war was going.

'I had a letter from Harry yesterday,' said Mona. 'I think he wants us to get wed when he comes home.'

'Me too.' Molly smiled at her friend. 'I mean, I had a letter too.'

'Hurry up, girls, there's another rehearsal,' a voice said behind them and they looked at one another. It was getting difficult for Molly to hold off Mr Dowson. He was always about when she came out of her work room, always next to her in the queue at the canteen somehow.

'We know, Mr Dowson,' said Mona, and gave Molly a meaningful grin. 'He's here again,' she whispered loudly.

'Shh!' hissed Molly.

'Call me Gary,' Mr Dowson said affably, and Mona could hardly control her giggles.

'Now then, our Mona, stop messing about. Do you want cabbage or not?'

Mona's mother was behind the counter, her hair done up in a net, a voluminous white overall wrapped round her. Mrs Fletcher was a widow. Mona's father had died only three months before the war started and his wife had been just under fifty so didn't receive a widow's pension.

'Quite right, Mrs Fletcher,' said Mr Dowson primly. 'Go on, girls. As I said, we have to rehearse.'

'OK, Mam, give us a spoonful,' said Mona. 'It looks all right, you cannot have cooked it, eh?'

Her mother made a threatening gesture with her serving spoon and Mona ducked, laughing. The girls took their trays to one of the long tables and settled down to eat fish and chips and cabbage followed by spotted dick and custard.

The days were getting longer. When Molly left the factory and walked along by the perimeter wall to where the buses were lined up near the station the sun was still shining; in the trees across the road birds were twittering as they got ready to roost for the night. She felt a surge of optimism. Summer was almost here. Surely it would be a good summer after the cold snows of winter? Was the sun shining on the boys in Belgium, or wherever they were?

Jackson and six of his men were lying just under the brow of the hill above the hamlet, watching the column of approaching Germans. The French Lieutenant was further along the hill, staring at the advancing column, looking as though he couldn't believe what he was seeing. But Jackson didn't wait for his orders. As soon as the column was within range he ordered his men to fire. The column slowed, halted for a minute or two, and then came on inexorably.

'Fall back!' called the Lieutenant. 'Fall back!' he cried in English to Jackson, but Jackson didn't hear. Rifle fire in his ears drowned out all else. When he looked across at where the Frenchmen had been, they were gone.

'I think we're on our own here, Sergeant,' said the

Private who had helped him with Harry earlier in the afternoon.

'You're not supposed to think,' snapped Jackson. 'Keep firing!' Suddenly there was a deafening explosion as one of the leading tanks in the column fired at the hill where they were concealed. Three of his men were thrown into the air and fell heavily, to be covered in a rain of grass tufts, soil and stones.

'Bloody hell!' the Private said, Jackson glanced at him. He was white and shaking with shock. He had dropped his rifle but picked it up quickly and turned back to face the Germans.

'Fall back to the gun emplacement,' said Jackson. 'Now!'

Only two of the men got to their feet. As the dust cleared, Jackson crept closer to the others. They were all dead.

Harry . . . He had to get back to Harry. What would Molly think if he let her brother fall into the hands of the Germans? With its even occurring to him how ludicrous the thought was when they were all likely to be taken by the enemy at any minute, Jackson picked up one of the dead men's rifles and carried it along with his own down the hill to the cluster of houses near the bottom.

Thank God there was a French ambulance standing there, they must be taking away the wounded. There were bodies all around, the German fire had taken a heavy toll of the French infantrymen.

'Harry?'

His friend was being brought out of the cottage, leaning heavily on the arm of a Red Cross man. He was white from loss of blood, but he was on his feet.

'I'm fine, Jackson, don't bother about me. I reckon this lot'll get me a nice fortnight back in Blighty.' He looked over his shoulder and winked at his friend as he was helped into the ambulance which was already crowded with wounded.

'Lucky beggar,' said Jackson. At least Harry was getting out of it, he thought as he turned away and began to climb back up the hill to the clump of bushes where the French ack-ack gun was, barrel trained on the skyline where the Germans would appear. The thing was to hold them back as long as possible, he told himself.

The French were falling back, only the gun crew were still there. But even as Jackson slid behind the sandbag barrier the Germans appeared on the skyline, inexorably moving nearer. The French were shouting to each other. The soldier manning the gun left it and moved back. Jackson realised they were going to abandon the position. But if they did, the Germans could easily overrun the ambulance, take them all prisoner, and then what about Harry?

'*Allez! Allez!*' he shouted, and took hold of the gun. With a quick glance behind him he waved them away, a gesture they understood more easily than his terrible French. He began firing at the enemy, succeeded in halting the first car, then the tank behind. He didn't pause but carried on firing until the ammunition was exhausted. When he looked behind him the French were gone, all of them, men and vehicles, including the ambulance carrying Harry, thank God.

Now was the time to get away himself, while the Germans were momentarily halted. Jackson slid away from the gun emplacement on his belly, got almost to a clump of trees by the now roofless farmhouse when an explosion rocked the earth once more. The gun he had been manning was flung into the air like a child's toy and he sank into oblivion.

Chapter Nineteen

'Middlesbrough bombed!'

The news spread fast around the Royal Ordnance Factory.

'Bloody hell,' the guard on the gate said as Molly showed him her pass to get in. 'Middlesbrough! Not a kick in the backside away from here, is it?'

Molly agreed. All of them felt a surge of disquiet at the news. It wasn't the fact that Middlesbrough was the first industrial town to be bombed so much as the thought of what would happen if a bomb dropped on this factory. Half of County Durham could be blown to smithereens.

'What the heck?' said Mona when they met during the break. 'They'll never find us, not with the fog down most of the time. Any road, we have to go sometime, haven't we?'

They were getting used to the feeling of danger, all of them. At the beginning of the war they'd all carried their gas masks everywhere but now fewer and fewer people did, though more might well after this latest event.

'No letter from Harry,' Mona said as they walked down to their places. For once she was solemn-faced. It had been on the radio that the Germans had broken through, were streaming into France. She looked at Molly questioningly.

'I haven't had anything either.'

Mona sighed. 'Oh, well, let's get on with it.'

Today at dinnertime they were to give their first show to the workers. Gary Dowson was full of himself, they moaned to each other.

'Don't forget, girls, straight in and go to the head of the queue. I've arranged it,' he said, hurrying past them. Though even then he still had time for an ingratiating smile at Molly, followed by a look which drank her in from head to toe, though her figure was hidden under the enveloping overall. Instinctively she folded her arms over her breasts.

'My Lord, Molly, you're going to have to watch him,' Mona commented as they paused outside Molly's door. She watched the foreman disappear around the bend in the corridor.

'Not so easy when we're singing a duet,' she replied.

They were singing 'The Indian Love Song' from *Rose Marie*, and Gary Dowson gave every indication of revelling in it. He was only acting, Molly assured herself. Don't be a fool, he knows you're engaged.

'Bring your heel down on his instep,' Mona advised. 'Or there are other moves I could teach you which will make him reach high C.'

'Oh, Mona!' said Molly. She was smiling as she went in to begin work.

The concert was a success, the canteen packed with their fellow workers. Everyone cheered and clapped with enthusiasm for the dancers, now not quite so ragged in their performance as they got into the swing of it. They cheered Gary Dowson and Molly when they sang their duet, Gary looking deep into Molly's eyes until she discovered she could fake rapture in return by staring fixedly at the Brylcreemed lock of hair arranged carefully on his forehead.

They fell about laughing when Mona recited her comic monologue, but it was when Molly stood on the improvised stage and sang the 'Love's Old Sweet Song' that they clapped and cheered the most. Her heart beat fast and her palms sweated so she had to rub them with her handkerchief and then keep it there, twisting it between her fingers as she began the song. But then the image of Jackson appeared in her mind's eye, his dark eyes smiling into hers, one eyebrow lifted quizzically, and she sang to him. It was so quiet in the canteen that she could have been all alone but for her dreams. And then the applause began.

Afterwards, brought down to earth by the need to get back to her work, she stood by the hopper filling shells, one after the other. Her workmates actually liked her, she thought. They did. A few of them had come up to congratulate her, clapped her on the shoulder. This was a new life for her in spite of the dangers of the war and the fact that her brother and Jackson were in France fighting. She felt that everything would turn out well, her bad times were surely over.

She was smiling softly to herself when there was a loud bang and the alarm sounded. For a second she was disorientated. She looked around at the door as the belt stopped its progress and the music halted on the wireless.

'Evacuate the building! Evacuate . . .' Molly rushed for the door, turning to see if Mona was there before realising that she wouldn't be. She had been transferred to the detonator section at the beginning of the week.

Joining the stream of people as they hurried for the emergency exists, Molly tried to ask what had happened but those around her had been working in closed off rooms themselves, and were as mystified as she was.

'Have we been bombed?' She caught sight of Gary Dowson standing by the door, but he was busy ushering them out and for once not willing to talk to her.

Outside groups of workers were talking in hushed voices as they went to their emergency stations, away from the danger. One of the First Aid team came out of a door and hurried down the street and everyone watched as though that would give them the answer to what had happened.

'What was it, do you know?' Molly asked Violet, a girl from her group.

'You know as much as I do, Molly,' she replied.

'Fifth columnists, I bet,' one of them said. 'Sabotage.'

The girls fell silent as they reached the perimeter wall and lined up by the emergency exit. The idea that a saboteur could get into the works and cause mayhem was sobering to say the least.

'It was the detonator shed,' a new voice broke in. 'I was working right close. I was deafened by the bang, I can tell you.' She put her fingers in her ears and wiggled them about, frowning. 'I never ran so quick in all my days.'

'Are you sure? I mean, that it was the detonator shed?' asked Molly anxiously, an awful dread creeping over her. She began looking round for Mona, her gaze going from group to group, but her friend was nowhere to be seen. A fire engine went by along one of the internal roads, followed by an ambulance.

'Was anyone hurt, do you know? Mona was working there, has anyone seen her?' Molly's dread was mounting. Her heart beat so fast it threatened to choke her. She went from group to group, asking if they had seen Mona but no one had. But it couldn't be true. Mona couldn't be dead. She was so alive, always laughing. Molly had a vision of her flicking her long blonde hair back from her forehead. Oh, she was so *pretty*. She couldn't be gone, blown to smithereens, of course she couldn't, the idea was ludicrous. Mona was her friend, her very best friend. Please God, not her.

Molly struggled to keep a hold of herself, fighting down the panic, the feeling that it was true and that it was all her fault. She had a jinx on her. Mona was her friend, ergo Mona had to die.

The group looked at one another, shook their heads. Molly chewed her lip. It seemed like an age before they could move away from the emergency exit. The ambulance drove away, not using its siren. Was that a good sign or was it a bad? The tannoy crackled and everyone looked up expectantly.

'Everyone to the canteen. Move to the canteen in orderly fashion, please,' a tinny voice ordered and the girls started to move away, quiet now, all of them wondering the same thing.

In the canteen Molly searched the faces behind the counter for Mona's mother. If anyone knew what had happened to Mona she would. But Mrs Fletcher wasn't there. Perhaps she was working in the kitchen, Molly thought. No, of course, she was probably not back yet. Even the catering staff would have had to go to their emergency stations.

There was tea from the urn but Molly couldn't face it. She sat at the table with the others while they drank and lit cigarettes. For the first time Molly wished she smoked, it seemed to release tension. Then the word went round the room, coming from nobody knew where: a girl had been killed working on detonators.

It still didn't have to be Mona, thought Molly, but where was she? The next minute her worst fears were confirmed as Mrs Fletcher was led out of the kitchens, supported on either side by members of the First Aid team. Head bent she was taken out, looking neither to left nor to right as she went. Molly was on her feet and pushing her way through the crowd to reach her but by the time she got to the door Mrs Fletcher was being helped into a car.

'Mrs Fletcher!' Molly called, and the woman looked up, her face white, her eyes staring. Molly ran to her.

'Is it –' But she couldn't say it, she couldn't. Mrs Fletcher merely nodded and began to get into the car.

'Are you a friend of hers?' someone asked, and looking up Molly saw it was the works doctor.

'A friend of her daughter's,' she said. And it was because of her that this had happened, she thought again. The numbness of grief crept over her, mixed with guilt. It was because of her own bad luck. It had rubbed off on her friend.

'You'd best go with her then,' he said. He was a middle-aged man with heavy jowls and thinning hair which was parted in the centre of his large head and plastered to either side with some sort of dressing. His eyes were dark brown and sympathetic. He had been a local GP for twenty years. Now his list was twice as big with the advent of this sprawling factory amid the green fields of central Durham.

Molly hesitated. 'I'll have to ask . . . get permission.'

Five minutes later she was sitting in the back of the car with Mona's mother. They didn't talk, there was nothing to say.

'I'll leave her with you,' said the driver. 'I'll be outside.' Not until they were inside the little terraced house in Ferryhill did Mrs Fletcher speak.

'Our Mona's not usually careless,' she said. 'I mean, she wasn't.'

'No! I'm sure she wasn't,' Molly answered. 'It must have been an accident, you know.' She looked around, hardly knowing what to do, or what to say. 'Would you like a cup of tea? I'll get you one, shall I?'

'No. I've had enough tea to sink a ship. Well, if she wasn't careless, how could it happen?'

'It does, these things do,' said Molly helplessly.

Mrs Fletcher looked at her. She seemed to accept Molly's assurances and changed tack. 'I mind when her dad died,' she said. 'It's funny, it doesn't seem real at first.'

'No,' said Molly, thinking back to the time when her own father was killed. Her heart ached for the older woman.

'I was that pleased when she got on with your brother. A nice lad, yes, a nice lad.'

'Yes.'

Molly looked about the neat kitchen-cum-living room. The linoleum on the floor was scrubbed and polished and covered with oblong clippie mats, just like most of the houses she'd known. The windows gleamed. Cheap cotton curtains hung there, lined with thick black-out material, the same as Maggie had at her windows, bought at the Co-op no doubt. A cinder fell to the enamelled plate covering the hearth. Automatically Mrs Fletcher got to her feet and scooped it up with the steel-handled brush and shovel which hung on the companion set by the side of the grate.

'Will you be writing to Harry?'

Molly looked back at Mrs Fletcher. Mona's mother sounded so polite. She sat on the edge of her chair, smoothing her skirt over her knees as though she had unexpected company.

'Yes. Yes, of course,' Molly said. The clock on the mantel ticked loudly. 'Are you sure I can't do anything for you?' she asked. 'Is there a neighbour I should call? Anyone else that I could get in touch with?'

'No, no, that's fine, you've been very good,' said Mrs Fletcher. She got to her feet. 'I'd like to be on me own now. It's not that I don't appreciate . . .'

And Molly found herself outside on the street, ushered out. She needed to be allowed to mourn, with Mona's mother, oh, she did. But she couldn't push herself forward, she wasn't wanted. Mrs Fletcher closed the door behind her, leaving Molly staring at it for a moment. A minute or two later the curtains closed too, leaving the windows looking strangely blind as the black cloth gave back her own reflection through the glass. The sign of a death in the family, a sign for the neighbours to walk past quietly, the children not to play too close, show some respect. It was always done.

Molly was surprised to find the car still waiting. She had supposed that she would go straight home from Ferryhill. As she approached it the driver got out and opened the door for her.

'All right, is she?'

'As all right as she's going to be,' Molly said shortly. 'Are we going back to the factory?'

'Those are my orders. To take you back to Administration.'

The Administation building was on the opposite side of the complex from where Molly had been working and when she came out it was only five minutes to the end of her shift. Instead of taking the internal bus she walked across to the station, glad of the fresh air.

The manager had asked if she was a friend of the family, told her the funeral would be taken care of, all in very business-like tones. He made notes on a piece of paper in front of him, looking up at Molly from time to time.

'Mrs Fletcher has a sister in Eden Hope,' he commented. 'Her only relation. She will have to be notified. Well, I think that's all.' He put down his pen and sat back in his seat. 'May I say how sorry I am about the death of your friend? By the way, how was Mrs Fletcher when you left her?'

'Shocked,' said Molly. 'I don't think it has hit her yet.'

'No, of course not.'

He looked uncomfortable as Molly stared at him, but what could he do? How was he supposed to act?

'Well, goodbye then, Miss Mason,' he said finally, standing up.

The funeral was small. There had been nothing in the paper about the explosion and workers weren't encouraged to take time off to go to the funeral. The powers that be didn't want a fuss made, nor did they want the public to think the works were unsafe. Molly did get the afternoon off. She went with Maggie, Mona's aunt and uncle to the Methodist Chapel at Ferryhill. A few of the girls from the concert party who were off shift went too. But it was a low-key affair.

What on earth was she going to write to Harry? How could she tell him that Mona had been blown up and the inquest returned a verdict of accidental death? They sang the twenty-third psalm and then the minister began to talk about Mona as a child in Sunday school, or telling jokes to the back row of the choir as a fourteen-year-old. And now she was buried in the wind-swept cemetery, only twenty-one years old.

Molly travelled back to Eden Hope with Maggie, Mona's aunt and uncle going back to the house with her mother. As soon as she got in, Molly resolved, she would sit down at the little table and write that letter.

It took a few sheets of spoiled paper before she felt reasonably satisfied. She told the bare facts and expressed her sympathy and in the end didn't try to write anything else. She put the letter in an envelope and addressed it care of the regiment. It would be forwarded to wherever Harry was from there.

'I'll just go to the post with this,' she said to Maggie. 'I'll be back in time for tea.'

As she walked past the newsagent's to the post office she saw the chalked notice on the billboard:

FRANCE CAPITULATES

The first thought which came into her head was that at least it meant Harry and Jackson would be coming home soon.

'They will, won't they?' she asked Frank when she got home and told them the news.

'Nay, lass, how would I know?' he replied. Seeing the look on her face and hearing her sigh, he went on swiftly, 'I'd say they stood a good chance of getting leave any road, when they get back this side of the Channel. We'll get it on the news.' He wheeled himself over to the wireless which stood on a table in the corner and began twiddling with the knobs, causing bursts of static before the voice of the BBC announcer came on.

Chapter Twenty

There was an epidemic of diphtheria in Eden Hope. The summer days were fine and hot. While there were often planes droning overhead, sirens wailing, dog fights in the sky, and the excited cries of bairns on the ground searching for bits of shrapnel for souvenirs, ambulance sirens were wailing too as they took small children to the fever hospital.

The panel doctor went to the schools to vaccinate the ones who were well while their teachers harangued them about the dangers of collecting shrapnel and of drinking from each other's cups.

In their houses people sheltered under the stairs or built underground shelters in the gardens. Others used the entrance to an old drift mine, putting in chairs and emergency supplies, a door across the opening made out of pieces of wood. That was until a bomb was dropped too close for comfort, the German pilot obviously mistaking it for a working mine.

The fumigating team was in the street as Molly came home one morning from night shift. They usually followed the ambulance after a diphtheria victim was sent to hospital.

'Little Annie Sutton,' said Maggie in answer to her query. 'There was an allowance of oranges the day at the Co-op store. One for each ration book. I sent them up for the other Sutton bairns. You don't mind, do you?'

Molly assured her that she didn't mind at all. She looked up at the mantelpiece but there was no letter. She sighed. She had even resorted to the old child's game of adding up the numbers on her bus ticket and dividing them by seven. It all depended on how many were left over.

One for sorrow,
Two for joy.
Three for a letter . . .

The rhyme went on and on endlessly in her mind, she had to make a conscious effort to stop it. It was just too childish altogether to think it might work. It showed how much she missed him, missed them both. Harry was on her mind a lot. She couldn't bear for anything to happen to him, he was all she had left of the family.

Men were filtering back from Dunkirk. It was on the wireless all the time about the army of little boats bringing them home. A triumph, they said, when the Germans thought they had had them trapped.

'They just don't know us British,' Frank said proudly. 'Just like in the last war. The Kaiser called our lads "that contemptible little army". But we showed them, didn't we, Mother?'

'Aye,' said Maggie absently. She had her baking things out on the table and was about to make a meat and vegetable pie, though it wouldn't taste like one of her usual pies, she told Frank crossly. 'Not with only half the fat, like.'

Most folk didn't care that they had lost their main ally. They'd manage better without the French, they told each other. There was an air of relief almost, they were on their own now.

'Well,' said Frank, who had been occupying his time reading history books from the library, 'we've been on our own afore now.'

'If I only had word of our Jackson I wouldn't care,' Maggie said wistfully. Frank was fiddling with the wireless, hoping for the racing results. He had a sixpenny bet on a horse in the one-thirty at Sedgefield. The bookie's runner still came to the end of the rows on racing days, slyly taking slips of paper wrapped round coins while keeping an eye out for the polis. To Molly it was amazing that racing and football or any kind of sports should go on just as though the war wasn't happening, as though Jackson and other mothers' sons weren't in danger.

'You're all strung up, lass,' said Maggie, seeing her exasperated expression. 'But folk like Frank have to have something to take their minds off the war.'

It was true, Molly thought as she ate her porridge sugarless, like the Scots did, and drank her tea sugarless too. Frank had a sweet tooth and they were saving sugar to make bramble jam in the autumn. It was strange coming in from work in the mornings to eat breakfast and getting up in the evenings to eat dinner before going out again. But she couldn't ask Maggie to cook things separately just for her.

Afterwards she took a few turns at the poss tub, thumping the stick up and down in the soapy water, watching the clothes twist and turn. It had a strangely soothing effect and when, later on, she washed and changed into her nightie and climbed into bed, the curtains drawn against the bright sunshine outside, she fell easily into a deep sleep.

It was still light when she woke but the sun's rays had left the front of the house, showing it must be afternoon. At first she didn't recognise the noise outside. It took a minute or two to realise it was the pit blowing the air raid siren. Soon there was a plane droning overhead. Molly wondered if it was British or German, if she should get up and investigate, even look for shelter. But her limbs were heavy with sleep. Instead she simply lay there. In the end the noise faded away, the plane evidently heading home, its bombs already dropped.

The chapel had been full on Sunday, people turning back to God who hadn't seen the inside of a church for years apart from weddings and funerals. Molly's thoughts wandered back to it. She had prayed for Jackson and Harry but all the while she couldn't help thinking that there must be women in Germany praying for their sons and sweethearts too. Ah, well. She sighed and climbed out of bed. She would go downstairs and see if Maggie needed a hand with the ironing. If only there was a letter when she came home tomorrow, if only she had some news.

Downstairs, Maggie was extricating Frank and his wheel chair from the cupboard under the stairs.

'I'm going in there no flaming more, woman,' he growled. 'If a bomb drops on us, we'll go any road, I've told you before. Besides, I want you to push me up to the corner, I have some winnings to collect.'

'I'll do it, if you like?' offered Molly.

'No, I'll go. I could do with a bit of fresh air,' Maggie replied.

After they had gone, Molly covered the table with an old blanket which Maggie kept for ironing and connected the gas iron to the outlet by the gas ring. Soon she was working away at the pile of clothes which she brought in from the yard, filling the overhead line which stretched across the kitchen.

It was hot working in the glow of the gas and the fire which had heated the oven for Maggie's pie. Molly paused and rubbed her brow with the back of her hand, then hung up the shirt she had just finished and turned to pick another from the pile. And through the open doorway saw the telegraph boy just coming to the door, raising his hand to knock.

Her heart dropped into her shoes. She felt sick and faint with dread. The telegraph boy meant only one thing nowadays, especially if you had a soldier in the family. Carefully she turned off the gas at the outlet, turned her back on the boy and stood for a minute or two, trying to tell herself it wasn't happening. Dear God, she'd prayed for a letter, not this. The boy interrupted her frantic thoughts.

'Missus?'

Molly turned slowly. The boy was holding out a yellow envelope. 'I'm sorry, Missus.' His face was solemn. He had done this before, of course he had, he must have done it countless times over these last few months. Molly took the envelope. It was addressed to Frank. It wasn't Harry then, she thought. Suddenly she tore it open, not able to bear the suspense any more.

'. . . regret to inform you that Sergeant Jackson Morley is missing, believed killed.'

'There'll not be a reply, Missus?' asked the boy. No one wanted to reply to the War Office.

Molly shook her head and he went off up the yard. He started to whistle in his relief to have it over, realised what he was doing and stopped, looking guiltily over his shoulder.

It wasn't true, of course it wasn't true. Missing he might be but he wasn't killed. Anyone as full of life as Jackson couldn't be dead. Molly was still standing there, the telegram in her hand, when Maggie came back with Frank.

Jackson's name was read out in chapel on the following Sunday along with half a dozen others. Molly stopped going to the services then. After all, she thought dully, they did no good. All these years of Christianity, all the centuries even, and there were still wars. If there was a God, He didn't care.

About a week later, there was a letter from Harry.

> I got your letter today. It had followed me around for weeks. Little Mona, I can't believe it. This bloody war. And you, Molly, you be careful, I don't want to lose you too. Can't you get a transfer or something? It doesn't seem right, lasses getting blown up, doesn't bear thinking about. I don't know where Jackson is, we got separated. But he'll be all right, Jackson knows what he's doing.

He didn't say much more, except that he was expecting leave and would try to get up to see her and the Morleys. Molly told Maggie but she didn't know whether the older woman had taken it in. She and Frank had withdrawn into themselves since the telegram came, sitting for hours in silence. Frank didn't even listen to the wireless now except for the news. In vain Molly told them that it wasn't definite. She felt in herself that if Jackson were dead she would have known, have felt it in her heart. But the next minute she was telling herself not to be a superstitious fool. There was no way, no way at all, she would be able to tell. And then Harry came home.

When Molly came back from the factory he was waiting for her on the corner of the rows, a tall, rangy soldier, a lock of dark hair falling over one eye, his forage cap stuck in his epaulette. He was leaning against the end wall of the last house and there was a ring of lads surrounding him, firing off questions, asking about the battles, about Dunkirk. When Molly saw him he had his back to her and was describing something, using his hands to draw in the air. For a moment she thought it was Jackson. Her heart leapt, her pulse raced, she could hardly see. But then her vision cleared and she saw it was her brother. And a surge of gladness and a wave of sorrow washed over her at the same time.

'Harry!'

He picked her up and swung her round then grimaced as he put her down. 'Oh, heck, I shouldn't have done that,' he said, putting a hand to his side.

'Why? What's the matter?' She gazed anxiously at the place.

'Nothing, just a nick, it's better now.'

Molly was desperately wondering if he knew anything at all about what had happened to Jackson. He had said nothing and she couldn't ask him in the street for fear of his reply.

They went into the house arm in arm. Maggie and Frank were by the fire in spite of the warmth of the day. They looked more alert than they had since the day the telegram came. Maggie had even made the tea, a salad with lettuce and scallions from next-door's garden, tomatoes and cucumber from the cold frame.

It was Frank who brought up the subject which was uppermost in Molly's mind. 'Harry thinks Jackson might be still on his way back. He might even be a prisoner-of-war, the lists haven't all come out yet,' he said. For the first time for days there was an air of hope about him.

Molly glanced quickly at her brother. 'You saw him?'

'We were attached to a French platoon,' he said. He dropped her arm, looked guilty somehow. 'I was wounded, came away in an ambulance while Jackson was left behind.' He was looking at the floor as he spoke. Suddenly he lifted his head and looked at them. 'I couldn't help it, honest!' he exclaimed. 'I was hit in the side, I would never have left him otherwise, I wouldn't.' He sounded on the defensive and the others stared at him.

'Nay, lad, of course you wouldn't,' said Maggie. 'We never thought it was your fault, not at all.'

At the weekend Molly took him to Ferryhill to see Mona's grave and pay his respects to her mother. It was an uncomfortable interview. Mrs Fletcher seemed surprised to see them and politely glad to see them go. There was simply nothing to say, thought Molly sadly.

Harry went back to barracks the following Monday. Molly was on fore shift and so she could go in with him to the station at Bishop Auckland. She smiled and waved as she stood on the platform and the train pulled away, but behind the smile she felt desperately alone. More alone than she had ever been in her life, even after her dad was killed in the pit. She went back to Eden Hope where Frank and Maggie had relapsed into sad apathy, hardly noticing her coming or going, not even listening to the news.

'He got away then?' Maggie did manage to say as she came in the door.

'Yes,' Molly replied. She went upstairs to toss and turn in Jackson's bed, getting up once to take his old coat off the hanger in the closet and lie cuddling it, breathing deeply, catching the essential scent of him. She slept fitfully, waking with a headache and that deep sense of loss which wouldn't go away.

Her days and nights were filled with the factory. She began working in the sewing room. Mrs Fletcher came back to the canteen, thinner and older-looking but as efficient as she had always been.

The battle in the air faded or moved away. The RAF had beaten off the Luftwaffe, people said, the threat of invasion was not so imminent. But Molly felt as though she was in a fog, it was all so unreal. Her wage packet became lighter. For the first time she had to pay income tax of eight shillings and sixpence in the pound.

'It's a flaming disgrace!' Jenny Johnson said when she sat down beside Molly in the canteen. She ate her Cornish pasty and chips rapidly then lit a cigarette. 'Fags going up an' all. They're making us workers pay for the war, all right.' She sat back in her chair and took a long drag on her cigarette, blowing out smoke through a round 'O' of bright red lipstick. Jenny was on Molly's band in the sewing room. They were sewing cordite bags for the navy today.

'Yes,' she said absently.

Jenny regarded her thoughtfully. 'You're going to have to come out of it, you know.'

Molly looked up in surprise. 'Out of what?'

'Look, there's more than you lost somebody in this war. I know it was rotten losing your friend *and* your boyfriend, but you have to pull yourself together. You've not been to the concert party rehearsals for weeks and we could certainly do with you. Most of us can't sing for toffee. We just go for a laugh and a bit of fun.'

'I can't. Anyway, rehearsal's after the shift and I have to get home.'

'Want to see if there's a letter? You're not still thinking your lad might be in a prisoner-of-war camp, are you?'

Anger bubbled up in Molly, rousing her from apathy, stinging her to a reply. 'You shut up! What's it do with you anyway? Mind your own business!'

Jenny got to her feet. 'Suit yourself.' She shrugged. 'I was only telling you for your own good.'

And Jenny was right, Molly admitted to herself as she ran the bags under the needle back at work after the break. She would go to rehearsals. She had to face the fact that Jackson wasn't coming back, he was never coming back again.

Chapter Twenty-one

Jackson tried to fight his way through the cotton wool clouds which enveloped him, but they were too thick. As fast as he thought he was getting out, the clouds thinning so that he could see shapes moving about, they closed in on him again. There was something he had to do . . . what was it? He had to watch out. There was danger, terrible danger, he knew it even if he didn't know what the danger was.

There were voices close by. He tried to listen but they were incomprehensible. He couldn't even make out what language this was. Where was he? His mind struggled with the problem. He had no time to waste, the sense of urgency was overwhelming. He tried to hold his thoughts together. The voices droned on. Then there was a prick in his arm and suddenly sleep, taking away the urgency. He fell into nothingness.

When he woke he was in a strange bed in a strange room. He moved his head to get a better view and winced as pain darted through him, searing in its intensity.

'Don't move,' a man's voice said, heavily accented, 'be still.' A face swam into view, a strange face with a black beret atop it.

'Where am I?' Jackson asked.

'Never mind,' said the man. 'You were hit in the head. Go back to sleep.'

'Hit in the head?' Who'd hit him?

'We're going to try to get you back,' said the man. 'You are a very brave man.'

Jackson looked blank. What was the man talking about? But thinking hurt too much, he was weary to death, thought slid away and he was asleep once again.

The Frenchman called to someone through the door, an older man perhaps in his sixties. He brought in clothes, a rough fisherman's jersey, baggy trousers and beret, and they dressed Jackson in them. He moaned once or twice as they moved him but didn't open his eyes.

'We'll have to go tonight, there's no moon,' the older man said. 'Do you think he'll be able to stand it?'

The younger one shrugged. 'We have no choice,' he replied.

A few minutes later the door of the cottage opened and the older Frenchman came out. He looked around and beckoned and the other followed him quickly down a path to a narrow beach. They were carrying Jackson wrapped in a blanket. They laid him in a small boat, similar to the cobles the fishermen of the Durham coast used when the mackerel were running, and climbed in beside him. They did not start the engine but rowed out to sea with long sure strokes which carried them through a channel they knew well, away from the dangerous undertow which could so easily tip and sink a small boat like this one.

In the bottom of the boat Jackson stirred. His eyes fluttered and his lips moved. He was in a nightmare again, one where danger was drawing nearer and nearer and he had to help . . . but who he had to help, he didn't know.

Some time later, it could have been days or even weeks, he woke up and his mind was clear. He turned his head, and though the movement made him wince it wasn't unbearable. He was in a hospital ward, he recognised it as such, two parallel rows of beds with pale green counterpanes, a screen around one of them.

'How are you today? Feeling more yourself, are you?'

A doctor was standing by his bed, an open file in his hands. He looked down at it and made a quick note.

'Fine,' said Jackson. 'Where am I?'

'This is a military hospital in Essex,' the doctor replied. 'Now, can you tell me your name, rank and number?'

Jackson tried to remember, it was there on the edge of his mind but oddly elusive. 'I don't know,' he had to admit in the end.

'Don't worry, it will come back to you.'

'But how did I get here?'

'As I understand it, you were smuggled out of France. The Frenchmen who brought you said only that you had held off a German assault virtually on your own. They insisted you were a hero.'

'I don't feel like one.' Jackson gave a small smile at the thought.

The doctor looked at his head, shone a light in his eyes and nodded with satisfaction. 'Well, you are definitely on the mend. Don't worry, it will come back to you. This often happens after a head injury. Don't push it, it will come.'

After he had gone, Jackson relaxed back on to his pillow. France . . . There was something about France . . . what was it? He puzzled and puzzled and then was seized by a violent headache and had to give up.

Molly was late coming out of rehearsal. They were practising for a *Workers' Playtime* programme for the wireless, and Mr Dowson had made them do the last song over and over again. She was bone weary. It was the end of a very long and hard week and she was looking forward to her free weekend.

Though she didn't have anywhere to go, she thought. But she would at least get out of the house in Eden Hope, she had to. The atmosphere there just made her more depressed than ever. Perhaps she would go the pictures in Bishop, she thought. Take in the matinee at the Majestic, do a bit of early shopping afterwards for already things suitable for Christmas presents were growing scarce in the shops. There was talk of bringing in ration coupons for clothes.

'That'll be the next thing,' Maggie had reckoned in a rare moment when she came out of her sombre mood and talked to Molly.

'Best get a move on if you want to catch the train,' said Mr Dowson. As usual he had contrived to be by her side as she came out of the gates. Sometimes she wished he would just leave her alone; other times it didn't matter, nothing mattered. She quickened her pace, however.

'Are you doing anything tomorrow night?' he went on, increasing his pace to match hers.

'I don't go out much in the evenings.'

'We could go to the dance at–'

'No, thanks,' said Molly, beginning to run up the platform, jumping on the train and leaving him behind. Why couldn't he take a hint?

The following afternoon as the lights went up in the cinema and they all stood to sing 'God Save The King', she saw him standing on the end of her row. Almost as though he felt her gaze upon him he turned and smiled at her, his hopeful, ingratiating smile.

When she came out he was waiting in the foyer, just as she had feared he would be. Molly sighed. She had sat through the film, one with Greer Garson and Walter Pigeon being heroic against all the odds and setting a fine example to the lower orders, though she couldn't remember much more about it than that. During the newsreel, with the cheerful voice of the news reader booming out over the audience, she had scanned the faces of troops whenever they came on, hoping against hope that Jackson would be there among them. But he was not and she was once more filled with melancholy. Hope was gradually draining away from her.

'Hallo, Molly. Did you enjoy the picture? I thought you might like to go for a bite. Maybe a cup of tea? My treat. We could go to the King's Hall, what do you say?'

He wouldn't be snubbed, she realised. He stood before her, smiling so hopefully, so persistent! Did he really feel for her as she felt for Jackson? Molly wondered as people milled around them and the foyer began to empty. No, of course he couldn't. Or was that a sort of arrogance on her part?

'All right,' she said at last.

They sat in the café at the King's Hall, eating toasted teacakes and drinking milky tea. The café was half empty, most of the afternoon shoppers had already gone home, Molly thought. And that was where she should be as well. She could stay in her room, keep out of the way of Maggie and Frank if they wanted to be on their own.

'I think I'd best be going now, Mr Dowson,' she said suddenly, picking up her bag and making as though to get up from her seat. 'Or I'll miss my bus.'

'No, no, there's no hurry. You don't have to catch the bus,' he exclaimed anxiously. 'I've got my car, I've enough petrol to take you home.'

She looked at him in surprise. 'You've got petrol?' she asked.

He winked and nodded. 'You can get the coupons if you're in the know,' he said. 'Any road, let's just say I've got it. I thought we could go for a spin.'

Molly was shaking her head and he looked crestfallen.

'Aw, come on, it won't hurt. You could do with some fresh air after breathing in that powder. We both could. What do you say, just a little run up the fell? Please, Molly, I promise to get you home early.'

She considered it, tempted. She thought of the sharp moorland air. It was ages since she'd been up the dale. And there was nothing to rush home for, nothing to hope for, there wasn't another post until Monday. And Maggie and Frank were so quiet, so wrapped up in each other and their grief just now, they hardly noticed if she was there or not. They had given up and she was beginning to feel the same way. Her thoughts shied away from that, she couldn't bear to think it.

'Righto.'

The car was a Morris four-seater with dark blue paintwork and leather upholstery, all polished to a high gleaming gloss. There were few cars in Eden Hope and those there were belonged to the management of the pit and the doctor. None of the ordinary people owned one. Once she was sitting in the front passenger seat with Gary Dowson pulling away from Newgate Street and heading for the ancient stone bridge over the Wear which a fourteenth-century bishop had had constructed to take him to his hunting grounds in Weardale, Molly couldn't help being shaken out of her apathy a little and started showing interest in her surroundings. The little car climbed gradually out of the valley and soon they were out in the open with great vistas of fields and tiny villages and woods. Down below them on their left she caught glimpses of the Wear, running back to Bishop and Durham and beyond. The war seemed to be an irrelevance as they caught glimpses of farmers gathering in the harvest. They were held up by a tractor chugging along the road with a load of straw, then an old cart pulled by a horse, straining forward, its muscles rippling as it hauled its load.

'We'll stop here, I think. I don't want to waste too much petrol,' said Gary. He pulled into the side along a winding track. They were past the fields now, close by huge swathes of heather, some of it still purple with summer flowers.

He sat there, not moving, and the tiny frisson of alarm which Molly had felt faded away. He didn't mean anything, he wouldn't do anything, no, of course he wouldn't. Anyway, she could look after herself, couldn't she? She was a woman now, an experienced woman.

She made herself relax too, staring out over the fells, wondering what it would be like to live in a remote place like the tiny farm, she could see half hidden in a fold of the moor some distance from the road. Gary offered her a cigarette from a gunmetal holder, lighting one for himself when she refused. He wound down his window and the sharp air came into the car, the muted baa-ing of sheep audible amongst the heather.

Molly relaxed into her seat, put her head back and closed her eyes. She let the evening sun play on her eyelids. Just for a moment, she told herself, just for a moment she would pretend it was Jackson sitting beside her in the little car, Jackson's warmth she could feel beside her.

'Molly?'

Her eyes flew open as Gary flung the cigarette end out of the car and turned to her. He put a hand to the nape of her neck and stroked it gently. She stiffened, didn't move. She could feel his fingers on her neck. She lifted her head to protest but his arm slid around her shoulders and he drew her towards him.

He kissed her on the lips, a soft, gentle kiss, becoming more insistent. Molly sat there, feeling the warmth of his lips, not thinking, just feeling.

'I love you, Molly,' he murmured against her ear, and her eyes flew open. She struggled upright. What was she doing?

'Gary,' she said, against his restraining arm. 'Gary! let me up!'

'Why? Don't you like it?'

'You know I'm engaged to a soldier – he's away in France, I can't do this.'

Gary sat up and lit another cigarette. He shook the match out, threw it out of the window. 'I've heard all about it. So he's away in France, is he? Molly, the soldiers are all back from France – all those who are coming, any road. The man's dead, he has to be. If he was in a POW camp you'd have heard by now, you know that, don't you?'

She stared at him. She wanted to shout, to tell him it wasn't true, Jackson *would* be coming back, there could be a letter any day now. What was she doing sitting beside this horrible, self-important little man on the moor where nothing else moved but sheep, where the sky was already darkening to night and they were miles from home? She fumbled with the door catch, managed to get it open, fling herself out of the car and to begin walking back towards Woodlands, the last village they had come through. The road was pot-holed and stony and she stumbled once or twice but kept on, tears streaming down her face, his words echoing in her mind.

For it was true, everything he'd said, she knew it. Jackson wasn't coming home, she wasn't going to feel the sweetness of his love-making ever again, never again, no. Blinded with tears she stumbled once more, fell against a snow pole and clung on to it as she lifted her foot and rubbed her ankle. It wasn't really hurt, the pain was lessening already, she could make it down into the village. Maybe there was a bus.

'Molly, don't be silly, pet.'

Gary had turned the car round. He pulled up beside her, got out and came to her. 'Are you all right? Have you hurt yourself?'

'Just turned my ankle, it's OK,' she managed to mumble, keeping her head down. She felt so foolish now, he sounded concerned and kind. Why on earth had she run away from him, thought she could get home on her own when she didn't even know if there was a bus? She turned to him, allowed him to put his arm around her, take her back to the car. She felt so confused.

'Sit in the back, pet,' he said, 'then you can put your foot up. It'll be better.'

There you see, she told herself, he was only concerned for your welfare. He *was* a nice man, no matter if all the girls scoffed at him. She was safe with him, he hadn't any dark designs on her, of course he hadn't. All men weren't like that horrible Bart Jones. And it did feel better to put her foot up.

'Comfortable?' He smiled at her, patted her arm as he bent over her. It was quite accidental that his hand brushed across her breast as he straightened up, she was sure.

'Yes, thank you,' she said, and managed a small smile.

'I'm sorry about your lad, Molly,' he said softly. 'But it's best you face facts.'

This almost started the tears again but she managed to hold them back. What a fool she was being!

He got into the driver's seat, switched on the blue-shaded headlights and drove carefully downhill to where a small bridge led over a stream. Then he pulled off the road on to a patch of gravel and took a clean handkerchief out of his pocket.

'I'll just wet this in the water,' he said. 'That's what they teach us at the First Aid post at work, isn't it? Cold compresses for sprains.'

'Oh, I don't think it's much of a sprain,' said Molly, startled. 'Why don't we just get on home?' But he was already scrambling down the little bank and dipping the hankie in the water.

The cool wet cloth against her skin was soothing, she had to admit when he came back and climbed on to the seat next to her and laid it against her ankle. She sighed, laid back against the window. Yes, he was a nice man really, thoughtful too. The feel of his fingers against her leg was pleasant. It was almost completely dark in the car now. He leaned over to her and kissed her on the lips and for some reason it felt like . . . it could almost have been Jackson. Oh, Jackson! Gary kissed her so gently, his lips fluttering over her eyelids, his hands touching her breasts, cupping them in turn, easing her blouse from her waist band, finding the warm flesh beneath.

Suddenly Molly was kissing him back, her body responding to his, remembering that other time.

'Oh, Jackson, my love,' she breathed, and Gary's hands stilled but only for a moment. The next minute he was pulling her cami-knickers aside, adjusting his position in the cramped back of the car, thrusting into her. And her treacherous body responded to every sensation. The pain in her ankle forgotten, she clung on to him and breathed her lover's name.

Chapter Twenty-two

Afterwards Molly couldn't believe it had happened, that she had acted like that. What sort of a girl was she? Were those who had called her terrible names after that night in West Auckland right? She remembered how she had felt only too well: the excitement in her blood, being swept along on it, helpless to stop. She couldn't bear to think of it. *Gary Dowson*? Dear God, it had to be just a terrible nightmare.

Afterwards she sat beside him as he drove down the dale. There were no twinkling lights from the villages along the banks of the Wear, only a slight glow from the chimney of Townhead colliery, a gust of sparks now and then to show that the black bulk further down was the town. Into it and out again, she sat looking dumbly out of the window. Even if there had been anything to see she would not have seen it. It was cold and Molly shivered involuntarily.

'You cold, pet?' asked Gary Dowson. Even now she couldn't think of him as Gary without giving him his surname, even after doing the most intimate things with him. Her mind shied away from the thought. He put a hand on her thigh, squeezing the flesh with a proprietorial air. Molly pulled away from him as far as the seat allowed.

'I'm fine!' she snapped.

He glanced across at her but of course there was nothing to see but the outline of her head. Perhaps he had imagined it. He didn't think she could be turning hoity-toity on him now, not after what she had let him do.

'You can let me out at the bus stop,' said Molly.

'Don't be daft, lass,' he said easily. 'I might as well take you all the way, it's practically on my own way home.' She opened her mouth to demur but he was accelerating out of Newgate Street, sailing past the bus stop, ignoring her desperate need to get out of the car and away from him. For how could he not feel it? The need was so strong she had to restrain herself from opening the door and jumping out while the car was moving.

The car drew up in Eden Hope, right on the end of the rows. At last she could get out and run up the back street to the gate.

'See you, pet,' Gary called after her, and Molly mumbled something in reply. She was never so thankful as when she had the back gate closed behind her and could lean against it, panting heavily as though she had run all the way from Weardale. After a moment she managed to gain some control over herself and walked up the yard and in at the back door.

'Mind, you've been a long time, lass,' said Maggie. But she didn't ask where Molly had been, why she was late. Maggie and Frank were still in a world of their own. There was no room for curiosity about anyone or anything, they were mourning their son still.

'I . . . I don't want anything to eat,' said Molly. 'I think I'll go straight up, if you don't mind?'

'Aye, lass,' Maggie answered, the tiny spark of interest she had shown dying away as she turned to stare into the fire as she had been doing when Molly came in. Frank hadn't even looked up.

Molly stripped off her clothes and poured cold water from the jug into the china basin which stood on the wash stand. She took the piece of flannel which hung over the rail and rubbed it with Sunlight soap, dipped it in the water. Then she scrubbed at herself, never minding that it was cold and her skin stung with the harsh rubbing. She scrubbed at the sensitive skin of her breasts and between her thighs, rinsed off the flannel and did it again. She pulled on her long flannelette nightie and climbed into bed, lying shivering, filled with self-loathing. She had betrayed Jackson. Her body had betrayed him. She was like a cat on heat, she told herself savagely. She couldn't understand why she had done it, she could not.

But gradually warmth seeped through her, her mind closed down, she fell asleep to dream of Jackson. He was calling her and she was running after him but somehow she couldn't reach him, he was too far away. She called after him, 'Don't go, please don't go, I didn't mean to do it!' But he went anyway and she woke up desolate. And somehow the reality of being awake was worse than the terror of the nightmare.

Molly dreaded going to work the following Monday. All day Sunday she wandered the lanes around Eden Hope avoiding anyone she knew, slipping into the fields if she saw anyone coming. The weather was turning cold but dry and the hedges still afforded some protection from the gaze of anyone on the road, still held some leaves. She ate very little, couldn't think of it.

'You'll be in for your dinner?' Maggie asked as she was going out of the door.

'No . . . I expect to be eating with my friend in Shildon,' Molly replied.

'You might as well take your ration card there,' Maggie said acidly. 'I mean, how does her mother manage?'

'Er . . . we'll eat in a café,' Molly replied.

'Aye, well, some folks cannot afford to eat in cafés,' was Maggie's parting shot. Their relationship hadn't been the same since the telegram came about Jackson.

Jackson, Jackson, Jackson. She could still hear his name over and over in her mind. Sometimes she had talked to him there but now she couldn't. Not after what she had done. On Monday morning Molly went into work, managing to avoid *him* all morning for now she was in the sewing room he was no longer her foreman. But she had to go to the canteen at dinner-time, had to pass the table where he sat with the other foremen. As she passed he looked up at her.

‘Now then, pet,’ he said. ‘Will I see you outside when you’ve eaten?’

‘I . . . I haven’t time today,’ said Molly, and he shrugged and turned to the other men, said something and laughed. The others laughed too, one or two grinning slyly at Molly. She blushed and hurried to catch up with Jenny, holding her tray high as she squeezed past tables in the crush.

‘I said that Gary Dowson liked you,’ Jenny observed as she sat down. ‘You want to watch him.’

‘Don’t be daft!’ said Molly, but she blushed vividly and bent her head over her plate to hide it. The talk turned to other things: how there were hardly any air raids now, the Germans giving them a rest.

‘Me mam does her turn fire watching down at the school,’ one girl was saying. ‘It’s just an excuse to sit in the headmistress’s study and have a natter with her pal, get away from me dad for a bit, have a sleep on the job.’

‘Well, they were kept well awake in the summer, though, weren’t they?’ said Jenny.

Molly listened with half an ear but she was still preoccupied with memories of Saturday. What would she do if Jackson came back now? Could she pretend it hadn’t happened? Many another woman had. She heard the talk in the factory about what some of the married women got up to. But not her, no, never again. She would tell Gary Dowson the first time she was able to talk to him alone.

The chance came as she walked back to the station one night the following week, a few yards behind everyone else for she had been last out of the sewing room.

‘What’s the matter with you, Molly?’ Gary asked with no preamble. ‘Why are you keeping out of my way? I thought we were going together, you and me?’

‘Going together? No, we’re not, of course we’re not. You know I was engaged to a soldier.’

‘Aye, I did. But you seemed to forget it that night up on the fells, didn’t you? I didn’t force you, you were willing enough. Any road, the fella’s dead, you can’t hanker after a dead man.’

Molly stopped walking and turned to face him. 'The telegram said missing, believed killed. It didn't say he was definitely dead. He could be anywhere – lying injured in a French hospital maybe or perhaps a German camp. He could . . .'

'Oh, don't talk so daft, Molly! We've been over all this before. And besides, if you feel like this, why did you go with me? An' don't say you didn't enjoy it, because you did!'

'Oh, go away, Gary Dowson, and leave me alone, will you? I tell you, I don't want to go with you!'

Molly marched off towards the train, leaving him standing on the track. 'You'll come looking for me afore I ask you again!' he shouted and turned on his heel and stomped off. Molly was the last to get on the train so she had to stand all the way in the corridor of the last carriage. The others there looked curiously at her but they were not people she knew and at least they left her alone.

A couple of weeks later Molly went into work and sat down at her machine, turning to take the thick, densely woven material from the box beside her. It was quiet in the sewing room, the wireless not as yet switched on, so that the sound of the new girl's voice rang out loudly and Molly turned to look at her.

'Well, would you believe it, it's Molly Mason!'

Molly's heart plummeted. She looked incredulously at the girl who had been on her way to the furthest machine but had stopped right opposite her.

'Joan,' Molly said faintly.

'That's right, it's me, Joan Pendle,' the girl said, and gave a smile which didn't quite reach her eyes. She looked around at the other girls. 'We know each other well. We should do, we were brought up next door to each other, me and Molly.'

'What are you doing here?' she whispered.

'Same as you, what do you think I'm doing here?' demanded Joan. 'I got a transfer from West Auckland. Well, it's more money, isn't it?'

Suddenly the wireless came on, the music drowning out

what she was saying. The other girls were bending over their machines. Joan grinned, came closer to Molly so that she could speak into her ear. 'I'll see you in the break, will I?' Her voice was heavy with meaning. Then she laughed and went on to her own machine.

Molly sewed automatically. Picking up the cut out material, sewing and oversewing, dropping it in the basket, picking up more material, repeating the process over and over. The Andrews Sisters were singing a popular melody, the other girls singing along with them, but it might as well have been a dirge for all it meant to Molly. Her mind was busy with what it might mean if Joan were to tell everyone about her past, the fact that she had been to prison. Well, she would just have to face up to it, she told herself when the whistle blew and the machines fell silent. Face it out. By this time she was almost past caring.

She got to her feet, squared her shoulders and followed the other girls on their way to the canteen. She queued at the counter and got her meal. Sausage and mash it was, two pale sausages and a pile of mash with a spoonful of processed peas. Jenny was sitting halfway down the room but Molly didn't go to sit beside her, instead taking a place at an empty table in the corner. Stolidly she began to eat, though for all she tasted it might as well have been cotton wool. She kept her eyes on her plate. Perhaps Joan would not see her, she thought dimly.

She did. 'Now then, Molly Mason,' she said as she slipped into the empty chair beside her. 'How've you been getting on then? Managed to keep quiet the fact that you're a thief and a gaolbird?'

Molly put down her knife and fork and sat up straight, squaring her shoulders. 'Just leave me alone, will you?' Joan laughed and began to eat her own meal, grimaced and put down her knife.

'Pass the brown sauce, will you?' she asked, and Molly handed it to her silently. 'That's not very friendly, is it?' Joan went on, shaking a dark stream of sauce from the bottle.

'You've not exactly been a friend to me!' she was stung into replying. Suddenly she was sick of talking. If Joan expected her to plead, she wasn't going to. Rising to her feet, Molly picked up her bag and turned for the door, feeling an urgent desire to get out into the fresh air.

'See you later then,' Joan called gaily after her.

Outside Molly had to skirt round a group of men lounging against the wall of the canteen. At least Gary Dowson wasn't among them, she thought. She walked along the road between the sheds, up to the top and back again, and then it was time to go back into work. Gary was waiting at the door, in spite of what he had said the last time they met.

'Don't forget there's a rehearsal tomorrow dinnertime. I thought we could meet tonight an' all, run through that duet . . .'

'I can't tonight. Anyway, I'm thinking of dropping out of the concert party,' Molly said, backing away down the corridor as she spoke. She felt panicky. She'd almost let herself be caught and dreaded the thought of his putting a finger on her now. She couldn't bear that.

Gary frowned. 'What do you mean, drop the concert party? You can't do that,' he called after her. He made as if to follow her but the whistle had blown for work to start, he halted and she ran, making good her escape.

Somehow she managed to elude both Gary and Joan for the rest of the day. She didn't see Joan on the train back to Bishop Auckland but that wasn't too surprising, there were so many people working at the munitions factory now. But the day's bad news wasn't finished for her yet. When she got in from work, Maggie was waiting for her.

'You look a bit peaky, lass,' she said, gazing intently into Molly's face.

'No, I'm all right, I'm fine,' she protested. 'I just had a hard day at work, that's all.'

'There were none of your monthly clouts in the wash,' observed Maggie. 'I wondered about it, that was all.'

Dear God, no! It was like a shout in Molly's mind. In fact, she couldn't believe she hadn't spoken it aloud. It couldn't be . . . could it?

'I'm not due 'til next week, Maggie,' she managed to say.

She folded her arms. 'I think you are.'

For goodness' sake, how could she know? thought Molly.

'I tell you, I'm just not myself. I think I'll go to the doctor tomorrow. Maybe I need a tonic or something.'

Maggie pursed her lips but said no more. Instead she began to ladle broth from the iron pan on the bar. Molly watched her. She couldn't understand the older woman. One minute she was showing not a bit of interest in her lodger and the next she was saying she knew when Molly's periods were due. Why was she so suspicious? She couldn't think that Molly might be having Jackson's baby, it was too long since that last time he had been home. It was almost as if she was jealous on behalf of her son, could that be it? But Molly was too tired even to think about it. She looked at the broth which Maggie put before her, saw the globules of yellow fat floating on the top and jumped out of her chair. She ran for the outside sink where she retched and retched. Bile came into her mouth, sour bile which stung the back of her throat.

'Aye, I think you should see the doctor all right,' Maggie sighed as she turned away and flopped into her chair.

Next morning Molly waited her turn to see the doctor in a waiting room full of women with pale children. Though the cold weather had seen off the diphtheria epidemic, the children who had survived it were debilitated and prone to other infections. In the yard leading to the waiting room a few men clustered, some sitting on their hunkers, wheezing and coughing. Cigarette smoke curled up into the damp air.

'You haven't been doing something you shouldn't, young lady?' was the first question Doctor Hardy put to Molly when it was her turn to go in and she'd stammered out her symptoms. His gaze was penetrating and she lowered her eyes as she replied.

'Yes, Doctor.'

The examination was brisk and brief and when she came out she knew her worst fears were realised.

Chapter Twenty-three

Molly felt numb with shock as she left the surgery, stumbling blindly through the waiting room. Outside she leaned against the wall for a few minutes with her eyes closed until she heard a woman's voice.

'Are you all right, hinny?'

'Yes, thank you, just dizzy for a minute,' Molly managed to reply and hurried off down the street and along past the pit to the open country beyond. What she was going to tell Maggie she had no idea. She shrank inwardly from saying anything at all to Jackson's parents. In the end she walked all the way to Shildon and went into a café in Church Street and bought a cup of tea and sat with it in a dark corner, not even drinking it, just moving the spoon round and round in it, hardly knowing what she was doing.

The day wore on. The woman behind the counter kept looking at her. In the end she walked over to where Molly sat.

'Do you want anything else?' she asked. 'Because I'll be closing in a few minutes.'

It was four o'clock, Molly suddenly realised, and she had to go to work on the night shift. She left the café and caught the bus back to Eden Hope.

'Where the heck have you been?' Maggie demanded in an injured tone as she walked through the door. 'Here I've been, worried to death about you!'

'Sorry, I went for a walk . . . to see a friend in Shildon,' said Molly.

'You didn't think about me and Frank, did you? Of course, I'm just your landlady . . .'

'Oh, Maggie, of course you're not, you know I'm fond of you both. It wasn't like that, really. Only the doctor said I need to get more fresh air so I thought I'd take the opportunity, that's all,' Molly protested.

'Hmmm. Well, what else did he say?'

Maggie stood with her hands on her hips, her expression showing only too plainly her suspicions, and Molly quailed before her.

'He said I was anaemic,' she lied on a quick inspiration. One lie begat another, she thought miserably, that was what her mother used to say. 'He gave me an iron tonic.' He had. She took it out of her bag now, showing the bottle of dark brown fluid to Maggie.

'He gives that to all them as has fallen wrong.'

'Does he? Well, that's what he said to me anyway,' Molly replied, and escaped upstairs to change for work.

'I'm doing some tatie hash for the tea. Only you'd best look sharp. It's nearly ready,' Maggie called after her.

'No, thanks, I'm not hungry. I had a bite in Shildon, at . . . my friend's.'

'Well, I'll keep it to warm up for you the morrow,' said Maggie. 'We can't afford to waste food. There's a war on, you know.'

Even the thought of warmed-up hash made Molly feel nauseous. She could feel the bile rising in her throat and made a desperate effort to keep it down. She sat on the bed and closed her eyes and after a minute or two felt better, able to finish changing her clothes. She stayed upstairs until it was almost time to go for the bus then went down, drank a cup of tea with Frank, asked about the day's news and escaped thankfully as soon as she could.

'You're going to be early for the bus,' Maggie observed, her face grim and expressionless, implying she hadn't been fooled one little bit.

'Well, sometimes it comes early,' Molly replied. She hated the atmosphere in the house now but didn't know what to do about it.

She stood at the bus stop, the only one there until a queue began to form behind her. The line chatted and laughed behind her but Molly heard nothing. Being first in the queue she got a seat and sat still and quiet though her thoughts were still whirling. She knew she had to tell Gary Dowson. He would surely offer to marry her, that's what always happened in this situation, but her mind shied away from the thought in horror. How could she possibly marry Gary? After all her hopes, her love for Jackson, all their plans. Oh, Jackson, she cried inside herself, why did it have to happen?

'I'm only sitting here because it's the last seat left on the bus.' Joan Pendle sat down beside her.

Molly jumped. Dear God, she thought, what did I do? What did I do to deserve this? She barely looked at Joan but stared out of the window instead.

'By, you're a stuck-up madam, you,' said Joan. 'I don't know why I bother to talk to you.'

'Well, don't then,' Molly was stung into replying.

Joan ignored that. 'But I wanted to ask you if you'd heard from Harry?'

'Harry?'

'That's what I said, Harry. Your brother, remember him?'

Molly was so surprised by the question that Joan's attempt at sarcasm went over her head. 'Why do you want to know?'

'I'm interested, that's all.'

Molly's attention was diverted. For a few seconds she forgot about her own trouble. 'I haven't as it happens, not since he went back last time. But I didn't really expect to. He said he was going on some sort of special duty.'

Joan sat quietly as the bus drew into Bishop Auckland, got off it with Molly and walked beside her to the station platform where the train was standing. They had joined the queue of workers before she spoke again.

'I could make it pretty hard for you at work. If I told them about you being in prison, and why.'

Molly waited for her to go on. Obviously Joan had more to say. Molly had been worrying about her past getting out ever since she'd come to the factory but her present trouble loomed even larger, more threatening. She felt quite detached as she waited. In a few months she would have to leave work anyway.

'You could write to Harry, you must have his address.'

'Come on, Joan, just say what you mean,' said Molly, though she was beginning to get the idea.

'You could tell him about me, say how we're friends now that we're working together.'

'Friends?' Molly's eyebrows rose. She couldn't believe what she was hearing.

'Yes. Say how I didn't tell on you, how I admitted I was wrong about you. Maybe say I was asking after him?'

Molly started to laugh. She couldn't help herself, the laughter bubbled up inside her. She laughed as she climbed on to the train so that people turned to gaze at her in astonishment; laughed until tears came to her eyes and she had to fish out a handkerchief to wipe them away. The compartments were full so she walked on, not looking behind to see if Joan had followed her. When she did stop at the end of the carriage she leaned against the window, blew her nose and smiled at those around her.

'Sorry, just a fit of the giggles,' she said. There was no sign of Joan. She must have found a seat. Joan was the sort who usually did, Molly told herself. She couldn't believe the girl. Oh, she had known that Joan still had feelings for Harry even though she went the wrong way about expressing them. But after all that had happened . . . Yes, Molly would write to Harry, through the regiment, tell him about it. He would have a good laugh and no doubt he could do with one. Especially now that Jackson wasn't there with him as he'd always been, ever since their schooldays. But for the minute Molly had other things on her mind.

When the dinner break came she sought out Gary at the table where he was sitting with a few of the other men.

'Can I have a word with you, Mr Dowson?' she asked. The other men looked at one another with knowing amusement. They obviously thought she was chasing the foreman. Had he said anything to them? she wondered.

Gary Dowson had finished his meal. He paused to light a cigarette, making a show of keeping her waiting. The men smirked. 'Oh, all right,' he said at last. 'Come on, we'll take a walk outside.'

They walked between the buildings, along the road to Admin, round the corner and back in a circle. They walked in the dark, no flashlights allowed in the grounds in case they attracted the attention of a stray bomber. Molly glanced sideways at Gary; there was nothing to see but the dark shape of him. Now they were out on their own she couldn't get the words out. This was the wrong time anyway, she thought.

'Can I see you when the shift is over?' she asked at last.

'I don't think I have anything to say to you,' he said carefully. She could feel the change in him and was bewildered. She stopped walking and peered at him in the dark, trying to make out what he meant. A shaft of moonlight caught his face. His eyes glinted coldly in it.

'Why? What's the matter?'

For answer he pulled her round the corner of a building and slammed her against the wall, holding her there with his body.

'Here, is this what you want?' he asked roughly, grasping her breast in his hand and pushing his knee hard between her legs so that she cried out at the sudden pain of it.

'Don't! Gary, don't!' she cried.

'Oh, come on, don't act the innocent with me, I know you better than that. You were panting after it the other week and then you pretended to hold me off. What do you take me for, a neddy?'

'No, no! What do you mean? I haven't done anything!' Molly cried.

'No, not lately you haven't. Though you thought you could

string me along, didn't you? Well, I've been hearing a thing or two about you from that lass what used to work with you at West Auckland. You never told me about what you did there, did you? About taking that poor fella for his dead wife's jewellery and landing up in prison.'

Too late, Molly realised what a fool she had been. She remembered Joan's venomous expression when she had laughed so uncontrollably on the train. Already she was spreading her poison around the factory.

'Whatever she's told you, it wasn't true,' Molly said at last.

'No? Then you haven't been in prison for leading your landlord on and robbing him?'

'No! Yes, I was, but I didn't do it! I didn't, really I didn't.'

'No. Well, they all say that, don't they?'

The buzzer went for the return to work. Automatically they turned and began to walk back. The words to tell him were in her mind, on her tongue, but somehow Molly had trouble uttering them. It wasn't until they were practically at the door of her building that she said them aloud and even then she wasn't sure whether she had or not.

'I'm expecting.'

Gary halted and caught hold of her arm, pulled her into the building and whirled her round to face him. The entrance was deserted, they were the only two who had gone out into the night.

'Say that again?'

'I'm expecting. Fallen wrong. Pregnant.'

'All right, all right, I know what it means. Are you trying to say it's mine?' His tone was hard, his pale eyes narrow.

'Of course it's yours. You're the only one . . .'

'Oh, aye? You'd say that any road, wouldn't you?'

Molly wrenched her arm away from his grasp and walked rapidly away to her own section, the sewing room. As she turned into the doorway she caught a glimpse of him still standing where she had left him.

Molly felt numb and just for the minute nothing else. This was a day for surprises all right, she thought as she took her seat at the machine, switched on the power, placed the bag she was sewing under the needle and began sewing. It was indeed . . . All of a sudden she had an urgent need to throw up. She left her work and rushed for the toilets, knocking over a basket of material as she went.

Afterwards she wiped her mouth with a piece of hard toilet tissue and leaned against the wall. There was a strong smell of Lysol so after a moment she went out into the corridor before she started gagging again. One or two people walked past and looked curiously at her but Molly hardly noticed.

It was no longer a question of whether she could bring herself to marry Gary Dowson, she thought. He didn't *want* to marry her. The idea that this might happen had simply not occurred to her. So much for that. She wasn't good enough for Gary Dowson. Well, at least that made her decision easier. Molly stood up straight and went back into the rest room, washed her face in cold water at the basin and dried it on a clean bit of the roller towel hanging in the corner. Then she went back to her machine and bent her head over her work, not lifting it until the buzzer went for home time.

'Were you not well earlier on?' asked Jenny, coming to walk by her side out of the gate before crossing towards the buses which took girls back to the eastern end of the county.

'Something I ate, I think,' said Molly. 'But I'm all right now.'

'You're not talking to her, are you?' Joan was close by, a hard grin of contempt fixed on her face as she glanced at Molly. 'Did you not know she's a gaolbird, a convicted thief? Oh, aye, I could tell you a few things about that one there,' she went on to Jenny, who looked bewildered.

'What's she talking about, Molly?'

'You may well ask,' said Joan. She drew closer to Molly and took hold of her arm, pinching. 'I'll show you, you bitch!' she said in an undertone. 'You won't laugh at me again in a hurry.' She smiled and nodded to emphasise her words then went on ahead to the station platform.

'Molly?'

Jenny was gazing at her, waiting for an explanation.

'It's true. I was in prison but it was a mistake, I didn't do anything,' said Molly. It sounded lame even in her own ears.

Chapter Twenty-four

'I am looking for my friend, Captain. His name is Sergeant Morley. Sergeant Jackson Morley, I understand he may be a patient here, sir?'

The middle-aged Captain pushed his chair a little way back from the desk and crossed his left leg over the right, swinging it once or twice. He put his hand up to his moustache and studied the soldier standing before him, a tall, upright man, obviously regular rather than enlisted.

'Ask my Sergeant to look through the lists,' he drawled. Why had the man been allowed to come in here pestering him? It had been a long hard day and it wasn't finished yet. Though no longer crammed with wounded from the Dunkirk evacuation as it once had been, the hospital was still full.

'He's not on the lists, sir, but still . . .'

'What are you talking about, man?'

'I think he may be the unidentified man brought in by the French a few weeks back. My friend was seconded to a French unit, sir, we both were.'

The Captain sighed. 'Evidently a few men were. How did you find out about him?' he demanded. 'Hell's bells, I'm sick to death of being pestered by people who think they might know who he is! I won't have him disturbed again–'

The Captain stopped, got to his feet and turned his back on Harry to stare out of the window.

'Sir?'

'Did your friend have any identifying mark?' The officer turned back to him.

'Like a birthmark?' He had been asked this question before. There were lists of unidentified men, both living and dead, and most had a mark – a mole, a birthmark, even a bad vaccination mark – somewhere on their bodies. 'Sergeant Morley had a mole on the back of his calf, sir.'

The Captain picked up a paper from his desk, scanned it quickly. He sighed again. 'OK, Sergeant.' He took a chit, scrawled something on it and handed it to Harry. 'My Sergeant will show you where to go.'

Fired with hope, he went out to the wards. This time perhaps it would be Jackson. He was in a fever of excitement. Had been ever since he had heard about the French fishermen who had rowed across the Channel in a tiny fishing boat which had never been out of French coastal waters before. They'd brought with them a wounded Englishman whom they insisted was a hero, nominated for the Croix de Guerre. A man who had held off a German attack with a French machine gun while its crew escaped over the border from Belgium.

There were three men in the side ward, two of them sitting in armchairs facing the windows which looked out on to sodden grass and dripping trees. They glanced up when Harry entered the room with little interest, then turned back to their contemplation of the landscape. Another man was lying in bed, his face white in startling contrast to his bright red hair.

None of them was Jackson. The disappointment was crushing. Harry stared at them each in turn in disbelief. He had been so sure Jackson would be there.

'You looking for someone, mate?'

The voice was of the North Country, and not just North Country but definitely County Durham. Harry whirled around and there he was, standing by the door.

'Jackson!'

Harry covered the few yards between them in two strides. His arms went out and he grasped his friend by the shoulders as though to embrace him, then saw something in the eyes and changed the gesture. He took hold of Jackson's hand and pumped it up and down in a fervour of recognition and joy.

'I knew it would be you! I knew you wouldn't let the bloody Jerries get hold of you. Too fly for that, you are, Jackson!' he cried, words falling over themselves in the emotion of the moment. At first he didn't realise that the hand in his was still not reciprocating. In fact, Jackson wasn't even smiling. He was looking at Harry as at a stranger, a polite half-smile playing around his lips.

'Who are you?'

Harry dropped his hand, stood back a pace or two and gazed into his face. For some reason it hadn't occurred to him that Jackson might not recognise *him*. After all, they had been mates since they were bairns together at school.

'I'm Harry, man, don't you know me?'

Jackson looked puzzled. 'I should do, shouldn't I?' he asked hesitantly.

'You should that,' agreed Harry. 'By, I've been looking all over for you.'

'You know who I am then?' Eagerness lit Jackson's face. 'For God's sake, tell me, man!'

Suddenly, it was Harry who was hesitant. Jackson looked so different. He had lost weight, his cheeks hollow, his uniform hanging slackly on him. And his dark hair, though as thick as ever, was flecked with grey now. Harry glanced at the door. A male nurse had appeared and was standing silently watching them. He stepped forward.

'Don't get too excited,' he warned Jackson. 'You know it brings on your migraine.'

Jackson threw him a look of contempt. 'I'm not a bairn!' he said, and turned back to Harry. 'Tell me, man. If you don't, I think I'll go stark staring mad!'

The two men sitting in the window had turned from their study of the garden and were watching Harry and Jackson, even showing interest in what was happening. One leaned forward to hear what Harry had to say.

'I'm your friend Harry,' he said simply. 'And you are

Jackson Morley – and I'm that glad to see you, lad, I could eat you! They'll be dancing a jig back home in Eden Hope tonight when I ring the post office to tell them!'

In Eden Hope Maggie and Frank were sitting as usual around the fire in the kitchen. They were on their own again for Molly had gone. That morning she had packed her straw box and left.

'You don't need me now, with Frank so much better. And I'll find somewhere nearer the factory where I don't have the travelling to work. It's hard sometimes, especially on first shift when I have to go in the dark.'

Molly could hardly look at Maggie and Frank as she made up all the excuses she could think of to get away. But how could she stay? What would her life be like when Maggie found out that what she'd suspected was true? Shame flooded through Molly as she stood by the door, her box in her hand, her new utility coat buttoned up to her neck against the December cold.

'But why, lass? Where are you going to stay?' Frank knitted his brow and looked from his wife to Molly and back again. He couldn't understand what was happening, in the way of most men hadn't even noticed any tension between the two women. But he could see there was something now. Maggie wasn't half so upset as he'd have thought she would be.

'Have you two had a row? Has the wife upset you, pet?'

'No, I haven't, Frank Morley, and I'll thank you not to blame me every time anything goes wrong,' Maggie snapped. She was knitting a striped jumper from odd pieces of wool which would once have ended up in her darning bag. Her needles clicked away fast and furious, cheeks flagged with bright patches of red.

'No, we haven't.' Molly shook her head in agreement with the older woman. 'It's like I said, I could do with living closer to my work and when an empty place came up at the hostel . . . Anyway, I'll always be grateful to you both for giving me a home when I needed one, I really will.' She paused, unable to go on. Was it only a few months since they had been so happy here, both she and Harry? He meeting Mona and falling for her, and she and Jackson . . . It seemed like a lifetime ago.

'I'll keep in touch,' she said. 'I've written to Harry to tell him.'

'Aye, well, *Harry* will always be welcome to a bed here,' said Maggie, and Molly flushed and turned away,

'I'll be going then,' she said. 'I don't think there'll be any letters but if there should be, you can send them to the factory.'

The conversation went round and round in her head as she sat on the bus to Bishop Auckland, then the train to the factory. When she arrived she put her box in the cloakroom. She would take it to the hostel after she had worked her shift.

It was almost as bad as the first time she had had to leave Eden Hope. Once again she was going to live among strangers only this time it was entirely her own fault. 'You deserve everything you've got!' she whispered fiercely to herself as she bent her head over the machine, stitching away at the tough cloth which left calluses on her fingers and broke her nails. She felt a sort of perverse satisfaction in that. When her working day was over she sat on the only chair in her tiny room at the hostel or lay on the bed, not reading or even relaxing, just in a kind of stupor. When a girl asked her to go down into the communal sitting room to listen to the wireless Molly refused, making weak excuses. After a few days the other girls stopped asking her and left her alone.

'Old misery guts,' she heard one of them whisper at work. 'Does she think she's the only one to lose her man in this damn' war?'

'She was always the same,' Joan Pendle assured them. 'Ever since I've known her.'

Mrs Fletcher called her to the end of the serving counter one day at lunchtime, a day when Molly was feeling sick and dizzy and had had trouble sewing a straight line that morning.

'I heard you were living in a hostel now, Molly,' the older woman said. She hesitated before going on, taking time to tuck a stray lock of grey hair up under her turban. Molly watched her. Surely Mrs Fletcher hadn't been so grey before? Poor woman, she thought compassionately, forgetting her own troubles for a minute.

'Yes, that's right, Mrs Fletcher.'

'Well, I just wondered . . . how would you like to stay with me? I have plenty of room in my house.' She bit her lip as she gazed at Molly, trying to gauge her reaction.

'Well . . .' For a moment Molly was unsure what to say, she was so taken by surprise. Since Mona's death her mother had been quiet as a mouse at work, simply getting on with what she had to do and keeping herself to herself.

'Like I said, I have the room and could do with a bit of rent coming in to help out with the rates and that,' Mrs Fletcher went on. 'It cannot be very nice in a hostel.'

Molly was shaking her head. 'I don't know, really I don't. I might be having to leave the factory anyway.'

Mrs Fletcher nodded, unsurprised. She cast a quick glance at Molly's stomach though she was sure there was nothing to see, not with the enveloping overall.

'Aye,' she said, 'I thought so. And you won't be able to stay at the hostel, will you?'

Molly didn't know what to say. She looked at the floor, at the food on her tray. Food she certainly didn't feel like eating.

'You'd be doing me a favour, it's lonely on me own,' Mrs Fletcher said. She put a hand on Molly's arm persuasively. 'And Mona would have liked me to help you out an' all.'

'Are you going to give me a hand or are you going to stand there all day gossiping?' the woman serving along the counter called.

'Sorry! I'm coming now,' Mrs Fletcher called back. Turning to Molly, she said, 'Look, come along of me home tonight, will you? I'll give you a bite of supper and we can talk. It'll be better than going back to that hostel, won't it? You can get the Ferryhill bus, can't you?'

She was already walking back along the counter so Molly nodded her agreement before carrying her tray to a table where she could sit on her own. She was even avoiding Jenny these days.

Why was Mrs Fletcher offering to help her? she wondered. She picked up her fork and forced herself to eat a few bites of Woolton pie, drank the cup of sugarless tea. As she walked back to the sewing room, Joan Pendle fell into step with her.

'I don't suppose you've heard from your Harry?'

'By, you're bold as brass, aren't you? After the lies you've told about me.' Molly could hardly believe Joan would come and talk to her. 'No, I haven't heard from him lately. He's off somewhere training for some new thing as far as I know.' She could hardly bear to think about her brother. What would he say if he knew how she had let the family down?

'I wondered, that was all,' said Joan. Molly glanced at her. The other girl wore such an expression of longing on her face Molly could almost feel sorry for her in spite of her meddling.

'If I hear from him, I'll let you know how he is,' Molly surprised herself as well as Joan by saying. She sat down at her sewing machine and began the monotonous work of sewing powder bags yet again. At least she had reason to look forward to the evening, she thought. Going to Ferryhill on the bus and having supper with Mona's mother was better than going back to her bare room in the hostel. Anything was.

It was a dark and stormy night when Molly got off the bus in Ferryhill market place and walked along the end of the rows of terraced houses until she came to George Street. Sadness flooded through her as she walked halfway down its length to the house where Mona had lived for all her short life. Molly was glad of her flashlight for the street was very dark, not a chink of light from the windows and of course not a street light lit. She played the beam of the torch on the number of the house to make sure she'd the right one and a passing air raid warden growled: 'Keep that light down!'

Hastily she lowered it and knocked at the door. 'Sorry, warden.'

Mrs Fletcher had been waiting for her. The door opened in a trice and Molly was ushered into the kitchen where there was a delicious smell of meat and onions.

'Sit yourself down, it's all ready,' the older woman said. She was bustling about from oven to table, cloth in her hands as she took out a shepherd's pie which even had a crust of cheese on the top.

'I don't want to take your precious meat ration,' said Molly, though in truth her mouth had begun to water embarrassingly. It was a long time since the canteen meal she had been unable to finish.

'Nonsense, get it down you, it's a pleasure to have you,' said Mrs Fletcher. She served the meal and sat opposite Molly. 'Tuck in,' she said. 'We can talk later. No use letting the food get cold.'

Later they sat by a blazing fire and drank tea from a pot which Molly suspected held at least two days' tea ration. Mrs Fletcher was putting herself out to be friendly, she thought. Completely different now from the silent woman who served them in the canteen at dinnertime. She had a look of Mona, thought Molly as she sipped her tea. And, yes, her hair had gone completely grey, she could see that now the turban Mrs Fletcher had to wear at work was removed. But the thing was, if she was to take up this offer, Molly had to tell her the truth, she owed her that.

'Mrs Fletcher–'

'Call me Dora, dear.'

'Dora . . . I would love to come and live here, I really would, but you should know I won't be at the factory for very long. I'm expecting a baby.' There, she'd said it. Molly hung her head in shame.

'I know. I can tell. There are signs, you know. That wet streak of nothing Gary Dowson, was it?'

'How did you know?'

'We hear things in the canteen, you'd be surprised.' Dora leaned forward and gazed earnestly at her. 'You can come here, I told you you could. Our Mona would have wanted it. And any road, I have the spare room now, don't I?'

Molly felt tears spring to her eyes. The back of her throat swelled up, thick with those unshed.

'But if I lose my job . . .'

'Why, there's nowt so sure but you'll do that,' said Dora calmly. 'Look, lass, you're not the first this has happened to, not by a long chalk. Many a lass has been taken down by a good-for-nowt. Aye, and let down after an' all. Now, I think we should be making a few plans, don't you?'

Molly could only smile tremulously and nod her head. At least her immediate worries were over, she told herself. Though a small voice within her said that *she* had not been taken down, she had been as willing as Gary Dowson though she still couldn't understand why. Oh, if only the father of her baby had been Jackson, her own dear Jackson, though she hadn't the right to call him that now. But if only! The two most poignant words in the language.

Chapter Twenty-five

There was another telegram from the War Office. Maggie gazed at it as the new telegram boy, a young lad of sixteen years whose one fear was that the war would end before he had a chance to register for the Royal Air Force, proffered it.

'That cannot be for us, lad,' she said.

'Aye, it is,' he said. 'Look you here. Mr F. Morley – it says, plain enough.' He hadn't been in the job long enough to know the hatred the sight of a lad in Post Office uniform with a yellow envelope in his hand could generate, so he was surprised by Maggie's joyful reaction.

'Frank! Come here, will you?' she cried and Frank rolled towards the door in his wheel chair.

'Who is it, lass?' he asked testily. He glanced at the boy, still holding the telegram. 'Aw, give it here, man,' he said. 'How do you expect to find out what it says if you don't open it?' he asked his wife. Tearing the envelope open with his third finger because the tip of his index finger and thumb had been chopped off in the pit, he drew out the thin sheet.

'Why, yer bugger! Yer bugger!' he said, over and over, before handing the sheet to his wife. 'Our Jackson's not dead at all, Maggie, now what do you think of that?' This last was a shout of triumph which made the telegram boy back away down the yard.

'There's no reply then?' he asked, before diving out of the gate and on to his bike.

Maggie and Frank didn't even hear him. They were clinging to one another, tears streaming down their faces.

'I told you he wasn't dead,' she asserted, though she'd told him nothing of the sort. 'I told you!'

'Eeh, lass, isn't it grand?' asked Frank, not bothering to contradict her. Maggie dried her eyes on the corner of her apron and ran down the yard and into the next where her neighbour was hanging out clothes.

'Our Jackson's not dead!' she cried, waving the telegram at the woman who stood, forgetful of the couple of clothes pegs sticking out of her mouth. 'He's in a hospital down south. Look, here's the name of it here.' She pointed to the piece of paper. 'He's not dead!' she shouted aloud.

'Mind, I'm right glad for you, Maggie,' the neighbour said after removing the clothes pegs and dropping them on top of the basket of clothes. 'Eeh, who'd have thought it, eh?' But Maggie was off down the row, calling her news out to anyone else who was there.

When she finally calmed down a little and returned to her own door, Frank was still sitting there. 'Give us another look at that, woman,' he said. 'I've been waiting for you.' Taking the telegram, he read it again. 'It doesn't say what it is that's the matter with him, does it?' he muttered. 'Just that he's been injured.'

The delight died from Maggie's face as she stared at him, visions of her lad being brought home in a wheel chair like his dad's filling her mind.

'I wonder, like,' said Frank soberly, 'why it's been so long? I mean, it's months since the lads got back from Dunkirk, isn't it?'

'What can we do, Frank?' She sank down on the rocking chair by the fire, the chair where she had sat for so many unhappy hours contemplating the fact that, barring miracles, they weren't going to see Jackson again, not in this life.

The pit hooter had gone for the first shift. Men were coming out of the mine when there was a second knock at the door.

'Mrs Morley, me dad says will you come? There's a

telephone call for you,' the little boy from the post office said. 'An' he said will you hurry? It's long distance.'

Maggie raced down the street after him and into the little shop at the bottom of the rows. The man behind the counter looked up as he saw her.

'Mind, I wouldn't allow this if it wasn't for the fact it's long distance and about your lad,' he said. 'It's not allowed, really.'

'Oh, thanks, Mr Dunne, thank you,' Maggie said humbly, still breathing hard from her exertions.

'Aye. Well, he said he'd ring back in ten minutes,' said the postmaster and looked up at the clock, kept on time by a phone call every morning from the exchange. On cue the bell rang and he picked up the receiver, handing it over to her.

'Mrs Morley? Is that you? This is Harry Mason here, I'm speaking from a hospital in Kent. I've seen Jackson, Mrs Morley, he's going to be fine! A knock on the head, that's all. Did you get a telegram from the War Office?'

'We did, lad, not long since. Are you sure now? I mean, are you sure he'll be all right? We wondered why it took so long . . .'

'I'll write and explain, Mrs Morley. Come home if I can next leave. Have you told Molly, Mrs Morley?'

'No, I haven't. She's–'

'At work, is she? Well, I bet she'll be pleased as punch.'

The pips sounded, an operator's voice cutting in. 'Your time is up, caller. Three minutes only for civilian calls.' The line went dead and Maggie handed the receiver back to the postmaster.

'Good news, eh?'

'By, it is, Mr Dunne, it is. The best news there is.'

'Aye, I thought as much.'

Maggie practically skipped up the rows, her head in the clouds, but as she neared her own back gate she slowed. Molly . . . She had to get in touch with Molly. In her euphoria she was prepared to forget her suspicions of her lad's fiancée. There were lots of things stopped a girl's courses. That blasted powder for one, the stuff which dyed all the lasses' necklines.

Maggie nodded to herself as she turned in at the gate. Jackson wouldn't thank her for losing touch with Molly again, indeed he would not. She would write now, catch the four o'clock post.

Frank was waiting, a thin white line of strain around his mouth. 'Well?' he asked.

'It's fine, Frank, really it is. That was Harry on the phone. He says our Jackson has nowt but a bump on the head!'

'When will he be able to travel home, Doctor?' Harry had waited at the door while the doctor examined Jackson, heard him pronounce approval of the way the patient had recovered physically. 'Good,' he had said, testing Jackson's reflexes. 'Yes, the wound has healed nicely. I think we should leave the bandages off now.' There was a vivid red line above Jackson's brow and disappearing into his hair, a puckering of scar tissue on his right temple and a patch where the hair had had to be shaven above his ear. The hair was grown again now, of course, except in one stubborn part about two inches long.

The doctor frowned at Harry, his expression forbidding. 'Patience,' he pronounced.

Harry had managed to get down to see Jackson for at least a short visit every week, but he knew this wouldn't be able to carry on. He was being posted shortly. He wasn't supposed to know where but the fact that he and his fellow paratroopers had been given an intensive course in Norwegian was a good pointer. And he dearly wanted to get Jackson home before then. Harry felt his friend looking gravely up at him and he smiled, his quick lopsided smile, his teeth gleaming white against a face still brown after so many years in the Indian sun. Just as Jackson's was. This visit he had been sure that the past was coming back to his friend. Sometimes he started to say something then stopped, wearing a frown of puzzlement.

'I will speak to you in my office, Sergeant Mason,' the doctor said now, and Harry had no choice but to go out into the corridor and along to the door marked 'Dr West'. He stood by the window of the office, staring out at the garden, waiting for the doctor, wondering how he could convince him that Jackson would be better among his own people. Surely there in Eden Hope, with the people he had known all his life and the familiar accents of home, Jackson would remember, wouldn't he?

'I wish to keep him under supervision,' Dr West said when Harry put this to him. Did he think that there were no doctors experienced in head injuries in the north? Harry clamped his lips tight together; he was a soldier and used to doing what his superiors told him to, no matter how wrongheaded.

'I know what I'm doing,' Dr West said, and smiled in perfect understanding of what was passing through Harry's mind.

'Well, couldn't he go north anyway? There are hospitals there too and he would be safer from the bombing, wouldn't he, sir?'

'That's true,' said the doctor, 'and don't think I haven't thought of it. He sighed. 'Look, I'll make enquiries, see if there is a place for him. But I'd have to travel with him. Hmmm . . .'

Harry watched him as he sat down at his desk and picked up a pencil, began to doodle on his blotting pad. Suddenly he threw down his pencil and stood up.

'Right, Sergeant. I'll see what I can do. Now, I have other patients to see to. I'll let you know of any developments.'

Harry had to be content with that. He wrote to Maggie and Frank, and also to Molly through them for he still hadn't had word of where she was staying. But he was sure that Maggie would see she got the letter.

> Don't worry, Jackson is in good shape physically. Evidently he must have been caught in some blast or something and it has affected his memory so the doctors want to watch him. You know what they're like, over cautious mostly. But he'll be fine. He's coming back up north as soon as there's a place for him. I'll try to get leave so I can come with him.

But Harry's own orders came through before Jackson got his place. Early one morning he and his men were driven to a quiet air strip where they boarded a plane and headed north themselves. They skirted London and the Midlands, flying over the West Riding and turning north-east over the North Riding and County Durham. If there had been a porthole Harry would have seen the broad sweep of Teesdale and Weardale, Wear Valley and its clusters of villages with pitheads standing proud above them. And then the city with its ancient cathedral, majestic above the curve of the Wear in the early-morning light. Then they were out over the grey North Sea, heading for the fjords of Norway.

In hospital in Kent, Jackson was dreaming. He was on a parade ground in India, one of a company of men, and they were marching forward in a perfect straight line, right to the end of the enormous, dusty ground, left turn and one, two, three, four, and about turn, two, three, four, forward again, back and forth over the ground. The heat was tremendous, the sun beating down on them. He could feel the sweat trickling down his back. The sun was so bright it made his eyes water, heat struck through the soles of his boots and still they marched, one, two, three, four. Until he felt himself falling. He was going to disgrace them all, he thought, and sank into a deep, black, bottomless hole.

'Howay, Jack, man,' said someone, and he knew the voice. He couldn't open his eyes because the sun was so bright if he did it would blind him, but he knew who it was only the name eluded him for the minute. Think, Jackson, bloody well think! he told himself. You're just not thinking hard enough. And then the name came to him.

'Harry, is that you?' he asked hoarsely. But there was no answer, only another voice then, a woman's voice like Harry's but not his. She needed him, he could tell. There was distress in her voice, panic even.

'Molly?' he called. 'Molly?'

With a tremendous effort of will he opened his eyes, braving the light from the sun, defying it. Only it wasn't the sun, it was an electric light directly above his bed where the sheets were damp with sweat. Jackson blinked and a face swam into view but it wasn't Harry's or Molly's, it was a woman in a nurse's cap that sat over her ears, covering all her hair.

'Now then, Sergeant,' said the nurse, 'stop shouting, there's a good boy. You must have had a nightmare. Why, you're sweating like a bull. Here, have a drink. It's nice cold orange juice.'

Jackson drank thirstily, thanked her and lay back on his pillow. He knew who he was now. It had come to him. 'My name is Jackson Morley,' he said.

Molly went into Winton Grange mother and baby home in June, 1941.

'Well, if you must,' Dora Fletcher had said, though it was not what she had wanted. 'You can have the baby and bring it back here afterwards. I'll look after the poor little mite, give up me job in the canteen, it'll be all right. You can go back to work, you've no need to worry.'

'I'm not,' said Molly. Not about having the baby she wasn't, not now. She sat in Mrs Fletcher's best armchair and put one arm protectively across her swollen abdomen, waiting to feel the slight movements the baby made. Ever since she had first been startled by the fluttering in her belly she had begun to think of the baby as real, a little person, one she was responsible for. 'I love you, baby,' she said beneath her breath.

'What? What did you say?' demanded Dora.

'Nothing, nothing at all,' Molly replied. She watched as Dora cast on a white matinee jacket. Molly had got the wool with the extra clothes coupons she was allowed for the baby; there was enough for three jackets. And a ball of pink which Dora had bought herself, using her own coupons.

'How do you know it will be a girl?' Molly had asked.

'I know, I just know,' Dora replied confidently.

Molly watched her now, feeling a slight sense of disquiet. Sometimes it seemed that Dora was taking over this baby. She seemed much livelier and happier these days. For the first time since her own daughter's tragic death she was putting on weight, her pale face showing a hint of colour high on the cheekbones. And she was always busy. She had brought down an old wooden cradle from the attic, cleaned it up, given it a coat of varnish. Now it stood, wood shining in the light, an old soft blanket cut down to fit, a muslin-covered quilt fashioned from Molly knew not what.

It all looked very nice, she had to admit, and everything Dora had prepared for the baby was good and sensible. She had even begged a wooden fruitbox from the greengrocer and padded it with the remains of the blanket, covered with a muslin frill.

'It'll hold the bairn's bits and pieces, talcum powder and such,' she had said to Molly, displaying it with an air of triumph. Working in the canteen, she got home earlier than Molly and had fitted up the box in the interval.

'Very nice,' said Molly, sniffing the air for any smell which would indicate a meal was being cooked, but there was none. And she felt empty suddenly, dizzy with hunger. It was a feeling that came on her often these days, ever since she had been carrying the baby.

'What's for tea, Dora?' she asked, sinking down into the armchair.

'Well, me being busy, I thought I'd just pop along to the fish shop when it opens.' Dora put the box down, frowning slightly. It was evident she was disappointed with Molly's reaction, had expected more enthusiasm.

'I'll go, if you like?' said Molly, though she was weary and all she really wanted to do was snuggle down in the chair.

'No, I'll do it. It's about time now any road.' She gazed keenly at Molly. Now that her attention was diverted from the baby box she noticed the deep shadows beneath the girl's eyes, her white face.

'You want to look after yourself better,' she reproved Molly. 'There's more than yourself to think of now. Goodness knows I do my best for you.'

'Yes, I know, Dora, and I'm grateful. I don't know what I'd do without you.'

'Aye, well, I'll just go along the fish shop now, see if I can get you a nice bit of haddock.'

After she had gone, Molly rested her head back against the cushion and gazed into the heart of the fire, one which was on every day no matter what time of year it was for it was the only means of cooking and heating the house. There was a small fireplace in the sitting room but it was never lit. Though Dora had plans for Molly to be confined in there, in which case it would be. She was uneasy still; it was as if every decision about the baby was being taken out of her hands.

As ever when she had a few minutes to herself Jackson came to the forefront of her mind. He was always there, of course, but pushed to the back, waiting. She could feel his presence no matter how busy she was, what else she had to worry about.

What am I to do, my love? she cried silently. What else can I do? If Molly left Dora's there was nowhere to go except the mother and baby home and she shrank from that. There had been so many whispered stories about those places, how awful they were, how the girls were made to work and not allowed to go out, slept with no wireless, nothing. A girl had come back to work at the factory after having her illegitimate baby there and she was changed out of all recognition. From a lively, outgoing girl she had become a silent, solemn-faced one, someone who rarely spoke to anyone, just sat like a frightened rabbit and got on with her work.

She had had her child adopted, Molly remembered. Oh, poor lass, she had thought at the time, how could she do it? She would never do that, no, she wouldn't, she vowed to the baby inside her. 'It's you and me, petal,' she whispered now, stroking her distended belly. And Dora was her best hope. She was the mother of the only real friend Molly had ever had, she wouldn't fail her, no, of course she wouldn't.

Molly got to her feet and filled the kettle, settled it on the fire. She spread a checked cloth on the table and laid out knives and forks, brought the milk and sugar from the pantry, spread margarine on bread. Her stomach rumbled and she took a slice of bread and ate it. There, she felt better for something in her stomach.

Dora was just excited at the prospect of a baby in the house after so many years, that was it. Of course she wasn't trying to take over the child.

Chapter Twenty-six

Molly had told no one at work that she was leaving. Of course she had had to hand in her notice, secure her release, for no one was allowed to leave for no good reason. But the manager had said nothing. So many girls were working at the factory now that one more or less made little difference. He simply took the doctor's note which Molly handed him, perused it briefly, didn't even look at her again and the following Friday she received her severance pay. As a pregnant woman she was exempt from war work.

It was strange handing in her pass and walking away from the factory gates. The other girls chattered and laughed among themselves. Jenny called goodnight to her, waving cheerily as she went off to meet her soldier who was home on leave. Molly watched them, a strange feeling of melancholy sweeping over her. She had been happy here, she thought, most of the time at least.

Joan went past, sniffed and looked away. Molly drew her loose coat around her, turning away, dreading that Joan would find out and tell everyone in Eden Hope about the baby. It was just as well she was leaving. Her loose overall had served her well up to now but it wouldn't cover her condition much longer, Molly was well aware of that. At least Gary hadn't told anyone, or she didn't think so. He had gone out of his way to avoid her lately. If he met Molly at all he looked away, embarrassment plain on his face.

What an escape she'd had from him, she thought. She would manage without him all right. Why, it was coming up to the middle of the twentieth century and what with the war and soldiers going away all the time there were many girls in her position. Though with more excuse, she told herself, feeling the by now familiar pang of guilty shame.

She had another job to go to, cleaning a school at Ferryhill. Then as soon as the baby was old enough she would go to another Royal Ordnance factory, the one nearer Darlington. It was easy to get to from Ferryhill. Oh, yes, she had everything planned. And when she had the baby she would have someone to love, someone who would be totally uncritical of her, a child of her own.

The work was hard at the school for the caretaker had gone to war and his replacement was a retired man. The hours were awkward too, early morning and evenings, but Molly didn't care. She went through her days scrubbing and polishing until the classrooms shone. If she worked hard she would be tired enough to sleep without dreams or nightmares of a future without Jackson. Sometimes the dreams were worse than the nightmares for she was happy in her dreams. Jackson was always there. Sometimes they were in the woods or on the path from Shildon, and it was summer and the sun was shining, and Jackson would have his arm around her and it was one of the magical times again, like the time he was home and they were planning to marry. Then she would wake up and be filled with devastating despair for those days gone forever.

'I have the baby to look forward to,' she told herself aloud in the empty classrooms. But she wouldn't have Jackson or even her brother Harry. She couldn't bear to think that he might find out about the baby. Oh, if only it had been Jackson's . . .

'You don't need to pay me any board, Molly, not now, not until after the baby comes,' Dora said one Friday night. It was only three weeks before the baby was due and Molly had given up work at the school. She would have worked on, but the headmaster had insisted she leave.

'After all, Miss Mason,' he had said, looking away from her

rather than at her noticeable bulge, 'you are not a good example to the children, are you?'

'Oh, go to hell!' Molly had replied. It was a Friday afternoon and she was bone tired. She had worked late the evening before and this morning had come in early rather than lie in bed sleepless. She had gone to sleep in the armchair in Dora's kitchen after scrubbing the place out and dulling the itching of the skin on her hands by rubbing them with olive oil and sugar. It was one of Dora's remedies.

'It's the soda as does it,' she had asserted. 'Me mam always rubbed olive oil and sugar into hers, it never fails.'

Dora came in from the canteen and found Molly asleep, slumped in the chair, legs sprawled out before her.

'Wake up, lass,' she had cried and Molly jumped up, her mind in a whirl, hardly knowing where she was. She hadn't been dreaming this time but in a deep, deep sleep and her head thumped with the sudden awakening.

'You'd best be away down for your pay,' said Dora. 'It's close on half-past three and the school will be empty if you don't.'

Out in the fresh air, birds singing and bright dandelions glowing from every little patch of grass, Molly began to feel better. Until the headmaster handed her her notice along with her pay.

'Go to hell,' she said again. 'Do you think they don't see their mothers like this most of the time?'

'That is irrelevant, Miss Mason,' the headmaster said stiffly. 'You are unmarried.'

'You're a bit of a bastard yourself, headmaster,' Molly replied and walked out, amazed at herself. It was the first time she had ever used such a word.

'It doesn't matter,' said Dora when she got home. 'You'll get dole or sick pay or something, won't you?'

'I'm not going down the dole office,' Molly said flatly. Not letting those mealy-mouthed clerks look at me as though I'm a whore, she thought. I'll starve first.

'Mind, you're in a mood with yourself, lass, aren't you?'

said Dora. She sniffed. 'How am I supposed to keep you and the bairn when she comes?'

Molly was just in the mood all right, ready to kick against the world and Dora in particular.

'I don't expect you to keep me,' she snapped, 'an' what's more I'll keep my own child, thank you.'

'Getaway! What will you do without me, eh? You're having the baby here, in *my* front room, and it's me is going to see to her an' all.'

'I'll see to her myself, I told you. I'm sick of you trying to take over. And anyway, what makes you think the baby will be a girl?'

'Of course she'll be a girl, it's the way you're holding her. Me mam always said–'

'An' that's another thing. I'm sick to death of what your mam used to say! And don't think I'm relying on you either. I'll go into the mother and baby home. In fact, I've decided that's what I'll do.'

'Molly! After all I've done for you. You wouldn't, would you?' Dora blanched.

'I will. I'll go into a home, I'm telling you, then I'm not beholden to anyone. I'll see the doctor tonight, ask if he'll arrange it.'

'Oh, Molly, don't! Please don't,' said Dora. She sat down heavily, looking stricken. But Molly was determined, though when she saw the effect on Dora she felt a pang of compunction. But she had been uneasy for a while about the way the other woman was taking over. Sometimes you could swear the baby was hers or at least that she was the grandmother. It would be best to get away for a while. And in the home there would be other girls like Molly.

'Look, Dora, it'll be for the best,' she said. 'I'm not saying I won't come back to see you, I will.'

'You won't,' Dora sniffed.

Molly sighed. 'Well, I'm away to the doctor's now, the surgery starts at five and I'll get a good turn.' Dora said no more and Molly put on her coat and went out in silence.

*

It was a beautiful day when she walked up the drive to the home. Dora had offered to take the day off and go with her but Molly had refused. At least Dora had accepted her decision to have the baby there, thought Molly. She had apologised for losing her temper and Dora had accepted gracefully. Only too pleased to, Molly realised. In the back of her mind she suspected Dora wanted the baby as a substitute for Mona, but what could she do?

She winced as the gravel from the path pressed through the thin leather of her shoes. Her feet were already slightly swollen and aching. The path undulated between what had once been lawns and were now potato patches. DIG FOR VICTORY said a poster seen everywhere, and most people obeyed. So instead of grass and roses there were yellow potato flowers, promising a good harvest of King Edwards in the autumn.

The baby in her belly moved and kicked. Molly winced, her bottom rib sore. This child would be a footballer, she thought wryly as the large redbrick house came into view. She rang the bell and waited. After a few minutes a tiny girl in an all-enveloping overall, like the one Molly herself had worn at the factory, opened the door and peered at her through thick-lensed spectacles.

'Aw,' she said, opening the door wider. 'You're the new lass. Howay in then.'

Molly followed her into the hall of the big house. The great curving staircase with the large window at the first bend testified to the former magnificence of the place, but now it was bare with the floorboards scrubbed and a great, empty stone fireplace. A damp cold struck Molly in contrast to the warmth of the summer's day outside.

'I'll tell Matron you're here,' said the girl, and scuttled to a door at the side where she knocked.

'Enter!' a voice boomed out, and something about that imperious command made Molly's heart plummet in despair. For some reason it reminded her of prison. She put a protective arm around her stomach though she hardly knew why she did it. Standing waiting in the hall, she told herself it was just something else to be got through. 'What can't be cured must be endured' sprang to her mind, a cliché often repeated in Eden Hope.

Molly was to repeat it to herself often before her baby was born. When she was on her knees scrubbing down the great staircase with her belly sometimes rubbing against the treads. Or mangling sheets in the ancient laundry where washing machines hadn't been heard of, or if they had were not considered necessary in this place. After all there was the free labour of the pregnant women or new mothers.

Vi, the girl who had answered the door to Molly on her first day, was a new mother though she hardly looked big enough to have carried a baby, let alone delivered one. In fact, she hadn't. Not a live baby that is.

'My baby was born dead,' she confided in Molly as they rubbed the banister with vinegar water before polishing it. Her little face was screwed up and her eyes invisible behind the thick lenses of her glasses.

'I'm sorry,' Molly said, pausing in her brisk rubbing of the mahogany rail, knowing her response was inadequate.

'Aw, I'm over it now, it was two months ago,' said Vi. 'But I was that pleased when Matron said I could stay on. I haven't got no mam or dad, like.'

'Me neither,' said Molly, feeling an instant kinship with this diminutive girl. 'How old are you, Vi?'

'Fifteen, I think.'

'What did your boyfriend say when you started the baby, Vi?'

She looked at Molly with transparent innocence. 'Eeh, I haven't got a boyfriend,' she said, and giggled. 'That's what Matron asked me but I told her the same as I'm telling you– I never did have a boyfriend, the lads don't look at me.'

Yet somebody, some man, had taken the girl down, thought Molly, and when she was just a kid. She herself felt only a weary resignation at the ways of the world.

'Well, me and you can adopt each other as sisters, what do you say? We can be family.'

Molly didn't know why she said it, she had enough problems of her own without taking on Vi's, hadn't she? But somehow the girl's simple tale had pierced the protective shell she'd adopted since the telegram came.

The regime at the home was hard and unremitting but Molly welcomed it. They were wakened at six o'clock every morning except Sunday when they were allowed to lie in until seven. Before breakfast they all had their allotted tasks; those not actually in labour or lying-in, that is. For Molly and Vi it was to the laundry where the bloody sheets and cloths from the labour ward which had been soaked overnight had to be put through the mangles, a task Molly found more and more exhausting. Vi, for all her small size, was surprisingly strong and turned the mangle with a will but Molly couldn't let her do it all herself.

At eight o'clock the gong went for breakfast and the girls, looking like maids from a bygone age in their overalls, with faces scrubbed clean and hair tied back 'like little orphan Annie' as one described it bitterly, went in to their porridge and fried bread. On Sundays they had their ration of one slice of bacon and a small pile of scrambled egg, which was really dried egg reconstituted.

The rest of the day was filled with housework, with a free hour in the grounds after tea, rain or shine. The obstetrician on call to the home believed in fresh air. Some of the girls grumbled but Molly was glad of it. She and Vi would stroll around, inspect the progress of the potato patches, go round to the back to the kitchen gardens where the girls who had already had their babies and were over their lying-in period looked after the carrots and cabbages, peas and sprouts growing there.

It was nice in the gardens. There were high walls that reflected the evening sun and blocked out the chill winds.

'You'll be working here soon, Molly,' Vi said to her wistfully. It was a day in July and pods of green beans were swelling on the thick stems.

'No, I'm going as soon as I'm allowed out,' said Molly absently. She was watching a late bee busy in a clump of hollyhocks that had escaped being dug up in favour of vegetables.

She wandered on up the path, at first not noticing that Vi hadn't followed.

'We'd better go in now,' she said as she reached the end of the path. 'Vi?' For she hadn't answered and when Molly turned round she saw the girl standing by the hollyhock clump, her shoulders hunched. She was crying.

'Why, what's the matter?' Molly asked, and went back to her.

'I thought you would be here another three months like the rest of them,' Vi replied, between sobs, hiccuping a little. 'What will I do when you've gone? You'll forget about me.'

'No, I won't, Vi, I promise I won't,' Molly tried to assure her, but the girl nodded her head.

'You will,' she asserted. 'Everyone does.'

'Well, I won't,' said Molly. She put an arm around the other girl's thin shoulders. 'You're the only sister I've got, aren't you? Didn't we adopt each other? I won't forget you. You can come and see me on your afternoon off. Come on now, pet, dry your eyes and blow your nose and we'll go in. We have to look after each other now.'

Looking only partly reassured, Vi did as she was told. Goodness knows, thought Molly, the lass has had few reasons to trust anyone so far. She would never let Vi down, she vowed silently, never.

That same night Molly woke with a deep, nagging ache in her back. She lay for a few minutes, unsure what to do. The baby wasn't due for another week. Perhaps this was another case of that false labour the other girls talked about frequently. But the ache deepened into a pain that made her gasp and at the same time she felt a gush of wetness between her thighs.

There was a bell at the head of the bed, there for just this sort of emergency, and Molly struggled to reach it. The pain was holding her in a tight clamp and at first she couldn't move. But reach it she did in the end and the bell rang out, loud and clear, so that the other girls in the ward, which was converted from the upstairs drawing room of the old house, stirred, a few lights went on and they came to crowd round the bed to see what was wrong.

'Get out of the way this minute, girls!' an authoritative voice snapped from the door and the crowd backed away to let the midwife on duty through. A capable woman, she was middle-aged with iron grey hair under a starched white cap and a bosom like a platform under her apron.

'Now, what's all the fuss about?' she said to Molly. 'Turn on your back and let me have a look at you.'

'Right, it's the labour ward for you,' she said after she had examined Molly. 'Though I've no doubt it will be hours yet before we see junior.'

In fact it was not the next morning when Molly made her final, desperate push but the morning after. And when the baby girl did arrive, crying with rage no doubt at the delay, Molly was a quivering wreck and all she felt was an enormous thankfulness that at last her ordeal was over. Half an hour later, when the child was washed and put into her arms, 'Only for a minute mind,' the midwife admonished, Molly looked down at the red face of her daughter and fell instantly in love.

Chapter Twenty-seven

'But why did she leave Eden Hope, Mam? I mean what possible reason could she have had?'

Maggie Morley gazed at her son, biting her lip. She couldn't voice her suspicions of Molly, not to Jackson, not when he was so obviously worried about her. She was aware that he had trusted her to do her best for his girl this time and she had failed him. And Molly too. She and Frank had shut her out from their private grief, not admitting she might have been hurting as well. What's more, Maggie was only too aware this wasn't the first time she hadn't spared enough thought for the lass. And it was only a suspicion she'd had that Molly had fallen wrong. Maybe she had been wrong. In fact, surely she would have heard by now if she'd been right? That spiteful cat Joan Pendle would have seen to it.

'She said she wanted to be nearer the factory so she could save money on fares. Time an' all. It wouldn't take so long to get there, especially when she was on nights.' Even as Maggie said it she turned away. He'd know they were only excuses.

Jackson shook his head in disbelief, automatically putting a hand up when the movement caused him a spasm of pain.

'Don't, lad, be careful,' his mother warned, forgetting about Molly. She put a hand out to him then took it back as he turned away and pulled a chair out from under the table.

'I'm all right, Mam,' he said, and sat down. Putting an elbow on the table, he leaned his aching head on his hand, using it as a prop.

'Eeh, you're not right yet, are you, son?' asked his mother, her face creasing in anxiety.

'I tell you, I am. I'm just upset about Molly.'

No, she definitely couldn't say anything to him yet, Maggie decided. If at all. Maybe she *had* been wrong about Molly, maybe she hadn't been expecting after all. Maggie sighed. She had had enough on her hands when Jackson was missing all that time. Oh, she never wanted to go through that again. No, indeed. And worrying about the way Frank had taken it. She had hardly been able to look at the lass, never mind take an interest in her. Molly had reminded her too much of Jackson, her lovely lad.

Then, when she had had the good news, she had told Joan Pendle to tell Molly and to give her the letter Jackson had sent. Well, Joan saw her at work, didn't she? Surely the girl would have done it? She wasn't as spiteful as all that, was she?

If in the back of her mind Maggie had wondered why Molly hadn't come straight back to Eden Hope to wait for Jackson, she hadn't had time to do much about it, she had been so busy turning the house out, getting ready for his return. She'd even saved the precious fat and meat rations so that she could make him a real old-fashioned steak and kidney pie. And now he wasn't eating it. It lay ignored on the table while he went on about Molly Mason. Maggie felt a niggle of jealousy. It was enough to make a saint swear, it really was.

Jackson had picked up his letters to Molly, two of them, both unopened. 'If I had her address, I'd go through. But I only have a few days, I have to report to the hospital on Monday.'

Maggie felt a pang of disappointment and dismay. Monday! And it was already Thursday evening. And if he was going to spend the little time he had chasing after the lass, what time did that leave for his mother and father?

'You're not going to rush off straight away, lad, surely not?' she protested.

'No, of course I'm not,' he said quickly, noticing the hurt

expression his mother wore. 'But I'll have to try tomorrow. I'll go to the factory, I think. After all, the weekend is coming up and she won't be there then.'

He couldn't understand why Molly had gone off without even leaving her address. Of course, she hadn't known he had survived and got back from France. But still, Harry might have been coming home on leave and she wouldn't have wanted to miss him. Though perhaps she had written to her brother? Goodness knows, he thought unhappily. Harry was off somewhere on a 'hush-hush' operation he had been told, when his friend didn't come back to see him at the hospital. There was no way he could get in touch with Harry just at the present. Poor Molly, she must think that she had no one at all. What good were he and Harry to her, always away at war?

'Howay, lad, eat up the pie. Your mother made it especially for you,' said Frank. He wheeled his chair up to the table next to his son. 'Don't blame her, lad,' he said in a soft undertone. 'She was at her wit's end about you, she was.'

Jackson smiled at him, tried to throw off his melancholy mood. 'No, Dad, I'm not blaming her,' he replied and looked across at his mother. He smiled at her and suddenly his face lit up, eyes crinkling at the corners, twinkling at her. And Maggie saw she had her lad back again and felt again the joy she had known when the news of his miraculous return from the dead reached her.

'Aye, lad, tuck in now,' was all she said, however. 'There's the best part of a week's ration of meat in that lot.'

Of course, Jackson couldn't get into the factory when he went in search of Molly. He couldn't get past the gate.

'But I want to see the manager,' he protested to the guard. 'I only have a couple of days before I have to go back to my unit. I must get in.'

'Not without a pass you don't,' the guard said stolidly.

'Well, ring the manager and ask him to come down here, will you?'

'No, I can't do that, not if it isn't urgent,' the guard replied.

'But it *is* urgent! I told you it was.'

'You told me nothing, Sergeant,' said the guard.

'It's my girl, she's in there . . . she thinks I'm dead.'

'If I did it for you, I'd have to do it for every soldier as comes looking for his lass, wouldn't I? Write a note and I'll give it to her when she comes out.'

'But it's only eleven o'clock in the morning. She won't be coming out until the end of the day, will she?'

'No, likely not,' the guard conceded. 'But you don't expect her to come out when she's supposed to be working, do you? The work here's important, like. There's a war on, you know.'

'Aye, I do,' said Jackson in exasperation. 'I'm a soldier or haven't you noticed?'

The guard bristled. 'I see you're wearing a uniform, but then any fifth columnist could get hold of a uniform, couldn't he?'

Jackson controlled his rising temper and dug into the breast pocket of his battledress for his identity card. 'There! Now will you get her?'

The guard took his time about examining the card then handed it back. 'Aye,' he said. 'Well, all right, you're a soldier on sick leave. Wounded in France, were you? Whereabouts?' The guard saw Jackson's look of exasperation and his voice hardened again. 'But like I said, I still can't bring her from her work. What's the lass's name, any road? I'll see where she's working and try to get a message to her. I can do no more.'

'Well, thank God for that,' breathed Jackson, who was getting to the stage where he was ready to punch the man in the nose. And that, he well knew, would get him nowhere.

'Molly Mason.'

The guard went back into his cubbyhole and began sifting through lists. He came back out, shaking his head. 'She's not here the day,' he said. 'Not any Molly Mason on this list. Mind, she might be on night shift.'

Jackson groaned. He hadn't thought of that. There was more time wasted until the night shift came on. After leaving a note for the guard to hand over to Molly, he walked back to the station and caught a train back to Bishop Auckland.

He was back at the factory gates when the night shift was going in. There was no sign of Molly though he was sure he hadn't missed anyone. He saw Joan Pendle coming along in the crowd from the station and managed to push his way through the throng to her. She turned as she heard him calling her name.

'Jackson Morley! Well, fancy meeting you here. I heard you were back.' She looked over his shoulder. 'Is Harry with you?'

'No, sorry. He's in the paratroopers now, I don't know where he was sent.'

Joan's face dropped. She started to walk towards the factory gate. 'Any road,' she said, 'where've you been? We all thought you'd been killed.'

He fell into step beside her. 'Well, as you can see, I wasn't. I was injured but I'm all right now. Is Molly on this shift? Did you give her Mam's letter?'

'How could I? She hasn't worked here for months,' said Joan. Jackson stopped and stared at her. The disappointment was shattering. For a minute he could think of nothing else and Joan walked on, almost disappearing into the crowd. He ran after her, caught hold of her arm.

'She doesn't work here?' he asked incredulously. 'But where's she gone? And why didn't you tell my mother?'

Joan shook her arm free. 'How the heck do I know where's she gone? She's no friend of mine. Do you think I keep company with gaolbirds, like?'

Jackson grabbed hold of her again. 'Don't you speak of Molly like that,' he growled, glaring down at her menacingly. 'What about the letter Mam gave you? I said. What did you do with it?'

'Aw, I can't remember now. Do you think I've nowt else to do but run messages for your mother?' But Joan's voice was rising; she felt a tremor of fear.

'Hey, you, leave that lass alone!'

It was the gatekeeper, a different one from the morning. Jackson looked up, realising they were right by the gate and the streams of workers had slowed to a trickle.

'He's hurting my arm,' cried Joan, appealing to the gatekeeper over her shoulder.

'Leave her alone, I said,' shouted the man. He even left his post and came out the few yards to where they stood. Jackson stared at him, his lips a thin line in his angry face. He had never hit a woman in his life but he realised he had come very close to doing that. His grip reluctantly relaxed and Joan pulled herself free once again.

'Don't you ever touch me again!' she shouted, retreating through the gate. 'I'll have the law on you, I will.'

'Get along then, Sergeant,' said the gatekeeper. 'You'd best be off.' Now the girl had gone he felt quite sorry for the young soldier. Some of these lasses got up to all sorts of devilry while their men were away fighting for their country, he knew that. He'd seen them throwing themselves at the Canadian airmen who were stationed out Darlington way.

'You're better off without her, lad,' he said kindly.

Jackson stared at him a moment or two before comprehension dawned. 'She's not . . .' he began and stopped. No point in trying to explain, he thought. In any case he hadn't the time. He might as well catch the train back to Bishop. He turned on his heel and strode off to the station.'

'Cheerio, then,' called the gatekeeper. 'Watch theeself, mind.'

Jackson half-turned and waved. 'Thanks. Cheerio.'

Back home in Eden Hope he sat around the house for the rest of the weekend, trying to think how he could get in touch with Molly, or at least find out what was happening to her.

'She'll be all right, lad. Likely she just got transferred somewhere else,' Frank said. He watched Jackson's pale face with the livid scar just showing under his hairline.

'I don't know whether the lad's so out of sorts because he cannot find Molly or because he still feels badly,' he confided to his wife.

She sighed. 'Aye, well, time will tell. Eeh, we were that glad when we found out he was alive and coming home, weren't we? I tell you, there's always summat to worry about. At least he's going to get a transfer to that convalescent hospital near Sunderland. We'll be able to go and see him there, won't we? And looking on the bright side, the war might be over before he has to go back, mightn't it?'

Molly had been directed to a munitions factory nearer Ferryhill. It was easier for her to get home now. Her life was centred round Beth, her little daughter, and work. Because she had a child she wasn't allowed to work where the bombs were filled or anywhere near explosives.

'I wouldn't anyway,' she said. She was sitting watching Dora bathe the baby, her own hands itching to take over. In fact she had already offered to but Dora had shrugged it away casually.

'You're tired after work, I'll do it,' she had insisted.

Molly watched as Dora lifted the tiny, plump and perfect little figure from the water, laughing and talking baby talk to her, Beth gurgling and laughing back. Dora had been the first one to see Beth smile; she had met Molly at the door to tell her. Beth followed Dora everywhere with her eyes, her smile disappearing when Dora went out of her line of vision.

'Let me hold her,' Molly said suddenly. 'I'll dry her and get her ready for bed.'

'No, it's all . . .' Dora stopped as she saw Molly's stubborn expression. 'Righto, then,' she said, and handed the baby over with obvious reluctance. Immediately Beth started to whimper.

'It's all right, baby. Look, it's your mammy,' Molly said softly, trying hard to smile though anxiety lurked in her eyes. If only Beth wouldn't cry, if only she would smile back at her then everything would be fine, of course it would. Beth was *her* baby, wasn't she?

Dora had got to her feet and picked up the kettle to fill it for the tea and Beth's bottle. But she was hovering about, watching Molly and Beth anxiously, making Molly more nervous. The baby sensed it and her whimpers turned into full-blown crying.

She arched her back and yelled at the top of her lungs with rage.

'Don't cry, Beth. Please, please, don't cry,' Molly whispered. Dora put down the kettle and bent over Molly's shoulder and clucked and chattered to the child. Beth wriggled more than ever, and being still wet was slippery so that Molly had to grasp her firmly. The baby was screaming loudly now, her little face red, the eyes screwed up, her fists waving in the air with frustration.

'Go on then,' said Molly, defeated. 'Take her, she likes you the best.' Dora stepped forward eagerly and held out her arms and Molly put the child into them.

'Howay, my bairn,' said Dora fondly, and gently patted Beth dry. The baby stopped crying immediately and leaned against her, snuffling now with just the occasional hiccup. 'You're a naughty girl, aren't you?' said Dora in a tone of voice which implied the exact opposite of what she was saying. 'Now just wait until Auntie Dora has your clean nappy on and your nightie and then you can have your bottle, can't you? Are you hungry, my flower? Of course you are, petal.' Her tone changed to a normal one as she turned to Molly. 'Put the kettle on, will you? This one will be shouting for her bottle next.'

Molly picked up the kettle and took it to the tap in the pantry. She felt like crying herself, she was so tired and frustrated and filled with resentment of Dora because the baby obviously preferred her to her own mother. It wasn't natural, really it wasn't. She settled the kettle on the fire and brought out the tin of National Dried Milk and sugar and began preparing it for the baby's evening feed.

'Put a bit more sugar in, Molly,' Dora ordered.

'No, I don't think she needs extra sugar.'

'Go on, she's growing that fast she needs it for energy,' said Dora. 'If you're thinking about the ration, I'll do without mine.'

'Of course I'm not thinking about the ration!' Molly exploded, tears pricking the back of her eyes. 'I–'

'Shh, never mind, you'll upset the bairn,' said Dora.

'Anyway, I always put a bit of extra sugar in, she's used to it now.'

'I should have been breast feeding her,' said Molly fretfully. 'It's more natural.'

'Well, you can't, can you? Not when you have to go to work at all hours an' all. No, it was much better to start bottle feeding her.'

Molly sighed and made up the bottle as the kettle boiled. She cooled it under the tap and brought it back into the kitchen.

'I'll feed her now.'

'Best not disturb her,' said Dora comfortably. 'She'll be asleep as soon as she's finished her milk and then we can have ours. There's a nice hotpot in the oven.'

Chapter Twenty-eight

'At least it's more money at the munitions factory,' said Dora. She had a proprietorial hand on the pram as though Molly couldn't really be trusted with pushing it, not when it held the baby. The bubble of resentment that seemed always to be present in her these days swelled a little more. Dora glanced up at her.

'You're not listening to me,' she accused.

'I am, really I am,' said Molly. 'You were saying how I made more money at the munitions factory.'

'Aye. Just as well when I had to leave work to look after my little princess, isn't it, petal?' The question was addressed to the baby who turned her head sideways to smile at Dora. A milky sort of a smile but one of delight that Dora was speaking to her. Her first word will be 'Dora', Molly thought sourly.

It was a Sunday morning, the time when Molly usually took the baby out on her own, a time she looked forward to all week. Only today Dora had declared her intention of coming with her.

'It's a nice crisp morning, just the sort I like,' she had said. 'Autumn is so lovely, isn't it?'

'It's still September,' Molly had replied shortly. But she couldn't say to Dora that she didn't want her company as she strolled down the lane away from the village and between the fields where the corn was being harvested. The fact was she needed Dora and she couldn't afford to antagonise her.

They strolled in silence for a few minutes then Dora started again.

'I mean, a house like mine has a big mouth,' she said. 'The winter coming on and coal to buy and the electric. A baby has to be kept warm in the winter, you know.'

'You mean, I don't give you enough money? Is that what you're saying, Dora?'

'Well, like I said–'

'I can raise it to four pounds a week, I suppose,' said Molly doubtfully. It was practically the whole of her pay, she thought. But she didn't need much for herself and if she did she would have to try to get more overtime, that was all she could do.

They called at the newsagent's on the way home, Dora buying the *News of the World* and Molly the *Sunday Sun*, the local North Eastern Sunday paper. Because the weather had taken a turn for the worse they didn't even look at the headlines, simply rolled the papers up and put them under the pram's storm cover before making a dash for home as the rain began coming down in earnest.

It wasn't until the dinner was cooked and eaten and the dishes washed and put away that the two women sat down before the fire to read their papers, Beth asleep in her pram.

It was the photograph that caught Molly's attention first, a grainy photograph on the inside page of a soldier with dark hair under his forage cap, dark eyes and an unassuming smile. A lop-sided smile like her brother Harry's but it wasn't him, oh, no, it was Jackson Morley. LOCAL HERO, it read in big letters beneath the photo.

Molly sat straight in her chair with a sharp intake of breath. It couldn't be, not after all this time!

'What's the matter?' Dora had noticed her agitation and leaned forward, full of curiosity. But Molly didn't hear her; her heart was beating so fast she felt as though she was choking. There was a mist before her eyes so that when she tried to read the text she couldn't, it merged and blurred before her eyes. Dora got to her feet and came round to the back of Molly's chair. 'What is it?' she asked again. 'By heck, you've gone as white as a sheet, you have.'

She leaned over Molly's shoulder to see what it was. 'Do you know that lad, like?'

'No,' said Molly, only half-attending. 'I mean, yes.'

'He comes from Eden Hope, I see,' said Dora. 'The Croix de Guerre, eh? That's French, isn't it?'

'Yes.'

'Eeh, why, fancy. I wouldn't have thought they'd have been giving out medals, not now, not when they gave in.'

Molly wanted to jump to her feet and scream at Dora, tell her to shut up, stop looking over her shoulder, go to hell or anywhere, she didn't care where. But mainly just to *shut up*!

Her vision was clearing now after the initial shock. Oh, yes, it was Jackson, My love, my love, my love is alive, her heart sang. A great thankfulness enveloped her whole body. 'Thank you, God,' she said aloud. 'Thank you, God.'

'What for?' asked Dora, mystified.

'It's Jackson, don't you understand? He . . . we are engaged to be married.'

Molly began walking about the kitchen with quick, jerky steps, over to the window, stopping, turning around and walking back.

'For goodness sake, lass, stand still, you'll have me dizzy,' said Dora. Molly picked up the paper again, stared hard at it as though she might have been mistaken the first time. Her fingers trembled so much the paper rustled. But it was still Jackson's face looking out at her. Blurred as it was, definitely him. And didn't it say so anyway? She read the text properly this time.

> . . . Sergeant Jackson Morley of the Durham Light Infantry, presented with the Croix de Guerre by General De Gaulle for bravery when seconded to a French unit in Belgium, in that he manned a field gun against a German advance so allowing the rest of the unit to escape with the wounded. In the action Sergeant Morley was wounded . . .

Molly dropped the paper. Oh, she had to go to Eden Hope, she had to find out where he was, write to him . . .

'I have to go to Eden Hope,' she said to Dora, and started towards the stairs. 'If I hurry I'll catch the bus to Bishop. Or maybe Merrington to catch the Eden bus. That'll be the best, I think.'

'An' what will he have to say about the bairn then?' asked Dora. She gazed at Molly, head on one side, an ironic half-smile playing around her mouth.

Molly looked blankly at her. 'The bairn?' She stopped in her tracks and turned slowly round. 'I . . . I . . .'

'I bet he doesn't know about our little Beth, does he? Innocent little babe that she is, he's not going to like it, is he?'

Molly looked piteously at her and Dora nodded her head.

'Aye, I thought as much,' she said. 'Oh, go on then, you go. I'll see to her. At least it'll put your mind at rest. But mind, don't build your hopes up because it takes a saint of a man to accept another man's bairn, I'm telling you that for nothing.'

'I have to go, Dora,' said Molly. She crossed to the pram and touched her child's face briefly; Beth slept on. Molly ran upstairs to change into her best costume, a grey flannel cut on the new utility lines with a short skirt and only one pleat and square military shoulders to the jacket. She brushed her hair until it shone, looked into the mirror and frowned slightly, added a touch of colour to her lips and ran back downstairs again.

Dora had abandoned the papers and was sitting with her feet propped up on the fender, staring into the fire.

'That didn't take you long,' she said, and sniffed.

'No, well, I have to catch the bus, don't I?' said Molly. 'I'll see you when I get back.'

'Oh, don't hurry on my account,' said Dora. 'Nor Beth's neither. We'll be all right, don't you worry yourself.'

'Dora–'

'Aye. Well, go on then. An' don't forget to close the door properly. It's getting cooler by tea-time now.'

*

It was only as she stood at the bus stop by the triangular green in Kirk Merrington that Molly allowed herself to wonder what Maggie's reception of her might be like. Had word got back to Eden Hope that she'd had a baby? Perhaps not, she thought. After all, no one knew her in Ferryhill apart from Dora and the immediate neighbours. And these days there were often strange folk about, especially young mothers and children evacuated inland from Sunderland or Hartlepool, even Middlesborough. As far as she knew no one in Ferryhill had asked who she was.

There was fifteen minutes to wait for the Eden bus. Molly, filled with excitement, couldn't stand still. She walked up and down, up and down. Gazed at the corner from which the bus would appear as though she could make it do so by the power of her will.

'I'm not going to tell her,' she said aloud on the corner. A door opened in one of the houses bordering the green. A young woman came out, glanced at Molly, startled, then decided she couldn't possibly have been talking to her and disappeared round the corner. Talking to yourself was a bad sign, thought Molly, and turned the other way and walked to the opposite corner.

She wouldn't tell Maggie about Beth, she decided. At least not before she told Jackson. Jackson . . . Would he be there, in Eden Hope? In his mother's house? Her pulse leaped at the thought and panic rose into her throat. She would have to tell him, wouldn't she? And she wasn't ready yet, oh, no. He would send her packing, he would too. Oh, God, if he should look at her with contempt, she wouldn't be able to bear it.

The sound of an engine impinged on her anxious thoughts. The bus was coming. She couldn't go, couldn't face Jackson with what she had done, not now. She needed more time.

What a fool she was, Molly told herself as she climbed on to the bus, she had to go, had to see him one more time even if he did reject her. The bus set off, winding its way round the farming communities and colliery villages, coasting down hills and creaking slowly round corners, drawing nearer and nearer to Eden Hope and her own personal Judgement Day. All the time Molly's thoughts whirled chaotically. One minute she was filled with wild elation that she could see Jackson at any minute and the next cast into despair, sure he would cast her off. She alighted at the top of the rows, her stomach churning, and walked the short distance to the Morleys' house on trembling legs.

'Molly! Well, who would have believed it? Frank, Frank – here's Molly come to see us.'

Maggie stood in the doorway, one hand on the door, her face breaking into a smile of surprised welcome. 'Why, yer bloke, we were just talking about you, wondering where you were. Why the heck didn't you keep in touch?'

'Hallo, Maggie, Frank,' said Molly as Maggie took her arm and drew her into a kitchen still redolent of Yorkshire pudding and boiled cabbage. 'Eeh, who would have believed it? We were just talking about you, wondering where you were . . .'

'Is it true? Is he alive?' Molly butted in, unable to wait any longer to ask. She gazed anxiously round at Frank in his chair by the fire; an ordinary chair now with crutches propped against the wall beside it, not his wheel chair she noted with one part of her mind. No Jackson, though, he wasn't here, she thought, and slumped in disappointment.

'He is, lass,' said Frank. 'And out of his mind wondering what happened to you. Where the hell have you been, any road? There's been no word from you in all these months, you never even told us you'd changed your job.'

Molly heard what he said, the words were there in her head, but for a second or two she was incapable of understanding anything but the first three. It was true, Jackson was alive, it wasn't some cruel trick the *Sunday Sun* had played on her. It wasn't some other Jackson Morley, it was *hers*.

'Where is he?' she whispered as Frank fell silent.

'A place out Sunderland way. A convalescent place.'

'He's hurt?'

'He was. Getting better now, though. He'll be back with his unit soon.'

Frank had instinctively answered her questions as tersely as they were given. Molly sat down again for she had risen to her feet when she had thought Jackson was hurt.

'You never even wrote, lass,' said Maggie reproachfully. But she was affected by Molly's obvious agitation, as was Frank.

'Put the kettle on, Maggie, make the lass a cup of tea,' he said now. 'She looks as though she could do with it.' She did an' all, he thought. By heck, she must love their Jackson all right. Well, mebbe this time there would be a happy ending to it. They deserved one, that was for sure.

'Near Sunderland?'

Molly looked as though she was ready to go there now, this minute. She sat on the edge of her chair, looked at the clock on the mantelpiece. Her clock it was, she thought suddenly. The clock that had come from her dad's house, the marble clock, still ticking away. Beside it stood a wooden clock from around 1930 that had stopped.

Maggie saw her glance. 'You don't mind, do you? But ours stopped and yours was upstairs doing nothing, so I thought . . .'

'No, of course I don't mind,' said Molly. She looked at Maggie, really looked at her for the first time since she had entered the house. Jackson's mother looked well, better than she had done for ages. The dullness had left her eyes, the corners of her mouth turned up as though she was ready to smile at any minute and there was a healthy colour in her cheeks. Very different from the last time Molly had seen her, when they had both thought Jackson was lost.

Maggie lifted the kettle and felt its weight before settling it on the fire. Then she began bustling about from the pantry to the kitchen table, laying a cloth and bringing out the best cups from the press.

'I'll help you,' said Molly, moving to do so.

'No, I can manage,' said Maggie. Then, realising she must sound short, she paused and smiled at Molly. 'Look, like I said, we'll forget the past, will we? I know I likely said things I shouldn't but I was near out of my mind about the lad. You an' all, I shouldn't wonder. I just didn't have room in me to consider how you were feeling.'

'It's all right, I know.'

'An' if I should have had suspicions I shouldn't, I'm sorry about that too,' Maggie went on.

'What the heck are you on about, woman?' Frank demanded.

'Nothing, it was nothing. I'm sure I took no notice,' said Molly hastily.

How could she say it like that? she asked herself. How could she take a forgiving tone when Maggie had been right all along and it was she herself who was in the wrong? By, she was a right bad 'un, she knew that. But she would tell Maggie the truth, she would really, after she had had a chance to explain to Jackson. If he forgave Molly, his mother would. But it was a blooming big if, indeed it was.

Suddenly the need to see him for herself, even if it meant he couldn't bear the sight of her after what she had done, was paramount, an all-consuming desire.

'How far away is it? The convalescent home, I mean?' Perhaps she had time to go there and see him tonight.

Maggie looked up from setting out a raspberry sponge filled with jam from the canes that grew wild on the old disused railway embankment. She saw at once by her expression what Molly had in mind.

'Eeh, you can't go there tonight, man, it's thirty miles or more. You have to get a bus to Sunderland from Bishop and another out to the place. No, don't be so daft. There's time for you, he'll likely be there a while yet. It's two or three weeks before he goes back to his unit.'

Molly's eyes dimmed. 'You'll give me the address, though?'

'Oh, aye.'

'We have some letters here from your Harry,' said Frank. 'Maggie, fetch them out for the lass.'

Molly looked at the writing on the envelopes. There were two of them, one written weeks ago and one just the previous week. 'I'll read them on the bus home,' she said, and stuffed them into her bag feeling guilty once again. She should have told Harry, she knew that. After all he was her only kin.

In spite of all her feelings of guilt and worry and foreboding for the future, Molly enjoyed the couple of hours with the Morleys before she left to catch the bus back to Ferryhill. For whatever her troubled thoughts there was one big underlying truth which shone in her mind. Jackson was alive. He was even in the county. He had been hurt but he was better or at least recovering. And he still loved her. He had come looking for her, hadn't he? Surely he would still want her, no matter what she had done? She would forgive him anything, anything at all, of course she would, because her love was big enough for it. And his too, she told herself. His too.

Chapter Twenty-nine

'Was he there then?' asked Dora when Molly arrived back in Ferryhill that Sunday evening. Dora looked agitated even though she was sitting in a chair knitting away furiously. She didn't lift her eyes from the work.

'No. He's in a convalescent home up Sunderland way,' Molly answered. 'But, oh, Dora, isn't it marvellous? He's alive!'

'Marvellous,' she agreed. Her knitting needles clicked busily on to the end of the row. She changed the needles round and straightened out the tiny garment she was making before relaxing her hands into her lap and looking hard at Molly.

'He might not want you back, you know, not with the bairn.'

The light died from Molly's eyes. Oh, she didn't need Dora to tell her that. She was unbuttoning her coat but now slumped down on a chair without taking it off.

'I know.'

Dora resumed her knitting, making the steel needles click hard like a tattoo. 'Not many men will accept another man's baby.' She nodded her head to emphasise her words.

'Dora, I know that, don't go on about it.'

'Aye, an' if he does, what then?'

'What do you mean?'

'What about me? What do you think I mean? After I stuck by you, gave you a home, looked after Beth like she was my own?'

Molly gazed at her. Dora's face was red, she had obviously been crying. As she knitted her lips worked continuously.

'I love Beth like she was me own an' all,' she burst out angrily before she stopped knitting abruptly and rolled the garment up, stabbing the ball of wool viciously on the end of the needles.

'I'll put the kettle on. We'll have our cocoa. You have work the morrow.'

'I'm on nights,' Molly reminded her gently. She didn't know how to deal with Dora's pain and fear. Surely the woman must have known that Molly and the baby might move away one day? After all, Beth was her baby, not Dora's.

'I'd like to go to see him one day this week. I could go during the day . . .'

'Best go tomorrow,' said Dora. She was mixing cocoa and sugar with dried milk; half a pint of fresh milk a day didn't allow for such luxuries as cocoa. 'You want to go tomorrow, don't you?'

'Yes.'

'Well then, I take it you don't want to take Beth?'

'No. Not this time at any rate.' Molly looked at her. 'Look, I'm sorry, really I am. But I don't know what's going to happen, do I? Or even if anything is. In any case you would still be able to see Beth, of course you would. I'll always be grateful to you, Dora.' She tried to put out of her mind all the times when she had not been grateful, those occasions when Dora seemed to be taking over Beth.

'There she is now, I'll go,' said Dora, and it was only after she'd said it that Molly could hear the baby whimpering. Either Dora had especially acute hearing or she was so attuned to the baby that she heard her almost before she started to cry. She rushed upstairs and Molly could hear her crooning softly, the baby's cries stilled. Sometimes Molly thought Dora was trying to put Beth in Mona's place. But perhaps she was reading too much into it.

Next morning Molly caught the eight-thirty bus to Durham and a connecting one to Sunderland. Her first glimpse of the town shocked her and she was surprised at the amount of bomb damage. There were great holes in some of the streets, single walls still standing even to third- and fourth-floor level. It was raining and water stood in exposed cellars; wind blew at a pair of green curtains hanging at a third-floor window with all the glass blown out.

A twinge of anxiety went through Molly. Surely the soldiers' convalescent home wasn't near this place where there was so much danger from air raids? She rummaged in her bag for the address: Barton Lodge, Washington Road. There was a post office nearby and Molly went in and asked for directions.

'Why do you want to know?' the postmaster asked with suspicion. 'How do I know you're not a spy?'

'My boyfriend is there. Do you want to see my identity card?' She wasn't a bit affronted, it was good that people were suspicious.

'Number 23 bus will drop you at the gates,' the postmaster said after looking at her identity card. Molly thanked him and hurried back to the bus stop. Her feelings were so mixed up by now, elated anticipation uppermost one minute then dread at what Jackson would say the next, that her stomach was churning. No matter what, though, she told herself, she had to see him, touch him. If he rejected her after that she would die; she couldn't bear to think of what she would do if his reaction was contempt.

'I would like to see Sergeant Morley,' she said to the young girl in mobcap and apron who opened the door.

'Who?' asked the girl, and Molly could have screamed at her. But instead she said again.

'Sergeant Morley. Jackson Morley?'

'You'll have to ask Matron.'

The girl pointed to a door at the side of the hall and Molly walked over to it and knocked.

'This is not visiting time,' said a thickset woman with hairs on her chin and an incongruous lace-edged cap tied under her chin with a large bow.

'I know, I'm sorry. But I have to work tonight. I'm on night shift at the munitions factory.'

‘Well, all right. Sergeant Morley is in the garden. The girl will show you where. He is expecting to be discharged today, after the doctor’s rounds. Now they’re at twelve o’clock sharp so you haven’t got long.’

The clock on the wall stood at half-past eleven. Molly went with the maid around the corner of the house to where there were long lawns running down to a stream. There were only one or two soldiers visible, one sitting on a bench in the shelter of a wall, another walking along by the stream. His head was bent, shoulders hunched. He stared at the brown, peaty water bubbling along over the stones as he walked.

‘Jackson!’

Molly took one look at him and all her doubts, all her misgivings, were forgotten as she ran down the slope to him. He lifted his head, gazing at her, opening his arms as she ran into them, holding her close. Her arms were round his neck, her face buried in his shoulder. She could feel the beat of his heart through his tunic, only a little slower than the fast wild beat of her own.

‘Molly . . . Molly,’ he whispered in her ear. ‘Oh my God, I was beginning to think I would never find you again.’

Tears were dropping from her eyes unheeded. She lifted her face and he kissed each eyelid, her cheeks, her chin, and at last her lips. A deep, satisfying kiss which yet conveyed all the loneliness of the last months, years even. He took out a handkerchief and wiped her face gently, gazed down into the deep brown pools of her eyes. She clung to him, never wanted to let go, could not even if she had wanted to.

‘Jackson . . .’

‘Whisht, my love, hush. Don’t talk, not now.’

Holding her close against him with one arm, he began walking her to the edge of the garden, a secluded corner where a large laurel bush screened them from any prying eyes that might be looking from the windows of the home. There he took her in his arms again, stroked her hair and held her against the lean, hard length of him. She lifted a hand against his brown cheek, twisted a lock of dark hair in her fingers, felt faint with love of him. She pressed closer to him, her breasts tingling, the tips hardening; felt the answering hardness of him against her belly.

'I want you,' he whispered in her ear. 'I want you now!'

'Sergeant Morley? Sergeant, where are you? The doctor is here, come in at once!'

They didn't hear it at first until the soldier who had been sitting on the bench by the wall, and had watched with interest as they took cover behind the laurel bush, added his voice to that of the nurse.

'Jack? Put her down and come out of there, you're wanted,' he called. 'Can't you hear the nurse?'

Jackson sighed, loosed his arms from Molly, though retaining her hand in his, and kissed her on the tip of her nose. 'Wait for me,' he said softly. 'I won't be long.'

As he walked back to the house, the soldier on the bench grinned at him. 'Lucky devil,' he said. 'How did you manage to get a girl like that?'

'Never you mind, Don,' Jackson replied. 'You find one of your own.'

They went to a hotel overlooking the beach at Roker for the need to hold each other, to touch and make love, was overwhelming. Molly hung back a little, sure the bored-looking woman behind the desk would guess they weren't married and tell them to go. But she didn't, merely reached behind her for the key to the room. She had lots of soldiers coming in with their girls or wives, she didn't care which.

'After all, there's a war on, the poor lads have to go somewhere,' she said to her husband as she went through into the office. 'And any road, we need the money.'

'I'm not saying nowt, am I?' he asked.

The room was fairly basic but clean, and in any case they weren't really interested in their surroundings. They undressed each other, carefully at first then with increasing haste, pulling off the inhibiting clothes, dropping them on the floor where they lay unheeded. Her arms were around his neck, her mouth on his. He lifted her up and she wound her legs around him and they fell on the bed, both lost in an ecstasy of pounding blood and rising excitement until Molly at least thought she would die of it. And when release came it was in such a crescendo of feeling that both of them cried aloud and collapsed in each other's arms. And a few minutes later it all started again.

It was Molly who woke first from a deep contented sleep. Her head was resting in the crook of his shoulder, his arm across her breasts. She felt herself deeply wrapped in his love, so bewitched that all her worries were as nothing compared to it. This was the real world, this was what mattered, nothing else in the whole world.

Jackson stirred, opened his eyes and smiled at her. His smile was perfect, eyes shining into hers so that she smiled back adoringly.

'We could stay here tonight,' he said softly. 'We'll stay in this bed until tomorrow. If we're hungry later I'll order a meal sent up. Will I do that?'

'Yes. Oh, yes,' she breathed into his ear, took the lobe between her teeth, nibbled gently at it. But then an image of Beth rose before her eyes, intruding on her Eden.

'No,' she said, moving away from him so that he protested and held on to her arm, trying to stop her. 'I have to get back, it's important.'

'Stay,' he insisted. 'What could be more important than this?'

It's not a what, it's a who, thought Molly. She tried to say it aloud, now, when it was a good time to say it, but she couldn't, not when they were so happy.

'I have to go to work,' she said lamely.

'Take a shift off,' said Jackson. 'Surely at a time like this you're entitled to a night off? Oh, come on, my love, stay with me.'

'I can't. I have to go,' Molly said, a catch in her voice. Oh, God help me, she thought, what am I going to do?

Jackson took his arm away, sat up in the bed. 'Then if you have to go, I'm coming with you.' He swung his legs out of bed, stood and went to the window. She watched him, loving his long, lithe body, the powerful shoulders, and the line of his hair on the strong column of his neck. Then his words echoed in her mind, she realised what he had said and sat bolt upright.

'No!'

He turned, raised an eyebrow in surprise. 'Why not? I have to know where you're living, I don't intend losing you again.' He strode to the bed, took her in his arms. 'Not ever again, do you hear me?'

Molly leaned her head into the curve of his shoulder and closed her eyes. She felt drunk with the proximity of him. It became harder and harder to think, but she had to.

'Why?' he asked.

'It's just that I'm living with a widow and she doesn't like men callers,' Molly said lamely, and Jackson put back his head and shouted with laughter.

'She doesn't like men callers! Which century is she living in? Is this the twentieth or not?'

Molly pulled away from him and got out of bed. She began picking up her clothes from the floor where they had been discarded in the urgency of their need. She went to the wash basin which stood in a corner of the room, ran water and began washing herself.

'What's wrong?' asked Jackson, watching her. He pulled on his underpants and uniform trousers, looked around for his shirt.

'Nothing. At least . . . I can't go back there now, I'll have to go straight to work or I'll be late.'

'All right, I'll come with you there,' he said. 'You can give me your address on the way. Or, better still, I'll meet you tomorrow morning at the factory gate and we can go back to Eden Hope, how's that?'

'No, I can't. I'll be altogether too tired, I will honestly. No, I'll have to go home myself in the morning.'

Jackson said nothing. He washed and finished dressing and was ready when she was. But the smile had left his eyes. He kept glancing at her with a puzzled expression which gradually hardened into resolve.

As they walked away from the hotel he took her arm and put it through his but the closeness of before was missing and Molly was acutely and miserably aware of it. They caught the Darlington bus which wound its way through the coastal villages before turning inland and sat close together, he holding her hand, saying little. He did not ask for her address again, but simply watched her with that questioning look.

The bus stop was about a quarter of a mile from the factory and they got off together and walked the rest of the way. Molly was more than an hour early for her shift so they found a café and drank weak tea and ate toasted teacake with plum jam. No butter, of course.

'I'll pick you up tomorrow,' said Jackson in a voice that brooked no argument. 'And I will go home with you. We'll tell your battleaxe of a landlady that we're going to be married next week before I go back to duty. If she says anything, anything at all, you'll come back to Eden Hope with me. Now, is that understood?'

Molly nodded, looking down at the half-eaten teacake on her plate. She was going to have to tell him, she thought.

Chapter Thirty

'We can't, you see,' said Molly, thinking: God forgive me, I'm lying through my teeth. 'Dora, that's my landlady, has gone to see her sister. So we might as well just go to Eden Hope. Did you tell your mam and dad?'

'Of course I did. And I told them we'd be coming to see them. I thought tomorrow, but we can go today. Did you ask for next week off work?'

'Yes,' said Molly. The morning was bright and sharp with that touch of frost that seems to clear the air so that the trees and bushes stood out against the pale blue sky. Strangely Molly felt not a bit tired even though she had worked all night, concentrating on the straight seams as she sewed the stiff cloth together into powder bags. She flexed her fingers at the thought; they were stiff and slightly painful.

The management of the factory was understanding, that was one good thing. Especially if you were marrying a member of the fighting forces. And in any case, she was owed the time off. Molly glanced up at Jackson and her heart melted within her. She couldn't lose him now, she told herself, forcing down the panic which threatened to rise and overwhelm her. No, she couldn't. But now was not the time to tell him about Beth.

Jackson looked down at her, took her hand, and they began walking towards the bus stop for Bishop Auckland.

'Don't look so worried, my love, nothing is going to go

wrong this time. I won't let it, I love you too much. Howay now, smile. I promise I won't lose you again.'

Molly smiled, enveloped in his love. Surely it was too strong for any revelation to break it? She would tell him tomorrow, she resolved. Yes, she couldn't marry him without confessing. And when he saw Beth he would be captivated by the baby, of course he would. She was so beautiful, he couldn't fail to be.

On the bus they sat close together, Molly leaning on Jackson's shoulder.

'That's right, pet,' he said. 'You have a snooze, you must be tired out. This afternoon you can have a couple of hours while I go to see the registrar about a special licence. We have arrangements to make.'

'I must go back to Ferryhill,' she said quickly. 'For clean clothes if nothing else.'

He frowned. Their time together was so short, he begrudged any of it being spent apart. 'Righto,' he said, 'of course. And I'll see you tomorrow morning and soon it will be the weekend and we'll be together.'

Molly walked up the yard of the Morleys' house.

'Come away in, love,' Maggie cried. 'I'll soon knock you up a bite of breakfast. And we've got a surprise for you . . . look who's here!' There, rising from the rocking chair by the fire, was Harry. He held out his arms and Molly went to him with a surge of delight and affection. He lifted her off her feet and swung her in the air.

'Now then, sis,' he cried. 'Where the heck have you been this time? I tell you, I can't take my eyes off you in case you disappear again!'

'Not any more,' said Jackson firmly, coming up behind Molly as her brother put her back on her feet and clapping his friend on the shoulder. 'You made it back then, mate,' he said. 'How much leave have you? A week?'

Harry pulled a face. 'No such luck,' he said. 'Seventy-two hours, that's all.'

'Still you'll be here for the wedding. I'm going down to

Bishop for the special licence today. Fancy coming with me? We haven't a lot of time to waste.' Jackson glanced at the marble clock which still stood on the mantelpiece though Molly noticed that Maggie's own was keeping good time now. She must have had it mended.

Harry followed the glance and grinned at Molly. 'You've still got the old clock, eh? Still going an' all.'

'Of course I still have it. It's all we've got left from the old house.'

Harry sobered for a minute. 'Aye,' he said. Then he smiled the lop-sided smile which was so like his father's.

'Well, we have to look forward now, haven't we? Soon you and Jackson will have a place of your own. When this flaming war is over, eh?'

'Time you settled down, Harry,' said Maggie. 'Have you not met a nice lass yet?'

'Lots of 'em.' He grinned and felt in the pocket of his battledress. 'By the way, here's me ration coupon. It's for three days.'

'Eeh, thanks, lad. I can't deny it'll come in handy.'

Molly listened with half an ear to the talk around her. Jackson was discussing the course of the war with Frank, who was wondering when the Americans would come in: 'For they will, late, just as they did the last time,' his father said.

'If only,' said Molly, surprising herself. She hadn't realised she was thinking aloud.

'They will,' Jackson insisted. 'But if they don't, what the heck? We've been on our own, backs against the wall, before now and come through. We can do it again, don't you worry.' And everyone nodded agreement.

Molly hadn't been thinking about the war, she had other things to worry about. By, she thought, leaning back in her chair and closing her eyes wearily for a few seconds, if it wasn't for Beth I would be so happy, I'd be out of my mind. With Jackson home, and Harry. Dear Lord, what was she thinking of . . . if it wasn't for Beth? What sort of depraved mother was she even to think such a terrible thing? Her lovely,

lovely Beth! Molly sighed and tears pricked the back of her eyelids.

'Come on, love,' said Jackson, taking her hand and pulling her to her feet, 'I think you'd best go and lie down for a couple of hours. I have to go into Bishop anyway, there's arrangements to make.'

'No, I'll go back to Ferryhill. I have things to see to as well, you know.'

'You're going to eat this first, though, aren't you?' asked Maggie. She had a pan of scrambled dried eggs in her hand; Frank was toasting bread before the bars of the grate.

'Thank you,' Molly whispered. They were so kind. Her eyes were wet with unshed tears.

'Sit down at the table, lass,' said Maggie. 'You'll feel better when you've got this inside you. You're tired, that's all. It's all been a bit much for you.'

Later, on the bus to Ferryhill, Molly felt almost too tired to worry about the situation at all. She dozed off time and time again, woke up with a start whenever the bus slowed to a halt at a bus stop, dozed off again when it lumbered into motion once again. When it turned into the market place at Ferryhill, she woke to hear the conductor calling, 'Terminus! Everybody off!' At least she couldn't go past her stop.

'What sort of a time is this to be coming home, that's what I want to know?'

Dora was sitting at the table with Beth in her arms, feeding the baby with a bottle in one hand and eating her own meal with the other.

'I'm sorry, Dora, really I am. I know I shouldn't have left you with Beth. I wouldn't do it with anyone else but I know I can trust you with her. But, oh, when I saw Jackson again I couldn't believe it, and you know how difficult it is to catch a bus these days. The time simply flew by –'

The baby was smiling at her, waving her fists in the air with excitement, and Molly's heart melted. How could she have gone all day yesterday without seeing her baby? She held out her arms and took her, cuddled her in, kissed the top of her head. Dora watched, unsmiling.

'Give me her back, will you? You'll make her sick, squeezing her like that. And if she doesn't finish her feed, she'll be fretful for the rest of the day.'

'I'll give it her, will I? Then you can eat your own meal in peace.'

'Hmmm. You never thought about how I was managing when you didn't come home, did you?' said Dora, but she didn't really sound angry. 'Oh, go on then, take her. I tell you, the poor bairn doesn't know who's her mammy. You don't, do you, my petal?' Her voice changed to a warm and loving tone as she spoke to the baby. And Beth looked at her gravely as she handed over the bottle to Molly. The child opened her mouth to receive the teat and recommenced the serious business of sucking.

Dora watched for a second or two and then resumed eating her own meal. 'I suppose you'll have to go to bed now an' all,' she said. 'I reckon you must be dead tired.'

'I am. But I'll stay up and watch Beth while you go to the shop, if you like.'

'Mind, that's blooming good of you,' said Dora, casting her a sarcastic glance. But Molly could see she wasn't anything like as angry as she had expected her to be.

Dora laid Beth down and went out to the shops. Molly bent over the baby, stroked the soft, downy cheek with a forefinger, smoothed the silky hair back from her forehead. By, she was a bonny bairn, she was. The baby stirred, whimpered slightly, and it was all the excuse Molly needed to pick her up, wrap a shawl round her and sit down in the rocking chair, cuddling her in. Beth slept on, a sweet, heavy bundle on her arm. She was growing fast, no longer a very tiny baby. Her eyelashes curled down on to her cheeks, dark and becoming thick. A beauty she would be, Molly thought proudly.

'I won't leave you, petal, not for any man in the world,' she whispered. And at the same time another voice was saying in her head, *But what about Jackson?*

'Each, Molly, put the bairn down, will you? She'll be sore with so much handling and then she won't sleep the night.'

Dora had come in without Molly even noticing. She came swiftly over to the rocking chair and took Beth from her; laid her back in the pram that was still used as a downstairs cot.

'Go on to bed, lass, you'll be no good for work the night if you don't get some sleep at least.'

Molly went upstairs feeling so tired she was past thinking any more about Jackson or Beth. She would be able to think better, she thought, when she had a clearer head. But when she woke it was with a headache and leaden limbs. Now she had to tell Dora she was getting married on Saturday.

'Saturday? Did you say Saturday?' Dora's voice rose. She stared at Molly with a shocked expression.

'Yes. Jackson was applying for a special licence today and he'll get one, him being a soldier and going back on duty.'

'An' what about me? What about this canny bairn?'

'I'll tell him, Dora. It'll be all right, I'm sure it will. Anyway, he'll be going off to North Africa won't he? That's where they're fighting now. Goodness only knows when he'll come back.'

Molly was looking down at her plate as she spoke, overcome almost by the prospect of Jackson's going away again. So she didn't realise that Dora was crying until she raised her head. Molly dropped her knife and fork and rushed over to the other woman.

'Oh, Dora, are you worried you won't see Beth any more? You will, I promise. Of course you will. I'll never forget what you did, you were such a friend when I needed one.' She put an arm around Dora's shoulders and hugged her.

'Aye, you say that now, an' you mean it, I know. But you'll take the poor little mite away and you'll forget all about bringing her back to see me, I know what it'll be like. I'll be losing another daughter, won't I?'

Dora sniffed, pulled out a handkerchief and blew her nose. She shrugged off Molly's arm and squared her shoulders.

'Oh, don't mind me, you'll go off with your soldier lad and

he'll forgive you and keep the bairn. You're a bonny lass, you know. You'll look at him with those big brown eyes and he won't be able to help himself, that's the top and the bottom of it all.'

No matter what Molly said Dora wasn't to be persuaded that she wouldn't be forgotten. In the end Molly had to leave her to get ready for work.

Molly and Jackson were married at the Register Office at Bishop Auckland. It was ten o'clock in the morning, a cold, damp day when the mist hung about so that the Methodist Chapel just along the road was partially obscured by it. She and Dora came in on the train without Beth, who had been left with a neighbour for a couple of hours.

At first Dora had refused to come, saying she couldn't leave the baby. And Molly had misgivings about her coming, too, dreading that she would say something to Jackson before she herself got a chance to explain about her little daughter.

She would have liked to have asked Vi to come to the wedding too. But Vi would almost certainly give her secret away to Jackson in all innocence. In fact when Molly thought of Vi she felt guilty; she had seen her only twice since she left the home, the last time weeks ago. But she dare not ask her to the wedding.

For she had not as yet told him. Throughout the last couple of days before the wedding she had set out to see him with every intention of telling him, but each time when it came to it she had not.

'You dither on much longer, my girl,' Dora remarked grimly, 'and you will really be in trouble. It's not right, marrying a chap and keeping a secret like that from him. It's bound to come out, you mark my words.'

But she was not angry or woebegone as she had been when Jackson first came back. Most of the time she had a faraway look in her eyes, or Molly would look up suddenly and find Dora gazing speculatively at her. She did not complain when Molly spent time with Jackson but looked after Beth as though she were her own. In fact, Molly sometimes had the uncomfortable thought that Dora did think of Beth as her own.

'I could adopt the bairn,' she had said abruptly the night before the wedding. 'That would be an answer, wouldn't it?'

Molly was horrified. 'No, of course you couldn't!' she cried. 'No, Dora really, everything will be fine, you'll see.'

In her heart Molly had grave doubts about everything being fine. But it just had to be, she told herself fiercely. And when she was with Jackson he was so loving towards her she began to believe it would be.

'I'll do anything for you, my love,' he'd whispered in her ear. 'Anything at all.' And Molly was beginning to believe it.

So she walked along Newgate Street towards the Register Office, past the Chapel where another wedding was in progress. She could hear the choir singing Charles Wesley's great hymn, 'Love Divine All Loves Excelling' and knew it was a wedding. A chapel wedding, that was what she had always dreamed of, Molly thought with only a faint twinge of regret. The important thing was to marry the one you loved, she told herself. And she loved Jackson. Oh, yes, she did.

He was waiting for her on the pavement outside the office, he and Harry. They kissed and made introductions, and Harry looked sadly at Mona's mother who glanced at him and looked away rapidly at a couple walking past on the opposite side of the road, then up the road, anywhere but at him. Harry had forced himself to smile, to laugh at something Frank said, and then they had all gone into the Register Office.

The ceremony was short, the office bare and dingily brown, and they were outside on the pavement again before Molly was properly aware she was at last married to Jackson. And she still hadn't told him about Beth.

Jackson had booked a photographer from Taylor's in Newgate Street and they stood together for the wedding photographs. But the photographer didn't take long; the other wedding party was emerging from the Chapel and he rushed along to it. A grand wedding it was, Molly could tell. The guests were laughing and throwing confetti which she could see was made up of chopped bits of newspaper for of course confetti was not available because of the war effort.

Harry had brought some too and Molly's heart swelled with affection for him, her brother in his red paratrooper's beret and khaki battledress. God keep him safe.

'All right, sweetheart?' Jackson had hold of Molly's arm and was bending down to whisper in her ear. He had noticed the look of anxiety which had flashed across her face as she studied Harry. Then they were laughing and trying to dodge as he threw the newspaper confetti.

They were going to the Wear Valley Hotel for a celebratory drink and walked along the road in a small group, the men with late roses from Frank's garden in their buttonholes and Molly with a spray of carnations from Hardisty's flower shop. The wedding party were moving away from the Chapel too, she saw, going towards the schoolroom where no doubt there was a spread from the Co-operative Store acquired with the special food points allowed for weddings and funerals.

At the Wear Valley Hotel they paused and Dora stepped away from them. Molly watched her; unconsciously her grip tightened on Jackson's arm so that he looked down at her, momentarily surprised.

'I'd best be getting back home,' said Dora.

'Won't you stay and have a drink first?' Jackson asked politely. He didn't press her, though, still thinking she must be something of a termagant after what Molly had said about her.

'No, I have to get back. I have the baby to see to.'

Molly felt faint. The dark day turned darker. A cold wind whistled down the neck of her grey utility costume. 'Dora?' she whispered, her brown eyes large in appeal.

Dora let her eyes roam over the company: Harry, holding on to Frank's wheel chair with Maggie beside him. Jackson in his Sergeant's uniform. He was smiling at her though his eyes were watchful. And lastly she looked at Molly.

'No, I'm sorry, I have to go. I'm minding a bairn for the neighbours. I promised, you see. I'll see you soon, will I, Molly?'

‘Yes, soon.’ It was all she could do to get the words out. The party stood and watched as Dora hurried over the road to Station Approach and disappeared into the station.

‘Molly, you look fair nithered,’ pronounced Maggie. ‘Come on, you two, shift yourselves. Let’s get in the warm.’

Chapter Thirty-one

The newly-weds wandered hand in hand through the park at Cockton Hill and along Etherley Lane until they came to the banks of the Wear. The clouds had thinned at last and the sun kept peeking through as they walked on to the path alongside the river. They didn't speak much, they were too happy just to be there together, forgetting the war and the fact that Jackson had to return to his unit by the following Tuesday morning, when Molly would also be back at her machine in the arms factory.

It had been a muted celebration in the Wear Valley Hotel where they had reservations for two nights, all the honeymoon they had time for. Now Frank and Maggie had gone back to Eden Hope while Harry had returned to camp. He was due back that evening. Jackson and Molly had seen him off at the station.

'Watch yourself, mate,' said Jackson. 'Though how you'll manage without me to look after you, I don't know.' He grinned and dodged Harry's mock blow. 'Anyway, I reckon I might join you in the Airborne Division. It's more money, isn't it? Aye, I thought that's what must have tempted you.'

'What else?'

Harry turned to his sister. 'You'll have to stand up for yourself with this one,' he said to her. 'Don't take any lip from him, mind.' He put out his arms and pulled her into a bear hug. 'Look after yourself in that factory, won't you?' he whispered, and she knew he was thinking of Mona. Poor Mona, killed so soon after she'd met her love.

Now as Molly and Jackson wandered by the river, which was brown and peaty after its run through the dale high in the Pennines, her brother was uppermost in her thoughts.

'I wish Harry would meet a nice girl and settle down,' she said to Jackson, who laughed.

'Married all of two hours and already you like it so much you want it for Harry,' he said, and put his arm around her to draw her to a fallen log by the side of the path. He kissed her lingeringly on the lips and small boys walking past whistled and cheered.

'Go on, soldier, give it to her!' one cheeky urchin cried. Jackson made a threatening move after them and they scattered and flew along the path and round the bend in the river.

Jackson smiled and turned his full attention back to Molly. 'I'll give you everything you've ever wanted, you'll see!'

Molly took a deep breath. Now was the time, she thought. He would forgive her, of course he would. He loved her. She wished she had told him straight away but she had not and now she couldn't let it go on any longer.

'Even your forgiveness?' It didn't sound like her own voice asking. She could hardly believe she had finally found the courage.

'Forgiveness? What could I possibly have to forgive you for?' Jackson laughed, his arm tightening around her. With one hand he tilted her chin, looking deep into her eyes. Oh, it was too hard. Molly coughed slightly, pulled away a little, looked in her pocket for a handkerchief.

'Well?'

'Dora had to go back to see to a baby, do you remember?'

'Yes?' Jackson was looking puzzled now.

'She said it was a neighbour's baby, but it wasn't.'

'No? Surely Dora hasn't got a baby at her age, has she? Has she had a secret love affair, is that it? The baby is hers? I don't believe you, you're joking!'

'No, I never said that. Oh, just listen to me, Jackson, and let me tell you.'

He sat back on the log, leaning against the low branch of an oak tree, a remnant of the forest that had given the town its name.

'You know, Jackson, when you were posted missing, believed killed, I nearly went mad, I think.' Molly sat forward, picked up a stick and began scratching in the dirt at their feet with it. Anything to occupy her hands, keep them from trembling. Anything to stop her heart from jumping up into her throat and threatening to choke her, the way it was doing now.

'I know it has been hard for you, love. But I'll make it up to you, I promise.'

'I was so low,' Molly went on. She was speaking deliberately now, the terror rising within her. She had to make an enormous effort to force her voice to work at all. 'And your parents . . . well, they were grieving so much, too, they closed in on themselves, didn't want me. Oh, I don't mean that in a grumbling sort of way. And I'm not making excuses for what I did either–'

'What you did?' Jackson sat forward suddenly, put his hands on her shoulders and stood up, taking her with him. 'What are you saying, Molly? Are you telling me the baby is yours?'

He held her away from him, the grip of his hands on her shoulders like iron. She couldn't bear to look at his eyes; they were so changed, so cold.

'Jackson, you're hurting me,' she whispered, but he didn't appear to hear. His relentless grip on her shoulders tightened.

'Whose is it?'

'No one's. Nobody important.'

'Nobody important? Are you telling me you went with some bloke but it wasn't *important*?'

'Yes! No . . . Oh, God. Jackson, let me go!'

'I'll let you go all right – you can go to hell! Or go back to your *unimportant* lover!'

'Jackson, it wasn't like that. I was out of my mind . . . I thought you were dead.' She tried to explain, her words falling over themselves in her hurry to get him to understand how it had been.'

'Don't make excuses, Molly,' was all he said. She looked up at him. There was a white line around his nostrils, his mouth was pinched and his eyes glittered.

'I'm not! I'm not making excuses . . . I'm just telling you how it was . . .'

'You couldn't tell me yesterday, though, could you? You couldn't tell me when I first came back, could you?'

Jackson released his grip, pushing her away from him violently so that she staggered and almost fell over the log they had been sitting on. The place where he had whispered so lovingly in her ear, where he had told her he would do anything for her. He turned and walked away, not even pausing to see if she had been hurt but striding along the path in the direction of the town.

'You all right, pet?' a kindly voice asked. It was a man returning from his allotment, a basket of vegetables in his hand. He paused on the path and looked at her with concern.

Swiftly Molly turned away, found her handkerchief and blew her nose. 'Yes, I'm fine, thank you. Just a cold, I think,' she said, her back to him, her head bent.

He regarded her doubtfully for a moment. 'Aye, well,' he said. 'If I were you I'd go home to bed, lass, you look terrible.' He went on his way.

Molly walked in the opposite direction, then paused to study the turbulent waters of the dam head. She was deeply shocked, in a kind of daze. The water were dark, deep and rushing, and for one brief moment she thought of ending it all, throwing herself into the depths, at last finding some peace. She couldn't believe Jackson had said what he had. He hadn't even asked why or how, had simply condemned her out of hand. His features had been transformed with hatred and jealousy. And now he never wanted to see her again. She swayed, dangerously close to the edge, almost hypnotised by the river, her eyes closing. Then a picture of Beth flashed before her eyes. Beth, her innocent baby, smiling at her as she had done that morning before Molly went out to her wedding. But maybe she would be better off with Dora . . .

'Come here!'

Molly turned, her heart suddenly fluttering for Jackson had come back! He was going to forgive her, he really was. But the hope died in her as she saw his face, still that of a stranger. He took her by the arm and marched her along with him, back down the path to the town and the hotel. He got the key to their room from a mystified receptionist who gazed after them curiously as they mounted the stairs, the soldier pushing the girl in front of him. A bedroom door banged shut above. The receptionist glanced at a waiter, who was hovering in the dining-room doorway, her eyebrows raised.

'By heck,' she said. 'Those two have soon started fighting, haven't they?'

Inside the room Jackson flung Molly on to the bed. He pulled at her suit buttons, sending one flying into the corner of the room so that she tried to undo the rest herself only to have her hands thrust away. Then she let him finish, undressing her. He pulled off her blouse, pulled down the straps of her bra so that her breasts were exposed, the nipples proud and the contours fuller since she'd had the baby. He pulled her skirt up around her waist and held her down with one hand while he pushed the wide-legged cami-knickers to one side.

Molly lay there, the roll of her clothes around her waist hurting her back, her legs spread-eagled so that the elastic of her suspenders stretched hard against her skin. His hands were rough on her breasts, squeezing, digging into the soft flesh. He has a right, she thought dimly. I married him under false pretences. Tears ran down her face and she didn't even know she was crying. She was nothing, less than nothing, she was worse than a whore, she knew it now, saw herself through Jackson's eyes and shrank from what she saw.

He was unbuttoning his flies; he wasn't even going to undress, she thought dimly. She wasn't worth it. She turned her face away and closed her eyes. Suddenly he stopped in the very act of pushing her legs wider apart. His hand was on her breast but he was still. Molly opened her eyes and looked up at him.

Jackson was staring at her reddened face, at the tears, with an expression of disgust. But the disgust was not for her, she realised as the next minute he was climbing off the bed, adjusting his clothing, pushing his hair back from his forehead.

'Cover yourself up,' he said, his voice ragged. He turned to the window and looked out at the darkening street, filled with shoppers making their way home. He couldn't do it, she thought. When it came down to it, he couldn't do it. A flicker of hope stirred within her to be instantly quashed as he spoke again.

'You can stop here tonight. The room's paid for. I'll go back to camp early. I don't want my mother and father to find out about this, do you hear?'

'Yes.'

Jackson turned and looked at her. She saw the suffering in his eyes and it was because of her and she couldn't bear it.

'I wanted to tell you, Jackson. Oh, dear God, I thought you were dead, don't you understand?' She sniffed, looked around for her bag, found it and searched inside for a handkerchief. A tiny blue lacy handkerchief which Dora had given her for luck. It was completely inadequate. He threw her a large khaki square and Molly wiped her eyes, blew her nose.

She pulled down her skirt and buttoned up her blouse, still conscious of the marks of his fingers on her breast, squeezing and twisting. She shrugged into her costume jacket and winced.

'I'm sorry if I hurt you,' he said. 'No, I'm not, what am I saying? Dear God in Heaven, you've done for me today, Molly. I was going to treat you like the whore you are, but when it came to it I couldn't.' Jackson sighed heavily and turned to the window, his back straight and unforgiving.

'I'm sorry,' she said, and he laughed mirthlessly.

'What was it, Molly? I gave you a taste for it, did I? Was it my fault, all of this?' She was shaking her head in denial but he wasn't looking at her, talking to himself. 'I know it's been happening a lot in this blasted war, I hear of it often enough.

What's it going to be like by the end, whenever that might be? Oh, God, I never thought it would happen to *me*!'

His voice was full of anguish and bitterness and Molly couldn't bear it. She moved towards him, to comfort him; put a hand out to him. But he shrank away from her touch as though it burned him. She moved quickly away, sat down on the only chair in the room and clasped her hands tightly together in her lap.

'I love you, Jackson,' she said. 'I'll never love anyone but you.'

'I know that really,' he replied. 'I know you thought I was probably dead. But you didn't know for sure, did you? So soon, Molly, it was so soon after I'd gone!'

'I was half-mad with grief.'

'Yes, I'm sure you were,' said Jackson heavily. He sounded so sad, so resigned, and Molly knew that he had decided, he wasn't going to change his mind, not now.

'I'll have to go back to my baby,' she said and rose to her feet.

'I don't want my mother and father to find out what has happened, not yet,' he said again. 'They've had enough grief. You'll have to pretend.'

'I can't stay there, Jackson. I have my baby. Dora looks after her when I'm at work, that's all.'

'Yes, well, you'll have to concoct a story, won't you? You're good at lying.'

There seemed nothing more to say. Jackson had been going straight from the Wear Valley to the train in any case; he did it now instead of a few days later. She knew he didn't want her to go with him to the station, of course he didn't, but she watched through the window as the train steamed away and felt as though her heart was being cut out of her body.

Molly stayed in the room that night, sitting sleepless in the chair, staring at the wall. She didn't eat; couldn't face the curious eyes of the women working in the hotel. On Monday, she packed her bag and went downstairs, said a dignified goodbye and went out to catch the bus to Eden Hope.

'I thought you weren't coming back until tomorrow,' said Maggie, surprised when she came in.

'I wasn't, but Jackson was called back early so I might as well go to work.'

'You'll be bringing your things here, will you?' Maggie studied her; Molly looked so white and there were huge shadows under her eyes.

'It's easier to travel from Ferryhill,' she said. 'Jackson sends his love and says he'll be seeing you.'

'By, I hope he doesn't have to go abroad again,' said his mother. 'In my opinion he's done his bit, it's somebody else's turn.'

'I'd like to take the marble clock, is that all right?'

'Oh, aye, it's yours, isn't it? I bet you're fond of it, what with it coming from your mam's house.' Maggie lifted the clock down from the mantelpiece and dusted it with the corner of her pinny, spotless and gleaming though it already was.

Oh, Mam, thought Molly. If you could see me now you'd be ashamed of me, and that's a fact.

'I'll be back to see you, you know that,' she said aloud. 'But, you know, we're going to be working overtime . . .'

Back in Ferryhill, the clock wrapped in newspaper under one arm, her going away case in the other hand, Molly walked down the street to Dora's door, knocked and went in.

'You've told him, then?'

'Yes.'

'And he left you. Well, I could have told you what would happen. You should have let me have the bairn and kept quiet.'

'I couldn't do that, Dora.'

Molly walked over to the sofa where Beth lay propped up between cushions. She was smiling and waving her arms, chirruping away to her mother to attract her attention.

'Hallo, my precious,' said Molly. She cuddled the baby tightly until Beth began to struggle and protest. Molly sat down on the sofa with her, jiggling her knees and turning the cries of protest into chuckles.

'You're all I've got now, petal,' she said softly. The baby burped and a dribble of milk ran down her chin and dripped on to Molly's skirt. Dora ran over with a cloth and began wiping it.

'Oh, leave it alone, Dora.'

'But it will spoil! It'll smell an' all. Clothes aren't that easy to come by these days,' she protested.

'I don't care. I'll never wear it again,' said Molly. 'Coupons or no flaming coupons.' She bent her head until her chin touched the soft curls of Beth's head and wept. The tears ran down and mingled with those of the baby who began to cry also, frightened by her mother's emotion.

'Give her here,' Dora commanded. 'You're tired out. Get away up to bed and get some sleep. 'I'll bring you a nice cup of cocoa. Once I've got Beth to sleep, that is.'

As Molly climbed the stairs she reflected that Dora looked happier than she had done since Jackson came home.

Chapter Thirty-two

It seemed to Molly that she was living in a kind of limbo. The weeks dragged on, one after the other, filled with going to work and sewing and coming home and sewing. The only bright spots, the only times she came alive at all, were when she was with Beth, her baby, watching her grow, sit up unaided, begin to crawl. The war passed her by apart from the fact that rationing tightened and the news was all of the Tunisian campaign with little maps on the front page of the *Northern Echo* illustrating the position of the troops; the line sometimes moving forward, sometimes back towards Egypt. Was Jackson among them? she wondered, anxiety for his safety rising in her.

'You look tired out, lass,' Dora greeted her one evening, a dark, cold evening with sleet slanting down the street as she walked home, drenching her skirt and bare knees for her last pair of stockings had 'gone home' as Dora put it. She should have worn her one pair of slacks, Molly thought dully, but the morning had been fine and sunny.

'I am tired, Dora,' she admitted. 'And I promised Mrs Jones that I would finish her skirt tonight.'

Molly took in sewing now. She had bought herself a hand-operated sewing machine and specialised in making over clothes from others bought before the war. Mrs Jones's skirt was cut out of a full-skirted coat, which had been her mother's. The style looked as though it could date from the last war. Still, it was a warm tweed and when the material was turned it looked quite good.

'Tell her you'll do it the morrow, lass,' Dora advised. 'Go on, have a night off.'

Molly shook her head, smiling. She couldn't, she needed the money. She received a small allowance from Jackson's pay every month but she didn't use it, of course. The slips were all in the top drawer of the chest in her room. Sometimes she opened the drawer and looked at them. They were the only link she had with him now. She thought back to the last time she had seen Harry.

He had come to see her on his last leave. He'd met her out of the factory and insisted on going with her to Ferryhill. He had nodded to Dora gravely and said hallo before going over to where Beth was lying on the couch, waving her arms in the air and cooing. Molly waited for his condemnation. He sat down beside the child, put out a finger and she clasped it tightly.

'Well, will you look at that?' he said admiringly. He put out his hands and lifted the baby in the air and she gurgled and tried to grab at the badge in his red beret. Obligingly he settled her on his knee and gave her the beret. The badge twinkled in the firelight and Beth smiled in delight, touching it with her tiny baby fingers.

'Mind, you're a bonny bairn, aren't you?' her uncle asked, and she chuckled and tried to pull off the medal ribbon.

Molly relaxed. Oh, he was the best brother anyone had ever had, he was indeed. 'Thanks, Harry,' she said, and he smiled at her, before turning his attention back to the baby.

'Well,' he said finally. 'We Masons have to stick together, haven't we?' He stood up with the baby on one arm and put the other round Molly's shoulders, kissed her on the cheek. 'You have had a hard time of it, little sister,' he said without looking at her. 'I don't blame you for anything. Mind, that bloody Joan is spreading her poison all over Eden Hope. Jackson's parents are bound to have heard.'

Molly nodded. Well, she thought, she couldn't keep Beth a secret forever and she wouldn't want to.

He tickled the baby under her chin and she gurgled, wetly, making a damp patch on his khaki shoulder.

Now, as she took out her sewing machine and set it up on the kitchen table, Molly thought back on that day fondly. She would always be grateful for Harry's love and support, but he had refused to talk about Jackson.

'I don't see him now,' was all he had said. Had she caused a rift between the two men or was it simply that they had been separated by the war?

'Are you going to Eden Hope on Saturday?' Dora asked. ' 'Cause if you are, I'd like to know now. I thought I might go to the pictures if you're here to look after Beth.'

Molly thought about it. She tried to go to see Maggie and Frank whenever she could but she was sick to death of pretending to them that everything was all right. Still, if Joan had been talking she wouldn't have to pretend. She would have to face them sometime. She quailed at the thought of going again, though. Sometimes she saw a letter from Jackson propped up on the mantelpiece and itched to take it down and devour it. But she couldn't, of course. She found it harder and harder to conceal the fact that he never wrote to her. She had to guard her tongue at all times, in case she should let slip something about the baby, so she always made an excuse to leave early.

'I don't think I'll go this weekend, Dora,' Molly said now. 'I have some jobs to do.'

It was true, she had half a dozen orders waiting for her in a pile in the corner of the sitting room. She glanced up at the marble clock and frowned. It had stopped, she couldn't think why. She had dragged it all over the place with her since her father was killed and it had never stopped before but now it didn't seem to run for five minutes after she had wound it before stopping again. She would have to take it to the clock mender's on Saturday morning, she thought.

Dora went off to the pictures on Saturday afternoon to see *Pride and Prejudice* with Greer Garson and Molly got on with her sewing. But her head ached for some reason and she was glad to have a break when Beth woke from her afternoon nap and demanded attention.

'We'll go for a walk, shall we?' she asked the child and Beth crowed with pleasure as her mother struggled to put on her siren suit. She had made the suit the night before from a remnant of cloth she'd found on the market; an all-in-one suit in yellow with a hood which she had trimmed with white. Siren suits had become all the rage since Churchill began to wear one, even for babies.

She pushed the pram along the road to the park that looked strangely denuded with its railings chopped off at the base and gone to make tanks or something. The trees were bare, the only bird about a dejected-looking robin pecking beneath an elm. Molly shivered. She was wearing her slacks under her coat and a headscarf over her head but the wind was cutting. Only Beth looked cosy and warm, sitting up in her pram in her siren suit with an old quilt that had been Mona's over her. She chuckled and talked in her own personal language to the bird, the trees, anyone who happened to pass. But Molly's headache was becoming more insistent, like a hammer pounding in her temples. She longed for a hot drink and a couple of aspirins.

Back home she was surprised to find Dora had returned from the pictures. Surely the big film wasn't over yet?

'I've got a headache,' Dora explained as she blazed the fire and put on the kettle for tea. 'I expect I'm getting that 'flu which is going around the village.'

'Is it? I hadn't heard.' Molly gazed anxiously at Beth, dreading the thought that she might get it. There had been an epidemic the month before but it had passed by their house, thank the Lord. Beth looked back at her, her smiles turning to howls of indignation for it was time for her tea too. She held up her arms to be taken out of the pram, pumping them up and down when Molly didn't immediately rush to do her bidding. But her yells were loud enough, her eyes bright, her cheeks flushed with health as well as temper. No, she wasn't sickening for anything, not Beth. And Molly herself was probably only suffering from eyestrain. She had sewed on late last night, trying to finish the siren suit.

'I'll tend to her. You make the tea, will you, Molly?' asked Dora. 'I have to stop her making such a noise, I feel my head might burst with it.'

Eventually the child was settled and peace reigned again. Dora and Molly sipped their tea and ate corned beef hash and cabbage, took some aspirin each. But it didn't seem to work as it should and in the end Molly stopped sewing and folded her work away.

'I think I'll have an early night,' she said to Dora.

'That makes two of us,' the older woman replied.

Jackson fingered his weekend pass and even now, after all that had happened, his pulse quickened at the thought that if he wished he could be on a train in half an hour and on his way to see Molly. He didn't want to see her, though, did he? Not after what she had done. It was what all the married and engaged men in his unit feared, and it had happened to him.

'Well, Sergeant?' The middle-aged Captain sitting behind the desk looked up at him impatiently. 'Do you want a travel warrant or not? Come on, make up your mind, I have men waiting.'

If he did go north he would see Molly, Jackson knew that, he wouldn't be able to help himself. And how was he going to tell his parents? Or had they found out already? He shied away from the thought. But he should see his parents, he told himself, there was no telling when he would get back to England. Not that they had been told where they were going but there had been a short, intensive course in everyday French.

'Sergeant?'

'Yes, sir. A travel warrant to Bishop Auckand, sir.'

Even as he boarded the crowded train with only minutes to spare and threaded his way through the troops sitting on their kitbags in the corridor until he found a space just large enough for him to dump his own small bag and stand beside it, he still wasn't sure if he was going to go to Ferryhill. He took off his red beret and folded it, buttoned his epaulette over it and turned to gaze out of the window. Not that there was anything to see. The night was dark and soot from the engine smeared the window anyway. There was only the reflection of him standing grim-faced and those reflections of the other soldiers and airmen lounging about in the crowded corridor. It was of course impossible to get into any of the compartments with seats, they had been taken up at King's Cross.

Jackson flexed his shoulder muscles. They had stiffened slightly since the morning when they had practised their jumping over and over again. He could still feel the pull of the harness as the parachute opened, the rush of air against his legs as he floated down to earth. He wondered if he would be posted anywhere near Harry this time.

The last time he had seen his friend was when he had told him he was going to volunteer for the Airborne Division. And about Molly and her baby. Jackson had watched Harry's face for his reaction. Condemnation of his sister perhaps.

'Do you think they're managing?' he had asked. 'Oh, why didn't Molly tell me?'

'Who knows?' Jackson replied. 'And don't worry, she'll be getting a wife's allowance, I haven't stopped that.'

'Poor Molly. She's had a hard fight of it since Dad died.'

'Yes, well, so have a lot of women and they didn't go completely off the rails, going with men, acting like a . . .'

'Don't say it, Jackson,' warned Harry. 'It's not true. Molly loved you, you know she did.'

'Only a few weeks after I was posted missing?' said Jackson. 'Oh, aye, I'm sure she must have loved me then.' Bitterness welled up in him; it was like bile in his throat. 'Well, I'm finished with her.'

'Poor kid. All on her own. What it must have been like for her.' Harry bit his lip, gazing at Jackson. 'I'll have to see her, first chance I get. I'll go up, seek her out.'

'She lied to me, Harry,' said Jackson. He felt almost on the defensive, as if it had been he who had done the unforgivable, not Molly. 'Well, not exactly lied but she married me without telling me about the baby.'

'Se must have been desperate,' said Harry. 'We let her down, Jackson. At least I did. I should have been there to look after her better. This isn't her fault, it's the fault of this bloody war.' He sighed. 'She must have been convinced you were dead. She was all alone, don't you see?'

'No, I don't,' Jackson replied.

'For God's sake, Jackson!'

He said nothing but turned on his heel and walked away.

The train was pulling into York where the platform was awash with people even though it was past midnight. Next stop Darlington, Jackson thought, and had to make up his mind what to do. Maybe he should go to see that Molly was all right, he told himself. He needn't even look at the baby, just find out how Molly was, see if she was in need. Then he would go home to Eden Hope and tell his parents that his marriage was over. That was his best course.

After all he would be away fighting by this time next week, he expected. He had to have his domestic problems sorted by then.

In his heart Jackson knew he was fooling himself as to his reasons for taking the Durham train from Darlington and alighting at Ferryhill station. But he couldn't seem to help himself.

He walked down the street to the house, stood irresolute before the door, his heart beating as hard and as painfully, perhaps more so, than on the occasions when he had faced the enemy. Squaring his shoulders, he knocked. And knocked again. There was no answer and he felt incredibly let down. In the distance a pit hooter sounded, signalling the end of a shift, the beginning of another. Fore shift, he thought, it must be just after twelve o'clock. Jackson knocked again, louder this time. No response. A straggle of miners in their pit black began walking down the street. One of them flashed his light over Jackson, inspected his uniform, saw the badge gleam on his red beret.

'Now then, mate,' he said respectfully, and a few of his marras spoke too. 'Wot cher.' 'Good luck, lad.' There was a lot of respect for the paratroopers among the miners. They wandered away down the street, talking to each other in low voices. A shaft of moonlight illuminated the group, which was thinning out as the men dropped away on reaching their homes. Jackson turned back to the door and raised his hand to knock.

Suddenly there was a cry from inside. At first he thought it might be a cat. It came again, not a cat but a baby. Well, that would wake Molly at least. He waited, listening for movement, but there was none. The baby's wailing was louder now, a continuous, furious crying out that no one was taking notice.

Jackson tried the door handle with little expectation of the door opening but to his surprise it did. He pushed it open and stood in a narrow passage leading to a kitchen-cum-living room. Closing the door after him because of the blackout, he struck a match and looked around. There was a light switch on the wall; there was electricity then. Upstairs the baby's wailing had subsided a little, was almost despairing.

'Molly?' he called. 'Molly? It's Jackson.'

The baby cried afresh. There was a thud as though someone had fallen. Jackson took the stairs two at a time and opened the first door he came to. A woman, it must have been Dora he thought, lay there, breathing heavily. Why hadn't she woken? But he hadn't time to think of that. He opened the other door and switched on the light. Molly was lying half in and half out of bed, her arms moving weakly as she tried to pull herself up.

Jackson's heart filled with dread. Running over to her, he picked her up in his arms, laid her back on the bed and pulled the covers over her. The atmosphere in the room was freezing, her face was blue-white with the cold. Oh, God, she wasn't dying, was she?

'Molly? Molly? Wake up, please, wake up!' he cried, laying his face alongside hers, cradling her in his arms. She opened her eyes and tried to move.

'Beth,' she said, her voice faint and faraway. 'I must get to her.'

'No, no, you can't! You're not well enough,' said Jackson. 'Oh, Molly–'

She looked at him properly for the first time. 'Jackson? Oh, Jackson!' she began to sob. 'I prayed you would come.' Exhausted, she lay back against the pillow, her breathing fast and shallow. She closed her eyes then opened them immediately. 'See to her, please . . .'

Reluctantly he stood up, adjusted the covers over her. 'I will, I will, don't fret.'

Going over to where an old brown-painted cot stood in the corner, he looked down at the bright red face of the baby. She had stopped screaming and was now sobbing quietly, looking up at him with Molly's dark eyes. The bedclothes had been kicked off; her feet were like ice. She lifted her arms to him and he picked her up.

Beth was wet, very wet. She must have been lying there for a long time. Jackson looked helplessly around, he had to do something. Beth hiccuped, waved her fist at him, and where it touched his cheek it was so cold he realised he had to do something. He laid her down again, found the safety pin in her nappy and released it, drew the sopping nightie over her head. 'Give her to me,' said a wavering voice he hardly recognised as Molly's and he took the baby over to the bed and laid her beside her mother.

'Warm milk,' said Molly, and closed her eyes as though the effort to speak had been too much for her.

'I'll get it,' he said and ran down the stairs. He chopped sticks from an off-cut of pit prop he found in the coal house, built a fire in the cold grate and fanned it to life by propping a tin blazer on the top bar. Milk now, he thought, and found a baby's bottle in the pantry and a saucepan on the shelf. He picked up a bottle of milk then saw the National Dried can of baby's milk beside it. He heated water, read the instructions on the side of the can, found two cups and Beth's boat-shaped bottle, and soon was carrying a tray up the stairs. He even had time to be amazed at how well he had managed.

Molly took a cup and drank thirstily then sank back on the

pillow as he took the baby in his arms, wrapped her in a large towel he had found on the rail over the kitchen range and offered her the bottle.

'It's not too hot?' croaked Molly anxiously.

'Do you think I'm daft?' he asked. But all the same he shook a few drops on to his hand before Beth took the teat in her mouth and sucked with the serious expression of a dedicated drinker.

It was when the baby had finished her bottle and pushed it away and was smiling up at him as though she had known him all her life that he caught sight of the other cup of milk. Giving Beth back to her mother, he took the milk into the next room. But Dora couldn't take the milk, she was deeply unconscious.

'Dora's very ill, Molly,' he said as he went back into the other room. But she didn't hear. She was sound asleep, breathing noisily, her mouth open slightly,

'Oh, God,' said Jackson aloud. 'Don't die, Molly, please don't die!'

Beth started to cry. She held out her arms to him and he picked her up and rushed downstairs and outside to bang on the door of the neighbouring house. Luckily there was a light on. A miner just returned from the pit answered. He was in his stockinged feet, braces hanging down. But he was quickly galvanised into action when Jackson gasped out his story.

'I'll fetch the doctor, lad.'

''Flu, that's what it was, followed by double pneumonia,' said the doctor. It was half an hour later and Jackson and he were in the kitchen waiting for the ambulance that was to take Dora away to hospital. 'A lot of it about, I'm afraid. I'll write you out a prescription for . . . the young lady.'

'My wife,' said Jackson firmly. He held Beth lightly to his chest with one hand and the baby tried to reach up to the shining badge in his cap. She seemed to have recovered already from her cold night. She chuckled and grabbed at the beret and, like Harry had a few weeks earlier, he took it off and gave it to her to play with.

'A shame about Mrs Fletcher,' said the doctor. 'I've had a few similar cases after this 'flu.' He paused and wrote something on his prescription pad. As he handed a torn-off sheet to Harry he added, 'Don't worry, your wife will be fine in a few days. And it looks like your little daughter has escaped it though she'll be to watch for a while. When are you due back?'

'Monday evening. But I'll ask for compassionate leave. It should be all right for a few days at least. Then there's my mother . . .'

The doctor sighed. 'So long as proper care can be arranged if you have to go.'

After he had gone and Jackson had dispatched a neighbour's son for the prescription, he started up the stairs with Beth on one arm. Sitting down on the edge of the bed, he took Molly's hand. Already she was looking more her old self.

'Mind, you gave me a heck of a shock,' he said. He bent and kissed her on the forehead, squashing Beth a little so that she protested loudly and he sat up straight.

'You're not going to come between us all the time, young lady,' he said to her, and Beth smiled and crowed and held out a hand to him. Obviously she was taken with him and by the look on his face the feeling was reciprocated.

Downstairs, the marble clock suddenly chimed. It must be going again, Molly thought, startled. Her hand beneath the bedclothes, she crossed her fingers.

'Is it all right now, Jackson?' she asked, holding her breath in case she had misread the signs. Was he being nice simply because she was ill? Oh, she couldn't bear it if it was that.

'I don't know. I don't know how I feel.'

In truth his emotions were in complete chaos. He looked at the baby and she gazed back at him, with Molly's eyes. She even tilted her head in the way Molly did. He couldn't hate her, of course he couldn't. None of this was her fault. In the back of his mind he knew it was nobody's fault. It was the war, the flaming war.

Molly said no more, she was afraid to. Instead she stared out of the window at the row of chimney pots opposite. But a spark of hope had been ignited and it was still flickering.

'Well, at least Dora is going to get better,' said Jackson. 'Though you won't be in a fit state to look after her when she comes out of hospital.'

He had been down to the telephone box to ring the hospital to enquire after Dora. Now he sat on the edge of Molly's bed again, dandling Beth on his knee. She was gurgling and smiling for all the world as though she had known him all her short life rather than a few hours. Molly, already feeling a little better, was propped up on pillows, a doting smile on her face as she looked from her man to her daughter and back again. She refused to think about tomorrow.

'At least she'll be all right. I'll manage somehow.'

'No, you won't, my love.'

Had the endearment just slipped out? Molly wondered.

'I know you're used to managing but I won't have you doing too much. You have this one to see to.' Jackson lifted Beth up in the air and jiggled her about and she crowed with pleasure.

'There's my mother . . .'

'But she has your dad in a wheel chair,' Molly reminded him.

'I'll ring up, ask for extended leave,' said Jackson. 'But I'm not sure . . .' After all, Molly was not in any danger now.

She suddenly sat bolt upright, her weakness forgotten. 'I know! I'll ask Vi.'

'Vi?'

'A girl who worked in the maternity home. I got friendly with her when I was there and I've felt guilty ever since that I hadn't asked her here at all. She has no family of her own and she loved Beth. Oh, I know she'll come! I'll ask Vi. Send her a card now. It'll catch the post, won't it?'

It was the following morning at nine o'clock, just half an hour after the post was delivered at the home, that Vi presented herself before Matron.

'I have to leave,' she said, her smile stretching from ear to ear. 'I'm going to help my friend, live at her house.'

'Are you sure of what you are doing?'

Matron gazed at the diminutive figure before her. She would be sorry to lose Vi, she thought. The girl was a good worker. Vi handed over the card from Molly.

'Molly Mason, is it?' asked Matron and Vi nodded. Matron sniffed. Molly Mason was a strong-minded girl. She had refused to put her baby up for adoption which was the only sensible course for a girl in her position. Still, she had been kind to Vi, Matron remembered that.

'Very well,' she said, handing the card back. 'You can take a week's notice.'

Vi lifted her head and gave Matron a determined look. 'Eeh, no, Matron. I'm going now,' she said.

'*The funny thing is*,' Molly wrote to Jackson a fortnight later, '*that Dora and Vi have taken to each really well. Dora is thinner and still weak but Vi couldn't look after her better if she was her own mother . . .*'

Molly stopped writing and looked over to where Beth lay on the rug. She rolled over on to her stomach and tried to push herself up, her head wobbling a little as she grunted with the effort. Her hands slipped from under her and she whimpered before trying again. Her mother went over to her and picked her up and sat down on the rocking chair with her. She crooned as she rocked back and forwards, the baby laid against her shoulder, and eventually Beth fell asleep.

Molly was supremely happy. She felt that she had never been so happy in her life. There was Maggie, of course, and Frank. They weren't nasty to her when they found out about Beth, not at all.

'They are my family now,' Jackson had said to them. 'Both Molly and Beth. I don't want to hear a word against them.'

'I wasn't going to say one,' said Maggie. She and Frank had exchanged a glance, each understanding what the other was thinking. They didn't want to lose Jackson again and were definitely not going to say anything to risk it.

'Any road, she's a fine bairn,' Frank had said.

Molly stood up and put the baby down in her cot and went back to her letter to Jackson.

' *'Til we meet again*,' she wrote. '*Watch yourself, my love*.'

Things might seem OK between them but she wasn't so soft as to think everything was as it had been before Beth. There were bridges to build still. And it was difficult to do it by letter. But when the war was over . . .

Come The Day

Una Horne

To the memory of
Tot and Cilla,
my parents

Acknowledgements

My thanks are due to Mr and Mrs Walker, my aunt and uncle, who live in Cowley, and their friend and local historian, Mr Hope, of Cowley. Also, I owe a debt of gratitude to Durham Records Office and Bishop Auckland Town Hall Library.

Chapter One

Hannah crouched in the kitchen, her younger brother and sister clutched tightly to her.

'Aah, aah, aah, Nora, Nora –'

The tortured voice coming from the front room rose higher and higher and Jane and Harry buried their faces in Hannah's skirts, their hands covering their ears and their bodies racked with sobbing. Hannah stared unseeingly out of the window, desperate to get away from the sound of Da's pain. But Betty had told her to keep the young ones in the kitchen, 'out of the way,' she had said. Betty was twelve and she was in the front room with Mam, in case she was needed for anything when the doctor came.

There was another voice in the front room now – the doctor, that was whose voice it was, Hannah realised, and she looked down at the heads in her lap

'Whisht now,' she said softly. 'Whisht. The doctor's here, he'll make Da better, he will, you'll see.' But suddenly there was a scream from the front room worse than anything that had gone before and Harry wrenched himself away from Hannah's grasp and ran to the back door and out of the yard.

'Harry, Harry!' she called, releasing Jane and racing after him and even though he was only four years old and she was ten, she didn't manage to catch him until he was halfway down the row.

'Harry! I told you you had to stay with me!' she cried, pulling him roughly to her and then Jane was there, hanging on to her skirt and shrieking with terror. 'You left me, you left me!' Jane cried and she and Harry set up such a bawling they could be heard all along the pit rows.

'Howay in along of me, hinnies.'

The calm, sympathetic voice caused all three children to look up. It was Mrs Holmes who lived in the end house, the official's house; she was picking Harry up in her arms and cuddling him in to her, not caring that his tears were staining her white pinafore.

'That's right, Phoebe, take them in. Just until the ambulance goes, anyroad.'

Hannah looked round and saw that a cluster of women had gathered round them, all clucking in sympathy.

'Your da will be all right, you'll see,' said one. 'Go on along of Mrs Holmes now, Hannah, take the bairns inside, that'll be best.'

In the distance there was the clanging of a bell, getting nearer and nearer. Hannah knew what it was; the Union ambulance, coming to take Da. She watched the end of the back alley and sure enough the green-painted ambulance went by, slowing as it turned into the front row.

'Howay, pet,' she said to Jane, and, taking the smaller girl's hand, she followed Mrs Holmes and Harry into the kitchen of the end house.

Mr Holmes was sitting in front of the fire, still black from the pit. The sight of him made Hannah close her eyes tightly but she couldn't cut out the vivid picture she had of her da, lying on a board on a flat cart as his marras, as miners called their workmates, brought him home from the pit, with Mr Holmes, the shift overman, walking in front of the pony as he tried to pick out a path which avoided any potholes.

'Now then,' said Mrs Holmes, 'sit ye down. I'd wager you haven't had your dinners yet, have you? Now I have a nice pan of broth on the bar keeping hot, you shall have a bowlful each.'

The children looked at her with round eyes, even Hannah. The broth smelled really meaty and they hadn't had anything to eat since breakfast. Harry's stomach rumbled; he glanced up at Hannah anxiously and Mrs Holmes noticed it.

'Howay, Harry, your mam won't mind you having something to eat in our house,' she encouraged him. 'I'll put a cushion on this chair so you can reach the table comfortably. Now, lasses, sit on the form at that side. Don't worry, I tell you, your mam won't mind. And after, I'll give you a can of broth to take home for the others. That'll help your mam out, like.'

The children sat round the table, Harry balanced on a fat, round cushion filched from Mr Holmes's chair, and soon they were tucking into bowls of Mrs Holmes's broth. At least, Harry and Jane were tucking in; Hannah's throat had closed in, she found she couldn't swallow after the first mouthful. She stared at the yellow globules of fat floating on the top but she wasn't really seeing them. Instead she was listening for the ambulance bell starting up again, taking Da away.

'It looks badly,' Mr Holmes said quietly to his wife but not so quietly that Hannah's sharp ears didn't hear. 'Poor lad's back's broke, I doubt.'

'A fall of stone, was it?' asked Mrs Holmes.

'Aye. The deputy had fired the shot all right, none could fault him; he'd got the men back out of the road first and the coalface came down. It was after the black dust thinned and settled and the men were returning to the face that it happened. Jake was the first back. He was always the first, always eager to get back to work. You know the name he had for hard work. Well, the shot must have disturbed a fault in the roof, loosened the stone, for suddenly there was a rumble and the men jumped back, away from the danger, they all knew what it meant, but Jake was caught when the stone came down. There wasn't a lot, the others soon got it off him, but the damage was done.'

Hannah stared at her broth, feeling sick. She looked up at the wooden beams of the kitchen ceiling, imagining them falling on her and Jane and Harry, and shuddered. Suddenly, she knew she was definitely going to be sick and she mumbled something to Mrs Holmes, and rushed out to the drain in the yard and retched and retched.

Mrs Holmes glanced at her husband, biting her lip. 'There, now, we shouldn't have said anything in front of the bairns,' she said. 'That Hannah's a sensitive lass.'

Jane and Harry had stopped eating and were gazing through the window at their sister who was crouched over the drain.

'Don't worry, now, she'll be all right,' Mrs Holmes reassured them. 'I'll fetch her back, poor lass.'

Hannah's eyes were watering and she was trembling violently when Mrs Holmes took hold of her shoulders and drew her back to the kitchen door.

'Howay, lass,' Mrs Holmes said, 'it's the shock, that's what. You have to be strong now, you big ones, for the sake of little Jane and Harry.' She offered Hannah a large handkerchief, a real one, not a piece of rag, which was what the Armstrong children usually used for a hanky, and Hannah wiped her face. They paused in the doorway as they heard a motor starting up, followed by the loud clanging of the bell on top of the union ambulance and Hannah's trembling increased until she was shaking uncontrollably.

'They'll be taking him to the County Hospital,' said Mr Holmes. 'Eeh, lass, you're shivering, come away in by the fire and have a warm.'

'Thank you, Mr Holmes,' Hannah said, surprising herself at how normal her voice sounded, 'but we'll have to get back. Betty said we had to stay in the kitchen, she'll be mad if she can't find us.'

'All right, lass, if you want to,' said Mrs Holmes. 'Wait on a minute, though, I'll give you that broth. It'll likely do for your mam and Alfred.'

Hannah stood quietly, with Jane and Harry hanging on to her skirt, as Mrs Holmes went into the pantry and brought out a large tin can with a lid in the form of a cup. Picking up the pan, she filled the can with what was left of the broth.

'Poor bairns,' Mrs Holmes said to her husband as she watched the children go down the yard and out into the back lane. 'Whatever's going to happen to them now?'

'Jake'll get compensation,' said Mr Holmes.

'Hmm!' His wife's expression showed plainly what she thought of the compensation rates for hewers who were injured in the mine.

'Where've you been?' demanded Betty as the children trooped into the kitchen of the Armstrong house. 'Mam's gone in the ambulance with me da and I have to get some dinner ready for Alf when he comes in from work. An' you let the fire get down, it'll be ages before it's hot enough to cook anything.'

Betty had one of her mother's aprons tied round her thin twelve-year-old body and drooping almost to her ankles. She was a tall girl, with fair hair and brown eyes, now red and strained-looking.

'Mrs Holmes took us in her house,' volunteered Jane. 'She gave us some grand broth, Betty, we've brought you some an' all.'

'You shouldn't take food off folk!' snapped Betty. 'You know Mam says we haven't to.'

Jane looked crestfallen and Hannah put the can of steaming broth on the table. 'Mrs Holmes said Mam wouldn't mind, not when we've trouble in the house,' she said. 'Didn't we take some to Mrs Gittens when Mr Gittens was hurt in the pit? Anyroad, it'll do nicely for Alf's dinner. Mam just made the bread this morning, it'll be grand and fresh for him with the broth.'

Betty looked undecided, she was very conscious of the fact that she was in charge of the household, if only temporarily, but she glanced at the smouldering fire and back at the can of broth on the table and made up her mind.

'Don't leave it on the table to get cold, our Hannah,' she said. 'Get the pan from the pantry and put it on the bar to keep warm. Alf won't eat it if it's cold, will he?'

Hannah rushed to do Betty's bidding.

It seemed to Hannah in the next few weeks that she was always rushing to do Betty's bidding. The moment she came in from school, even as she walked down the yard, Betty was issuing her instructions. 'Fetch a bucket of coal in', 'Peel the taties', 'Go to the shop' – even little Jane had to do her share. For Mam was busy with Da, who had been sent home from the hospital in a boxlike bed on wheels, unable to sit up or move his body from the chest down. He lived in the front room now and it was Alf who came in black from his work on the screens where he cleaned the coal of stone. Alf sat in Da's chair by the fire though he was only fourteen years old, and waited for Hannah to fill the tin bath with hot water from the boiler by the fire and demanded his dinner on time. For Alf was the only one bringing in a wage now, even if it was only four shillings a week.

'Seventeen and tuppence,' said Mam the first time Alf brought home Da's weekly compensation. 'It'll be fourteen and ninepence when they take off the war money an' they'll be doing that, sure as shot, now the war's over and done with. An' we can't live on that, there's only one thing for it, we need another wage coming in.'

'Mam! I can't go to work, I'm not thirteen yet,' said Betty, suddenly looking very young and vulnerable.

'Not you, pet,' answered her mother. 'Our Robert'll have to come home.'

Hannah sat beside Jane and Harry on the horsehair sofa and all three gazed at Mam. What was she talking about? thought Hannah. Robert wouldn't want to come home, he didn't like it in Winton. Why, the last time he'd come he'd told her that he was going to work on the carriers with his uncle Billy when he left school. Robert lived with Grandma Armstrong, miles away in Consett; they hadn't even seen him for almost a year.

'Robert's only thirteen, Mam,' said Betty.

'Aye. Well, he can take the leaving exam like Alf did. If he knows his letters and his figuring, the gaffer will take him on, he's sure to when his father broke his back in the pit. You and Alf will have to look to your da on Saturday, Betty, while I go to Consett and tell your grandma. Best not put it in a letter. I'll away up to see the manager now, see about getting him a job.'

Nora Armstrong looked the three younger children over critically.

'Hannah, wash Harry's face, you three are coming along of me. It won't hurt to show the manager I've got bairns to feed an' all,' she said as she looked in the mahogany-framed mirror which hung over the high mantelpiece. She smoothed her dark hair away from her forehead, then, satisfied with her appearance, went to the middle door which led into the front room.

'I'm going up to the colliery office, Jake,' she said. 'You'll be all right for a while, will you?'

'Aye, I'm fine. I'm enjoying the rest, lying here,' came the sardonic reply.

'I'll only be half an hour,' Nora said. 'I'm taking the little ones; Betty will be here, though, if you want her.'

'Well, get away, woman, if you're going,' Jake answered irritably.

Nora took her shawl from the hook on the back door and wrapped it round her.

'Are you not going to wear your Sunday coat?' asked Betty, sounding surprised.

'No. It's better not to let them think I'm well off, a shawl's the best thing,' said Nora.

They walked up the row, Nora holding Harry's hand and Hannah behind with Jane. The children were quiet; even Hannah was nervous of meeting the colliery manager, while Jane and Harry looked white and strained. It wasn't far to the pit yard and the colliery office was just inside the gates, a red brick building with steps leading up to the entrance. Parked beside the steps was a motorcar and sitting in the passenger seat was a boy of about fifteen, a boy in a suit with a Norfolk jacket and a proper collar and tie and his dark hair slicked back over his ears.

'Look, Hannah, a motorcar,' cried Harry, grinning with delight. 'By; isn't it grand? What does it say, Hannah? Those letters on the front, I mean.' Harry was fairly dancing round the car; he touched the gleaming coachwork and the bright silver of the headlights. 'When I grow up I'm going to have a motorcar just like this,' he declared.

'Sunbeam, that's what it says,' said Hannah. She was almost as entranced by the machine as Harry was.

'Sunbeam coupé,' said the boy and he climbed out of the car. All three children quietened and Harry drew close to his mother.

'He talks funny,' Harry said in a whisper which nevertheless was heard by them all. The boy smiled.

'Would you like to sit in my seat for a minute?' he asked Harry.

'Eeh, no,' said Mrs Armstrong, pulling the child to her.

'Mam!' said Harry, his eyes bright with hope, and she gave in.

'All right, but just for a minute. We have to see the manager before he goes home,' she decreed.

'Oh, my father's with him now, he won't be going home yet,' said the boy. He held the door open for Harry, who clambered on to the padded leather seat and sat quietly, gazing at the dashboard with its knobs and dials, happiness oozing out of him.

The boy looked down at Hannah, smiling, and she smiled back shyly. By, he was a grand lad, she thought, letting Harry have a go in his car. She reckoned he was about the same age as Alf, but he was so tall and good-looking and his clothes were so clean. Even his hands were clean, she saw, there were no scars or black bits under the skin, his hands were soft and white. He didn't work on the screens, she decided. He had kind eyes, though. Was he a prince? A prince like in Cinderella?

Hannah looked up, startled, as the office window opened and a man stuck his head out.

'Timothy! Get that boy out of there at once. At once, do you hear? God knows what dirt and disease he might be carrying, not to mention fleas. I told you to sit in the car until I was ready, did I not, sir?'

'Come on, Harry, we have to go in now,' said Nora. She had turned a fiery red and kept her head bent as she lifted Harry out of the car. Hannah was mortified, she burned with the shame of it. Her family didn't have fleas, nor nits either. Everybody in the rows knew Mam was spitting clean – why, didn't she rake their heads every night with the small-tooth comb? Just in case they picked anything up at school, that was.

'We haven't got fleas, Mam, have we not?' she said as Jane and Harry began to whimper.

'No, we have not!' snapped Nora. 'We're as clean as anybody, we are.'

Hannah stoke a glance at the boy, who was sheepishly climbing into the car.

'Dust the seat before you sit down, Timothy,' roared the man at the window.

'Yes, Father,' the boy mumbled. He took a blue duster from the tray under the dashboard and rubbed it over the seat.

'There'll be no dirt on it,' hissed Hannah and Timothy looked at her, his eyes shamed.

'Howay, Hannah,' snapped her mother and Hannah followed her up the steps and into the office.

There was a desk just inside with a clerk sitting behind it. Through the partition window behind him, Hannah could see the man, Timothy's father, talking to the manager.

'Yes, what do you want?' demanded the clerk. 'It's almost closing time, you've left it a bit late, whatever it is.'

'I'm Mrs Armstrong,' said Nora, holding her head high. Two bright spots of colour still burned in her cheeks. 'I've come to see the manager.'

'Oh, yes, it was your man who was hurt by that last fall of stone, wasn't it? Well, you can't see the manager now, he has

Lord Akers's agent, Mr Durkin, with him. You'll have to come back tomorrow.'

The clerk gave a dismissive nod and shuffled the papers together on his desk, but Nora was not about to go.

'I'll wait until I can see him,' she insisted, her voice rising. 'Surely he'll see me, when my Jake's had his back broke in the pit?' The incident with Harry and the car had filled her with resentment, stiffening her resolve.

'My good woman –' the clerk began, but he was interrupted by the manager, who opened the door to the inner office and poked his head out.

'What's the commotion, Robinson?' he asked testily.

'It's Mrs Armstrong, sir, the wife of the hewer who was injured in that last roof fall. I told her you were busy.'

'Get her to come in, Hudson, I might as well hear what she has to say while I'm here,' a voice called from behind the manager. Harry shrank into Hannah's skirt, whimpering once more.

Hannah patted his head. 'It's all right, Harry,' she whispered.

'Yes, of course, Mr Durkin,' said the manager and held the door open for Nora and her children.

They stood before the desk, Nora, Hannah and the two little ones between them. They were not offered seats though there were a couple of chairs by the wall besides the comfortable armchair occupied by Timothy's father.

Hannah gazed at him in awe. It was bad enough having to come to see the manager, but Mr Durkin was like no one she had ever seen before. She looked at the smooth black cloth of his suit, his highly polished shoes and white spats. He held a shiny walking stick with a silver top in one hand and was tapping it idly against one leg of his chair. He was tall and elegant and his shirt collar was snowy white against the pale skin of his neck. She watched him as he looked the children over, his face expressionless.

'Well, what is it, Mrs Armstrong?' asked Mr Hudson, who had returned to his chair behind the desk.

'Well . . .'

Nora was suddenly tongue-tied.

'Come along now, Mrs Armstrong, we haven't got all day,' Mr Hudson said briskly.

'She's been getting weekly compensation, hasn't she, Mr Hudson?' Mr Durkin put in.

'Yes, sir, seventeen shillings and twopence,' answered the manager.

'Well, then, that's all right.'

'I was wanting to ask you if you'll set our Robert on, on the screens, I mean,' Nora said, finding her tongue at last.

'Robert? Is that your son? We already have one son of yours working on the screens, haven't we?'

'Yes, sir. Alf. But Robert's turned thirteen and he'll sit the test to leave school. We need the money, sir, seventeen shillings doesn't keep a family, sir.'

Mr Durkin stopped playing with his stick and stared at her, frowning. 'What do you mean, it's not enough? I'd have you know, it's all you're going to get. The trouble with you people is you don't know how to handle money correctly. Remember, the Compensation Committee haven't decided on your husband's case yet. There's some question as to whether it was his own fault, and if that is the decision they come to, you are not entitled to anything. We are paying you now and we don't have to, you know. And we're allowing you to stay in the colliery house when we could put another workman in.'

Nora gasped. Her face whitened and she leaned forwards, putting her hands on the desk to prop herself up. She closed her eyes for a moment.

'Are you feeling faint, Mrs Armstrong?' Mr Hudson got to his feet hurriedly and brought Nora a chair. 'Would you like a glass of water?' He poured some water into a glass from the carafe on the desk and offered it to her and she took a sip.

The agent watched the little drama curiously but with little obvious concern. When Nora sat back, the colour returning to her cheeks, he spoke again.

'Come now, Mrs Armstrong, I only said the committee hasn't decided yet. There's no need to take on.'

'I don't know what we'll do without compensation,' said Nora. 'We can't hardly manage as it is.'

'I did not say there would be no compensation, I simply said we as a company may not be liable. But Lord Akers is a benevolent employer, I think you'll find. Now, come, we have work to do here. I think we have allowed you enough time.'

Nora got to her feet, looking and feeling defeated. Hannah looked up into her mother's face and saw the misery there; then she looked at Mr Durkin and she hated him. She hated the way he talked to her mother and most of all she hated the way he spoke, fancy like but frightening, like the wicked man in the pantomime she'd seen at chapel last Christmas. She took hold of her mother's hand and squeezed it in an effort to comfort her as they turned for the door.

They were in the outer office, almost outside altogether when Mr Hudson followed them and spoke to the clerk.

'Robert Armstrong. Put his name down to start on the screens next week,' he said. Without looking at Nora, he turned on his heel and went back into his office.

Chapter Two

Hannah was playing house in the yard with Jane when Robert came home. The two girls had their mother's wooden clotheshorse open in a V and an old blanket thrown over it to make a tent. Inside the tent was an old clippie mat and Harry lying down on it pretending to be a baby. Harry didn't want to be the baby, he wanted to be the father, but he gave in when the girls insisted.

All three children abandoned the game and scrambled out of the tent when they heard their mother's voice at the gate.

'Now then, Robert,' Nora was saying, 'you're a big lad now, it's time you went out to work. Anyroad, we need the money so that's the end of that. Now stop making a fuss, there's a good lad.'

'Gran calls me Bob,' muttered Robert, 'and so does Uncle Billy.'

Hannah stood in a row with Harry and Jane, watching her mother and Robert curiously.

'Righto, then, we'll call you Bob if that's what you want,' said Nora as she led the way up the yard. 'Now, come and say hallo to your sisters and brother.'

Three pairs of dark eyes looked solemnly at Bob as he stood awkwardly before them. He was a tall, ungainly boy with the same shock of dark hair as they all had. It was almost two years since they had last seen him, and only Hannah had any remembrance of him at all. The little ones were shy of him and huddled in Hannah's skirts.

'Hallo,' said Bob, looking down at the brick-paved yard. He

scuffed the hobnails of one boot back and forth over the bricks.

Hannah suddenly felt sorry for Bob. His face was flushed and his eyes full of unshed tears. She smiled at him, while Jane and Harry hung their heads, overcome with shyness.

'Clear that mess up, our Hannah, and mind, don't forget to fold that blanket up properly and put it away. Right, then, Bob, let's away in. Betty will have the tea ready,' Nora said briskly. She went inside, followed after a second or two by Bob and the two younger children. Hannah was left to dismantle the tent.

The family were already sitting round the table when she got in after putting the clotheshorse back in the wash house in the yard.

'You bide with me, our Bob,' Alf was saying in his 'big brother' voice which Hannah knew so well and resented almost as much. 'You'll get on all right on the screens tomorrow if you do what I say.'

Bob looked down at the meat-paste sandwich on his plate. Hannah could see that his fists were clenched so hard the knuckles were white. She took a bite out of her own sandwich and chewed it carefully. He looks so unhappy, she thought.

'Did you not want to come back home to live, Bob?' she asked. 'It's nice here, you know, there's the bunny banks and sometimes there's the magic lantern at chapel. And –' Hannah meant to make Bob feel at home and tell him of all the nice things about Winton. But all she did was to cause his pent-up feelings to burst out. He stood up from the table and glared at her so hard she dropped her sandwich.

'This isn't my home!' he shouted. 'I live at Consett, that's my home, with Gran and Uncle Billy. I'm going back an' all, I'm going back to school and then I'm going to help Uncle Billy in his carrier business, that's what I'm going to do. I'm not going down the pit, I'm not. I don't care about your stupid bunny banks – what sort of a name is that for a rabbit warren, anyway?'

'Robert! Sit down!'

The roar came from the open door of the front room where Da was lying in his box bed. All the children gazed at him in shock. It was the first time they had heard Da shout since the accident. Robert subsided into his seat and there was a moment's silence.

'Bob,' Nora said. 'Bob, you have to stay here, pet. I know you love your gran, but you're needed here.'

'I don't care,' answered Bob, though this time he kept his voice low. 'I'm going back. You didn't want me when I was little, why should I come back now? Gran's been my mam.'

Hannah stared at him, wide-eyed. She tried to imagine what it would be like if she had to go and live in another place and go out to work doing something she didn't want to do, but it was hard to imagine such a thing.

'Bob, Bob, it wasn't like that. We did want you, son, but Betty came along and you were nought but a babby yourself. Times were bad, pet, your father was on short time. Your gran could look after you and feed you better, your grandda was an overman and they only had Billy left at home. Try to understand, Bob, there's a good lad.'

Hannah watched her mother as she talked. Mam looked as distressed as Bob was himself. A lump formed in Hannah's own throat. She looked down at the sandwich on her plate, suddenly she didn't feel hungry any more and the sandwich looked enormous. If she didn't eat it now, she would get it for her supper, she knew that well enough.

She'd been looking forward to seeing Bob again. It had not occurred to her that he wouldn't want to come. Everything had changed since Da hurt his back in the pit, she thought. If only they could go back to the way it was before.

It was Christmas before Jake's claim for permanent disability compensation was allowed by the committee. Hannah came running in from school on the day before the Christmas holiday, clutching the green paper Christmas tree she had cut out in class together with a multicoloured paper chain and a hat made out of newspaper.

'Look, Mam, look,' she said, 'we made them in school. Can we put them on the wall?' She was excited and didn't at first notice that Mam was smiling for the first time in months and Da's 'chariot', as he had begun to call his wheeled bed, had been brought out of the front room and was by the settee.

'Why, they're grand, pet,' declared Mam. 'We'll hang the paper chain round the mirror, what do you think, Jake? And the tree, why, it's almost like a real one, isn't it? We'll stick it on the wall, eh?'

'Aye,' said Da. Hannah looked at him, he too was smiling.

Forgetting about the paper tree and the chain for a minute, Hannah looked from one to the other. Her mother was relaxed and happy-looking, and so was Da. For a minute she had a wild hope that Da was going to get better and everything would soon be back to normal.

'Are you a bit better, Da?' she asked anxiously, fearful of his answer.

'A bit, pet, a bit,' he said. 'All the better for getting my compensation through, I am.'

Hannah smiled. The tiny hope that her father was going to get back to his normal health died, but the money made her mother and father happy and that was good. The atmosphere in the house had changed and she responded to it eagerly. 'Can Bob go back to Consett now?' she asked and her mother's smile faded. 'No, no, pet, he'll have to stay here and work. He'll be all right, you'll see, he'll get used to it. All the lads have to go to work.' She looked down at Jake and bit her lip. Bob wasn't settling down as they had hoped; he still hankered after going back to live in Consett.

Hannah felt a twinge of sadness for Bob but it was soon forgotten in the excitement of decorating the kitchen for Christmas. Jane had a paper chain from school too, and there was some holly which Alf had garnered from the hedge by the bunny banks and with bits stuck on the frame of Jake and Nora's wedding picture which hung on one wall, and the red paper bell which came out every year hanging from the gas light, the kitchen soon began to look quite festive.

Hannah had made a star from silver paper culled from Da's cigarette packet, and was pinning it to the top of the paper Christmas tree when Robert and Alf came in from work.

'Hurry up, Hannah, and get the bath in for the lads,' said Betty. 'I'm busy tonight.' She had been ironing a great pile of clothes on the table and now she rushed to get the ironing out of the way so that the table could be laid for the meal.

Obediently, Hannah went out into the yard and reached up to take the bath down from where it hung on a nail.

'Do you see my Christmas tree, Bob?' she asked brightly as she lugged the bath in and put it down before the fire. She smiled as she ladled hot water out of the boiler into the bath ready for Alf, who always insisted on being the first to wash as he was the oldest. She was thinking the Christmas tree was just the thing to cheer Bob up, he was always so glum.

Bob looked at the cut-out tree stuck on the wall with its star slightly lopsided on the top of it.

'Uncle Billy bought a real one from the market last year,' he said. 'That's just a bit of paper.'

Hannah was crestfallen. Suddenly the tree didn't seem quite so festive as she had thought it did.

'Eeh, a real tree?' Harry asked Bob, round-eyed. 'A big one, like at the Sunday-school party?'

'Of course, a real tree,' snapped Bob, 'a big one an' all.'

Harry was snubbed; the light faded from his eyes and he looked down at his boots. He was still a little in awe of his new-found brother and easily put down by him.

'Bob, what's the matter with your face?' Da asked all of a sudden, and everyone turned to look at Bob.

'Nothing,' said Bob.

'Oh!' cried Hannah, distressed, 'you've hurt your eye, I didn't see it at first.' Bob's left eye was swollen and bruised purple and there was a small cut and a streak of dried blood along the cheekbone underneath.

'Who did that to you, Bob?' asked Mam quietly. She had come out of the pantry carrying a tureen for the potatoes which were simmering on the bar. Putting the dish down on the table, she put her finger under Bob's chin and lifted it so that she could look at the bruise in the gas light. Even though his face was covered in black smears from the coal dust, the black eye was becoming more obvious all the time.

'Nobody,' said Bob, twisting his face away.

'It was Ralph Cornish, Mam,' said Alf. Alf was already kneeling before the tin bath, stripped to the waist and lathering himself with a bar of carbolic soap.

'Ralph Cornish? But he's a full-grown man!' exclaimed Mam. 'Whatever did he do that for?'

'He said our Bob was cheeky,' said Alf. He bent over the bath and dipped his head under the water, rinsing off the lather before reaching for the towel which Hannah was automatically holding out to him.

'An' were you, Bob?' Mam asked quietly.

There was a low growl from Jake. 'If he was, do you think

that gives a ruffian like Ralph Cornish the right to hit a bit lad like Bob? What are you thinking about, woman?'

'I didn't say anything, Mother,' said Bob. He was the only one to call Nora Mother. 'We were just coming out of the pit-yard gate and he pushed me out of the way and I asked him who he thought he was pushing, that's all.'

'I told you to keep out of his way,' said Alf. 'He takes after his da, that one, they're both of them bullies.'

Jake swore. 'By God,' he said, 'if I only had the use of my legs I'd go up there now and show him what for. Like his da, do you say? He hasn't got a da, that one, or if he has, nobody knows who it is. Wesley Cornish took up with his mother when Ralph was a bairn. Aye, and left his own wife and bairns to God and Providence an' all, he did. That Ralph's a bas–'

'Jake!' Nora cut him off sharply. 'The children are listening. Don't use bad language in my house.'

Hannah and Jane were indeed listening, wide-eyed. Their father's head was moving restlessly from side to side in agitation on the pillow of the 'chariot'. Harry got under the table and stuck his thumb in his mouth.

Hannah's brow creased in puzzlement. What did Da mean, Ralph Cornish hadn't got a da? She couldn't understand that at all.

'Why, man, it's enough to make a saint swear,' said Jake, but his voice was quieter though still bitter. Nora shook her head at him and turned back to Bob.

'Let's get that face washed, lad,' she said. 'Betty, come on, we'll empty the bath and fill it with some fresh water.'

'It's cold water that eye needs,' counselled Jake. Before his accident he had started a first-aid course as part of his training to become a deputy. An ambition which was lost now, 'like snow on the oven top', as Nora had commented sadly.

'You'll have to wash up the dishes tonight, Hannah,' said Betty. 'I've got enough to do with the mending and darning.'

'But we have to go to the choir practice, it's the last one before the carol singing,' said Hannah, dismayed. Hannah loved the chapel choir. She had a fine voice, pure and strong for her age and already showing signs of deepening to mezzo-soprano.

'If you hurry you can still go, it's not until six o'clock, is it? I can see to your da after that,' said her mother, and Hannah relaxed.

'We're going carol singing all round the village on Sunday night,' she announced happily. 'Mr Hodgson says we're even going up to the manager's house, even to Mr Durkin's house an' all. We're taking the little harmonium too, if it doesn't snow, like.' She was torn between wanting it to snow for Christmas and wanting to sing with the accompaniment of the harmonium.

Nora's face hardened at the mention of Mr Durkin. She had not forgotten the humiliation she had had to endure from him at the colliery office.

'You'll not get much out of the agent,' she observed tartly. 'And his house is a mile and a half away from the village an' all, it'll be a long way to walk for nowt. Still, I dare say Mr Hodgson reckons he knows best, he's the choir master, after all.'

The snow came during the night, but left only a thin covering, which crisped into ice crystals soon after it fell. There was a little more on Sunday morning, as the children sat in Sunday school, and Mr Hodgson, who was a Sunday-school superintendent as well as choir master, had a harder time than usual keeping order. The children were excited to see the soft flakes falling past the high windows. They sang 'In the Deep Mid-Winter', and Hannah threw herself into it heart and soul, imagining to herself the Baby in a cold, draughty stable with snow falling outside just as it was falling in Winton now.

By the time the Sunday school was out, the snow had stopped and a strong, freezing wind was blowing down on them from the fells to the west.

'I'm cold,' whined Harry. Hannah tied his muffler in a cross over his chest and fastened it at the back.

'We'll have a race home,' she said. She and Harry went whooping along the row and into the house, with Jane trailing behind them looking white and cold.

'Does Father Christmas come tonight?' Harry asked his mother as he'd asked her every day for a week.

'Only to good boys and girls,' said Nora.

'Father Christmas!' said Bob scornfully, but his mother quelled him with a look.

At seven o'clock, the choir assembled outside the chapel. Hannah stamped her boots on the frozen ground and tucked her chin in her mother's shawl which was tied over her coat, but she was so excited she didn't really feel the cold. This was the first year she had been allowed to sing with the grown-up choir, not just with the Sunday-school singers, and she held her candle carefully even though it was not yet lit, not here under the street-lights lit by gas from the colliery. The candle was for when they walked out to the manager's house in Old Winton and then on up to Durham Road, where Lord Akers's agent, Mr Durkin, lived.

'You stick close to me, mind,' Betty admonished. 'I don't want you dancing off on your own like you do.'

Betty was more bossy every day, Hannah reflected as she moved her fingers about inside her mitts in an attempt to warm them up. The mitts were really a pair of Da's socks but they were nice and warm, each sock folded over on itself to make a double layer of wool. There was a burst of male laughter and she looked over to where Alf was standing with a group of men and boys. He was holding his hand in a funny way, she thought; staring hard, she saw the tiny red glow and realised he was holding a cigarette, turned back into his cupped hand to hide it. Quickly, she moved to stand between him and Betty. If Betty saw Alf smoking she would be sure to tell Da.

When Mr Hodgson came out with Laurie, his son, who was the organ player, they were carrying the tiny harmonium between them. At last the singers were off.

'By, it's grand, isn't it, Betty?' Hannah cried as they trudged away from the rows of miners' cottages to the village. They had sung two carols at each end of each row. Alf and his friends had rattled their collecting boxes labelled 'METHODIST MISSION TO THE POOR' and almost every household in the rows had contributed a penny; Mr Holmes had put in sixpence. Hannah crunched the thin, icy layer of snow beneath her boots, fairly dancing along as she wondered what it would be like to be 'the Poor' and not have any money at all, not even the compensation, nor a house to live in. She gazed up at the clear starry sky and wondered which one was the Star of Bethlehem.

'It'll be grand when we get back home,' said Betty dourly. Hannah's excitement dimmed a little, but only for a minute. They had just reached old Winton and Mr Hodgson halted before the Black Boy. The choir gathered round the harmonium under the swinging sign with its picture of a little pit lad with a candle in his hat.

'Once in Royal David's City' rang through the air and men tumbled out of the inn, some with tankards of beer in their hands. Hannah knew a lot of them, for they were neighbours and friends of her father's. There were some disapproving looks among the choir but the collecting boxes were satisfactorily heavier by the time Alf and his friends had done the rounds of the drinkers and she was glad for the sake of the Poor.

However, farther along the street the choir met with the opposition. The vicar and his party of waits from St Martin's, the village church, were out carol singing too. After the first clash of hymns, Mr Hodgson decided the best thing to do was take his choir elsewhere.

'We only show them up with our singing, anyroad,' he said. 'Howay, lads and lasses, we'll away up to Durham Road to the agent's place.'

'Mebbe you'd better go home, our Hannah, it's a long way to Durham Road,' said Betty.

Hannah gasped with dismay. 'I want to come,' she cried. 'I can walk, I'm not tired.'

'Let her come, Betty,' said Alf, 'lest we never hear the last of it.'

'Well, all right,' Betty conceded, 'but you'd better keep up, mind.'

Durham Road was really nearer to Bishop Auckland than Winton and the party set off on the short cut across the fields. It was quite a climb in places but Hannah forced herself to keep well to the front of the party, just to show Betty she could manage.

At last they reached the house and trooped up the drive. The laughing and talking quietened as they approached the house, most of them walking more slowly as they got near to the imposing stone pillars before the front door.

'Now then,' said Mr Hodgson, 'light your candles now. Don't step on the grass, mind, keep to the gravel.'

Guilty feet shuffled off the grass and the choir clustered round the harmonium, their uplifted faces lit by the glow of the candles. Hannah gazed at the light shining through a chink in the curtains and her heart began to beat rapidly. She was frightened of Mr Durkin – would he chase them away? Mr Durkin didn't like pit folk, he'd said so that day at the colliery office.

The harmonium started up and the choir sang 'Oh Come All Ye Faithful'. Suddenly they were bathed in a light which put the candles to shame as the curtains were drawn back.

'Electric,' breathed Hannah. She'd seen electric light before, but only in the shops in Newgate Street. She forgot to sing as she gazed into the room, at the red plush armchairs and the huge Christmas tree in the corner, twinkling with gold and silver ornaments and topped by a big fairy with shining silver wings. And then she forgot about the Christmas tree as she saw Timothy, the boy who had been in the car, standing by the window, smiling straight at her.

The choir finished their carol and the door opened. Hannah shrank back against her sister but it was not Mr Durkin who came to the door, it was a stranger, tall and haughty, dressed in a funny sort of black jacket and striped trousers.

'The master says you're to come into the hall, and mind you wipe your feet,' he announced grandly, looking over the heads of the choir as though he was speaking to the trees at the end of the drive. Hannah looked uncertainly at Mr Hodgson but he was moving forwards quite unperturbed and the choir was following him.

They were ushered into a large hall, all gleaming, polished wood and with a red carpet in the middle. At one end there was a wide staircase and there was even carpet going up the stairs, not a strip of linoleum like they had at home.

Mr Durkin and Timothy came through a door at the side and Hannah was thankful to see that the agent was smiling.

'Good evening to you all,' he said and they all mumbled a reply. Hannah smiled shyly at Timothy and he smiled back.

'Can you sing "Still the Night", do you think?' asked Mr Durkin.

'Yes, sir, of course.' The choir master beamed. He glanced down at Hannah and hesitated. 'I wonder, sir . . . our little Hannah here, she has a lovely voice and she's been rehearsing it for the Sunday-school party. Would you like to hear her sing the first verse, sir? Then we'll all join in the second.'

Hannah's throat closed up and she stared up at Mr Hodgson, her dark eyes filled with fright. Surely he wasn't going to make her sing for Mr Durkin! But Mr Hodgson chose not to see the appeal on her face; instead, he took hold of her shoulder and drew her to the front of the choir.

'Now then, pet,' he encouraged her, 'just pretend you're singing in the chapel. Sing it just like we practised.' Drawing a tuning fork from his waistcoat pocket, he struck the note, and Hannah opened her mouth obediently, though she was sure she wasn't going to be able to sing at all.

But sing she did, faltering a little over the first few notes but then losing herself in the lovely old carol. Her pure tones gained strength and rang out over the choir and the well of the staircase lent resonance to the music. The choir joined in the second verse and after a while Hannah was conscious of a new voice. Looking across at Timothy, she realised it was his baritone she could hear.

There was a moment's silence after the hymn before Mr Durkin finally broke it. 'Very nice,' he said. 'Timothy, fetch some mince pies from the kitchen.' He took a gold watch out of his waistcoat pocket and peered at the dial pointedly. 'Well, good night to you all and a merry Christmas.' He turned and went back through a door at the side of the hall, not even noticing the collection box held up by Alf. Mr Hodgson sighed.

Timothy came back and handed round a plate of mince pies and the choir ate them quietly. Seeing the collection box, he fumbled in his pocket and put in a sixpence.

'You have a lovely voice,' he said to Hannah, and she smiled shyly.

'You an' all,' she answered.

'Well, we'd better be going, we still have to go to the manager's house,' said Mr Hodgson and he ushered the choir out of the hall and down the drive.

Hannah looked round just before they got to the gates and saw Timothy standing at the window, watching them. On impulse, she gave a little wave and he must have seen her for he lifted his arm and waved back. Hannah felt a tiny glow of happiness. Was he lonely in that big house with his father and the snooty man, she wondered.

Chapter Three

Christmas 1920 was the best one Hannah could remember. 'Like magic,' she breathed to Jane when Grandma came with Uncle Billy on Christmas morning and Bob's face lit up at the sight of them. That was the second good thing to happen. The first had been coming downstairs that morning to find that the stockings they had pinned to the mantelpiece valance were bulging.

'Father Christmas came!' Harry shouted. Betty reached up, unpinned the stockings and handed them round. Besides the usual apple, orange and handful of hazelnuts, each stocking held a bag of sweets; black bullets and humbugs. For Harry there was a hand-carved wooden truck and Jane had a wooden doll with real clothes.

'Father Christmas brought it because I've been good,' said Harry thickly, through a mouth bulging with humbug. He clutched his truck to his chest as though someone were going to snatch it from him.

'They had a gathering for Da in the pit,' said Alf prosaically. Luckily, the two youngest children didn't hear this.

Grandma had brought a chicken to go with the piece of belly pork Mam had in the oven. She put it down on the table, kissed Bob and asked him how he was getting on and then went into the front room to see her injured son. After about ten minutes she came out again.

'Howay, Hannah,' she said and her voice was so trembly that Hannah looked up at her with quick sympathy. 'We'll start the dinner, eh? Let Betty have an easy morning for a change.' Grandma's eyes were wet and her hands were trembling as she took the chicken out of her basket and got it ready for the oven.

'You can chop the sage with the onion, Hannah,' she went on. 'Now mind, breathe through your mouth so the onions don't make you cry.'

Hannah kept chopping away at the onions and mixing the dried sage and breadcrumbs in with them, but she remembered to breathe through her mouth so they didn't make her cry and it was Grandma who had to keep taking out her handkerchief to wipe her eyes, not Hannah.

'I forgot to breathe properly,' said Grandma once. She blew her nose and smiled tightly at Hannah.

The dinner was grand. Mam brought Da out of the front room and they were all together for the meal. Hannah beamed as she looked round at them all; even Da was smiling.

After dinner, Uncle Billy took all the children for a ride in his cart. They went round the rows and up into the old village, doing a circuit which led back to the house, with the children waving to all their friends. Harry wanted to go again but Uncle Billy explained that the pony would have to have a rest before taking them back to Consett after tea. Reluctantly, Harry allowed himself to be lifted down. Uncle Billy let him help unharness the pony and showed him how to fit on his nosebag, and then Bob went off for a walk up the bunny banks with his uncle. And later there was spice cake for tea, and a glass of ginger wine for everyone.

'Tomorrow will be even better,' breathed Hannah as she settled down in the iron-framed bed she shared with Jane. 'Tomorrow is my birthday and the Sunday-school party and there's to be a magic lantern.'

The house was quiet. Grandma and Uncle Billy had left soon after tea, and the family had watched the lantern bobbing on the side of the cart until it disappeared. Hannah had gazed anxiously at Bob, standing beside her watching the cart. She had caught hold of his hand and squeezed it.

'They'll be back, Bob,' she had said softly.

Bob had shaken off her hand. 'Aw, leave me alone, Hannah,' he had said. 'I'm all right, man.' And he had stumped off up the yard to the back door.

Hannah put her arm round the thin body of her little sister and snuggled in to her. Eleven! I'm eleven tomorrow, she thought as she drifted near to sleep. And, unexpectedly, into her mind popped the image of the boy, Timothy Durkin, so lonely he had looked in that great house in Durham Road. 'I hope he had a lovely Christmas too,' she whispered to herself and snuggled into her pillow.

'The demand for coal is slackening,' said Daniel Durkin moodily. Timothy, sitting opposite him at the dinner table, watched his father as he played with his wine glass, twirling it round and round in his fingers.

'It is?' asked Mr Abbot, the vicar. Mr Abbot had only recently been appointed to the living of St Martin's; he was a bachelor not yet thirty years old and knew nothing whatsoever of the coal trade, coming as he did from a farming community in Yorkshire.

Timothy sat quietly, wishing the interminable dinner were over so that he could excuse himself and go up to his room. Maude, the housemaid, brought in the steaming Christmas pudding and the men were quiet as she placed it before Daniel along with a dish of brandy butter.

'That will be all, thank you, Maude,' said Daniel. 'I can manage.'

'Thank you, sir,' said Maude and went out.

Timothy gazed at the enormous fruit-filled pudding and felt slightly sick. He remembered the Christmas pudding his mother had made four years before.

'Have a stir, Timothy,' she had cried to him. 'Make a wish, Timothy.'

And he'd taken the wooden spoon in his hand and stirred and knocked the bag of flour over with his elbow and the table and floor had been covered in the fine white dust.

'We'd better clean it up or Mrs Bates will be cross with us for making a mess of her kitchen,' his mother had said, but she was smiling as she said it, not angry at all. But when Christmas came and the pudding was placed on the dining table, his mother was dead. Timothy forced his mind away from the memory of it and looked up at his father.

'None for me, thank you,' he said as Daniel took up the serving spoon.

'Don't be silly, Timothy,' his father said sharply. 'You don't want to hurt Mrs Bates's feelings, do you?'

'No, of course not, Father,' said Timothy and accepted the plate the vicar passed him.

'You were saying, the coal trade was slackening,' said Mr Abbot. 'I'm afraid I know very little about it, myself.'

Daniel ate a spoonful of pudding before replying. 'Very good,' he pronounced. 'I must congratulate Mrs Bates.'

'Oh yes, indeed,' said Mr Abbot.

'Hmm. Well, perhaps I should not have mentioned business on a festive day like this,' said Daniel. 'But I do have it on my mind, I'm afraid. Demand was bound to slacken some time now the war is over, but try telling the men that.' He shook his head and took another spoonful of pudding before putting down his spoon and wiping his mouth with his napkin. 'It's the wages bill, you see.' He sighed. 'Between you and me, it will have to be cut.' He looked across at Mr Abbot earnestly. 'Miners are well paid, you know, compared with, say, agricultural labourers. Most farmworkers only get forty-six shillings a week. Some of our hewers can earn four pounds a week.'

'The men should be thankful they have work,' said the vicar. 'After all, they have their coal allowance, too. Some of the labouring population in the south are hard put to pay for coal. And there are ex-servicemen still out of work, or so I understand. After all, the miners didn't have to fight, or most of them didn't.'

Timothy looked surprised. He remembered the victory parade when the soldiers had come back from France and marched through Winton. Surely they were miners? But the vicar was talking of parish matters now, and he could not interrupt to ask about it. Instead Timothy turned his attention to his food, looking down at the lump of pudding on his plate. He took his spoon and stirred it around, trying to make it look as though he had eaten some of it. A coal fire blazed in the grate of the ornate marble fireplace and he felt uncomfortably hot. Mr Abbot did not like the miners, he thought, remembering how the vicar had replied when Daniel had asked him how he liked living in Winton.

'To tell you the truth, Mr Durkin,' Mr Abbot had said, 'I would never have come had I known there were two flourishing Methodist churches here, besides the Congregationalists and the Roman Catholics. We are outnumbered, I fear. And as for the miners, either they waste their wages on drink or they are ranting teetotallers and I find it hard put to tell which is worst.'

The door opened and Mr Bates came in with the decanter of port. Timothy breathed a sigh of relief.

'May I be excused, Father?' he asked and at his father's nod he escaped to his room and took off his jacket. Thank goodness another Christmas was almost over, he thought as he stood by the window, gazing out over the trees to where the winding wheel and chimney stacks of the colliery towered over the colliery rows. Another two weeks and he would be back at school in Barnard Castle. At least he had friends at school, there was no one here.

Looking down on the village reminded him of the chapel choir, and in particular of the little girl wrapped in a shawl which reached down to her knees and up over her head so that only her small face peeped out, pink with cold. He remembered her from the time she had come to the colliery office with her mother and little brother, and he still felt hot with embarrassment at the way his father had spoken to them.

When she had come with the choir she had stood beside what was obviously her older sister, for they both had dimples in their chins and dark eyes fringed with black lashes. It must be nice to be part of a big family, Timothy mused. And then, when she sang, such a large, pure voice had emerged from such a little girl that he had been enchanted and drawn to sing along with her.

A germ of an idea was forming in Timothy's mind. There were some days left before he had to go back to school. Tomorrow he would go down into Winton and find the chapel, maybe he could make some friends and even join the choir. He always enjoyed singing at school, though when he had asked to take singing lessons his father had stated that they were a waste of time and money and so he had given up the idea.

Next evening Timothy told his father he was going for a pre-dinner stroll and set off through the fields to Winton Colliery. As he approached the small, cramped houses, the rows practically on top of one another, he almost turned back at the smell, he had forgotten about the smell. The air was laden with sulphurous fumes from the cokeworks and ashes and coal dust from the colliery waste heap mingled with the stink from the ash closets in the narrow back alleys. He wrinkled his nose, breathed through his mouth and went on to the tall stone building which was the Methodist chapel and schoolroom, standing alone on a patch of waste ground midway between the village and the pit.

The windows of the schoolroom were ablaze with light and he could hear children laughing and shouting. Timothy hesitated for a few minutes, fearing they would think he was intruding. In the end he walked in through the open side door into a hall strung with paper chains and a platform at one end with a woman sitting at an old upright piano. Over the platform was a huge painted sign, 'SUFFER THE CHILDREN TO COME UNTO ME.'

The children were sitting in a large ring on the floor and playing 'pass the parcel'. There was a great deal of noise and confusion as the parcel went round the circle, being dropped by hands too eager to pass it on and picked up hurriedly, while the lady on the platform banged out a tune he couldn't recognise. No one saw him at first, not until the music stopped suddenly and it was Hannah holding the parcel. Her face registered her disappointment but she handed over the parcel to her neighbour and left the circle. As all eyes followed her, they caught sight of Timothy inside the doorway and suddenly there was a hush. Mr Hodgson, from his position as referee in the middle of the circle, gazed blankly at the intruder before remembering his manners and rushing to greet him.

'Master Durkin! How nice of you to come,' he cried.

'I . . . I heard the merriment and wondered . . . I hope I don't intrude,' Timothy faltered.

'Indeed no, everyone is welcome in the Lord's house,' said Mr Hodgson grandly. 'The children have had their tea but I'm sure there will be some Christmas cake left for you. Will you stay? There's to be a magic-lantern show and then Father Christmas is coming with gifts for the children. This is their day, you know.'

'Thank you, I will,' said Timothy and he looked down at Hannah, and smiled and she forgot her disappointment at not winning the parcel and smiled back into his deep-blue eyes. Mrs Roberts brought Timothy a slice of cake and he and Hannah sat at the side of the hall and watched as the game continued, the circle dwindling until at last there was a winner and it was Harry. Timothy shared in Hannah's delight as Harry brought his prize to be admired; a colouring book and a packet of crayons. All the children crowded round to see, forgetting their shyness of Timothy. Then it was time for the magic lantern and the flickering pictures of black children in Africa with the Methodist missionaries their collected pennies had helped to send out to teach the heathen. Father Christmas came after that and Hannah had a pretty, lace-embroidered handkerchief, delicate and white.

'It's my birthday today,' she confided to Timothy and blushed in embarrassment when he fished in his pocket and brought out a shilling.

'I didn't mean . . .' she said unhappily.

'No, of course you didn't, I never thought that,' he assured her. 'But please take it, I want you to have it.' And Hannah stowed the shilling along with her lace handkerchief in the pocket of her dress.

'I just meant that it always feels like the Sunday-school party is my birthday party too,' she explained earnestly.

The party finished with the children singing carols. Timothy joined in unselfconsciously, his baritone ringing out over the voices of the rest. He was enjoying himself hugely.

As they all filed out of the schoolroom, Mr Hodgson stopped him.

'Come back any time you like, lad,' he said. 'The choir could just do with a singer like you.'

'Thank you, I will,' answered Timothy. He waved to them all and in particular to Hannah before striding off over the fields to Durham Road.

'You're late, sir,' snapped Daniel as his son let himself into the house. Daniel was standing in the doorway of the dining room, frowning heavily.

'Sorry, Father,' said Timothy. 'I won't be a moment changing.' As he washed his hands and face and combed his hair ready to go down to dinner, he found himself smiling into the mirror; he felt happier than he had done during the whole of the holiday and not the least bit sorry.

Chapter Four

'Hannah! Hannah, get up out of bed now, will you?'

Something in Betty's voice made Hannah jump up immediately, her feet landing on the icy cold linoleum, at which her toes curled up in protest. She hurriedly found her boots and crammed her bare feet into them, then pulled her dress on over her nightie and raced downstairs.

Betty was standing by the fire with the heavy kettle in her hand, pouring water into the teapot. Hannah blinked. It was only six o'clock, she could see by the wall clock, yet the kitchen was already warmed up as though the fire had been on for hours.

'What's the matter, Betty?' Hannah asked as she went up to the fire and held her hands out to the blaze.

'The baby's come,' said Betty.

'The baby? What baby?' Hannah had been bending down to tie her bootlaces but she straightened up and stared at her sister.

'What baby do you think?' Betty snapped, but Hannah could see she was not really cross for she was smiling. 'We've a new baby brother,' she added, her tone softening. As though to verify her words, the sound of a baby crying came from the front room, and Mam's voice hushing it.

Betty laughed at Hannah's astonishment. 'You mean you didn't know Mam was having a bairn?' she asked, using that superior tone of voice which Hannah hated. 'Why did you think she was getting so fat, then?'

Hannah blushed; she hadn't even noticed Mam was fat. She bent her head and finished tying her boots.

'Hurry up, you'll have to stay off school and see to the

breakfast and everything. I'll have enough to do, seeing to Da and helping Mam with the baby,' said Betty. 'Now, take some tea in for Mam, she could do with a cup now it's over.'

Obediently, Hannah took the cup of tea and pushed open the door to the front room. The room was warm in spite of the snow falling outside, for the fire was lit in the black-leaded grate and the old wooden cradle was drawn up beside it. Da's box bed was pulled up by one side of the double bed and in the bed there was Mam, sitting up with a bundle in her arms and smiling at Hannah.

'Eeh, thanks, pet, I could just do with that,' said Mam softly. 'Howay, come and see your new baby brother. Quiet now, your father's just got back to sleep.'

Hannah stared down at the tiny, red-faced mite wrapped in the faded crochet shawl she could dimly remember from when Harry was a baby, and she fell instantly in love.

'By, he's bonny,' she whispered. 'What's his name, Mam?'

'We think we'll call him Walton, after your grandfather. Now, will you put him in his cradle for me? Careful, now.'

Hannah took the baby in her arms and carried him to the cradle, laying him down and covering him with the tiny flannelette sheet she remembered Mam making from the corner of an old, torn, full-size one. She gazed down at the sleeping baby, reluctant to leave him.

'Go on now, pet, go and help Betty,' said Mam. 'Be a good lass and do what she says. I think I'll have a rest now, while the bairn's asleep.'

For the next few weeks, while the wintry weather turned to spring, Hannah's days were filled with peeling vegetables and boiling puddings, possing clothes in the wooden wash tub and helping Betty to iron them with the flatirons heated on the bar of the kitchen fire. And helping with baby Walton. That was what she liked to do, she would change his nappies and cheerfully wash them out and hang them on the line in the yard. She hovered anxiously over him whenever Jane asked to hold him. And when Hannah managed to catch threepence in a wedding 'hoy-out', when the groom throws a handful of copper into the street for good luck, she bought a hank of white wool and laboriously knitted him a tiny cap. But then the kiddy-catcher came and Hannah had to go back to school.

At first, she worried about Walton and would hurry home from school to make sure he was all right. But Mam was stronger now and could see to both Da and the baby herself. In April there was something else to worry about; the owners locked the men out of the pits until such time as they should see sense and agree to new terms.

'At least we have your father's compensation money coming in,' said Nora. 'Now the pit's idle some folk'll have nothing.'

'Nay, lass,' said Jake, 'there's the relief, if anyone's starving.'

Nora snorted. 'Not for a man on his own, there's not. The board reckons too much has been paid out to them as isn't in proper distress. And anyway, those who do get it have to pay it back when the pit starts up again. I read it in the *Chronicle*.'

'The *Chronicle* said Peter Lee's petitioning Parliament,' Alf volunteered. 'He says some of the men won't have much more than two pound a week if they go back on the new terms.'

'Aye. Well, we've got fourteen shillings and ninepence, now the war rating has been taken off us and you and our Bob's laid idle.'

'The union's giving out credit notes for the Co-op store,' said Betty. 'To be paid back after, like.'

'Aye, that's the nub of it,' said Nora. 'How would we pay anything back? Your da's not going back to work. And the lads don't get that much on the screens.'

No matter how they talked round it, Hannah thought as she trudged to school with Jane, they didn't have enough even though they had the compensation. She looked up at the colliery winding wheel, so still and quiet. The gates of the pit yard were closed and locked and the yard itself was deserted. It began to rain, the water coming down in hard sheets which soon had tiny rivulets of water black with coal dust running under the gates and out over the pavement to the gutter.

'Mind you don't step in the water,' she said sharply to Jane. 'You know you haven't to get your feet wet, it makes you cough.'

Jane sniffled miserably, hunched her chin down between her shoulders and dragged her feet. 'I want to go home, I feel bad,' she whimpered.

'Well, you can't,' said Hannah. She put an arm round Jane's shoulders and hurried her on. 'Come on, it's not so far now and maybe the teacher will have some cocoa for us.'

That was something else Mam had seen in the *Chronicle*. The teachers had recommended that breakfast and dinner should be provided for the children. And as the two girls came to the gates of the school yard they both began to quicken their steps, for there, drawn up to the main door, was the motor van belonging to the Co-op store. A man was lifting out boxes and carrying them into the school.

'Now then, girls.' Miss High, the headmistress, stood on the top step of the girls' entrance. 'Form your lines now. We're going into school early today, there's cocoa and bread for everyone.'

The children were not to tell twice. In record time they had formed lines according to which class they were in and stood patiently waiting for the order to march forwards. The only sound was that of the man from the store whistling as he went backwards and forwards to the van; the children knew better than to talk in line.

'We've had our dinners, Mam,' cried Hannah when she got home after school. 'We had bread and scrape and cocoa for breakfast before we started our lessons. And then we had soup at dinnertime. And Miss High says we're to have our breakfast and dinner every day, even Saturday and Sunday.'

'That's grand pet,' said Nora absently and Hannah's face fell.

'I . . . I thought you would be pleased,' she said.

'Eeh, I am, I am,' said her mother. 'It's Jane, though, she's come home poorly.' Jane was still in the junior section at school and got out half an hour earlier than Hannah. She was lying on the settee wrapped up in Nora's shawl. Hannah hadn't thought anything of it when she came in, for Jane often had a rest when she came in from school. Now she looked at her little sister properly and felt a sick alarm at what she saw. Jane had a high colour in her cheeks and her eyes were wide open and shining brightly but she didn't seem to be seeing anything.

'Jane?' Hannah whispered, but Jane didn't appear to know her or even see her.

'Come away, Hannah, she can't hear you. Now, I want you to run down to the doctor's with this note. I'm feared for the bairn,' said Nora, handing over a folded piece of cheap writing paper.

Nodding dumbly, Hannah turned and ran through the rows and on up the road to the doctor's house in Old Winton. By the time she reached the large stone-built house she was panting heavily and a stitch in her side caused her to double up, but she followed the instructions on the notice by the gate, 'Patients and messages through the yard at the back'. At the sight of her white, anxious face, the men squatting on their haunches around the door, in the way of all pitmen used to working in cramped seams, moved quickly to allow her passage through. Inside, the wall benches were full of women gossiping in hushed voices as they waited their turn to see the doctor, but Hannah went straight to the hatch in the far wall where the dispenser stood before his rows of medicine bottles and handed him her note. He peered at it, then looked over his half-spectacles at her.

'The doctor's busy just now, don't you know it's surgery time?' he said.

'Our Jane's very bad,' Hannah persisted. He frowned before deciding. 'Well, I'll have a word with him when he has a minute.'

Hannah licked her dry lips and cast a desperate glance around at the women watching her. 'Can you not have a word with him now?' she asked, fear for Jane making her bold.

'No, I cannot,' said the dispenser, who was also the man who came round on Friday evenings to collect the 'panel' money, the fourpence a week Mam paid for the doctor's services.

'Why, man, can you not see how worried the bairn is?' a voice said from the benches. Hannah looked round and saw it was Mrs Holmes, the overman's wife. The dispenser transferred his attention from the girl to the woman.

'Everybody in their turn, Mrs Holmes,' he pronounced. 'Why didn't they send for the doctor before the surgery started, anyway?'

'Likely there was no one to send, you barmy sod,' said Mrs Holmes. She looked away from him dismissively and spoke to Hannah. 'Go on, pet, you can ask the doctor yourself if *he* won't. It's my turn next and you can go in along of me.'

'No need for that, Mrs Holmes,' said the dispenser huffily. 'If it's urgent I'll go in to him now.' After a deferential knock he went through the door which connected the dispensary with the surgery.

By, she was a nice woman, Mrs Holmes, Hannah thought as she sped home. A grand woman. But as she ran up the yard she forgot about Mrs Holmes, for through the lighted window she could see Mam bending over the settee while Harry was standing crying and sucking his thumb by the table.

'He's coming, Mam, the doctor's coming –' Hannah stopped short as Nora stood up and Hannah saw the towel she was holding was covered in blood, bright-red blood. Jane was lying still and white and quiet, and dread rose up in Hannah's throat.

'What is it? For God's sake, Nora, what's the matter?'

Da, shouting from his box bed in the front room, could hardly be heard for the noise of Harry's sobs and the baby Walton woke and added his terrified screams.

'Whist, Harry, whisht,' said Hannah, moving to her little brother and putting her arm around him. 'Howay, now, come into the front room, I have to see to the bairn.'

'Oh, God,' Nora was moaning as she snatched the clean tea cloth from the brass line under the mantel shelf and used it to wipe the beads of sweat from Jane's face and neck. 'Oh, God, oh, God, where's our Betty? Where's the flaming doctor?'

'If by the flaming doctor you mean me, I'm here,' said Dr Short as he came in and, taking in the situation at a glance, strode over to the settee. 'Now, send the children out of the room, this is no place for them. And pull yourself together, Mrs Armstrong, I need your help while I examine the lassie.'

Hannah dragged Harry into the front room and closed the door before taking Walton from his cradle and cuddling the wet bundle into her chest. Harry went to his father's bedside and, leaning over, buried his head in the pillow.

'Now then, stop blubbing, Harry, you're a big lad now,' said Jake and patted his son's head. 'What happened with Jane?' he asked Hannah. 'I thought she just had a bad cough or maybe the influenza.'

Hannah couldn't bear the anxiety and frustration in his face and she looked quickly down at the baby in her arms. 'Our Jane's spitting blood,' she mumbled as she sat down and began to unpin Walton's sopping nappy.

Jake looked relieved for a minute but then his eyes narrowed. 'How much blood?'

A vivid picture of Mam holding the blood-sodden towel came

to Hannah and she bent to her work of changing the baby, unable to answer at first. Walton was still crying and she desperately wanted him to stop so that she could hear what the doctor was saying in the kitchen.

'How much blood, Hannah?' Jake raised his voice.

'A lot, Da.'

'Oh, my God!'

Hannah lifted the clean and dry baby and leaned him against her shoulder, rocking him gently. After a few moments, his sobs subsided. She stole a glance at her father, who was lying with a curiously blank expression on his face as he absently patted Harry's head.

'I'll ring for the ambulance as soon as I get back to the surgery,' she heard the doctor say. 'In the meanwhile, keep her quiet and don't give her anything to eat or drink.'

'Maybe Jane has scarlet fever,' whispered Hannah. She remembered the time the year before when May Martin in the next row had scarlet fever and she and Jane had watched as the ambulance came to take May to the fever hospital. 'Touch collar, never follow, don't come to our door,' they had chanted, fingering their collars, but the charm hadn't worked, for now the ambulance was coming for Jane.

'I doubt it's not scarlet fever, pet,' said Da. 'Put the baby in the cradle now and go and help your mam, our Betty's not back from work yet.'

Hannah did as he bid her, fetching in a pail of cold water from the pump on the end of the row to soak the bloodied clothes in, fetching a clean nightie for Jane from the chest of drawers upstairs. All the time, Jane lay still and quiet and Hannah could not bear to look at her.

When Betty came home from her work at Mr Hudson's house and she and Mam stood huddled together whispering. Hannah couldn't hear properly but she did catch the word 'consumption' and her eyes widened anxiously. 'Consumption' was a word to be whispered, never spoken aloud.

Jane didn't go to the fever hospital, she went to the sanatorium, which was high in Weardale where the wind was fresh and bracing and would blow the germs away in no time, or so her father told Hannah. But the days and weeks dragged on and Jane didn't come home. Mam went to visit her once during the lockout, walking into Bishop Auckland and catching the train from there. She took six large oranges given to her by Mr Nelson, who was a greengrocer and a chapel man, and a little purse with a string to hang round her neck which Hannah had made for Jane out of a piece of bombazine left over from two years ago when Nora had made her good dress. But it was becoming more difficult every day to find money to live and the fare to Weardale was just too much.

Hannah had an idea. The school hall was so crowded at dinnertime, surely no one would notice Harry? Anyway, he was almost five and would be starting school in a few weeks. So why couldn't he have his dinner with the other children? After all, it was Sunday and after dinner they all went home again, they didn't have to stand in line and go back into their classrooms.

'It'll be all right if you stand close to me and keep on the side away from Mr Carney,' Hannah warned Harry as they waited in the queue by the school gates. Harry nodded and moved in closer to his sister among the crowd of children. His mouth watered; he could smell the beef even at this distance from the school hall.

'Will there be meat, Hannah?' he whispered, his eyes shining. Yesterday he had had a bowl of soup from the soup kitchen, broth thick with vegetables but with little trace of the ham which was said to be in it.

'Whisht!' Hannah hissed, glancing quickly at the gate which Mr Carney, the school caretaker, was unlocking to allow the children in. Mr Carney knew the Armstrong family too well, he was aware that Harry was not yet at school. The children surged forwards as the gates opened, heading for the hall.

'Walk, don't run!' shouted Mr Carney. 'Anyone who runs will go to the back of the queue.' He lifted his chin and glared officiously at a small girl who was doing a little skip of delight in her anticipation of the food. She dropped her head and blushed scarlet.

Hannah managed to get Harry past Mr Carney and into the hall without the caretaker seeing him. She hustled him to a seat beside her on the long forms by the trestle table. Harry's eyes shone, for not only were there boiled potatoes on the plate in front of him but also a slice of meat – not pressed brawn or cow heel either, but proper boiled beef. He picked up his knife and fork at once, took a bite and chewed blissfully.

'Wait, Harry!' Hannah whispered urgently. 'Miss Dunne has to say grace.' Luckily, Miss Dunne, the duty teacher this Sunday, was not taking too much notice of what the children were doing. She was resentful of having to come in to work on a Sunday and wanted to get the meal over with so that she could go home.

'For what we are about to receive, may the Lord make us truly thankful,' she intoned rapidly.

'Amen,' said the children, and there was a clatter of tin cutlery on pottery plates as they dived into the meal. There was no chattering among them, no laughing, no mischief; simply a steady concentration on eating the food on their plates. Within ten minutes all eyes were turned to the server at the head of the table, for sometimes on a Sunday some children had gone to grandparents, there might therefore be some food left. This time they were lucky, for at a nod from Miss Dunne the server began to dole out an extra potato each.

'Harry Armstrong, what are you doing here?'

Both Hannah and Harry jumped in their seats and looked round in horror. They had been watching the server, the caretaker's assistant, coming nearer and nearer and hadn't realised that Mr Carney was also approaching from the other end of the hall. He grabbed hold of Harry, tucked him under his arm, kicking and screaming, and dumped him in front of Miss Dunne.

'Leave him alone!' shrieked Hannah, practically falling over the form as she rushed to follow her brother. She put her arms around him and he buried his face in her skirt, his screams fading to a thin, hiccuping wail.

'This lad isn't five yet, he's not a scholar here,' said Mr Carney, his mouth pulled down in frowning outrage.

'He's five next month,' Hannah asserted. 'He's nearly old enough.'

'Hannah Armstrong,' snapped Miss Dunne, 'don't you dare speak until you're spoken to. You know the rules: the meal is for the schoolchildren and the boy isn't at school yet. Did you bring him in here?'

'He was hungry!' Hannah cried. 'What difference did it make anyroad? There was dinner left over today, I knew there would be on a Sunday.'

'That's as may be, my girl,' said Miss Dunne, 'but now I'll have to go and see your mother, she will have to pay for what the boy ate. That will be threepence.' The teacher was very angry for it meant that she was going to be late home if she had to go down into the miners' hovels. Besides, she had her new dress on, ready for her afternoon walk with her intended, and she would likely get it marked.

'Threepence!' Hannah gasped. By, she would catch it from Mam now and Betty an' all. And what would Da say if they didn't have threepence left from the compensation money and they had to admit it to snooty Miss Dunne?

'Can . . . Can I bring it tomorrow, miss?' she asked desperately, trying to put off the time when the money would have to be forthcoming.

'No, you can't,' snapped Miss Dunne. 'The rules are quite clear: if a child not on the school register manages to get a free meal, then the parents must be charged. I have to collect it immediately.'

Harry felt his sister trembling and his wails grew louder, punctuated by enormous, gulping hiccups.

'Stop that bellowing boy,' shouted Miss Dunne, losing her patience altogether. She grabbed hold of his shoulder and pulled him round to face her. 'You are a very naughty boy, do you hear me? What you did was stealing. Perhaps it will be a good thing when you do start school, it's very obvious that you need discipline. Now, come with – Oh!' Miss Dunne released her hold on Harry and jumped back in horror for suddenly the boy vomited beef and potatoes and gravy all over her new dress. As the teacher stood frozen for a moment, watching his heaving shoulders, Hannah took her chance. She grasped Harry's arm and raced from the hall, his feet barely touching the ground as she flew along, to a chorus of giggles and chatter from the rest of the children.

Chapter Five

'*The Beggar Prince* is on at the Hippodrome in Auckland, Mam,' said Hannah. She was reading from a copy of the *Auckland Chronicle* which Mrs Holmes had given her to light the fire; the Armstrongs could no longer afford a newspaper. She was silent for a moment as she tried to picture a beggar prince in her mind – someone like Timothy Durkin, she thought, tall with blue eyes and black hair. Except that Timothy Durkin was no beggar, being the agent's son, she reminded herself.

'Hurry up with that fire, I want to melt some soap to wash the woollens through,' Mam interrupted her thoughts.

'It says here that you should buy Rinso, it's a soap powder, then you won't have to boil soap,' said Hannah. '"Rinso, the cold water washer, less waste, more comfort,"' she quoted.

'Oh aye, does it tell you what to use for money to buy it? Will they take fresh air?' Nora smiled grimly and carried on grating the bar of hard brown soap. Hurriedly, Hannah crumpled the paper, laid it in the grate and criss-crossed it with sticks garnered from the bunny banks. There were no pit-prop offcuts for the lads to bring home while the pit was still idle, they were Norwegian pine and made the best fire sticks. She piled cinders and a few lumps of coal on top of the sticks and lit the paper with a match before standing well back from it. The day was uncomfortably warm and the fire added to the discomfort immediately, but it was the only means they had of boiling water or cooking. A flame curled lazily upwards and the sticks settled, causing a charred piece of paper to fall on the hearth.

'"Considerable damage to the denes by miners seeking fuel,"' she read aloud as she picked it up. 'We could do with some of that, the coalhouse is almost empty.'

'Aye,' said Nora, sighing heavily. 'What we'll do then I don't know.'

'It's not fair, Mam, is it?'

Nora knew what Hannah meant; even if they were not locked out of the pit, Alf and Robert were too young to get a coal allowance so the Armstrongs, along with the widows in the village, were dependent on their neighbours, most of whom gave them a couple of buckets of coal when their own allowance came. But now the neighbours were short themselves.

'Nowt's fair in this world,' she said wearily. 'Now go on up to the allotment and see if Alf has any vegetables ready for the pot. I could make a dinner if I had some vegetables. You can take Walton, he could do with some fresh air.'

Hannah put Walton in the black pram which had served all the Armstrong children when they were babies, though it had been second-hand when it was bought for Alf. One of the wheels was a bit rickety but it still could be pushed along fairly easily. The hood had broken off years ago but that didn't matter either unless it rained. Today was a lovely June day and there was no chance of rain. Her heart lifted as she walked along the row to the path leading to the allotment gardens, daydreaming as she went. Walton lay on his back gurgling peacefully. He was late in trying to sit up but Mam said he would do it in his own good time.

Hannah watched him, fantasizing that he was her very own baby and she was pushing him along with her husband by her side. She soon became engrossed in the fantasy, holding an imaginary conversation with the shadowy man by her side, discussing the pros and cons of lace curtains for the parlour window and whether to paint the bathroom pale green or cream. 'We must be sure which we would like best,' she said under her breath, 'for it may have to last a long time.' Hannah had borrowed a book from the school library only last week, full of helpful hints on how to be a good housewife and mother. She tried to follow its advice with regard to Walton. 'Babies need plenty of fresh air,' the book had said, and Hannah felt virtuous as she remembered it. Walton looked up at her and smiled. Suddenly her attention was caught by loud voices coming from the allotment gardens.

'It was you. You've pinched the last of my spring cabbage!' shouted Alf.

'Aye, and what are you going to do about it?' a jeering voice answered.

Hannah rose up on her toes to peer over the hedge. It was Lancelot Cornish, standing with his hands on his hips and grinning at Alf. Hannah bit her lip. Lancelot was the same age and build as Alf, but she could see his older brother Ralph lounging on the path, holding Bob easily with one hand and carrying a stick in the other.

Enraged, Alf flung himself at Lancelot with his fists flailing and Lancelot fell back for a moment, his grin fading. But Ralph had thrown Bob aside and in two strides he reached Alf and pulled him off Lancelot. Holding him off with one hand, he felled him with a blow from his fist. Alf lay dazed as Ralph turned to Bob and instead found Hannah. She rushed at him, kicking him on the shins and pummelling him with her small fists.

'Leave my brothers alone, you great bully!' she screamed at him. Luckily for her, miners working at the other end of the allotments had heard the commotion and came running up to separate the two families. 'What's going on here?' shouted a burly hewer at Ralph. 'You fighting with bairns and lasses now, Ralph Cornish?'

'It's her went for me,' Ralph said, the bullying tone gone from his voice all of a sudden. 'And anyroad, Alf hit my little brother.'

Alf was picking himself up and fingering his jaw, which was swelling up alarmingly. 'They took my cabbage,' he mumbled thickly.

The hewer became even angrier and the other miners muttered among themselves. Stealing food was a serious offence at any time but stealing food during a lockout was heinous.

'I have a good mind to tell the polis!' one of them shouted. 'I will if you don't give the lad his cabbage back. Howay then, where have you got it hid?' The miners advanced on the Cornish brothers purposefully.

'Aw, I only meant to have a bit of a laugh with him,' said Lancelot. 'I'll get the bloody cabbage.' He walked over to the Cornish allotment, a patch of ground which was as untidy and full of rubbish as the Cornish house. He picked up the cabbage from behind a stand of stinging nettles and thrust it in Alf's face.

'Try that again and you'll have us all to answer to,' said the burly hewer. 'An' them wi' their da with a broken back an' all.' He spat on the ground at Ralph's feet to show his disgust and, satisfied, began to walk back to his own allotment. Lancelot shot a murderous look at Bob and Alf but in the end decided it was best to leave matters as they were, at least until he could catch one of them on his own. He contented himself with a snarled 'I'll fettle you later!' and sloped off after his half-brother Ralph.

Hannah felt herself shaking with the reaction, and she grasped the handle of Walton's pram as hard as she could and gritted her teeth so that her brothers wouldn't see how upset she was. But if she had looked up she would have seen that neither of them was watching her, they were grim-faced as they gazed at each other.

'Best not let yourself be caught on your own, lad,' Alf advised Bob, and Bob nodded. 'Howay then, let's be off home,' Alf went on. 'Hannah, put the cabbage in the bottom of the pram.' So the Armstrongs made their way back down the bath and cut on to the road for the village.

'You're just going to have to keep out of the way of those Cornishes,' Jake said heavily when told the story. From his bed in the chariot, he gazed keenly at the side of Alf's face, which was swelling up and turning purple. 'You'll be all right if you keep with the other men and don't let them catch you on your own.'

'That's what I told our Bob,' agreed Alf.

'There's a band concert on in the bishop's park this afternoon,' Nora put in. 'Why don't you all go together? You an' all, Betty, I can manage myself this afternoon.'

'Eeh, I don't know,' Betty started to object but Hannah could see by her face that she would really like to go. The concert was a big one, all the colliery bands for miles around were playing, for it was in aid of the locked-out miners and their families. And Betty loved to hear a brass band.

'Go on. It's Saturday, after all, there's not a lot to do, I can manage. And if you all stick together, those Cornish lads will leave you alone,' Nora urged her.

Hannah looked up anxiously at her mother, 'Can we go, Mam, me and Harry?'

'I don't know, I haven't forgotten the time you sneaked him in to school dinner and it cost me threepence I couldn't afford,' Nora said sternly and Hannah hung her head.

'Let them go, Nora, they get little enough enjoyment,' said Jake. Hannah flashed him a grateful glance.

'I'll give you a piggyback,' Alf offered Harry, and the little boy beamed. 'Mind, you'd best not be a nuisance or we'll leave you to find your own way home,' Alf threatened.

'I won't, Alf, honest,' Harry said earnestly.

They set off along the road to the footpath which led into the town of Bishop Auckland. Betty and Hannah walked together in front, laughing and talking, and Bob and Alf, with Harry on his shoulders, followed. They were not alone on the path. Quite a number of miners and their families were making their way to the bishop's park and for once the lockout seemed to be forgotten: there was a great deal of light-hearted banter as groups came together for the walk. By the time the children reached the town and turned into the straight length of Newgate Street which led down to the marketplace, the pavement was fairly taken up with miners and their families, good-naturedly jostling each other.

Hannah gazed around her, her eyes shining. It was a long time since she had been in this main shopping street and she loved it. She stopped to read one of the bills posted up on the walls between the shops.

CANADA WANTS
Men for farmers
Women for domestic work
Boys and youths to train as farmers

Apply Canada Chambers.

There was an address in London but she didn't have time to read that for Betty was looking back and calling her.

'Come on, Hannah! Don't dawdle, you know Mam said we had to stick together.'

Hannah hurried after them, her thoughts filled with what it would be like to go to Canada to work, to leave her family and friends and maybe never see them again. But then her attention was diverted by a handbill for the Hippodrome picture house. It was a cowboy film, *A Fighting Fool*, with Tom Mix, plus the story of Shackleton's expedition to the Antarctic – 'British pluck and endurance,' it said, and Hannah's heart swelled with pride. But then they saw a board outside a newsagent's which told them of Sinn Féin causing great havoc on the Durham coast with incendiary devices and explosives, and she shivered as though a cloud had passed over the sun.

The marketplace was full of stalls selling all kinds of goods; there were even some fishwives from Shields, selling cod, caller herrings, shrimps and mussels. She listened to them calling, 'Caller herring! Caller herring! Kippers, twopence a pair!' in their singsong accent, which showed they were from farther north. They saw her interest and one called over to her encouragingly, 'Come buy, hinny, twopence a pair kippers, ha'penny, a bag of shrimps.'

But Hannah shook her head and hurried after Alf, who was striding towards the castle gates with Harry on his shoulders, the little boy wriggling with excitement until Alf lost patience and put him down on the ground to walk. Hannah had only a halfpenny and much as she liked shrimps she had to keep her money to put into one of the collecting boxes in the park.

The crowd of miners walked under the stone arches of the castle gates on to the broad gravelled path which led past the castle walls to the entrance of the park. The gate in the inner castle wall was open and the people from the pit villages looked in on this other world, the green lawns and carriageway which led to the ancient castle with its mullioned windows and stone portico. But they didn't stop to gape. In the distance they could hear the sound of a band playing, too far away to recognise the tune but close enough to make Harry skip along beside his big brothers. For, of course, on a family outing like this, Harry would stay with the lads; Hannah was abandoned to walk with Betty.

There was something of a bottleneck at the old iron kissing gate which led into the park proper, but at last they were in and free to run down the grassy banks to where the bands were playing.

'By, it's grand, Hannah, isn't it?' said Harry, his eyes bright with excitement so that he forgot for a moment that he was with the lads.

'It is, pet,' Hannah agreed. She wandered over to where the Dean and Chapter colliery band from Ferryhill were playing. A small, thin young man, smart in the navy blue and red of the band uniform, was playing a trumpet solo, pure and sweet with the deeper tones of the larger horns coming in to harmonise. She was soon lost in the music. The solo was followed by brisk Souza marches and then more local tunes, 'Bobby Shafto' and 'Blaydon Races'.

The afternoon was warm and soon Harry had joined a crowd of children paddling in the stream which ran along the bottom of the little valley on its way to join the river Wear. Hannah watched, thinking it would be nice to feel the cool water over her feet herself, but Betty vetoed it.

'You're too big now to be plodging with the bairns, our Hannah,' she said sternly, so Hannah contented herself with sitting, by the side of the stream and dangling her hand in the cool water, and Betty sat beside her.

'Well, will you just look at the snooty Armstrong lasses, playing with the bairns,' a voice said behind them. Hannah's heart sank. Not another confrontation with the Cornish family, she thought, not twice in one day. This was Kathleen Cornish sneering at her and Betty, she knew that even before she looked round.

Kathleen Cornish was standing, legs apart, hands on hips and grinning from ear to ear. She had her mother's bold good looks though her hair, a brassy red, was only slightly darker than that of her father, Wesley Cornish. She was wearing a short red dress which clashed oddly with her hair and when Hannah looked closer she realised that Kathleen was wearing rouge on her cheeks and her lips were smeared unevenly with lipstick.

'Get away from us, Kathleen Cornish,' said Betty harshly.

Hannah looked up at her sister in surprise; she had never heard Betty speak so rudely to anyone. Betty's lips were compressed in a straight line and her eyes were flashing. Hannah jumped up to range herself beside Betty, though she wasn't at all sure why she was doing it.

'Ooh, think you're better than I am, do you, Betty Armstrong?' Kathleen had lost her bantering tone and she thrust her head forwards as she spoke to Betty.

'I wouldn't have to be much to be better than you,' Betty said evenly and Hannah gasped. Though she hadn't a notion what this was all about, she bunched her fists, thinking that this was fighting talk and the taller, stronger Kathleen would go for Betty so she'd better be ready to help her sister. But Kathleen looked away from the two Armstrong girls to where Alf and Bob were standing with a few of their friends on the top of a nearby knoll.

'I'm not going to belt you, I've got better things to do,' she smirked, changing her attitude completely. 'Anyroad, your Alf doesn't think he's too good for me; he likes me, he does.'

'An' you're a big liar, Kathleen Cornish,' snapped Betty. 'Alf wouldn't touch you with a bargepole, he wouldn't.'

Kathleen only smiled knowingly and minced off up the hill to where the boys were gathered, her hips swaying scandalously from side to side.

'She's a disgrace to Winton, that one, her and her mother, both,' said a woman who was sitting on the grass watching her two toddlers playing in the water. 'Eeh, it's a good job they live in Winton village, if they were still in the colliery rows the men would run them out.'

Hannah turned startled eyes on the woman and recognised her as Mrs Hutchinson, who lived a couple of streets away from them.

'Our Alf wouldn't have anything to do with her,' Betty said again, speaking for Mrs Hutchinson's benefit, Hannah could tell. From the top of the knoll came the sound of male voices laughing and mixed in with it was the high giggling of a girl.

'Alf! Bob! Howay now, we have to be going if we want to get home. Harry's tired, he'll be asleep before we get there if we don't get a move on.' She walked to the water's edge and dragged a reluctant Harry out of the water.

'I don't want to go home,' wailed the boy but it was no use, Betty was drying his feet with the large piece of rag which was her handkerchief and forcing them into his boots.

'We have to go,' she repeated. 'Now come on, be a good lad.'

Alf and Bob were walking slowly down the bank to them. 'I don't know what the hurry is,' Bob grumbled.

'It's time Harry was back,' repeated Betty. 'You know we said we'd all stick together so you'll have to come with us.'

The bands were still playing as the Armstrongs straggled up the bankside to the path.

'Piggyback, Alf,' cried Harry, 'piggyback.'

'It's our Bob's turn,' Alf replied surlily. Bob knelt down on the ground so that Harry could climb on to his back.

'I'm not carrying you all the way, mind,' he warned, but he set off jauntily enough.

Hannah and Betty were left bringing up the rear. As they emerged through the castle gates into the marketplace, they could see that some of the market traders were packing up for the day. The fishwives from Shields had already gone to catch the train, leaving a strong smell of rotting fish around the stall.

'What did you mean about Kathleen Cornish?' Hannah asked Betty as they walked along Newgate Street. They were a few feet behind the boys and unlikely to be overheard. 'Did she do something bad?'

Betty laughed shortly. 'Oh, never mind, you're too young to know,' she said, infuriating her sister.

'I'm nearly thirteen,' said Hannah, lifting her chin and sticking out her chest. 'I will be left school altogether a year come Christmas, won't I?'

Betty glanced at her brothers, who were striding out, lengthening the distance between them. She came closer to Hannah and lowered her tone.

'Her and her mother have been working in the marketplace, earning a bit extra, like.'

Hannah gazed at Betty in bewilderment. 'Well, they're lucky to get work, aren't they? What's wrong with that?'

Betty sighed and leaned even closer to Hannah's ear. 'Dafty, I mean they've been going with men for money!'

Hannah blushed scarlet, as much with embarrassment at showing her ignorance as anything else. She quickened her step to catch up with the boys for she didn't want to hear any more. She knew what it meant: it meant Kathleen and her mother were whores and harlots. And she knew because the minister had read a lesson from the Old Testament about whores and harlots and she had looked the words up in the dictionary at school and it said a harlot was a woman who hired herself for sexual intercourse, so she had looked up 'sexual intercourse' and Miss High had caught her at it and rapped her knuckles with the ruler. Hannah pushed the thought of that day from her mind. Miss High had made her feel dirty, somehow.

The family trudged home, taking much longer than they had to come into the town earlier in the day. Bob got tired of carrying Harry and made him walk once they got to the footpath through the fields, but Harry went to sleep on his feet and had to be carried anyway, Bob and Alf taking turns. When they got to the gate of their house at last, Alf didn't come in.

'I'm going out,' he said and disappeared up the row.

Chapter Six

Hannah woke up in the early dawn bathed in sweat. The wall clock in the kitchen below chiming four o'clock had brought her out of her dreams. She remembered she was in her own bed at home, and not standing in the station at Bishop Auckland waving a tearful goodbye to Alf, who was going away to Canada to be a farmer. She turned over on to her back and flung the sheet from her body and lay allowing the slight draught from the open window to cool her through her nightie. Gradually, the feeling of loss left her and her heartbeat returned to normal. Alf wouldn't go to Canada, of course he wouldn't, she told herself, it was just that advertisement in Newgate Street which had preyed on her mind.

Downstairs in the front room the baby began to cry hungrily and through the thin boards which served both as bedroom floor and kitchen ceiling, she heard her mother moving quietly about, the murmur of Da's voice and Mam's soft answer. Beside her in the bed, Betty turned over in her sleep. No one was going anywhere, Hannah told herself sleepily, there was no reason to. The lockout would be over soon and the lads would go back to work and everything would be all right again.

She began to think of the choir practice to be held in the evening and the concert next week in the big chapel in Bishop Auckland. Maybe Timothy Durkin would be there, she thought. The last time he was home from school he had come to the meeting at Chapel and he had come to choir practice too.

She liked Timothy, she mused, he always spoke to her as though she was a person and not a tiresome little girl, as Alf so often did. Though Mr Hodgson insisted on calling him Master Durkin and the rest of the choir fought shy of calling him anything at all, Hannah thought of him as Timothy, in her mind at least.

She dropped into a doze and her dreams were brighter now; she was singing with Timothy before a huge audience, a duet she'd never heard before yet was singing in perfect harmony with him and he was looking down into her eyes and smiling and he looked as grand in his fine suit, tall and dark and broad-shouldered –

'Hannah? Hannah, will you wake up now? Come down and see to Walton. I'm busy with your da.'

It was her mother's voice cutting into her dream. Hannah opened her eyes and found it was broad daylight already. Betty was gone from the bed, she had to be at work in Mr Hudson's house by eight o'clock, and Hannah could smell the smoke from the kitchen fire, lit to boil the kettle for breakfast.

Jumping up, she tossed off her nightie and pulled on her shift, stiff drawers and cotton dress. The day was going to be another warm one, from the bedroom window she could see the sun shining on the field which lay by the end of the rows and the slight haze on the higher pasture. She paused for only a second and gazed out at the pit ponies grazing there, moving slowly along with their heads down and their tails swishing rhythmically against the flies. They were having a fine holiday, she thought, now they had got accustomed to the sunlight. Picking up her boots, she ran down the cool linoleum which covered the stairs and into the hot kitchen.

'The bairn's just woken up, I let him lie because he had such a bad night. I think he's cutting a tooth, poor babby,' Mam greeted her. She had filled a bowl of water from the set pot in the range and was taking it into the front room to give Jake a bed bath.

'I'll see to him then,' Hannah answered. She bent over the pram where Walton was struggling against the belt which they used to tie him in now he was getting big enough to move about; any time now he would be sitting up by himself. The baby was soaked, not just his nappy and nightgown but the blanket and sheets down to the waterproof jaconet sheet which protected his mattress, but he smiled angelically when he saw Hannah and, as usual, a wave of love washed over her.

'Come on, pet, let's have you comfortable,' she said softly as she lifted him up, and he crowed with delight. She soon had him lying naked on a towel on the rag rug where he kicked his tiny legs and watched her preparing the tin bath for him. By the time she had him washed, dressed and sitting on her knee as she fed him arrowroot mixed with a little diluted condensed milk, Nora had finished getting Jake ready for the day and she came into the kitchen to share a cup of tea with Hannah.

'I wish we could afford to buy proper milk for the bairn, he needs it,' she said wistfully. Her tone caused Hannah to look critically at the baby. He seemed fine to her, maybe a little pale but she put that down to the heat.

'He's all right, isn't he, Mam?' she asked.

'He'd be better if I could feed him myself or if I could buy fresh milk for him,' answered her mother. 'I wouldn't like him to get rickets.'

Alarm rose in Hannah. Anxiously she stared at Walton's legs lying on her lap; they seemed like any other baby's legs to her, a little bit bent, but so had Harry's legs been and they were straight enough now. But Harry had been breast-fed for his first year, whereas Mam's milk had failed when Walton was only two months old. She thought of the children she knew at school, whose legs were bowed or knock-kneed with the rickets, and she definitely didn't want it to happen to Walton. One way or another they would have to get fresh milk from the farm if that was what he needed.

'Eeh, don't look so worried, Hannah,' said her mother. 'This lockout can't go on for ever. When the lads go back to work we'll be better able to afford things.'

When the lockout's over, thought Hannah as she poured fresh water into the tin bath and grated Sunlight soap into it to make a lather. She remembered when she was small and grown-ups were always saying, 'When the war is over, this or that would be better,' but somehow it never was. She rubbed vigorously at the baby's clothes before flinging them into a bowl of blue rinsing water and wringing them out. Though the day was warm and dry, it was Sunday and no one hung washing out on a Sunday, so she draped them over the brass line under the mantelpiece instead.

Afterwards she wheeled Walton's pram up the track to the

high pasture so that he could watch the pit ponies in the field. She had no sugar to coax them to her but she pulled a few choice dandelions from the trackside and a sturdy Shetland pony of no more than ten hands came to her and delicately took the juicy stems from her hand. Below her in the village she could see children wending their way to chapel for Sunday school. Momentarily she felt guilty, she would go to chapel and choir practice in the evening, and she couldn't leave the baby for Mam to see to in the morning as well as the evening, not when she had Da to see to. And Betty had to work at the manager's house on Sunday mornings.

Hannah looked across the field to the farmhouse and buildings, idly wondering what it would be like to belong to a farmer's family and have lots of fresh milk and eggs. The thought put an idea into her head. She would ask Farmer Burton if he had any odd jobs she could do in exchange for milk for Walton, or maybe Mrs Burton would let her help in the house or with the children. After school, of course, or maybe on a Saturday. And when she wasn't needed to see to Walton.

'Nay, lass, we have no jobs going for girls,' said Mr Burton when she reached the farmyard. A big man with a red, weather-beaten face and kindly eyes, he paused in his work of sluicing down the milking shed to look at Hannah and Walton in his decrepit pram. 'Anyroad, aren't you still at school?' he went on.

'It's nearly the summer holidays,' Hannah pointed out. 'And I meant odd jobs, something I could do after school or maybe on Saturdays,' said Hannah.

'Nay, I'm sorry, lass,' the farmer repeated. He turned off the water hose, and took a large broom and began to sweep the water from the flags with the long, slow movements of the countryman. Hannah watched him for a moment and then tried again.

'Mr Burton, do you think Mrs Burton might have some odd jobs I can do? I don't need pay, just a can of milk two or three times a week for the bairn.'

The farmer paused again. 'I don't think so, lass,' he said, but then he saw Hannah's disappointed expression and added, 'Look, lass, this farm belongs to Lord Akers, same as the mine. While your da's on strike, I'd be in trouble if I gave you work, do you see?'

'My da's not on strike,' said Hannah.

'Well, locked out then. When he goes back to work it will be different.'

'He's not locked out, his back's broken,' said Hannah.

The farmer stopped what he was doing and walked over to where she was standing holding Walton's pram.

'Are you Jake Armstrong's lass?' he asked, and Hannah nodded. Mr Burton shook his head sympathetically, tut-tutting aloud. 'I was right sorry when I heard about your da's accident,' he said. Hesitating for only a moment, he went on, 'Just you go on up to the dairy and tell the wife I say to give you a can of milk for the bairn.'

'I'll have to work for it, though, we're not to take charity, Da says.'

'Aye, well, I'm sure Mrs Burton will think of something you can do. Now go on, like I tell you.'

Hannah turned the pram round in the dusty yard, which smelled so strongly of manure it was almost as hard on the nostrils as the coke ovens, and pushed the uncomplaining Walton over to the dairy on the side of the house. She didn't have to ask, for Mrs Burton had heard her voice and had come to the door of the dairy to see who it was.

'Give the lass a can of milk, Dot,' called Mr Burton.

'But –'

'Go on, give her a can of milk,' he repeated when his wife hesitated. 'It's Jake Armstrong's bairn, you know, the one what had his back broke in the pit.'

'I'll do some odd jobs for you, Mrs Burton, I'll do anything,' Hannah said eagerly. She stood at the door of the dairy, hesitating to go in on the clean floor with her dirty boots.

'No need,' said the farmer's wife as she dipped a shining steel measure into a bucket of milk.

'I have to, Mrs Burton, or I can't take the milk,' Hannah insisted.

The woman folded her arms across her ample chest and pursed her lips as she looked down at her. 'Well, I suppose you can turn the butter churn while I scald out the milk cans,' she decided. 'Mind you clean your boots before you come in, there's a scraper by the wall if you look. Will the bairn be all right if you leave him outside?'

'Oh yes, he's asleep, Mrs Burton,' Hannah said happily and hurried to do what she was told.

'Did you go asking Farmer Burton for milk?' demanded Nora when Hannah came home and triumphantly put the can of fresh milk on the kitchen table. 'Haven't I told you we take no charity here?'

'It's not charity, Mam, I helped Mrs Burton with the churning and she gave me the milk in payment. And she says I can go up three times a week after school and I can take the baby an' all, if I like.'

'Well, I don't know . . .' Nora was doubtful at first. 'It doesn't seem much to do in return for two gills of milk.'

'It is, Mam,' Hannah reassured her. 'It's quite hard work, really. And it means we have milk for Walton and maybe some to spare to make a barley pudding or maybe even rice pudding, doesn't it?'

Nora nodded her head. It was true, fresh milk would allay her fears for Walton and a milk pudding might even stimulate Jake's appetite. He was taking less and less nourishment these days, sometimes he wouldn't eat anything at all and he was becoming thinner every day, his skin taking on a translucent, bluish hue which frightened her. She had asked Dr Short if there was nothing more he could do, or if Jake should go back into the county hospital for tests, but the dour Scottish doctor only shook his head gravely. Still, she hoped against hope that one day Jake's shattered back would begin to heal and the nerves knit together. The thought was the only thing which saved her from complete despair.

Timothy Durkin was already in chapel when Hannah took her place beside Betty. She returned his quick smile of greeting shyly, suddenly conscious of the fact that her Sunday dress of faded blue cotton was a hand-me-down from Betty and was beginning to be tight round her chest. It didn't matter, she told herself, that the skirt was short too, short skirts were fashionable. Wasn't Amy the doctor's daughter, wearing a skirt which barely covered her knees?

'Stop looking over at the lads,' Betty whispered fiercely. 'You'll catch it from Alf if he sees you making a show of yourself.'

Hannah blushed and looked down at her hymn book as the preacher announced the first hymn. They were soon standing to sing 'Summer suns are glowing', but she could hear Timothy's baritone above the rest, and she was conscious of him all through the prayers and sermon.

Betty went home after the service while Hannah stayed behind for choir practice. She stood quietly in her place, waiting for Mr Hodgson to call the choir to order, but Mr Hodgson seemed in no hurry tonight. He and the other men were discussing the lockout. Prayers had been said during the service for an early end to the dispute.

'The labourer is worthy of his hire,' said one man, 'doesn't it say so right here in the Bible? We're only asking to keep what we've got; why, man, if they get their way we won't have a living wage.'

'I doubt some of the men cannot last out,' said another. 'There is a great deal of distress in the whole coalfield. It's not for ourselves – we could manage, I think – but it's the women and the bairns.'

The men were nodding their heads in agreement when Mr Hodgson noticed Timothy standing nearby, well within earshot. 'Now then,' he said, 'this is not the time to be discussing politics. We're here to practice for the concert next Saturday night in Bishop Auckland.' He nodded meaningfully in the direction of the agent's son and Timothy lifted his chin and stared right back at him, a challenge in his eyes. 'I am not a spy, I would not tell anyone of anything I heard in chapel,' he said.

'No, no, of course, not, Master Durkin,' Mr Hodgson replied. 'Now, come along, choir, get into your places, we have a full programme to go through tonight. There is only one more rehearsal, that's on Tuesday evening at six o'clock, and I expect everyone to be on time.'

Soon they were deep into rehearsing the hymns and songs which formed the programme for the concert. Mostly hymns, of course, but one or two sacred songs and even a couple of local songs, for the concert was expected to draw in the townspeople, not just their own people. They practised for an hour and a half until at last Mr Hodgson called a halt.

'That's enough for now, then,' he said. 'Master Durkin, perhaps you'd be so kind as to stay behind with Hannah and we'll go through your duet. It won't take long, I'm sure Hannah knows it well by now and you'll pick it up quickly, you always do.'

They were to sing 'Count Your Blessings' and Hannah did indeed know it well; she had been singing it at least once a day since it was given to her by the choir master. But she found it sounded altogether different when Timothy's voice was joined to hers, and soon forgot her shyness of him as she lost herself in the music. All too soon Mr Hodgson pronounced himself satisfied and they were free to go home.

'If you wait a moment while I lock up, I'll walk you home, Hannah,' said Mr Hodgson. 'It's a mite late for a young lass to be out on her own.'

'I'll see Hannah safely back to her house,' Timothy offered.

Mr Hodgson hesitated for only a moment before agreeing. 'Very well, Master Durkin. It's very good of you, I'm sure. Well, goodnight, then. Goodnight, Hannah.'

Once outside, Hannah's shyness overcame her and she walked along by Timothy's side, desperately trying to think of something to say, anything.

'You don't have to come all the way to the door,' she ventured at last. 'It's just along the road here.'

'It's no bother,' said Timothy. he drew a paper packet out of his pocket and offered it to her. 'Won't you have a caramel?'

'Thank you,' said Hannah, awkwardly taking one of the sweets. She unwrapped it, put it in her mouth and then wished she hadn't, for how was she going to be able to talk to him with her mouth full of toffee?

Timothy was asking about the chapel in Bishop Auckland. 'Is it a large place? Will there be a big congregation?' he wanted to know.

They had arrived at the gate of the yard and Hannah paused, swallowing hastily. The sticky toffee seemed to clog her throat so that when she tried to speak her voice came out huskily.

'It's . . .' She coughed and tried again. 'It is big,' she began, but then she caught sight of Mam looking out at her from the kitchen window.

'Is that you, Hannah? Who's that with you, is it Mr Hodgson? Bring him in, do, don't keep him standing at the gate.'

'No, Mam, it's Timothy Durkin.'

'Who? Bring him in, whoever it is. If he's been good enough

to walk home with you, he's good enough to bring in and thank properly.'

'I don't think – Timothy began, but Hannah was already walking up the yard and, after a moment's hesitation, he followed.

'Timothy is in the choir, Mam,' said Hannah as they went inside. She looked around the kitchen, seeing it with new eyes as she remembered the hallway of the Durkin house where the choir had sung carols last Christmas. The old wooden table had a worn cover of American oilcloth and behind it was a mahogany press which had belonged to Nora's mother and had seen better days. The black-leaded range shone brightly enough but now that the dinner was over the fire had been allowed to go out; there was coal only for cooking during the lockout so the iron kettle was not in its usual place, singing on the bar.

She saw her mother's face was a fierce red and suddenly Hannah remembered that the last time Mam had seen Timothy was in the pit yard when his father had so humiliated her.

'Timothy brought me home from the choir practice, Mam,' she said lamely.

'I'm sure it was very good of Master Durkin,' Mam said, not looking at Hannah but staring hard at Timothy. 'I'm sorry we can't offer you a cup of tea, Master Durkin. As you can see, we have no coal for the fire.'

Timothy looked as embarrassed as Nora. 'No, no, don't think of it, I must be on my way home. I have to be . . . I must get back . . . Goodbye, Hannah, Mrs Armstrong.' He turned and almost ran down the yard to the gate.

'Why did you bring a lad like that in here?' Nora demanded.

'But you said to bring him in, Mam,' Hannah answered. She was mortified, for she had seen the shabby kitchen as Timothy saw it, poverty-stricken, and she had seen the shock in his eyes. Miserably she stared up at her mother. 'He was just helping Mr Hodgson, bringing me home.'

'You could have come home yourself, it's nobbut a stride,' snapped Nora. 'Now get away up to bed, Betty's been there this last half-hour. What the agent's son wants coming to our chapel I don't know. Why doesn't he stick to his own kind?'

'He likes to sing in the choir, Mam, he's a good singer,' said Hannah.

'Aye, well, do they not sing in their church, like?' retorted her mother. 'Now go on, away to bed with you.'

Timothy was walking through the fields to Durham Road, his mind full of conflicting images. In all his seventeen years he had never been inside one of the miners' cottages until now, even though he had lived on the outskirts of Winton all his life. He was shaken by the poverty he had seen. To be unable to boil a kettle because there was no coal in the coalhouse? A miner's coalhouse? Of course, he knew by what his father had said almost every day since he came home from school for the holidays, that it was their own fault, the men were on strike, even though they themselves disputed the fact, saying they were locked out. But how could Hannah's father be on strike? Wasn't he disabled, injured in the pit? Surely he should have a coal allowance?

Timothy left the fields behind him and walked up the metalled road which led to Durham Road and his home. For the first time he was beginning to question his father's views.

Chapter Seven

The evening of the concert was fine and dry so the choir could walk into Bishop Auckland from Winton without fear of getting their feet wet, an important thing from Hannah's point of view because her boots had got too tight and she had to walk in sandshoes. The chapel in Cockton Hill was thronged with people for all the seats had been sold. She had been worried that Timothy wouldn't come and she would have to sing the duet with Hodgson, but as she walked up the path with the other girls of the choir she saw his tall figure standing in the porch waiting for them. There was not much time for greetings; the stewards were hurrying them into position along with the other choirs. There was to be an address by the minister before the concert and it was almost time to begin.

'Hallo, Hannah,' Timothy found time to say. 'You were right, it is a big chapel, almost as big as St Andrew's.'

Hannah smiled at him in relief, not only because he had actually turned up but also because he seemed the same as ever. But she couldn't say anything for Mr Hodgson was hushing them into silence and in the main body of the church the murmuring of voices had stopped as the audience looked to the front expectantly.

Mr Hughes, the minister, began with a short prayer and thanked everyone for coming before getting to the main business of the evening.

'As you know, this evening's proceeds are for the relief of the distress in the town and surrounding villages. Consequently, if anyone finds it in their hearts to add a little extra to their ticket money, there will be a retiring collection plate by the door as you leave after the concert. As the good Lord has blessed you, so we ask for your donations to this worthy cause. Now, with no more ado, we will do our best to entertain you and earn your contributions.'

Hannah's heart fluttered with nervousness as the organist began to play the grand organ with its silver pipes reaching to the roof. But somehow she forgot her misgivings as the choirs went from hymns to sacred songs interspersed by soloists. The choir from Winton sang 'Bobby Shafto', the lament of a young girl of long ago who lost her lover when he sailed away to London to become the Member of Parliament for Durham. And then it was time for her duet with Timothy.

There was a rustle of surprise when they went to the front, the girl in her shabby blue dress and the tall boy in his fine broadcloth suit. Quite a few people recognised him and there were some raised eyebrows in the pews. They sang 'Count Your Blessings' and, for an encore, an old miner's song, 'The Caller', their voices ringing out clear and true, each the perfect complement for the other. The song was about a knocker-up man who went round the miners' houses, calling weary men who were due to go on shift from their beds.

'Ho, marras, 'tis the Caller cries,
And his voice in the gloom of the night mist dies.'

It was the third and fourth verses that affected the audience, as Mr Hodgson had thought they would when he included them in the programme. The clear young voices filled the crowded chapel.

'The collier sleeps e'en now he's dreaming
of a pure bright world, and loved ones there.
He basks in the rays of fortune beaming
In some far land full and fair.

Dream on, thou poor and ill-used collier,
slaves may have visions bright.
There's one above who deems thee holier
than the wealthiest in His sight.'

As Mr Hodgson had hoped, the song was a great success and the collecting plate was full when the crowd left the chapel.

Hannah was only thankful she hadn't forgotten her lines. Afterwards, when the choirs were invited into the schoolroom to partake of the supper laid on for them, she found herself overwhelmed by the number of people who wished to congratulate her and Timothy. There was only one thing which marred the occasion for her. Timothy suddenly decided he had to go home early.

It was just after a distinguished-looking gentleman came up to them. 'Well, Timothy,' he said, a rather puzzled expression on his face. 'I didn't expect to see a Durkin here, let alone one taking part in the concert. Though you sang very well, my boy, very well indeed.'

'Thank you, sir,' Timothy answered, and after a moment the gentleman moved on.

'I have to go, I'm sorry,' Timothy blurted and hurried out before Hannah could even say goodnight to him.

'Well, sir, what do you think you are about?'

It was a few days after the concert and as Timothy came down to breakfast he found his father waiting for him, in such an angry mood that he didn't even bother to greet his son, merely barking the question at him.

'Good morning, Father,' Timothy said. He helped himself to bacon and eggs from the hotplate on the sideboard, more for something to do than because he felt hungry. In fact, his appetite had left him as he realised that Mr Hall, the gentleman who had greeted him on the evening of the concert, must have spoken to his father, as he had dreaded he would do.

'Well, damn you, what have you to say for yourself?' demanded his father. Timothy was granted a few minutes' grace to gather his thoughts as the housemaid brought in a fresh pot of coffee.

'Thank you, May,' he said to her as she picked up the empty pot and took it out of the room.

'I'm waiting,' said Mr Durkin, once she had closed the door behind her.

'I'm not sure what you mean, Father.'

'You know what I'm talking about all right. What sort of a fool do you think I looked when old Hall told me my own son was taking part in a concert at the Primitive Methodists' and not only that, he actually sang some damn fool song about the poor miners?'

Mr Durkin's face had been getting redder and redder and his voice rose angrily until he was almost shouting.

Timothy looked down at his plate but he hardly saw the congealing food there. Mr Hall hadn't taken long to rush to his father with the story, he thought bitterly. A businessman in the town, Timothy had been surprised to see him at the concert, he had thought none of his father's friends would be there.

'You'd better answer me, my lad, or by God I'll take a strap to you, big as you are!'

Timothy put down his unused knife and fork and stared his father straight in the eye. 'I joined the choir at Winton Chapel,' he said. 'You know I enjoy singing and they have a good choir for a mining village. I'm not hurting anything by going there.'

'Not hurting anything? Why, you've made me the laughing stock of the club! My son going to a Methodist chapel, I'll not have it, do your hear? Church of England, that's the only church for gentlemen of our class and don't you forget it. How dare you shame me by going to that bloody place?'

'It's perfectly respectable, Father, else why was Mr Hall there?' Timothy was stung into replying, rashly, as he saw by his father's face, which was turning from red to purple.

'Where Mr Hall goes is his business! But you will not go there again, do you hear me? And of all things, you not only go to a concert in aid of the wretched miners, you have to take part in it! When you know of this dispute? How on earth do you expect us to get the stubborn fools to be reasonable and go back to work at a realistic wage if people are for ever giving them handouts? The wages bill was crippling the industry, haven't I said it time and time again? These people don't seem to realise how well off they are, nothing to worry about but putting in a fair week's work and getting paid for it.'

'They don't seem to be very well off to me,' Timothy muttered.

Mr Durkin practically exploded. 'No, of course they're not now, but whose fault is that? All they have to do is go back to work and earn their pay, haven't I just told you?' He stood up from the table, upsetting his coffee cup over the damask tablecloth. Striding over to the fireplace, he turned with his back to it, the better to be able to glare down at his son.

Unhappily, Timothy watched the brown stain spread on the cloth. He thought of the poverty he had seen in the village, especially in Hannah's house, where her father lay, injured in one of the pits his father was responsible for. He remembered the shock he had been hard put to hide when he entered the kitchen of the house, a house without even the means to boil a kettle now the mine was laid idle. But his father was talking again.

'We could handle the miners, even the leaders and trouble-makers. Or I could, at least, and most of the other agents and owners too. All you have to do for some of them is give them free beer. Aye, we could handle them all right if it wasn't for these damn left-wing, teetotalling Methodists.'

'Father, a labourer is worthy of his hire.' Timothy quoted a saying which he'd heard often in the chapel the last few times he had been there. This only enraged Mr Durkin further.

'Get out of my sight!' he yelled, causing Mary, who was just coming in to clear the breakfast table, to drop the tray with a tremendous clatter, which served to emphasise his words. 'Go to your room, sir, how dare you presume to judge me? Get out this minute! You won't get another chance to defy me, you'll go to my brother's house in Yorkshire until it's time for you to go back to school. And think yourself lucky I don't throw you out of the house now, without a penny to bless yourself with! Get out!'

It was hard to tell whether the last 'Get out!' was directed at Mary or Timothy; the poor girl turned and ran for the kitchen in a flood of tears and Timothy had no option but to retire to his room.

He was not allowed to stay there long. Mr Durkin lost no time in getting in touch with his brother by telephone, and Timothy was packed off on the afternoon train for York, there to spend the rest of his summer holiday in the gloomy house of his father's elder brother.

Hannah never knew why Timothy stopped coming to chapel or choir practice. She was unhappy about it at first, but she was so busy during the summer, what with seeing to baby Walton and doing odd jobs for Mrs Burton, the farmer's wife, that she had little time to think about anything else. By reading snippets from the old *Auckland Chronicles* which Mrs Holmes gave the Armstrongs, she knew that the miners wanted a National Wages Board but the owners would not agree to it. The owners insisted that the men give in and agree to their terms before they would be allowed back to work. Peter Lee, the Durham miners' leader, told a *Chronicle* reporter, 'Some of our men, if they went back at the price offered, would have very little over two pounds a week.'

But the men knew they had little chance of holding out and despair hung like a cloud over the pit rows, lightened only by the pit-pony Derby which was held one hot afternoon, in aid of the miners' families. Mr Hodgson and the other Methodists frowned on such a way of making money but there was no doubt it was a great success, with the ponies being ridden by their drivers. The mine managers turned a blind eye to the proceedings for, after all, the ponies were getting fat and needed exercising and, in any case, they knew that they were winning the dispute.

Alf and Bob came home full of excitement about the races.

'There was a Lockout Handicap and a Workingman's Club Stakes,' Bob told his mother and Hannah. 'And I had a threepenny bet in the Aged Miners' Cup and I won at three to one so I had a shilling back.'

Hannah was slightly scandalised that her brother should have had a bet on a horse, even though it was only a pit pony, but she smiled delightedly at him nevertheless. 'That's grand, Bob,' she said, and meant it. At least, she thought, Bob seemed to be settling down with the family now and there had been no more trouble with the Cornish brothers, thank goodness.

The following week, the miners had to give in to the owners' demands and go back to work on reduced wages. The dispute was over and everyone felt that it would be a good job when 1921 was over, it had not been a good year. There had not even been a Miners' Gala in Durham city that July, for the pit folk had nothing to celebrate.

'Kathleen Cornish and her mother are coming down the row,' reported Harry as he came in from playing cricket in the back lane with his friends. He carried the fire shovel with him, for it had been the bat, and the stumps were chalked on the wall of the coalhouse.

His mother looked startled. 'Sally Cornish? I didn't think she had the brass to show her face in the rows after the way those two carried on during the lockout.'

It was Harry's turn to look surprised. 'What did they do, Mam?' he asked.

'Never you mind,' was all Nora had time to say before she saw Sally and her daughter Kathleen turn into the back yard and walk up to the door.

'Are you there, Mrs Armstrong?'

Sally didn't wait for an answer before marching into the kitchen. The family were all home except for Alf, who was on shift at the pit, and Betty, who was at her work at the Hudson house. Alf had graduated from the coal screens and now worked as a putter underground on the adult shift system. Mrs Cornish looked round the room and nodded at Jake in his chariot in the corner.

'How are you, Jake? I was meaning to come and see you but you know how it is when there's a family to see to,' she said, her tone full of solicitude. Nora gasped at it. It was almost a year since Jake had been injured and none of the Cornish family had even enquired after him. And they would not have been welcome in the rows if they had.

Hannah, who was sitting with Walton on her knee while she fed him mashed potatoes and gravy, paused with the spoon halfway to his mouth and stared at Kathleen. The older girl looked different from the last time she had seen her; her face was devoid of make-up and her carroty hair hung lank and dull. Baby Walton lifted his hand to the spoon and cried at this sudden cessation of his feeding and Hannah hastily put the spoon to his mouth.

'What do you want, Sally?' asked Nora, her voice grim.

'It's not me, it's our Kathleen, poor lass. She's fallen wrong with a bairn and I want your Alf to do the right thing by her.'

Hannah stared at her. What on earth had it to do with Alf? She'd known other girls in the rows to be expecting a baby before they were married, but usually all it meant was that they married their sweethearts a bit earlier than intended. But Alf was not Kathleen's sweetheart, of course he wasn't. Alf was only just sixteen and Kathleen was almost twenty.

'Alf? It has nothing to do with our Alf!' said Jake, echoing Hannah's thoughts.

'Aye but it has!'

Mrs Cornish put her hands on her hips and glared determinedly from him to Nora. Beside her, Kathleen nodded her head vigorously to support her mother's assertion.

'Don't you come here with your tales about my lad,' Nora warned them, her cheeks turning pink and her eyes flashing. 'Hannah, take Harry and the babby into the front room out of the way. Whatever lies these two are saying are not for young ears.'

'Aw, Mam, I'm hungry, I want my tea,' Harry wailed, but his mother cut him off short.

'Do as you're told, go on with Hannah,' she snapped. 'Take a piece of bread and dripping if you're hungry.' Hannah picked a slice of bread from the plate on the table and smeared beef dripping on it for Harry. She closed the door to the front room behind her and sat down by the fireplace with the baby leaning on her shoulder sleepily. Even with the door closed her sharp ears could pick up everything that was said in the kitchen.

'Our Alf hasn't been with your lass,' Mam said flatly.

'Well, she says he has,' retorted Sally Cornish. 'An' I believe her an' all. If our Kathleen says the bairn's Alf's then that's whose it is. And I want to know what he's going to do about it.'

'Nothing, that's what he'll do,' said Mam, her voice rising. 'Why, by all reports she has been with all sorts down in the marketplace at Auckland. I dare say she could name any amount of lads as could be responsible for her condition, but Alf is not one of them, do you hear me?'

'Don't you shout at me. I'm as good as you are, I'm as good as any of the Armstrongs. I'll set our Wesley on to you, that I will do, and our Ralph an' all.'

'Oh, aye, like the big bully set on Bob, a lad half his size. If you think we're feared of you or your bullyboys, you're sadly mistaken. You're no better than you should be yourself. Don't think you weren't seen plying your mucky trade in the town, there's many a one from the rows saw you.'

Against Hannah's shoulder, the baby stirred restlessly, disturbed by the anger in his mother's voice, and Hannah cuddled him, rocking him in her arms. Harry came and stood close to her; the raised voices had upset him too.

'Well! You bloody evil-minded old –' Sally began, but she was interrupted by Kathleen.

'Mam, don't, you know I need Alf,' she said.

'Aye, I bet you do,' Jake said grimly. 'Eeh, if I could only get up from this damn bed –'

'Whisht now, Jake, don't take on,' Nora put in swiftly. 'It's bad for you to get upset, you know it is. I won't let them get away with this, don't worry now.'

'We're not wanting to get away with anything,' said Sally, changing her tone altogether. 'But my lass has been taken down and your Alf is responsible. All we want is for him to face up to his responsibilities, own up and give the bairn a father. It's no more than anybody would expect, you can't always have your fun and get away scot-free.'

'Get out of my house, the pair of you, and don't come near us again!' Jake suddenly roared. 'Whores, the pair of you, the lass as bad as her mother! What do you take us for, bloody fools? If the lass has no father for her bairn, that doesn't mean she can name the first lad she thinks of. Anyroad, she's no worse than her mother, is she? You came back here to Winton with Ralph a nameless babby and no sign of a father for him. An' worse, you took Meg Cornish's man away from her, leaving her to bring up her bairns on her own; don't think the folk round here have forgotten about that. Not that Wesley Cornish amounts to anything, big nowt that he is. Get out of my sight, I'm warning you, and if you send your lads round here I'll set the polis on them.'

Hannah was sitting with one arm round Harry by now and the other holding the baby. Her heart was beating painfully against her ribs. She was sure Ralph and Lancelot Cornish, even Wesley, would be coming round and forcing Alf to marry Kathleen somehow, and if he wouldn't do it they would get their revenge on the Armstrongs.

'We're going, we're going,' she heard Sally say, sounding less sure of herself all of a sudden. 'But we're not beaten yet. You ask Alf if he's been with our Kathleen when he comes in. He'll be a bloody liar if he says he hasn't.'

It was very quiet after Kathleen Cornish and her mother had gone. Harry moved away from Hannah's protective arm, remembering that he was a big boy now and old enough to go to school. Hannah laid the sleeping baby in his cot and after hesitating for a short while, she opened the door which connected the front room with the kitchen.

Jake was lying, white and silent, his eyes closed. Her mother was in the act of lifting the iron pan on to the fire to warm up the boiled meat pudding which would be Alf's dinner when he came in from the pit.

'Is my dinner ready now, Mam?' Harry asked, his fears forgotten as his hunger returned.

'Yes, sit down at the table, it's waiting in the oven,' his mother said quietly. In the distance they heard the sound of the hooter at the pit, signalling the change of shifts. 'Hannah, bring in the bath tin, Alf will be here in a minute.'

'Yes, Mam.'

Hannah went into the back yard and took the bath down from where it was hanging on a nail on the wall. She brought it in and placed it on the clippie mat before the fire and got the ladle tin, ready to ladle the water from the boiler as soon as Alf walked in the door. If his bath wasn't ready for him, Alf was usually so hungry he would eat his dinner in his pit dirt, which meant that Hannah had to wait until he had had his bath so that she could empty it and clear away any mess, and that made her late in going up to Burton's farm. But as it happened, she need not have bothered. As soon as Alf walked into the house, her mother turned to her.

'Go on, Hannah, get away up to the farm now. I can see to Alf's bath and put the little 'uns to bed. Anyroad, Betty will be coming in just now, she'll give me a hand.'

Hannah didn't argue, she knew her parents wanted her out of the way while they talked to Alf. 'Righto, I'll be as quick as I can,' she said. 'I think there'll just be the eggs to wash tonight, Mrs Burton might give me a few to bring home an' all.' She took her coat down from the hook on the back door and went out quickly without looking at Alf. But not too quickly to miss Harry's eager question to his brother.

'Alf, Mrs Cornish says you took their Kathleen down. Did you, Alf? What's taken down mean, Alf?'

Chapter Eight

'You've been a proper fool, Alf,' said Jake.

It was the week after Kathleen Cornish and her mother had visited the Armstrongs and by now the news was all over Winton, even the children in school were saying that Alf Armstrong would have to marry Kathleen Cornish. For the trouble was that Kathleen and her mother had retired from their trade when the pit was working again and, what was more, someone had seen Alf with her up among the bunny banks. So no one bothered any more about telling Hannah to leave the room when the subject was being discussed.

Alf hung his head, his face the colour of beetroot. 'Aye, I know, Da,' he muttered.

'Well, I still think she's blaming you for another lad's work,' said Nora. 'An' I don't see why you should marry that piece. So I've been thinking. You should go away to work, I hear there's work in the south, you can go there. Why, if you look in the *Northern Echo* you can see loads of advertisements for strong working lads.'

Hannah felt a sudden tightening in her chest – was Alf going to have to leave Winton? Agitated, she turned to the baby in his pram so her back was to the others and they couldn't see how dismayed she was.

'What, leave the pit?' Alf was startled enough to raise his face and look his mother straight in the eye, something he hadn't wanted to do these last few days.

'What's wrong with that? The pit hasn't done this family any favours, has it? No, you'd be better off in a nice clean factory, I saw one on the news at the pictures the last time I was there.'

'But, Mam, what'll you do without my money?' asked Alf. 'We're hard put to manage as it is.'

'An' how much do you think I'd see of your money once that lass gets her claws into you?' demanded Nora. 'No, me and your da's been talking it over and we think that's the best thing for you to do.'

'I don't want to go away,' Alf said miserably.

'Aw, don't go like a soft bairn on us now, lad,' said Jake. 'If you were man enough to go with a woman you're man enough to go away to work. You'll be able to come home sometimes, the lasses do it all the time, go away to place and come home for a summer holiday every year.'

Which is true enough, thought Hannah. She was dreading the day when she might have to go away herself in search of work, for there was precious little in Winton or even in Bishop Auckland.

'It's not right,' said Bob hotly, 'If one of us can leave the pit and go away it should be me. You know I want to work with Uncle Billy on the carrier wagon, don't you?'

Nora looked at his flushed face sadly. 'I'm sorry lad, I am,' she said. 'It's just the way things have turned out, isn't it? It's nobody's fault but that lying Kathleen Cornish.'

Bob looked from his mother to Alf, a picture of frustration, then he muttered something which Hannah didn't catch and, picking up his cap from the side table, he planted it on his head and rushed out of the door.

'He'll get over it,' his mother commented as she watched him leave the yard.

Alf and his mother went into Bishop Auckland to the Labour Exchange to see what sort of jobs were available in the south of England, though Alf had to be persuaded into it. But the weeks were passing by and Kathleen's belly was getting bigger, perhaps bigger than it should have been if it was conceived when she said it was, Nora hinted darkly to anyone who would listen. Mrs Cornish lay in wait to catch Nora on her way to the store so she could demand to know when Alf was going to do right by her lass. And in the pit, Wesley Cornish was making sarcastic remarks, whenever Alf was near, about lads that wanted their fun but didn't want to pay for it. So far, Nora had managed to be vague about setting a date for the wedding but she knew she couldn't keep it up for ever.

'You'll likely be able to make good money,' she encouraged him as they boarded the bus which nowadays went all the way into the marketplace in Auckland. 'You'll be able to get decent lodgings and still send us a bit home.'

He gazed at her, his normally open face full of trouble. But it was an altogether brighter Alf who came home a couple of hours later.

'We're to go to Oxford,' he said. 'There's a party of us going down to be apprenticed to the Morris Car Company. Just think, I'm going to make cars. And the pay is good when you've learned the job, and they find you lodgings an' all.'

Hannah beamed at him. Alf liked cars, he always watched them with great interest on the rare occasions when one came into the village, other than the bull-nosed Morris coupé which belonged to Dr Short. She could see her brother was thrilled to be actually going to work where cars were made.

'Aye, well, keep it to yourself for now,' warned Jake. 'You don't want it to be getting about that you're going, do you? Best if it doesn't get back to the Cornishes.'

Alf looked worried. 'But there's a group of us going, Da, about twenty, they might hear of it. Though luckily I'm the only one from Winton.'

'It'll be all right, you'll see,' said Nora. 'Everything will turn out champion.'

Bob muttered something which Hannah couldn't catch and she looked across the table at him enquiringly.

'What did you say, Bob?'

'I said I think I'll go over to Consett and see Grandma this weekend,' he replied, staring hard at his mother as if challenging her to say that they couldn't afford the fare. But Nora merely nodded in understanding.

'Aye, that's a good idea, Bob,' she said. 'It's a while since you went over to see her.' She would just have to put off her visit to Weardale to see Jane until she had saved the fare again, she thought. Maybe when she went to the Co-op store she would buy a pretty card and send it to her, the stamp would only cost a halfpenny.

Hannah went to bed that night sad that Alf was going away. 'At least he's not going to Canada,' she whispered to herself remembering the poster in Newgate Street. 'Not halfway across the world.' But what with Jane going away to the sanatorium and now Alf leaving home, she felt the family was breaking up, though she knew it was silly to think like that. Alf would come home some time and so would Jane as soon as she was better. And she *would* get better, Hannah told herself, the sanatorium would make her better, even if it did take a long time to do it.

So Alf went to Oxford, or rather to a place called Cowley, Oxon. Hannah puzzled about that until she could look it up in the atlas at school and found that Cowley was to Oxford rather as Winton was to Bishop Auckland, a separate place really but almost a suburb. And Oxon was to Oxford city as County Durham was to Durham city, it was just a different way of putting it.

He managed to get away without the Cornish family finding out until it was too late, and their fury was a sight to behold.

'Your Alf's done wrong by my lass,' screamed Sally. She had marched round to the Armstrong house as soon as she heard about Alf's going and now she stood at the back door, her hair falling over her red face and her once blue dress stained a patchy black. The floral-print apron tied round her waist was, if anything, even dirtier than her dress and her feet were thrust into an unlaced pair of men's boots. She bunched her hands into fists as Nora went to the door, and, seeing it, Hannah hastily put the baby in his cot pram and went to support her mother.

'I wasn't going to let you blame Alf for something he didn't do,' Nora said determinedly and she took hold of the door with one hand and pushed it shut so that Sally had to jump back hastily.

'Close the door on me, would you?' she bawled, spittle spouting from her mouth and dribbling down her chin. She took her fist and banged loudly on the door till Hannah thought she could see it shake.

'Hey, what's all this?'

Hannah looked out of the window and saw that the noise had brought their neighbours to the gate and Mr Holmes, the overman, was walking up the yard.

'These bloody Armstrongs think they're better than the rest of us,' shouted Sally. 'There's my Kathleen so badly she cannot get out of bed, all because that Alf Armstrong's deserted her.'

'You come away this instant, woman, or I'll call the polis,' said Mr Holmes and Hannah blessed the fact that he was the night shift overman and so happened to be at home when the ruckus started.

Sally faltered for only a moment when he confronted her, then she appealed to the crowd at the gate. 'What about my lass, abandoned and with a bairn on the way? By, if she was one of yours, you would make sure right was done by her, I dare swear.' But she stopped when she realised that the onlookers were hostile to her, not to the Armstrongs.

'You should be ashamed of yourself, coming round here, Sally Cornish!' shouted Mrs Hardy from next door. 'I thought we'd chased you from the rows long since, you brazen-faced hussy! And now you come pestering a family where the man's lying with his back broke. Get away from here, or I'll send you on your way meself.'

'No need for that,' said Mr Holmes. 'Just go and get Mr Parry. I'll stay here and see she does no more harm.'

Sally gasped. 'Do you mean to say you'd set the polis on me? When you know it was Alf Armstrong?'

'Aw, you never fooled anybody,' jeered a voice from the back of the crowd. 'Why, man, the lad's only sixteen, good luck to him, I say, even if he did do it. I'm pleased he's got away from here. There's nowt for the young folk here and that's the truth.'

Sally suddenly stopped blustering and started to cry, great drunken sobs which made Hannah realise for the first time that she had been drinking, even though it was only the middle of the afternoon.

'Come on, Mrs Cornish,' said Mr Holmes, 'you'd best away home.' He spoke quietly now for he could see that she was defeated. Gulping, she wiped her eyes on her filthy pinafore and started down the yard without a backward glance at the house. Mr Holmes walked with her though with a couple of yards between them for the rank smell of her had been somehow intensified by the scene. The crowd at the gate parted silently to allow her through. Her unlaced boots flopped up and down on her ankles as she walked up the row. Cautiously, Hannah opened the door and went to peep round the gate. When Sally was almost to the end of the row and when she got there she turned to face the crowd still lingering in case there was anything more to see.

'Right!' she bellowed. 'Right! I know none of you likes me and mine though what I ever did to you I don't know. But we'll get our own back, me and mine, just you wait till my Wesley finds out about this.'

Hannah's heart beat fearfully as Sally stumped off round the corner. Not that she was frightened for herself, but for Bob she was, he was on his own now without even Alf to stand by his side. What might Lancelot Cornish or Ralph do to him if they caught him on his own?

'Please watch out for yourself, Bob,' she pleaded with him when he came in.

'Aw, I'm not frightened of Lancelot Cornish,' he boasted. 'Anyroad, who could be frightened of a fellow with a cissy name like Lancelot?'

But Hannah wasn't taken in by her brother's bravado and she noticed that when he went backwards and forwards to the pit he always managed to be in among a crowd of others, mostly older men, and he rarely went out at night on his own.

The warm weather gave way to the sharp northeast winds of autumn and the days became steadily colder. In Winton the pit was working normally though not all the seams reopened. The winding wheel buzzed round busily and the smell from the cokeworks was as sulphurous as ever.

'Farmer Burton says I can begin potato picking for him on Monday, Mam,' Hannah said as she came in from the farm one Saturday evening.

'What about school?' asked Nora wearily.

'It'll be all right, there are always some people take the time off to go potato picking, Mam. And I can earn six shillings if I work the week.'

'Well, there's no doubt it will come in handy. I had a postal order for five shillings from Alf this morning, he's a good lad, he sends the money every fortnight, bless him. But it's not the same as having him at the pit.'

'Well, there's talk of some seam closure there,' Bob put in. He was sitting in the rocking chair before the fire, in the seat which had been his father's, then Alf's, and which Bob had now inherited. 'Some of the putters are expecting getting laid off.'

Nora sighed. 'Aye, these are bad times, Christmas coming on an' all. Everybody is hard up. It's paying back the five shillings a week to the Co-op store to pay for the groceries they had during the lockout that's the trouble. If things don't get any better they'll be paying till Kingdom come. Thank God we owe nobody anything.'

'Aye, but we have nothing, either,' grumbled Bob.

Hannah gazed sympathetically at him. He was fed up, she knew, because he hadn't the fare to go to Consett for the weekend. The last time he had been there he came home full of tales of how Uncle Billy had let him drive the wagon from the station with the parcels for Walter Willson's, the grocery store and the Meadow Dairy too.

'That's what I'll do one day, Hannah,' he said, determination making his boyish features seem older. 'When I'm twenty-one I'll be able to do what I want to do.'

Hannah knew what she wanted to do also, though she kept it to herself, fearing that if she told anyone it would never happen. She wanted to go to night school in Bishop Auckland as soon as she left school altogether; she wanted to better herself. 'I'll learn shorthand and typing,' she promised herself, 'as soon as I can save the money for the fees.' She felt sure that a bright girl with ambition and office skills could rise to great things in Auckland, maybe in a bank or the Co-op store. The only trouble would be finding the fees for night school but, one way or another, she would get the money. Hannah was determined she was not going to go into service, neither locally in Bishop Auckland nor away from home.

But 1921 was not yet finished with the Armstrongs. Before the year was out tragedy struck.

It was in the cold hard days of December, when an icy wind whistled through the crack in the back door and played havoc with Nora's rheumatism, that Jake Armstrong died. Hannah was lying in bed, snuggled against her sister to preserve the warmth under the bedclothes, when she heard her mother's terrible cry.

'Jake! Oh, my God, Jake!'

Both Betty and Hannah jumped out of bed and flung themselves down the stairs to the open door of the front room.

Their mother was leaning over the box on wheels which was Jake's 'chariot', her arm across his thin chest and her head buried in the pillow beside the still, gaunt face. The girls moved into the room, automatically going one to either side until they were standing close.

Hannah looked down at her father's face, and even in her grief she noticed that the lines of pain which she had become used to seeing in his face had smoothed out somehow, he was lying as though asleep. For a moment she thought her mother was mistaken, he seemed so peaceful, but then she realised how still he was, his mouth dropped slightly open in death, his eyes not properly closed. There was no breathing, none at all.

Nora's wild keening stopped and she got to her feet, only one convulsive sob racking her frame before she picked up a towel which she had brought in ready for Jake's morning wash and dried the tears from her face. 'What will we do, Jake, what will we do without you?' she asked softly now, and her daughters began to weep together quietly, tears running down their faces. In the corner, Walton awoke and for once Hannah did not run straight to him so that his cries became louder and louder and he struggled to a sitting position in his pram and glared at his mother and sisters in outrage.

'See to the bairn, Hannah,' his mother said quietly and Hannah dried her eyes and went over to the baby.

The rest of the day went in a blur for her, feeding and changing Walton and helping Betty clean and tidy the house in readiness for the visitors who would be coming to pay their respects. A telegram had to be sent to Consett to tell Jake's mother of his death, the doctor had to be fetched and Mr Hudson, the colliery manager, had to be informed; these were all tasks which Bob could do. The house was busy until the funeral, filled with visitors coming and going, and Hannah was expected to keep Harry and the baby out of the way for most of the time.

The funeral was held on the Wednesday before Christmas and it was on the morning of the funeral that the envelope came from Mr Hudson containing a voucher for six pounds to pay for the funeral expenses and a letter explaining that in accordance with the agreement reached by the Coal-Owners' Association, no more compensation was due, since Mr Armstrong was not deemed to have died from his injuries following the accident as he had lived more than one year after it had happened. Nora stared at it, her expression unreadable, then she put it away in the top drawer of the press.

It was a fine day, cold but sunny, when Jake Armstrong was buried in the churchyard of St Martin's. Mrs Holmes looked after the two youngest Armstrongs so that Hannah and Betty could follow their father's coffin to chapel and from there to the churchyard. Grandma was down from Consett and she walked dry-eyed with Nora, followed by Alf who came up from Oxford on the train. The houses in the rows drew their curtains as a mark of respect until the funeral party had passed, and most of the men off shift were waiting respectfully at the doors of the chapel to follow the family inside. Afterwards, the Co-op Funeral Service supplied a tea of ham sandwiches and cakes, all included in the six pounds.

What amazed Hannah, who was still a mass of pain and jangling nerve endings, was the hearty way the guests put away the feast, the plates being emptied so rapidly she began to fear there would not be enough. At last everyone appeared to have eaten their fill and drunk all the tea they needed. And they sat back and began to reminisce about her father, what a good man he had been, a good father to his bairns, a good and reliable worker for his marras in the pit, how he had borne his injuries with such fortitude. So gradually, as the afternoon wore on, the memory of Jake began to acquire a saintly overlay which Hannah couldn't recognise.

A great weariness was overtaking her and when she looked at her mother she could see that she too looked wearied to death. The guests seemed to have realised it too and, one by one, they began to leave until only the family were left and they could all relax around the kitchen fire.

'How are you off for money, Nora?' asked Grandma. 'I know it's not the day to be bringing it up, but I have to go back to Consett the morn. And it's something that has to be talked about. Now I can spare a bit if you're short. Was there any insurance on Jake?'

Nora shook her head. 'No, I couldn't manage to keep it up. But at least the funeral's paid for. I'll have my widow's pension and there was another gathering at the pit, twenty-three pounds that is, a fair bit. I know there are eight hundred men but times are hard, I could expect no more.'

Hannah, sitting in the corner with Walton on her lap, guzzling away at a bottle of milk dropped in by Farmer Burton, felt dimly outraged. How could they sit there, talking about money, when Da was dead? She rocked herself and the baby to and fro as he sucked steadily and gazed up at her with large, unblinking brown eyes. Misery rose in her like a tide, swamping her throat and choking her, swamping her eyes so that she could hardly see the baby on her lap.

Her mother's eyes were sharp and she saw Hannah's expression and understood. 'Life goes on, lass,' she said softly. 'We have to live and there's two little lads to feed and care for till they are old enough to see to themselves. Your da would understand, pet, and so will you when you're older.'

Chapter Nine

'Our Betty's got a lad,' Harry announced as he came in from school, late as usual, his seven-year-old face alive with mischief. 'Me and Billy seen them when we went up the lane looking for conkers.'

'So that's where you've been instead of coming home for your tea,' his mother observed wearily. She finished ironing Bob's best shirt and hung it on the clotheshorse by the fire before taking another garment from the pile on the end of the table.

'Saw, not seen,' said Hannah. She was standing at the opposite end of the kitchen table, which had been covered by a folded flannelette sheet as a makeshift ironing pad, helping her mother with the ironing.

'Eh?' said Harry, looking from his mother to Hannah, disappointed that his news wasn't having much of an effect on them.

'Billy and I saw them,' said Hannah who was taking a course called English for Secretaries in Bishop Auckland twice a week. Next year she was going to take shorthand and typing and hoped to get a proper office job the year after that. She took her cooled flatiron back to the range and exchanged it for one of those heating on the bar. She picked up the hot iron with a folded rag to protect her hand and spit on it judiciously. It hissed satisfactorily and she took it back to the table and inserted it into the steel 'iron protector' and fastened the pin across it.

'Billy and I saw them,' said Harry in an affected voice. He put his hand on his hip and minced round the kitchen repeating it over and over.

'Harry, behave yourself or you'll get no tea at all,' Nora

snapped. Hannah looked across the table to her, seeing how tired her mother's face looked, the droop to her shoulders.

'Mam, sit down and have a rest. I'll finish this lot off, I have plenty of time before I go back to the farm.'

'I think I will, pet, if you don't mind,' answered her mother. She finished the nightie she was ironing and returned her flatiron to the bar. Sighing, she sank down in her rocking chair and stretched her legs out on the steel fender.

Hannah watched her anxiously. It was almost three years since Jake's death and in that time, her mother had seemed to age ten years. She had hit on a scheme to supplement her widow's pension: she went into Auckland every Saturday, bought in a few groceries as cheaply as she could and sold them at a modest profit in a makeshift shop in the front room. Of course, her customers were mostly housewives who ran out of supplies and wanted just enough to last them until they could get to the Co-op store, maybe a quarter pound of sugar or two ounces of lard. Today it seemed that everyone in the rows had run out of something, usually when she was busy with something else. And she couldn't afford to turn away custom, no matter how small the purchase.

Hannah had now left school but there was no full-time work for her in the district, all she had was the small amount of money she earned by helping out at Farmer Burton's. And Bob, though he was almost a man now, could only get datal work in the pit and was on a bare subsistence wage, for day labouring paid poorly. Alf still sent money home but the intervals between the postal orders were becoming longer and longer and Hannah guessed that he was courting a lass.

'Where's my tea, Mam?' demanded Harry. 'I'm hungry.'

'Stay there, I'll get it, Mam,' Hannah said quickly. She used the rag she had wrapped round the handle of the iron to lift a plate of potatoes and cabbage doused in pork dripping she'd bought at Manner's butcher's shop in Newgate Street on her way to her class the evening before. She brought the wooden stool which had been Da's cracket when he worked in the pit – the cracket which he used to sit on or lean against when hewing coal crouched in a low seam – and put it on the mat before the fire. Placing the dinner on the cracket, she brought him a knife and fork from the dresser.

'You'll have to kneel on the mat and eat it there,' she said. 'I need the table for the ironing. If you'd come straight home from school you could have eaten at the table like a Christian.'

Harry made no demur but fell to with a will. Walton, who had been playing under the table, came out and stood beside him, absorbed in watching him eat. At two and a half, Walton was tall and thin for his age and always hungry.

'Leave Harry alone, you've had your tea,' Nora said to him, and his face crumpled. Harry offered him a potato on the end of his fork and, after a quick glance at his mother, the toddler took it and crammed it into his mouth, chewing noisily. Nora leaned forwards and pulled him on to her lap, cuddling him in to her chest.

'Come on, my chick,' she said and began rocking gently, crooning a nameless tune to him.

Hannah had finished the ironing and was folding the flannelette sheet when Betty came in. The whole family gaped in astonishment as they saw the man who was with her. There was something familiar about his face, though Hannah couldn't think what it was, and he was so tall he had to stoop as he came in the door. Although it was the middle of the week, he was wearing a good suit and his reddish hair was slicked back smoothly from his forehead, not covered by a cloth cap such as everyone else in the rows wore.

'Mam,' Betty began, her voice sounding high and nervous. 'Mam, this is Thomas Cornish.' She flashed a brief smile at the man who was hovering in the doorway, unsure of his welcome. 'Everybody calls him Tucker.'

'Cornish? Did you say Cornish?' Nora sounded as though she couldn't believe what she was hearing and Hannah too stared at him, dumbfounded. Now she knew why he looked so familiar; he had the same colouring as the Cornish boys, the same fair, freckled skin and light reddish hair. But he was different from them at the same time, with his fresh, clean clothes and open, honest face. Was he a cousin?

'I telled you that our Betty had a lad,' observed Harry with a look of self-justification.

'Told,' Hannah whispered automatically, still watching the stranger. Betty's uncertain smile slipped and she glared at Harry for a quick second before turning back to her mother, but before she could speak Tucker himself intervened.

'Cornish, that's right, Mrs Armstrong,' he said, stepping forwards and extending his right hand to Nora. 'Though I'm sometimes called Grizedale after my stepfather.' His hand was still outstretched, almost forcing the issue with her, so that in the end her natural politeness won through and she put down Walton and took it, though she never had thought to shake hands with a Cornish. Then light dawned.

'Eeh, Tucker Cornish! You're Meg Maddison's lad, aren't you? By, the last time I saw you you were a little lad. There were two of you, weren't there? Now, were you the oldest or was it – what's his name?'

'Christopher, though he gets Kit. No, I'm the second one.'

'Well, come in, lad, come in and I'll make a pot of tea. How's your mother? Do you know, I always liked her, I thought that Wesley Cornish treated her rotten.'

Nora, her tiredness forgotten, busied herself in filling the kettle and making tea. Betty led Tucker to the horsehair settee, where they sat side by side as though both of them were company.

Hastily, Hannah got the Sunday tablecloth out of the dresser drawer and laid the table. Harry grinned with delight as he was sent into the front room to fetch ginger biscuits from the large, square tin in the 'shop'. It wasn't very often that the Armstrongs got to eat any of the biscuits his mother sold.

'Now then,' said Nora, when they were all settled with their tea and Harry and Walton were nibbling round the edges of their ginger biscuits, seeing whose would last the longest. 'Tell me how your mother and the others are getting on now, and afterwards you can tell me about you and our Betty. 'Cause I have to say that she's never even mentioned you to her family.'

Betty blushed. 'Oh, Mam,' she said, putting down her cup and staring at it as though it were responsible for her embarrassment, 'there wasn't anything to tell, really there wasn't.'

In front of them all, Tucker took her hand and squeezed it and Hannah gasped. Such an open display of sympathy and affection was practically a declaration of intent to marry. She looked at her sister with new eyes and realised Betty was attractive; the pink blush on her normally white skin looked very pretty against her dark hair. Hannah put up a hand to her own cloud of hair, the same colour as Betty's, just as their complexions were the same. Did that mean that she herself was as pretty as Betty was?

'Hannah, stop dreaming and get away out to your work. You're going to be late tonight as it is,' her mother said briskly.

Reluctantly, Hannah got to her feet and went to the door, looking back in astonishment when Tucker half rose and said goodbye.

'I'll see you again, Hannah,' he went on courteously.

She went up to the farm, hurrying now to make up time, but her thoughts were back in the kitchen with her family. She was desperate to know what was being said so she could find out more about Tucker and what he was doing in Winton.

'Eeh, I remember Meg Maddison well,' said Nora. It was the following morning and Hannah was tidying up after Bob's bath while her mother chopped up vegetables for soup. She had managed to get a ham bone from the butcher and had it simmering slowly on the bar. 'Poor motherless lass, she was, always working for her family, her brothers and sisters. Then she had to go and marry that Wesley Cornish and get two lads of her own. Though, you know, when he was younger he wasn't so bad as he is now, dirty drunken beast that he is, though he was spoiled rotten by his mam. But then Sally Hawkins got her claws into him and Meg and her bairns were left to God and providence. Not a penny piece could she get out of him. But still, she fell on her feet in the end, got on with Jonty Grizedale from up at the Hall. A proper gentleman he was – and still is, I should suppose. Of course, there was precious little money left, Jonty's da had run through that, but Tucker said they went away to the coast, Marsden, I think he said, Jonty has a farm there.'

The front door opened and Mrs Hutchinson from the next row called out, 'Are you there, Mrs Armstrong? I'm only wanting a fresh egg if you've got one, I thought I'd do some egg and cheese in the oven for the bairns' dinner. I haven't time to go to the store.'

Nora put down her vegetable knife and went through to serve her with the single egg. 'A penny, that'll be,' she said.

'They're only eightpence a dozen up at the store,' grumbled Mrs Hutchinson.

'Well, you're welcome to try to buy an odd one there, if you can make the time to go, that is,' said Nora evenly.

'Nay, nay, I'll take it, I didn't mean nothing.'

'Some folk think I should be doing this for nothing, just the good of my health,' Nora observed as she came back into the kitchen and picked up her knife to finish off a carrot. 'Now, what were we talking about?'

'Tucker Cornish and his family,' said Hannah, impatient to hear more about her sister's boyfriend. 'It must be grand to live on a farm beside the sea, don't you think so, Bob?'

'I like the moors better,' said Bob from his chair by the fire. Bob was seventeen now and his shoulders were beginning to broaden out with the hard muscles of a labourer in the pit. He shook his head in wonderment. 'Are you sure Tucker Cornish is serious about our Betty? I mean, all the lasses will be after him, him being an undermanager. An' then, he's getting old now, he must be nearly thirty. Nobody gets to be an undermanager lest they're getting on a bit, never mind how clever they are. And Betty is a daft bit of a lass, she's only sixteen.'

'Well, he is a clever lad, anybody can see that, an' a good worker too, I have no doubt. And if he suits our Betty, he suits me,' Nora said firmly.

'Aw, Mam, if our Betty's courting the undermanager I'll never hear the last of it. The lads'll say I've gone over to the bosses,' Bob protested.

'Don't talk barmy, Bob,' said Mam, quite unconcerned and Hannah noticed that as she tipped the vegetables into the pan on the bar and added salt and pepper, that she was smiling softly to herself. She's pleased that Betty's lad is an official, she thought, and guessed why. It would be a little bit of security, because officials don't get locked out of the mine ever, nor had she heard of them going on strike.

'Tucker wants to get married at Christmas,' Betty confided as she lay in bed beside Hannah a few weeks later.

'Christmas? But you've only been courting for a month or two,' said Hannah, surprised. 'What will folk say? They'll think you have to get married.'

'Well,' answered Betty with some spirit, 'if they can add up they'll find out they're wrong, won't they? Anyroad, he's got the undermanager's house to go into, you know the one that's on the road past Old Winton. And he wants me in it, he says now he's met me he wants a proper home with me in it, he's sick of living in lodgings. He had to live in lodgings when he first left home and went to Horden and now he's got this job he wants to settle down. With me,' she repeated, as though she had to remind herself it was all true.

Hannah could hardly imagine Betty living in the under-manager's house, it was so big, set in a garden with lawns and fully grown trees. But these last few weeks Betty had blossomed and as Hannah thought back she realised it had begun to happen ever since the day her sister had met Tucker at Mr Hudson's house. Now it was a seven-day wonder in the rows that a Cornish was the undermanager and, what was more, he wanted to marry Betty Armstrong. Betty had a diamond ring to prove it and that was another wonder, for in these hard times a girl was lucky to get a wedding ring, let alone an engagement ring.

Wesley Cornish was mad as all get-out to find him and his lads working under Tucker, the son he had abandoned all those years ago. Bob said Ralph and Lancelot were hard put to be civil to him but they had to be to keep their jobs. Hannah would have given a lot to be in the pit and see those two have to take orders from their half-brother. She smiled to herself in the dark as she thought of it.

She lay quietly, her thoughts returning to her sister and her lover, wondering what it was like to be in love as they were. She thought of the lads in the village, Bob's marras, some of them, and others she had been to school with. But none of them sparked any feelings at all in her, let alone love. She loved Bob and Harry and little Walton, and she couldn't imagine leaving them to go and live with someone else and what's more, do so blithely in the way Betty was obviously prepared to do. No, the sort of love that made Betty look so bright-eyed and gormless whenever she saw Tucker was a mystery to her. Though she had to admit that Tucker was special, so handsome and kind and rich an' all, she knew no one at all who could measure up to him.

Betty had fallen silent and Hannah guessed she was asleep by her deep and even breathing. Restlessly, she turned on her side and closed her own eyes, trying to will herself to sleep. And eventually, she slept and dreamed that a young and very rich businessman in Bishop Auckland came courting her and when she looked up into his face it was Timothy Durkin, the agent's son.

The dream came back to her as she scrubbed the kitchen floor the following day and she smiled wryly. Some chance of any one coming courting her, she thought, let alone Timothy Durkin. It was two years since she had seen him in any case, and he had probably forgotten all about her. No doubt he had just taken the choir up to amuse himself that summer, he must have been bored. But he had dropped it soon enough when something better had come along, and he never came into the village now.

Sighing, Hannah finished her scrubbing and took her pail of dirty water to the outside drain to empty. Well, anyone can dream, she told herself ruefully as she dried her hands on her sacking apron.

Chapter Ten

'Not a bad little motor, this, Tony, don't you think?' said Timothy, 'even if it is a prewar model.'

The young man sitting in the passenger seat of the 1912 Austin tourer nodded his head in agreement. Indeed, as he was well aware that the car was his friend's pride and joy he had to agree, it was not in his nature to offend a friend.

They were just edging on to the Great North Road on the second lap of their journey home for Christmas. That is Timothy was going home; though Tony's family had an estate near Durham, his father being Lord Akers, their main residence was in London, Park Lane, to be exact. But his parents were spending the winter in Cannes and when Timothy asked him to accompany him home for Christmas, Tony accepted with alacrity.

The two young men had known each other slightly since they were boys, Lord Akers being the owner of the estate and its mining interests and Timothy's father his agent, though it was not until they bumped into each other at Oxford that their friendship had developed. Their two families were almost as far removed socially from each other as were the Durkins and Armstrongs, yet it didn't seem to matter in the enclosed world of the university, and they had discovered during their first year that they had many things in common. Both had had essentially lonely childhoods and both had hated boarding school, though Tony had gone to Eton and Timothy to a smaller school in Barnard Castle on Durham's border with Yorkshire.

'Where shall we stay tonight?' Timothy asked now. 'Or do you want to rush on to Bishop Auckland without stopping? We will if you like, I think the old bus is up to it. She ran pretty well yesterday.' They had set out the day before and done almost ninety miles before looking for somewhere to spend the night, finally deciding on a tiny country inn. They had been the only guests but their rooms were clean and adequate and the food good.

'Let's do that then,' said Tony. 'Though won't your father be expecting us tomorrow rather than today?'

'It won't matter,' Timothy answered, thinking to himself that his father would hardly notice what day he came home. The fact that the son of Lord Akers was coming with him would make a difference, Timothy had no illusions about that.

'There's a long, long trail awinding into the land of my dreams,' Tony carolled as they sped northwards, touching forty miles an hour in places, for Timothy wanted to show what the old car could do. He had bought it the week before and this was the first time he had had the chance to put it to a real test and in spite of his apparent confidence he was slightly anxious; after all, the journey was the best part of two hundred miles. But the engine was responding to him beautifully and he relaxed after a while and added his baritone to his friend's.

By one o'clock they were on the outskirts of Doncaster and sitting in the Miner's Arms with a pie and a pint while the tourer had a rest. It was Tony who had caught sight of the shabby little pub and suggested they stop there.

'Most appropriate, my boy,' he said grandly to Timothy as he led the way in to the bar. 'Doesn't it remind you of home?'

Timothy had never been in a working-class pub in his life, let alone one at home in Auckland. In Oxford the pubs he and Tony frequented were all given over to students.

As they went into the bar, which was half filled with men, most of them miners and some still black from the pit, the buzz of conversation stilled. Timothy, sensitive to the atmosphere, hesitated, but Tony didn't appear to notice. He moved through them to the bar, nodding a greeting.

'Afternoon, landlord,' he said in his booming upper-class accent. 'Two pints of bitter, please, and a couple of those pies you have there. Pork pies, are they?'

'Lamb,' said the landlord, not bothering to return the greeting.

One of the men standing at the end of the bar hawked loudly

and spat into the spittoon at his feet. Tony showed no sign of noticing anything, he was absorbed in watching the landlord drawing the foaming pints of beer.

'Come on, Tim, we'll sit over there,' he said, a pint in one hand and a plate with two pies on it in the other, and led the way to a table in a corner. Only when they were sitting down and tucking into their pies did the other men in the bar turn away and resume their conversations.

Timothy looked round the dingy bar with its walls and ceiling darkened to a deep brown with tobacco smoke. The floor boards were bare and pitted with tiny dents caused by the studs in pit boots, at least he thought it must be that for most of the men were wearing pit boots whether they were dirty from the pit or not.

There was the unmistakable smell which Timothy remembered from the times he had accompanied his father to the mine offices, the smell of coal and coke ovens mixed with strong tobacco. It brought to his memory the time he had seen the miners step out of the cage as they came to bank at the top of the shaft and immediately light up pipes and cigarettes and begin coughing and spitting to clear their tubes of the dreaded coal and stone dust. For, of course, smoking was strictly forbidden down the mines, the danger of explosions was ever present.

Timothy polished his pie off quickly, finding he was hungry. He drank some of the strong beer and looked over to a group of men talking by the bar, catching one man staring at him, his expression unreadable. Timothy acknowledged him with a slight nod to the head and the man immediately looked away and took a large swallow of beer. His clothes were stiff and black with coal dust and he was still wearing leather knee protectors.

'Have another, Tim?'

'No, I don't think so, thanks,' Timothy answered. He watched the miners, becoming aware that whenever he or Tony spoke they paused in their conversation and listened, making no effort to hide the fact. He began to feel uncomfortable, ready to go. But Tony was already on his feet and heading for the bar. Silently, the men made way for him.

'You men all work in the same mine?' Tony's ringing, aristocratic accent sounded loud and clear and utterly foreign to the thick South Yorkshire accents of the workmen. But he was bending benignly to the group nearest him, his face expressing a genuine interest.

'Aye, we do, those of us who haven't been laid off, that is,' replied one at last, the one who had been watching them earlier.

Tony nodded his head sympathetically. 'Trade's bad, I know,' he said sagely, delving into his pocket and pulling out a handful of coins to pay the landlord. The change jangled as he dropped it back in the pocket and the miners all looked towards the sound.

'Oh, aye? An' tha'll know all about it, would thaa?' said the miner, lifting his chin aggressively to Tony. He was a short man, barely five foot six, but his shoulders were broad and powerful even against Tony's rugby-playing bulk. Tony seemed oblivious to it and remained standing at the bar, smiling down at the men.

'I know a little,' he answered. 'After all, my father's in the mining business.'

Oh, Lord, thought Timothy helplessly, is he going to tell them his father's a mine owner? He knew from his own father how bitter the men were as their condition gradually worsened over the last few years; he had no reason to think that the miners here were any better off than those in Durham.

'Have you been on the dole, mister?' a man was asking, his voice flat and unemotional.

'Well, no, of course, I'm still a student,' admitted the Honourable Anthony Akers. 'I haven't actually –'

'Naa,' said the man, turning to the bar and picking up his pint. 'Naa, thaa hasn't.' He drained his pot, replaced it on the bar and wiped his mouth with the back of his hand.

'Well,' said Tony reasonably, 'I suppose it does give you a bit of a holiday, doesn't it? And times will get better, they always do, and in the meantime, you have the dole, haven't you? I mean, if you can afford to drink beer in the middle of the day –' He faltered as he caught the expression on the faces of the miners. As a man they stepped forward, an angry growl coming from more than one throat.

'Coming into our alehouse . . .' Timothy heard one say, while another butted in, 'An', "a twopenny pair of kippers is good enough for any working man's dinner", is that it?' he said, quoting from a well-known Tory minister's speech of the week before which had made all the papers.

'Now then, lads, I'll have no trouble here,' said the landlord, but before he had finished his warning Timothy was on his feet and had hold of Tony's arm and was drawing him outside.

'But I haven't finished my beer,' Tony protested, though he allowed himself to be drawn.

'Yes, you have,' said Timothy as he propelled his friend through the door to the kerb and the waiting car. 'That's if you don't want to be lynched.'

'But I said nothing to antagonise them,' Tony said indignantly as Timothy cranked the engine with the starting handle and, as it burst into life, jumped into the driving seat.

'No? Well, just look behind you then,' said Timothy, indicating the open door of the pub where miners were standing, staring after them.

Tony shook his head in wonderment as they drove through the quiet afternoon traffic of Doncaster. 'There was no arguing with them, in any case,' he said. 'How can you argue with a man who suddenly begins to talk about kippers?'

But by the time Timothy had explained the relevance of smoked herring to the argument, Tony's interest had waned. He was singing once again as they hit open road on the far side of the town and began to pick up speed.

'Let the whole wide world keep turning, just so long as I have you,' he sang, only slightly off key, Timothy was glad that the car was open-topped for all the cold day, at least most of the noise was carried away with the wind.

It was already dark by the time the car pulled up in Durham Road. Tony jumped out to open the gates so that they could drive up to the front of the house. As he stopped the engine, he saw the portly figure of his father standing in the lighted window of the dining room and when they got out of the car and lifted their luggage from the dicky, he opened the door and came down to greet them.

'Timothy, my boy,' he cried, smiling broadly. 'I wasn't expecting you until tomorrow. And you, Anthony, let me welcome you. As I told your father on the telephone only the other day, we are delighted to have you with us for Christmas.' He held out his hand to Tony, who had perforce to put his suitcase down to shake hands with his host.

'Don't worry about the luggage, dear boy, the servants will bring it in,' Mr Durkin went on, sweeping Tony up the steps and into the house. Timothy smiled grimly to himself as he followed.

Arrangements for the wedding of Betty and Tucker were almost finished. The chapel had been booked for the Saturday before Christmas and Mr Hughes, the minister, had had his usual little talk with the happy pair. The reception, paid for by Tucker at his insistence, would be held in the chapel schoolroom. Alf was coming home from Oxford and Tucker's mother, Meg Grizedale, was coming with Hope, her young daughter, and Kit Cornish, her eldest son.

'I hope you don't mind that Tucker's father won't be able to come,' Meg wrote to Nora. 'I'm afraid he can't leave the farm for a whole day. However, we are both delighted for Tucker and Betty. He has worked so hard to get where he is and I know Betty is just the girl to help him.'

Tucker had taken Betty over to the coast to see his parents one weekend at the beginning of December. Afterwards, as she and Hannah lay in bed together, the place where all their confidences were shared, Betty had told her sister all about the farm by the sea and the family living there.

'Oh, it's lovely, Hannah,' she said. 'It's an old stone farmhouse and when you lie in bed at night you can hear the sea, it's like a lullaby. And Tucker's mam is lovely, she hasn't put on any airs, she talked about how it used to be in Winton and how sorry she was to hear about Da, she knew him, you know. And Mr Grizedale, you would never think he came from Grizedale Hall, he talked to me so ordinary somehow, yet he's a proper gent, so polite.

But Kit, now, oh, it's sad to see him, Hannah, it really is. He was hurt in the war, you know, left for dead in the trenches, Tucker says. He has a gammy leg now, though he manages to get about, help on the farm. But it's his mind that's funny, he's very quiet and seems to get on better with the dogs and other animals than with people. It was his experiences in the war, Tucker says, he was all right before.'

Hannah lay awake a long time after her sister fell asleep, trying to visualise the farm by the sea and the family that lived there. Poor Kit, she thought, what horrors he must have experienced to make him as he was.

Nora had baked the wedding cakes herself. There were three of them: a large one which was to be cut at the wedding feast, a smaller one which was for Mrs Grizedale to take home and give out to Tucker's friends and relations, and a small one which was to be saved for the christening of the first baby. When they were put together in tiers, supported by silver-coloured pillars and with a tiny bride and groom made of sugar, bought in Auckland for a scandalous five shillings and elevenpence halfpenny, little Walton couldn't take his eyes off them.

The wedding was at eleven o'clock and even though it was but a short walk to the chapel from the rows, Tucker had hired a grand, open-topped car with gleaming black paint, a Humber, with plush leather upholstery and floating white ribbons decorating the bonnet.

It made three journeys round the rows, going up and down every one before heading for the chapel. The first time it held Nora, resplendent in mauve crepe, and Bob, in a dark serge suit and stiff white collar which was obviously uncomfortable for he kept trying to insert a finger behind it to ease it from his neck. On the second journey there was Hannah, in a new dusty-pink satin dress with a low waist and hemline which dipped to a point on one side and a coronet of Christmas roses on her head, showing off the dark gloss of her hair. With her she had Harry and Walton, both unrecognisably clean and tidy in new suits. The people of the rows came out to watch the grand sight; Harry, from his seat beside Hannah, bowed, smiled and waved his hand as he had seen the Prince of Wales do on the newsreel at the pictures, and Walton imitated him until a bump in the unmade road caused him to fall off his seat and tears threatened. Hannah had to put down her posy and pick him up, promising him a piece of wedding cake if he didn't cry.

Nora had drawn all her dividend from the Co-op store to help pay for the new clothes, determined that Tucker should not have all the expense, even though it meant she had nothing to fall back on if things got worse. And as Hannah travelled along so grandly in the motorcar, she couldn't help thinking that she had to get some work soon, her mother couldn't afford to keep her with only the small amount she made at the farm coming in. But still, it was Betty's wedding day, not the time to worry about money, she told herself as the car drew up before the chapel and she helped her little brothers out.

It took only ten minutes for the car to return with Betty, even though it had gone round the rows. Hannah's heart swelled with pride as Betty got out with Alf, who was to give her away. Alf looked handsome and prosperous and so much like his father had been before the accident in the pit that she felt tears prick the back of her eyes. He was the only one of the Armstrongs to have been able to afford to buy his own suit for the wedding. But Betty, in her white satin gown with a lace veil over her dark hair, drew gasps of admiration from the group of onlookers round the chapel gates.

'By, you look grand, Betty,' Hannah whispered, as she hurried to arrange the satin train of the dress so that it would flow smoothly down the aisle after her sister. Then Betty took Alf's arm and the organ played 'Here Comes the Bride' as the bridal procession started down the aisle to where Tucker, flanked by Kit, his brother, was standing waiting.

It was afterwards, at the reception in the schoolroom, Hannah met Tucker's family. As bridesmaid, she was sitting beside Kit who was best man, but apart from a brief hallo when Tucker introduced them properly, he hardly opened his mouth during the whole of the meal, either to eat or to talk. He sat there, staring at his plate for most of the time, answering in monosyllables when she tried to start a conversation until in the end, Hannah decided to give it up. And when the meal was ended and the blackcurrant cordial poured into the glasses for the toasts, it was his mother who rose to toast the bridal pair.

Hope, Tucker's half-sister, sat quietly beside her mother, watching everything with obvious interest. She was perhaps a little younger than herself, Hannah noted, yet looked quite self-possessed and smart in her cherry-red costume and cloche hat which fitted over her ears so that only wisps of her fashionably cut hair showed below it. She looked across and saw Hannah watching her, and smiled so that Hannah found herself smiling back.

Meg Grizedale was also dressed smartly yet simply in a similar costume to her daughter's, though the skirt was longer and the material was dark green edged with white. Once the meal was over and people began to move around, Meg went to sit beside Hannah's mother and the two women began to talk amicably. Beside Meg's costume, Nora's mauve crepe didn't look quite so smart as Hannah had thought when her mother first put it on. Suddenly it was obvious that the crepe was cheap, would probably shrink the first time it was washed, and there was something odd about the cut, it dragged slightly over her mother's thin hips.

'Hallo, may I sit beside you?' someone said in her ear.

Hannah turned to see Hope beside her, already sliding into the chair that had been Kit's. Hannah hadn't even noticed he had gone.

'I think we should be friends, don't you?' Hope went on, her warm smile lighting up her face. Before Hannah had time to reply they were interrupted by a commotion at the door of the schoolroom. Hannah heard Ralph and Wesley Cornish shouting belligerently.

'I've come to see my lad get wed,' said Wesley, his words slurring into one another.

Mr Hughes, who had been standing chatting to Meg and Nora, strode to the door. 'Now, come on, Mr Cornish,' he said reasonably. 'You've been drinking, don't you think you should go home and sleep it off?'

Wesley pushed past him roughly and took a few steps into the room, closely followed by Ralph. The guests looked at him, unsure what to do.

'Why wasn't I invited to my lad's wedding?' Wesley demanded and those closest to him moved back, away from the stench of beer and rum. 'Didn't I have a bloody right, me, his own father? Where's he at, Tucker, where the hell are you? Coming over here so that you can lord it over me down the pit and then not even asking me to your wedding?'

Tucker stepped forwards with Alf close by his side, ready to back him up if necessary. 'You weren't invited, so why don't you get out of here?' he asked quietly.

'I have a bloody right to be here, I have as much right as anybody else, I'm telling you. Don't you go telling me what to do, we're not down the pit now, you know,' shouted Wesley.

Tucker moved forward, grasped him by the lapels of his filthy suit and lifted him off his feet. 'You have no rights over me at all,' he said, his voice low and passionate. 'You did nothing for Kit and me when we were bairns, it was left to my mother to bring us up with no help from you at all. Don't talk to me about rights.' He dropped Wesley on his heels so that he stumbled slightly and had to struggle for a moment to regain his balance.

Ralph stepped forwards, waving his arms and shouting. 'Hey, leave him alone or you'll have me to deal –'

He got no further, for Mr Hughes and Mr Hodgson each took hold of him by the upper arms and dragged him backwards to the door and outside. But while everyone's gaze was diverted to his stepson, Wesley had got his eye on Meg and stepped towards where she stood, her face white and expressionless, her head held high.

'Well, see here if it isn't that frozen-faced bitch who took my lads away from me in the first place. Will you look at her? Butter wouldn't melt in her bloody mouth. Thought she was too good for me, did you know that? But not too good to play the whore with that Jonty Grizedale, was she?'

Meg stood still as he swayed close to her, spittle dribbling from his mouth, and Nora stepped forward and took her arm to draw her away. The next moment Alf and Tucker had hold of Wesley and were yanking him back, away from the women.

'Don't you ever speak to my mother again, do you hear?' yelled Tucker. 'If you do, so help me I'll –'

'Please, Mr Cornish, please, let's have an end to this unpleasantness,' said Mr Hughes, who was just coming back into the schoolroom. 'Remember where you are.'

'Sorry, minister,' Tucker muttered, relaxing his grip on Wesley. As he did so, Wesley stumbled over Alf's foot, falling heavily on his side on the floor. There was the ominous sound of breaking glass and a strong smell of rum filled the air of the room, which had never before smelled of strong liquor. Wesley squealed loudly and scrambled to his hands and knees. Beneath him the rum spread, staining the scrubbed white boards of the schoolroom floor.

'You've done for me, you bloody sods, I've been stabbed, I'm bleeding to death,' he cried, gingerly feeling down his side with one hand. 'Fetch the polis, somebody, will you? And the ambulance, I need the ambulance.'

Tucker bent down and hauled Wesley to his feet. Bits of broken glass dropped away from his trousers to the floor, where they glistened against the wood. Wesley howled at him to let him be, his face bright red with rage where it was not covered with greyish-black stubble.

'I'm only looking to see if you really are hurt,' said Tucker as he undid Wesley's belt and dragged his shirt up to expose the flesh, still black from the night before's pit dirt. As he did so, he released a strong stench of body odour combined with the peculiar smell of body lice and the men around, who were used to bathing every day when they came off shift, stepped back, making audible signs of disgust.

There was a tiny trickle of blood where a piece of bottle glass had scratched him, but otherwise Wesley looked unharmed.

'There's nothing the matter with you,' said Tucker, letting him go. 'Now, get out of here before I throw you out.'

But Wesley, once he was assured that he was unhurt, regained his aggressiveness. 'I'll go when I –' he began, but the men around him had had enough. Three or four of them caught hold of him and carried him to the doorway and out into the unmade-up road, where they dropped him in the gutter. He lay there beside his stepson, who had collapsed into insensibility, a dark stain slowly creeping along his trouserleg where he was in the process of wetting himself.

Hannah and Hope, along with most of the rest of the wedding guests, had followed the men out to the door with Meg and Nora close behind.

Hope, catching sight of her mother, went to her and Meg put her arms around her. 'Can we go home now, Mam?' she asked, her voice that of a small girl and Hannah knew she had changed her mind about making friends now.

Hannah didn't hear Meg's reply, her gaze had been drawn to a motorcar which had stopped on the opposite side of the road. It was an Austin tourer and sitting in it were two young men surveying the scene, one of whom she recognised instantly.

'Well, my boy.' The ringing tones of the Honourable Anthony Akers sounded loud and clear to the cluster of wedding guests at the door of the chapel schoolroom. 'You said you would show me how pitmen lived but I think I've seen enough, don't you? Shall we be on our way to Durham now?'

Hannah and Timothy stared for a brief moment into each other's eyes and she shrank at the contempt she saw in his. Then he deliberately looked away to the road ahead without a flicker of acknowledgement.

'Certainly, Tony,' he said and the car glided on down the road.

Chapter Eleven

'You can please yourself which you do, Hannah,' said Nora. 'But you know yourself you cannot stay at home, not now. You've got to earn your own living, haven't you?'

Hannah looked down at her hands which were clenched in her lap, she knew that her mother was right, of course she did. If only she could get work in Bishop Auckland or even Shildon, she thought miserably. It was ironic that Bob, who still desperately wanted to go back to Grandma's in Consett and work with Uncle Billy, had to stay at home to help his mother financially while Hannah had to go away for the very same reason.

'There's only Harry and Walton needs seeing to now, Hannah. I can manage on my own,' her mother went on. 'And Betty will be living close anyroad. But we don't want to have to take money from Tucker, do we? Not when you're old enough to take a job.'

'No, Mam,' said Hannah, almost inaudibly.

'Well, I told you about the housemaid's job I saw advertised in the *Chronicle*,' Nora went on. 'Harrogate's not so far and it's thirty-six pounds a year, not too bad for a young lass.' Her heart ached as she looked at the bowed head of her daughter and she almost told her she didn't have to go, she could wait a little while longer to see if she could get anything nearer home. But Hannah had to start earning a living; she was almost sixteen and earning a few coppers at the Burtons' farm was not enough, even though she often brought home eggs and milk.

'I don't want to go as a housemaid, Mam,' said Hannah at last. 'If I can go back with Alf to Oxford, I'd rather do that.' At least there would be one other Armstrong near, she thought.

'You might still have to go into service,' warned Nora but Hannah didn't answer. I'm not, she vowed silently, I'm not going to be a housemaid, I don't care what. A place like Oxford, there's bound to be night schools I can go to, I'll ask Alf.'

Alf, when he came in from Bishop Auckland, where he had been to the pictures with Bob to see Tom Mix in the latest cowboy film, was a bit taken aback at first to think he was to have the job of taking Hannah back with him to Cowley and helping her to get lodgings and a job. But after a few minutes he agreed.

'There's plenty of work in Oxford,' he said, 'good paid work an' all, even for girls. Better than round here, at any rate. I'll ask Ma if she has a spare room for her.' But then he remembered that Ma, which was the name given by all the lodgers in the house to the landlady, Mrs Prendergast, just took in boys. 'Girls cause trouble,' he had heard her say often enough. He looked at his sister but he really couldn't see that she would cause any trouble with his fellow lodgers, she was too skinny for a start and her unfashionably long hair hung down her back tied with a plain black ribbon. And then there was her dress, down over her skinny knees and with a little girl's round collar.

'I hope she has a better dress than that,' he said. 'I don't want her to show me up in front of my mates, do I?'

Hannah flushed with anger and indignation. 'If there's anyone showing anyone up it'll be you shaming me,' she burst out, her fists clenching by her sides.

'You needn't take it like that, I didn't mean anything,' said Alf calmly. 'It's just you don't know what it's like down there, man, it's a different world.'

Hannah remembered that expression as she sat on the bus which was taking them from Oxford railway station to Cowley, Alf by her side, and her basketwork box containing her clothes balanced on their knees. She gazed out of the window, fascinated by everything she saw. The busy streets were thronged with people, most of them well-dressed and prosperous-looking; not a single corner with unemployed men sitting on their hunkers depressed and shabby as it was at home. The shops were filled with customers and they all seemed to be buying.

And the streets were filled with motorcars of all kinds, she even saw two or three like the one Timothy Durkin had been driving on the day of Betty's wedding.

'Usually the place is full of undergraduates,' Alf volunteered. 'Luckily they don't come back to pester everyone else for a week or two yet.'

Timothy is a student, thought Hannah, is that an undergraduate? But she didn't show her ignorance by asking Alf, she would find out in time. They passed high stone walls with entrances through which she glimpsed grass lawns and buildings similar to Auckland Castle, or perhaps Palace Green in Durham, where the castle was on one side and the cathedral on the other. Only here, they passed one after another.

'Queen's,' said Alf laconically, and a bit farther on, 'Magdalen, the choir boys sing on the roof there on the first of May.'

Hannah peered through the window, trying to see the roof. How did choir boys stay up on that sloping slate? But again, she didn't ask. Alf was sitting back looking out of the window with an expression of boredom on his face and she told herself this was an everyday experience for him and she didn't want to make a nuisance of herself by asking questions. She knew her brother, in the ordinary way of things he would never have had her trailing round after him.

'This is the Cowley Road,' said Alf, and Hannah watched eagerly as the buildings began to thin out, giving glimpses of marshy ground. There was a church with a cemetery attached and several scattered cottages; briefly, a stream not unlike the Gaunless which flowed by Winton Colliery on its way to the Wear; then more houses; and suddenly Alf was getting to his feet.

'Come on, look sharp,' he said, tugging the box from her lap so that a loose piece of basket weave snagged on her dress and he had to wait impatiently while she freed it and it left a tiny tear. They got off the bus and walked away from the main road. Despite the weight of the box on his shoulder, Alf strode on ahead so that she had to keep breaking into a little run to keep up with him.

'Rymers Lane,' she read out loud, delighted with such a whimsical name.

'What?' Alf looked back at her without slowing his stride.

'Come on, Hannah, it's getting late. If Ma won't take you we'll have to find somewhere else for you to stay before dark.'

Hannah hurried after him and they passed the steam-plough works and turned the corner into Hockmore Street, where there were a few shops and houses. Having rounded another corner, Alf stopped before the gate of a terraced house with a small front garden with bare rose bushes and shrubs giving it the forlorn air of a winter garden anywhere. But under the bushes, Hannah could see snowdrops and the green shoots of crocuses which surprised her for the new year was barely a week old. Alf had a key to the front door and he unlocked it and motioned Hannah inside, where she found herself in a small hall with a door to their right and a staircase with a carpet patterned in roses. At the farther end of the hall, by the well of the staircase, was an open door to the kitchen; she could see a white sink and painted cupboards.

'Ma, are you there?' he called and a plump, middle-aged woman came out of the door to their right.

'Oh, hallo, Mr Armstrong,' she said, though she was not looking at him but at Hannah. 'You're back then. Just in time for tea, too. And who's this then, your young lady? You know I don't allow young ladies in the house.'

Hannah looked down at the rose-patterned carpet which ran along the length of the hall, over a brown linoleum. She felt very embarrassed.

'This is my sister, Ma, she's come down to look for work.'

Mrs Prendergast regarded Hannah, her gaze unsmiling. 'Your sister, eh? Well, you know the rules, Mr Armstrong, you'll have to find somewhere else for her to stay.'

'But couldn't she stay here just for tonight, please? We've been travelling all day and she's tired.'

They were talking about her as though she wasn't there, thought Hannah. The landlady hadn't even said hallo to her yet. She drew herself up and stepped forwards, looking into Mrs Prendergast's face.

'Don't worry about me,' she said. 'I'll find somewhere. I'm sure I don't have to stay here.'

'She's only a slip of a girl,' Mrs Prendergast observed. 'Are you sure she's old enough to be seeking work? Looks more like she should be at school to me.' She was still addressing her remarks to Alf.

Hannah was furious. 'I am almost sixteen, Mrs Prendergast,' she snapped, stretching the truth a little for she was only just turned fifteen. 'I am quite capable of earning my own living. I'm a good worker, all I need is a start.' All the lessons in English grammar and pronunciation which she had learned at night school went into this speech; she even remembered to round off her vowels.

'Well,' said Mrs Prendergast, 'at least your accent is not so bad as your brother's was when he first came down. Couldn't understand a word he said, most of the time.'

Hannah picked up her box by the leather strap which held it closed. 'You have your tea, Alf,' she said. 'I'll just go down to that little shop we saw at the end of the road. There were cards in the window, I'm sure some of them were wanting lodgers.'

'Don't be daft, Hannah,' said Alf. 'I'm not letting you look on your own, I'll come with you –'

'Never mind,' said Mrs Prendergast, suddenly changing her mind. 'She can stay here, for a short while at any rate. I've been thinking, I could do with some help in the house, my charlady is off nursing a sick husband and my back's not what it was – this damp, cold weather gives me gyp. If she helps me out with the scrubbing and such, she can stay for now. It will only be for a week or two, though.'

'I'm not looking to be a housemaid,' said Hannah.

'Oh, hoity-toity!' retorted Mrs Prendergast. 'Please yourself, I'm sure.'

'Hannah, don't be daft, it'll tide you over till you get something.' Alf turned his back on his landlady and whispered urgently to his sister. She looked up at him, her anger dying away. She hadn't much choice but to accept Mrs Prendergast's offer, she knew. She put the box down again on the floor.

'Thank your very much for your kind offer,' she said. 'So long as it is only a temporary arrangement I will be pleased to stay here and help you.'

Mrs Prendergast nodded, placated. 'So long as you understand I won't have you making eyes at the lodgers. This is a respectable house.'

'Hannah is a respectable girl, Ma,' said Alf in an offended tone of voice.

'Well, I didn't mean to imply she wasn't,' the landlady

answered him, relaxing into a smile. 'Come along now. Leave your luggage in the hall, Hannah. There's no room at the dining room table for you but I will set you a place in the kitchen and when you've eaten I'll show you your room. It's only the attic but the bed is comfortable enough.'

In the days that followed, Hannah's opinion of Mrs Prendergast softened until she came to like the older woman. She was strict with her, not allowing her to mix with her young men, as she called them, apart from Alf, but she was fair and only expected Hannah to work in the mornings so she had the rest of the day to look for work and a place of her own to live. Ma was a widow, her husband had worked at the John Allan Steam Plough and Engineering Company and when he died she had begun taking in lodgers to supplement her pension. She was a good cook and her house soon acquired such a good reputation that she rarely had a spare room to let. Hannah didn't mind the attic; it was somewhere clean and warm to sleep, and if she rose early enough she had the bathroom to herself before the lodgers wanted it.

Hannah revelled in the bathroom with its iron bath enamelled white and the white porcelain hand basin with a mirror above it. She revelled in the fact that the water from the hot-water tap ran truly hot, though the geyser had to be lit first. It was very like the bathroom in the undermanager's house where Betty and Tucker now lived, though the water there was heated from a coal-fired boiler in the scullery. This was the first time Hannah had lived in a house with a real bathroom and she was delighted with it. When she had said so to Alf he had told her not to be so obvious about it, she was showing him up, acting as though she had never seen a bathroom before. She tried to hide her feelings but she loved popping into the bathroom at every opportunity to wash her hands, and this was easy to do for it was downstairs, off the kitchen.

The water closet was built into the house though the door was outside, side by side with the back door. She loved that too, it was so different from the ash closet at the end of the yard at home, a place which was always smelly no matter how clean her mother tried to keep it.

'It's like living in paradise,' she said softly to herself one day shortly after she had arrived in Cowley. It was afternoon and she was walking along Rymers Lane to catch the bus into Oxford. It was a fairly warm, sunny day for January and the air was fresh and invigorating. She was going to see about a job she had seen advertised in the *Oxford Mail*, a job in a newsagent's shop near the railway station.

'Much better wait till you get something in Cowley,' Ma had counselled, but Hannah didn't want to work in Cowley. She wanted to work in Oxford itself where life seemed so much more exciting, even if she had fares to pay for the bus into town.

The bus was coming up to the stop and she had to run the last few steps, but soon she was sitting in a window seat gazing out as it picked up speed along the Oxford Road. Paradise, she thought again dreamily, enchanted with the clean streets and made-up roads thronged with cars and people milling about, looking as if they had somewhere to go and something to do when they got there, not like at home. It was hard to believe they were in the same country as Winton Colliery, where dejection hung heavy in the air along with the coal dust and smells from the ash closets.

Paradise, except for the dull ache inside her for home, for the sight of little Walton running towards her with his thin little arms outstretched for her to lift him up and hug him, and Harry coming in late from school once again, and her mother standing at the kitchen table, washing up in the chipped enamel bowl and putting the pots to drain on the tin tray. Suddenly her eyes dimmed and a lump rose up in her throat. Fiercely, she clenched her hands in the lap of her good dress, the warm serge dress which her mother had found the money from somewhere to buy for her. The dress had seemed fine enough when she first put it on in Winton but in a place like Oxford it looked what it was, a dress bought for warmth and durability rather than style or fashion, and the material was rough and scratchy so that it irritated her skin and prickled between her shoulder blades. And the three-quarter coat she wore over it hung loosely for it had been one of Betty's and Betty was a bigger girl than she was altogether.

'Carfax,' shouted the conductor and Hannah stumbled from the bus, determined to walk the rest of the way to clear her head of silly low notions. Holding her head in the air, she walked along pretending to herself she was wearing a dress she had seen in the window of the shop opposite the bus stop, a dress of lime-green wool with a chic little jacket and a cloche hat of the same colour. After a moment or two her momentary bout of homesickness receded and her natural buoyant spirits returned.

She found the newsagent's shop without any trouble and went in, reminding herself to watch how she spoke, to keep her vowels nicely rounded and, above all, not to let a hint of North Country idiom creep into her speech.

'Mr Ridley?' she said primly to the man behind the counter, a man of about forty-five with a Kaiser Bill moustache and streaks of grey in his bushy hair. He looked at her enquiringly and she went on, 'I've come about the job as sales assistant.'

'Have you now,' came a woman's voice from the back of the shop. 'You've never come all the way from Durham today for a job in our shop, have you, pet?'

Hannah watched, startled, as a hand drew aside the curtain which screened the back shop from the customers and a stout little woman with a merry grin on her face stepped into the shop. Her accent was pure Geordie, with the singsong tones of somewhere near Sunderland, or so Hannah guessed.

'No, no, just from Cowley, I came down last week. I'm staying in Cowley, my brother works there,' said Hannah, wondering how the woman had known she came from Durham when she had taken such pains to disguise her accent. Mr Ridley laughed heartily.

'Nay, lass, the wife didn't really think you'd come down specially for the job. She's one for a little joke, that's all.'

Mrs Ridley held the curtain up and beckoned to Hannah, her smile widening so that her eyes almost disappeared in the fold of flesh between her plump cheeks and brow.

'Howay through here, hinny,' she said. 'I'll put the kettle on and we'll have a nice cup of tea while we talk.'

It was a happy, triumphant Hannah who took the bus back to Cowley a couple of hours later. She fairly skipped down Rymers Lane in the gathering gloom of a wet winter evening and round the corner to Mrs Prendergast's boarding house, going up the path by the side of the house to the back door.

'I've got a job, Ma,' she cried as she went in. 'I start tomorrow.'

'Just as well,' said Mrs Prendergast. 'It's time you were moving out of here. I've noticed the way the boys look at you and I want no trouble in my house.' She closed the door of the gas oven where she had been basting a shoulder of lamb and straightened up to look at Hannah, who was opening her mouth to protest. 'Oh, I don't say it's your fault, I'm sure you don't encourage them, I will say that for you. But boys being what they are, it's best you go and the lady what does for me is coming back tomorrow in any case, I don't need you any more.'

'Ma!' cried Hannah, all her elation draining from her. Where was she to go? She hadn't looked for another place to live yet – what was the point until she was earning? She had banked on Ma letting her stay, at least for another week.

Chapter Twelve

'Well, don't look so worried,' said Ma, 'I'm not going to throw you out on the street. You'll just have to start looking for somewhere else, there are lots of people that take in boarders. You can have a couple of days to look around.'

When Alf came in from work he was quite philosophical about it. 'You'll get somewhere,' he said. 'Anyway, I haven't time to talk about it tonight, I'm going out.' Straight after tea he rushed upstairs to get ready, whistling as he went, and Hannah guessed he was seeing a girl again, the same girl he had already been out with twice since he came back only a week ago. No wonder he can't afford to send Mam much money home, she thought. Still, Mr Ridley had promised her twenty shillings a week and extra if she worked overtime; she should be able to spare some of that to send home, she told herself optimistically.

But there was the problem of how she was going to keep herself and pay fares into Oxford and pay for a room as well out of the tiny sum of money she had left. She had only brought two pounds with her and it was alarming how quickly the money had disappeared. She went up to her attic room and carefully counted out what she had left as she sat on the bed. Eleven shillings and threepence. She counted it again to make sure but the sum remained the same.

There was nothing else for it, she would have to ask Alf to help her out, and that meant that he would have even less to send home, or spend on his girlfriend. The homesickness which always lurked in the back of her mind, grew larger and larger, casting a dark shadow over her mind, and she lay down on the bed, for the first time allowing it to take over. Alf would help her, she knew that, he was her brother, wasn't he? If there had been some urgent need for money at home then everyone in the family was expected to help all they could but here there was only Alf. And Alf, she suspected, was courting and his thoughts fully occupied with the girl, whoever it was.

Well, she thought, sitting up on the bed, moping wasn't going to do any good. She had to get out and do something, look at the cards in the corner-shop window for a start.

But when she did, she found there were none at all advertising for a girl lodger.

Next morning, the sky held only a few red-streaked clouds, promising a bright day, though with a chill wind blowing along Oxford Road as she waited at the bus stop. It was only half past seven, for she was to begin work at eight o'clock, but there was a queue of people all going in to work. She caught the eye of the girl standing next to her and smiled, and the girl smiled back warmly. She looked only a little older than Hannah, a pretty girl with blonde curls and friendly blue eyes, wearing a bright-red hat with a feather in the brim. When the bus came along, Hannah found herself standing beside the girl, squashed up against her in fact, for the vehicle was crowded with people. She had to bend her head quickly to avoid getting the girl's feather in her eye, and the girl saw it and moved her head backwards out of Hannah's way.

'Murder, isn't it?' she said to Hannah, pulling the corner of her lips down in a mock grimace.

Hannah nodded.

'Going to work, are you? Do you live round here?'

Hannah admitted that yes, she was indeed on her way to work and she was living just off Hockmore Street.

'My name's Gloria, I work in Timothy White's,' the girl said and looked enquiringly at Hannah. She was so warm and friendly that Hannah quite forgot to try to hide her accent and answered her quite naturally.

'Hannah. Hannah Armstrong,' she said. 'I've just come here to live and I've got work in Ridley's newsagent's, that's near the station.'

'Oh yes, I think I know it,' cried Gloria, sounding as delighted as if she had found out they were long-lost cousins. By the time the journey was over and they were stepping off the bus, it felt to Hannah as though she had known Gloria for ages; they were chatting together like old friends.

'I'll see you on the bus tomorrow, Hannah,' Gloria called merrily as she went on her way, the feather in her red hat bouncing with her every step.

Hannah was still smiling as she approached the door of the newsagent's and went in, all her troubles forgotten, for she felt that she had found a friend.

'Good morning, Mr Ridley,' she cried cheerfully to the man behind the counter, who was busy stacking a shelf behind him with cigarettes.

'What cheor,' he answered and she grinned. Mrs Ridley had told her the day before that they had lived in Oxford since 1912, yet his Geordie accent and way of greeting had not altered one jot.

'Gan on through and put the kettle on, will you?' he asked. 'The missus will be coming in a minute with my breakfast and I'm fair clemmed for it. I've been here since five o'clock and mind, I've been right busy.'

'Yes, Mr Ridley,' said Hannah obediently and went through the curtain to the back shop, where there was a rickety table with a gas ring on it and some cups, saucers and cutlery. She hung her coat on a hook on the back door alongside Mr Ridley's, took down an overall and put it on as she had been told to do the day before when Mrs Ridley had issued her with instructions. It was evident that the overall belonged to the older woman, Hannah could easily have wound it twice round herself, but she bunched it at the back to make it look better from the front and tied the belt fairly tightly to keep it in position. She filled the tin kettle from the single cold tap over the sink in the corner and put it to boil on the gas ring. There was a cracked mirror hanging above the sink and she peered into it; seeing her hair was windblown, she tidied it up as best she could with her hands and was ready to go back into the shop. She must bring a comb tomorrow, she thought.

'The prices are on everything,' said Mr Ridley. 'An' if they're not, you just have to ask.'

The shop was filling up with people on their way to work and impatient for their morning newspaper, Hannah was soon working hard selling Woodbine and Park Drive cigarettes, matches, mints and magazines along with the papers. It wasn't difficult, she found; she had a good head for figures and soon was remembering prices without having to check all the time.

Mrs Ridley came in just as the kettle began to boil and fried bacon and eggs on the gas ring in the back shop for Mr Ridley's breakfast. The smell of the bacon hung about for a while but it was not unpleasant. So the morning went on, customers coming and going at intervals, mostly according to when the trains got in. Hannah had half an hour for lunch, which she ate in the back shop with Mrs Ridley, who had brought sandwiches enough for them all and to spare.

'I'd take you in myself, pet,' she said when Hannah, rather hesitantly for this was, after all, her first day at work, asked if she could go early to look for somewhere to live. 'But we only have a tiny flat. All our money went on the shop, d'you see, an' though we mebbe could manage to buy a house now as the business is a good little earner, we've settled where we are, it's nice and handy and big enough for the two of us. But you go off at half past four, we'll manage. Anyroad, you're not going to be any use to us if you haven't got a place to live, are you? But why don't you look in the *Oxford Times*? There'll likely be a place in there. Though the ones in the town will be too dear for you, you'd best try for a room in Cowley.'

At half past four, Hannah was standing on the bus stand waiting for the bus, the folded paper clutched in her hand, an address in the Accommodation to Let column underlined in pencil. And within half an hour she was ringing the bell of a house in Cruel Lane, only a short distance from Mrs Prendergast's. But there was no reply, though she rang the bell three times and she checked the address in her paper again, but it was right enough, 39, Cruel Lane.

Disconsolately, Hannah walked away and up the lane to Mrs Prendergast's. She let herself in the back door and went straight up to her room, hoping to avoid seeing Ma Prendergast, but the land-lady had heard her come in and followed her up the stairs.

'Have you found a place to stay?' she asked, with no preamble at all. Hannah looked at her uncompromising face and wished Alf was back from work to stand beside her. She felt very young and alone and her longing for home was more intense than ever.

'Not yet,' she admitted. 'But I have picked a place out of the paper, only they were out when I called.'

'You'd best go back after tea, then,' said Mrs Prendergast. 'In the meantime, as you're home early you can help me with the vegetables. I'm a bit late with them, as it happens.'

Hannah sat down on the edge of the bed, 'By,' she said aloud to the empty attic, 'for two pins I would walk out of here and never come back, even if I had to sleep on the streets. That woman! I don't know where I am with her, I don't, one minute she's all right and the next minute she's . . . she's . . .' Hannah couldn't think of the right adjective to describe what she thought of Ma Prendergast. Sighing, she got to her feet, went down the stairs to the kitchen and attacked a mound of carrots with the vegetable knife.

She managed to catch Alf on his own after tea and poured out all her worries to him. He stood leaning on the doorpost of his room, for Hannah wasn't allowed inside even though he was her brother, and gazed indulgently down at her.

'Oh, go on,' he said. 'Ma was just trying to get you to hurry up and find somewhere, she'd never put you out. Anyroad, if she did, she'd find she'd lost me an' all and she wouldn't want to do that, I've been with her since I came down to Oxford and she knows I'm a good payer.'

'But she doesn't like me,' said Hannah, her voice all forlorn.

'It's not that,' Alf reassured her. 'It's just that the last girl lodger she had got herself into trouble with one of the men and Ma was frightened she would get a reputation for a disorderly house. It's nothing to do with you.'

'A disorderly house?' said Hannah and her eyes flashed and two flags of colour stained her cheeks. How could Ma think she was that sort of a girl?

Alf saw her look of outrage and grinned. 'Oh, I told you, it's not you, it would be the same with any girl living in the house. But you're just a kid, I don't know why she should be worried about you.'

Hannah was about to retort when she remembered she needed Alf's help, so it was best not to get into an argument with him. He wasn't rushing out tonight, she observed, he seemed quite happy to stand about talking to her.

'I have an address in Cruel Lane, I got it from the *Oxford Times*,' she said to him. 'Will you come with me to see it? Only I'm a bit worried I won't have enough money to pay the first week's rent if I get the room, what with my fares into town too. Will you be able to help me out?'

Alf shrugged, resignedly. 'Oh, all right,' he said. 'Just wait a minute while I get ready.'

They walked up the road side by side to number 39 and Hannah was relieved to see that there was a light in the window. Alf rang the bell and after a moment the door opened and a middle-aged man stood there, dressed in his shirtsleeves and braces and holding a newspaper in his hand. he peered over a pair of glasses enquiringly.

'Good evening,' said Hannah. 'I've come about the room.'

'Gloria!'

The man stepped back and shouted in the direction of the kitchen and after a moment a girl came out, wiping her hands on a teatowel.

'There's no need to yell, Dad,' she said crossly, 'I can hear perfectly well – oh, hallo, you're the girl I met on the bus this morning, aren't you?'

'Yes, Hannah Armstrong, I've come about the room,' said Hannah, her strained features relaxing into a smile. 'And this is my brother, Alf,' she said as an afterthought.

'Do come in,' said Gloria. 'I'll just take this teatowel back to the kitchen, I'll be with you in a tick. This is my father, John Morgan. Take them into the sitting room, Dad.'

Obediently, Mr Morgan led the way into a pleasant front room with a square brown carpet on the floor surrounded by linoleum. He motioned them towards seats on the comfortable-looking chesterfield and Hannah sat down beside her brother. In a minute or two, Gloria came into the room with a tray of tea and biscuits.

'You'll have a cup of tea, won't you?' she said and handed round dainty china cups and saucers. Her father sat in a chair by the fire, watching her proudly, his forgotten newspaper still in his hand.

'You've come about the room?' said Gloria when they were settled.

Hannah looked at Alf nervously. She was beginning to think

there was no way she could afford a room in this house, she could see that it was newly decorated and the furniture and curtains were of the best quality. But Alf was looking at Gloria as though he had never seen a girl before, he seemed to have forgotten why they had come.

'I can't afford to pay very much,' Hannah mumbled at last.

'Oh, we're not charging a lot,' Gloria exclaimed, 'are we, Dad?'

'Well . . .' said Mr Morgan.

'No, we thought ten shillings a week, that's all, with breakfast and evening meal. That's not too much, is it? Oh, do say you'll take it, we'd love to have you.'

Hannah did a quick calculation in her head. If she paid ten shillings a week for her board and her fares to work were three shillings and sixpence a week, that left six shillings and sixpence. If she saved half-a-crown a week and sent home ten shillings every month, then she had four shillings for her clothes and everything else, including lunches – she couldn't expect Mrs Ridley to provide her lunch every day. Still, she could eat a good breakfast and maybe manage on a sandwich or an apple at lunchtime.

'I'll take it,' she said, glancing at Alf for approval, and he nodded enthusiastically. 'Er, do you need a week's money in advance?'

'Well,' said Gloria, looking doubtfully at her father. 'Can you manage it? I know you said you were only starting work.'

'Of course we can manage it,' said Alf grandly, speaking for the first time. He stood up and dug into his trouser pocket to bring out a small fold of ten-shilling notes, perhaps thirty shillings, Hannah guessed. He handed over a note to Gloria, who took it and held it in her hand, smiling happily.

'Oh, I'm so glad you're coming, I liked you as soon as I saw you this morning at the bus stop,' she said to Hannah. 'Now let me see, it's Wednesday tomorrow and my half-day, can you come tomorrow night? I'll have the room ready by then.'

So it was agreed. Mr Morgan had taken no part in it at all, he'd left everything to his young daughter. But Hannah, sipping her tea and watching Gloria over the rim of her cup, thought she understood why. Gloria was so self-assured, so businesslike and so pretty, all the qualities she felt she lacked herself. And now the business was over with, she chatted on composedly about this and that, how there were only three of them living in the house, there was an older brother who was working nights, and she wanted another girl to live with them to be company for her.

'My mother is dead, you see,' she said.

'Oh, I'm sorry,' said Hannah, and Alf tut-tutted his sympathy too.

'It was a long time ago, four years,' said Gloria, a shadow wiping out her smile for barely a moment before she shook her pretty curls and picked up the plate of biscuits to offer them round again.

'Thank you, but we'd better be going now,' said Hannah, rising to her feet, and a reluctant Alf put down his cup and rose also. Gloria saw them to the door.

'I'll see you tomorrow then,' she said, standing on the doorstep rubbing her arms against the cold winter's breeze. Nevertheless, she stayed on the step with the door open until brother and sister were rounding a bend in the lane.

'Mind, she's a bonny girl,' said Alf, and Hannah grinned.

'Yes. You looked a bit bedazzled,' she answered. 'Gormless an' all.'

'Why, you cheeky young imp, I'll knock your block off,' said Alf, lifting his hand to her in mock rage, and she ducked and danced on ahead of him. When they got back to Ma Prendergast's, she sought her out in the kitchen immediately and told her she had found a place and would be out of the house the next day.

'So you see, you need not have worried about me,' she said proudly. 'I am not the sort of girl to bring trouble to a house in any case.' She turned on her heel and went up to her attic room and wrote a long letter to her mother and Betty, telling them how well she was doing.

'I've got a job, Mam, working in a newsagent's, and the owners are from Shields and very nice. And I have a nice room just along the road from Alf and there's a very nice girl there, called Gloria.'

Hannah paused and chewed her pencil. It had just occurred to her that she hadn't even seen the room. But she shrugged the thought away; the room would be fine, she knew.

Chapter Thirteen

Hannah soon settled in to working in Ridley's, travelling with Gloria every morning on the bus into town and coming home every evening to the house in Cruel Lane where Gloria reigned supreme. Reggie, her easy-going brother, and Dan Morgan, her doting father, seemed unable or unwilling to cross her at all. Gloria was charming and sunny-tempered most of the time and Hannah loved having her for a friend, someone who knew her way around. Her first year in Oxford fairly flew past. And suddenly, Alf was paying his sister more attention than he had ever done, turning up most evenings, 'to see how she was getting on', he would explain, though when he got there he spent more time chatting with Gloria than with Hannah.

'Aren't you going out with your girlfriend tonight then?' Hannah asked him pointedly one evening, when she and Gloria were having a serious discussion about boys and their peculiarities and Alf turned up and spoiled it.

'What girlfriend?' he asked, frowning quickly at her before turning to Gloria and smiling. 'I haven't got a girlfriend, not at the moment.'

Then he became friendly with Reggie and they would discuss the relative merits of the cars they were going to buy as soon as they had a little more money saved. Alf was all for getting a bull-nosed Morris – after all, he could get one for less than a hundred pounds with his staff discount – whereas Reggie would have to pay a hundred and twenty for the Austin Seven he fancied.

It made Hannah unhappy to hear Alf talk so grandly of acquiring a car when things were so bad at home in Winton. But life was so different in Oxford, there was an air of prosperity about the place and it was seductive, anything was possible, all you had to do was work a little harder, do some overtime and there would be the money to buy what you fancied. Alf wasn't even in a union; the Morris workers got good money without a union, he explained to her, and in any case, to join a union was to court dismissal.

'Dad only gives me five pounds a week for the housekeeping, you know,' Gloria grumbled one day. She was looking longingly at a costume in a shop window, with a pearl-grey short skirt and long jacket with dusty pink collar and cuffs and piped round the edge of the jacket. 'Just the thing for the summer,' she said.

Hannah gazed at it. It certainly was smart and would look great on Gloria, but it cost six pounds. Six pounds might as well be sixty, she thought, it was a waste of time yearning for something so expensive. She herself had her eye on the pretty print dresses in a shop near Ridley's, twenty-nine and eleven they were and in the latest style, cut severely straight and without sleeves.

The girls separated and went to their work. Even though Hannah was used to Gloria's way of speaking now, she couldn't help a wry smile as she remembered the way she grumbled, about having only five pounds a week for the housekeeping. That was more than twice as much as Mam had at home in Winton.

The shop was full and Hannah hurried through to the back to change into the overall which Mrs Ridley had made for her. It was a good job she had made it a size too big, Hannah reflected, for she was putting on weight and her bosom was developing at last. A quick flick of the comb through her hair, cut in a bob by a hairdresser in Hockmore Street, and she was ready to take her place behind the counter with Mr Ridley. Trade was steady and she was kept pretty busy for most of the morning, but as usual there was a small hiatus round about half past eleven, just before the lunchtime rush. Hannah was replenishing the stocks of cigarettes on the shelf behind the counter while she had a spare minute or two when Mr Ridley nudged her.

'Do you see that chap over there? He's been looking at that magazine for ten minutes – what does he think this is, a reading room? I'll be having a word with him just now.'

Hannah looked over her shoulder at the man, obviously an undergraduate, and as she did so he looked up and caught her eye.

'Hallo, Hannah,' he said. 'I thought it was you.'

Hannah blushed a bright scarlet. All she could think of was the last time she had seen him, sitting in a car with his supercilious friend looking over the Cornish men drunk in the gutter outside the chapel at Winton on Betty and Tucker's wedding day. In her mind's eye she could still picture his expression of contempt and disgust as he had started the car and driven away.

'Oh, if he's a friend of yours,' said Mr Ridley. 'I didn't realise.' He nodded affably to Timothy, who stepped towards the counter. But Hannah had found her voice and her pride.

'No, no, not a friend,' she said calmly. 'I'm surprised he even remembers my name.'

Timothy halted abruptly, his smile of greeting fading. 'Well, of course –' he began and then thought better of it. Fishing in his pocket, he pulled out some coins. 'Er, how much is this?' he asked.

'One shilling,' said Hannah and held out her hand for the money.

Timothy put the copy of the *Strand* down to sort two sixpenny pieces from the change in his hand and gave her them. He paused and glanced over at Mr Ridley, who was regarding him stolidly, then he spun round on his heel and walked to the door.

'Mr Durkin, Timothy!'

He turned back as Hannah called to him, but she was simply holding out his magazine. He took it and left the shop.

'What was that about, pet?' asked Mr Ridley. 'Who is the toff?'

'Oh, nobody. Well, he is, he comes from home, not Winton exactly, but outside. His father is the mine agent.'

'Oh aye, is he now,' commented Mr Ridley, lifting his eyebrows mockingly to show how impressed he wasn't. Coming from Shields, he was well aware of a mine agent's importance.

Hannah didn't see Timothy again that summer of 1925 and she told herself that she didn't want to either. But sometimes, when she walked past one of the colleges and peeped through the entrance to that other world, she fancied she did see his tall figure at the distant end of the quadrangle. Or sometimes, when there was a quiet moment in the shop and the doorbell tinkled, she looked up quickly, thinking it might be him. But it never was, yet she was always aware of the fact that he was in the city, somewhere close. Not that it mattered to her at all, she told herself.

In August, Hannah, Gloria and Alf travelled north on the train for a week's holiday. Gloria stood on the platform with her arm linked through Alf's, holding her hand so that the sun sparkled on the tiny diamond in the gold ring on her finger. She looked so pretty and smart in her grey and pink costume, for Mr Morgan had given her the whole of six pounds she needed to buy it. Hannah, in her print dress and plain cardigan, had a few misgivings about what Gloria would think of Winton, with its towering winding wheel, slag heap, narrow rows of colliery houses and no tarmac on the roads. But then she felt disloyal; Winton was a grand place, she told herself, the folk were grand and the countryside around the village was grand, much better than Oxfordshire.

But when they arrived at Bishop Auckland and had to walk down Newgate Street to catch the bus, Hannah was dismayed to see the air of decay and poverty which hung over everything like a grey fog. Even the bigger shops looked poor things to those she remembered from Oxford, and in Kingsway there was a great long queue at the Labour Exchange. Even though the weather was warm, the men all wore cloth caps pulled down over their heads and their hands in their pockets.

Hannah watched Gloria covertly as they descended from the bus and walked the last few yards to the colliery rows, past a group of unemployed miners sitting on their hunkers by the wall of the chapel. She was waiting to see the horrified reaction she was sure would come to Gloria's face, the girl from Oxford wouldn't be able to help it. But apart from a slight tightening of her nostrils as they passed by the ash closets, Gloria appeared to be delighted to be there and had eyes only for Alf.

'It's a bit different to Oxford,' Hannah ventured as she determinedly led the way to the front of the house as though they weren't family – family always went in by the back yard. But she had forgotten that Mam had the front room turned into a shop and when they opened the door a bell tinkled and her sister

Jane came out from the kitchen, ready to serve a customer.

'Jane! You're home at last,' Hannah cried, forgetting all about Gloria and Alf in her delighted surprise. 'When did they let you out?'

Jane didn't reply for a moment, she was busy calling to the rest of the family in the kitchen. 'Mam! Bob, come and see, our Hannah's back an' Alf an' all.'

Suddenly they were all there, hugging and kissing each other and laughing and crying together and Hannah was exclaiming at how much Walton had grown, why, he must be almost ready for school. Harry, taller and thinner now, his pale face looking more and more like his brother's, was hanging back shyly, watching Gloria as though she had dropped in from Mars.

'This is Gloria, Mam,' said Alf proudly. 'Gloria, this is my mother, and my brother Bob and sister Jane, and the little 'uns are Harry and Walton.' And Gloria was charming and pleasant to everyone, even shaking hands with little Walton.

'There's parkin for tea,' he informed her solemnly, 'and stotty cake and best butter, not margarine or dripping.'

'How lovely!' said Gloria, though Hannah was quite sure she had never eaten margarine or dripping in her life before, and she silently blessed her future sister-in-law for being so nice. Now that Gloria had actually seen the worst, as it were, Hannah felt she could relax and enjoy her homecoming.

They sat round the kitchen table and ate bread in the form of stotty cakes hot from the oven with butter melting over it and followed up with ginger parkin. Gloria swore that it was the best tea she had ever tasted.

'You are a wonderful cook, Mrs Armstrong,' she said, full of admiration. Nora blushed and mumbled something about it being easy to be a good cook if you had plenty of the right ingredients.

'Oh, I'm sure I'll never be able to cook like you,' said Gloria. 'What a comedown it will be for poor Alf.' Alf smiled fondly at her and everyone knew he didn't believe that at all.

'Well, Bob,' Alf said at last, man to man, like, for Bob had taken no part in the conversation so far. 'How's things at the pit?'

'Badly,' Bob said shortly. 'It's a three-day week we're on now. And expecting to be laid idle altogether by the autumn.'

'It's going back to the gold standard that's made it worse,' said Alf sagely. 'I was reading about it in the *Oxford Times*. But I thought with the government subsidy the pits would keep on working.'

'Aye. Well, Mr Durkin is playing it canny, he reckons Lord Akers can only keep half the pits open, there's no demand, he says. If there's no demand, why does he want us to work an extra hour every day and for no more pay? Tell me that. Anyroad, Lord Akers can afford to go gallivanting all over the world an' all, he shows no signs of going bust. An' this government's on the side of the owners, if it hadn't been for the unions there would have been no subsidy neither.'

Bob was in full flow, his bitter voice went on and on and Hannah could see that Gloria's smile was slipping.

'Alf says they have no need for a union at the car works,' she intervened. 'Isn't that right, dear?'

'Well,' said Alf, glancing at Bob, 'it's different at Morris's.'

Bob shot him a look of contempt. 'Aye, different,' he snapped. 'But what happens when everyone has a car as wants one? Will it be different then?' His voice rose passionately and he stuck his head forward so that the frayed edge of his collar became all the more noticeable, a collar which Hannah could see had already been turned once.

'Now, lads, let's not have any arguments today. I've been looking forward to seeing the family all together again, don't spoil it,' said Mam, and a fraught silence fell.

'Come on, Gloria, we'll walk up to the bunny banks,' Alf said at last, jumping up and holding his hand out to her. 'It's nice up there, you'll like it.' With an air of relief, Gloria went with him to the door and paused before going out, flashing a hesitant smile at the family grouped round the table.

The bell tinkled from the front room and Hannah started to her feet. 'I'll go, Mam,' she said, 'you have a rest.' She went into the 'shop' and weighed out a pennyworth of yeast for a tired-looking woman with a mewling child hanging on to her skirt.

'Hallo, Hannah,' the woman said and Hannah, who hadn't recognised her when she first came in, looked more closely and was surprised to see it was Mrs Hutchinson, looking at least fifteen years older than when she had last seen her. They chatted for a minute or two and then Mrs Hutchinson went on her way, saying she had to get the bread laid down to rise or there would be none for the morning.

Back in the kitchen, there was only Jane and her mother. Bob had gone out and Harry and Walton were playing in the back lane.

'It's lovely to be back,' Hannah said, 'really great to see you home as well, Jane. Are you home for good, now?'

'Oh yes, I'm cured, they say,' Jane answered. At fourteen, Jane was a quiet, reserved girl and acted almost like a guest in the house, Hannah noticed, thinking sadly that it must have been the years in the sanatorium that did it. The old, close relationship they once had was completely gone.

When Hannah suggested that the three of them should call in the boys and walk up to see Betty and Tucker, Jane demurred, saying she would rather stay in by herself and read, 'while I have the house quiet and to myself,' she said. So Hannah, her mother and the two children walked up the row and out of the village to the undermanager's house.

Looking at the house as they went through the flower garden, full of the scent of roses and phlox, Hannah was surprised at how different it was from her memory of it. Oh, it was still grand next to the cottages in the miners' rows, but in comparison with the new houses being built in Cowley it wasn't so grand at all. But she forgot all that in the delight of greeting Betty, seven months pregnant and huge with it so that she had to lean forward to kiss Hannah's cheek.

'You look well, Hannah,' she said. 'At least you're not so skinny as you used to be.'

'Thank you,' said Hannah dryly. 'I can say the same about you.'

The three women talked for an hour while Harry and Walton played in the garden, they had so much to catch up on. Betty was happy in her marriage and looking forward to the baby and just about everything she said was prefixed by 'Tucker says' or 'Tucker likes', but Hannah could see there was a shadow of anxiety about her nevertheless. Mam was very happy sitting with her two daughters, discussing how grand it was in Oxford and how nice Alf's girl was. 'Not a bit of side to her,' she said. So Hannah didn't want to ask what it was that was causing the shadow over Betty's happiness, she didn't want to spoil the moment.

'I'll come up and see you during the week,' Hannah said as they were leaving. 'It'll be good to have a proper chat, just like we used to when we shared a bed at home.'

'Oh yes, do that,' said Betty rather quickly, glancing at her mother who was in the garden rounding up the boys for the walk home. Harry and Walton ran on ahead down the dusty road and Hannah and her mother strolled arm in arm in the warm August air. The cokeworks were busy filling the air with the stench of sulphur and coal gas, but to Hannah the smell was not so bad, it was simply the smell of Winton and home. At intervals they stopped and had a word with neighbours and friends who came out to greet Hannah and exclaim over how well she looked and Nora would glow with pride as she told them how Hannah had a good job in a shop owned by Geordies and how Alf too was doing well in the motor works. All in all, a happy first day home, thought Hannah as she climbed into the bed she was to share with Gloria for the holiday.

'Things are bad, Hannah, they couldn't be worse,' said Betty sadly. It was the following Tuesday and the two sisters were sitting in the garden of Betty's house, drinking home-made lemonade.

'I can see that,' said Hannah, 'the whole place looks poverty-stricken. But the pit's gone through bad times before, it usually gets going again.'

'Yes, but Tucker says the slump is set in this time. He heard Mr Durkin telling the manager that costs have to be cut and that means the wages bill, there's no other way. And you've seen the folk in the rows, they're on starvation wages now and a lot of them are on the dole. Tucker's worried about the future, he thinks the owners have been conniving with the government and stockpiling coal now because they want to have a showdown and break the unions.'

'Do you think there'll be another strike?' asked Hannah. 'Bob thinks that there could be a general strike, he thinks that the workers of the country will support the miners this time.'

'Tucker thinks a strike will come, maybe not yet but soon. Or if not, a lockout to force the men to accept the owners' conditions. Do you think the other unions will support them?'

'I don't know.' Hannah shook her head, thinking of the people she knew in Oxford and Cowley; the mines were so remote from most of the country and she suspected most people knew very little about them as did the people of Oxford. 'Will Tucker be affected if there is a strike?' she asked.

'He will, though not like the men; he'll still get his salary though it may be reduced. But it's Bob and the others like him I worry about.'

'Well, there's nothing you or I can do, Betty, so what's the use of worrying?'

'I don't know, Hannah, but if all the young people think there's no future here and move away like you and Alf did, what will be left? A wasteland, that's all. I don't want my baby to be born into a wasteland.'

Hannah thought about Betty's words as the train carrying them back to Oxford pulled into the station. She followed Alf and Gloria out of the station and looked around her; the contrast between the people here and those at home in Winton or even in the town of Bishop Auckland could not be more marked. The two worlds of Oxford, both town and gown, were indeed so remote from the world of the pit villages of Durham that they might as well be in Timbuktu.

Hannah left Alf and Gloria to go back to Cowley on their own while she went in to see Mr and Mrs Ridley in the newsagent's shop.

'By, am I glad to see you back,' Mrs Ridley said as she went in. 'Now I can put my feet up for an hour, they're killing me.'

Hannah was taken aback. She hadn't expected to begin work immediately – after all, her holiday wasn't over until Monday – but she saw the look of strained tiredness on the older woman's face and decided not to mention that she still had another day's holiday due.

'You've been busy then,' was her only comment.

'Busy? We've been rushed off our feet,' Mr Ridley put in. 'The place is full of visitors, all coming in off the trains and coming in here for a newspaper. Not that I'm complaining, mind, God forbid; the time to complain is when we're not busy.'

'None of the shops at home looked busy,' said Hannah sadly

as she went into the back shop to don her overall.

'Aye, we've heard it's bad,' said Mrs Ridley. 'I bless the day we decided to move down here, I do. I thank God every single night.'

Yet even for Hannah the troubles of the distressed mining areas receded into the background as she became immersed in her life in Oxford. The summer turned into autumn and the autumn into winter and her mother wrote that the pit had not, after all, closed down but that Bob was again working a full week. Betty's time came and she had a baby girl, and Hannah knitted a matinee jacket in pink and white and sent it off with her monthly postal order for her mother. But there were days now when she didn't think of Winton at all, she was so busy at the shop during the day, and the evenings were never lonely for Alf was round most of the time to sit on the chesterfield in the lounge with Gloria, holding hands and planning the wedding. And Hannah would willingly wash the dishes and clean up the kitchen while Dan sat at the table reading his *Oxford Chronicle*, exiled from his own lounge. Sometimes Hannah and Reggie made up a foursome with Alf and Gloria to go dancing the one-step and the palais glide or the new American dances they saw at the pictures such as the black bottom or the Charleston.

Hannah liked to go to the Palais, she loved the freedom of the new dances, though sometimes she wondered what Mr Hughes or Mr Hodgson would think if they saw her swinging her legs about in the ultrashort skirts which were the fashion.

But it was almost 1926, these were modern times, she told herself, there was no harm in dancing, how could there be? It was lovely to start the 'gentlemen's excuse me' quickstep with Alf and know that Reggie would tap her brother on the shoulder after they'd done one round of the room and sometimes another boy would tap Reggie's shoulder and he would frown but stand aside nevertheless. And she would feel attractive and popular, like Gloria, who always had three or four partners for this dance and only laughed at Alf's objections.

So she was delighted on Saturday night when she and Reggie were flying about the room to the lively beat of the 'Twelfth Street Rag', to see out of the corner of her eye that someone was tapping Reggie's shoulder and he was slackening his hold on her, though his frown this time was particularly black as he muttered something about 'blooming university blokes'.

She stood looking up into Timothy Durkin's deep-blue eyes, stupid with the shock of seeing him there, while the other dancers wove round them and the mirrored glass ball hanging from the ceiling reflected a myriad tiny lights. Then she felt his arms around her and as she automatically put up her own and followed his steps she could feel the steady beat of his heart against hers.

He swirled with her, round and round, saying nothing but smiling faintly down at her, and though she tried to stare straight in front of her at his shirt front she found that her eyes were drawn to his as the music changed. Her step faltered but he held her a little tighter and the singer with the band began to sing through a megaphone.

She saw Reggie approaching through the dancers determinedly but Timothy saw him too and expertly swung her through the double doors of the refreshment room.

'You'd like some lemonade, wouldn't you?' he said as he led her to a table.

Chapter Fourteen

Hannah watched Timothy, feeling slightly dazed, as he caught the waitress's eye with ease and ordered the lemonade. Then he sat back and smiled easily at her across the table.

'How are you, Hannah?' he asked.

'I must get back to the dance floor,' she said instead of answering his question.

'But why? We're not doing anything wrong, sitting here waiting for a nice glass of refreshing lemonade. The dancing has made me thirsty, aren't you thirsty?'

The waitress came with the drinks and Timothy searched in his pocket for change to pay for them, providing a few seconds for her to study him. He was so different from Reggie and Alf, she thought, so self-assured. She glanced around quickly and saw Reggie in the doorway, frowning fiercely at her and jerking his head to one side to indicate he wanted her to come away from the toff. She glared at him, forgetting that a moment before she had been going to leave of her own accord. What right had he to tell her what to do? She picked up her glass and took a sip of lemonade, enjoying the sweet yet tangy taste, and smiled at Timothy.

'Why were you so offhand with me when I saw you in Ridley's shop?' Timothy asked her softly. 'I felt quite hurt, I thought we were friends.'

Friends, she thought, gazing into her glass. She hadn't seen him for years until the day of Betty's wedding and then he had looked at her as though she were dirt, the memory of it was still painful. 'We were never friends,' she said scornfully. 'How could we be? Me a pit lass from the rows and you the agent's son.'

'Oh, now, it was never like that when we sang in the choir at chapel.' He reached out across the table and put his hand over hers. His low, clear voice brought back the remembrance of his baritone mingling with her mezzo-soprano as they sang 'Gethsemane' that Easter, so many years ago. But he had gone, left the chapel without a word, and though she had only been a child at the time, that had hurt too.

She pulled her hand away and started to rise but stopped as she heard Alf's voice, taut with anger.

'Howay, Hannah,' he said, his aggression making him return to the idiom of his native northeast. 'Get back in the dance hall, you promised this dance to Reggie.'

'But it's the interval,' she said, surprised. When she looked up and saw her brother's hard expression and Reggie standing just behind him as though to back him up, she understood and flushed with resentment.

'I don't care if it is the interval, come away with us,' Alf insisted.

'I'm staying here,' she answered evenly. 'I haven't finished my lemonade yet.'

Alf glared at her. 'You'll do what I say,' he snapped. 'I won't have my sister sitting with a university chap, a stranger.'

Timothy had been sitting without saying anything, just looking from Alf to Hannah, but now he intervened. 'I'm no stranger, we're old friends, Hannah and I. Don't you know me?'

Alf stared down at him, his face set. 'Oh aye, I know who you are mister. But that doesn't mean to say I want to know you, if you see what I mean.'

Timothy got to his feet, keeping his expression pleasant though his eyes were watchful as he replied, 'Well, I'm not all that sure I want to know you. But that has nothing to do with Hannah and me. If she wants to enjoy a drink with me, she has that right. She's not in purdah, you know, this is 1925.'

'Hannah, get out of here when I tell you,' Alf barked, his fists bunched to within six inches of Timothy's nose. Reggie stepped forward just behind him. When Hannah looked into their faces she saw all the enmity there of town for gown which she had heard had existed for centuries but had had no experience of until now.

But Alf wasn't from Oxford. And besides, he knew Timothy Durkin, he had sometimes been in chapel when she and Timothy had sung their duets. Alf had no right, she told herself angrily.

A man was stepping in front of her brother and Reggie. 'We'll have no trouble in here,' he warned, and a murmuring rose from the other tables. Hannah looked round to see that two or three large young men had ranged themselves beside Timothy, standing quietly doing nothing, their eyes as watchful as his. Everyone else in the room was looking at the confrontation too, and the murmuring from the tables grew louder.

'Coming in here after our girls, think they can do what they like –'

'Treat them like dirt, they do –'

She heard the comments and was alarmed. The atmosphere was becoming charged with anger and the bouncer standing between the two groups looked from one to the other.

'I said, we'll have no trouble and I meant it. Mary,' he called to the waitress, 'go and get the manager.'

'No, no, there'll be no trouble,' Hannah stammered. 'I'm coming with you Alf, let's all go home.' As she spoke she rose to her feet and pushed her way to the door, looking neither to left nor right, her face scarlet with humiliation. She rushed through the dance hall to the cloakroom for her coat, and was buttoning it up with shaky fingers when Gloria came in.

'What was that all about, Hannah?' she asked. 'I missed it, I was powdering my nose and when I came back I saw the boys were crowding into the refreshment room and then you came running out as though the devil was after you.'

'Nothing, it was just Alf making a fuss,' said Hannah. 'We're going home now.'

'But the dance isn't half over,' Gloria started to protest but thought better of it as she saw her friend was struggling to control her emotions. 'All right,' she said, 'I'll just get my coat.'

Nothing was said as the four of them walked to the bus and during the short ride, but the moment they reached the house, Alf turned to Hannah.

'Don't you show me up like that again,' he said. 'All my mates there an' all, and you making up to a student.'

'I wasn't!' Hannah retorted. 'It was an excuse-me dance, wasn't it? Timothy had a perfect right to cut in if he wanted to.'

'They have no right coming to our dances, that lot,' said Reggie. 'They only come round to pick up our girls and the girls are soft enough to let them.'

'But I know him, Reg, he comes from near Winton, he was just being friendly,' Hannah protested. 'What's wrong with having a drink with someone you know?'

'Nothing's wrong with having a drink, but it wouldn't have stopped there, would it? Do you think I couldn't tell what he was after? Grow up, Hannah,' said Alf.

'Alf, leave her alone, there was no harm done,' Gloria tried to intervene. 'She's only a kid, she just doesn't understand.'

'Keep out of it, Gloria,' said Reggie, taking hold of his sister's arm and drawing her away.

'You didn't keep out of it,' Gloria retorted.

'Oh, why can't you all mind your own business?' cried Hannah, thoroughly roused. 'I don't need your help, Gloria, this is between Alf and me, though it's none of his business either, I wasn't doing anything wrong.'

'Don't talk to Gloria like that,' Alf shouted, took hold of Hannah by the arms and shook her. It was so unexpected that Hannah was taken by surprise and her head flicked forwards and backwards painfully.

'Alf!' cried Gloria with a muttered oath, Alf flung Hannah down on the chesterfield couch.

'Now then, what's this all about? You're not fighting, are you?'

Dan Morgan came to the bottom of the stairs dressed only in crumpled, striped pyjamas and stuck the top half of himself round the door. 'What's going on?' he demanded when no one answered him the first time.

There was a moment's silence as Reggie and Alf looked at him, not knowing what to say.

'It's all right, Daddy.' It was Gloria, as usual, who found her voice first and spoke to him quite normally. 'They were just horsing around, I told them they would wake you up. Alf's going home now in any case.'

Dan gazed around uncertainly. 'It sounded like you were having a bust-up,' he said. Fortunately, he couldn't see Hannah properly because Reggie had moved to stand with his back to her, hiding her as she sat with her head hanging down, trying to fight off the sick dizziness which Alf's shaking had brought on.

'Go back to bed, Dad,' said Gloria. 'We're sorry we woke you up. We won't be long, we'll see everything's locked up after Alf goes.'

'Goodnight, then,' said Dan, satisfied, and he closed the door and padded off upstairs.

'Oh!' cried Hannah, jumping up the minute the door was closed and running out to the toilet. Bending over the toilet bowl, she promptly vomited, her head thumping, retching and retching until at last the spasms subsided and she straightened and leaned weakly against the distempered wall. The taste of bile was bitter in her mouth and she searched in the pocket of her dress for her handkerchief but it wasn't there.

'Here, use mine,' said Gloria who had followed her out, full of concern. 'Come on in now and sit down, you'll feel better in a minute or two.'

'Thanks,' said Hannah shakily. 'I think I'll stay outside, though.'

'No, come in, it's too cold. Alf's going now. If you don't want to see him again tonight, go into the bathroom till he's gone.'

Hannah nodded, then winced, even that small movement was painful. She went through the kitchen to the bathroom and locked herself in. Filling the hand basin with water she washed her face and neck, then held the flannel, soaked in cold water, against her forehead.

'Hannah? Are you all right?'

She jumped as Alf called through the door, then stared at her reflection in the glass above the basin. Her dark eyes were wide in her pale face, dull and shadowed, and her hair was all over the place.

'Leave me alone, Alf.'

'I'm not going to hurt you, Hannah, I'm sorry I shook you so hard. But I got so mad, seeing you with that –'

'Go away, Alf. I'll see you tomorrow.'

Hannah opened her tin of tooth powder, picked up her brush and began to clean her teeth. The clean, minty powder took away the sour taste of bile and refreshed her somewhat; the thumping in her head began to fade. As she turned off the tap she heard a whispering outside the bathroom door, then Gloria's anxious voice.

'Are you feeling better, Hannah?'

'I'm all right. Has he gone?'

'He's going now.'

'Goodnight, Hannah, I'll see you tomorrow,' said Alf.

Hannah waited until she heard the back door close behind him before she came out of the bathroom. There was only Gloria in the kitchen; she was sitting at the table pouring cocoa into two cups.

'Come and drink this, it'll make you feel better to have something in your stomach,' she said as Hannah emerged. 'Lordy, Hannah, you look terrible. Will I get you a couple of Aspros?'

'No, just the cocoa, thank you, Gloria.'

'I told Alf he shouldn't have touched you. There is no need for it, if he ever touched me like that I'd leave him, I told him straight.' Gloria picked up her cup in two hands and sipped from it, her face solemn and unhappy.

'Oh, Gloria, he didn't mean to hurt me. He didn't hit me, he just didn't realise how hard he was shaking me, he's a strong man,' said Hannah. This was the first time she had ever heard Gloria criticise Alf and if there was a rift between her brother and his fiancée it would be all her fault.

'He's not a violent man, Gloria,' she tried again. 'He would never hurt you, he adores you.'

Gloria looked across the table at Hannah and smiled, 'Oh, come on, Hannah,' she said. 'You look as though you're dead on your feet. Let's drink our cocoa and go to bed before we wake Dad up again.'

The next day was a Sunday and Hannah decided to go for a walk to clear her head.

'But what about your lunch?' asked Gloria. She was cooking sirloin of beef and Hannah had mixed Yorkshire puddings to go with it. 'Dad and Reg have gone to meet Alf at the Cowley Workers' Club but they'll be back for two o'clock, I thought we'd have a nice family afternoon. After all, we will be a real family after the wedding, it's not long now.'

'I don't feel much like eating a big meal. Don't bother about me, I'd rather walk,' said Hannah.

'But Reggie will expect you to be here.'

'Oh, he won't care if I'm here or not, why should he?'

'Well, because he likes you, I can tell.'

'Gloria, don't talk soft,' Hannah said briskly. 'If he does, he certainly fooled me last night.'

'Oh, it's because you don't want to see them,' Gloria looked relieved. 'Don't worry, they won't say a word to you, I won't let them. You did something foolish but now it's over and done with, we'll all forget about it.'

Hannah opened her mouth to protest that she hadn't done anything but changed her mind, there was no sense in getting into an argument with Gloria.

'Yes, but I think I'll still go for that walk,' she said. 'I need the exercise. I'll see you all later.'

'I'll keep your dinner warm in a low oven then,' Gloria replied as she turned back to her preparations, and Hannah knew she was slightly offended. Shrugging helplessly, she let herself out of the house and set off briskly along Cruel Lane to the junction with Hockmore Street. She turned left and left again into Church Street. The weather was very damp with a low, overcast sky which threatened rain and a cold wind which soon whipped colour into her cheeks, so she decided not to take to the fields but to stick to the streets, for her shoes were thin leather with open fronts and a buttoned crossbar. She had bought them in the July sales and was trying to make them last until January, when she hoped to find some brogues in the winter sales.

Walking past St James's Church and vicarage, she looked over curiously to try to catch sight of the cows which Gloria had told her the vicar, Georgie Moore, kept. Hannah knew him by sight, he was a large man who drove a pony and trap around Cowley.

'He has been known to marry people with his cow boots on under his surplice,' Gloria had said. 'I hope he remembers to take them off for my wedding.'

The wedding was to be in March, Alf and Gloria had decided. The couple would live in Dan's house at first, just until the new houses being built up the road were finished, then they hoped to rent their own home; they even talked ambitiously of buying, all in good time, of course.

Hannah turned left past the vicarage and left again, to walk up Cruel Lane. But she felt the walk had been too short so she hurried past the house and on to the end of the road, turning right along Hockmore Street. She kept on past the shops, turning corners as the fancy took her, not really caring where she went. She felt restless and unsettled somehow. Her night had been disturbed by bad dreams and long, wakeful periods. She saw the sign, Junction Road, and was thinking of turning back down Temple Road when she noticed the Methodist chapel. The lights were on inside and she could hear the sound of the organ and singing. On impulse she went in and slid into an empty pew near the back.

It was the first time Hannah had been inside a chapel since she came to Cowley. If Alf had kept it up, no doubt she would have gone with him, but he hadn't, and on her own she had not got around to it.

The chapel was very different from the plain, undecorated meeting house in Winton; this one was all polished wood and carvings and bright stained glass in the windows. But the organ music and the singing were the same, even though the minister wore a gown like a vicar. So it made a link with home somehow and Hannah resolved to come more often. The warmth in the church after the cold outside began to make her feel sleepy and during the sermon she dropped off to sleep, awaking with a start as the last hymn began. She got to her feet feeling woolly-headed, thinking at first that she was back in Winton and that Mr Hodgson, who kept an eagle eye on the younger members, must have seen her lapse. But then she remembered where she was and slipped out before the benediction so that she didn't have to talk to anyone.

Outside, the rain had started in earnest so that by the time she got back to the house in Cruel Lane, she was soaked to the skin and her thin shoes were sodden. She went in the back door and Gloria popped her head out of the lounge, exclaiming when she saw the state she was in.

'Hannah! You'll catch your death of cold. Look, I'll run you a bath and you get straight into it and you can have your dinner afterwards, I've kept it hot in the oven.'

'Nothing to eat, please Gloria, I'll have something later,' said Hannah, but she was only too pleased to strip off her clothes and soak in a hot bath, letting the heat seep into her bones. And afterwards she slipped through the hall dressed in Gloria's lounging pyjamas, which her friend had thoughtfully brought down for her. Hearing the drone of men's voices behind the lounge door, she went upstairs to her room, glad of an excuse not to face Alf and Reggie for a while at least. Changing into her nightie, she got into bed, pulling the covers up to her chin. And then, lying watching the raindrops slide down the windowpane, she at last allowed herself to think about Timothy.

'Something up?'

The Honourable Anthony Akers dumped his glass of beer on the table where Timothy was sitting by himself, morosely staring into the middle distance. The bar was full of undergraduates, noisily celebrating or debating.

Timothy shook himself out of his reverie and smiled at his friend. 'Hallo, Tony,' he said. 'No, what could be wrong? I was just sitting here having a quiet drink, that's all.' To illustrate this he took a long swig of his beer before putting his glass down on the table and staring at it as if fascinated.

'You could have fooled me, old son,' said Tony cheerfully. 'If I were asked to diagnose what's wrong with you I'd say woman trouble. Am I right?'

'No, you're not,' Timothy snapped. 'I told you there was nothing wrong. Now, if I'm too quiet for you, why don't you join that lot at the bar? They're noisy enough even for you.'

'Ooh, quite a temper,' observed Tony equably. 'It wouldn't have anything to do with that little girl who almost caused a riot on Saturday night, would it? The one Rupert Rowlands was telling me about? You know, the refugee from the wastes of the industrial north?'

Timothy rose to his feet and, picking up his glass, drained it before replying. 'I can see there's to be no peace in here tonight,' he pronounced, sounding only a little pompous. 'If you don't mind, I'll be off now.'

Tony whistled. 'I say, you really are smitten by this girl, aren't you? Come and sit down and tell your Uncle Tony all about it.'

But Timothy was gone, the door into the street swinging after him. He walked back to his rooms through the gloom of the early December day, then, when he was almost there, he turned round and walked away again. He told himself that he was simply in need of fresh air, even though rain was already falling from a lowering sky. And as he walked, Hannah was in his thoughts, how lovely her face had been as she gazed at him across the table in the supper room of that cheap dance hall, he couldn't remember its name. Her great dark eyes, such eloquent eyes, did she know they mirrored her thoughts so plainly? And the flawlessness of her skin, so fresh and creamy; the entrancing way her dark hair framed her face; the dimple in her chin he had been tempted to put his finger over. He could picture her so well now. But of course he wasn't really smitten by her, as Tony had said he was, Tony was always jumping to the wrong conclusions about everything. It was just that he was interested in her, of course – hadn't he known her years ago when she was a skinny little girl with a large voice? Not that she was skinny now, he mused, oh no. Even in the straight, rather shapeless dress she was wearing he could see how her figure had rounded out, the way the cheap fabric was strained a little over her breasts, and when he had held her to him in the dance he had felt her tiny waist and the voluptuous way her hips swelled beneath. Oh no, she was no longer skinny.

It would be pleasant to talk to her for a while without that loutish brother and his pals interrupting, he thought. He would be interested in finding out what she and her brother were doing in Oxford, so far from their native northeast. He had always thought miners liked to stay in the pits, were born to the work almost, though he had only the vaguest idea of how the girls made their living, before they were married, that is. Of course, some of them became servants, he knew.

With a shock, Timothy came to a halt by the railway station, just across the road from the newsagent's shop, the shop where he had seen Hannah that day, for the first time since she was a child. What on earth had made him walk all the way here? he wondered. Oh, well, he decided, he might as well go in and get an evening paper. Crossing the road he went in.

'Yes, sir?'

It wasn't Hannah behind the counter, but a middle-aged woman with a lilting Geordie accent.

'Umm, the *Standard*, please,' he said, mentioning the first paper which came into his head.

'Twopence, that is, sir,' said the woman and he delved into the pocket of his Oxford bags for the money. He hesitated for a moment and she looked at him, eyebrows raised.

'Anything else, sir?'

'No, thank you. That is, er, there was a young lady in the shop the last time I was in, can you tell me if she still works here? A small girl, about seventeen, I think.'

Mrs Ridley looked him up and down, compressing her lips, her usual merry smile missing. 'I'm sure I don't know who you mean, sir,' she said. 'Now if you don't mind, I am rather busy –'

'A girl from County Durham, perhaps a relation of yours?' Timothy persisted.

'What do you want with this girl?' Mrs Ridley demanded. Timothy had no time to reply for the curtain at the back of the shop was lifted and Hannah came out.

'It's all right, Mrs Ridley,' she said. 'I know Mr Durkin, he's from Bishop Auckland.'

Chapter Fifteen

They sat in a small café near the station, the sort of place which was not quite what Hannah would call scruffy but on the other hand, it didn't pretend to be a genteel tea room either. But the counter and the tables were clean and so were the thick cups and saucers. She had thought of it as a good place to meet for it was tucked away round a corner and so in the unlikely event that Alf or Reggie should come by the station they wouldn't see her.

Timothy had brought cups of muddy brown tea from the counter and now they sat facing each other in the almost empty room. The café was used mainly during the day; at this time of early evening, there were few customers.

'I'm sorry if I caused you any trouble on Saturday evening,' he said softly. She watched him stirring sugar into his tea, two spoons of sugar, she noted abstractedly, he has a sweet tooth. Briefly she thought of Alf's angry reaction when he had found her with Timothy, the way he had shaken her and shouted at her.

'It doesn't matter,' she said.

'The truth is, I was so pleased to see you there I didn't think,' he said. 'I just knew I wanted to dance with you and talk to you, find out what you had been doing during all these years.' He sat back in his seat and smiled at her. Somehow, the smile excluded the people hurrying by on the pavement outside the window and the waitress standing behind the counter wiping pots with a grey tea cloth and watching Timothy and Hannah curiously. It excluded everything; the smile built a world of their own and there were just the two of them in it.

'Look at me, Hannah,' he commanded.

Startled, she looked up into his eyes and a melting sensation crept up from her toes. Beneath it there was a warning voice telling her to be very careful, to hang on to her common sense; he was the agent's son, upper middle class, and as such as far out of her reach as the son of Lord Akers. But all of that was of no account against the way he was looking at her.

'Hannah, why were you so unfriendly that day I found you in Ridley's? I was so pleased to see you and you made me feel like a worm.'

'I don't know,' she mumbled, her face pink as she thought of the reason she had acted that way.

'Did you think I was just trying to pick you up? I know that's what your brother thought at the dance hall that night, though it wasn't that at all. But I was so surprised and pleased to see you after so many years, and in Oxford of all places. Why did you leave home?'

'For the same reason my brother did, to put myself in the way of earning a living,' said Hannah. 'There was no work for either of us at home.'

Timothy was embarrassed, he could have kicked himself. Of course, it was obvious. To cover up he pressed on. 'But why Oxford, of all places?'

'Alf came to work at the motor works, and I followed because he could help me get settled.'

Hannah took a sip of tea and put the cup down hurriedly, it was stewed. She stared out at the rain, wondering what she was doing here with a man like Timothy Durkin who had to have it pointed out to him that girls in her position had to leave home to find work. Sadly, she was becoming more and more aware of the gulf between them, it seemed impossible to cross.

'I'd better be getting off home now, they'll be wondering where I am,' she said, rising to her feet. Timothy automatically stood up too.

'Oh, do you have to? I thought we could go to the pictures or something, maybe have a meal somewhere. We haven't had a chance to talk yet.'

'I must go.'

He saw she was determined and shrugged in disappointment. 'Oh, well, if you must. I'll run you home, the motor is parked just around the corner in the station yard, it won't take me a tick to get it.'

'No, I'll get the bus, it drops me at the end of the road,' she said, shaking her head decisively. Alarm showed in her face for a moment as she thought what would happen if she drove up to the house with Timothy and Alf saw her, or even Reggie or Gloria.

Seeing it, Timothy immediately capitulated, half guessing the reason. 'I'll walk with you to the bus, then,' he said. But even though it was only a short distance to the bus stop and the evening was dark and wet, illuminated only by foggy pools of light under the street lamps, she was nervous, looking around all the time, and he could sense it and cursed her lout of a brother for making her so.

'I'll call for you tomorrow evening, same time,' he said softly as they waited at the bus stop.

'Better not,' said Hannah.

'But I want to,' cried Timothy, 'and you like me a little bit, don't you? So why not, we're not hurting anyone?'

The bus was pulling up to the stop and Hannah moved forwards to the step, feeling confused, not knowing what to say. She paused for a moment and the man behind her said, 'For God's sake, girlie, make up your mind, before the bus goes without us.' She climbed up, not looking behind her at Timothy, and moved down the bus, only to find that he was with her, taking the seat next to hers.

'What are you doing?' she whispered urgently, glancing around to make sure no one she knew was aboard.

'I'll come all the way with you unless you agree to meet me tomorrow,' he replied and she knew he meant it.

'All right, all right, but wait outside Ridley's for me, six o'clock. Don't come in and don't let Mrs Ridley see you,' she answered and he smiled triumphantly. He picked up her gloveless hand and kissed the tips of her cold fingers for anyone to see before getting to his feet and ringing the bell.

The bus came to a halt just as it turned into the Cowley Road; he jumped off and waited until it started up again, to give her a jaunty wave through the window. Blushing, she glanced round at her fellow passengers. Two girls sitting opposite were watching her, their eyes alive with curiosity and something else, was it envy? She looked away quickly, folding her hands in her lap, still feeling the touch of his warm lips on her fingers. Dreamily, she gazed at her reflection in the window until the bus sailed past her stop and she had to walk all the way back, feeling very foolish.

But she had decided on one thing. Maybe she was a fool, but she loved being with Timothy, she loved the way he made her feel special and she was going to stop letting thoughts of the gulf between them get in the way of her being with him. She would meet him as often as he wanted to even if that was only until he tired of seeing her. And he would tire of her, her common sense told her he would. But till then, she had this lovely new exciting feeling to cherish and she could pretend it would last for ever and not worry about afterwards. 'Sufficient unto the day is the evil thereof,' as Mr Hodgson had been so fond of quoting.

'Oh, I meant to tell you, I've joined the choral society and there is a practice tonight. Don't bother about any dinner for me, Gloria, I'll get a snack after work. There isn't time for me to come home for anything, the practice starts at seven.'

Hannah rose from her seat on the bus where she had been sitting with Gloria and rang the bell to get off and Gloria followed her.

'But why didn't you tell me?' asked Gloria, looking slightly injured. 'I have a casserole all ready for tonight and Reggie promised to light the oven at three o'clock when he gets up. And Alf is coming round, we were going to have a nice family evening together before Reggie goes to work. He'll be disappointed if you're not there.' Gloria was becoming more domesticated by the day as her wedding day approached, she loved to play at happy families.

Hannah turned to her contrite. 'Oh, I'm sorry, I didn't think,' she said. 'I arranged it at lunchtime yesterday and it completely slipped my mind. Still, you don't need me to enjoy yourself, not when Alf will be there.'

'It's Reggie, though; he likes you, Hannah, and he's beginning to think you're avoiding him. You're not, are you?'

'No, of course not,' Hannah said quickly, moving away as she spoke. 'Look, I have to go, Gloria, or I'll be late.' She hurried off to the shop, guiltily thinking of how she was deceiving her friend.

'I'm not doing anything wrong,' she told herself for the umpteenth time as she went into the shop and greeted Mr Ridley. And anyway, she did intend to join the choral society. But not tonight, tonight she was meeting Timothy. The thought of it brought a light to her eyes and a spring to her step. She changed into her overall and began to serve the stream of customers, happiness bubbling up and spilling over into her work so that many a customer went out with a lighter heart than when he came in.

During her lunch hour, Hannah wandered round the shops, wishing she could afford one of the smart outfits she saw in the shop windows, just so that she would look nice for Timothy. But it was only a passing wish, she was level-headed enough to know that her most pressing need was for winter shoes and she had seen just the pair she wanted in a little shop just off Carfax. Dark-brown brogues, stout enough for the winter weather, yet fashionable too. Now she was waiting for January and hoping they would be reduced in the winter sales. Twenty-nine shillings and eleven pence was just too much for her, she reckoned, looking down at the shabby, thin-soled shoes she was wearing. They were beginning to let in water, but she hardly thought they were worth the expense of taking to the cobbler; the last time it had cost her five shillings and she would rather save the money towards a new pair. So she had cut out insoles from a cardboard box, hoping to make them last, it was only a week or two now, she told herself.

Thinking she had just enough time to go and look at the shoes again, she hurried over to the shop where she had seen them. There they were, on a stand in the window. 'Best-quality brogues,' the notice said. 'Snug and warm for the winter.'

'Here's a bonny sight, enough to brighten any winter's day,' said a voice in her ear, and she jumped round with a surge of gladness she couldn't hide.

'Oh!' she cried. 'Hallo, Timothy.' Taken by surprise like that, she forgot that she was guarding against letting him see how she felt about him, and all of her heart was in her eyes. 'I was just window shopping,' she added.

Timothy glanced in the window at the display of shoes, a

slightly speculative glance, before he turned back to her.

'I'd offer to walk you back to the shop but I know you would turn me down,' he said, twisting his lips a little discontentedly. He was becoming impatient with all the secrecy, she was aware.

'We'll see each other tonight,' she reminded him. 'Now I must go or I'll be late.' She walked quickly away from him before he could say any more, turning to wave as she came to the corner. But she felt a flutter of dismay as she saw he wasn't watching her till the last possible moment as he usually did. Instead, he was staring moodily into the shop window.

'That friend of your brother has been in to see you,' said Mr Ridley when she got back to the newsagent's. 'He said he'd call back.'

'Reggie?' Hannah was surprised. 'But he's on nights, he should have been in bed.'

'When a man gets out of bed to come and take a girl to lunch, he means business,' said Mrs Ridley, winking at her husband. 'I reckon he's taken a shine to you, lass.'

'He was just being friendly, I expect. He probably had to come into town for something else and thought he might as well eat with me,' said Hannah.

'Right disappointed he looked when you weren't here. Are you sure he's not your sweetheart?' Mrs Ridley grinned knowingly.

'No, he's not, I haven't got a sweetheart,' said Hannah, rather too quickly.

'Nay, lass, for a lass what hasn't got a sweetheart you show all the signs. You're on edge on a night to get off on the dot, then waste time prettying yourself up in front of the mirror in the back. An' when I saw you wearing your good dress underneath your overall, I says to George here, our Hannah's got herself a boy, sure as eggs is eggs. Well, the lad's well enough to look at and seems to have a good job, why keep it a secret?'

'Reggie is not my boyfriend,' Hannah repeated as she went into the back shop to change into her overall, leaving the curtain which usually screened the room from customers half drawn back. Combing her hair, she saw through the mirror Mr and Mrs Ridley looking at each other, Mrs Ridley's usual smile absent. As she put down her comb, the older woman followed her into the back shop and drew the curtain properly.

'Hannah,' she said, 'I hope you don't think I'm an interfering old woman but we neither of us want you to do something you will regret. I mean, about this chap from the university, it's not him you're keen on, is it?'

Hannah didn't answer, she didn't need to; the look of dismay did it for her. Mrs Ridley nodded, her suspicions confirmed.

'I thought as much,' she said. 'Oh, pet, think what you're doing, that sort's not for such as us. It's only in fairy stories that the king marries the beggar maid, you know.'

'I'm not exactly a beggar maid, nor is he a king,' said Hannah.

'But you know what I mean. Oh, I know, he's likely a nice lad an' he mebbe thinks a bit about you, but when it comes down to it, he'll not marry you, pet, bonny though you might be – an' you are, you're pretty as a picture. That's mebbe the trouble, he fancies you, that's all. Aw, lass, don't cheapen yourself, not you, I'd be that sorry to see you hurt.'

All the time Mrs Ridley was speaking, Hannah kept her eyes on her clenched hands; she was quivering with anger and humiliation and at last she could keep quiet no longer. Drawing herself up, her eyes flashing in her pink face, she kept her voice low as she replied.

'Don't worry about me, Mrs Ridley, I'm not doing anything to be ashamed of and neither is Timothy. And he's not like that at all, he likes me for what I am. And as to marriage, well, what makes you think I want to get married yet anyway? I'm too young to get married, for a start.'

Mrs Ridley gazed sadly at her. 'Well, pet, if that's how you want it, all right. I'll say no more.' But as Hannah turned to go into the shop, she couldn't help adding, 'Just be careful, though, hinny, will you? Me and George have none of our own and we're fond of you, you know.'

Hannah smiled, albeit a bit shakily for she felt all churned up emotionally. Mrs Ridley had put into words all her own unspoken doubts and fears. Before she could reply, Mr Ridley called from the shop.

'Is anyone coming out here to give me a hand or do I have to do all the work around the place myself?'

Thankfully, Hannah went into the shop and began serving the usual stream of afternoon customers. Later, when the stream dried up, she took a duster and began the business of cleaning the shelves, keeping herself busy until it was time to leave.

Pulling the wine-red cloche hat over her head, Hannah stood back from the mirror to admire the effect. She felt safe enough doing it in the back shop for Mrs Ridley had gone home to start the evening meal and Mr Ridley never noticed such things. Nevertheless, Hannah drew the curtain that screened off the room before she pulled a tube of lipstick from her bag and applied it rather inexpertly to her lips. But the colour wasn't right with the hat, she saw, and she rubbed it off again, feeling guilty because it had cost a shilling in Timothy White's, the chemists, last payday. And the hat itself had taken five shillings and eleven pence of her savings, but it had looked so pretty she hadn't been able to resist it. In any case, she told herself, it was a good felt and it kept her head warm.

'Goodnight, Hannah,' said Mr Ridley as she went through the shop. 'Have a good time. You know Mother didn't mean to upset you this afternoon. She worries about you, that's what it is.'

'She didn't upset me,' said Hannah. 'Goodnight then, Mr Ridley, I'll see you in the morning.' But as she went out into the cold, damp evening, she acknowledged to herself that Mrs Ridley's plain speaking had touched a raw nerve. She knew it was foolish to hope that anyone like Timothy could possibly be serious about her. She pushed the disagreeable thought away; she was going to meet him because she couldn't help herself, she was desperately in love with him and it didn't matter whether he was serious about her or not, all that mattered was that he was interested enough in her to want to go out with her.

As she opened the door of the café and saw him sitting at their usual table, she couldn't help smiling at him with her heart in her eyes.

She sat down opposite him and he put his hand over hers, slipping his thumb underneath to her palm, caressing gently. It was a gesture he usually made on greeting her and, as always, it sent tiny shivers of excitement up her arm.

'You're not expected at home, are you?' he asked, a small furrow between his eyes. Too often they had met like this and she had said she had to get back after only half an hour of their being together.

Hannah shook her head dreamily, still bemused by the feel of his thumb on her palm. 'I said I was going to choir practice, that I'd joined the choral society,' she admitted, and he laughed out loud.

'You didn't! You little devil,' he cried in mock horror. 'Oh, Hannah, how shocking, telling fibs like that.' They grinned at each other in complete accord.

'Actually, it's not a bad idea, that. It would give us somewhere to meet legitimately, wouldn't it? We'll have to think about it. But for now I have a great idea. There's a hotel I know out on the Banbury Road, we could go there for dinner tonight, what do you say? It's only half an hour's drive.'

'Well, I don't know . . . I'm not dressed for anything grand.' Hannah had never been out to dinner in a hotel in her life. She glanced uncomfortably down at her coat, of a dark-brown wool mixture. Her mother had taken a club out at the co-op store to buy the coat for her first winter away from home and it was definitely showing signs of wear. But the main problem was her shoes.

'Oh, come on, Hannah, you're so pretty no one will notice what you're wearing,' said Timothy. 'But I promise you, we'll find a secluded table away from everyone else if you would rather. Aren't you hungry?'

'Oh, I am,' said Hannah, almost without volition for she was very hungry indeed. All she had eaten at lunchtime was a chocolate bar she'd bought from stock; the walk over to see the shoes had taken up too much of her dinner hour to leave time for a meal.

'Well, come on then,' he said briskly and led the way out to his car. He settled her in the passenger seat, solicitous about wrapping the travelling rug around her and tucking it in carefully, even though the hood was up, and Hannah felt warmly cherished. He went round the car and climbed into the driver's seat and then he turned and kissed her, a gentle, tentative kiss. Hannah lifted her lips to his and kissed him back.

'Sweet little Hannah,' he murmured and put his arms around her and held her close, a little awkwardly in the confined space of the car. Despite this, Hannah's arms found their way around his neck and she breathed in the fragrance of him, masculine and fresh with a faint tinge of something else, something that smelled expensive. His arms tightened around her and he lifted her chin and kissed her again, this time a more demanding kiss, and her mouth opened naturally to his probing tongue.

It was only a few seconds before he let her go, groaning audibly and straightening the rug, which had become disarranged during the embrace.

'Oh, Hannah, you don't know what you do to a man,' he whispered. 'We'd better go before I lose my head altogether.'

Hannah's eyes were still half-closed dreamily and she savoured the taste of him. As he drove out from the shadows of the station yard into the lighted street, she looked up at him wonderingly. At that moment she would have gone anywhere with him, done anything he wanted, no matter what the consequences or what Mrs Ridley or Alf or anyone else thought.

They drove out of the town and along a country road lined with dark, bare hedges. There was very little traffic, just the road, closed in by the hedges, curving and twisting ahead of them, and their tiny enclosed world of the car. For a few minutes, Hannah fantasised that they were truly isolated from everyone and there was no one else to care what they did. Then Timothy was turning into a wide gateway, a gravelled drive, and pulling to a halt by wide stone steps leading to an imposing front door.

'We're here,' said Timothy.

Hannah stayed where she was, reluctant to leave the cosy intimacy of the car, until Timothy got out, walked round the car and opened her door.

'Come on, Hannah,' he said, holding out his hand to her. 'I thought you said you were hungry?'

She got out and waited while he picked up a parcel from the back seat and they walked up the stone steps and into the hotel entrance. Warm air met them as they opened the door and light twinkled from the electric chandelier and bounced off the gilt-framed mirrors on the walls so that Hannah blinked at the brightness. She stood uncertainly but Timothy led her forward and a stately man in evening dress came to meet them.

'Good evening, sir,' he said. 'Mr Durkin, isn't it? We have your reservation,' and he beckoned to a waiting girl to take their coats.

Hannah fumbled with the buttons nervously but Timothy

lifted it from her shoulders and the coats disappeared through a door on the left with the girl. Hannah glanced down at her plain dress and was relieved to see it wasn't creased even though she'd had it on under her overall all day at the shop.

'Shall I take your parcel, sir?' asked the man, but Timothy shook his head.

'I'll keep it with me.'

'Very well. This way, Mr Durkin.' And with only a flicker of an eyebrow in Hannah's direction the head waiter – for Hannah had realised that was who he was – led them into the dining room, an old, oak-panelled room with many secluded corners and crannies. Timothy had chosen this hotel well, it was indeed the ideal place for a private meal. Their table was hidden in a corner by the window, the only table there, so that the only indication of other diners was a slight murmuring of voices.

'Do you like it?' asked Timothy and she nodded her head wordlessly. Timothy put the parcel on the floor by his chair and she looked at it curiously. What could be so important about what was in the parcel that he had to keep it with him? But Timothy had noticed her interest and grinned at her.

'You'd like to know what it is, wouldn't you, Hannah?'

'Well, I wondered, that's all,' she replied, blushing.

Timothy waved away the hovering waiter and picked up the parcel and handed it over to Hannah. 'Open it,' he said.

'Oh, no, I'm not that curious,' she answered, blushing even more furiously.

'But it's for you,' he murmured softly and she looked up, startled. 'Go on, open it,' he went on.

Hannah tried to undo the knotted string but the knots were too tight. After a moment watching her, Timothy picked up a knife and sliced through them impatiently. Hannah opened the parcel to reveal a shoe box and straight away guessed what was inside. She looked at the lid, thoughts racing through her head of what her mother, Alf or even Gloria would think of her taking such a gift from a man she was not even engaged to.

'Go on, open it,' Timothy insisted and she looked up at him solemnly so that for a moment he stopped smiling and looked anxious.

She took the lid from the box and there they were, the brogues she had been admiring in the shop window. Tucked in the side of the box was a cellophane packet and through the cellophane she could see a pair of sheer silk stockings. Her toes curled up in her old thin shoes, uncomfortably wrinkling the cardboard insoles. She had never had a pair of silk stockings in her life before; in fact, the only pair she had seen was the ones Betty had had for her wedding. She stared at them for a long moment, the shoes and the stockings, and imagined what it would be like wearing them. Then she looked up at Timothy who was watching her with the indulgent expression she had seen on her mother's face when she had been able to give the children some rare treat. And she remembered how her mother had refused to allow Tucker to give Betty just such a gift as this before they were properly engaged. 'Only loose women take presents like that,' Nora had stated firmly.

'I can't take them,' she said boldly. 'It was nice of you to think of it, but I can't take them.'

Chapter Sixteen

'I'm sorry,' said Hannah as Timothy reached across the table for the shoe box and put it back on the floor at his feet.

He looked at her unhappy face and smiled. 'Don't be,' he said. 'If you can't take them, you can't. Now let's have something to eat before we starve to death altogether.' He picked up the menu and handed it to her. 'What would you like?'

She glanced at the bewildering array of dishes and gave up immediately. 'You choose,' she said and he looked across the room, and magically the waiter was there to take their order. They ate asparagus soup and dainty portions of plaice and the main course was duckling in a delicate orange sauce. Hannah had been sure she would not be able to eat after the misunderstanding about the shoes, but Timothy tucked into his meal so matter-of-factly that she felt less embarrassed about refusing the shoes and her appetite returned and she ate well. But she always waited until he lifted up the correct knife and fork and copied him, just as the advice column in *Woman's Weekly* advised. And only a few days before she had found a second-hand booklet on etiquette in a box outside a bookstore. It had cost her sixpence but now she knew not to hold her knife like a pen, a piece of advice which had been one of the many little gems she had found in the book.

The white wine Timothy had ordered made her feel a little light-headed after only half a glass so she prudently refused any more. Still, by the time they had eaten their way through several courses and were sipping strong, black coffee, which was so bitter that she hastily added two spoonfuls of sugar, she was intoxicated without the benefit of more alcohol. Simply sitting there with Timothy, talking of nothing in particular and eating good food in such an atmosphere of rich comfort was enough. It was with a sense of loss that she realised that the meal was over and it was time to go.

She slipped out to the ladies' cloakroom and when she came out into the hotel entrance, Timothy had paid the bill and was ready. He was holding her coat for her to put on when the waiter came after them with the shoe box. 'You forgot your parcel, sir.'

Timothy tucked it under his arm with a murmured 'Thank you'. In the car he threw it on the back seat without a word and concentrated on tucking the rug round Hannah. And, still intoxicated by the whole evening, she put her arms around his neck and drew him to her and kissed him.

'Thank you for understanding,' she whispered.

'Oh, Hannah,' he said, lifting his head and looking down at her.

It was a very dark night, there was only the faint light of the lamp which hung over the door of the hotel, and all she could see was just the outline of his head, haloed against the lamp as he bent it to hers. She felt his lips on the nape of her neck and somehow her coat was open and he was cupping her small breasts in his hands. Such shivers of emotion ran through her that she felt she couldn't bear it, the intensity of her feelings taking her completely by surprise.

'I could get a room,' he said, his voice hoarse. 'Not here, they know me, but we could go nearer home, I know just the place.'

And all the warnings and moralising which had been drummed into Hannah at home and in chapel, all the talk of strumpets and whores and the dangers of falling into sin were nothing compared with the compelling necessity of being with Timothy, truly with him. She nodded, wordlessly, and sat quietly under her rug as he turned the car in the drive, drove back along the Oxford Road and pulled into the forecourt of a small inn with a notice in the window, 'ROOMS TO LET', a place much smaller and less grand than the hotel they had just left. She waited quietly as he booked a room, explaining to the sleepy landlord that he and his wife were driving north for Christmas, taking it in easy stages as 'the old bus won't be pushed'. And the landlord didn't appear to notice that they brought no luggage into the inn with them or that she kept her left hand firmly in her coat pocket, just in case he should notice the absence of a wedding ring. He handed over the keys the minute Timothy had signed the book.

'First door on the right at the top of the stairs, bathroom at the end of the upstairs hall,' he told them. 'What time would you like breakfast, sir?'

'Oh, we may sleep late, we're in no hurry,' said Timothy casually, for all the world, thought Hannah, as though he had done this often in the past. Even this thought didn't disturb her; she followed him upstairs and into the tiny room, which was taken up almost in its entirety by an enormous double bed covered in a flowered chintz counterpane. She couldn't take her eyes off the bed as she allowed Timothy to take her coat and hang it in the minute wardrobe alongside his. Then he started to undress her, taking off the brown wool dress and hanging that up too before pulling the ribbon of her camisole so that it dropped from her shoulders and revealed her firm, high breasts. All of her being now focused on him and the intensity of her feelings for him. Feelings which flooded her whole body until she felt she would drown in them.

Hannah woke in the dark winter's morning with a feeling of euphoric contentment. Timothy lay beside her, his head resting on her shoulder, breathing evenly as he slept, one leg bent up over her thighs and an arm flung over her waist. She lay quietly for a while, savouring the closeness of him, the feel of his skin against hers. It must be six o'clock, she thought, twisting her head to try to read the dial of his wristwatch, which was the only thing he was still wearing, but it was too dark to see it properly. Inevitably, the euphoria was seeping away from her as thoughts of the coming day crept into her mind. Sighing, she tried to slip out from under his leg but it lay too firmly across her thigh and she reached carefully down to lift it, she instead encountered his manhood. Wondering, she left her hand touching it, so flaccid now, so different last night. Cautiously, she moved her hand so that her fingers encircled it and at once it sprang up, almost as though it had a life of its own. Hannah pulled her hand away hastily, but not hastily enough – Timothy was awake, his arm tightening around her, his lips nuzzling her ear.

'Timothy, I must go, I'll be late for work,' she said urgently.

'Not now, you can't do that to a man and just go,' he replied, lifting himself on to his elbow and gazing down at her face, barely outlined on the pillow in the gloom of the dawn. But Hannah was thoroughly awake now and beginning to panic.

'I must, Timothy, please take me back, I have to be in the shop by eight o'clock. Oh, Lord, what am I going to do?'

Timothy sat up in bed. 'All right, don't panic, of course I'll take you back. But I had thought you might take the day off today, ring in and say you're sick or something. Don't you want to stay with me? We have hours yet before we have to get up, then I'll order breakfast – we can't go without breakfast, can we?'

Hannah was reaching into the wardrobe for her coat to cover herself while she went to the bathroom. Her hand stayed for a moment, but then she took out the coat and pulled it on before going to the light switch by the door.

'You don't understand anything, do you?' she said flatly. 'What do you think my brother is going to say if he finds out I've been out all night? He'll likely break my neck, can't you see that? And my job, I can't simply take days off, it's my living, what would I do if I lost my job?'

'Oh, don't be so dramatic, Hannah, I wouldn't let you starve. Now be a good girl and come back to bed.'

Hannah gazed at him as he lay back down on the pillow and lifted the bedclothes invitingly. Without speaking, she opened the door and went out to the bathroom. Locking the door, she gazed at as much of herself as she could see in the mirror over the hand basin. Her breasts felt sore and swollen but as far as she could see they looked no different from how they had looked yesterday, nor did anything else about her except perhaps her lips, swollen they certainly were. Still, she didn't look like a fallen woman, though she wasn't sure what they would look like, just that there would be a difference. She thought about running a bath but decided there was no time, it was already getting lighter outside and if she didn't hurry Mrs Ridley would be in the shop and be wanting to know why she was late. So she ran water into the basin, washed herself all over and, shivering, dried on the skimpy towel provided. Still damp, she pulled on her coat and hurried back to the bedroom.

He was sitting on the edge of the bed waiting for her, his trousers on but his chest still bare. 'Sure you want to go back now?' he asked.

'Sure.'

'Righto then.'

She dressed quickly behind the open door of the wardrobe and with her back to him. When she turned round he was still sitting on the edge of the bed, grinning.

'What –' she began and stopped, blushing, as she noticed that her reflection in the mirror on the inside of the wardrobe door was repeated on the wall mirror opposite so he had had a perfect view of her as she put on her clothes.

'Oh, come on, Hannah, it's a bit late for false modesty, isn't it?' he teased.

'Timothy, please, I have to go,' she pleaded and he jumped to his feet, suddenly businesslike.

'I'm ready, I can bathe and shave when I get back. I'm ready, see, just hand me my coat.' He pulled on his shirt and jacket and flung his overcoat on the top. 'Come along now, don't dawdle, you go out to the car and I'll pay the man.'

They drove along the road to Oxford in a line of morning traffic but just as they reached the outskirts of the city, Timothy pulled into the side and turned to her.

'Timothy, I must get on,' she exclaimed.

'I know, you have to get to work, you told me. But first I want to know – you looked so cross this morning, flying about, desperate to get back – are you sorry it happened?'

Hannah looked away from him, down at her hands, out of the car window at the houses lining the road, anything. She wasn't sure how she felt. Everything was so different in the daytime.

'Hannah? Look at me, Hannah. Don't be sorry, please. It was wonderful and natural and nothing to be ashamed of at all, not when we love each other.'

Something in his voice, something young and vulnerable, made her turn to him. His eyes were very blue and questioning and the faint shadow of stubble on his cheeks and chin paradoxically seemed to accentuate his youth. And she knew, no matter what trouble she had to face during the day, no matter even if she lost her job and Gloria threw her out of the house, she loved him and she wasn't sorry.

'No, I'm not sorry, Timothy, I'm glad,' she said.

'I love you, Hannah,' he whispered and kissed her gently. Restarting the engine, he swung the car out into the morning traffic and headed for Ridley's shop, pulling up a few doors farther on.

'I'll wait for you this evening,' he said.

'Well, I won't be able to stay long, I must go home,' she answered, sounding doubtful.

'I'll wait for you, the usual place,' he repeated, getting out of the car to open the door for her. As she got out, he kissed her again, insistently. Two girls passing by on their way to work blinked at them, startled, before going on their way, giggling.

'Timothy! Suppose someone I know sees us,' she protested.

'Would it be such a disaster?'

'Yes, it would,' she replied, her tone quite sharp with exasperation. But she didn't have time to say any more; already people were pouring out of the station and many of them were going into the shop. With a muttered goodbye she hurried away, leaving him gazing after her.

'And what time do you call this, young lady?'

Her spirits sank as she saw that Mrs Ridley was working behind the counter alongside her husband. As his wife put the question, Mr Ridley paused as he counted out change from the till and stared solemnly at Hannah. She looked away, flushing guiltily.

'I'm sorry I'm late, I won't be a minute getting ready,' she mumbled and hurried to change into her overall. When she came back into the shop, Mrs Ridley finished serving her customer and then went behind the curtain. For perhaps fifteen minutes, the shop was busy, giving Hannah a chance to compose herself, though she still hadn't the faintest idea what she was going to say to them, or rather to Mrs Ridley, for it would be she who demanded an explanation.

'Breakfast, George,' called his wife from the back shop, and Hannah was left on her own for a while. But inexorably the time came when Mr Ridley came back and took her place.

'The wife wants you,' he said, flicking his head towards the curtain and Hannah went through.

Mrs Ridley handed her a cup of tea and picked up her own, and they sat down to drink as they did every morning. But this morning she didn't start chatting about a customer or how the warehouse had let them down or what trouble she was having with her knees.

'Right, lass, out with it,' she said bluntly.

Hannah took a sip of tea and swallowed nervously. 'I'm sorry I was late, I'll make it up tonight,' she began. 'I missed the bus –'

Mrs Ridley snorted and put her elbows on the table. Holding her cup in both hands, she glared at Hannah. 'Don't lie to me, lass,' she said. 'I saw you get out of that car, it was that student's, wasn't it? Eeh, I'm right disappointed in you, that I am, telling me lies an' all. You didn't try to catch the bus, did you?'

Hannah sighed. Mrs Ridley was right, what was the point in telling her lies when it must be obvious to her what was going on?

'No, no, I didn't,' she admitted. 'Timothy brought me. I'm sorry. I'll make sure I'm not late again.' She looked across the table anxiously. 'You're not going to give me the sack, are you?'

'Nay, lass, of course not, you're a blooming good worker, what would we do without you? I just wish you'd mind me when I tell you you're making a mistake about this chap. Stick to your own kind, that's what I think, it's always best in the long run.' Mrs Ridley finished her tea in one gulp and took the cup to the sink and rinsed it out under the cold-water tap. Picking up the teatowel she dried the cup slowly before putting it down and turning back to Hannah.

'I suppose nothing I say will make any difference to you, though, I might as well save my breath to cool my porridge. But be careful, lass, that's all. I'll say no more about it. If it's him you want, then you must do what your heart tells you to, that's all. But don't forget, pet, I'm here if you need me, me and George, both of us. We've gotten fond of you and you're a good little worker like I said, we'd do badly without you now, I'll say that. Just try to get in on time and as far as we're concerned that's an end to it. All right?'

Hannah got to her feet and hugged her, feeling close to tears. For a moment, Mrs Ridley was stiff and unbending, then she held the girl to her and patted her shoulder.

'There, pet, it's all right. Now you'd better get back to the shop before George comes looking for you.'

'Thank you,' whispered Hannah. 'I do love him, you know.'

'Aye, pet, I know you do, that's the nub of it,' Mrs Ridley answered.

The morning wore on and a steady stream of customers kept Hannah busy till at last it was one o'clock and she was free for an hour. She had decided that she would seek out Gloria at her work so, pulling on her coat and hat, not bothering to look in the mirror to check if it was on straight, she rushed out of the shop. Walking along in the cold, grey afternoon, Hannah almost bumped into Gloria coming the other way.

'Oh, I was just coming to see you,' she exclaimed, a smile faltering on her lips.

'Were you indeed?' said Gloria. Hannah's heart sank as she caught the other girl's tone, which was almost as cold as the day. 'Well, we'd better go in here and have a hot drink. I think you owe me an explanation.'

Meekly, Hannah followed Gloria into a small café and they sat down at a table. 'Two hot chocolates, please,' Gloria said to the waitress. She pulled off her leather gloves with the fur-trimmed cuffs which Alf had bought her for her birthday and loosened the top button of her warm tweed coat. As usual, Hannah thought, Gloria was neat and smart from the crown of her brown velvet cloche with the tiny mink ornament over one ear to her elegantly crossed ankles clad in artificial silk stockings (one and eleven a pair in Marks and Spencer's and too dear for Hannah) and her neat shoes with the decorative tongues over the laces. Hannah could see the shoes peeping out to one side of Gloria's chair and instinctively she pulled her own ill-shod feet out of sight.

'You look terrible,' said Gloria, startling Hannah into glancing up. 'Your hat is on crooked and you look tired to death, you're all eyes. Have you looked in a mirror today?'

Hannah remembered that she hadn't and put her hands to her hat to straighten it.

'Oh, for goodness sake,' snapped Gloria, 'do it in the ladies' after we've had our chocolate.' She fell silent as the waitress served the drinks, waiting until she had gone back behind the counter at the end of the café to take someone's money. Then Gloria launched into her attack.

'Where were you last night? I was worried to death, I laid

awake half the night waiting for you and then when I found out you still weren't back this morning I didn't know what to think. It's just as well Reggie's on nights and Daddy never notices anything. I can tell you, they wouldn't like to think you stayed out all night.'

'Er, I stayed with a friend,' said Hannah, not looking at Gloria.

'A friend? What friend? Some one you met at the choral society?' demanded Gloria, and Hannah nodded her head eagerly.

'Yes, it was getting late when the practice finished and it was so cold out, so when my friend offered to let me stay with her –'

'What's her name? I presume it is a her?'

'Er, Jane,' said Hannah, giving the first name which came into her head.

'And I suppose it never occurred to you that I might be worried. I almost went along to see Alf this morning before I came to work, I thought he might know where you were.'

'You didn't, though, did you?'

'No, I didn't, I thought there was no sense in us both worrying about you. He had enough to think about, I wasn't going to upset him when he had a day at the works ahead of him. I've got more consideration for him than that.'

Gloria picked up her spoon and stirred her hot chocolate and Hannah watched her set face, the usually pleasant expression gone.

'He's picking up his new car today, did you remember? It's a big day for him, I didn't want to spoil it. Though naturally, I was worried. Supposing you hadn't gone in to work today? Supposing you'd disappeared for good? He would have blamed me for not telling him straight away, wouldn't he?'

'Picking up his new car?' said Hannah, more to change the course of the conversation than anything.

'Yes, you didn't even remember, did you? You don't take any interest in anything Alf or I do nowadays. I'm that disappointed in you, Hannah, I really am.' Gloria picked up a glove and pulled it on over her carefully manicured and pink-painted nails, then followed suit with the other glove. She sighed heavily.

'Well, I suppose I should be thankful that you're all right. I was imagining all sorts of things had happened to you, you'd been run over and were lying in a hospital bed or taken by white slavers or something,' she said. 'I'd better be getting back now, or I'll be late. Are you coming home tonight? Because if you're not, kindly tell me now, it's only civilised behaviour, you know.'

Hannah rose to her feet, leaving her cup of chocolate untouched. 'Yes, I'm coming home tonight, Gloria. And I'm sorry, I really am, I'm sorry I worried you and everything. Thank you for not telling Alf, I promise I won't stay out again, not unless I've told you beforehand.'

'Oh, come on, walk to the end of the street with me. We won't fall out about it, not this time. I was worried about you, like I said, that's all.' Gloria's expression relented.

Hannah felt miserably guilty as she walked back to the shop. She felt she was entangling herself in a great web of lies, one lie leading to the next and then another and another. If only she had someone to confide in, she thought, someone close she could talk to. Gloria might have been the very person but for her engagement to Alf. Hanging up her coat and hat in the back shop, Hannah remembered her future sister-in-law's comments on her appearance and looked in the mirror. There were dark smudges under her eyes and the only colour in her face was that of her lips, still slightly swollen and bruised. She splashed cold water over her neck and face, dampening the front of her hair, before taking a comb to tidy her short bob. At least she looked a little better now, she thought, studying her reflection before going out into the shop.

'By, I'm pleased to see you back, pet,' said Mr Ridley. 'This has been a long morning, I can tell you. I'm ready for a rest.'

Hannah looked at him, shaken out of her preoccupation with her own troubles, for he sounded even more tired than she was herself. There was a grey look to his face, she saw, and a tiny tic at the corner of his mouth.

'Why don't you take a long dinner hour?' she suggested. 'I can manage fine here, that is until the teatime rush.'

'Aye, I reckon I will,' he answered heavily. 'I feel a bit off colour, mebbe it's the flu coming on. You sure you can manage?' He wrapped a long muffler round and round his neck and pulled his overcoat on over it. Taking a checked cap out of his pocket, he pulled it forward over his face and turned up the collar of his overcoat so that all Hannah could see of him was his nose.

'See you later then, pet,' he said and went out.

The afternoon stretched ahead of Hannah, seemingly endless. As the short December day darkened into evening, there were few customers and she kept herself busy checking the stock and writing a list of things needing to be replenished when the wholesaler's representative called. Four o'clock came, then half past, and still no sign of Mr Ridley, but Hannah wasn't worried. It was half an hour yet before the evening rush began as people dropped in for the evening paper on their way to the trains.

But at half past five, he still hadn't returned and the trickle of customers had increased to a flow and there was an impatient queue forming at the till. And then it was six o'clock, the time Hannah usually finished work, but there was nothing she could do but carry on serving customers and hoping one of the Ridleys would turn up to relieve her soon.

'Hallo, Hannah. Got a packet of Park Drive, have you?'

She had been mechanically taking money for papers, cigarettes and matches and hardly seeing faces, only hands, the grubby hands of workmen and the pale hands of academics and businessmen, typists' hands stained with typewriter ink and some with faint traces of oil under the nails and round the cuticles, just like this pair in front of her now. She looked up and saw it was Reggie.

'Oh, hallo, Reggie. Yes, of course.' She handed him the packet of cigarettes and took his sixpence and gave him two pennies in change.

'I've been doing my Christmas shopping,' he said, holding up a brown paper carrier.

'Oh?'

Hannah smiled at him as she took coppers from a customer beside him and dropped them in the till. Desperately, she wished he would go, Mr Ridley would be coming in any minute now and she would be free to run round the corner to the café where Timothy would be waiting for her. But Reggie simply moved to one side so that other customers could take his place at the counter.

'Yes. So I thought I'd call for you, we can go home together.'

The shop was empty of customers for the moment and she started to tidy the piles of papers on the counter; it was something to keep her hands busy while she thought of an excuse. There was the obvious one, of course, she realised.

'I can't leave the shop until Mr Ridley comes back. He's very late, I'm afraid he may be ill.' As if on cue, the door opened and a small boy came in with a note in his hand.

'You Hannah?' he asked, and when she nodded he held out the note. 'Mr Ridley asked me to give you this and I'm to wait for an answer.'

Hannah opened the envelope and read the note and her heart sank.

'Look, Reggie, you might as well go. Mr Ridley's poorly, I have to cash up and lock the shop and take the keys and cash over there.'

'I'll wait for you, we'll go over there together,' Reggie said quickly. 'I'm in no hurry.'

'But Gloria will have a meal ready. If neither of us turn up on time, she'll worry.'

'No, she won't. Don't you remember Alf got his car today? He said he was going to surprise her, pick her up at work and take her for a drive. We'll eat later.'

Hannah couldn't think of any other way of getting rid of Reggie short of telling him the truth. She would just have to stand Timothy up. Surely he would understand when she told him what had happened.

'Well, go and sit in the back, I won't be long cashing up,' she said, giving up.

Slipping the bolt in the door and changing the sign to 'CLOSED', she pulled down the door blind and began counting the money out of the till and putting in the cloth sack Mr Ridley used to transport it. She had almost finished when there was a knock at the door.

'We're closed,' she called, but the knocking went on, becoming more imperious as she called out again. Sighing, she went to the door and opened it just a little. When she saw who it was, she flung it wide. She was so glad to see Timothy that she forgot all about Reggie, sitting in the back shop.

Chapter Seventeen

'What's wrong? Why didn't you come to meet me?' asked Timothy.

Before she could answer him, Reggie came from behind the curtain, walking out into the body of the shop to where she stood with Timothy.

'The shop's closed, didn't you hear? Hannah called it loudly enough,' he said. 'Now if you don't mind, we'd like to get home.'

'Who are you?' asked Timothy. 'And what has it got to do with you if I want a word with Hannah? Isn't Mr Ridley here?'

'No, he isn't, Hannah's closed the shop and we are going home now so please leave.'

'Oh, yes, I remember you now. You were with Hannah's brother at that dance hall, weren't you?' Timothy became hostile as he recollected where he had seen Reggie before.

'And I remember you too,' retorted Reggie. 'But I didn't think you'd still be pestering my girl. Has he been bothering you, Hannah?'

Hannah stared at him, dumbfounded – what did he mean, *his* girl? For a moment she couldn't think what to say, so there was a tiny silence as Timothy turned to her.

'Tell the man, Hannah, go on, tell him, have I been pestering his girl?' Timothy's face was a mask of jealous rage, yet he spoke softly, almost calmly. 'Whose girl are you, Hannah?'

'Timothy, please don't make a scene. Reggie is my brother's friend, his sister is engaged to Alf. I live with Gloria and Reggie and their father.'

'How convenient that must be for you, so cosy,' he replied with heavy sarcasm.

'And just what do you mean by that?' demanded Reggie stepping between them, his fists bunching. 'Hannah's a good girl, she is, I won't have anyone even hinting such things about her.'

'What do you think I mean?' asked Timothy but he was unprepared for what came next for the next moment he was on the ground, flattened by a clumsy swing from Reggie, which nevertheless connected with his jaw. Timothy scrambled to his feet with a growl of rage and made to charge at Reggie but Hannah somehow got between them and clung on to him so that he couldn't carry out his obvious intention of returning the blow.

'Timothy, don't. Please go, I'm in enough trouble as it is, please,' she cried, and he looked down at her, the anger dying away from his eyes.

'Oh, I see, you want me out of the way, is that it?'

Hannah looked from Timothy to Reggie and back again, helplessly. Oh, why had Reggie chosen tonight to come to meet her?

'Reggie, please go and wait for me in the back shop,' she said at last.

'I'll do nothing of the sort,' he replied, glaring from her to Timothy. 'I'll not leave you with this rotter, didn't you hear what he was implying about you? I've a good mind to knock him flat again –'

'Reggie! Wait for me in the back shop, I tell you.' Her voice rose as her temper finally snapped. 'You can wait for me in the back shop or get out of here, now.'

Reggie paused, frowning unhappily, then he walked backwards towards the curtain. 'Righto, I will. I'm not leaving you alone with him, though, don't forget, I'm just behind the curtain.'

'Reggie, just go,' she said wearily, and he ducked into the back shop, the curtain swishing behind him. Hannah looked at Timothy, his eyes cold in his set face. He was like a stranger. She couldn't imagine that she had really spent the night with him, it must have been a dream. 'Come to the door,' she said, keeping her voice low, and silently he followed her.

They looked at each other and Hannah could see that he

wasn't in any mood to be understanding, but she had to try to explain. 'I'm sorry I couldn't get away to meet you,' she began. 'I was busy.'

'Yes, so I see,' he replied, glancing at the curtain.

'No, you don't. Mr Ridley took ill, I had to take over. That's where I'm going now with the day's takings. Reggie was –'

'Oh, save it, Hannah, you don't have to tell me about Reggie. It's plain to see he's in love with you. It must be quite cosy for you two to live in the same house. You were careful not to tell me about that, weren't you?'

'You never asked me about where I lived,' Hannah pointed out, stung. 'And even if you had, there was nothing wrong, nothing to tell. I don't even know why we're fighting, why you're so different to what you were this morning.'

'Don't you, Hannah? No, perhaps you don't, that's the trouble. I come in here and find you with him and he tells me you're his girl and you don't know why I'm angry. Didn't last night mean anything to you? Well, I congratulate you, you certainly had me fooled with your air of innocence. That was a good move, saying you couldn't take the shoes. What was it, were you hanging out for something more expensive? Well, it's too late now, you've been rumbled. Goodbye, Hannah.' Pulling open the door, he strode away into the gloom, leaving her staring after him in complete disbelief.

'Gone, has he? Not before time,' said Reggie, coming up behind her, and she turned on him furiously.

'What do you mean, acting as though you owned me?' she shouted at him. 'Why did you tell him I was your girl?'

'But Hannah, I thought you were! Haven't we been going out together?'

'No! No, we haven't, except to make up a foursome with Gloria and Alf. That didn't give you any rights over me. I've never given you any reason to think I was your girl, no reason at all.' Hannah lowered her tone as she saw how stricken Reggie looked, his earlier aggressiveness had completely disappeared. 'Oh, Reggie, why did you say it?'

'I don't know, I suppose I just wanted it to be true,' he mumbled. 'I saw red when I saw that university chap hanging round after you again. Hannah, he only wants one thing, can't you see that? They're all the same, these students.'

Hannah stared at him, realising it was a waste of time losing her temper with him. He would never understand how it was between Timothy and her and he would never understand what he had done. She wondered what Reggie would say if he knew she had spent the night with Timothy in a hotel, but her imagination stopped short at that. The thought flashed through her mind that if Reggie was right and Timothy had only been after 'one thing', as he called it, then he had succeeded. But Reggie was wrong, oh yes, he was wrong, Timothy loved her, he did. And when he got over his fit of jealousy he would come back to her, she knew he would.

'Oh, come on, let's get locked up,' she said. 'We have to go over to the Ridleys' place yet. Alf and Gloria will be back from their drive before we get back home at this rate.'

It was only a short walk to the Ridleys' flat, which was a second-floor walk-up above a row of shops. Mrs Ridley opened the door to Hannah's knock.

'Oh, you're here,' she said, looking relieved. It was a measure of her preoccupation that she didn't even cast a speculative glance in Reggie's direction. 'I was beginning to wonder if you'd had a last-minute rush,' she went on.

'Not really,' said Hannah, handing over the cloth sack of coins and reaching into her handbag for the roll of one-pound and ten-shilling notes. 'How is he?'

'The doctor's just been. It's that new flu, he says. He has to stop in bed, though. We'll have to manage the business between us. Do you think you can open up in the mornings for a while? It's six thirty, though, that's the rub, can you get in in time? Is there a bus? We'll pay you extra, like.'

'Of course I can, don't you worry,' said Hannah.

'Keep the keys then, I'll come in when I can to give you a break.' Mrs Ridley glanced behind her as the sound of coughing came from the bedroom. 'Poor George, he sounds badly, doesn't he? I'll have to go and see to him. You know what men are like, proper babies when they have anything the matter with him. I'm grateful, Hannah, I really am; thank God we have someone we can trust to take care of the shop. You won't be the loser, I promise you, pet.'

'Mother? Where are you at?' Mr Ridley called, his words punctuated by a fit of coughing.

'You'd better go. Don't worry, I'll see to everything,' promised Hannah.

'I wanted the telephone put in the shop but George was against it,' Mrs Ridley fretted. 'Now I'll be kept busy going backwards and forwards.' She was already backing towards the bedroom. 'Well, I'll see you tomorrow then.'

It was almost eight o'clock by the time they got back to Cowley, but Gloria and Alf were not back from their drive.

'I don't know, no one seems to care about me getting my dinner on time any more,' grumbled Dan Morgan as soon as they went in. He was sitting in the lounge with the evening paper, looking disgruntled.

Hannah went into the kitchen and checked in the oven. There was a rabbit casserole there just waiting to be warmed up and a pan of potatoes on the ring; Gloria usually left something prepared just to finish off when she came in from work. Hannah lit the gas and went back into the lounge.

'It'll only be twenty minutes, Dan,' she said and he grunted and rustled his paper angrily. Reggie sat down and fiddled with the wireless set, making it whistle and whine before he got it properly on station. American dance music filled the room and Hannah went upstairs to check if the water was hot enough for a quick bath before the meal was ready. Luckily, Dan had lit the geyser and she spent a blissful ten minutes soaking in water as hot as she could bear it before reluctantly drying herself and pulling on an old skirt and jumper. She was combing her hair when she heard the front door open and the excited voice of Gloria over the lower tones of Alf. Bracing herself apprehensively, even though Gloria had said she would say nothing to Alf, she went downstairs. The other girl was in the kitchen.

'Oh, bless you, you've got the dinner on,' she greeted her. 'Dad is moaning on about it, he hates his dinner to be late. We called for a drink and now I'm absolutely starving. Oh, Hannah, the car's lovely, it really is, goes like a dream. You'll have to slip out and see it after we've eaten.'

'It's a bit dark for that,' said Hannah, thinking that Gloria must have kept her word about not saying anything or Alf would have been in the kitchen now 'playing war' with her, as they said back in Winton. And Gloria seemed to have forgotten her earlier annoyance with Hannah.

'Alf parked it under the streetlight on purpose so that he could show it off,' she said now, laughing. 'You'll be able to see it all right.'

By the time they'd eaten and Hannah, Reggie and Dan had admired the bull-nosed Morris and Hannah had explained about Mr Ridley going down with the flu, it was already ten o'clock.

'You go on up to bed, I'll do the washing-up,' said Gloria. 'You have all my sympathy if you have to get the six-o'clock bus every morning, I think you want well paying for that.'

Hannah was only too pleased to slip away, she felt so weary she could hardly climb the stairs. She'd had nothing to eat all day through worrying about what Alf would say when he found out she'd been out all night and consequently had eaten a little too well of the rabbit casserole and that made her sleepier still. She pulled off her clothes and put on her warm flannelette nightie, shivering in the cold bedroom. Snuggling down under the bedclothes, she lay curled up on her side, listening to the murmur of voices from downstairs. She'd been lucky not to be found out, she thought, very lucky, she would not be so lucky again. But then, with an aching sense of loss, she thought it wouldn't be happening again. She and Timothy were finished, he'd made that very plain to her. Timothy didn't want her any more; he believed Reggie when he said she was his girl.

Chapter Eighteen

'For heaven's sake, Tim, pull yourself together,' Tony advised. 'What sort of a Christmas are we going to have with you mooning over a little shop girl the whole time?'

'I'm not mooning over anyone,' said Timothy. 'And if you don't want my company I can easily go back to Oxford or even home to Durham. Just say the word and I'll be off.'

Tony sighed. 'Dear me, you are prickly today, aren't you? Not at all your usual cheerful self. In my experience that means you have woman trouble, deny it as much as you like. And the antidote to woman trouble is more women, so get out and enjoy yourself. Now it's the season of good cheer and here were are in London with the house to ourselves except for the servants. I for one intend to have a high old time. Pull yourself together, old chap, we're partying tonight and tomorrow night after that. Don't forget it'll be noses to the grindstone in the new year, with finals looming.'

Timothy gazed out of the window which overlooked Park Lane and the park beyond, only half hearing his friend. He shouldn't have come, he thought, he just wasn't in the mood for jollification. But when Tony had suggested he spend part of Christmas with him in London as Lord and Lady Akers were in New York for a few weeks, he had thought it was just what he needed to take his mind off Hannah. Besides, it was a good excuse not to go home to that increasingly gloomy house in Durham Road to spend a lonely Christmas with his father, who was always preoccupied with business. The only people invited to the house were business friends or members of the Coal

Owners' Association and they would have grave discussions over the dinner table about the blind intractability of the miners and their communist leaders.

Besides, Timothy mused, Durham Road was too near Winton and Winton reminded him of Hannah. He would run the risk of meeting her in Auckland if she went home for Christmas. He didn't want to see her again, at least not until he was sure he was properly over her.

'Tim? You're not taking a blind bit of notice of me, are you?' demanded Tony in a tone of outrage. He was normally of a pleasant nature but he was not used to being ignored. Timothy turned from the window.

'Sorry,' he said. 'I was miles away.'

'Yes, I know, that's just what I was talking about,' said Tony crossly. 'Mooning over that girl again, I'll be bound. Now, come on, we're supposed to be at Lady Cynthia's in half an hour for cocktails before the theatre. Then we're all going on to Rupert's place to dance the night away. That should be enough to take your mind off that girl.'

Trouble is, thought Timothy as he struggled with his bow tie before the mirror in his dressing room, nothing seems to be enough to do that. For the last three or four nights they had followed the same hectic round of cocktail parties and theatre parties, supper parties and dancing parties, where the girls were all pretty and sophisticated and dressed in the latest fashions. Every time he had found himself comparing them with Hannah in her cheap little dresses and worn shoes, and it was always Hannah, with her grave, dark eyes and translucent skin, who had the best of the comparison, though she had never seen the inside of a beauty parlour. He thought of the shoes he had bought for her that day. Having seen the wistful look on her expressive face as she gazed into the shop window he had thought he would surprise and delight her with them and the silk stockings too. But he had been mistaken in that; he just didn't understand Hannah, that was the trouble.

'Ready?' asked Tony through the open door. Timothy wrenched his mind away from thoughts of Hannah and followed his friend out to the waiting car, determined to at least try to enjoy the evening ahead.

* * * *

Back in Oxford, Hannah was kept busy from early morning until evening in the shop, every day of the week except Sunday, when she worked until one.

'The doctor says George has to stay away from work for another couple of weeks,' Mrs Ridley reported, a week before Christmas. 'I've tried to get a girl in, temporary like, but you know what it's like at this time of year, all the shops want extra help.'

It was still a novel idea for Hannah that there should be more jobs available than workers, even though she had been in Oxford long enough to realise it for herself. She put her hand in her overall pocket and felt the letter from her mother which had been waiting for her when she got home the evening before. 'Things are bad, Hannah,' Nora had written.

I know they are always bad, but this year they are worse. Half the pits are on short time and that means traders in the town are doing badly too, so there's no work at all for the lasses. Poor Jane, she's talking about taking a job on the coal screens, she's desperate to earn a bit, but I worry she's not strong enough for it. I know she's cured of the consumption, but the screens are lads' work really. We're managing, though, I've got my pension and the bit the shop brings in. Folks are living from day to day, they can't afford to get food in any amount from the big shops, it's all they can do to buy for the next meal and that's where I come in handy. As long as I don't have to ask Tucker to help out and I'm determined not to. It wouldn't be fair, not when they've got baby Simon now, it would be taking advantage.'

Betty's baby Simon had been born at the beginning of October and Hannah had knitted a matinee jacket and sent it for him.

Hannah took the money for the *Oxford Times* from a customer and he went out, leaving the shop empty for a few minutes. This was a good time to suggest what she had in mind, she thought, and turned to her employer.

'Mrs Ridley, I've been thinking,' she began.

'Yes, hinny?'

'My sister Jane, she needs work. You know what it's like back home, there's nothing for her at all. But she'd come down here to work like a shot if she was sure of a job.'

Mrs Ridley pursed her lips, considering. 'I don't know, Hannah. The job would only be temporary like, just until George gets on his feet, it wouldn't be fair to bring a lass down for that. And anyroad, where would she stay?'

'She could sleep in my room, that wouldn't be any trouble,' said Hannah. 'And if she was here she would get work after Mr Ridley is better; you said yourself there's plenty of work so folk can pick and choose. It's just that first chance she needs.'

'I don't know, I'd have to speak to George,' Mrs Ridley said doubtfully. 'I don't suppose we could pay much, and then there's the money for her ticket. Would she be able to come straight away?'

Hannah smiled. The battle was won, she could tell by Mrs Ridley's tone. 'She could get the money for her ticket all right,' she assured the older woman. 'And I can ring up my sister, she has the telephone in the house because her husband is the under-manager.'

'Really? Oh, well, I'll speak to George this dinnertime and let you know when I come in at four o'clock. Now, go and get a bite to eat while I'm still here.'

Hannah was pretty sure that George would agree to anything his wife proposed, and in the event she was right. That evening, after closing the shop, she rang Betty from the telephone box in the station.

'Hannah!' cried Betty, immediately apprehensive when she heard her sister's voice. 'Is there something wrong?' It was the first time Hannah had ever telephoned her, for long-distance calls were so expensive.

'No, no, nothing, Betty. How are you? Mam said in her letter that you and the baby are blooming.'

'Oh, we are. Baby Simon's growing fast and do you know, Hannah, he's the image of Tucker. I've just put him down for the night, he's such a contented baby he sleeps all the way through but for his ten-o'clock feed. I wish you could get away for a few days and come up and see him, Hannah. He's quite grown out of that little jacket you sent. But are you ringing for something special?' Betty became businesslike as the operator came on the line, advising that more money should be inserted, and Hannah pushed in another precious sixpence. Quickly, she explained about the job for Jane.

'If she can come the day after tomorrow, there's work here for her at least until the end of January. Then I'm sure she'll get something else. Mam said Jane is desperate for work, and she can sleep with me till she gets a place. Do you think she'll come?'

'Oh, she'll jump at it. And don't worry about the fare, Tucker will see to that. I'll go down to see her now – Tucker's in, he'll keep an eye on Simon. Can you ring tomorrow night, just to make sure?'

'Yes, same time,' said Hannah, just as the operator's voice cut in again with a request for more money. Thankfully, she put the phone down, thinking it gobbled up sixpences at an alarming rate.

Going home to Cowley on the bus, Hannah remembered she had yet to ask Gloria if it was all right for Jane to stay with them, it was a bit cheeky arranging it without asking her nominal landlady. Still, she was fairly sure Gloria would agree.

In the event, Hannah was right about Gloria's consenting to Jane staying, at least in the beginning. And two days later, a Sunday, Hannah stood on the platform waiting for the train bringing Jane. The train was due in at two thirty so Hannah hadn't bothered to go home when she closed the shop at one o'clock, instead she had made herself a cup of tea in the back shop and eaten a sandwich she had brought with her to while away the time until the train from the north came in.

There was a chill wind blowing along the platform but the afternoon was bright and sunny and Hannah was reminded of the day she had come down herself. Of course, she hadn't had to travel on her own, Alf had been with her. But Jane was fifteen now, only a little older than she had been. Jane's sure to be homesick, she thought, remembering the agonies she had suffered herself in the beginning. She would have to help her to feel at home. After all, she and Jane had been very close as children, before Jane had gone away to the Sanatorium in Weardale.

The tinny voice announcing the imminent arrival of the train came over the loudspeaker and Hannah watched as it steamed into the station and the doors began to open. She saw Jane at once, clutching the strap of a basket-weave box just like the one which Hannah had brought with her, an age ago, it seemed now.

'Jane! Jane!' she called and ran down the platform to her sister, ready to throw her arms around her, but when she saw Jane's composure she was suddenly shy and simply kissed her on the cheek.

'Hallo, Hannah,' said Jane. 'It was good of you to meet me.' She was small and thin, too thin, Hannah thought, and pale too. Two spots of colour brightened her cheeks, standing out against the white skin like rouge, but Hannah knew they were not artificial.

'Come on, I'll take your box, you must be tired after the journey. It's only a short bus ride to Cowley.' Hannah picked up Jane's box in one hand, took her arm with the other and led the way out of the station and there was Alf, just getting out of his car.

'Oh, good, I've caught you,' he cried, taking the box and heaving it into the back seat before grabbing Jane and hugging her, not at all put off by the way she shrank back, looking stiff with embarrassment. 'Come on, jump in, we'll be home in two ticks and Gloria is making a slap-up tea for us all.'

All the while, Jane had hardly spoken, simply murmuring her greeting. Hannah got into the back seat of the car beside the luggage and Jane climbed sedately into the front seat. She's tired, thought Hannah, and perhaps a little overwhelmed by the suddenness of the change; after all, everything had happened so quickly.

'Look, there's the shop,' she said, leaning forward and pointing out the single-storey lock-up shop with the sign across the top of the window, 'Ridley's Newsagents'. 'I have to come in early tomorrow to open up, six o'clock. You can come with me for the first day, though usually you'll be starting at eight.'

Jane looked over at the shop, her face expressionless. 'Will I be paid for the extra time?' she asked, and Hannah looked astonished.

'Oh, I don't think you should ask for that. After all, it's just that I can show you the way into town and what to do when you get here,' she replied.

'I just wondered, that's all,' said Jane.

Alf laughed. 'You start as you mean to go on,' he said. 'You should be paid for the hours you put in.' He turned briefly and winked at Hannah, obviously tickled by his young sister's business acumen. Jane said no more, she just stared out of the window at the streets, quiet on a Sunday, especially when the students had gone down for the Christmas break.

'It's a bit different from Bishop Auckland, isn't it?' Hannah tried to keep a conversation going as they turned into Cowley Road but Jane just nodded. Giving up, her sister sat back in her seat. The afternoon was darkening into evening already. Alf switched on his sidelights and began to whistle, cutting through the silence in the car with his rendering of 'Good King Wenceslas'. And then he was pulling up before the house and Gloria came out to welcome them.

'Had a good journey?' she asked. Jane nodded again, but somehow her quietness wasn't quite so noticeable as Alf was explaining how he had nearly missed them at the station and Gloria was saying they must be starved and she had tea cakes under the grill all ready to be toasted and buttered, and wasn't the weather foul? Gloria had set the table in the lounge with the best embroidered teacloth for Jane's first meal with them and Jane sat, quietly eating, saying nothing unless she was spoken to and then very little. Hannah was thankful to see that Reggie was out for the afternoon; she was getting tired of the way he seemed to take it for granted that they were a couple, even though she had told him again and again that they were not.

Later, when it was time for bed, Hannah took Jane up to the bedroom. It felt as if she was sharing with a stranger.

'It's not very big, is it?' said Jane, eyeing the bed. 'Not much room for us both. I always had a bed to myself at Weardale, and when I came home.'

'But it's only supposed to be until you can get something for yourself,' said Hannah. 'It was the only thing we could think of for now. You and I used to share a bed before, I thought you wouldn't mind.'

'We were children then,' said Jane.

Hannah looked at her, helplessly. 'When you get a permanent job, we'll find you a room somewhere close,' she said.

'But I'll be on my own then, won't I?' Jane pointed out. 'Couldn't *you* get another room? You're older than me.' Before her sister could reply, Jane went out to the bathroom.

Hannah lay awake long after Jane had gone to sleep and the rest of the household was quiet. She was wondering if she had made a mistake in bringing Jane to Oxford. What on earth had changed her little sister into this quiet, self-possessed young woman who was nevertheless so watchful of her own interests? But then she thought of the years Jane had had to spend away from the family in the sanatorium and of the weeks that would go by when Mam would not be able to find the fare to visit her daughter. Jane must have been very lonely and homesick, more so than Hannah had been when she had come to Oxford, she thought. And Jane had been a young child at the time. No wonder the experience had changed her. Hannah resolved to try to be more understanding with her.

Next morning, Jane was ready before Hannah, wearing a dress which Hannah recognised as one of Betty's, taken in at the sides by Nora, she guessed. Straight with a low belt, it fitted nicely round the hips and looked fine but for the neckline, which was slightly baggy. Jane had fastened a little flowered rayon scarf round her neck which partly disguised the badly fitting neckline. She was standing very still, waiting for her sister to finish her tea and toast. Hannah, trying to keep in mind her conclusion she had come to the previous night concerning her sister's attitude, thought Jane was holding her shabby imitation-leather bag a little too tightly and she was very white, apart from the two flags of crimson in her cheeks.

'Aren't you going to have some breakfast, Jane?' she asked. 'At least have a piece of toast.' She held out a slice of buttered toast and after a moment's hesitation Jane took it and ate it daintily.

'There's nothing to be nervous about, you know. The Ridleys come from our part of the country and they are very nice people to work for,' Hannah said but was rebuffed immediately.

'I'm not nervous,' said Jane, finishing her toast and rinsing her fingers under the sink taps. 'Are you ready now?'

A funny girl, thought Hannah later in the day. Jane was quick to learn and listened attentively to everything she was told, and by the late afternoon was serving customers and tidying shelves as though she had been doing it for years. She was like a different person when dealing with other people, especially Mrs

Ridley, helpful and bright and smiling. Mrs Ridley was delighted with her.

'I'm so pleased you thought of her, Hannah, she's just what we needed,' the older woman confided as she put on her coat to go home after the evening rush. It was six o'clock and Jane had been sent home already, though she protested she would stay if necessary.

'No, you go, I'm sure it's been a long day for you, your first day an' all,' Mrs Ridley had said kindly. 'Hannah will close up, won't you, Hannah?' Mrs Ridley had got into the habit of taking the day's takings with her when she went, leaving Hannah to hide the small amounts she could take in the last hour somewhere in the back shop.

'I only hope we can get her settled in a permanent job,' said Hannah.

'I wouldn't worry yet. I've been thinking, it might be good for George to have extra help when he comes back, at least at first, give him chance to ease into the routine again. Anyroad, Hannah, the doctor's coming tomorrow morning, and I might stay at home to see what he says, I never get a proper story from George. You and Jane can manage, can't you? Tell her she needn't come in early with you, eight o'clock will do fine.'

After Mrs Ridley had gone, Hannah sat behind the counter for a while. The shop was empty of customers and the streets outside looked deserted too. Rain pattered on the window and the glass door and she watched it run down, glittering in the electric light. Tiredly, she pushed her fingers through her short, thick hair, lifting it from her scalp and pushing it back from her temples. She rose to her feet and walked to the door, gazing out at the rain. Jane was going to be all right, she thought, she was a good worker. Maybe she was just naturally quiet when relaxing with her family. I'm too fanciful, thought Hannah, absently tracing the trickle of a raindrop down the glass pane with her fingertip, imagining she dislikes me when she is just reserved. She'll be all right when we get to know each other properly again.

She looked at the clock; another half an hour before the London train was due and the usual half-dozen customers came in for their evening papers. When they had gone she could close up for the night. While she waited she went into the back shop and sat down to change her old shoes for the new brogues she had bought with the money she had earned for the extra hours she had worked. They weren't quite like the ones Timothy had bought for her that day, but they were similar.

The sound of the shop bell tinkling made her jump to her feet, her heart pounding – was it him? It was just such a night as this the last time she had seen him, the night when they had that awful row about Reggie.

'Shop!'

The disappointment when she heard the female voice was as sharp as a pain. Fool, she told herself and went out into the shop to serve the customer with a bar of Cadbury's chocolate. The London train came in and with it the small rush of late customers and Hannah was free to lock up the shop.

Without acknowledging to herself what she was doing, she slowed her movements so that she missed the bus home. She decided she might as well go to the little café and have a cup of tea in the warmth while she waited for the next one. At the same table she had shared with Timothy, she sat and drank some of the muddy brew. But no one else came into the café and in the end she had to go for the bus.

After all, she told herself miserably, it was the Christmas break and all the students had gone home for the holiday. Why should Timothy stay in Oxford? It was time she stopped thinking about him and organised her life without him; she was finished with men. As soon as the holidays were over, she would enrol in night school, perhaps do book-keeping and accounts instead of shorthand and typing. One day, if she worked hard and saved hard, she would have her own business, she vowed, run her own life.

She was so busy planning that brilliant new life that she missed her bus stop and had to walk twice as far as she normally did, and by the time she got home she was soaked to the skin.

It was on Christmas Eve, just as she was closing the shop, that he came. The perpetual rain had swelled the wood of the door and she was having trouble getting it to close properly so that she could turn the key in the lock.

'Here, let me,' he said.

She paused, still glaring at the door, holding the key in the lock. She'd misheard, she thought, it had to be someone else, some passer-by who had seen her difficulty. But then his hand was taking the key from her and he reopened the door, closed it firmly and the key turned easily in the lock.

'Hallo, Hannah,' he said.

Chapter Nineteen

'I give up,' Tony had said when he came down to breakfast and found Timothy moodily stirring cream into his porridge. 'Here you are again with a face like a wet week. The worst of it is, when the girls see you looking all melancholy and forlorn, doing your Lord Byron act, they flock round you, forgetting all about me. And it's not as if you're interested in them at all, you make that pretty plain – I suppose that's half the attraction. No, Timothy my lad, I think it's time you got that girl out of your system. Where is she, still at Oxford?'

'I don't know, I suppose so. Unless she's gone back to Durham for Christmas,' said Timothy. 'Look, I'm sorry, you're right, I'm not much company for you here. I'll clear out if you like.'

'Well, I don't mean to be inhospitable, old chap, but I have to say that's an excellent idea. With you gone, maybe I'll get a look-in with Lady Cynthia. As it is, she's like all the others, eyes for no one but you. Go on, find your little shop girl and turn your charms on her. I'm sure she'll fall into your arms, swooning with delight, and then when you've had enough of her you'll come back to your senses once again.'

'Hmm, I'll have to take the train,' said Timothy, not listening to his friend now as he made his plans, which was just as well for his plans were very different from what Tony thought they were. 'I'll go to Oxford first, I'll have to pick up my car if I'm to go on to Durham.'

They had driven to London in Tony's car, so his own was still in Oxford. But if Hannah wasn't there he would drive home to his father's house and seek her out, he decided, realising it had been in the back of his mind for a while, it had only taken a small push from Tony to decide him. Now his mind was made up he moved briskly and within an hour he was on his way, with Tony acknowledging he was pleased to see the back of him.

There was a feeling of inevitability about it when Timothy came out of the station at Oxford and saw the light go out in the paper shop and Hannah struggling with the door lock. When she turned to face him and he saw the gladness in her eyes, he knew he had done the right thing in coming.

They went first to the little café round the corner but found it had already closed for the Christmas holiday. They stood for a moment in the side street, which was quiet but for the hum of traffic coming from the main thoroughfares close by. A group of late Christmas shoppers went by the end of the street, laughing and talking and then they were gone and it was quiet again. The rain had stopped, but an icy wind sprang up and Timothy drew Hannah close to him protectively as they walked to the car, which he had parked in the station yard.

'What do you want to do?' he asked. 'I can't take you back to my rooms but we could go to a hotel – oh, only to have dinner and a chance to talk,' he added hastily. They sat in the car and as Timothy wrapped the rug around her, Hannah felt the warm remembered intimacy of the tiny enclosed space. She felt her whole body was coming alive after weeks of numbness, and when his hand touched hers her palm tingled in anticipation. But he moved away and sat back in his seat with no attempt to take her in his arms. In the light from the streetlamp she saw he was watching her gravely.

'Well, what do you want to do?' he said again.

'I have to go home, Timothy. I can't just go off again, there'll be a terrific bust-up if I do. It's Christmas Eve and I was going to go to the carol service at chapel with my sister Jane, she's here now.'

Timothy nodded. 'Very well, I'll take you home,' he said. 'I've finished with this hole-in-the-corner business, I'll come in and tell them about us. And I'll come to the carol service with you and tomorrow – you're not working tomorrow, are you?'

'No, not on Christmas day, but Timothy, you can't, Alf will go mad if he sees you with me.'

'He'll get over it.'

'No, but –'

Timothy had already got out of the car and was turning the starting handle. The engine burst into life and he got back in and turned the car in the direction of the Cowley Road.

'Please, just drop me off, Timothy, I'll meet you tomorrow,' she begged. Instead, Timothy pulled the car into the side of the road and turned it round and headed back towards the city.

'What are you doing, where are we going?' she asked. 'I want to go home, take me home.' But he didn't answer, driving straight to the High Street, where many of the shops were still open to attract last-minute Christmas shoppers and he stopped in front of a jeweller's shop.

'Come on,' he said, jumping out of the car. 'If we don't hurry, the shop will close.'

Hannah stared at him. 'What are you doing? You're not going to buy me a present, are you? I told you I can't accept –'

Timothy took hold of her hand and drew her out of the car; banging the door shut, he marched her into the jeweller's. Hannah felt sick, her mind raced; he was going to try to dazzle her with an expensive gift, she knew it.

'I won't take anything, not even for a Christmas present,' she blurted, her voice wobbling.

'Not even an engagement ring?' he asked.

Timothy and Hannah were married by special licence in the chapel in Junction Road on the first Saturday in January 1926.

'But why so soon?' asked Hannah, when he told her he wanted to marry as soon as it could be arranged. 'I thought, perhaps a summer wedding, back home in Winton.'

Timothy looked alarmed. 'Oh no, we'll get married here in Oxford and this is the perfect time during the vacation. We'll have a few days for a honeymoon before I go back.' He took her in his arms and kissed her, his kiss gentle at first but then more demanding. 'I'd get married tomorrow, wouldn't you? I can't bear to wait; you don't really want to wait, do you, Hannah?' And, of course, she did not.

The only guests at the wedding were Alf, Jane and Gloria. Dan Morgan and Reggie were asked but declined, and Mrs Ridley was helping George in the shop for he still wasn't up to par. The Honourable Anthony Akers was best man. In the chapel beside Timothy he stood looking round with an air of disbelief that he should be participating in this unlikely event.

'I didn't mean for you to marry the girl,' he had said, when Timothy rang him up at his parents' home in Park Lane. 'Look, you're not yourself, Tim, old boy. I'll come back today and we'll find a way to get you out of this.'

'I don't want to get out of it, Tony. I love her. Now will you be my best man or not? I've got a special licence, it's at the chapel in Cowley on Saturday.'

'The chapel? What chapel?'

'Just come, Tony, I'll show you,' Timothy had said. And Tony had come, though he had protested that he couldn't see what the rush was all about. 'I have my reasons,' Timothy had said and would not be drawn further.

Tony suspected it had something to do with Mr Durkin senior, who had not been invited to the wedding and, as far as Tony knew, didn't even know it was taking place. But Timothy was of age, he didn't need his father's permission; and he had an income of his own from his mother which had come to him when he was twenty-one. Nevertheless, Tony could visualise the almighty row which was likely to erupt as soon as Daniel Durkin found out about the marriage. He had seen and recognised the elder Durkin's snobbery and contempt for the working class, especially the miners and their families, and he was glad he wouldn't be there to see the confrontation between Timothy and his father. Tony couldn't abide any sort of unpleasantness.

Hannah walked down the aisle on the arm of her brother, past rows of empty pews towards the small party at the front but she didn't notice the empty pews or anything else. All she really saw was Timothy, standing there waiting for her, and her heart swelled within her. Her thoughts were a good match for Tony's; if anything, her disbelief of what was happening was greater than his. Ever since Christmas Eve when she and Timothy walked into the house in Cruel Lane and told them they were to be married and she had held out her hand to show them the diamond ring, she had felt as though it was all happening to someone else. It was like watching Greta Garbo at the pictures and pretending it was happening to her. As she saw Alf turn to watch her progress up the aisle, the scene returned to her clearly.

Alf had started up from his seat at the supper table when she went in with Timothy; she had seen the anger rising swiftly in his face and his ugly expression. And then he had frozen, half risen, looking at them with his mouth open. Reggie had pushed his chair back and gone out without a word. Jane had stared at them, her dark eyes, so like Hannah's, wide and unreadable.

'I'm going to marry Hannah so you may as well accept it,' Timothy had said. Hannah would always be grateful to Gloria for the way she had jumped to her feet immediately, rushed over to Hannah and kissed her, and offered her hand to Timothy, congratulating them loudly. Somehow it had relaxed the atmosphere and made it easier for Alf and Jane to follow Gloria's example, and after that everything was fine.

Hannah and her brother reached the end of their walk down the aisle; Alf stepped back as she took her place beside Timothy and the ceremony began. Her dreamlike state persisted and she barely heard the minister speak at all, let alone ask her the vital question, though she knew she must have given the correct response for Timothy was slipping the gold band on her finger and they were married.

Afterwards, they drove out to the same hotel where they had had dinner only a few weeks before, though it seemed like an age ago to Hannah. They ate a hastily arranged wedding lunch and drank champagne. Tony talked easily with Alf about the relative merits of various motorcars and was gallant with Gloria and Jane. And then it was time for the newlyweds to head for London, where they were to spend the last few days before the new term at Tony's parents' house in Park Lane.

'Nonsense,' Tony had said heartily when he had offered the house and Timothy had demurred. 'The place will be empty in any case. I'm invited to Cannes for a few days with a party which includes the divine Cynthia – at last she has begun to notice that I'm around, thanks to you disappearing from the scene, so I owe you something for that.'

Hannah accepted everything, as one does in a dream, for it was still a dream and fervently she hoped never to waken. She was even oblivious to the way the servants looked askance at her whenever she opened her mouth and spoke, her northern accent showing through no matter how she tried to cover it up. She went shopping with Timothy during the day and bought day dresses, evening dresses and all the accessories needed to go with them, and pairs of silk stockings by the dozen. Every evening they would dine in, go to bed early and rise late, and fill the hours in between with long, sensual loving. There were times, very occasional though they were, when Hannah would wake in the night with a gasp of fear for she had dreamed that something was threatening their dream, something or somebody was waiting to drag them back to the real world. When she searched her mind frantically for the source of the threat, she would think of Timothy's father, that stern mine agent who had frightened and intimidated her so when she was a child. And though she had not talked about him to Timothy, she guessed he had not been told of their marriage, so in the night she would be beset by fear for the future.

Then she would cling to Timothy and he would waken aroused and they would make love, quickly and urgently as though it was the first time, and then she could sleep once again, her fears smothered under her love.

'We'll rent a flat in Oxford,' said Timothy, on the morning after their wedding. 'Though I must stay in college as soon as the term begins, it's only for a little while, darling, just until the finals are over. Then we'll be together all the time.'

'But –' Hannah started to protest; she was puzzled, she couldn't understand why it had to be like that. Other married students lived out, she knew they did.

'Trust me, Hannah, it will all work out,' he said quickly. 'I just think it's best if no one knows about us for a while.'

Tony knows, thought Hannah, and my family knows. But she didn't say anything, not yet; the questions were there and they would have to be asked but not now, not until they got back to Oxford. In the meantime, the world was filled with Timothy and their love. And Hannah would not have been human if she had not been entranced with other things about her new life, not least of which was the fact that for the first time in her life she did not have to turn every penny over twice before spending it. It seemed to her that her husband was fabulously rich and

Timothy, seeing her delight in buying good clothes, could not bear to disillusion her.

When they got back to Oxford and Hannah was installed in a small flat just off the Cowley Road in Princes Street, the dream began to dissolve around her and reality crept in.

Chapter Twenty

'I'll come over as often as I can,' Timothy said as he kissed her in the tiny vestibule of the rented flat he had found for them. 'You understand how it is, don't you, darling?'

Hannah nodded mutely though she didn't understand at all why he couldn't come home to her every evening. What she did understand was that he was determined to keep her and his marriage apart from his life at the university and there was nothing she could do about it, not yet.

'It'll only be for a few months, Hannah, just until I graduate. Come May I'll be free of the university and we'll be together all the time. We'll leave Oxford and go north again if you want to.'

She wanted to ask him about his father then – did his father still not know about her? What would he say if they turned up on his doorstep and announced that they were married? But now was not the time to talk about anything, not when Timothy was rushing off to college. She lifted her face for a second kiss.

'I don't care where we live so long as we're together,' she whispered, and Timothy smiled.

'We'll always be together,' he promised.

After he had gone, she looked round the flat. When she had first come with Timothy the day before, she had been enchanted with the tiny rooms filled with dark furniture and the tiny kitchen and bathroom, complete with water closet. It was to be their own little love nest and she knew they would be ecstatically happy in it. In the light of the shaded electric lamps it had looked warm and inviting. But now, on her own and in the light of day, she saw that the plush of one brown armchair was worn down, showing the coarse weave of the backing, and that the curtains, which had looked a pleasant plum colour the night before, were really a dingy purple. She stood fingering them absently as she looked out into the street, where a pale January sun was shining on the heads of the people scurrying by on their way to work or the shops, and she felt miserably lonely. The long hours stretched out in front of her without even the surety of Timothy coming home in the evening to look forward to. After the excitement of the wedding and honeymoon in London, there was already a flatness about her new life which came over her the moment Timothy left the flat. And it was so unexpected she thought it must be a fault in her – wasn't she married to the man she loved and ecstatically happy about it? Boredom had no place in her life.

'Well, Hannah,' she said briskly to herself, her voice sounding loud in the empty flat, 'best make a list of what to do.' Turning from the window with an air of determination, she looked in her bag for a pencil and something to write on. There was only the envelope which had contained her mother's letter and written consent to the marriage. The sight of her mother's even handwriting with the carefully rounded letters and straight loops, which she had been taught in National School, made Hannah think of Nora and the little house in Winton Colliery and she paused for a minute, forgetting the list she was about to make out. Mam hadn't understood the need for the hasty wedding; after all, Alf and Gloria had been engaged for months now and their wedding was not to be until the spring. Still, Mam had given her consent and Hannah was grateful that she had not asked if the reason was the obvious one.

'I know you are a sensible girl, Hannah,' she had written. 'If you are in love with him then I won't stand in your way.' But Hannah had known that her mother was hurt at not being given the time to arrange to come down to Oxford for the wedding, and she was hurt at being asked not to spread the news of it about. 'I don't know why it is such a secret,' she had written. 'But of course I will do as you say, no doubt you will explain when you come home.'

Hannah sighed, if only she knew what it was all about herself, she would gladly explain to her mother. Her own family were all so open with each other, she had difficulty getting used to having secrets. But her marriage was so new and wondrous to her that when she was with Timothy he was all she could think about, and she still couldn't get over the fearful conviction that it wouldn't last. He would wake up one morning and realise he had made a mistake in marrying a girl like her, a pitman's daughter, and she couldn't bear to do or say anything that might bring that day any nearer. Hannah pushed the thought to the back of her mind and turned over the envelope to make her list, imagining how Mam would scorn the idea that she had nothing to do but wait for her husband to come home and feel the long, empty hours stretching ahead of her endlessly, Mam had no patience with such notions.

'Get going,' she used to say, 'there's always something to be done. Don't tell me you're bored. If you've finished your work, take the bairn out for an airing. The fresh air will do you both good and it'll mebbe brighten your ideas up.'

Hannah smiled as she sat down at the table with her pencil and the envelope and started on a list of things she would do.

First, she would go to see the Ridleys. At this time of day Mrs Ridley was likely to be in the back shop making breakfast for George, and Hannah wanted to make sure they were not offended by the way she had left so hurriedly to get married. And she would see Jane, too. Her brow knitted as she thought of Jane; they were like chance acquaintances rather than sisters, or at least Jane acted as though they were. Hannah licked her pencil and wrote, 'Try to have a talk with Jane.'

Then she would go shopping, buy in some food just in case Timothy came home unexpectedly, something which could be cooked quickly. And she would go to the library and find some good books, books that she could discuss with Timothy and so prove to him she wasn't completely uneducated. Maybe she could even take some classes during the day, when he was in college – that was a good idea. The thought made her jump up and run into the bedroom to comb her hair and take her new camel coat from the wardrobe. As always, she ran her hand down the nap, it was so soft and warm and when she put it on it made her look so smart. So it should, of course, the money it had cost Timothy in Harrods. But he had a private income, she told herself, he could afford it and he liked her to look smart. Smiling as she turned off the gas fire which made the flat so warm and cosy, she went out and ran down the stairs into the street.

Outside, she was glad of the warmth of the coat, for though the sun still shone there was a biting north wind and she stepped out briskly. She had intended to walk to the station but when a bus came along she was glad to board it for the short distance involved. She got off right opposite the newsagent's shop. When she opened the door and went in, she saw it was full of customers and Jane and Mr Ridley were working at full stretch.

'Hallo, Mr Ridley, hallo Jane,' said Hannah, smiling a little uneasily when she saw how busy they were. After all, she thought guiltily, she had left very suddenly and when her sister had barely had time to get to know the work and Mr Ridley wasn't up to par. Jane affected not to hear Hannah at first but she had to acknowledge her sister when Mr Ridley looked up and smiled a welcome.

'What cheor, lass, it's grand to see you,' he cried heartily. Pulling the curtain to the back shop aside briefly, he called to his wife, 'Mother! Come and see who's here. It's our Hannah back from her honeymoon and a grand married lady now.'

Mrs Ridley came out of the back shop with a beaming smile on her face which would have warmed the coldest January day.

'Eeh, lass, it's you,' she said. 'Come away into the back and we'll have a bit of a natter while I make George his breakfast. This rush will soon go and then he'll be demanding his bacon and eggs, as you know.'

Hannah followed the older woman behind the curtain, loosening her coat as she went, for the heat from the gas ring filled the back shop and the smell of frying bacon with it. Mrs Ridley picked up her fork and turned the bacon in the pan, then she looked Hannah up and down.

'Mind, lass, you don't half look smart in that coat – what is it, camel hair? By, it's lovely, it is. Best take it off and hang it up, though, you don't want to get any grease splashed on it, do you?'

Hannah placed the coat on a hanger on the door beside Jane's and then she turned back to Mrs Ridley.

'I've been wanting to tell you I'm sorry I left in such a hurry. I know you were annoyed about it and you had every right to be,' she said. 'I would have waited until Jane had a bit more experience, or at least until Mr Ridley was properly better –'

'Nay, Hannah, think no more of it, it worked out all right,' said Mrs Ridley. 'I must admit I was a bit huffed at first when you went off like that, but your Jane's very good, you know, she's nearly as good as you already. And George has got over his flu so there was no harm done.' Deftly, she lifted the slices of bacon from the pan and broke a couple of eggs into the sizzling fat. Turning the gas down low, she waited for them to set.

'I was wrong, wasn't I, pet?' she said. 'This time the prince did marry the beggar maid, didn't he? And it couldn't have happened to a nicer lass, that's what I said to George, you ask him.' Carefully, she slid the eggs onto the plate beside the bacon and put the kettle on the gas ring.

'I'll tell him it's ready,' said Hannah, going to the curtain. She was relieved and happy now that she knew Mrs Ridley bore her no ill-will, it was something that had been bothering her.

'Breakfast is ready, Mr Ridley,' she called. Then she saw that there were still half a dozen customers waiting to be served.

'Aye, and I'm ready to eat it, only trouble is, I'm too busy for the minute,' said George. 'Tell Mother to keep it hot for me, there's a good girl, Hannah.'

'No, go on, you get your breakfast, I'll help Jane,' she replied, moving in behind the counter.

'If you're sure you don't mind.' He hesitated, but Hannah waved him away.

'Go on, eat it while it's hot.'

The sisters worked steadily away until the shop was clear of customers, about fifteen minutes later. Hannah was alone with Jane in the shop at last and she smiled at her younger sister, noticing that Jane seemed to have put on a little weight and seemed much healthier than she had been when she first came to Oxford.

'How are you liking it here, Jane?' she asked. 'Mrs Ridley says you're doing well. Do you like living with the Morgans?'

'It's all right. At least I have the room to myself now you've gone,' Jane answered.

'I'm glad,' said Hannah. There was a silence between them for a few minutes, then she tried again. 'Have you heard from Mam lately? I haven't had a letter since just before the wedding.'

'There was a letter this morning, I didn't have time to read it before I came out.'

Automatically, Hannah began to straighten out the piles of newspapers which were laid out on the counter, feeling slightly uncomfortable at the lack of response from her sister. She wondered how Jane could bear not to open a letter from home the instant it came. From the back shop they could hear the voices of the Ridleys chatting together. Jane stood behind the counter with her arms folded and a slight smile on her face as Hannah moved from the papers to the rack of magazines and straightened them.

'It must be nice to come in here and play working,' she said suddenly, making Hannah glance across the room at her, startled. Jane hadn't sounded hostile exactly but her tone was not friendly either.

'Oh, I'm not, it's just that I've done it for so long,' said Hannah. 'I wasn't thinking, really.'

'I thought you were checking whether I'd laid them out the way you like them,' said Jane, and there was definitely a sarcastic note in her voice this time.

'Oh, Jane, I don't know why you're annoyed with me,' said Hannah. 'We used to be such friends when we were small, why can't we be friends now? We're family, aren't we?' She kept her voice low so that the Ridleys wouldn't hear.

Jane shrugged. 'What's family? It doesn't mean anything, really. When I was in the sanatorium none of you bothered to come to see me, the nurses were more to me than family.'

'Jane!' gasped Hannah, forgetting all about the Ridleys in the back shop. 'You know we hadn't the money for fares to Weardale. And Mam came to see you whenever she could, you know she did.'

Jane's face twisted in disbelief. 'Do I? Maybe she did. All I can remember are the times I was expecting her and she didn't come. The fact is no one came to see me for weeks at a time and after a while I stopped expecting it.'

Mrs Ridley pulled back the curtain and came into the shop, looking from one girl to the other. 'There's nothing wrong, is there?' she asked.

Jane's whole demeanour changed, and she smiled at the older woman vivaciously. 'No, no, we were just talking of old times back home,' she said. 'Now, shall I have my break now? I thought if we weren't busy I could clean the shelves afterwards.'

'Thanks, pet, you're a good girl.' Mrs Ridley relaxed, obviously thinking she had been mistaken in feeling there was tension between the girls.

'Well, I'll be on my way, then. I have to do the shopping for tonight's meal,' said Hannah awkwardly. She walked to the door, then thought of something and went back to the curtained doorway of the back shop.

'Jane,' she said, 'will you come up to see me at the flat one night next week? For a meal, I mean? Then we could have a proper talk.'

Jane looked at her over her teacup. 'Oh, I don't know. What about Timothy? You don't want me there, really.'

'Yes, I do,' Hannah insisted. 'And Timothy would, too, you're my sister, after all. Anyway, Timothy isn't home every night so there could be just the two of us, we could talk over the old days.'

'Oh, well, if you're lonely and want someone to talk to, I'll come,' said Jane with an air of conferring a favour.

'Tuesday, then, will that be all right?' asked Hannah, hoping Tuesday was indeed an evening when Timothy would not be in. She felt she had to try to get on better terms with her sister; she had to show her that she had not been pushed out of the family when she had had to go into the sanatorium.

Jane put down her cup and stared at Hannah, her expression unreadable. 'If you like,' she said She picked up a day-old newspaper from the pile ready to go back to the wholesaler and became immersed in something on the front page. Hannah watched her for a moment but Jane did not look up again.

'See you on Tuesday, then,' she said at last and went out through the shop.

'Don't forget to come back and see us,' called Mrs Ridley from behind the counter.

'I won't,' Hannah replied, closing the door after her to the tinkling sound of the bell.

She wandered around the town, her spirits dampened by the insight into her sister's feelings which Jane had revealed. Was Mam aware of Jane's bitterness, she wondered, absently staring at a poster on a telegraph pole; one corner had come unstuck and was flapping in the wind. MFGB it said along the bottom edge, and she read the poster properly. It was the Miners' Federation of Great Britain, how could she not have recognised it straight away? It was something which was talked about almost daily back home in Winton Colliery. But here in Oxford she knew it meant nothing to most folk, why should it? Sighing she read the rest of it. Arthur Cook, the secretary of the federation, was going to address the Oxford City Labour Party at the Corn Exchange.

'Come and hear the truth about conditions in the coalfields today.'

Hannah looked at the date; Wednesday evening, the day after tomorrow. Oh, well, she thought, Timothy would probably be home on Wednesday evening and she wouldn't be able to go to the talk, but if she was free, she would like to hear what the miners' leader had to say. She went on her way to the butcher's and bought a pound of stewing beef, thinking she would make a beef casserole for supper. She could keep it in the oven on a low gas if Timothy was late in, and it would be fine. At the greengrocer's, she bought carrots, onions and potatoes, and then caught the bus home. It was only when she was getting off the bus that she remembered she had been going to call at the library. Never mind, she told herself, she would start her course of self-education tomorrow.

Back in the flat she made herself a sandwich and a cup of tea and ate it before the gas fire in the tiny sitting room. Arthur J. Cook, she thought, Bob used to talk about him, Bob thought he was a great man. 'A marvellous orator' was what Bob had said. 'If anyone can put across the case for the miners, Arthur J. Cook can.' The last time she had been home, Bob was becoming very involved with the Miners' Federation. She could remember him rushing in from the pit and rushing out to a meeting of the union as soon as he had washed and changed and bolted down his meal. She would have liked to hear this great orator, Arthur J. Cook, she thought, lazily stretching her feet out towards the fire, luxuriating in the warmth, even though it did not have the same cheerfulness of a coal fire.

At eight o'clock she began to give up hope of Timothy coming and went into the kitchen to lift the casserole out of the oven. Might as well eat her own meal, she thought dismally, though her appetite had disappeared under the growing disappointment. Delicious smells filled the room when she lifted the lid of the pot, but they only served to make her feel slightly sick.

Putting the lid back on the dish, she left it on the stove and went back into the sitting room and sat down only to get to her feet almost at once. A brisk walk was what she needed to restore her appetite, she told herself. She had nothing to feel discontented about, nothing at all. Hadn't Timothy told her he might not get home this evening? Nevertheless, she was feeling very down in the mouth.

She changed into her outdoor shoes, grabbed her coat and went to the front door of the flat just as a key turned in the lock. The door opened and there was Timothy.

'You're going out?' he asked, his eyebrows lifted in surprise. She hardly noticed, she was so pleased to see him. Happiness bubbled up in her, her whole being seemed to sparkle as she threw herself into his arms.

'Oh, I thought you weren't coming,' she cried as he stepped into the flat, still holding her, and closed the door with the back of his foot.

'I wasn't going to, I shouldn't be here, really,' he said as he picked her up bodily and carried her to the sofa in the sitting room. 'Truth is, I couldn't stay away, not tonight. Tomorrow night, maybe.' He buried his face in her hair and undid her coat, then the buttons of her dress, stripping them from her and dropping them there on the hearthrug and his own hastily shed clothes on top of them. And Hannah forgot all about her own doubts and worries and everything else in the surge of feeling which engulfed her.

Later, much later, she reheated the casserole and they ate quickly and ravenously at the kitchen table as though they hadn't a moment to spare. She began to gather the dishes to stack in the sink but he took her hand and drew her into the bedroom.

'Do them tomorrow,' he commanded. 'Plenty of time when I've gone.'

A shiver of apprehension ran through her and the light faded from her eyes. When he was gone, when he was gone; the words ran through her head almost prophetically. It was as though he meant he would be gone permanently. But then he was taking her in his arms again and the phrase was blotted out of her consciousness by the feel of his body against hers.

Chapter Twenty-One

Two evenings later, Hannah was on her way to the Corn Exchange to hear Arthur J. Cook. She hadn't told Timothy she was going, she hadn't had the chance, for Timothy had not been home since he went back to college the morning before. She had waited for him yesterday evening, even though he had warned he might not make it but in the end she had put the pork chops she had bought for supper back in the meat safe and gone to bed without bothering to cook one of the chops for herself. She was not expecting him back this Wednesday evening either, for he had said he had an important meeting, and the day had seemed endless to her.

Hannah stared out of the bus window; there seemed to be an awful lot of people on the streets. Although it was half past six, the High Street was almost as busy as during the day, with many students, in their short undergraduate gowns, hurrying along in groups, either walking or cycling. She wondered if they were going to the same meeting that Timothy was attending. Maybe she would catch a glimpse of him going along with his friends, she thought hopefully, then smiled to herself at her own naivety. Obviously, in a large university such as Oxford there would be lots of things going on in the evening and it was very unlikely she would see him.

She alighted from the bus as it came to a halt near the Corn Exchange and walked the last few yards, hurrying, for she was late. Once inside, she took a seat near the back and sat quietly to listen to the speeches, which had already begun.

'Is it right that men who have what must be one of the dirtiest and most dangerous jobs in the country should be earning wages at below the subsistence level?' a man was saying. 'Brothers, I appeal to your sense of fair play. The miners need our support.'

There was a burst of applause from the audience and the speaker held up his hand. 'We have with us today someone who can put the case for the miners to you much better than I can, that great champion of the miners' cause, the secretary of the Miners' Federation of Great Britain, Mr A. J. Cook.'

He doesn't look anything special, thought Hannah as the miners' leader stepped forward. He wouldn't have been out of place living in the rows of Winton Colliery. Of course, she reminded herself, he had been a miner from the South Wales coalfield for years before he became the secretary. She gazed at him expectantly, trying to see what Bob saw in him.

He didn't speak at first, simply waited quietly for his audience to settle down and within a minute or two, the hall was quiet.

'Comrades –' At last he began to speak, but the moment was spoiled for Hannah as noise of talking and laughing came from behind her. She looked over her shoulder to see undergraduates filing into the room, quite a large number of them, talking among themselves as they began to walk down the aisles.

'Comrades,' Mr Cook repeated, raising his voice, 'I have come here this evening to appeal to the working men of Oxford.' His next words were unintelligible to Hannah as loud talking broke out close to her and she turned to see that undergraduates were all around her, some with the student magazine *Isis* under their arms.

'Communist!' one shouted. 'Why don't you go to live in Russia?'

Arthur Cook heard the jibe and he began to answer, 'This country belongs to the working people –'

'Come on, men, we'll de-bag him,' Hannah heard someone shout, and there was a general surge towards the platform. Hannah jumped to her feet, her heart beating painfully as she tried to see over the heads of people in front of her. Arthur Cook was standing his ground and grim-faced men at the front of the hall were turning to face the threat and joining together to form a barrier round the speakers. Then her view was cut off by the crowd.

'Cowards!' she cried, though her voice was lost in the general hubbub. 'Let him speak.' She was jostled and pushed as she struggled to reach the aisle, and frustrated outrage flooded through her. At that moment she hated the students around her with their well-fed faces and strong, healthy bodies more than she had hated anyone in her whole life. If she had had a weapon in her hand she would have lashed out at them regardless of the consequences and felt it as revenge for all the ground-down poverty of the mining folk at home, the men injured in the pits, the children with rickets, her dead father. She hardly felt the weight on her foot as one man stood on it as he went by or the pain in her ribs as an elbow caught her a glancing blow.

'Come with me.'

She heard the voice in her ear but she ignored it until an iron grip took hold of her upper arm and she found herself dragged through the crowd to the back of the hall and the exit, though she fought furiously to free herself.

'Let me go, do you hear me?' she screamed and kicked out at the man's shin. He deftly avoided the blow and then they were outside and he was pulling her away into a side street. As the cold air hit her and cleared the fog of furious hate which had blurred her vision, she glared up at him as he towered over her, ready to fight against whatever he was going to do to her. And it was Anthony Akers.

'You bloody little fool,' he said, still holding on to her arm though she strove to pull herself away. 'What were you doing in there? Where's Timothy? What's he doing, allowing you to go there?'

'Allowing nothing,' Hannah snapped. 'I go where I like. And I haven't seen Timothy since yesterday morning when he went back to college.' Anthony had relaxed his grip and she backed away from him. 'It was a perfectly orderly meeting until your loutish friends came in. I wanted to hear what Mr Cook had to say, I was interested. I thought this was a free country, a man should be allowed to speak without being attacked by a gang of hooligans.'

'We weren't going to attack him, just de-bag him, teach him a lesson,' said Anthony mildly. 'He won't be hurt.'

'De-bag him? Humiliate him like that, a man who is just trying to get a living wage for the men in the pits? Why, you rotten –' Hannah stopped as a thought struck her. 'Timothy's not in there, is he? He's not one of them?' She waited for his answer, dreading what she might hear. Oh God, she thought, Timothy's not like them, he isn't.

Anthony stared at her grimly. 'No, he isn't. Which is just as well. What do you think he would have thought if he'd seen you in there at a communist meeting?'

'It's not a communist meeting,' she shouted at him. 'It's a Labour Party meeting, don't you know the difference? Why does anyone who fights for the working man have to be a Communist?' She stamped her foot to emphasise her point.

Anthony stared at her in silence, his normally pleasant face grim and baffled-looking. 'Come on, I'll see you home,' he said at last. 'My car's just around the corner. Don't worry, I won't say anything to Tim about you're being at that meeting.'

'You can if you want to,' Hannah said sharply. 'I'm not ashamed of going. I come from a mining family, I wanted to hear Mr Cook speak, why wouldn't I? Not that there was much chance of him being heard, not with your university friends there.'

'Timothy is an undergraduate too,' he reminded her as he opened the car door for her, and Hannah was silenced.

It was true, Timothy was a student just like those others, she thought. No, not like them, he was different, he would never try to humiliate a man by trying to take his trousers off in public. Timothy cared about people's feelings. She stole a glance at Anthony as he drove along the road. He had been at the meeting and he was Timothy's friend. Yet he was a pleasant, harmless enough chap. Would he have joined in with the others if he hadn't seen her and come to get her away from the hall?

'Do you think they will have managed to de-bag Mr Cook?' she asked.

'Oh yes, I think so,' he replied cheerfully. 'After all, there were two or three rowing blues there, not to mention the rugger players. I don't think they were about to be stopped by those communists.' He glanced at her, seeing her anxious expression. 'Oh, don't worry, they wouldn't hurt him. It's just a lark to most of them, really it is.'

'Let me out. Stop the car and let me out now,' said Hannah, taking hold of the doorhandle. She was so furious she was spluttering, and if she had managed to get the door open she would have flung herself out of the moving car.

'I say, don't do that, you'll fall and hurt yourself.' Alarm sharpened Anthony's tone and he leaned across her to drag her hand from the handle. 'You're being silly, Hannah. I told you they wouldn't hurt him, what are you making such a fuss about?'

'Let me out, Tony. If you don't, I'll jump.'

Tony hastily pulled into the kerb, but as soon as the car was stationary he grabbed hold of her arm. 'Look, what's the matter with you? Timothy would never forgive me if I let you walk home. Now be a good girl and sit still, you'll be home in a couple of minutes.'

Hannah turned a furious face to him. 'What's the matter with me? What's the *matter*?' She was practically screaming now. 'How would you like it if a gang of young miners tried to take your trousers off in public? How would you like it if they did it to your father? I suppose he will be about the same age as Mr Cook. And you say they weren't going to hurt him?'

'Oh, I say, Hannah, you're taking it all too much to heart,' he said. 'I told you, it was just a bit of a lark. Hannah –'

But Hannah was out of the car and running along the road. He poked his head round the windscreen and called after her but she ignored him. All she wanted to do was get away from him and from anyone who thought like him. An opportune bus came alongside her, slowing down as it came towards a stop, and she raced after it, managing to catch it before it pulled away again. It was half empty and she flung herself down on the nearest seat and stared unseeingly out of the window. Her mind was seething so that even her thoughts were incoherent; her emotions had taken her over completely and she felt physically sick with rage.

The short walk from the bus stop to the flat calmed her down a little. The air was so cold and damp that it penetrated through her clothes and by the time she was home she was shaking more with cold than with temper. Shedding her outdoor clothes, she turned the gas fire up high and made herself a cup of cocoa then pulling the armchair close to the fire, she sat sipping her drink and mulling over the night's happenings in her mind. She hadn't even heard what Mr Cook had had to say, she thought, remembering the grinning students as they surged forwards in the hall, 'for a lark' as Anthony had said. She felt so alienated from them that they seemed like a different species. How could they be so unfeeling about the suffering of their fellow human beings?

'I'll go and see Alf and Gloria tomorrow,' she said aloud, suddenly feeling the need to be with her own people. 'Alf will understand when I tell him about tonight.' She hadn't seen her brother since her marriage – during the day he was at work and in the evenings she usually waited in, in case Timothy should come home. Except for this evening, she thought and shifted restlessly in her chair at the memory. She yawned suddenly and glanced at the clock on the mantelpiece. Ten o'clock, a bit earlier than her usual bedtime but the emotional stress had tired her. Maybe she would have an early night. Rising to her feet, she stretched luxuriously before carrying her cup into the kitchen and rinsing it under the tap.

The sound of a key turning in the lock made joy shoot through her. She dropped the cup in the sink and flew into the hall.

'Timothy, oh, Timothy, I'm so glad to see you,' she cried. 'I thought you weren't coming tonight. What a lovely surprise.' Flinging her arms around his neck, she hugged him, not noticing at first that he did not hug her back. But her joy faded as he took hold of her by her upper arms and held her away from him, and when he looked up she saw he was very angry, his blue eyes hard and glittering and his mouth drawn into a thin line.

'Timothy?' she faltered.

'Where have you been?'

'I . . . I went to hear Mr Cook at the Corn Exchange. I wanted to hear his speech. Were you here earlier? I thought you weren't coming home tonight, you said you had a meeting, I would have stayed in if I'd known.'

'No, I wasn't here earlier. I had a meeting with my tutor, I told you. Then I was studying in my rooms when Tony came in.'

'Oh. The Honourable Anthony Akers. I suppose he told you what happened? Well, I wasn't in any danger, really, but he forced me to leave.'

Hannah turned and walked into the sitting room before continuing. 'It was disgraceful, Timothy, those undergraduates were acting like hooligans. I thought there was supposed to be freedom of speech in this country. I was so –'

'Hannah!'

She looked up at him quickly, her eyes widening as she saw his expression. 'I told you, I was all right, were you worried about me? Is that why you've come home?'

Timothy strode into the room and faced her. 'You may be all right, that's not the point. You could have been hurt, you could have been trampled on or caught in the crush. What on earth possessed you to go to a Labour Party meeting? You're my wife now, did you not think you might have asked me before attending a meeting of communists? What do you suppose my friends would think?'

'They are not communists. And your friends don't even know you're married,' cried Hannah, her temper rising.

'They would have found out soon enough if you had been caught up in a disturbance and arrested, or even if you had been hurt and taken to hospital.'

Hannah gasped. 'Well, you seem to know which would have been the worst thing from your point of view,' she snapped.

Timothy sighed. 'Oh, don't be a fool, Hannah! Of course I was more worried that you might have been hurt than anything else,' he said. 'But Tony said you were fine, he got you out before there was any trouble. In any case, I found out that it all fizzled out in the end, the stewards got Cook away somehow so nothing happened at all.'

'No thanks to your friends,' she said bitterly. 'I never thought you would side with them, I thought you had some sympathy for the miners and the way the coal owners are trying to force them to accept a cut in wages when they are poor enough as it is.'

'I do, I do, Hannah, but you have to realise it's a question of simple economics. The coal industry is losing money, it can't go on –'

'Oh, no, of course not,' Hannah flared. 'Poor Lord Akers might have to sell one of his estates, or even his house on Park Lane, and we can't allow that to happen, can we?'

Timothy stared at her for a long moment, then he shrugged his shoulders and went back into the hall. 'There's no talking to you when you're in this bitter mood,' he said, taking his coat from the stand where he had flung it when he came in.

'You're not going back tonight, are you?' Hannah asked anxiously, she couldn't believe that that was what he intended to do.

'There's no point in staying here to argue and in any case, I have an early tutorial tomorrow,' he said.

'I'm surprised you found time to come out to see me at all,' said Hannah bitterly.

'Have you sufficient money?' asked Timothy, ignoring her last remark as he pulled out his wallet. 'I may not be back for a day or two, I'd better leave you some.' He put a five-pound note on the hall table.

'But why?' cried Hannah, pain making her voice almost shrill. 'Please don't go now, not now, I'm so upset, you've no idea how what happened tonight affected me, I feel so low.'

'I have to,' he said, 'please understand, Hannah.'

'I *don't* understand, Timothy. There must be other married students, why do we have to be so secretive about it? Is it just your father? Or are you ashamed of me? That's it, isn't it? You're ashamed of me.'

Timothy took a step towards her. 'No, don't think that,' he said. 'Look, I have to go, I don't want the proctors after me. I told you, Hannah, it's only for a short while; come the summer I'll be finished with the university. Now I have to go, I'm sorry.' He opened the door and was gone, leaving Hannah staring at the closed door.

Dully, she went into the bathroom, washed her face and brushed her teeth. She felt icy cold in spite of the gas fire in the sitting room so she filled a hot-water bottle and took it to bed with her. She lay between the cold sheets, hugging the hot-water bottle but still shivering. After a while she got up and went to the sideboard where Timothy kept a bottle of whisky. She poured herself a glassful and drank it down, choking as the unaccustomed spirit burned her throat. But it did bring some warmth into her and she carried the bottle and glass with her back to bed, putting them down on the bedside table. It's not going to work, she thought as she climbed back between the sheets, my marriage is over already. I should have known it wouldn't work. No matter what he says, I know he doesn't want his friends to know about me because he's ashamed of me, what other reason could there be? He's not dependent on his father for money, it can't be that.

Her mind went round and round endlessly and she began to feel dizzy and slightly sick. She was just considering getting up to go to the bathroom when at last she fell into an exhausted sleep, filled with unformed nightmares.

Chapter Twenty-Two

There was a persistent noise of hammering somewhere in the middle distance. Hannah stirred restlessly in her sleep and turned on her back. Then a bell began to ring, buzzing over and over again, and she opened her eyes, puzzled what it might be. Suddenly she sat bolt upright and pushed her hair away from her face. It was the front door bell – Timothy must have come back.

Jumping out of bed, she pulled on the kimono she had bought a few days before, wincing as her head began to pound painfully. Quickly she looked in the mirror and groaned. She looked awful, her eyes were red-rimmed and puffy and her hair was all over the place – where was her hairbrush? The hammering on the door began again, each blow shooting knives through her head and she gave up the search for her hairbrush and went to answer the door.

'Timothy,' she said shakily as she pulled it open, 'I'm so glad you came back.' Pushing the tangle of hair back from her face, she looked up at the man standing there, though the hall swam around her with the effort. It settled into place with a jolt as she saw it was not Timothy but his father standing there.

'Mr Durkin,' she said faintly, and stood back for him to enter.

Daniel Durkin pushed past her without speaking and strode into the dim sitting room, where he stood with his back to the unlit gas fire.

'You know who I am, then,' he said.

'Yes, of course,' she said as she followed him and hurriedly drew back the curtains at the window. Anyone brought up in Winton knew Daniel Durkin, she thought, and blinked at the light, for even though it was still midwinter, the sun was shining brightly in the street. Confusedly, Hannah wondered why it was so bright so early in the morning. It couldn't possibly be past eight o'clock, she never slept later than that. But when she looked at the clock she saw it was midday.

Mr Durkin was looking her up and down, not even trying to hide his contempt. Flushing, she realised that her kimono was open and her nightie was low-cut over her breast. She pulled it together and tied the belt tightly to keep it in place. Taking the matches from the mantelpiece, she lit the gas fire before turning to face her father-in-law.

'Won't you sit down?' she asked. She was fighting to still the tremor in her voice.

'No, I will not,' he answered. 'I can say what I have to say standing up. It won't take long.'

Hannah's toes curled into the hearth rug as she saw him glance at her bare feet, then bring his gaze slowly up her body to her flushed face and tangled hair.

'Well, do you mind waiting until I get dressed? It won't take me long,' she said stiffly, the tremor gone and a spark of anger taking its place. Still, she strove to keep her tone pleasant even though his manner reminded her vividly of that humiliating day so many years before, when he had looked at her mother and Harry with that same expression. She had been young at the time but she would never forget the scene in the colliery yard on the day she had first met Timothy and his father.

Daniel glanced through the open door of the bedroom to the unmade bed and saw the bottle and glass still standing on the bedside table.

'Go ahead,' he said. 'No doubt you'll need another drink to fortify you before hearing what I have to say to you.'

'Another drink –' Hannah gasped. 'What do you mean? I don't drink.'

Daniel raised his eyebrows sardonically. 'Oh, no? What's in that bottle in there, then? Looks like a pretty famous brand of single malt to me.'

'It's –' she began hotly and then shook her head. No, she told herself, she wasn't going to let him provoke her into losing her temper and her head. She needed all her wits about her if she was going to hold her own against him. 'I won't be a moment,' she said meekly and closed the door of the sitting room behind her. She splashed cold water on her face in the bathroom and cleaned her teeth; her tongue felt as though it was like a lump of soggy cotton wool but at least her head was beginning to settle down and the painful thumping had dulled. Going into the kitchen, she put the kettle on to boil while she was dressing. She refused to let the thought of him waiting in the sitting room make her hurry.

'Of all the days for him to come,' she muttered to her reflection in the dressing-table mirror. Why on earth had she drunk that glass of whisky after Timothy went off last night? It wasn't as if she liked the stuff, it tasted awful and look how it had made her sleep late this morning. She stripped off her nightie and put on her underclothes before looking in the wardrobe for something to wear. She was hesitant, for she was unsure of herself and her judgement and dreading the confrontation awaiting her. Who had told Daniel about her, she wondered, was it Anthony? But surely, if it was Anthony, why had he waited until now? He had known all along about her marriage to Timothy. Unless he had telephoned the evening before, he had been pretty fed up with her then, she thought suddenly. He could have phoned and Mr Durkin could have travelled down overnight. Or even set off early this morning, she admitted to herself wryly, remembering how late in the day it was.

She took out a plain woollen dress in a deep shade of blue, simple but well-cut, and pulled it over her head. She had bought it in London and the price had made her gasp in disbelief but Timothy had insisted she have it.

'It looks beautiful on you,' he had said and, remembering, Hannah smiled and took heart. Timothy loved her, didn't he? That was the main thing. There was a narrow leather belt which sat on the hips and she fastened it loosely before sitting down at the dressing table to comb her hair. Her bob was getting a bit long, she saw, it was time she went back to the hairdresser's. A lock of hair kept falling over her eyes so she fastened it back with a plain blue slide over one ear. Pinching her cheeks to bring some colour into them, she stood up and slipped her feet into low-heeled pumps the same colour as her dress. Now she was ready to face him. Timothy's father and now her father-in-law, she reminded herself, squaring her shoulders. It was natural for him to think she wasn't good enough for Timothy. But he couldn't do anything about their marriage, not now, it was too late no matter how enraged he was. Taking a deep breath, Hannah went into the sitting room.

'Would you like a cup of tea?' she asked Daniel pleasantly, as though he were a friend who had just dropped in unexpectedly.

'No, I would not,' he said impatiently. 'I –'

'Well, I'm sure you won't mind if I have one myself, will you? I like to start the day with a cup of tea.' Without waiting for him to answer she went into the kitchen, prepared a tray and carried it back with her. Mr Durkin had sat down in an armchair and she noted it with a tiny feeling of satisfaction. He was saying something about this being a fine time to start the day but she ignored it. Carefully she poured herself a cup of tea and added milk and a spoonful of sugar.

'Sure you won't have one?' she asked and he exploded with wrath.

'Young woman, I haven't come here to drink tea, nor did I expect to be kept waiting all this time by a chit like you,' he roared, getting to his feet once more and towering over her. Hannah picked up her cup with a steady hand and took a sip of tea, though her heart was beginning to pound as painfully as her head had done earlier. Carefully, she replaced the cup in the saucer and looked up at him, aware that her control was dangerously near to breaking.

'Why have you come here, Mr Durkin?' In spite of herself, her voice trembled slightly as she said his name. Abstractedly she noted how Timothy resembled him physically, though Daniel was of a stocky build whereas Timothy was slender. As she looked up at him now, she noticed how his cheeks were mottled with purple and his eyes were lighter than his son's, and harder, much harder.

Daniel glared at her. 'Don't be pert with me, young woman. It won't get you anywhere. I've come to put an end to this ridiculous so-called marriage. How much do you want to leave my son alone?'

'It's not a so-called marriage, it is a true marriage. We were wed in the Methodist chapel in Cowley and I have the certificate to prove it,' she said evenly. 'In any case, it's too late. Timothy is of age, he had a perfect right to marry whoever he wanted to.' Hannah was doggedly hanging on to her temper. 'And he loves me,' she added as an afterthought.

He laughed shortly. 'Wedded in a damn chapel, were you? To think a son of mine should marry in chapel, it's beyond belief. And you think I can't do anything about it, do you? Well, let me tell you, Hannah Armstrong –'

'Hannah Durkin.'

'Hannah Armstrong, I said, and that's who you are,' he repeated, his tone becoming vehement. 'You'll never hold the right to the Durkin name, believe me, I'm telling you and I mean it. Now stop this pretence, you and I know you're just in this for what you can get out of it. Good God, girl, you didn't think I would agree to my son ruining his life on a damn drunken pitman's brat, did you?'

'Pitman's brat? Pitman's brat? You say that as though you were talking to scum.' Hannah jumped to her feet, upsetting the tea tray so that the cup and saucer fell to the floor and milky tea spilled out over the carpet and hearth rug. But neither of them appeared to notice. 'Let me tell you, my father was a decent man and a hard worker until he broke his back in the pit. He wasn't a criminal and he was never drunk in his life, he didn't drink hard liquor. What gives you the right to talk about him like that?' Her voice was rising until she was almost screaming at him.

Daniel laughed. 'That's right, my girl, when you forget to play the lady it's easy to see where you come from. And no doubt Timothy will see it too before long, once he's a little less besotted with you. And then where will you be? Now come on, be sensible, let's get this sorry story done with. How does five hundred pounds sound to you? You can have it in your hand once I have your signed statement agreeing to an annulment and your promise not to get in touch with my son ever again.'

Hannah stared at him. He stood before her so arrogantly, sure that the offer of so much money would dazzle her into agreeing to his terms.

'Five hundred or five thousand, I won't take it,' she said at last. 'Can't you understand that Timothy and I love each other? We will not let you separate us.'

Daniel's expression turned ugly. 'I wouldn't be in such a hurry to turn it down if I were you,' he said, 'or you might end up with nothing. For this marriage is finished, Hannah Armstrong. You may depend on it, there is plenty I can do to persuade you of it.' His eyes narrowed as he glared across the brown stain on the hearth rug. 'I dare say you're as stubborn as that brother of yours, Robert Armstrong, him and his damn union. But I'll get the better of both of you, you'll see. Now I'll go and leave you to think things over. I'll be back tonight.'

'Don't bother,' Hannah replied. 'We Armstrongs are stubborn, you're right there. I think you'll find I am as determined to make this marriage work as you are to break it up.'

He gave her a superior smile, not deigning to answer her, and she had to grasp one hand with the other to stop herself slapping him across the face. Instead, she lifted her chin and stared at him with an arrogance to equal his own as he walked out. Only then did she crumble into a heap in the armchair, waves of humiliation washing over her.

After a while she got to her feet and tackled the mess made by the spilt tea. She fetched soapy water and a cloth and rubbed away at the stain on the hearth rug until her arms were tired, but the physical activity didn't stop her from thinking.

Did Timothy know his father was here, she wondered. Mr Durkin had seemed so positive that he could have the marriage annulled – what if he really could? Timothy had been so angry with her for going to hear Arthur J. Cook, he had gone off in such a temper that night before. Perhaps he would be glad to get out of the marriage, perhaps he saw it as a disaster himself now. Hannah felt sick at the thought. Though she had sipped only a little of the tea, it had left a sour aftertaste in her mouth. What she needed was food, she decided. She went into the kitchen, buttered a slice of bread and forced herself to eat it.

Suddenly the tiny room made her feel claustrophobic and she went back into the sitting room, but that only reminded her of Daniel Durkin for the smell of him hung about, a combination of cigars and some kind of shaving lotion, she supposed. Whatever it was, it made her feel sick again and in desperate need of fresh air. Grabbing her coat from the bedroom, she rushed out into the street and took great gulps of the freezing stuff. Without thinking where she was going, she headed off into the town at a brisk walk.

'Hallo, what are you doing here?'

Hannah looked up, startled, to find she was in the Corn Market, the street where Gloria worked. And there was Gloria, just coming away from the shop.

'Oh, Gloria,' she said dully.

'What on earth is the matter with you?' asked Gloria. Her gaze was full of concern. 'No one would take you for a bride, you look more like a deserted woman.'

'Oh!'

Hannah's eyes widened as she realised that that was exactly how she felt, Daniel had done his work well, she thought bitterly.

'Oh, don't look like that, Hannah, it can't be as bad as all that,' said Gloria. 'Look, it's my half-day, let's go somewhere and have lunch. I was just going to have a boiled egg at home, you know how it is, we're saving for the wedding. But it's ages since I had a meal out, we'll splash out on a proper meal, shall we? You look as though you could do with it.'

Hannah felt a surge of gratitude to Gloria; she was a good friend even though they had sometimes had a disagreement. And she was just the tonic she needed. Gloria would never let herself be humiliated by anyone, not even a man like Daniel Durkin. An afternoon with her was just the thing to take her mind off her troubles.

'Oh yes, that'll be great,' she said. 'I'll pay, though. What would Alf say if he knew you were throwing your money away on a restaurant meal?'

'I'll spend my money on what I want to spend it on,' Gloria asserted stoutly. 'Come on, I could just fancy a nice hot dinner I haven't had to cook myself.'

They ate steak-and-kidney pie in a small restaurant in the High Street where the food was plain but well cooked and didn't cost the earth. Gloria chatted on lightly about the wedding and Alf. Hannah had only to put in the occasional comment and by the time she had finished her pie she was beginning to feel more herself.

When their coffee came, Gloria sat back in her chair and regarded Hannah seriously. 'Now, tell me all about it,' she said. 'Have you been fighting with Timothy already?'

'No, not really. Well, yes, we did have an argument, but that isn't what's the matter.' Hannah hesitated for a moment before deciding to tell Gloria about her father-in-law's threats. Gloria was the only real friend she had in Oxford, the only one who would understand, and she had to tell someone.

'It's Timothy's father,' she began, and out came the whole story of Daniel's visit. She told it flatly, without embellishment, but even so Gloria gasped with indignation more than once.

'The cheeky sod,' she commented when Hannah had finished. 'Who does he think he is?'

'Well, he *is* Timothy's father.'

'That may be, but he has no right to talk to you like that.'

Gloria spooned sugar into her cooling coffee and stirred it angrily. 'You shouldn't have let him say such things, Hannah, you should have thrown him out, that's what I would have done.' She nodded her head to emphasise the point.

'It's difficult, though, Gloria. After all, he is my father-in-law. And then there's my family back in Winton, he could make things very awkward for them, you've no idea how powerful he is there. You know, if Bob were to lose his job, that would mean Mam would lose the house. He could blacklist Bob and he wouldn't be able to work in the pits if that happened. I don't think you know what it's like in a mining area.'

'No,' said Gloria thoughtfully. 'But surely he couldn't be so vindictive as to put a widow with two young children out of her house? Not when her husband was killed in the pit? This is the twentieth century, people don't stand for that sort of thing.'

'Not in Oxford, they don't,' said Hannah sadly. 'It's different in Winton Colliery.'

'My God, he's like the wicked squire in a pantomime. He didn't really threaten you with that, did he?'

'Well, no, not really. But I think it was implied.'

Gloria shook her head. 'Oh, go on, he was just trying to frighten you. He can't do anything really, not if Timothy loves you. And he does, anyone can see that. Does he know his father's here?'

'I don't think so. I think Mr Durkin came directly to me when he found out, though for the life of me I don't know how he learned about our marriage. We have been so careful to keep it quiet, the only one of Timothy's friends who knows is Anthony Akers and I don't think he would tell, not after being best man and letting us use the house in London for our honeymoon.'

Gloria looked thoughtful. Finishing her coffee, she pulled on her gloves before she said any more and then it was about something completely different.

'Have you seen Jane since you came back?'

Hannah looked surprised. 'I have, as a matter of fact. I went in to see the Ridleys on Monday and she was there. She seems to be doing well, at least they are satisfied with her. I asked her to come over to me for the evening, next Wednesday. Why do you ask?'

'Oh, no reason. She's a funny girl, isn't she? Keeps her thoughts to herself. It's not the same thing having her in the house instead of you, not the same at all. I can't talk to her like I can talk to you.'

Hannah sighed. 'I know she's quiet and shy and it makes her a bit abrupt sometimes, that's all it is. You know, she had to spend such a lot of time in hospital when she was younger, I think that was what made her as she is.'

Gloria nodded. 'Yes. Well, let's go back to my place. We can have a nice long chat on our own before the others come in. You can stay for tea too, Timothy won't be coming in until later, will he?'

If he comes in at all, Hannah thought, but she smiled warmly at Gloria. 'I'd love to. I've been meaning to come to see you all any way. But you won't mention anything about Mr Durkin to Alf, will you? I'd rather he didn't know, not yet anyway. I don't want any of my family to know.'

'I won't say anything,' Gloria assured her.

The family were sitting round the table in the kitchen when Jane came in, all except Reggie who had a date, or so Gloria said.

'She's that plump blonde who works in the baker's in Hockmore Street, do you remember her?'

Hannah did and was pleased. She was cheerful and uncomplicated, probably just the sort of girl for Reggie. Hannah had felt slightly guilty about Reggie even though she hadn't done anything to encourage him. Now she could forget about it.

Jane came into the kitchen. Giving a comprehensive nod of greeting, she sat down at the table, leaving Gloria to jump up and fetch her dinner from the oven.

'Is there any brown sauce?' she asked after the other girl had sat back down.

'Yes, of course.'

Hannah watched as Gloria left her own meal once again and went to the cupboard for the bottle of sauce. Jane must know perfectly well where it was kept, why didn't she fetch it herself? Her sister was not acting like a member of the family as Hannah had done, rather like a paying guest with the emphasis on the paying. She wasn't fitting in as she should have done.

When Alf came in to spend the evening with Gloria, Jane went up to her room without even excusing herself. Her sister's bad manners embarrassed Hannah, but Alf didn't seem to notice. Hannah resolved to speak to Jane about it on the following Wednesday when she came to visit. Maybe she didn't even realise she was being rude. She sighed, Jane was a problem all right. Perhaps it had been a mistake to bring her to Oxford.

Hannah glanced at her wristwatch. 'I've had a lovely time, Gloria, it's been grand. But I'd better be going back now.'

'I should think so an' all. You've got a husband to look after now, my girl,' said Alf, grinning. 'What will he think if he comes in from a hard day's studying and you're not there with his slippers all warmed and his dinner ready? You'd better be running along or he might take a slipper to you. We men have to keep our women in line, you know. That's true, isn't it, Gloria?'

'The first time you take a slipper to me will be the last, my lad,' Gloria warned.

He laughed and put an arm round her waist. 'Oh yes, and what will you do about it?' he asked.

Gloria accompanied Hannah to the door. 'Let me know what happens,' she whispered. 'And don't worry, Hannah, it'll be all right, Timothy won't let you go. I'm sure he's man enough to stand up to that rotten father of his, so don't let the sod intimidate you.'

'I won't,' promised Hannah. 'I would still like to know who told him, though. If he hadn't found out about me until after Timothy left Oxford . . . I think that's what Timothy thought, too, it would have been easier to break it to him if Timothy was working and fully independent.'

She was standing with the door half-open and the night was bitterly cold. A few snowflakes were blowing about in the wind and she watched them against the night sky. 'I'm as miserable as the weather, aren't I?' she asked with an attempt at a grin. 'I'm sorry, Gloria, I didn't mean to dampen your day.'

'Don't be daft,' said her friend.

'Close that blooming door, will you?' Mr Morgan called from the sitting room. 'The draught's enough to freeze us all to death.'

'I'll go. Bye for now,' said Hannah hurriedly and slipped out, closing the door behind her. She was hurrying up the street when she heard her name called and turned to see Gloria running after her.

'I had to tell you, I know I shouldn't really, your sister's post has nothing to do with me and I shouldn't have been reading the envelope . . .'

'What envelope?' asked Hannah. 'Come on, out with it, Gloria. Look at you, you're shivering. Why did you come out without your coat?'

'I . . . Jane had some letters to post, Hannah, and she put them on the sideboard and I saw the name on the top envelope. It caught my eye because it was addressed to a Mr Durkin, the same name as yours, and I read the address and it was somewhere in County Durham. I'm sorry, Hannah, I don't know why she would do such a thing.'

Chapter Twenty-Three

Timothy and his father glared at each other across the table.

'How did you find out? No one knows but Anthony and he wouldn't tell you.'

'Never you mind, I was bound to hear of it some time. And I'm telling you now, do something about that girl or I will see to it that your allowance is stopped.'

'You can't do it. The money's mine, I know I can't touch the capital before I'm twenty-five but in my mother's will she said I was to have full use of the interest when I reached eighteen.'

'With the proviso that it was to be used for your education.' Daniel laughed and the sound was full of derision. 'I have no doubt the pit lass educated you all right, girls of her class –'

'Don't speak about her like that, Father,' warned Timothy.

'I'll speak about her in any damn way I wish,' Daniel snarled, his temper flaring. 'What is she but a lass from those filthy hovels in Winton? What the hell do you see in her, a common miner's daughter? Why you couldn't have had your fun and left it at that I don't know, no one would have blamed you for that. But to actually marry –'

Timothy started to his feet and leaned over the table, taking his father's lapels in his fists and drawing him half out of his chair.

'I said, do not speak of her in that way. In fact, do not speak of her at all. Hannah is my wife.' He did not raise his voice but his father could not mistake the menacing tone. Timothy held the position for a moment or so, his face only six inches from Daniel's. Then he let go abruptly and resumed his seat.

Daniel straightened his coat and tie, giving himself a brief time to compose himself. Timothy watched him coldly.

'You're wasting your time here, Father. Hannah and I are married and we are going to stay that way. I don't believe you can do anything about my inheritance but even if you could, do you think that would make me abandon her? Why, I will graduate this spring, I can work for a living. Hannah will understand if we have to live carefully for a few months.'

'Oh, she will, will she? But will she understand if I cut you off altogether? For not a penny will you get from me if you keep on with this ridiculous marriage, and I'll do my damnedest to see you get no more from the fund set up by your mother. Have you forgotten that Brown-Robinson and I are the executors of the trust? Believe me, Brown-Robinson will do what I say; he's like all solicitors, he knows which side his bread is buttered.'

'Hannah is not interested in money, she loves me. You don't even know her.' A disquieting thought stuck Timothy. 'You don't, do you? You haven't been to see her, upsetting her, have you?'

'No, of course I haven't,' Daniel lied. 'I came to see you, I'm not interested in that trollop.'

'Get out of my rooms, Father, before I throw you out. I swear I will do it if you say any more.'

Daniel stalked to the door, his face grim. His hand was on the doorknob when he decided to try one thing more.

'What do you think Lord Akers will think of this marriage? I tell you this, it will spoil your chances of ever getting a position with him. And good positions are not so plentiful these days. You are jeopardising your whole career, man.'

'I don't think Lord Akers is as class-conscious as you are, Father, but even if he were, I don't expect to have too much trouble gaining a position somewhere. I stand a good chance of a first, you know. And even if I should only achieve an upper second, why, a degree in mathematics is something to base a career on. I'll even teach if I have to.'

Daniel snorted. 'Then to the devil with you!'

He flung the door open and went out, and Timothy could hear him stumping down the stairs. He pulled a textbook towards him and opened it, staring unseeing at the page. In spite of his words, he was rattled by what his father had said. If his allowance was stopped he would have trouble paying the bills he and Hannah had run up on their short honeymoon in London. But Hannah's wardrobe had been almost nonexistent before their marriage, he had had to renew it. And she took such a delight in nice things that it had been a pleasure to buy them for her. Only now the bills were piling up at a rate which surprised him and there was the expense of renting a furnished flat to make things even worse.

Hannah thought he was rich and indeed he was by her standards, he mused. He turned over a page in the textbook before realising that though his eyes had followed the words on the previous page, he hadn't actually taken them in, so he had to go back. But it was no good, he couldn't think about his work. He closed the book and flung it across the table. Going to the window, he stared out at the long shadows the afternoon sunshine was making on the grass of the quadrangle and his thoughts went back to the evening before.

It was the first quarrel he had had with Hannah and he could picture the pain on her lovely face as she stood up to him in the poky flat. He had been hard and unfeeling with her, he realised that now. But he had been worried she would be hurt and when she accused him of being more interested in what his friends thought than in what happened to her, he had lost his temper.

I'll go this evening and make it up with her, he thought. It was a waste of time trying to work until he did. Poor Hannah, it was rotten for her having to spend so much time on her own. How could he have blamed her for going to hear that chap Cook at the Corn Exchange? She was a loving, loyal girl, and of course her sympathies were with her own folk. He wouldn't love her so much if she was any different.

At least his father didn't know where she was; Timothy shuddered to think of what it would do to her if she had a visit from Daniel in his present frame of mind.

There was a knock on the door and he turned to face it, subconsciously squaring his shoulders. If his father had thought of something else to try to persuade him to give Hannah up, he really would throw him down the stairs, he thought grimly. But it was Tony who slipped his head round the door.

'Hallo, Tim. Am I mistaken or did I just see your father walking across the quad?' he asked. He pulled a wry face as he saw Timothy's expression. 'I thought he looked a bit thunderous. Found out about the nuptials, did he?'

His friend nodded. 'I'd like to know who told him. It wasn't you, was it?' Tony glared at him, affronted, and Timothy went on, 'No, of course not, sorry.'

'I thought no one else knew.' Tony looked thoughtful. 'There's Hannah's family, of course.'

'I don't think it could have been one of them. Most of them hate my father, they wouldn't give him the time of day. They blame him for everything that has happened in the coalfield since the war.'

Tony nodded. 'Your father and mine, actually.' He sat down before the fire and stretched out his long legs. 'I suppose your dear papa is threatening to cut you out of his will.'

'Worse than that, he says he can stop me using the interest on the money Mother left me. That will leave me in a hole until I graduate and land a job.'

'Well, at least you're pretty sure you'll get through your finals this year, which is more than I am,' Tony commented. 'My tutor reckons I'll be lucky to get a third. But as for money, you can rely on me, old son. I can spare the odd copper to help you out, you know.' He hesitated, looking curiously at Timothy. 'That is if you are absolutely sure about Hannah.'

'I'm sure. How many times do you need to be told? I'm not going to give her up, I'll find a way, just you wait and see.' Timothy's tone rose and took on a note of anger, and his friend lifted his hands in mock surrender.

'All right, all right, I just thought I'd ask. Now come along to my rooms, I've got some muffins, we'll have them toasted for tea. Forget about your father, there's not a lot he can do if you're determined, you'll see. In the end he'll have to give in.'

'Hmm, I hope you're right.'

They went to Tony's rooms and toasted muffins before the fire. Tony laughed at his own jokes and Timothy joined in politely, but it was obvious that his mind was on other things.

'I think I'll spend the evening with Hannah,' he said after a while.

Tony nodded. 'You may as well, your thoughts are with her, they certainly haven't been here with me,' he said. 'But then, I'm used to it by now.' He gazed at the ceiling and said piously,

'Lord save me from becoming entangled by a woman's wiles.'

Timothy didn't hear him. He was already on his way back to his own rooms to collect his overcoat.

I'll have to have a telephone installed in the flat, he thought to himself, his money worries forgotten for the moment. Then I can telephone and let her know when I'm coming. And another time, when I can't make it, I will be able to ring and explain why. Poor Hannah, she must be very lonely there on her own all day. In this contrite mood he went out to the car.

There was a flower seller on the corner and he stopped and bought a bunch of violets to give her as a peace offering. Though they were glass-house flowers, their sweet smell filled the car and brought the promise of spring to the cold winter's evenings, and his spirits lightened. He parked outside the flat, not taking any notice of another car standing in the shadows a little farther up the street. Bounding up the stairs with his key already in his hand, he opened the door and went into the tiny hall.

'Hannah? Hannah, where are you?'

There was a strip of light showing under the sitting-room door. She must be in, he thought, but why wasn't she running to meet him as she always did? Because of last night, that was what it was, she was still upset and annoyed. And rightly so, he thought contritely.

'I've brought you a peace offering,' he began and froze. Hannah was not there; it was his father who was sitting in her chair by the gas fire, a glass of whisky in his hand.

Chapter Twenty-Four

Earlier in the evening, Hannah had been returning to the flat in east Oxford. It was a bitterly cold evening but she hardly noticed it for she was so unhappy. As she came to the entrance, she glanced at her wristwatch. This time yesterday, she reflected, she had been going to the meeting in the Corn Exchange. How could twenty-four hours make so much difference in her life?

Jane – the sister she had watched and worried over when they were small. How could Jane have changed so much? Hannah had not gone back into the house with Gloria to confront Jane, she couldn't bear to see her, not yet. On Wednesday, perhaps, she could ask her sister about it when Jane came to visit, but now she was filled with a sense of betrayal. She couldn't begin to understand why Jane had done it. Was it envy of her good fortune in marrying someone like Timothy?

The ache inside her intensified at the thought of Timothy, and desperately she wished that she hadn't fought with him the evening before. She thought of his father's words that morning. Would she really hold Timothy back as his father had said? And, would he be so ruthless as to threaten to blacklist her brother, even throw her mother out of her home? Had he done that? Well, even if not in so many words, that was what was implied, she was sure of it. Timothy, Timothy, she pleaded silently, please come tonight, please tell me your father can't hurt us.

A car was parked outside the flat and as she came near the door opened. Her depression deepened as she saw it was Daniel Durkin.

'At last. I've been waiting for you,' he said, not bothering with a greeting.

'What do you want?' Hannah was equally brusque as she walked past him and climbed the stairs. She had intended to go straight in and leave him outside; she really thought she could take no more from him, not tonight. But her fingers were numb with cold for she had forgotten her gloves and she had to fumble about in her bag before she managed to locate her key. By that time he was beside her on the landing.

'I have a message for you from Timothy,' he said.

'Timothy? Then give it to me.'

'It's not written down, he asked me to tell you myself.'

'Go on, then, you can tell me here, there's no need for you to come inside.'

Daniel sighed heavily. 'Oh, come now, Hannah, let's be civilised about this. Let me in and I'll give you the message.'

'I don't want you in my home.'

'I won't be long, just say what I have to say and then I am going. I have to be back in Durham tomorrow morning and it's a long drive, especially at this time of year.'

'Oh, very well.' Hannah capitulated and opened the door. She went into the sitting room, lit the fire and flung her coat on the back of a chair. Then she turned to face him.

'Well? Why would Timothy give you a message for me? I was expecting him to come himself.'

Daniel took out a cigar and lit it without asking her permission. He sat down and blew the pungent smoke out into the room before answering her.

'I don't think Timothy will be coming again, not after what I have told him. He's a soft-hearted boy, but he's not as soft as not to know what he has to do if he wants to go on living a comfortable life. Believe me, my dear Hannah, there was no contest, not when I explained the alternatives to him.'

'What do you mean, the alternatives?' Hannah's scepticism showed plainly on her face.

'You don't believe me?' Daniel laughed. 'I assure you, it's true. When I told him there would be no more money forthcoming unless he agreed to end this disastrous marriage, believe me, he began to listen to reason.'

'He wouldn't! No, he wouldn't, I don't believe you. You're lying.'

'Am I? Well, time will tell, time will tell. Quite soon, too, I should think; in fact, as soon as the rent on this place runs out.'

'But Timothy has his own income, he told me his mother left him money.'

'That's true. But I am the executor and I can stop his income, believe me.'

'But even if he hadn't a penny, Timothy wouldn't do this without telling me himself. He's too good a man to do a thing like that.'

'That's true, he is good, too good sometimes, and, as I said, soft-hearted, else why would he marry a girl like you in the first place? That's why he didn't want to face you. As I told him, a clean break was best and I would see you were taken care of. He wavered a bit, but he's weak, you see.'

'He's not weak! I don't believe –'

'Well, you don't know him as well as I do,' Daniel interrupted smoothly.

Hannah stared at him, longing to contradict, but knowing that in this at least, Daniel was right. She had first met Timothy long ago but they had been children, and in the intervening years, she had only seen him once or twice. Their meeting in Oxford had been only a few short weeks ago. They had rushed into marriage at Timothy's instigation and she had agreed because she believed he loved her as much as she loved him and was impatient to make her his wife. And that was all that mattered to her at the time. She had believed that they could overcome the difference in their backgrounds; after all, she was young and reasonably intelligent and willing to learn. But now she remembered the times when she had been unsure what Timothy was thinking; in particular, she remembered how angry he had been the evening before because she went to hear Arthur J. Cook. She remembered how he had talked of the economics of the situation and the bitter way she had answered him. Maybe she didn't know him after all, because she hadn't thought they could have disagreed so much on such a subject.

Suddenly her knees felt very weak. She slid down into the chair opposite Daniel and bent her head so that he couldn't see the weary defeat in her face.

'You will be blighting his life if you insist on your rights, Hannah.' Daniel pressed home his advantage; he hadn't spent years negotiating with union men not to know when he had his opponent cornered. 'You don't want to do that, do you?'

'No,' she said, almost inaudibly.

'Well then, be sensible. This is what I propose. You will be out of Oxford tonight, I'll run you to the station.'

'Out of Oxford? How can I do that? There's no need anyway, I can go to my brother in Cowley.' Hannah felt as though she was on a runaway tram like one of those in a Buster Keaton moving picture. Why did it have to be done so soon? 'I want to see him just once more. I want him to tell me himself!' The words burst from her almost of their own volition.

'Now, that wouldn't be very sensible, would it? He's made his decision, he doesn't want to see you again. And you don't want to run the risk of meeting Timothy accidentally, do you? Not when he feels as he does. No, I think you should go now and as far away as possible.' He reached into the inside pocket of his jacket and pulled out a cheque-book. 'Now don't be silly about this, you will need money to start again somewhere else. Five hundred pounds, I think I said this morning?'

'I don't want your money.'

'Oh, come now, I said don't be silly.'

Silly, thought Hannah. That just about covered the way she had trusted Timothy. A suspicion came to her; had Timothy insisted on keeping their relationship secret because he was ashamed of her? If so, she had been even sillier than she thought. Lifting her chin, Hannah stared at Daniel.

'You're right, I was being stupid. I do need money and why should I scruple to take it from you? Five hundred pounds, you say. Well, it's not enough, I want seven hundred and fifty at least.'

'Seven hundred and fifty? Very well, but in return I want you to sign for it. Just a simple declaration, that's all.'

'What sort of declaration?'

'Just a receipt, really. I'll make it out for you along with the cheque. In the meantime, why don't you pack your stuff and I'll take you to the station.'

The tram was racing downhill with a vengeance now, she

thought, as panic rose in her throat. But she gave no outward sign of it. Numbly, Hannah went into the bedroom and put the suitcase she had bought for her honeymoon on the bed. She threw in her clothes, not bothering to fold them properly. She would have dearly loved to leave everything Timothy had bought her but she didn't, she had very little else to wear. So her new purchases went in higgledy-piggledy, shoes, skirts, hats, everything. Forcing the locks closed, she lugged the suitcase into the hall, went back into the sitting room and picked up her coat.

'Oh, you're ready? That was quick. Well, here you are then, here's the cheque and here's the receipt for you to sign.'

Hannah glanced briefly at Daniel as she took the pieces of paper. He was all geniality now he had got his way, she thought bitterly, so bitterly she couldn't trust herself to speak. She folded the cheque, put it in her purse, took the pen he was holding out to her and signed the receipt.

'Received, a cheque for seven hundred and fifty pounds signed Daniel Durkin in consideration of which I promise not to try to get in touch with Timothy Durkin ever again.'

Well, she thought as she signed it 'Hannah Durkin, née Armstrong', that's that. She was totally calm, as though this was happening to someone else; she felt no anguish, no pain. She was beyond that.

Daniel looked at his watch as he stowed the paper away in his pocket. 'Right then, I'll take you to the station and then I'll be on my way. It's only seven o'clock, you have plenty of time. Where do you want to go?'

'That is none of your business,' Hannah answered, thinking, only seven o'clock! I have ended my marriage, all but the legalities, in less than an hour. He shrugged indifferently and walked out with her following. She did not even look back as she left the flat which had been her home for so brief a time.

Daniel was back in the flat in under a quarter of an hour, having made sure he got the key from Hannah before she left. He poured himself another whisky and sat down, content with his day's work. It had been a bit of a gamble – well, a hundred-to-one gamble – but he had pulled it off and now he felt as triumphant as he did after besting any of those damn union men.

Curse of the nation, they were, trying to tell their betters how to run their business.

He had taken the chance that Timothy would not walk into the flat before he got the chit away, and he had been lucky. Now all he had to do was convince his fool of a son that Hannah had taken the money and gone. He had to admit, he thought as he lit another cigar, he had expected to have more trouble with her. But in the end, breeding had told; like all her kind, she couldn't resist the money when it was waved under her nose.

He leaned back in his seat, willing himself to keep calm as the door opened and Timothy came in. Indeed, it had been a close-run thing; he grinned as he realised how close.

Hannah sat in the overnight Edinburgh express as it clickety-clacked its way north. She was going home, of course, where else would she go? I'll write to Gloria and Alf, she thought, just a note to let them know I'm all right. Maybe it's just as well I haven't time to go to see them, I might run into Jane and if I do there's no knowing what I might do to her.

Restlessly, she gazed out of the window at the dark landscape, lit at intervals by the occasional streetlights. She was deathly tired, every bone in her body was aching, but though she had the carriage to herself she couldn't sleep. She looked awful, she saw by her reflection in the window; her hair was unkempt and there were great, dark circles under her eyes. She took out her comb and tidied her hair, then counted the change in her purse. Two pounds, fifteen shillings and threepence halfpenny, that was all. It would be enough for her needs, though, at least until she had the cheque deposited in Barclays Bank in Market Place in Bishop Auckland.

She hadn't said she wouldn't go back to Winton, she thought. And Daniel would never know she was there, he had a contemptuous disregard for anything that went on in the colliery villages. Closing her eyes, she leaned back in her seat. It would be hours before the train reached Darlington, with so many stops in between. She willed herself to relax.

'York. This is York.'

The train chuntered to a halt and Hannah woke up with a start. She couldn't believe she had slept as far as York, surely she had misheard? She peered out at the almost deserted platform – yes, it was York all right. Blinking, she rubbed the sleep from her eyes and glanced at her watch. Three o'clock in the morning, she couldn't believe it. They would be in Darlington in under an hour. Then she would have to wait for the first train to Bishop Auckland, she thought, but what did it matter? Nothing mattered very much, not any more. She had the rest of her life to get through without Timothy.

Opening her purse, she looked at the cheque. Seven hundred and fifty pounds was a lot of money, a fortune, but for the life of her she couldn't remember what it was that had made her agree to take it. Perhaps she should tear it up. Her head ached dully and so did her back and neck, no doubt from sleeping slouched against the side of the seat.

The train started to move slowly out of the station and Hannah rose to her feet and went out into the corridor. One of the windows was slightly open and cold air was blowing in. She stood for a moment, until the draught made her shiver, then went into the toilet and splashed water over her face and neck. Refreshed, she returned to her seat and began to consider what to do.

'Eeh, our Hannah, whatever are you doing here? Look, Harry, see who's here.'

Nora sprang up from the table, where she was spreading dripping on toast for Harry and Walton. Harry, who was squatting down, holding a long-handled toasting fork to the fire, jumped to his feet, forgetting all about the toast, and grinned in delight.

'Mind, you're a sight for sore eyes, all right,' Nora continued as Hannah dumped her case just inside the door and went to hug her mother. The feel of Nora's thin body against her own almost undid her; it took a supreme effort of will to hold her composure.

'But what are you doing here, pet? Eeh, I am pleased to see you, though. Do you know, I was thinking about you all day yesterday, couldn't get you off my mind.' Nora stood back and looked searchingly into Hannah's face. 'You don't look so good, our Hannah, you're not badly, are you? Mebbe a baby on the way?'

'No. No, I'm all right, Mam. It's just that I travelled up on that overnight train, that's all, I'm missing my sleep.'

'And where's that husband of yours? Had to go to his father's place, has he? By, it was nice of you to come to see us before you went there. Howay, take off your coat and we'll have a nice cup of tea, I dare say you could just do with one.'

Nora went to the fire and stirred it with the poker before settling the kettle on the coals, ignoring Harry's protests that she was spoiling it for his toast.

'How long have you got before your man comes for you?' she asked as she returned to the table.

Hannah looked round the kitchen, the familiar kitchen with its faded walls and the black-leaded range with its high mantelpiece surrounded by a cloth she had embroidered herself in sewing class at school. She saw Harry gazing at her, his grin turning to a puzzled frown, and Walton looking at her, his eyes large in his pinched little face as he tried to remember just who she was. She stared at the white-scrubbed boards of the table and the clippie mat on the floor before the fire. A new one, she thought, Mam must have put it down for Christmas. It had a bright red circle in the middle and Hannah recognised the cloth from an old coat of her own. She tried hard to keep her mind on the mat, looking to see if she recognised any other pieces Mam had cut up for it.

'Mam, is it our Hannah?' asked Walton suddenly. 'She looks a bit like our Hannah, I think.'

The question broke something in her and she looked up, caught her mother's eye, and then the tears came.

Chapter Twenty-Five

'Four hundred and fifty pounds, Miss Armstrong, and a bargain at that,' said Mr Eddy. 'And stock at valuation, of course.'

'Offer four hundred and thirty,' said Hannah, 'and we'll talk about the stock.'

She glanced composedly round the walls of the estate agent's office. They were painted a peculiar shade of buff with a brown dado and brown skirting boards. Bills advertising property were pasted to the walls along with a printed notice of terms and a framed certificate which stated that Mr Eddy belonged to a professional body, she couldn't quite make out which.

'I am not empowered –' he began saying. She pulled on her gloves and put her handbag over her arm as though preparing to leave.

'Of course,' she said briskly, 'there are other properties which will do just as well. Quite an interesting one in Spennymoor and not too far away.'

'Of course, I can always ring and put your offer to Mr Smith,' said the estate agent. Hannah smiled and drew off her gloves as he picked up the telephone receiver and waited for the operator to answer.

Hannah had been home a month. In the beginning, she had thought every knock at the door was Timothy. Surely he would seek her out, it must all have been a mistake. She bitterly regretted allowing Daniel to persuade her to leave so precipitately; if only she had insisted on seeing Timothy first, she agonised. During the day she watched for him all the time. When she went up to see Betty and little Simon, she hurried home just in case he was waiting for her, parked outside the back gate. If she went into Auckland she saved her bus ticket, added up the numbers and divided them by seven, just as she had when she was a child. The remainder was the important number, 'One for sorrow, two for joy, three for a letter, four for a boy.' And her heart would beat faster if the right number came up, a two, or three, or four. But no matter what the remainder, Timothy did not come.

The nights were the worst. At night, she lay sleepless in the double bed she shared with her mother, for now the family was so much reduced, the boys had the large bedroom. She ached for Timothy through the long nights, and after she fell into an exhausted sleep, more often than not when it was almost time to get up, she dreamed of him.

Mam watched her, full of concern. 'You shouldn't have left your man,' she said once. 'No good will come of it. You promised to love and obey him no matter what happened.'

'I had to leave, Mam. He didn't want me. He sent his father to tell me he didn't want me. So you see, I am obeying him.'

'Hmm,' said Nora.

Hannah did not tell her mother everything that had happened, and Nora forbore to question her too closely. Her face had hardened at the mention of Timothy's father and she turned back to her cooking, muttering with impotent rage, 'Come the day, Hannah, come the day. By, if ever a man needed to get his comeuppance it's that one, but God is good, Durkin will come to a bad end, you'll see.'

Hannah watched as her mother pounded the bread dough, lifting it up and flinging it back in the bowl with all the strength in her thin, wiry arms.

A few nights before Hannah went into Bishop Auckland to see the estate agent, she had come to a decision. She would go into business for herself, that way there was no boss to put you down. And the only business she knew anything about was the newsagent business. Consequently, she scoured the *Northern Echo* and *Auckland Chronicle* For Sale columns and found that a number of newsagent's shops were available. The depression in the mining industry affected all the trade in the area and most shops were struggling. She could have picked up a leasehold shop for almost nothing but she was determined to buy and she wanted a shop with living accommodation, in Bishop Auckland for preference.

So here she was, sitting across the desk from Mr Eddy. She knew him well, if only by sight, for she had often seen him about the town or driving his car on the road past Winton Colliery. Of course, he didn't recognise her, she was just a girl from the mining villages which surrounded the town. He finished his conversation and replaced the receiver in its cradle.

'Mr Smith is willing to negotiate with you concerning the stock,' he said, beaming. 'Would you like to make an appointment? Tomorrow afternoon, perhaps – I will be available to go with you at two o'clock, how will that suit you?'

'Thank you, Mr Eddy. I think I would rather go now. After all, it's just up the street and as I'm here, I may as well. Of course, if you're too busy, I can easily go by myself.'

Mr Eddy coughed and glanced at his watch. 'Well, I have an appointment in half an hour, Miss Armstrong. Tomorrow –'

'This is a cash sale, Mr Eddy. I have the money ready and waiting in Barclays Bank.'

'Er, yes, of course, Miss Armstrong. I'll just have a word with my secretary and we'll go. Perhaps I should ring Mr Smith and tell him we're on our way.'

'Don't bother.'

Mr Eddy rose to his feet, looking somewhat put out. This was a very forthright young woman, he thought. As they walked up Newgate Street he stole a glance at her. She had dressed carefully for this interview, and clothes like her smart camel coat and stylish cloche hat were not often seen in Auckland, especially not in these hard days. She walked confidently, her chin up, showing her flawless skin and striking dark eyes. Mr Eddy wondered where she had come from – a young lady obviously well-off, suddenly appearing in the town and wishing to buy a newsagent's. Her accent puzzled him: cultured, but with a northern tinge to it.

His speculations ended as they reached the shop and went in. There were a few customers inside, Hannah noted with satisfaction. She had chosen this place because it was the nearest to the station and even in a small market town such as Bishop Auckland, there were some travellers who liked to buy a paper before a journey or as they came to work.

Mr Smith was behind the counter, a small man, coming up to retirement age, she judged. Good, that meant there was a genuine reason for selling. The shop was dingy and, even on this dark late-February day, lit with only one light bulb. There were fewer magazines on the shelves than there had been in the Ridley's shop in Oxford and only one or two national newspapers.

'I'll only be a minute,' the newsagent said, nodding to Mr Eddy, and they waited as he served the customers with local papers and packets of Woodbine cigarettes. It did not take long and then he turned to Hannah.

'Yes, miss?'

'This is Miss Armstrong, the lady I telephoned you about.' Mr Eddy stepped forward and introduced them.

Mr Smith had a firm handshake and held her hand a fraction longer than necessary as he gazed into her face. 'You are very young to be buying a newsagent's,' he remarked.

'That may be, but I assure you I know what I'm doing.'

He nodded, evidently satisfied her offer was a serious one. 'I'll close the shop and we can talk.'

'It need only be for a little while,' said Hannah. 'I know that this can be quite a busy time in a newsagent's. But I would like to see the accommodation if I may.'

There were two bedrooms and a bathroom upstairs and a living room and kitchen at the back of the shop, together with a yard containing a coalhouse and lavatory – a water closet, not an ash closet. Some decorating needed to be done and she would have to furnish the place, but on the whole, Hannah was pleasantly surprised at the condition of the property. By the time she had inspected everything, including the broom cupboard under the stairs, she had decided she would take it.

'Four hundred and fifty including the stock,' she announced.

'But the stock is worth more than twenty pounds,' protested Mr Smith.

'Do you think so?' asked Hannah sceptically. She stared round at the shelves lining the shop walls, some of them covered rather sparsely with boxes of bootlaces and other sundries. There was a stack of cigarettes behind the counter but Hannah had seen no back-up stock such as the Ridleys had in their store room and she suspected there was none. It looked to her as if Mr Smith had been running down his stock in anticipation of a sale. Apart from the newspapers and periodicals, which would most likely be on a sale-or-return basis, there were only a few novels which appeared to have been on the shelf for quite a time, judging by the dust on them.

'Well . . .' Mr Smith had followed her glance and realised she knew what she was talking about.

'Perhaps you should wait a while before committing yourselves,' Mr Eddy interjected. He looked somewhat put out, no doubt at having taken so little part in the negotiations.

'My mind is made up,' Hannah replied briskly. 'Now, what do you say, Mr Smith?' She took out her brand-new chequebook and opened it. 'Of course I will give you a deposit, shall we say fifty pounds?'

Mr Smith glanced at Mr Eddy. 'I'll take it,' he said.

'This is all highly irregular,' said Mr Eddy. 'Make the cheque out to me, Miss Armstrong. My customers' account.'

'But where did you get all that money? From the Durkins? Timothy?'

'Yes.'

Nora gazed at her, eyes wide with astonishment. 'By, but it must have cost a fortune to buy a shop in Auckland. Are you sure it's all right spending Timothy's money like this? He will likely come for you yet, you know, then what will he say?'

'He won't come now, Mam.'

Nora bit her lip at the hard note in Hannah's voice. 'Why, man, you're a bit young to give up on your marriage, you've not given it a chance.'

'It's over, Mam. Don't worry, the money is mine to do what I like with.'

'But why didn't you tell me? You kept very quiet about this, didn't you?'

'I wanted to surprise you. I thought you and the two bairns could come to live with me over the shop. Oh, you'll love it, Mam, there's a bathroom upstairs and a water closet in the yard. I might even have a passage built from the back door to the lav, then we won't have to go out in the cold.'

'Me? I'm not leaving here pet. What about our Bob? He needs

me to look after him. And then there's the little 'un, what about school? Eeh, no, pet, there's me shop in the front room an' all, it's building up nicely. But if it's what you want, I'm pleased for you. I hope you make a go of it, I do.'

'Oh, Ma, you can help in the shop in Auckland, it'll be far better than the front room.' Hannah argued. She was disappointed, she'd been so sure her mother would go with her. But Nora was adamant.

'Nay, lass, I think I'll just stay here. Mind, it was nice of you to offer, don't think I don't appreciate it.'

At least there was somewhere for the family to live if Daniel Durkin did evict them, thought Hannah. For Tucker and Betty would not be able to help, Tucker's job would be at risk if they did.

When she told Harry, his reaction was much more positive. 'I can be a paper lad, Hannah. I can, can't I? How much will I earn if I deliver papers?'

'I'm not sure if you can,' she answered. 'After all, you would have to walk into Bishop Auckland and deliver the papers and still be back in time to go to school. I think it would be too much for you.'

Harry was deflated. 'I could do it if I had a bike,' he said wistfully. 'I could be in Auckland in no time at all if I had a bike.'

'That's true,' said Hannah. None of the Armstrongs had ever had a bicycle except Alf. He had had a second-hand one, bought in the days before Da's accident. Since then, there had not been enough money. How much did bicycles cost? When she went into Auckland to see her solicitor, she would see about buying a bicycle.

The following afternoon when Harry came in from school, there was a second-hand bicycle waiting for him in the yard. Though it was full-size, Harry was growing quite tall and Hannah reckoned he would be able to manage it.

'Eeh, ta, Hannah, ta.' Harry touched the bicycle reverently, he could hardly believe it was really there.

'Do you know how to ride it?'

'Aye, oh, aye,' he breathed. 'Well, I had a go on one once, I'm sure it won't take me long to get good at it. Eeh, thank you, Hannah, you're all right.'

'You have a week or two to practise before I get into the shop. Mind, be careful or you'll have to answer to me.'

'I will, Hannah, I will. I'll just take it out now. By, it's grand! My marra's eyes'll pop out when he sees it.'

'Mebbe you shouldn't have let him play with it, not if you want it for the deliveries,' Nora observed as he went out of the yard with the bicycle. She and Hannah walked to the gate and watched him as he climbed on it and wobbled down the row.

'Let the lad have his pleasure, he's had little enough,' said Hannah. 'I can always buy another for the shop, Mam, it was only twelve and sixpence.'

'*Only* twelve and sixpence. That's as much as my pension,' Nora commented as they went back into the house.

February turned into March and March into April; Harry learned to ride the bicycle without wobbling and became quite nonchalant about it. He also learned to ride it downhill with both feet on the seat or sometimes with no hands and his feet on the handlebars, but luckily, his mother and sister never found out about that.

At last the time came to collect the keys to the shop from Mr Eddy. It was a Saturday morning in April, a fine spring morning, and Hannah decided to walk into Bishop Auckland. Harry rode his bicycle by her side, flying past her for a few hundred yards before turning and coming back. She reckoned he must have ridden nine miles instead of three by the time they got to Newgate Street. Nora and Walton were coming in later on the bus, Nora was going to help her clean out the living quarters.

Hannah couldn't describe how she felt as she unlocked the door and entered the shop. For a short while, the perpetual ache for Timothy disappeared in her pleasure at having her very own shop. Even as she was closing the door behind herself and Harry, a customer came and looked in.

'You're not closed, are you?'

'Just for the weekend. I'm the new owner and I'll be open for business on Monday morning.'

'I only wanted a packet of Woodbines,' he grumbled.

'Oh, well, in that case I can let you have them. How many, five or ten?'

'Five.'

She went to the stack behind the counter and brought him the cigarettes, and he handed over three halfpence and went on his way. A good omen, she thought happily as she put the money in the till.

The rest of the day went by in a whirl of activity as she and Nora cleaned, scrubbed and lit fires in all the rooms so they would be dry by the time the furniture arrived. Hannah had bought most of it at the second-hand salerooms, good plain furniture at a fraction of the cost of new. They hung new curtains at the windows and Harry swept the yard and swilled the flags with washing-soda water to get rid of the green mould.

'Can I stay here the night, Hannah?' he asked when the furniture was in place and the curtains drawn, shutting out the sight of the snow which had started to fall at three o'clock.

'It depends on Mam,' said Hannah diplomatically. 'But there are the papers to go out tomorrow, I couldn't risk having them miss a day.'

'It's snowing an' all, I might not be able to come in on my bike,' said Harry. Both of them looked at their mother for her reaction.

'Aye. Mebbe it would be for the best,' she said reluctantly.

'Me an' all, me an' all,' Walton pleaded. He had been dozing in the large leather armchair which Hannah had picked out in the saleroom and which was now drawn up before the fire.

'Eeh, no, pet, you'd better come home with me,' said his mother.

'We could all stay, just for tonight,' Hannah suggested.

'And what about our Bob? Have you forgot he's to see to?'

'No, but –'

'We'll be going, then, me and the bairn.'

Walton snivelled in protest but Nora had her way and Hannah saw them to the bus stop. The snow was melting as it fell, damp and cold. She went back through the shop into the room made cosy by a bright coal fire in the grate.

'I'm famished, our Hannah. What's for supper?' Harry was sitting in the armchair vacated by his brother, reading a comic he had filched from the shop.

'Harry, I didn't say you could have that,' said Hannah sternly.

'But it's last week's, nobody's going to buy last week's *Beano*,' he said reasonably.

'Maybe not. But I'll thank you to ask another time.' She took her purse from the slate mantel shelf and took out a shilling. 'Now, how about slipping down the street for some fish and chips while I boil the kettle?'

There was a letter from Alf, Harry brought it on the Wednesday morning when he came in. It had come to her mother's house the day before. Hannah looked at the envelope with her name written in Alf's firm handwriting and the Oxford postmark. Oxford, she thought, where Timothy was. A wave of misery swept over her, so intense she leaned back against the counter and closed her eyes.

'Hannah? You're not badly, are you?'

At the sound of Harry's anxious voice she pulled herself together and managed a smile. 'No, just tired, that's all. Five o'clock is a little early to start the day. No, I'm all right, you go on out with the other boys.' Hannah had kept on the two paperboys, Billy and Dave, who had worked for Mr Smith, and Harry was learning the routes from them. Afterwards, she hoped to build up her business so that she could keep on all three of them.

Satisfied, Harry went out with his bag of papers slung across his chest. There was usually half an hour before customers began to trickle in, so Hannah went into the living room behind the shop and opened her letter. She had written to Alf and Gloria in March and this must be the reply.

Dear Hannah,

I thought I would let you know that Timothy came to see me last night. He wanted to know where you were living. It's not the first time; he came the night after you went away. He was looking for you and mind, he was in a hell of a temper.

Hannah's heart leaped within her. Timothy *had* come looking for her after all, he did want her back! Why hadn't Alf written earlier? Or if not Alf, then Gloria? She read on, eagerly.

I told him that I knew nothing about it, you went away in such a hurry you didn't even let us know. I might tell you, both Gloria and I were pretty upset about that.

She told me what Jane had done and there was a great row

and I told Jane she should have minded her own business, not that I hold with keeping secrets in families, mind. In the end, I told the little sneak to find somewhere else to live. You needn't worry about her, though, she's all right, the Ridleys found her a room near them. No doubt she told them a pack of lies and they felt sorry for her.

Hannah looked up from her letter as the bell over the shop door tinkled, and she went to serve the customer. Jane had not written to Mam to tell her she had changed her address, she thought. But then, Jane did not often write home. With the shop once more empty of customers, she went on with her letter.

Anyroad, as I was saying, Timothy came back and demanded to know where you are. I didn't tell him, but it's only a matter of time before he finds out. The thing is, I think he wants a divorce.

Hannah's hopes plummeted. Numbly, she put the letter in her pocket. Gloria had added a postscript, but she hadn't the heart to read it now – later, but not now.

Of course, it was no more than she had expected. She rubbed the fourth finger of her left hand. Her wedding ring had been worn for such a short time that there was not even a mark on the skin. Now it was in the top drawer of her dressing table, she couldn't bear to get rid of it altogether. Hope springs eternal, she thought bitterly. She would write again to Alf and Gloria and apologise for the fact that she had left so abruptly. But she would not mention Timothy. No doubt if he wanted to he could find out where she was.

It being Wednesday and half-day closing, Hannah decided to go home to Winton to see her mother. She had thought she would begin the painting of the shop walls but the letter had made her restless. She decided to walk; the snow of the weekend had been the last flurry of the winter and the wind had veered to the southwest, bringing warmer weather and sunshine. At last it was spring.

Locking up the shop, Hannah took the path past the iron foundry which led to a wood and the open fields beyond. The sun shone brightly and there was even some warmth from it, though under the trees the air was still cold and dank. But there were crocuses, bright yellow and purple, under the trees, and the scent of wild garlic by the stream which ran through the wood. Coming out on the far side, she could see the old village in the distance with its stone church tower and the winding gear and engine house of Winton Colliery towering over the miners' cottages and standing out clearly against the sky.

Too clearly, she realised suddenly – where was the smoke from the chimney stack, where was the steam and sulphurous fumes from the coke ovens? Hannah quickened her pace as she skirted the enormous slag heap and approached the village. The winding wheel was still and on the end of the rows, groups of men in their pit clothes, with leather protectors strapped to their knees, were sitting on their hunkers, talking little. An air of despair hung about them; Hannah could practically feel it. Though they were wearing their working clothes, these were not men just up from fore shift and having a natter before they went home, their faces were too clean for that.

'What cheor, Hannah, lass,' and, 'Now then, lass,' one or two greeted her as she went past, but the greeting was automatic, there was no real interest in it. She nodded and hurried on to the end row and home.

Bob was sitting at the table in his shirtsleeves, writing.

'What is it?' she asked him. 'Is something wrong? Why has the pit shut down?'

'Have you been walking round with your eyes shut these last weeks, our Hannah?' Bob demanded. 'What do you think has happened? The same as what happened in '21, that's what!'

'You mean it's a lockout?'

'Aye, that's what I mean exactly. But they won't get the better of us as easily as they did then, I'm telling you that.'

Hannah sat down on the settee, memories of the 1921 lockout filling her mind – the hunger and distress there had been in the rows, the pinched faces of the children. She thought of the time she had smuggled Harry into school so that he could have a free meal and the humiliation they had both felt when the caretaker saw him and told the teacher. What straits they had been driven to!

'No,' Bob was saying. 'This time the country is behind us, the workers won't stand for it. The railway men and the transport workers are on our side, we'll show the bosses what's what.

Why, man, we haven't a living wage now, how can we agree to a cut in our wages again? And then they are insisting on an extra hour on the working day with nowt extra to show for it.'

Hannah stared at him. He had never been out of County Durham in his life, he didn't know any other workers. She remembered the night that Arthur J. Cook was in Oxford, how close he had been to being humiliated. And she knew that the prosperous car workers weren't interested in unions, they were well enough off without.

'It'll be a general strike, that's what,' said Bob. 'The country will support us.'

Maybe it will, thought Hannah. Or maybe it won't.

Chapter Twenty-Six

'GREAT STRIKE BEGUN' said the headlines in the *Daily Journal*, one of the few newspapers that Hannah had for sale. Even that was greatly reduced in size. She stood behind the counter in the deserted shop and considered her position.

Her bank account held just under three hundred pounds and she had no bills outstanding. She suspected that she was in a better position to sit out the strike than most of the other shopkeepers but she wanted to conserve her resources until the strike was over. For she had seen the mood of some of the people in Oxford and was aware that if the rest of the country thought the same way as they did, the general strike would not last long. Then how long would the miners last? Hannah feared a repetition of 1921 and she wanted to be in a position to help the family if need be.

The doorbell tinkled and she looked up to see Bob entering the shop, his face thunderous.

'What the hell are you doing, keeping the shop open? Have you joined the bosses now? You soon jumped from worker to capitalist.' He strode up the counter, glaring at her.

'I'm not . . . I haven't . . .' She was taken by surprise. For some reason she hadn't looked on opening the shop as breaking the strike.

'What do you think you're doing, then?'

'Don't you think the people will want to know what's happening? How else are they to know if there are no papers?'

'Aw, Hannah, use your brain. The papers that tell the truth will be on strike anyway, there'll only be the Tory press spouting their propaganda for the bosses. The *Daily Herald* is definitely out.'

'Well, I think it's stupid, the papers should have been your best weapon.'

Now that Bob had pointed it out to her, Hannah realised that she should have closed up the shop to show solidarity with her own folk, but his belligerent attitude had put her back up. She would close in her own time, not his, she thought rebelliously.

'Aye, you could be right there,' Bob conceded. 'Anyroad, we've brought out own own news-sheets. The lads are selling them on the streets now.'

'I doubt they'll sell many on Newgate Street,' Hannah said shortly. She walked to the door and looked down the road, straight as an arrow as when the Romans first built it, to the entrance to the marketplace. There were very few people to see and even fewer when she glanced the other way, towards the station. Most of the railwaymen were on strike, not just the station staff, but also those who worked at the railway wagon works at Shildon. Sighing, she closed the door and turned back to Bob.

'Oh, come on through the back for a minute,' she said.

'I haven't the time, it's my job to go round and check who's working and who isn't. And here I find my own sister's a strike-breaker.'

'How can I be on strike against the boss when I'm the boss?' she asked. 'No, never mind, don't answer that, I'm not going to fight with you. But do you want me to refuse to sell cigarettes and chewing baccy?'

'Essential supplies are different,' Bob began, and Hannah laughed.

'Oh, come on, you can spare the time for a cup of tea and a sandwich. I boiled some bacon yesterday, a nice juicy bit.'

Bob wavered and fell. 'All right then, just ten minutes, though.'

While Hannah was preparing the food, her brother talked enthusiastically of the strike. 'By, it's going to be different this time, pet. The country's behind us, I told you it would be. The government will have to give in. Reports are coming in from all over the place. I tell you, everything's going grand, the strike's a success.'

The shop bell sounded and Hannah put down the knife she had been using to cut the bacon. 'Mash the tea, will you, Bob?' she said over her shoulder as she went to answer it.

The customer was Mr Eddy, immaculate in pinstripe trousers, black coat and a high stiff collar on a snowy shirt.

'Good morning, Miss Armstrong,' he said, glancing at the few newspapers and periodicals on the counter. 'It's a sad day, a sad day indeed. And such a shame, just as you are starting up. I do hope this emergency won't last long, I do indeed. But you'll see, the working class is all the same, when their beer money runs out and they find the government isn't going to pay them to idle their time away, the workers will come to their senses, I guarantee it.'

Hannah gazed at him and said nothing but he didn't appear to notice her silence.

'I've come for a paper, I thought you would have some in the shop. I suppose your delivery boys are on strike?' He shook his head at the foolishness of boys aping their misguided elders. 'I'll take a *Journal*, I think, as you have no *Times*.'

'I'm sorry, Mr Eddy, I'm afraid I can't sell you a newspaper,' said Hannah.

'What do you mean?' Mr Eddy looked surprised. 'There's one here, why can't you sell it? It's not reserved for anyone, is it?' He picked up the paper and fished in his pocket for coppers to pay for it.

'It's not reserved for anyone, no. But I can't sell it, nevertheless.'

Mr Eddy's eyes widened as he glanced behind her and saw Bob standing in the doorway leading to the sitting room.

'This man is not intimidating you, is he, Miss Armstrong? Just say the word and I'll send for the police.' The colour of his skin above the stiff, white collar had deepened to red and his eyes snapped with indignation.

'Send for the police, would you?' Bob stepped forwards and growled, and Hannah was startled at how dangerous he sounded. Hastily she interposed herself between the two men.

'There's no need for that, Mr Eddy,' she said. 'Of course he isn't threatening me. Bob is my brother.'

Mr Eddy's face hardened. 'Oh, I see, Miss Armstrong, I see,' he said haughtily. 'Your brother, you say. Yes, well, I'll bid you good morning, Miss Armstrong.' He turned and walked smartly out of the shop and Hannah could just imagine him heading straight for his office so that he could telephone his cronies from the Gentleman's Club to tell them that Miss Armstrong was not such a mystery after all. What was a puzzle was how a lass from a pit village who looked hardly eighteen had got the money to buy a freehold business in the town's main shopping street. Oh yes, thought Hannah, she knew well how his mind would be working. Mr Eddy would find out who she was easily enough and soon Daniel Durkin would know where she was and what she was doing.

Not that it was a secret, she thought as she locked the door and went through the shop to the living room. She hadn't promised she wouldn't come home to Auckland.

'I've closed the shop,' she said to Bob. 'I think I'll catch the bus out to Winton to see the family. I can walk up to the farm and see the Burtons, too, I haven't seen them yet.'

'Aye, I'll be on my way an' all. Mind, I think you'll have trouble catching a bus, they're all on strike.' Bob grinned as he pulled his cap down over his head. He was a handsome lad, like all the Armstrongs, Hannah thought as she watched him, with dark eyes and almost black hair, though the colour could be seen only in the short fringe over his forehead for he wore his hair close-cropped like most of the miners. When hair had to be washed every day it was easier that way.

'I'll just have to walk home then, won't I?' she commented as she weighed out a two-ounce packet of black bullets for Harry and one for Walton, to take with her. They went out together, Bob to go to the baking-powder factory to check on the workers and Hannah taking the path for Winton.

A miner stood on the corner of South Church Lane, a bundle of papers in his hands. '*Northern Light*' he called at intervals. 'A penny for the paper by the workers for the workers.'

Hannah fished a penny out of her purse and handed it over.

'Bless you, miss,' he said and gave her the thin sheet, poorly printed and obviously the work of amateurs. As she walked through the wood, Hannah glanced through the bulletin. There was an air of optimistic determination about it, something like a wartime spirit. There was a job to be done and they were going to do it; the workers of the country had risen and would not be denied. The message was reiterated throughout the paper with accounts of how different groups of workers – railwaymen, transport workers and others – had obeyed the call.

'EVERY MAN BEHIND THE MINERS!' was proclaimed. 'AN INJURY TO ONE IS AN INJURY TO ALL!' And the miners' slogan, the phrase which encapsulated their refusal to take any more cuts in wages or work longer hours for the same pay, 'NOT A PENNY OFF THE PAY! NOT A MINUTE ON THE DAY!'

Hannah sighed, filled with foreboding. Why could the men not see that the government and the bosses were so much better able to stand a long strike than they were themselves? The miners in particular had nothing behind them to sustain their families during a long strike. She folded the paper up and put it in her handbag as she left the wood and fields behind her and headed up the road for Winton Colliery.

'Well, will you just look at her, Miss High and Mighty Armstrong?'

Hannah had been lost in thought but now, as she walked along the road by the bunny banks, where the whinny or gorse bushes were blooming bright yellow against the green broom, she looked up in surprise at the jeering voice. It was Sally Cornish and Kathleen. Sally, as filthy as ever in a bombazine dress which, even in its present ruined state, Hannah could see had once been someone's town dress, stood before her, arms akimbo, grinning widely. The few teeth she had left were black and rotting and her hair was so dirty it was impossible to tell what colour it was.

Beside her was Kathleen, a girl only a year or two older than Hannah, though she gave the appearance of a woman of thirty or forty. She was wearing a lavender gown, much befrilled and ribboned, but in places the frills were coming adrift from the dress and there were food stains on the bodice and worse on the skirt. They must have bought the dresses on one of the second-hand stalls on the market, Hannah decided.

'Hallo, Mrs Cornish, Kathleen,' she said and sidestepped to walk round them, but the Cornish women were having none of it. They moved with her.

'Who does she think she is, Mam?' asked Kathleen, rubbing a hand under her left nostril to remove a drip. 'Walking along with her nose in the air like the Queen of Sheba.' She put out a filthy hand and fingered the material of Hannah's hip-length jacket. 'Dressed to kill an' all, isn't she? Who bought you this, Hannah? A fancy man, was it?'

Hannah stepped back almost without thinking, she couldn't bear either of the two to touch her. 'You know full well who I am, Kathleen Cornish,' she said. 'Now get out of my way.'

'Ooh! Get out of my way, is it?' Sally's jeering tone turned ugly and she caught hold of Hannah's arm roughly and pulled her close so that the stench from her body filled the girl's nostrils and it was all she could do to stop herself from gagging. She pinched in her nose and held her breath and at the same time struggled to pull away, but Sally was surprisingly strong and held on with vicelike fingers. 'I'll get out of your way when I'm ready, my lass. You're just like all the other bloody Armstrongs, think you're too good for the likes of us.'

'She's no different from us, Mam, else where do you think she got her fancy clothes and such? Been on the game, she must have been, that's what, down south where the men have more money to chuck about than the lads round here. Mebbe she's found herself a canny old man to keep her, mebbe she's found more than one, what do you think? Did your fancy man chuck you out, Hannah? Is that why you've come home to your mother?'

'Leave me alone,' said Hannah through clenched teeth. 'Leave me alone or I swear I'll make you pay, see if I don't.' Her anger was rising, lending her strength. With a supreme effort, she wrenched herself away and managed to get past them and fly up the path, only to run straight into Lancelot Cornish as he stepped out from behind a tree.

'Hey, now, not so fast,' he cried and held her fast and the stink of him was even worse than that of his mother and sister.

'Let me go!' she screamed at him in outrage. 'I'll . . . I'll lay you in to the polis! I'll have you up for assault, you hacky, mucky brute!'

Lancelot laughed. 'An' who's going to believe that? Why, lass, everybody knows what you've been doing to come home as flush as you have. It won't hurt you to let me have a bit, now will it? I mean, I'm not exactly going to damage the goods, am I? Not if you're nice to me, that is.'

'Aye, go on, lad, show the bitch what Cornish men are made

of,' Sally shouted and Kathleen hooted with laughter. For a moment, Hannah was paralysed with fear. Out of the corner of her eye she could see Sally jumping up and down, laughing and egging Lancelot on. She gazed up at him, at his unshaven chin and wet lips, as his head swayed down towards hers. And even as she watched she saw movement in his dank, greasy hair. Twisting sharply, taking him by surprise, she dragged the heel of her shoe down his shin and he jumped back, releasing her as he grabbed one leg and hopped about on the other, shouting expletives.

But Hannah wasn't there to hear, she was off racing along the road to the village and she neither stopped nor looked back until she got there, though she was panting and she had a painful stitch in her side. There were a few men idling by the end row and they looked at her curiously.

'Is summat the matter, Hannah? There's no one chasing you, is there?'

An older man stepped forward with a look of concern and Hannah saw it was Mr Holmes. She slowed to a walk and struggled to catch her breath.

'No, I'm all right, Mr Holmes,' she managed to say. 'I just thought I needed some exercise so I ran some of the way.' She laughed shakily. 'I suppose I'm not as fit as I thought I was.'

'Hmm,' said Mr Holmes. 'For meself, if I get the feeling I need some exercise I lie down until it wears off.' And he guffawed at his own wit.

Hannah smiled politely and went on to her mother's house. Nora was in the back yard, as she usually was on Mondays when the weather was fine, bent over a tub of soapy water, her sleeves rolled up over her elbows. She was pounding the clothes in the tub with the poss stick, a wooden implement with three short paddles at one end and a cross-bar handle at the other. She gave a delighted smile of welcome when she saw Hannah.

'Eeh, lass, I didn't expect you today,' she exclaimed. Leaning the poss stick against the side of the tub, she dried her hands on her apron, pushed a lock of hair back from her forehead and adjusted a hairpin to hold it. Hannah saw with a touch of concern that her mother seemed tired and was breathing quite heavily from the hard work.

'I've closed the shop. There weren't many papers to sell anyway,' she said.

'No, I suppose not. It's a rum business, isn't it?' Nora's face sobered as Hannah's words reminded her of the strike and she sighed. 'Well, go on and put the kettle on, I won't be long finishing this lot.'

'I'll do it, it's ages since I gave a turn to possing. Just lend me a pinny.' Hannah took off her jacket and handed it to her mother before rolling up the sleeves of her blouse. In a minute or two, wrapped in a pinafore which her mother brought for her, she was possing away, up and down, up and down, watching the water swirl round the tub and slap against the sides. It reminded her of schooldays when she would come home at four o'clock and finish off the last of the possing while her mother got the tea. Smiling sadly, she put the clothes through the mangle and dropped them in the blue water in the tin bath.

When the washing was finished, she slung a line across the back row and hung out the clothes, and propped the line up with a wooden clothes prop, out of the way of anyone walking by. The wind caught them and they fluttered like a row of flags in the sunshine.

'They'll be dry by teatime,' said Nora contentedly, watching from the yard where she was emptying the poss tub.

Hannah gazed up at the white shirts and pinafores; there was something satisfying in pinning clean clothes up to dry after all the hard work of washing day. She thought of the encounter she had had with the Cornish family earlier in the day and shuddered as she remembered the filthy state of their clothes and the stink of them too. Turning back to the gate, carrying the tin bath which had held the wet clothes, she saw Mr Hodgson, the Sunday-school teacher, watching her covertly as he went by.

'Hallo, Mr Hodgson.' She smiled, prepared to have a few words with him, expecting him to ask how she had got on in Oxford, and was surprised when he mumbled something and went on, almost running down the street. Shrugging, she went in, thinking he must have been in a tremendous hurry. It just wasn't like him to go off without a word, especially when she had been away for so long. Though she had been back a few weeks now, she hadn't been to chapel and this was the first time she had met him outside. Perhaps his eyes were going, poor man, he was getting on a bit.

The boys came in from school and Bob from his day in Auckland. He was jubilant, the strike was a great success, he reckoned.

'There's nothing to crow about, not with a strike,' said Nora. 'It's my experience that the coal owners always win, no matter what.'

'Aw, Mam, it's different this time. I've told you, we're going to win, it'll only take a week or two. An' it's not just the miners, the country's behind us, we can't lose.'

Nora said no more, but Hannah saw her face was shadowed as she set about frying up a pan of potatoes and onions to eat with the cold meat left over from Sunday.

'I'll walk up to see the Burtons before I go back,' said Hannah when the simple meal was finished. 'I haven't seen them since I got home.' She handed out the packets of sweets to Harry and Walton, enjoying the way their faces lit up with delight at the unexpected treat.

'You spoil those bairns,' said Nora, but it was something she said automatically every time Hannah gave them anything so no one took any notice.

A cool wind had sprung up as Hannah walked up to the farm and she was glad of her jacket. Mr Burton was in the cowshed, she could hear the swish of water as he swilled down the stalls. She would see him after, she thought, best not disturb him when he was busy. Walking up to the kitchen door of the farmhouse, she knocked and opened it. As she had thought she would be, his wife was in the kitchen.

'Hallo, Mrs Burton,' she called and, sure of her welcome, stepped inside and pulled the door to behind her.

The farmer's wife looked up from the table where she was ironing, a newly ironed shirt in her hand. Deliberately, she turned her back on Hannah and hung the shirt carefully on the airer which was strung on a pulley from the ceiling. Only when she was satisfied that it was hanging straight did she give her attention to the girl.

'Now then, Hannah,' she said, her tone neutral.

Taken aback, for a moment, Hannah couldn't think what to say. Normally she would have gone farther into the kitchen, maybe even sat down on a chair by the fire, but instead, she hovered by the door, looking uncertain.

'I . . . I thought I would walk up to see you, it's such a long time since,' she said at last.

'Hmm.'

'I hope you are feeling well. And Mr Burton too.'

'We're well enough, thank you.'

Hannah was beginning to feel very uncomfortable and bewildered. What on earth was wrong? Mrs Burton carried on ironing.

'Is there something the matter?' Hannah asked after a lengthy silence.

'Not with us there isn't.'

Mrs Burton licked her finger and touched the flatiron. Dissatisfied with the heat of it, she exchanged it for another, which had been heating up on the bar of the fire. As she turned back to the table, she gave Hannah a level stare.

'That's a nice jacket you're wearing,' she said. 'Not a bad dress neither, I bet it cost you a bob or two.'

Hannah looked down at her dress. It was only of cotton but pretty and well cut.

'You must have had a blooming good job to be able to afford clothes like that.'

'Well, I . . .' Hannah faltered, realising she couldn't say how she had been able to afford such clothes without telling of her marriage to Timothy. And she wasn't ready for that, oh no, that subject was still too raw.

'Of course, there are other ways young girls get money,' said Mrs Burton.

Hannah stepped back to the door. 'I'm sorry you should think that of me, Mrs Burton, I thought you knew me better. But I can see I'm not welcome here so I'll be saying goodbye.' Walking rapidly out, she did not see the look of uncertainty which flitted across Mrs Burton's face.

'I didn't mean –' the farmer's wife began but she was too late, Hannah had closed the door behind her and was striding off down the track.

She didn't go back into Winton, she felt too full of emotion for that. Instead she cut through the fields and went into Bishop Auckland the other way, a route which led past Durham Road into the marketplace. So that was what everyone thought, even

Mrs Burton, was it? she mused bitterly. Well, let them. She hurried on, past Durham Road and up Gib Chare into Newgate Street. She did not lift her head or glance to left or right, all she could think of was closing her own door behind her.

Chapter Twenty-Seven

My Lord,

I beg to acknowledge receipt of your letter of the 2nd inst. I have to agree that the strike is deplorable. There is little unrest among the men, they appear to be simply obeying their leaders. However, by next Saturday, their last wage packet will be exhausted and they will be finding it difficult to pay for their beer and then we will discover how firm is their resolve.

Arrangements have been made this morning for the bringing-up of the pit ponies and placing them out to grass. As to the safety men in the pits, contingency plans have been put into action.

Let us hope the government stands firm and refuses to give way to the TUC or this country will never recover.

I have the honour to be

Your Lordship's obedient servant,

Daniel Durkin

Daniel stood at the window of his first-floor study as he dictated the letter, looking out over the fields. A girl was walking up the path which led on to Durham Road. She was too far away for him to see properly, but there was something about the way she walked that reminded him of something.

'Fetch my field glasses, Davidson, will you?' he asked. 'They are downstairs by the dining-room window.'

'Yes, sir.'

The secretary left his typing immediately and brought the

binoculars. It was Hannah all right, Daniel was just in time to see before she turned the corner for Gib Chare. He frowned heavily. As though he hadn't enough on his mind without that little chit coming back here, he thought angrily. Well, he would just have to find out where she was staying and what she was doing. If she was just playing a waiting game, hoping Timothy would come home before she was discovered, she was to be disappointed. No doubt she thought she would be able to use her wiles to entrap him again. It was a good thing Timothy was still embroiled in his final examinations, he wouldn't be home for another month. And not even then if Hannah was still here, Daniel swore. But she wouldn't be, oh no, not if he had anything to do with it. It hadn't taken him long to get rid of her before and it wouldn't take long now. Turning back to his desk, he picked up the telephone.

Half an hour later, he sat back in his chair, a smile of satisfaction on his face. So she had taken a newsagent's in Newgate Street, had she? Stupid girl, did she really think he was going to let her stay?

'Was there anything else tonight, sir?' Davidson broke into his thoughts.

'What? Oh, no, you can go. Goodnight to you.'

'Goodnight, sir.'

Left on his own, Daniel allowed himself to remember that night in Oxford when Timothy had come into the flat and found him there and Hannah gone. It had taken all his powers of persuasion to convince his son that Hannah's greed had proved stronger than her love.

'I don't believe you,' Timothy had said flatly. 'What lies have you been telling her?'

'None at all, I simply pointed out that your inheritance would be forfeit if you stayed married to her. And she would be much better off taking the money on offer. Girls of her class are easily dazzled by the prospect of a good sum of money.'

Daniel had paused while he lit a cigar; so far the day had gone well and it would be silly to spoil it all by rushing the last hurdle.

'Hannah is not easily dazzled by money,' Timothy said doggedly. 'Why, she would take nothing from me before we were married.'

Daniel laughed. 'No, of course she wouldn't. She was playing for higher stakes. But once I showed her what the alternatives were, she knew where her best interests lay. Though I've got to say I admire her nerve, she wasn't bought cheaply.'

Timothy lunged at his father, taking hold of him by the lapels, and knocking the cigar out of his hand in the process. 'God damn you, Father, I hate you for this. I don't believe that's all that was said, you must have threatened her with something else. Now what was it?'

'Take your hands off me, Timothy, or I will –'

'You'll do what? There's nothing you can do to me now, nothing. You've done it all. I'll never forgive you for this. But I'll find her, mark my words, I will, and then you can go to hell!'

It had been an idle threat, thought Daniel as he left his study and went into his dressing room to dress for dinner. Timothy had stayed at Oxford and by all accounts had thrown himself into his work. No doubt he had come to his senses once the girl had gone and could no longer influence him. Marriage to someone from the inferior classes just did not work. Look at what happened to Ralph Grizedale when he married that girl – what was her name? Hope, that was it, something Hope. He'd taken to drink and the fortune his father had built up had been dissipated. And his son hadn't been any better, he'd run off with a married woman from Winton Colliery with two children.

The younger Grizedale was now a small farmer over by the coast, or so the gossips said. Not that he was so young, must be middle-aged by this time. And no doubt wished he had his time over again now he had to work the farm like a common labourer. Daniel's thoughts returned to his own son.

Better Timothy suffered a little love sickness now than spent a lifetime regretting a bad marriage, Daniel thought as he strolled downstairs for dinner. Meanwhile, there were more pressing problems to deal with, this strike for one. But it would be dealt with, he had confidence it would, and dealt with successfully. There was a stockpile of petrol and other necessary goods hidden away for just such an emergency as this, every precaution had been taken to enable the owners to withstand a lengthy strike. These left-wing unionists would find they were no match for Daniel Durkin and his fellows, indeed they would.

Mrs Bates brought in the roast beef and he carved himself a hefty slice and tucked into it with a hearty appetite. He had had a busy day, he deserved his dinner. He began planning the strategy for dealing with the pickets at the gates of the collieries within his jurisdiction.

'Will Edwards has been sentenced to three months' hard labour for selling the *Northern Light*,' said Bob gloomily. '"Actions likely to cause dissatisfaction among the civil population," the judge called it.' He rose from his seat by Hannah's fireside and walked to the door of the shop where his sister was standing behind the counter.

'We've been betrayed, Hannah, betrayed by our own class.' He stood in the doorway, his hands in his pockets and his cap pushed to the back of his head.

The general strike was over, it had ended on 12 May. That was it: the railwaymen, transport workers, printers and all the others who had joined in to stand behind the miners were going back to work. It had all happened just as Hannah had feared it would.

'Well, we are determined not to give in, we will carry on the fight for a decent living,' Bob went on. 'The miners will never give in.'

'Oh, Bob, get off your soapbox, you're not giving a speech now,' said Hannah wearily. 'Don't you remember 1921? Why, man, some of our folk haven't paid the Co-op back for the groceries they were advanced then.'

'The union is paying out twelve shillings a week per adult. We will manage,' said Bob stoutly.

'Yes. And for how long do you think the union will be able to carry on paying even that? Don't be so dense, lad.'

Bob stalked to the door. 'Well, if you're going to look on the black side all the time, I'm off home,' he said loftily. From behind his ear, he removed the cigarette butt he had put there earlier, and felt in his pocket for a match.

'Wait a minute, Bob, here, have these,' said Hannah, taking a packet of Woodbines from the shelf and holding them out to him.

'I don't want any charity,' he said, but she could see the hesitation in his eyes.

'Now you're being daft as well as dense. Since when was accepting a packet of cigarettes from your sister taking charity?'

'Aye, thanks, pet.' He smiled wryly and stowed the packet in his pocket. 'I'll be seeing you, then.'

After he had gone, Hannah sat down on the stool she had placed behind the counter for use when the shop was slack. It had been well used in the past ten days and no doubt would be well used in the coming weeks if the miners didn't give in, she mused. But the railwaymen were back at work, at least the ones the management had deigned to take back. People would be coming past the shop on their way to and from the station. Picking up a copy of the *Northern Echo*, she read an account of a train derailment in Northumberland. Some miners had removed a section of rail and then signalled to the train to stop, but instead it continued at a reduced speed. 'The fireman was a medical student, a volunteer,' the article read.

Hannah put down the paper and stared out of the window. She thought of the students she had seen in Oxford, a happy-go-lucky lot on the whole with no idea of how miners lived. Had Timothy driven a train or a bus in Oxford during the strike, she wondered, and the thought of him brought the old familiar ache. How could she have been so mistaken in him? She would have been willing to live with him on a miner's wage if need be. But he had not thought like that, he had preferred life without her if it meant he could keep his comfortable style of living. And how could she blame him? He had been born to comfort and security, unlike her.

She remembered the letter she had had from Alf saying Timothy had been looking for her. Even though Alf had said Timothy mentioned divorce, it had kindled the hope that he would come back, that somehow, magically, everything would come right. Yet at times like this, when she was feeling low, her emotions were so mixed up she didn't even know if she wanted that to happen. She certainly didn't want to be a drag on him, she'd die first. But she loved him, oh yes, and she wanted him. She probed the ache for him in her mind and it grew to unbearable proportions, yet she felt she would be nothing without it, so she nursed it, wallowed in it.

The shop doorbell rang and she glanced up resentfully, not wanting any interruptions to her mourning for her love. The next minute, she was on her feet and facing the man who had just entered the shop, her heart beating painfully in her breast and a slight sweat of fear breaking out on her skin.

Daniel Durkin did not waste time in any preliminary greeting. 'What are you doing here?' he demanded.

'Earning a living, what do you think I'm doing? I put the money to good use and bought a business, as you can see.'

She held out her hands expressively to the counter and loaded shelves.

'I mean, what are you doing in Bishop Auckland?' He twisted his lips impatiently as he spoke.

'I come from here, my family is near. Where else would I go?'

'This was not in the bargain. I expected you to go somewhere else, somewhere away from both Durham County and Oxford. How can Timothy come back here if you are here? No, my girl, you have to go, sell up and get out.'

'You can't make me,' said Hannah. 'The paper I signed promised I would not get in touch with Timothy. It said nothing about keeping away from my home town.'

'You may be from around here but you're not going to stay, believe me. Now why don't you be sensible, put the shop up for sale and go elsewhere? Liverpool, Australia, anywhere as long as it's far enough away.'

'I'm staying here.'

'Right, my girl. We'll see about that, shall we?' Daniel turned for the door but before he opened it he had more to say. 'Timothy won't be home for some time. After his finals, he is going to France with his friend, so you have a month or two to do what I say. And you will do what I say, girl, I'm telling you.'

Hannah stood as stiff as a board with her chin in the air until the door closed behind him. Well, she thought numbly, Timothy is going off on a holiday, probably with the Honourable Anthony Akers. That's how much he cares about me. She did not think about Daniel's threats, they meant next to nothing to her. All she could think of was Timothy and his apparent indifference, and she began to tremble with the pain of it.

She spent a restless night, falling asleep only as the dawn brought streaks of light into the bedroom through the chinks in the curtains. Harry's persistent knocking woke her barely half an hour after she fell asleep.

'By, you take some waking,' he remarked. 'Here's the papers on the step and me and Billy waiting to take them out. What's the matter with you, our Hannah?' He looked critically at her puffy eyes and tousled hair, her kimono tied untidily over her nightgown. 'You're not having a babby, are you?'

'No, I'm not, you cheeky little imp!' she was impelled to cry out with embarrassment as she glanced sideways at the grinning face of Billy. 'What on earth made you say such a thing? I'll tell Mam about you being so brazen, I will!'

'Eeh, Hannah, I was just asking, like,' he said, chastened. 'Only you couldn't wake our Betty up when she was having Simon, I remember it well. She was always dozing.'

'Yes. Well, come on, bring the bundles in and I'll soon have them ready to go out.' She hurried into the living room, combed her hair back and straightened her kimono before going back into the shop to sort the papers. The boys were soon on their way and she went back upstairs to wash and change. While she ate her breakfast, she glanced at the small ads in the local papers.

A small lock-up shop in Winton was to let. She had a mind to expand her business now that the general strike was over. She had hesitated before, thinking that Daniel would find out she was home sooner if she took a shop in the colliery village. But that didn't matter now. The shop was to let at the end of the rows, she had seen the handwritten notice in the window when she had last been in Winton. In these hard times she would probably be able to pick it up at a very reasonable rent, it was privately owned, it did not belong to the colliery. Sure enough, the shop was there in the paper, in the For Rent section. On Wednesday, half-day closing, she would see about taking it. She had known the owner all her life, and didn't anticipate any difficulties. She had to keep busy, that was the thing, she had to stop thinking about Timothy.

'You mean you're setting up in opposition to me, our Hannah?' Nora demanded.

'No, no, Mam, I want you to manage it. You can carry on selling bits and pieces like you do now, but in the shop. And there'll be a newstand there as well.'

'But how can I look after all that and keep the house for the lads an' all? Nay, lass, I'm better off as I am, can you not see it?'

'Mam, think about it. You don't have to do it all yourself, you can give a few hours' work to one of your friends. I'm sure there'll be no shortage of people wanting it, not when the men are on strike.'

'Eeh, I don't know. You know there's the paper shop in Old Winton, is there room for two in the villages? Though, I've got to admit, it'll be nice to have my front room back to myself. I get a bit fed up of folk treading in the muck from the street.'

'There you are then, it's a bargain,' cried Hannah triumphantly.

'What is?' Bob demanded as he stooped to come into the kitchen from the yard.

'Our Hannah's taken the shop on the corner for me,' said Nora, and Hannah could swear she heard a note of pride in her mother's voice.

'We're going to sell papers as well as groceries and sweets,' she told her brother.

Bob laughed shortly. 'Why, Hannah, what sort of trade do you think you'll do in Winton with the men still out on strike? Who can afford a paper to read or a few sweets for the bairns here? It's more than they can do to put a bit of food in their mouths, let alone toffee or black bullets. Before you know it, you'll be bankrupt.'

'No, I won't, you'll see. I've still got a bit behind me and the pit won't be idle for ever. And don't you see, it'll help, it's bringing a bit of enterprise to the place. I intend to sell cheap at first, especially necessities, not much above cost.'

'Can you afford it?' he asked, astonished.

'I can, for a time at least.'

'Oh, well then, lucky for some,' said Bob, but he said it good-naturedly rather than enviously. She was reminded of the time he had hankered to join Uncle Billy in his carrier business. Did he still keep in touch with Uncle Billy? She was about to ask him but he was on his way out. To one of his eternal meetings, no doubt, where they swore solidarity against all the bosses and Daniel Durkin in particular.

Hannah laughed aloud as she thought of Daniel Durkin and what he would think if he knew to what purpose his money was about to be used. The joke was on him, all right. Shoring up the strike, she supposed he would say it was, but she called it relieving distress among her own folk. For now she warmed to the idea, she was determined that even if it took all the money she had left as well as what she could raise on the shop in Auckland, she was going to help her own folk.

'What are you laughing at, Hannah?' asked Walton. She picked him up and waltzed him round the kitchen until he was chuckling with delight.

'Dance to your daddy, my bonny laddie,' she sang and he joined his treble to hers. 'Dance to your daddy, my bonnie lad.'

'Give over, Hannah,' Nora scolded. 'There's no need to act so daft, is there? Folks'll think we've got a loony in the house. What are you laughing at, anyroad?'

'Oh, nothing, Mam, nothing,' said Hannah, subsiding into a chair with Walton on top of her. 'I'm happy, that's all.'

'Well, I'm glad to hear it. I think it's the first time you've said that since you came home from Oxford,' snapped Nora. And the smile faded from Hannah's face as she was reminded of Timothy once again. No matter what she did or whom she was with, the ache for him was always there, waiting to pounce.

Chapter Twenty-Eight

'When the men were at work at least we got our coal allowance,' grumbled Mrs Brown, a miner's wife from the far end of the rows. She stood with her arms folded over a spotless white pinafore, shaking her head and pursing her lips to emphasise her words. There was a small group of women in the corner shop; these last few weeks it had become something of a meeting place. The women would slip out there for a breather after finishing the morning's cleaning and before starting the dinner, under the legitimate excuse of getting the messages.

'You're right there, mind,' agreed one of the other women. 'Though at least the weather is warmer now, we only need a bit of fuel for cooking. It's a grand day the day, isn't it?'

'Oh, aye, the weather's all right,' Mrs Brown allowed as she held out her hand for the two penn'orth of brawn which Nora had been weighing out for her on the new set of scales Hannah had bought for the shop. The brawn had been cooked by Nora on a gas ring at home and it was much in demand. So much, in fact, that Mrs Holmes, who had just entered the shop, watched anxiously as it slowly disappeared into shopping baskets.

'I hope you have some more of that brawn, Nora,' she remarked. 'Our Jack's real fond of a bit of your brawn.'

'You're all right, Mrs Holmes, I have some more coming. Hannah's just gone back to the house for it.'

'That's all right then.'

'You get twice as much for your money here than you do at the butcher's in Old Winton,' asserted Mrs Brown. 'I don't know how you do it and still make a profit, Mrs Armstrong.'

Nora smiled and said nothing. The truth was, the profit they were making was negligible on such items as brawn, even though they saved money by buying pigs' heads at a slaughter-house in Bishop Auckland and cleaning them and cooking the meat themselves.

Hannah came in carrying the covered tray of meat and the women stood back respectfully for her to pass. Somehow, the gossip about how she came by her money had died down. Knowing she was making a success of the shop in town as well as this one, they assumed she must have been in business in Oxford too. Their understanding of business affairs was hazy in any case, most of them had no experience of anything but life in a pit village.

Even the Cornish family kept quiet on the subject of how Hannah came by her money. They were keeping their heads down altogether lately, for if they had been the scandal of the rows before, they were more so now. Sally and Kathleen had been taken up for soliciting in Auckland and been sentenced by the magistrates to a month's hard labour at the beginning of June. No sooner had they returned to the filthy cottage in Old Winton, both of them somewhat cleaner and thinner after the harsh regime of prison, than Lancelot had been arrested for being drunk and disorderly in the marketplace. He had compounded the offence by pulling a knife and stabbing a policeman. Luckily, he wasn't seeing very straight at the time and merely inflicted a shallow wound in the arm rather than the body of the policeman.

However, this had incensed the mining communities, for the national press had picked up the story and there had been banner headlines. 'STRIKING MINER ATTACKS POLICEMAN WITH A KNIFE,' said one and 'ATTEMPTED MURDER OF LAW OFFICER' another. Afterwards, there had been editorials calling for the army to be on call in the coalfields to deal with any disorder. After all, the case had shown that the miners were turning violent and taking up arms to further their claims for more money.

Hannah had read the reports with some disquiet; this was just the sort of thing that would turn the country against the miners, she was sure.

'I'll go now, Mam, if you can manage,' she said now. 'I'd

better get back so Betty can come home.'

'Righto, pet, thanks for bringing the supplies,' Nora replied.

Betty and Tucker, though not as badly off as the ordinary pit folk, were feeling the pinch nevertheless, and Betty sometimes looked after the shop in town while Hannah went to the wholesalers or took supplies out to Winton. Her sister insisted on paying her the proper hourly rate.

Hannah had bought a little van, a Morris, and Tucker had taught her to drive on the back lanes around Winton. The van was parked outside the shop and when she went out there was a knot of children standing round it as usual, hoping for a ride round the rows.

'Oh, not today, pets, I have to get back,' she said, but they knew her resolve was easily weakened and set up a clamour of disappointed wails.

'Please, miss, just up the rows, we'll walk back,' entreated one little urchin with great blue eyes in a pinched white face. And of course she capitulated. After all, she told herself, they get few enough treats in these hard times.

'Just up the rows, mind, and you'll have to sit in the back, I can't have you jostling me when I'm driving.'

They crowded in among the boxes and she drove up the row and down the next, going fairly slowly so as to prolong the ride. But she couldn't take too long, Betty would be waiting for her, so as they came to the last row she slowed to a halt and, reluctantly, the passengers got out.

'I'll be coming back at the weekend,' she promised them, and from the brown paper bag which was lying on the passenger seat she gave them each an apple.

'Eeh, ta, miss,' they chorused.

'Stand back now, I don't want to run you over,' she warned, and they retreated to the side as she set off along the road to the town.

Betty was serving a customer when Hannah got back to the shop.

'Oh, good, you're back,' she said as she handed over three halfpence change and a packet of cigarettes to the man, a porter from the station. 'I'm pleased, I want to go down to the store for new shoes for Simon.'

The porter went out and the sisters had the shop to

themselves. Betty waited until the door closed after him before turning to Hannah.

'It's lovely to be able to go and get the bairn what he needs without having to ask Tucker for the money. Don't think I don't appreciate it, Hannah. He has enough worries as it is, what with trying to keep the pit right. He goes down every day with the safety men, you know, it's not an easy job, though you'd think it was the way he's had to take less money. And Simon's growing apace now, his clothes don't last him any time at all. But I wanted him to look nice today.'

'He's a big lad all right, he's going to make a big man like his da,' Hannah agreed. 'But don't be grateful to me. If it wasn't for you being willing to step in for me, I'd only have to employ someone else, wouldn't I?'

'And you'd have no trouble finding somebody these days,' said Betty grimly. 'I don't know what's going to happen, I don't. Tucker's worried the men might get violent and stop the safety men going down the pit to keep it right. If that happens there'll be no pit left for anyone to work in when they do go back and Tucker would be out of a job an' all.'

'They won't do that, Betty, they're not violent, you know they're not. It would be against their own interests, anyway.'

'I expect you're right,' her sister replied, sounding none too sure. 'I'll be off then, cheerio. I promised Tucker's mother I would take Simon to Marsden to see them all today, I'll take the teatime train and stop the night at the farm. Father Grizedale hasn't seen Simon for ages, it's time I took him. I'll likely be back tomorrow.' She walked down the sunlit street, a plump, matronly figure in her simple print dress and low-heeled shoes.

Hannah watched her from the doorway of the shop for a moment or two before going in and picking up a copy of the *Journal and North Star* to read in idle moments behind the counter.

'TRAIN WRECKERS SENTENCED' it proclaimed. 'CRAMLINGTON MINERS SENT TO PENAL SERVITUDE. WOMEN FAINT AND SOB.' Hannah sighed. Eight of the men had been sentenced to penal servitude, three for eight years, two for six and the rest for four, though some of the prisoners asserted they were simply walking by the line when the incident occurred.

This sort of thing did not help the cause of the miners, she thought sadly. She put the paper down as the door opened and the short dinnertime rush began. This evening she would have to make time to do the books, she decided. Since the end of the general strike the shop had been making a modest profit, which was just as well, because the purchase of the van had made a considerable hole in her small capital.

The shop at Winton wasn't doing so badly either, much to her surprise. Some of it had to do with the shortage of fuel for cooking in the village, especially since Daniel Durkin had decreed that any miner caught riddling the waste heap for small coal would be prosecuted for theft with all the force of the law. It had been a good idea to sell home-cooked food in the shop even at such low prices, it brought in customers. Folk didn't like to use the soup kitchens every single day.

Daniel had not been back in the shop since that time in May, just about when the miners' lockout began. In fact, Hannah had heard nothing from him at all and here it was already August. She did not suppose that he had forgotten about her, though, not for a minute. She could only think he was busy with other things, such as petitioning the government to hold out against the miners. And if Timothy was still away on the continent, well, then, Daniel would think there was plenty of time to deal with her.

There was no way Daniel could force her to leave, Hannah told herself. She owed no one anything, he had no hold over her – except for the family in Winton. The thought niggled. There was Bob, he was a prominent local worker in the Miners' Federation, no further excuse was needed to get rid of him.

The afternoon turned into evening and one or two customers wandered in, but by seven o'clock the street was deserted. Hannah locked the shop door and went through to the living room. The heat was oppressive, and she flung open the window and door to the yard to create a draught. Taking a chair out into the yard, she sat for a while by the covered passageway she had had constructed to connect the outhouses to the main house. It was pleasant sitting there, the only sound the hum of a late bee busy around the flowerpots she had placed around the yard, geraniums and nasturtiums in full bloom. Maybe she would leave the books for another evening.

She was still sitting there, thinking lazily that she ought to get up and prepare something for supper, when there was a thunderous knocking on the shop door. It made her jump to her feet, startled. She glanced at her watch in the gathering twilight; it was nearly ten o'clock. Who could it possibly be at this hour?

The house was almost completely dark and she had to switch on the light before going through the deserted shop. The knocking started up again and she called out as she fumbled with the bolts, 'All right! All right! I'm coming. I can't open up any faster than I am doing.'

At last she got the door open and Harry stumbled in.

'What on earth's the matter? Nothing's happened to Mam, has it?' she cried.

Harry was panting and struggling for breath. He must have run all the way from Winton, she thought, thoroughly alarmed by now. He shook his head and swallowed hard. 'No, no, Mam's all right, but she wants you to come, Hannah, she wants you now.'

'But why? What's happened? Can you not tell me?'

'It's our Bob, she's past herself worried about our Bob, he's ran off. The polis came to our house and Bob ran off!'

'The polis? But why? Bob hasn't done anything wrong. It's not a crime to be in the union now, is it?'

'No – I don't know. Aw, come on, Hannah, I don't know what's happened but something terrible has. And Tucker's down the pit with the safety men and Betty's away so I came for you, Mam's in such a taking, I've never seen her like this before.'

Harry stared in earnest appeal at his sister, his eyes wide with a fear of something, he didn't know what. 'You'll have to come, Hannah, hurry up, will you?' He was desperate to convey the urgency he felt.

'Yes. Yes, of course, I'll come now, I'll just get my coat. I'll only be a minute.'

Harry turned to run back the way he had come and she caught him and pulled him back.

'Wait, it'll only take fifteen minutes in the van. Don't you go running back, you'll make yourself ill. Where's your bike, anyway?'

'Puncture. Eeh, I'm glad you have the van.' His face cleared.

Hannah bit her lip, reminding herself he was barely ten years old. It was easy to forget his agc sometimes, he always seemed such a responsible lad, and had proved to be an excellent paperboy. But he must have been in a panic all the time as he ran the three miles or so from Winton to the shop. What on earth was it that had brought the police to the house? Hastily, she went into the living room for her bag with the van keys in it, switched off the light and locked the shop door behind her. Harry was waiting outside by the van, hopping from one foot to the other with impatience.

'Don't worry, Harry, it must be a mistake of some sort. You know Bob isn't one to do anything wrong,' she said, trying to reassure him as she unlocked the vehicle. 'Hop in and we'll soon be on the way.'

Getting into the van herself, she checked it was in neutral and pushed the starter button. The engine flared into life and then died immediately.

'Come on, come on,' she said tensely and tried again with the same result.

'It's not going to start,' said Harry.

'Yes, it is, I'll use the starter handle. It'll only be a jiffy.'

'Maybe I'd better run back, Mam might want me to see to Walton,' said Harry.

'Don't be silly,' snapped Hannah. 'Sit still when I tell you to.' She found the starter handle on the floor by his legs, got out of the car and began cranking the van. It shuddered and burst into life, only to fade yet again. Hannah was almost sobbing with frustration.

'Please, God? Please?' She lifted her eyes to the darkening sky and prayed. And as if in answer, she realised that in her panic she had forgotten to switch on the petrol – of course the blinking thing wouldn't go. Lifting the bonnet, she pushed the switch over and got back into the van.

'Will it go now?' asked Harry.

'Yes!' she said emphatically, and pressed the starter button once again. The engine purred into life and this time it kept on going. Fumbling with the gear lever to find first gear, she forced herself to control her trembling limbs.

'Get a hold of yourself, girl,' she muttered. The gear lever slipped into place and she edged the van away from the kerb. Though it was still dusk, the night was approaching fast. She had never had occasion to drive in the dark before and was surprised at how difficult it was to see.

'Put the headlights on, our Hannah,' said Harry, 'the polis will be after *you* next.'

Heaving a sigh at her own stupidity, she found the right switch on the dashboard and turned on the lights. After that it took only a little more than ten minutes to reach Winton Colliery. As she turned into the row, she saw a police car parked outside the house and a cluster of neighbours around the back gate. She parked the van behind the police car and, without waiting for Harry, ran into the house.

Her mother was standing before the fire, clutching Walton to her and looking strained and anxious. Just inside the door stood a policeman, not the local bobby who lived in Old Winton, but a stranger.

'What is it? What's happened?' she cried, going up to her mother. Nora gazed at her and burst out sobbing.

'It's Mr Durkin. He's been killed. And the polis is saying our Bob had a hand in it. They're after him, Hannah, they're going to take him to Durham Gaol.'

Chapter Twenty-Nine

'Don't, Mam, don't, you're upsetting the boys,' said Hannah. She put an arm round her mother's shoulders and led her to the settee, with Walton still hanging on to her skirts and sobbing as hard as she was. Every few minutes he cast a fearful glance at the policeman standing impassively just inside the back door, and the tears fell even faster.

'You're right, I'm sorry, I am.' Nora made a great effort to pull herself together. 'Harry, bring me a hankie, pet, will you?'

Harry went to the top drawer of the press, took out a large white handkerchief and gave it to his mother. She dried her eyes and blew her nose, then took Walton on her knee to comfort him.

'Whisht, pet, whisht, I'm all right now, I am. Howay, be quiet now,' she whispered in his ear, and he put his arms around her neck and hid his face in her shoulder. She patted his back and after a while he stopped sobbing.

'Come into the sitting room,' Hannah urged. 'We can be on our own in there, you can tell me all about it.'

Nora looked at the police officer standing by the back door. 'No, we can't there's another one like him just inside the front door.'

Hannah was annoyed. 'Can't you stand outside in the yard?' she asked the policeman.

'Sorry, miss,' he replied, 'my orders are to stand here.' She turned away from him impatiently.

'Listen, Mam, have the bairns had their supper? No? Well then, I'll make them some cocoa and sandwiches and get them to bed. They'll be better off upstairs out of it.'

'Yes, that's right, of course it is. I don't know what I've been thinking of. Fancy me going to pieces like that, I've never done it before. I didn't do wrong to send Harry for you, did I? Only I forgot to give him his bus fare.'

'No, you did the right thing.'

It was true, she couldn't remember her mother in such a state, thought Hannah, as she warmed milk on the gas ring and cut bread for sandwiches. Not even when Da had his accident, not even when Jane had to go away to the sanatorium in Weardale.

But Bob, well, he was different. Hannah was well aware that her mother still felt guilty about letting him go to his grandmother in Consett to be brought up. And even more guilty because she had needed him back home when he was old enough to go down the pit.

Where is Bob? That was the question uppermost in her mind. Why had he run when the police came if he hadn't done anything wrong?

'Our Bob wouldn't do what they say, he wouldn't do anything against the law, you know him, Hannah, he wouldn't.'

Hannah looked up in amazement. It was almost as if she had asked the question aloud and her mother was speaking in answer. But no, Nora was washing Walton's face and hands in an enamel dish she had placed on the cracket by the fire.

'Is the polis going to put our Bob in gaol?' asked Harry. Hannah could have killed him.

'He's not, is he, Mam?' Walton's face began to crumple once more.

'No, he's not, like I said, our Bob hasn't done anything wrong!' Nora snapped, and Harry looked down and flushed. Already washed and dressed in his nightshirt, he was sitting at the table waiting for his supper. Though his eyes were shadowed and his face still strained, he was much calmer now he had his big sister here to help him support his mother. Even her reproof did not upset him really; rather, it reassured him.

'Hurry up and eat your supper, you're going to be very late getting to bed tonight. I'd better call one of the other lads in to do your rounds in the morning.'

'I can do it,' Harry protested.

'No, you can't. Anyway, I want you to stay with Mam, you can run messages for her and mind Walton. I'll go in and get the deliveries under way, then I'll close the shop and come back.'

'Eeh, Hannah, I expect it'll be all straightened out before then,' said Nora.

'It doesn't hurt to plan, just in case,' her daughter insisted.

The boys were soon packed off to bed and Hannah and her mother left alone, apart from the man at the door, that is. She made tea and automatically offered the policeman a cup, but he refused, so she sat down in Bob's rocking chair by the fire opposite her mother, and with her back to the stranger at the door. She had decided the best thing to do was pretend he wasn't there.

'Have you any idea what this is all about, Mam?'

Nora shook her head slowly. She held the cup of tea in both hands, low on her lap, making no attempt to drink it. Gazing into the dead ashes of the fire, she chewed her bottom lip worriedly before answering.

'All I know is Harry came running in saying there were policemen coming up the street and our Bob took off through the front door. I don't know where he went, I hardly had time to think. But you know they've taken ever so many of the lads to prison – look at that one who was just selling a pamphlet on the street. Three months, he got, and all for selling a bit of paper. And Will Lowther, you know, the Durham miners' leader, they took him to Durham Gaol an' all. So our Bob being active on the committee, he always thought they might take him. But we never imagined they would want him for murder, never. I mean, you know our Bob, he couldn't do a thing like that, he couldn't,' she repeated once again.

'Drink your tea, Mam. I've put plenty of sugar in it, it's good for shock,' Hannah counselled. Somehow in this situation she felt like the mother to Nora rather than the other way round.

Obediently, Nora sipped her tea before continuing. 'I cannot think that it's anybody from the colliery rows as killed Mr Durkin, though mind, he wasn't liked. I well remember that time after your father had his back broke in the pit, how that man spoke to me. You'd think we were dirt, you would. I know he was your Timothy's father –'

Hannah glanced quickly over at the policeman and saw he was listening to her mother, his head cocked on one side and an alert expression on his face. She leaned forward and touched her mother's hand, a warning touch, cutting into Nora's words.

'Don't talk about that here,' she said meaningfully. Nora sat up straight, reminded that they were not alone.

'Anyroad, the polis said that Mr Durkin had been killed in his car. But it could have been an accident, couldn't it? I mean, why should they think he was murdered?'

'I don't know, Mam. We'll have to wait till we find out the whole story. I –'

Hannah stopped as there was the sound of footsteps coming up the yard and both women turned towards the door. Was it another policeman coming to tell them they had caught Bob? The fear and apprehension was plain to see on her mother's face as she was sure it was on her own. But no, the door opened and it was Tucker.

'I'm sorry, I have to know who you are before I can let you come in, sir,' said the man on the door.

'My name is Thomas Cornish, I'm the undermanager and this lady's son-in-law, constable,' said Tucker sharply. 'Now move aside, if you please.'

'Just doing my duty, sir.'

'Yes, well, that's as may be.'

After this short exchange, Tucker, after a brief nod to his sister-in-law, went immediately to Nora.

'How are you, Mother?' he asked. 'Now, don't make too much of this, I'm sure they'll find the man who really did it.'

'Yes, they will, won't they, lad,' whispered Nora. But she was twisting her hands in her lap now, twisting and twisting, wrinkling the material of her dress. Tucker glanced at Hannah.

'I heard what had happened when I came up from the pit, I had to go down this afternoon. The safety men reported some trouble with the supports in one of the seams, and I had to inspect them for myself – the best thing to do, I always think. I came as soon as I heard, I mean, when I came to bank. Betty's over at Marsden, I don't expect her back until tomorrow night.'

'They think Bob's had a hand in murder, Tucker, how could anybody think such a thing?' Nora held out her hand to him and he took it and held it as he hooked a foot round a wooden chair and pulled it over so that he could sit down beside her. He was still in the working overalls he wore when he had to go down the mine and there were streaks of coal dust on his cheeks and darkening his fair hair. Watching him, Hannah thought he looked so strong and dependable, she could hardly believe that he was the son of Wesley Cornish. How could he bear to keep the same name? In his position she would have changed it to Grizedale, that of his stepfather.

'No one who knows him will believe Bob did it, so don't worry any more,' Tucker was saying reassuringly. 'They'll catch the real culprit, you'll see. Now why don't you lie down for a while? You need your rest, you know, the lads will need you tomorrow. Sitting up worrying isn't going to help anything, is it?'

'Eeh, no, I couldn't sleep. No, I'm all right sitting here, Tucker.'

'Can you tell us what happened?' asked Hannah. 'All we know is that Mr Durkin has been killed and Bob's run off.'

Tucker glanced at the policeman by the door and moved his head closer to the two women. 'Well, when I got out of the cage at bank, the pit yard was swarming with police. There's been one on guard since the beginning of the lockout but there must have been a dozen there tonight. It seems that the one who had been on guard went up to the fish shop to get something for his tea; after all, everything has been quiet round here and I suppose he wasn't expecting any trouble. But while he was away, the powder shed was broken into.'

'The powder shed?'

'You know, the locked store we keep the powder in. Well, it's a paste really, the deputies use it to crack up a length of coalface so that the hewers can bring it down more easily. Anyway, some paste was missing and detonators an' all. Mr Hudson thought someone might be going to try to sabotage the mine buildings, or maybe even Lord Aker's place over by Durham, so the special police were called out to guard both places.' Tucker was silent for a moment or two before adding, 'I suppose the powers that be never thought of Mr Durkin being in any danger. With Lord Akers being away in London, the agent was deputising for him at a meeting of the coal owners in Newcastle. He came back this evening. And now there are two men dead.'

'Two?'

Tucker nodded. 'Yes, his chauffeur, a Mr Bates, was driving the car.'

Mr Bates, yes, of course, thought Hannah. Timothy had mentioned the name once, saying how Mr Bates and his wife had been so good to him after the death of his mother.

'But do you know where it happened? Or how?'

'The entrance to his drive, just inside the gates, so the police said. An explosion.' Tucker's brow knitted. 'Though how anyone knew he would be coming home round about the time he did, I don't know. I mean, I didn't even know there was a meeting today in Newcastle. And how did they get the trap laid without anyone seeing them? It isn't so easy to cause an explosion with black powder as all that, you know. Whoever it was knew what he was doing.'

'Like a deputy overman or a shot firer,' said Hannah thoughtfully. 'Our Bob was just a hewer. But you know lots of folk could have read about the meeting, the *Northern Echo* reported it was going to be held.'

'Yes, that's right!' her mother put in, suddenly animated. 'I mean, about our Bob just being a hewer. He couldn't have done it, I told you he couldn't.'

Tucker and Hannah looked at each other and away again. They both realised that Bob must have seen a deputy use the explosive lots of times, he was bound to have some idea of its properties.

'I'll make some more tea,' said Hannah after a moment.

The night wore on; three o'clock, four o'clock. One or two birds began to sing and the cockerel in the henhouse at the bottom of Mr Holmes's garden crowed once or twice. Hannah got up and drew back the kitchen curtains, letting in the dawn light. Mercifully, Nora had fallen asleep on the settee, her head resting against the raised end, and Hannah had covered her with a blanket.

'I must get back to the shop by six to take in the papers,' Hannah whispered to Tucker. 'Why don't you go home and have a bath and change? You'll feel better then.'

Tucker hesitated. 'Betty would never forgive me if I left your mother to face anything alone,' he demurred.

'She won't be alone. If you nip along now, I'll wait until you come back; you're not going to be very long, are you? And I've got the van, it only takes a few minutes to drive to Auckland.'

Tucker got to his fect, stretching himself, and yawned. 'I will then, I won't be long. If I'm clean and dressed and looking like a member of the managerial class, maybe the police will tell me more.'

Hannah stared out of the window after he had gone. The pink streaks which had dyed the sky only a few minutes before were already disappearing, it promised to be a beautiful day. She sagged against the wall. Oh, yes, she thought wearily, a beautiful day, a glorious day. A day which could see the complete downfall of the Armstrong family.

A policeman turned in at the gate and she jumped, her pulse pounding. But it was only the relief for the constable on the door, she had forgotten he was there. The relief came in with a cheery 'Now then' for his colleague. She hushed him with a finger to her lips and a fearsome frown and nodded to the sleeping form of her mother. He muttered something of an apology and took up his friend's former position by the door.

Hannah's mouth tasted vile from too many cups of tea and lack of sleep. Why didn't something happen? This waiting was intolerable. She wished Alf was here, or Betty, both of them older than she. She felt very young and unable to support her mother, should someone come through the gate and tell them that Bob had been charged with murder and taken to prison. She felt she would not be able to bear it.

'Hannah?'

She whirled round to see her mother pushing herself upright on the settee with one hand, the other over her forehead. Nora looked pale and ill with great dark shadows under her eyes.

'I must have dropped off for a minute or two. By, my head's fit to bust,' she said. 'Oh, but how could I have slept when our Bob is in so much trouble?'

'You didn't sleep for long, Mam. Anyway, you must have needed it, I reckon it was nature's way of giving you a break.'

'You could be right, I suppose. There's no news, is there? Where's Tucker?'

'He's just gone home for a bath, he's coming straight back. No, there's no news, Mam.'

'I could do with a wash meself,' said Nora wearily.

'Well, I'll put the kettle on the gas ring and you can have one,' said Hannah. Nora glanced at the policeman meaningfully.

'I'll put the basin in the pantry for you,' Hannah suggested.

'You don't want to go upstairs, you might wake the lads and there's nowhere else private.' She caught the officer's eye and he looked away and blushed. Picking up the kettle, she filled it at the tap in the pantry and put it on the ring. That was another inconvenience caused by the lockout, she thought, there wasn't enough coal to heat water in the boiler which formed part of the range, so every drop had to be heated on the gas ring.

By the time Tucker came back, freshly shaven and wearing a clean shirt and smart suit, and with his fair hair still wet from his bath, it was a quarter to six. She just had time to get to the shop before the paperboys if she left immediately.

'I won't be long, Mam, just an hour, I think.' she said and rushed out to the van. The police car which had been there the evening before had gone, as had the knot of onlookers, so the row was deserted.

'Come on now, no histrionics,' she muttered as she got into the driver's seat, remembering as she did so that she hadn't turned off the petrol the night before. Were there dire consequences if the petrol was left switched on overnight? She couldn't remember what Tucker had told her about that. Well, she would never know unless she tried it, she thought, and pressed the starter button. The engine burst into life and she sighed with relief. Soon she was driving along the road to Bishop Auckland.

'Can you run and fetch your brother Tom?' she asked Billy, who was waiting for her, propped against the shop door, one leg crossed over the other and his cap pushed to the back of his head. Billy was almost fourteen and would soon be looking for a proper job. He hoped to follow his father into the railway wagon works at Shildon. That left only Dave and Harry, and Harry's round was kept deliberately small because of his age. Tom might be just the lad she needed. If Bob was taken it was more important than ever that she make a success of this business.

Billy's face brightened. 'Aye, I will, miss,' he said. 'Our Tom's a good lad, are you thinking of taking him on regular?'

'I might. We'll see how he goes, shall we?'

Billy nodded eagerly. 'We won't be long, miss, I promise.'

As he ran off, Hannah made a start on sorting the papers, marking them for the houses they were meant for and putting them in the correct piles to go into the boys' bags. By the time she had finished, Billy and Tom were back and Dave had arrived, so she was able to send them on their way.

'Throw the bags over the wall into the back yard when you're finished,' she told them. 'I have to go out.' She hesitated about what to do about the customers who called every morning for their papers, but in the end, she put a pile on a stool in the doorway and a tin beside it with a label stuck to it, MONEY IN HERE. The chance of losing the money was outweighed by that of losing customers because they couldn't get their *Northern Echo*. As an afterthought, she picked up one of the papers and took it with her. Until then, she had avoided looking at the headlines.

She sat in the van and opened up the paper. 'MINING AGENT MURDERED,' she read.

> Daniel Durkin, mining agent for Lord Akers, was last night murdered in his car on his way back from a meeting of coal owners in Newcastle. 'An arrest is imminent,' the police inform us.
>
> Daniel Durkin was one of the most respected men in our community.
>
> 'A dastardly deed,' said Lord Akers when contacted in his London home. He was too shocked to say any more for the time being. Timothy Durkin, Mr Durkin's only son, is believed to be holidaying on the continent with the Honourable Anthony Akers. The police are trying to get in touch with him.

Hannah folded the paper with shaking hands and laid it on the passenger seat. So Timothy was still away in France, she thought numbly as she started the engine and set off to Winton.

It was seven o'clock when she parked the van by her mother's gate in the back row once again. There was no one about; in these long months of lockout, the miners and their wives had got into the habit of sleeping till eight or nine o'clock; after all, there was little to get up for. The sun shone on the paving bricks from a cloudless sky and Mr Holmes's cockerel, newly released from the henhouse after the night, stepped arrogantly about the end of the row, black feathers and bright red comb gleaming. As usual, he was accompanied by his harem of dowdy brown hens.

Hannah pushed open the gate, walked up the yard and went in. There was no policeman standing just inside. No one but her two small brothers, sitting at the table eating bread smeared with treacle, and her mother standing by, her face grey and set.

'Has something happened, Mam?'

Nora looked up at her but didn't answer.

'Mam, has something happened? And where's Tucker?'

Harry answered instead. 'They've caught our Bob, he was hiding up the bunny banks. And Tucker's gone to the police station to see about it.'

Nora gave a shuddering sigh and sat down abruptly. Walton gave her a startled glance and then stared at his plate. Licking his finger, he pressed it on a crumb of bread and treacle and transferred it to his mouth. Hannah moved quickly to her mother's side and put a hand on her shoulder.

'It'll be all right, you'll see.'

'Will it?' Nora put a weary hand to her forehead and rested her elbow on the table. 'I'm not sure of anything any more.'

Chapter Thirty

It was twelve o'clock when Betty walked in. 'I came as soon as I could, Mam,' she said, going straight to Nora's side. 'Tucker rang the farm first thing and told us all about what had happened. Have you heard any more? The paper lads in Sunderland were shouting that someone had been arrested.'

She glanced from her mother's face to Hannah's and slumped into a chair. 'Do you know, I was telling myself all the way here that they must have arrested someone else and Bob would be back here, safe and sound. But it was him, wasn't it?'

'It wasn't Bob that did it!' Nora flared.

'No, no, I didn't mean that. I meant it was him they'd arrested. I know Bob didn't do it, Mam, of course I wouldn't think that.'

'Yes. Sorry, pet, I know you do; I'm tired, that's all.' She tilted her head and looked behind Betty. 'Where's the bairn? Where's Simon?'

'I left him with his grandma. She offered to keep him for a while, just till we get things sorted out here. I thought it was best if he was over there, away from all the trouble. And it leaves Tucker and me with more time to help.'

'Aye. Well, Meg always was a good woman, do anything for anybody, she would.'

'She said to send Harry and Walton an' all, for a week or two at any rate.'

'Eeh, I couldn't do that, our Betty. I wouldn't put on the woman's good nature, no, I couldn't.'

'Well, I'd think about it if I were you,' said Betty. 'After all, the school's on holiday this month and it would be a good thing for them to go somewhere you'll know they'll be properly looked after. And we won't have to worry about seeing to them as well as everything else. It's really a good idea, Mam. I'm sure Walton and Harry would love a holiday by the sea.'

'A holiday? At the seaside?'

The women turned as Walton came through from the sitting room where he had been playing a game of snakes and ladders with Harry. His face was shining and his eyes round with hope as he gazed up at Betty. Harry came up behind him.

'What did you say, Betty?' he asked.

'Mrs Grizedale wants you both to go to her for a holiday. You'd like that, wouldn't you?'

Harry grinned a grin of pure delight which made him seem as young as Walton. But the next minute the grin faded and he looked at his mother.

'Eeh, no, Betty, I'd better not go. Walton can, though, can't he? I'll stay here, Mam might need me.'

This was enough to make Nora's mind up for her. 'No, lad, you go with Walton, you can give an eye to him, help Mrs Grizedale. And Simon an' all, the pair of them will keep you busy.'

'But I want to stay here and help you, Mam,' he protested.

'Yes, well, the best help you can give me is to go with your brother. Go on, lad, you know you like going to the seaside with the Sunday-school trips. Well, this time you can go for a whole fortnight and live on a farm, an' all.'

Harry wavered and, in the end, nodded his head.

'I'll pack the clothes for them,' said Hannah. 'It's a good job I have the van, I can take them over there this afternoon.' At least she could help by taking the boys, she thought, as she found the old straw luggage basket and set about filling it with shirts, shorts and the other things they needed. She was glum with a feeling of impotence at having to hang around the house doing just about nothing. Yet she couldn't bear to go back to Bishop Auckland and open the shop as though it was just another day.

Driving back along the coast road after leaving the boys at the farm, Hannah hardly noticed the sun shining on the sea or the gulls swooping about the sky. The sun beat on the roof of the van and the heat penetrated the thin cotton of her dress, making her feel hot and sticky. She was glad of the breeze from the sea as she drove along, past Whitburn, Seaburn and Roker. All she could think of was getting back to Winton to see if there was any more news.

Striking inland through Sunderland, she took the road for Durham, and found the streets of the city were baking hot and stifling. She was glad to get away from them and out on the open road, heading for Spennymoor. Hannah was beginning to feel very tired indeed. She had had little sleep the night before and the drive to Marsden had taken two hours of the hottest part of the day. The afternoon sun was shining on the windscreen, dazzling her and making her head ache. As she came to the end of the houses of Spennymoor, she pulled into the side of the road and stopped the van. Leaning back in her seat, she closed her eyes. Just for a few minutes, she told herself, just until the sun dropped behind the line of trees on the horizon.

She awoke with a start as a loud bang reverberated round her, and fumbled for the door catch of the van. Her stiff fingers wouldn't work at first and another bang made her panic. Someone was trying to blow up the van with her in it, she thought confusedly. Images of black powder and detonators flashed through her mind. At last the door swung open and she practically fell out into the road and ran to the grass verge.

The light was almost gone, only a greenish glow in the sky. How long have I slept? she wondered. It must be late. The next moment, lightning slashed vividly through the sky and a great splash of rain fell on her face. A thunderstorm, that was all it was; she must have been dreaming. Drops of water were coming down fast now and she ran back to the car. Seven o'clock, said the watch on her wrist – where had the last two hours gone? A sudden wind gusted through the open window of the van and she shivered in her thin cotton dress. Best get on, she thought.

The engine had gone cold and the starter button refused to work. Hannah looked out at the pouring rain. There was no help for it but to try the starter handle. She had no jacket; the newspaper she'd left on the passenger seat early that morning was the only protection there was. Picking up the handle and the paper, she got out into the rain and held the paper over her head with one hand as she tried turning the handle with the other, but she wasn't strong enough. Oh, well, she thought, dropping the paper, two hands it is. It seemed to take ages before the engine finally came to life and, thankfully, she climbed back in the van and set off once again.

Of necessity she went along the road at a snail's pace for water was streaming down the windscreen and the wiper was making little impression. But at last she reached Parkhead Bank and there, magically, the rain stopped and the sun appeared, gleaming between the trees on the far horizon. Hannah coasted down the bank into the valley and up the other side to the ridge which marked the beginning of Bishop Auckland. On impulse, instead of turning off for Winton Colliery, she carried on to Durham Road.

She just wanted to see where Daniel had been killed, she told herself. She would just drive past and look in. As she neared the entrance to the drive she slowed to a halt and gazed in horror at the hole blasted in the ground and the shattered glass and gravel in the gutter. One gatepost leaned slightly to one side and the gate, though still attached to the post at the bottom end, leaned the opposite way. Something attracted her gaze to a window on the first floor – a figure of a man, was it? But a drop of water suddenly fell from her hair on to her eyelashes and obscured her vision and when she had rubbed it away, the figure was gone. Probably a trick of the light, she thought.

'Move along there, miss.' A policeman standing by the hedge waved his arms at her and she put the van back in gear and went on her way. Poor Timothy, she thought, how awful it would be for him to be told of his father's death when he was so far away from home. Perhaps he had been told already, perhaps he was on his way back this very minute. She wished she could be with him to comfort him, he had no one now, just the housekeeper, Mrs Bates, and she would be mourning her husband.

'Fool!' she told herself as she went up Gib Chare into the town. He wouldn't want her to comfort him, of course he wouldn't. All he wanted from her was a divorce. She must forget about him for the moment, she had enough to think about with Bob and the trouble at home. And then there was the business. Now she was in Auckland, she might as well go up Newgate Street and check on the shop.

There were two or three newspapers still on the stool with the tin box she had put there for the money on top of them, half full of pennies and halfpennies. Well, she thought as she picked up the papers and the box, people are honest. Lots of folk must have walked past the shop and seen the money but no one had touched it as far as she could see.

Upstairs she took off her wet dress and petticoat and rubbed her skin and hair dry with a towel. She didn't take time for a bath for she was eager to know what Tucker had managed to find out in the police station. Instead she pulled on clean clothes and brushed her hair. Picking up a jacket, for the storm had cooled the air, she ran back down the stairs. In the sitting room, she took her bank books from the bureau drawer and slipped them into her bag. If Bob was going to be charged, he would need a good solicitor and lawyers cost money, a lot of money. She only hoped the family could raise enough.

'You took a long time, did the storm slow you down?' asked Betty when Hannah walked into her mother's house. 'I was just beginning to worry about you.'

'I'm sorry. No, I went in to the shop to check everything was all right.' She looked around; there was no sign of her mother or Tucker. 'Is Tucker not back? Where's Mam?'

'I persuaded her to go to bed for an hour or two. She needed the rest and there's nothing she can do here.'

'And Tucker?'

'Yes, Tucker's back. He had to go in to work, though, Mr Hudson sent for him.' Betty looked down at her hands, her face troubled.

'Did he find out anything? What's happening about our Bob?'

'They took him to Durham Gaol, Hannah,' Betty answered, her voice low and full of pain. 'Tucker protested – after all, Bob hasn't even been charged with anything. How can they charge him when they haven't got any proof? And they haven't, I know they haven't, they couldn't have. But the magistrates said they couldn't take the risk of keeping him in the police cells at Auckland, they're frightened there might be a riot.'

'A riot?' Hannah was stupefied.

'Aye. Well, the lads are angry, you know, they think the powers that be are trying to make Bob a scapegoat, him being a union man. But his marras say he was at a meeting last night down at the workingmen's club, there's a host of them ready to swear it, he'd just come in from there when the police came for him. But the bobbies wouldn't take the men's word for it and some of the lads started saying they would get him out themselves if he wasn't set free. It was only wild talk but it was enough for the magistrates to send him to Durham.'

'We'll get him a solicitor. I was thinking about it on my way home. I have some capital left and I could raise a mortgage on the shop.'

'I hope it doesn't come to that, Hannah. But if it does, the Miners' Federation will pay, surely. If they have anything left after this lockout, that is.' Betty sighed and changed the subject. 'Have you thought what all this means for you, pet?' she asked. 'I know no one but the family knows that you're married to Timothy, but if the newspapers find out about it they'll try to make something of it.'

'What do you mean? The marriage is over, you know that. This has nothing to do with my relationship to the Durkins.'

'The police might think it has. While I've been sitting here on my own it went through my mind, they might think our Bob had another motive for murder, apart from the lockout.'

'What do you mean? Oh . . .' Hannah put her hand up to her mouth in horror as she realised what her sister was saying. 'They wouldn't think that, Betty, no, no, they wouldn't.'

'I hope for our Bob's sake they don't, pet.'

Hannah walked to the window and stared out at the dark yard. Oh, God, she prayed, don't let them find out about me and Timothy, not before they discover who it was killed Daniel. Please, God, what would I do if Bob was convicted because of me?

'Mebbe I shouldn't have said anything, pet.' Betty bit her lip as she saw how her words had affected her sister. 'It's daft speculating, anyway. Like I said, only the family knows you two were wed and we're not going to say anything, are we?'

'There's Anthony Akers,' said Hannah tonelessly. 'There's Jane an' all. What if they go to Oxford and ask questions there?'

'Jane? Jane wouldn't say anything, of course she wouldn't, how could you think such a thing?'

'No, of course not,' Hannah answered. She drew the curtains against the dark and turned back to her sister. 'Well, as you say, it's daft speculating. There's more sense in starting supper, Tucker will be coming here when he's finished work, won't he?

He'll be ready for something to eat.'

She went into the pantry, brought out potatoes and onions and began to peel and slice them for a dish of panhackelty – layers of potato, onion and strips of bacon, cooked in meat stock. It was a dish which, once prepared, could be left to itself in the oven. Bob loved his panhackelty, she thought sadly as she worked. And there hadn't been much opportunity to cook it for him since the stock of coal ran so low, most of the miners' coalhouses had been swept bare for months. But Betty had lit a fire with coal Tucker had brought down from their own house earlier in the day, as Nora complained of the cold after the storm. So now it was a good chance to use the already warm oven.

Tucker came in, bringing with him a copy of the *Evening Despatch*.

'Any news?' The sisters asked the question almost in unison as soon as he opened the door.

'Nothing much,' he answered. 'Mr Durkin's son has come home, he and Anthony Akers flew from Le Touquet to London, and then up to Durham with Lord Akers in his private aeroplane. It's marvellous what they can do nowadays, isn't it?'

Betty took the food out of the oven and began dishing it up. 'I suppose it is,' she said, dispiritedly. 'Hannah, should we call Mam or let her sleep?'

'What?' Hannah gazed at her but there was a faraway look in her eyes betraying her inattention.

'Mam, Hannah, should we get her up for supper or let her bide where she is?'

'Oh let her sleep, I think.'

Picking up the paper which Tucker had thrown on the table, Hannah gazed at the front page. There was a picture of Timothy with Lord Akers and Anthony in the background. Timothy's face looked impassive and, stare as she might, she couldn't read anything in his expression. His cheeks were more hollow than she remembered – was he eating properly? Absently, she rubbed her forefinger over the picture.

'It doesn't look like him,' she said.

Betty glanced quickly at Tucker, who raised his eyebrows. 'Newspaper photographs never do,' he remarked. 'Come and get your supper, pet, before it goes cold.' Obediently, Hannah put down the paper and sat at the table. Taking a forkful of potato and bacon, she put it in her mouth and chewed it, then another.

'Poor lad, it must be awful for him to have to rush home like that, his father dead an' all,' said Tucker. 'We've tended to forget about that what with worrying about Bob.'

Hannah put down her fork and glared at him. 'I didn't,' she said flatly. 'I didn't forget him at all, or how he must be feeling.'

Tucker looked embarrassed and suddenly showed an animated interest in his meal. 'This is nice, Betty, a nice surprise. I wasn't expecting anything cooked.'

'Hannah made it.'

The three lapsed into silence until they had finished their meal. Afterwards, Betty and Tucker went back to their own home.

'I have to be near the telephone in case there's any trouble at the pit,' Tucker explained. 'We'll be back first thing so you can go in and see to the papers. Or Betty will be if I can't.'

Hannah smiled at him gratefully. Tucker was such a tower of strength, what would they have done without him? She lay down on the settee when they had gone and pulled the blanket Nora had used earlier over her. It promised to be a long night.

'Howay, Hannah, wake up, pet, it's nearly half past five. Are you going in to the shop?'

Hannah woke with a start to see her mother standing over her, shaking her shoulder gently. She sat up dazedly and glanced at her watch, but she must have forgotten to wind it; it had stopped.

'What time did you say?' she asked Nora.

'Half past five. Look, it's plain enough on the clock.' Satisfied her daughter was awake, Nora turned to the range and picked up the kettle, shaking it to judge how much water it held. Going to the tap in the pantry, she put in more and placed the kettle on the gas ring.

'I'll have to go, the lads will be waiting for me,' said Hannah as she wound her watch.

'Are you not having a cup of tea first?'

'I'll get one there, Mam.' She took a comb out of her bag and dragged it through her hair, looking at Nora as she did so. 'You look better, Mam, did you sleep well?'

'I did,' replied Nora, 'and I am better, I feel more meself. I'm more hopeful an' all, things will come right, you'll see.'

'Course they will.' Hannah gave her mother a swift hug and went to the door. 'Look, I might be a bit late getting back. But Betty's coming down and Tucker as well if he can manage it.'

'Don't worry, I'll be all right now,' said Nora. 'Go on, you have your work to go to.'

Hannah was soon in Newgate Street and seeing to the newspapers for the delivery boys. After they had gone on their rounds, she lit the geyser and when the water was hot she washed her hair and took a bath. She lay in the steaming water, going over her plans for the morning. First of all, she was going to try to see Timothy. And after that, she was going to do something else. She picked up the soap and soaped herself while she tried to think what it was she was going to do next, but it was no use. She simply could not think of anything beyond going to see Timothy.

Chapter Thirty-One

Timothy was not able to sleep at all; his thoughts were whirling around in his head the whole night. Unable to forget the horror of his father's death, he kept going to his bedroom window and staring out at the hole in the drive, trying to make sense of it all. Just as he had been staring out of the first-floor window at the little van parked on the road the previous afternoon, or rather at the face of the woman who was sitting at the driving wheel. He had closed his eyes tightly and opened them again; she was still there and, yes, it was Hannah. The dull ache in his chest which had been there since she left Oxford expanded, rising up into his throat and threatening to choke him.

I'm a fool, he told himself savagely. She doesn't want me, she made that plain when she took the money from my father and ran. He had watched as the van pulled away from the house. Why had she not at least made the effort to come in and see him? She was still his wife, for God's sake! His chaotic thoughts veered endlessly from his father to her and back again to his father's senseless death.

He thought about Bob, her brother, his father's murderer. Somehow he couldn't believe it, not of Bob, not Hannah's brother. They were too gentle a family altogether, surely it could not have been Bob? That he was a union man he knew, but what other evidence did the police have? The inspector at Auckland had seemed so sure, though.

'Bob Armstrong is a deputy, he's well used to explosives. And whoever broke into the powder shed knew what he was after, all right. He knew exactly how much paste he needed and where the detonators were kept and how to do it. I understand from the manager that it's a low-grade explosive and needs an enclosed space and someone who knows what he's doing to get it to blow a hole like the one in your drive, Mr Durkin. Oh yes, I think we have the right man.'

But Timothy wasn't so sure. After all, a lot of men would know how to cause such an explosion, he thought. The fact that Bob was active in the Miners' Federation didn't automatically mean he was a violent man, though some of the owners thought it did.

The night shadows were beginning to give way to a grey, misty dawn. Timothy pulled on his clothes and went down into the garden. There was still a policeman stationed at the entrance to the drive.

'Morning, sir,' he said as Timothy came up to him. 'A fine morning too.'

'It is,' said Timothy. 'Look, why don't you go into the kitchen? I'm sure Mrs Bates will find you a cup of tea. She's up, I heard her as I came through the hall.'

'I don't know, sir. My orders were to stay here, just in case there was any trouble,' said the policeman doubtfully.

'Oh, go on, no one will know. I'll stay here until you get back. I'm sure you could do with a cup of tea,' Timothy said persuasively. The officer nodded and headed for the back of the house.

Left to himself, Timothy walked to the edge of the hole in the drive. It was quite a sizeable hole, he thought, not for the first time. Leading away from it, the line could be seen where the wires had been uncovered by the police. Whoever did it must have been hiding behind the mock-orange bush over by the hedge. He crossed over the grass towards the bush, feeling the dew soaking through the thin soles of his house shoes. Surely there must be some sign of who had been hiding there?

The police must have been over the ground more than once, he told himself; it was stupid, really, expecting to find anything. Still, he searched the ground, looking at every blade of grass, every little patch of soil under the bushes. There was nothing to be seen. Timothy went as far as the boundary wall of the garden and turned and walked back, still staring at the ground. Nothing, there was nothing. Doggedly, Timothy went back over the same ground once again. He was standing by the boundary wall when the constable came back from the kitchen.

'Everything all right, sir?'

'Yes . . . yes, everything's fine, officer.' Timothy glanced up to see the policeman regarding him curiously. 'I was just looking at the garden,' he added lamely.

'It's all been checked, sir. You'd best go in now, your feet are wet through. Been a heavy dew overnight, sir. Thank you for keeping an eye out for me, sir.'

Timothy walked down by the boundary wall towards the house, feeling dispirited. His shoes were squelching, so instead of going in the front he decided to carry on round the side of the house to the back door. He was surprised to find his way blocked by a large black retriever dog, lying across the back entrance with something in his mouth, a tin of some sort. Mrs Bates was there, too, a bone in her hand.

'I didn't know you had a dog, Mrs Bates,' said Timothy, and she blushed.

'He belongs to next door, sir. I hope you don't mind me feeding him? He comes through the hole in the hedge yonder. He's company, like.'

'No, of course I don't mind, why should I?'

Mrs Bates relaxed. 'His name's Black Boy, you know, after the pit near Eldon. Come on, Black Boy, here's your bone. Shoo now, go home and take it with you.'

Dropping the tin, the dog got clumsily to his feet, his tail wagging slowly. He looked over at Timothy and evidently decided he was a friend, for his tail carried on moving from side to side. Licking Mrs Bates's hand in thanks, he gently took the bone from her and sat down again, slavering.

'I said go home, Black Boy,' said Mrs Bates.

The dog paused and looked up at her before rising once again. He tried to pick up the tin to take with him but only succeeded in dropping the bone; he tried again but dropped the tin. Mournfully, he regarded it.

'Come on, boy, I'll throw that over the hedge for you,' said Timothy and picked up the tin. It was an oblong box, much marked now with Black Boy's teeth. There was some lettering on the side – what was it? It looked like 'R.C.' though the short leg of the R was barely decipherable. Timothy turned it over in his hand. 'Winton Colliery' was stamped on the undersurface.

The tin had to have something to do with the explosion.

'Sorry, Black Boy,' he said to the dog. 'I'm afraid I need to keep this myself.'

'What is it, sir?' asked Mrs Bates, her face alive with curiosity. 'I noticed he had an old tin, but I thought he must have dug it up somewhere.'

'He very likely did, Mrs Bates,' said Timothy. 'As to what it is, that's something I mean to find out. Will you have a look at it for me, see the lettering on the tin?'

Mrs Bates took the tin in her hands and turned it over, examining it carefully. 'I think that's an R,' she said after a moment. 'It's definitely a C, anyway. And something to do with the colliery, isn't it?'

'It is,' replied Timothy. 'Do you think you would remember it if you saw it again?'

'Oh yes, of course, sir. With those teeth marks on it an' all.'

'Thank you, Mrs Bates. I have to go out now, I'll just go up and change my shoes.'

'But what about breakfast? You can't go out with nothing on your stomach,' the housekeeper objected.

'Don't worry, I'll get something in town if I'm hungry.' Already on his way through the kitchen to the stairs, he called back to her over his shoulder.

Mrs Bates stared after him, mystified. But she wasn't really that interested in what Timothy was doing just now, with the weight of misery lying across her chest since her husband was killed in the car along with Mr Durkin. Sitting down at the kitchen table, she poured herself a cup of tea and spooned sugar into it, stirring the spoon round and round, hardly knowing she was doing it.

'Can you tell me anything about this tin, Mr Holmes?'

Mr Holmes, the overman who lived in the end house of Winton Colliery, blinked as he opened the door and saw young Mr Durkin standing there, holding out the battered, oblong tin. Behind him, the clock on the kitchen wall was just striking eight. Why, he hadn't even finished his breakfast! His braces were still dangling round his waist and his face unshaven. What was the young fellow doing, banging on his door at this time of a morning and then not even greeting him properly but rushing straight into stupid questions.

'Eh?' he said.

Timothy looked impatient for a moment, then he remembered his manners and began again. 'Good morning, Mr Holmes,' he said. 'I wonder if I could come in for a minute.'

Mr Holmes stood back in automatic courtesy and at the same time fumbled for his braces and pulled them over his shoulders. Too late now to do anything about his bristles or his lack of a collar.

'Aye, lad, of course, come in and have a bite of breakfast.'

'Thank you, Mr Holmes, very kind of you. But I won't have anything to eat, just a cup of tea if that's all right.'

'Sit yourself down and I'll get one for you. Mother's having a lie-in the day. She's not been feeling over grand lately.'

'Oh, I'm sorry to hear that,' said Timothy. He cradled the tin in one hand and accepted tea in a china cup which Mr Holmes took out of a glass-fronted press. He contained his impatience until the older man had sat down himself and picked up the pint pot which held his own tea.

'Now then, lad – Mr Durkin, I mean, no disrespect, like. What is it you're after?'

Timothy held out the tin. 'Do you know what this is, Mr Holmes? It's a bit battered, I know, a dog's had hold of it.'

Mr Holmes took the tin but needed only a cursory glance to recognise it for what it was. 'Why, it's a powder tin from the colliery,' he said positively. 'Where did you find it? It's the sort the men have to keep the black powder in in the pit. They have their own, you know, the initials is on them. See here, I can't read it properly, what do you make of it?'

'I think it says R.C.,' said Timothy.

'Oh aye, I think you're right. Now who could that be? There's Robert Clary, but I doubt it would be his, he's too careful, he wouldn't lose his tin. An' then there's Ralph Cornish –'

'Ralph Cornish?'

Timothy remembered Ralph Cornish, everybody knew the Cornish family, they were notorious for miles around. Mr Holmes was nodding his head.

'Where did you say it was?'

'I didn't but as a matter of fact, I found it in the garden at home. I reckon whoever set the bomb must have dropped it.'

'I wouldn't put nowt past that Ralph Cornish, him nor his dad. So-called dad, like, he was born six months after his mother came back from service at Grizedale Hall. Funny that, he's more like Wesley Cornish than the rest of the brood. But I say, I've just tumbled, if we can prove that tin belongs to Ralph Cornish and it was found in your garden, that means Bob Armstrong –' Mr Holmes stopped abruptly and his eyes gleamed.

'Exactly, Mr Holmes. Now I'm going to see this Ralph Cornish and confront him with it.'

Mr Holmes jumped to his feet and reached for his jacket, which was hanging on the back of the chair. 'Wait on, lad,' he said, his voice full of determination. 'I'm coming with you. You'll likely need somebody to back you up at that place.'

Filthy and ragged curtains were still drawn across the grimy windows of the Cornish cottage when the two men arrived in Old Winton village. If anyone was in they were either drunk or dead, for no matter how hard Timothy banged on the door, no one came to answer. Frustrated, he stepped back and glared at the house.

'They'll be in there all right,' Mr Holmes observed grimly. Cupping his mouth in his hand, he yelled up at the front bedroom window, the bellow issuing from his mouth astonishingly loud. 'Wake up, you lot in there! Ralph Cornish! Wesley! You're wanted down here.'

A couple of doors down the street, the landlord came out of the Pit Laddie and strolled over to them. Two or three other cottage doors opened and curious neighbours began to gather.

'They'll still be pallatic drunk, them two,' the landlord said grimly. 'The lasses now, they went off on the early bus for Bishop Auckland, I saw them get on it. I don't know about Lancelot, though. I used to think he was a canny lad but he's getting just like his dad an' all.'

'Have you seen Ralph lately?' asked Timothy.

'I have that,' said the landlord. 'I had him to throw out of the bar last night, causing a ruckus, he was, him and Wesley. Shouting something about getting the old bastard at last, no other bugger had the guts to do it.' He glanced quickly at Timothy. 'Begging your pardon, sir.'

'Was he now?' said Timothy, pursing his lips.

'I was going to mention it to the polis when he comes round

this morning. I would have sent for him last night but I thought mebbe Ralph was just bragging in his cups.'

Behind them, the door of the Cornish cottage was pulled open at last.

'What's all this bloody noise about?'

Timothy whirled to face Ralph and almost gagged at the blast of fetid air which came out of the open door of the cottage. Ralph himself smelled strongly of stale sweat and vomit, traces of which could be seen down the front of his clothes. When he saw Timothy he grinned and, putting a hand inside his shirt, lazily scratched himself.

'Well, look at the young gaffer,' he drawled. Clearing his throat noisily, he spat at Timothy's feet.

Timothy saw red. Stepping forwards he lunged for Ralph's throat.

'Leave my lad alone!' Wesley yelled and flung himself into the fray, but he was easily felled by a blow from Mr Holmes. Howling, he tried to get to his feet, but the overman promptly sat on him. Murmurs of appreciation came from the couple of locked-out miners and their wives who were looking on.

'Gan on there, Holmsey,' one called. 'It's time the old bully-boy got what's coming to him. Land him one for me!'

Ralph's fists were flailing wildly at Timothy but to no avail, Timothy easily evaded them and knocked him to the dirt alongside his father. In doing so, the powder tin fell out of his pocket and one of the miners picked it up.

'Hey, look 'ere,' he said, showing it to his fellows. 'What's this?'

Before anyone could answer him, the village policeman arrived. Whether someone had called him or he had seen the scuffle from his window, Timothy didn't know.

'Righto, righto, now, break it up. I'll have no fighting 'ere!' he said importantly. Then he noticed Timothy. 'Oh, it's you, sir, is it? I didn't see you there. What's this all about?' As he spoke he was hauling Ralph to his feet and securing his hands behind his back with handcuffs.

'What are you doing?' yelled Ralph. 'I didn't do nothing, I was minding my own business when he set on me! Isn't that right, lads?' he appealed to the bystanders but no one backed him up. He turned vicious. 'By, it's one law for the rich and one for the bloody poor, that's what it is!' His eyes grew wilder as the policeman began to drag him along the street to the police station, and he began to scream out curses at the crowd. 'I'll make you pay, see if I don't! You canna back your own against a bloody gaffer – cowards, the lot of ye! None of you would have the guts to get rid of the old bastard, it took a real man to do that! An' I'll get the better of the young 'un an' all, see if I don't!'

His voice faded as he was hustled into the station and after a few minutes the policeman reappeared and came back to them.

'Right, then, I'll take the old 'un,' he said calmly. Mr Holmes rose from his sitting position on Wesley's chest.

'You'll likely have to fumigate the cells after you've had them two in,' he commented, and the policeman grimaced with distaste as the full odour of Wesley's body reached his nostrils.

'Aye, well, it won't be the first time I've had it to do after this lot,' he remarked. 'Let's hope it's the last, that's all.' He looked round at Timothy and Mr Holmes. 'I dare say the inspector will be wanting a word with you about this.'

'Certainly, officer. I'll just go home and change first. I'll come back for you and run you in if you like, Mr Holmes.'

'Aye, well, I'd best go back to Winton Colliery and let the missus know what's happening, then,' said the overman.

Timothy nodded and was about to go for his car when he remembered the powder tin. 'Oh, I forgot,' he said to the policeman. 'I think your inspector will be interested in that tin, it's evidence. You'd better take it for him. I'll explain when I get there, tell him.'

Chapter Thirty-Two

Hannah parked the van at the bottom of Gib Chare and walked up the hill to the Durkin house. The morning was much fresher than the previous day; the rain had cooled the air besides washing away the dust. She wore a long white cardigan over her simply cut white dress. Her shoes were low-heeled, brown with a bar over her instep and fastened with a button, and she carried a brown handbag to match. She had decided against wearing a hat, simply combing out her bob and clipping it back at the side with a brown and white clip. She had put a lot of thought into what she should wear to meet Timothy, changing her mind more than once before finally deciding. Should I have worn a more sombre dress? she wondered now. But no, Timothy had liked her dressed in white.

Approaching the gate which still leaned drunkenly away from its post, her heart began to thud uncontrollably and her breath quickened.

'Take a hold of yourself!' she muttered, standing still and forcing herself to take great mouthfuls of air into her lungs, holding it for a few seconds before releasing it. Slowly her heartbeat quietened and she resumed walking. The policeman standing guard on the gate had been watching her approach and he stepped forwards as she made to turn into the drive.

'Sorry, miss,' he said. 'No one is to go in.'

Hannah gazed at him levelly. 'I am a relative,' she said firmly. 'I wish to see Mr Timothy Durkin, is he at home?'

'I'm sorry, miss, I was told no one was to be allowed in, no one at all.'

'But I told you, I am a relative! Now, if Mr Timothy Durkin is at home I wish to see him,' she snapped imperiously in the best accent she could manage.

'He's not at home, miss,' he answered uncomfortably. 'But you understand, I couldn't let you in anyway, this is a very bad time. My orders are –'

'Constable, let her through, it's all right.'

Both Hannah and the policeman turned in the direction of the aristocratic voice, the policeman jumping to attention. Anthony Akers was standing before the open front door, his face grim.

'Yes, sir.'

Hannah walked up the edge of the drive, avoiding the shallow hole in the middle, trying not to look at it. 'Hallo, Anthony,' she said, and he nodded gravely.

'Come in. We can talk in here.' He indicated a door to the side of the hall and she went into a room furnished as a sitting room.

'Do sit down,' he said formally and as she sat, he took the chair opposite and leaned forwards with his elbows on his knees and his hands clasped together. 'This is a bad business, a very bad business.'

'My brother had nothing to do with it, Anthony, you must believe me. He was at a meeting, he couldn't have done it.'

Anthony gazed at her. 'I understand he ran from the police, though,' he said.

'Only because there have been trumped-up charges against the Miners' Federation men. You must know a lot of innocent men have been imprisoned.'

Anthony jumped to his feet and walked to the window. 'Let's not go into that, Hannah. Communists have to be dealt with harshly, we want no revolution here,' he said, his voice cold and remote.

'My brother is not a communist.'

Anthony shrugged his shoulders and Hannah looked down at her hands, twisting them on her lap, trying to summon up the courage to ask after Timothy. She felt she was choking, and swallowed hard. After a moment she gained control of her voice enough to put the question, the all-important question.

'Is Timothy here?'

Anthony answered without turning round. 'No. He's gone

with my father to examine new evidence the police have about the murder.'

'How is he?' The anticlimax was almost unbearable for her.

Anthony whirled abruptly and stalked up to her, stopping only a yard away with his hands clasped behind his neck. Suddenly he looked very much like his father; the same imperious lift to his chin, the same arrogant gaze.

'How do you expect him to be? Don't you know what you have done to him? These last few months, since you walked out on him, he has been in a terrible state. How he got through his finals I'll never know. Timothy is my friend, he had been my friend ever since we went up to Oxford, but I tell you, he's not the man he was, not by any manner of means. It's been like trailing a nobody around after me. No sense of humour, no bright ideas, no nothing. Just a face like a wet week, he had no interest in anything. And then this had to happen. How do you think he is?'

'I didn't leave him, he sent me away! He sent his father to tell me he was finished with me, he couldn't even tell me to my face.'

Anthony stared at her. 'Well, it's easy enough to blame his father now, isn't it? Now Daniel Durkin can't answer back, can he? He was my father's agent and a damn good one at that. Come on, Hannah, you'd better go. I think you've said enough.'

'I'm not going, I want to see Timothy. I don't care what you think about me, I'm telling the truth. And our Bob is telling the truth an' all, he is, I tell you,' she cried, slipping back into the local idiom. She hung on to the arms of the chair as though she thought Anthony might eject her physically, and gazed up at him in desperation.

He stared back at her and gradually his expression softened and he sat down abruptly. 'I don't know, Hannah, maybe I shouldn't have said what I did. I have to admit I was against Timothy marrying you in the first place, but when he did he seemed so happy. I always thought you were a nice girl, I couldn't believe it at first when he told me you'd taken the money and run.'

'I thought I was a drag on him, Daniel said I was. He said Timothy would never get a position worthy of him while he was married to me, a pitman's daughter. I understood that he would lose his inheritance if he stayed with me, even that from his mother. And so he decided to send me away. That's what I was told. You can believe me or not.'

Anthony's eyes opened wide and he whistled soundlessly. 'His father said that?' he asked. 'Oh, surely you must have misunderstood.'

'Well, I don't think so, that's the gist of what he said.'

They sat a few minutes in silence. Suddenly the telephone bell rang in the hall, making them both look up expectantly. Hannah waited for him to answer it but it didn't seem to occur to him. After a moment it rang again, stopping abruptly as a girl's voice answered it. Of course, she thought, Anthony was used to having telephones answered for him. There was a soft knock at the door.

'Come!' called Anthony.

'A telephone call for you, Mr Anthony,' said the girl's voice.

He made his excuses and went out into the hall. Hannah rose to her feet and walked to the window, gazing out over the fields towards the village and winding gear of Winton Colliery. What was happening there? she fretted. She should have tried to engage a solicitor for Bob before she came here, that was what she should have done. But was the Miners' Federation doing that? Perhaps they were; surely they had enough money left in the funds to provide legal aid for their own officials, especially those wrongly accused of a crime.

Hannah felt very tired and confused and guilty. She had given way to her impulse to see Timothy and attempt to put things right with him, when her first priority should have been her brother. When Anthony came back she would tell him she had changed her mind, she wouldn't wait to see Timothy, not now. Now she had to see if Tucker was home and talk to him about hiring a lawyer for Bob.

'That was my father,' said Anthony, coming back into the room and interrupting her thoughts. 'He wants me to go down to the police station in Bishop Auckland.' He paused and bit his lip. 'He says further evidence has come to light, the police are ready to prefer charges. He wants me to be there to give my support to Timothy if he needs it. We don't know how the miners will take it.'

'Oh! Oh, I must go home, I must find Tucker,' she cried and

ran past him into the hall and out by the front door.

'Hannah! Come back, it's not . . .' But Hannah was gone, racing over the fields towards Winton, forgetting all about the van parked in the road. Anthony reached the front door just in time to see her disappearing behind the hedge. He hesitated; should he go after her? But his father had said it was imperative he come immediately. Sighing, he went back inside.

'Was there some news, sir?'

Mrs Bates was standing by the door which led to the kitchen, her face wan and pale. She had lost her husband in the explosion, he reminded himself, of course she should be told the news. She had a right.

'Yes, Mrs Bates, I'm glad to say the police have caught the men who murdered your husband and Mr Durkin.'

'Yes, sir, but I believe they caught him yesterday, sir,' she said. 'Do you mean they now have the evidence to secure a conviction?'

'They have; my father says the man has actually confessed. But it's not the man they took into custody yesterday, Mrs Bates. No, it's someone else entirely, in fact, there are two of them, father and son, so I was told. Now I'm going to the police station. They are sending an extra policeman out to guard the house, so please don't worry about anything.'

Chapter Thirty-Three

Hannah burst into the kitchen, flinging the door open so violently it swung on its hinges. 'Have you heard?' she cried.

Betty and her mother were standing by the dresser, Betty with her arms around Nora's shoulders. Nora was sobbing as though her heart would break and as Betty was comforting her, neither answered Hannah at first.

So they have heard the bad news, she thought wearily. The stitch in her side, which had been nagging at her for the last half-mile, spread across her chest and she bent over double, panting for breath. She could hear muffled sounds of distress from her mother and Betty. What could she say to them to give them hope? Tucker, I need to speak to Tucker, she thought, we need to see a lawyer. The stitch eased a little and she straightened up.

Mam and Betty were watching her, and though there were still signs of tears on Nora's face, they were laughing, actually laughing. Had they gone mad?

'Haven't you heard the news?' she demanded.

'Yes, isn't it grand? Tucker just came in and told us,' said Betty. 'He's been down to the police station and knows all about it.' She glanced round for her husband. 'Where's he gone? Oh, there you are. Come and tell Hannah all about it, she looks a bit flummoxed.'

Tucker came out of the pantry carrying the kettle he had been filling. He looked pensive but when he saw the girls were watching him, he too grinned.

'I'll just put the kettle on. If a man wants a cup of tea and a bite round here, he has to get it himself.'

A wild hope was stirring in Hannah; perhaps Anthony had got it wrong, perhaps Bob hadn't been charged. 'Tell me!' she demanded. 'Pull yourselves together and tell me what's happened. I think I must have it wrong, I thought it was bad news.'

'Eeh, no, it's not. I'm sorry, pet,' said Nora, 'we thought you would know. It's our Bob, he's coming home. I told you he couldn't have done it, didn't I? I knew all along everything would be all right.'

Betty caught Hannah's eye and they burst out laughing and Nora joined in. Bob was coming home, he wasn't going to be charged with murder. Hannah repeated it to herself; after all the worry it wouldn't sink in properly.

'Tell me, Tucker,' she repeated.

'Yes, of course I will, pet.' Tucker sobered and his tone took on a hard note. 'We might have known who actually did it. I mean, who is it causes all the trouble round here?'

Wesley Cornish, thought Hannah. She sat down on a chair by the table and leaned on it with one arm. Oh, dear God, how awful for Tucker! Even though there was nothing between them now and Wesley had never been a true father to him, hadn't he brought enough shame on Tucker without this?

'How did they find out?' she asked.

'Well, I can see I don't have to spell out the name,' said Tucker bitterly. 'They found out easily enough. If they hadn't come looking for Bob soon after it happened and if Bob hadn't tried to get away, they would have found out sooner.' Tucker sighed and Betty put a sympathetic hand on his shoulder.

'I'm sorry I laughed, lad,' she whispered. 'It was the relief, you know, I didn't think.' He patted her hand and held it there for a moment. 'No, I know, it's all right, Wesley's nothing to me,' he reassured her before turning back to Hannah.

'Yes, it was Wesley Cornish and Ralph, they planned it between them, no one else was in on it, they've said so. In fact, I heard it on the quiet from the manager that they were actually boasting about getting rid of the agent themselves and landing the blame on Bob. "Nobody else had the guts to do it," Ralph told the landlord in the Pit Laddie last night. But it was Timothy Durkin who went looking for them, he'd found something belonging to Ralph in the garden. There was a fight in the old village about it, Timothy waded into them.' He watched Hannah carefully and when she went white he led her to the settee.

'Sit down, lass, it's all over now,' he said.

'He's all right? He's not hurt?' Hannah remembered all the bullying and fighting the Cornish men had been involved in over the years; they were hard men. She began to tremble.

'Eeh, lass, of course he's all right,' Nora put in quickly. 'He made short work of that Ralph, I'm telling you. By, I'll never forget what he's done for us.'

Nor me, nor me, thought Hannah and her heart yearned for Timothy. She felt utterly confused.

The kettle began to sing and Nora moved automatically to set the table. 'There's nothing much in the house to eat,' she said. 'I've not thought of getting any messages in.'

'I'll go to the corner shop,' suggested Hannah, standing up. She was anxious to get a few minutes on her own, she had to straighten out her thoughts. 'We'll just have to have sandwiches, that's all. What do you fancy, corned beef or sardines?' She heard herself saying the mundane words but she felt detached from them somehow. She walked out of the house and up the street to the corner, not seeing anything about her at all, not even hearing when a neighbour said how glad he was Bob had been cleared. The neighbour stared after her until she turned the corner and then went in to his wife.

'That Armstrong lass is suffering from shock,' he commented to her.

Hannah was remembering what Anthony had said about Timothy's bitterness towards her. Maybe he was finished with her altogether, she thought dismally as she picked up a tin of corned beef and one of sardines for good measure. Could she bear to return to the house on Durham Road and try to see him again? What would she do if he refused to see her? No, no, she couldn't bear that to happen, she couldn't. If Timothy did want to see her he would seek her out, wouldn't he? And if he didn't come, well, then . . . She didn't want to think about how she would feel if he didn't come. But he had cared enough to find out the true murderers and clear Bob's name, hadn't he? Had he done it for her? Or was it just a coincidence that the man he cleared was her brother?

During the afternoon, one person after another came in to congratulate the family on the news of Bob's innocence. Mr Holmes and his wife came in about three o'clock.

'Bear up, Nora, it won't be long before the lad's home,' said Mr Holmes. 'I'm right glad an' all, it makes you think there's some justice in the world, doesn't it?'

'They're still keeping him, though, aren't they?' said Nora. 'I can't understand why, not now, he's done nothing. Why don't they let him come home?'

'He'll come, you'll see. It'll just be the formalities,' said Tucker.

'Aye, well, we all knew he hadn't done it,' said Mr Holmes. 'That's why the lads were up in arms, they were all for marching to Durham and setting him free themselves. But it's quiet now. I was talking to Tommy Hutchinson a minute or two ago, he was getting off the bus from Auckland. He said the crowd outside the police station this morning had dispersed. I could see myself when I went in with young Mr Durkin they were pretty angry, all sorts of rumours were going round. But then Tucker came out and told them Bob was to be let go free, it was Wesley and Ralph Cornish that blew up Durkin's car. I tried to tell them myself but they were not in the mood to listen to me. They listened to Tucker, though, and Tucker told the lads to go home, Bob would be released. So that's what happened, they all came away soon after I left. By, Nora, Mr Timothy stood up to Ralph Cornish all right, he did well for your Bob.'

'I wonder why they did kill Mr Durkin. After all, Wesley's not even active in the union,' Nora mused aloud.

'Brooding about Lancelot getting put in gaol, I should think,' said Mrs Holmes. She tossed her head. 'By, I always said those Cornishes were a disgrace to the community.'

'Whisht, woman!' said her husband and she blushed.

'Eeh, I didn't mean you, Tucker, you know I didn't.'

'No. Don't worry, Mrs Holmes, I know,' he answered.

Hannah walked up to Durham Road after tea to collect her van. At least, that was the reason she told herself she was going. After all, she needed it and she couldn't leave it on the main road for long. But she knew that was partly an excuse, she really wanted to see Timothy. She couldn't bear to think of him only a mile or two away and not seeing him. She had forgotten all about her resolve to wait and see if he sought her out.

A workman was filling up the hole in the drive when she arrived.

'Now then, Miss Armstrong,' he greeted her and she looked up in surprise. Her head was so full of Timothy, she hadn't realised she knew him. It was the colliery mason from Winton. Of course, this would be a company house, she thought. Timothy would have to leave it in due time to make way for the new agent. It was a strange thing, almost equating him with the families of pitmen who had to leave their houses when their man was killed, or died naturally.

'I was pleased to hear the good news about Bob.' The mason leaned on his shovel and pushed his cap on to the back of his head, smiling. 'Has he got home yet?'

'Not yet, but he will,' she replied. Nodding, she passed on up the drive and knocked on the front door, half expecting to see Anthony. Instead, it was the maid, Mary, who opened it.

'May I see Mr Timothy?' she asked.

'Can I take your name, miss?'

'Just say it's Hannah. He'll see me, I think.' Hannah stepped firmly into the hall, though Mary looked uncertain. The house was very quiet; of course, it was a house of mourning.

'Wait here, please, miss.'

Hannah waited in the silence, and from nowhere there flashed into her mind a memory of years ago, when she was a child and had come here with the chapel choir, carol singing. She remembered how she had gazed around in wonder at the furnishings, which had seemed opulent to her eyes. And she remembered the tall young boy who had gazed at her as though she was a real person, not a thing, as his father had done that day in the pit yard. And he had listened attentively when she sang and even joined in one of the carols. 'Still the Night', was it? She could almost see him now, in the doorway of the sitting room, the room she had sat in only that morning.

'Hannah.'

He was at the top of the stairs looking down at her and she tried to read his expression but his face was in shadow and she couldn't see it properly.

'Hallo, Timothy,' she said and he walked down the stairs, not rushing but taking each step deliberately. And then he was there beside her, looking down at her, and she still couldn't see what he was thinking.

'Come into the drawing room,' he said quietly, his voice neutral, and led her into the same room she had been in earlier. Of course it was a drawing room, she thought abstractedly, what else would it be? She walked in and sat in the chair he indicated.

'How are you, Timothy?' she asked politely. 'I was very sorry to hear about your father.' For all the world as though she were paying a courtesy visit on someone in the village who had been bereaved.

'Were you?'

She glanced up at him and away again. 'Yes, of course,' she said. 'And I am so grateful for what you did for Bob.' She wished he would sit down, she wished he would put out his hand and touch her, say something human. But he merely nodded. His hands were clenched at his side; she gazed at his right hand, it was clenched so tightly the knuckles were white. He's just lost his father, she thought and remembered how she had felt when Jake died. A wave of sympathy washed over her; poor Timothy, poor lad! Almost without thinking she put out a hand and touched the white knuckles with her fingertips. He jumped back violently as though her touch had burned him.

'Don't do that!'

Hannah pulled her hand back into her lap, clasping it tightly with the other. He couldn't bear to feel my touch, she thought miserably.

'Why have you come here? And don't say it was to offer your commiserations for I won't believe you.'

'I . . . I wanted to see you, thank you for what you did for Bob and offer my sympathy for your father . . .'

Her words trailed off as she realised how ridiculous they sounded. I'm a fool, she thought, I shouldn't have come. I should get up and go, say I made a mistake, I shouldn't have come. She rose to her feet and moved towards the door and still he didn't speak. When she got there, she turned to face him.

'Alf said you wanted a divorce. Do you?'

Timothy shrugged. 'Do you?'

It was like walking on eggshells, thought Hannah and reached for the door handle. With it in her hand, she paused. If she went out now, she would never have the courage to come back. And she had to hear him say it himself.

'If you don't want me any more I will divorce you. Or you can divorce me, I don't know how these things work. But you just have to say so, Timothy.'

'Hannah, don't go yet. I'm sorry I was so abrupt, I can't seem to say the right things.'

She whirled to face him, hope flaring for a brief instant. He took a step towards her and stopped. 'This isn't the time to talk about anything. There's the inquest and the funeral and a thousand other things to see to. Later perhaps, but not now. Let's not rush into anything, we learned our lesson last time,' he went on.

'No, it isn't. You're right,' she replied. Of course this wasn't the time to discuss divorce, she squirmed at her own insensitivity. 'I'll go.'

Timothy walked with her to the door. 'I'll be in touch,' he said.

She walked to the van, not even noticing the mason filling up the hole. Well, she thought. I knew he didn't want me before I went, so nothing has changed. Taking out the starting handle, she started the engine and drove into the town, up Gib Chare and into Newgate Street and the shop. On a sheet of foolscap, she wrote out a notice and stuck it in the window.

Open for business, it read. *We apologise for any inconvenience to our customers while the shop was closed. The closure was unavoidable, due to pressing family business.*

Then she went inside and stood behind the counter, ready to serve the men who would be coming on the train from Shildon wagon works.

Hannah was standing on a stool, dusting the top shelf in the shop, when the bell rang. It was September and as the door opened, it let in a cold draught which ruffled the papers on the counter and turned over the cover of the *Beano* on the shelf nearest the door.

'I won't be a minute,' she said without turning round, 'there's just this last bit to finish. Close the door, will you? There, I'm finished.' Jumping down from the chair, she went behind the counter. 'What can I do for you?' she asked and looked up.

It was Timothy.

'That depends on you,' he said.

Hannah stared at him dumbly. His face was pale and tired-looking and the blue of his eyes seemed deeper, almost a navy blue, and set in dark shadows. He has come to see about the divorce, she thought. Well, she had known he would, now that the funeral was over and a new agent was installed in the house on Durham Road. She'd read all about it in the *Auckland Chronicle* and *Northern Echo*, and she had been expecting him to come. But even so, it still came as a shock and her heart began thudding against her ribs. She couldn't speak, all her being was concentrated on making herself act normally and not throwing herself at him and begging him to take her back.

'Can we go somewhere we can talk?' he asked, his voice neutral.

'What? Oh, yes.'

She looked at her watch; it was almost closing time. 'I'll just shut the shop,' she replied. 'We can go into the sitting room.' As she walked to the door and locked it and turned the notice in the window to CLOSED, Hannah was intensely aware of him watching her, and her hands trembled. She didn't look at him, she dared not, for she still felt unsure of her self-control. Timothy held open the door to the living room for her and she was very careful not to brush against him as she passed.

'Would you like a cup of tea?' she found herself asking.

He shook his head impatiently.

'You've come to see about the divorce?'

There, she'd said it. Well, it was over now, all she could do was try to hold on to her dignity.

'No. Well, not exactly.'

Abruptly, Hannah sat down on the settee. Timothy hesitated a moment, then turned the armchair towards her and sat in that. He leaned forwards so that he was barely a foot from her and clasped his hands together. She gazed at his hands, so clean and well cared for, not at all like her brothers' hands. She thought of the feel of Timothy's hands on her body and looked quickly away. She wasn't hearing him correctly, she decided, she'd misunderstood, that was it.

'Sorry, what did you say?'

'I . . . oh, Hannah, what did my father tell you? Anthony told me something of it, but how could you go off without a word like that?'

'I had to. He said I would ruin your future; he said when it came to a choice between your inheritance and me, I came a bad second.'

'And you believed him?'

Timothy's voice rose in anger and he jumped to his feet and caught hold of her by the shoulders, pulling her up too. She looked up at him, her eyes wide, feeling his fingers digging into her flesh, hurting.

'I didn't, not at first, but then he repeated that your life would be ruined if I stayed. And I thought how angry you were when I went to hear Mr Cook at the Corn Exchange, how you didn't understand how I felt when the students tried to humiliate him. You were like a stranger. All that secrecy about our marriage an' all, I didn't understand that, I thought you were ashamed of me.' Hannah bit her lip, trying not to cry. 'I wanted to see you, I wanted you to tell me to my face that you didn't want me. But he said . . . he said . . .' Her head dropped and she found herself staring at the lapels of his linen jacket.

'Hannah, look at me.'

His fingers relaxed their hold on her shoulders and he spoke quietly and calmly. He drew her close, so close that her head went back automatically. He bent his head to hers and his arms tightened as he lifted her off her feet and sat down on the settee with her on his lap. At least, that was the position she found herself in when he moved his lips from hers. Her body began to clamour for him, insistently, her mouth was full of the taste of him, all she could see or smell was him for she had been denied him too long.

'Oh, Hannah, I've missed you so much,' he whispered thickly and the surge of her body's responses rose high and overwhelmed them both. They forgot about explanations for a while, they didn't matter, all that mattered was that they loved and the sensuous delight they took in their love.

Some time later he bought fish and chips from the shop down the street and they ate them in the yard in the September twilight, shielded from the eyes of neighbours by the high stone walls.

'I needed to keep our marriage quiet, Hannah,' he said,

pausing in the middle of his meal and gazing at her soberly.

'Shush,' said Hannah, 'it's over now.'

'But you have to know. I couldn't let Father spoil it for us, I knew he would if he found out. And when he did, I just wasn't prepared for the way he went about separating us. I shouldn't have believed him, I'm sorry.'

'Oh, love, can't we forget about it now?'

Hannah moved round the table and bent her head to his. The meal was left unfinished as their need to make love again became so imperative that they forgot their hunger and hurried upstairs and fell on the bed clasped in each other's arms.

Insistent banging on the shop door woke Hannah. Carefully, so as not to wake him, she moved from under Timothy's arm and picked up her watch from the table by the bed. Six o'clock. She looked dreamily at Timothy's sleeping face on the pillow, closed her eyes tight and opened them again. He was still there, though she couldn't rid herself of the feeling of unreality. Tentatively, she touched his cheek with the tip of her finger and he moved a little.

'Hannah?'

The way her name was bawled out made her jump. It was Harry calling up to the bedroom window. She'd better let him in, she thought lazily. Slipping out of bed, she pulled on the nightgown she had discarded some time the night before and covered it with her kimono before going downstairs to let her brother in.

'By, our Hannah, I don't know what's the matter with you,' Harry grumbled as he picked up a bundle of papers and brought them into the shop. 'We're going to be late now and I wanted to go down the dam head with Dave and Billy for a swim after. It's a good job they aren't here yet an' all, when you haven't got their bags ready for them.'

'Well, you can still go for a swim, can't you?' she pointed out. 'The school's still on holiday, isn't it? Come on, we'll soon have the papers ready if you give me a hand.'

Harry looked at her disapprovingly. 'Are you not going to comb your hair even? You're not going to serve in the shop without getting dressed properly, are you?'

'I will soon get dressed, in a minute, after we've got the

papers ready,' she replied, pushing her hair back with her fingers.

'Well, you'd better hurry up –' Harry broke off and his mouth fell open as Timothy appeared in the doorway from the back shop, his feet bare and his hair even more tousled than Hannah's. Hannah forgot her brother as Timothy slid his arms around her waist and drew her to him.

'Good morning, my love,' he murmured and kissed her earlobe, and Hannah's eyes closed as she leaned against him.

'Our Hannah! I'll tell me mam of you carrying on an' in the shop an' all. Why, man, anybody could come in and see you!'

Hannah opened her eyes and there was Harry, his hands on his hips and his chin thrust forward. His frown was that of an outraged father.

'Has that man been here all night?' he demanded. ''Cos if he has, I'm telling you, me mam'll have a fit!'

Chapter Thirty-Four

'Lord Akers has offered me a position,' said Timothy. He placed the letter he had been reading back in its envelope and gazed at Hannah across the breakfast table, concerned how she would take the news.

'Not here, not in charge over Winton –' she began, panicking, but he interrupted her quickly.

'No, not here, in the head office in Durham. There's a period of training, of course, and some of that will be in the field but it will be north of here. His estates cover a large area, as you know.'

Hannah glanced down at the piece of toast in her hand and placed it carefully back on her plate. She looked about the small room; they had been so happy here. Oh, she had known that Timothy would not be content to live in the cramped accommodation behind the shop for ever, how could he be? It was just not what he was used to. But these last few weeks it had been their own private heaven, a refuge from the sadness and despair which pervaded the very air in Winton Colliery and spilled over into the town. And how could she leave the family now, just as the miners were defeated? She shivered slightly, and Timothy noticed immediately.

'Are you cold, my love? I'll build the fire up, these November days can be so dark and damp and the cold so penetrating. I don't want you catching a cold.' He half rose in his chair but she shook her head.

'No, I'm all right, not cold at all, just sad. I don't know why. Well, I do really, I was thinking how happy we've been here.

And about my mother and Bob and the boys, it will be hard to leave them. How are they going to manage?'

'We're only going to Durham, love,' he pointed out. 'And they have Tucker and Betty, and Bob is a grown man, after all. Oh, I've been happy here too, but we have to move on.'

Hannah looked into his eyes, so full of concern and understanding. 'I am a fool, aren't I?' she said. 'I can visit Winton from Durham easily, it's only half an hour's drive. But this shop will always be special to me, it's hard for me to let go.'

'It doesn't have to be sold,' said Timothy. 'Why can't Bob run it? Didn't you say he's always hankered after a little business?'

'But that was when he was a boy. Bob's a miner, not a shopkeeper!'

'Oh, Hannah, my love, you know as well as I do it will be a miracle if he ever gets work in the mines again. None of the union men will be taken on, not while any miner who took no active part in the strike is out of work. The Owners' Association are agreed on that.'

'It was a lockout, not a strike,' she reminded him flatly.

'Sorry, I meant lockout,' Timothy said quickly. He looked uneasy. Usually he was very careful not to comment on the troubles of the last few months for Hannah felt so deeply about them. Naturally so, he mused, remembering the shock and horror he had felt when he first saw for himself the extent of the poverty and distress in Winton. And Winton was just one of many pit villages in the same position.

The long months of the stoppage had devastated them and he could hardly believe it was the same world as the one he and his friends inhabited. It was as though the coalfield had taken a step back in time to the early nineteenth century and the social conditions of the Industrial Revolution. Still, the miners were back at work now and surely conditions would improve as the coal trade picked up. And it would pick up, he was certain.

Hannah had a faraway look in her eyes as she thought of her brother and how he had looked when he was released from Durham gaol. He had been imprisoned for only a few days but those days had changed him so much. He seemed to have lost his belief that the men would win in the end because their cause was just. He was quieter and began staying away from the meetings of the Miners' Federation, instead he spent hours sitting in the kitchen and staring into the cold grate. And when the men capitulated and went back to work, forced at last to accept the conditions laid down by the owners, he did not even comment on it. He put on his pit clothes and went with the rest to the colliery office, only to be turned away and told there was no work for him.

Timothy came round the table and lifted Hannah into his arms, holding her close. 'Please, my love, don't look so sad. If it's going to make you unhappy, I won't take the position.'

Hannah snuggled into his shoulder, feeling the steady beat of his heart against hers. The clean scent of his skin filled her nostrils and the now familiar feelings of love and contentment rose in her and overwhelmed her, cutting out everything else from her thoughts and mind. She put up a hand and felt the crisp hair on the back of his neck, and his arms tightened around her.

'Hannah?' he asked, his voice husky. She lifted her head from his shoulder and looked up into his face, her mind made up. He was ready and eager to start on his career and she had no right to hold him back, he had to come first with her.

'No, Timothy. You must take the position,' she said softly and offered her lips for his kiss.

Author's Note

The May 1926 General Strike in support of the miners lasted for ten days. The miners struggled on alone for seven months, but by November they had to admit defeat. The long months of stoppage availed them nothing; rather, it brought a great deal of distress and suffering, often the mothers and children suffering most. The Poor Relief and soup kitchens organised by the Miners' Federation and other philanthropic bodies prevented outright starvation in the pit villages and there were few instances of physical violence by the men. Labour Party members and other miners' leaders were often branded as communists and some imprisoned.

In the end, Durham County branch of the Miners' Federation of Great Britain, along with most other districts, recommended a return to work though a majority of the men wanted to struggle on. Some of these men, especially those who were considered to have been leaders, were not to obtain work again until the advent of the Second World War.

The miners who returned had to accept conditions that were worse than those they had had to endure before the lockout.